STAR WARS™

THE NEW JEDI ORDER

THE UNIFYING FORCE

JAMES LUCE

arrow books

Published by Arrow Books in 2004

13

Copyright © Lucasfilm Ltd. & ™ 2004

James Luceno has asserted his right under the Copyright, Designs and
Patents Act, 1988 to be identified as the authors of this work

First published in the United Kingdom in 2003 by Century
Arrow Books Limited
The Random House Group Limited
20 Vauxhall Bridge Road, London, SW1V 2SA

www.starwars.com
www.starwarskids.com
www.randomhouse.co.uk

Addresses for companies within The Random House Group Limited
can be found at: www.randomhouse.co.uk/offices.htm

The Random House Group Limited Reg. No. 954009

A CIP catalogue record for this book
is available from the British Library

ISBN 9780099410522

Penguin Random House is committed to a sustainable future for
our business, our readers and our planet. This book is made from
Forest Stewardship Council® certified paper.

Printed and bound in Great Britain by Clays Ltd, St Ives plc

ACKNOWLEDGMENTS

The Unifying Force owes something to everyone who has helped give shape and continuity to the Expanded Universe—from Alan Dean Foster to Tim Zahn to Matt Stover; and from Bill Smith to Stephen Sansweet to the hundreds of fans who have devoted countless hours to detailing the esoteric. I would, though, like to single out a few people whose help and encouragement were invaluable: Shelly Shapiro and Sue Rostoni, for their editorial magic; Greg Bear, Greg Keyes, Sean Williams, and Shane Dix, for their commitment to keeping things consistent; Troy Denning, for his many suggestions; Dan Wallace, Rick Gonzolez, Mike Kogge, Helen Keier, Eelia Goldsmith Henderscheid, and Enrique Guerrero, for their tireless work on the entire New Jedi Order series. Most of all, thank you, George Lucas, for creating a universe that continues to expand . . .

THE STAR WARS NOVELS TIMELINE

DRAMATIS PERSONAE

Nom Anor; executor (male Yuuzhan Vong)
Wedge Antilles; general (male human)
Nas Choka; warmaster (male Yuuzhan Vong)
Kyp Durron; Jedi Master (male human)
Jagged Fel; pilot (male human)
Harrar; priest (male Yuuzhan Vong)
Traest Kre'fey; admiral (male Bothan)
Cal Omas; Chief of State (male human)
Onimi; Shamed One (male Yuuzhan Vong)
Danni Quee; scientist (female human)
Supreme Overlord Shimrra (male Yuuzhan Vong)
Luke Skywalker; Jedi Master (male human)
Mara Jade Skywalker; Jedi Master (female human)
Han Solo; captain, *Millennium Falcon* (male human)
Jacen Solo; Jedi Knight (male human)
Jaina Solo; Jedi Knight (female human)
Princess Leia Organa Solo; diplomat (female human)

PART ONE

ACROSS
THE STARS

ONE

Selvaris, faintly green against a sweep of white-hot stars, and with only a tiny moon for companionship, looked like the loneliest of planets. Almost five years into a war that had seen the annihilation of peaceful worlds, the disruption of major hyperlanes, the fall and occupation of Coruscant itself, the fact that such a backwater place could rise to sudden significance was perhaps the clearest measure of the frightful shadow the Yuuzhan Vong had cast across the galaxy.

Immediate evidence of that significance was a prisoner-of-war compound that had been hollowed from the dense coastal jungle of Selvaris's modest southern continent. The compound of wooden detention buildings and organic, hive-like structures known as grashals was enclosed by yorik-coral walls and watchtowers that might have been thrust from the planet's aquamarine sea, or left exposed by a freakishly low tide. Beyond the tall scabrous perimeter, where the vegetation had been leveled or reduced to ash by plasma weapons, rigid blades of knee-high grass poked from the sandy soil, extending all the way to the vibrant green palisade that was the tree line. Whipped by a persistent salty wind, the fanlike leaves of the tallest trees flapped and snapped like war banners.

Standing between the prison camp and a brackish estuary that meandered finally to the sea, the jungle combined indigenous growth with exotic species bioengineered by the Yuuzhan Vong and soon to become dominant on Selvaris, as had already happened on countless other worlds.

Two charred yorik-trema landing craft, not yet fully healed from recent deep-space engagements with the enemy, sat in the spacious prison yard. Shuffling past them came a group of humans, bald-domed Bith, and thick-horned Gotals, carrying three corpses wrapped in cloth.

His back pressed to one of the coralcraft, a Yuuzhan Vong guard watched the prisoners struggle with the dead.

"Be quick about it," he ordered. "The maw luur doesn't like to be kept waiting."

The camp's prisoners had argued vehemently to be allowed to dispose of bodies according to the customs of the deceased, but graves or funeral pyres had been expressly forbidden by order of the Yuuzhan Vong priests who officiated at the nearby temple. Their ruling was that all organics had to be recycled. The dead could either be left to Selvaris's ample and voracious flocks of carrion eaters, or be fed to the Yuuzhan Vong biot known as a maw luur, which some of the more well-traveled prisoners characterized as a mating of trash compactor and Sarlacc.

The guard was tall and long-limbed, with an elongated sloping forehead and bluish sacs underscoring his eyes. The light of Selvaris's two suns had reddened his skin slightly, and the planet's hothouse heat had turned him lean. Facial tattoos and scarifications marked him as an officer, but he lacked the deformations and implants peculiar to commanders. Bound by a ring of black coral, his dark hair fell in a sideknot to below his shoulders, and his uniform tunic was cinched by a narrow hide belt. A melee weapon coiled around his muscular right forearm, like a deadly vine.

What made Subaltern S'yito unusual was that he spoke Basic, though not nearly as fluently as his commander.

The prisoners paused briefly in response to S'yito's order that they hurry.

"We'd sooner see their bones picked clean by scavengers than let them be a meal for your garbage eater," the shortest of the humans said.

"Make the maw luur happy by throwing yourself in," a second human added.

"You tell him, Commenor," the Gotal beside him encouraged.

Shirtless, the prisoners were slick with sweat, and kilos lighter than when they had arrived on Selvaris two standard months earlier, after being captured during an abortive attempt to retake the planet Gyndine. Those who wore trousers had cut them off at the knee, and likewise trimmed their footwear to provide no more than was needed to keep their feet from being bloodied by the coarse ground or the waves of thorned senalaks that thrived outside the walls.

S'yito only sneered at their insolence, and waved his left hand to disperse the cloud of insects that encircled him.

The short human cracked a smile and laughed. "That's what you get for using blood as body paint, S'yito."

S'yito puzzled out the meaning of the remark. "Insects are not the problem. Only that they are not Yuuzhan Vong insects." With uncommon speed, he snatched one out of the air and curled his hand around it. "Not yet, that is."

Worldshaping had commenced in Selvaris's eastern hemisphere, and was said to be creeping around the planet at the rate of two hundred kilometers per local day. Bioengineered vegetation had already engulfed several population centers, but it would be months before the botanical imperative was concluded.

Until then, all of Selvaris was a prison. No residents had been allowed offworld since the internment camp had been grown, and all enemy communications facilities had been dismantled. Technology had been outlawed. Droids especially had been destroyed with much accompanying celebration, and in the name of benevolence. Liberated from their reliance on machines, sentient species might at long last glimpse the true nature of the universe, which had been brought into being by Yun-Yuuzhan in an act of selfless sacrifice, and was maintained by the lesser gods in whom the Creator had placed his trust.

"Maybe you should just try converting our insects," one of the humanoids suggested.

"Start with threatening to pull their wings off," the short human said.

S'yito opened his hand to display the winged bug, pinched between forefinger and thumb but unharmed. "This is why you lose the war, and why coexistence with you is impossible. You believe we inflict pain for sport, when we do so only to demonstrate reverence for the gods." He held the pitiful creature at arm's length. "Think of this as yourselves. Obedience leads to freedom; disobedience, to disgrace." Abruptly, he smashed the insect against his taut chest. "No middle path. You are Yuuzhan Vong, or you are dead."

Before any of the prisoners could reply, a human officer stepped from the doorway of the nearest hut into the harsh sunlight. Thickset and bearded, he wore his filthy uniform proudly. "Commenor, Antar, Clak'dor, that's enough chatter," the officer said, referring to them by their native worlds rather than by name. "Carry on with your duties and report back to me."

"On our way, Captain," the short human said, saluting.

"That's Page, right?" the Gotal asked. "I hear nothing but good things."

"All of them true," one of the Bith said. "But we need ten thousand more like him if we're ever going to turn this war around."

As the prisoners moved off, S'yito turned to regard Captain Judder Page, who held the subaltern's appraising gaze for a long moment before stepping back into the wooden building. The body bearer had spoken the truth, S'yito thought. Warriors like Page could snatch victory from the jaws of defeat.

The Yuuzhan Vong held the high ground in the long war, but only barely. The fact that a prison camp had had to be grown on the surface of Selvaris was proof of that. Normally a battle vessel would have served as a place of detention. But with the final stages of the conflict being waged on numerous fronts, every able vessel was deployed to engage hostile forces on contested worlds, patrol conquered systems, defend the hazy margins of the invasion corridor, or protect Yuuzhan'tar, the Hallowed Center, over which Supreme Overlord Shimrra had now presided for a standard year.

In any other circumstance there would have been little need for high walls or watchtowers, let alone a full complement of warriors to guard even such high-status prisoners as the mixed-species lot gathered on Selvaris. At the start of the war, captives had been fitted with manacles, immobilized in blorash jelly, or simply implanted with surge-coral and enslaved to a dhuryam—a governing brain. But living shackles, quick-jelly, and surge-coral were in short supply, and dhuryams were so scarce as to be rare.

Were S'yito in command, Page and others like him would already have been executed. As it was, too many compromises had been made. The wooden shelters, the disposal of bodies, the food . . . No matter the species, the prisoners had no stomach for the Yuuzhan Vong diet. With so many of them succumbing to their battle wounds or malnutrition, the prison commander had been forced to allow food to be delivered from a nearby settlement, where the residents plucked fish and other marine life from Selvaris's bountiful seas, and harvested fruits from the planet's equally generous forests. Against the possibility that resistance cells might be operating in the settlement, the place was even more closely guarded than the prison.

It was said among the warriors that Selvaris had no indigenous sentients, and in fact the settlers who called the planet home had the look of beings who had either been marooned or were in hiding.

The sentient who delivered the weekly rations of food was no exception.

Covered with a nap of smoke-colored fur, the being walked upright on two muscular legs, and yet was graced with a useful-looking tail. Paired eyes sparkled in a slender mustachioed face, the prominent feature of which was a beak of some cartilaginous substance, perforated at intervals like a flute and downcurving over a drooping polar mustache. He was harnessed to a wagon that rode on two yorik coral wheels and was laden with baskets, pots, and an assortment of bulging, homespun sacks.

"Nutrition for the prisoners," the sentient announced as he neared the prison's bonework front gate.

S'yito ambled over while a quartet of sentries busied themselves removing the lids of the baskets and undoing the drawstrings that secured the sacks. He sniffed at the contents of one of the open bags.

"All this has been prepared according to the commander's instructions?" he asked the food bearer in Basic.

The being nodded. The fur on his head was pure white,

and stood straight up, as if raised by fright. "Washed, decontaminated, separated into flesh, grains, and fruits, Fearsome One."

The honorific was usually reserved for commanders, but S'yito didn't bother to correct the food bearer. "Blessed, as well?"

"I arrive directly from the temple."

S'yito glanced down the unsurfaced track that vanished into the high jungle. To provide the garrison with a place of worship, the priests had placed a statue of Yun-Yammka, the Slayer, in a grashal grown specifically for use as a temple. Close to the temple stood the commander's grashal, and barracks grashals for the lesser officers.

S'yito lowered his flat-nosed face to an open basket. "Fish?"

"Of a kind, Fearsome One."

The subaltern gestured to a cluster of hairy and hard-shelled spheres. "And these?"

"A fruit that grows in the crowns of the largest trees. Rich flesh, with a kind of milk inside."

"Open one."

The food bearer inserted a hooked finger deep into the seam of the fruit and pried it open. S'yito gouged out a fingerful of the pinkish flesh and brought it to his broad mouth.

"Too good for them," he announced, as the flesh dissolved on his thorn-pierced tongue. "But necessary, I suppose."

Few of the guards accepted that the prisoners couldn't tolerate Yuuzhan Vong food. They suspected that the alleged intolerance was a ploy—part of an ongoing contest of wills between the captives and their captors.

The food bearer placed his hands, palms raised, just below his heart, in a position of prayer. "Yun-Yuuzhan is merciful, Fearsome One. He provides even for the enemies of the true faith."

S'yito glowered at him. "What do you know of Yun-Yuuzhan?"

"I have embraced the truth. It took the coming of the Yuuzhan Vong to open my eyes to the existence of the gods. Through their mercy, even your captives will see the truth."

S'yito shook his head firmly. "The prisoners cannot be converted. For them the war is over. But eventually all will kneel before Yun-Yuuzhan." He waved a signal to the sentries. "Admit the food bearer."

In the largest of the wooden huts, all of which had been built by the prisoners themselves, there was little to do but tend to the sick and dying, pass the daylight hours in conversation or games of chance, or wait ravenously for the next meal to arrive. Harsh coughing or the occasional laugh punctuated a grim, broiling silence. The Yuuzhan Vong hadn't required any of the captives to work in the villip paddies or anywhere else in or outside the yorik coral walls, and thus far only the top-ranking officers had been interrogated.

A diverse lot, most of the prisoners had been taken at Bilbringi, but others had arrived from worlds as distant as Yag'Dhul, Antar 4, and Ord Mantell. They wore the tattered remains of starfighter flight suits and combat uniforms. Their battered and undernourished bodies—whether hairless, coated, sleek, or fleshy—were laminated in sweat and grime. They had Basic in common, and, more important, a deep, abiding hatred for the Yuuzhan Vong.

That they hadn't been killed outright meant that they were being saved for sacrifice—probably on completion of the worldforming of Selvaris, or in anticipation of an imminent battle with Galactic Alliance forces.

"Chow's here!" a human standing at the entrance said.

A rare cheer went up, and everyone capable got to their feet, forming up in an orderly line that spoke to the discipline demonstrated ceaselessly by the captives. Eyes wide, mouths salivating at the mere thought of nourishment, several of the prisoners hurried outdoors to help unload the food wagon and carry everything inside.

A Twi'lek with an amputated lekku studied the short being who had delivered the food, while the two of them were hauling sacks and pots into the hut.

"You're Ryn," the Twi'lek said.

"Hope that doesn't mean you won't touch the food," the Ryn said.

The Twi'lek's orange eyes shone. "Some of the best food

I've ever tasted was prepared by Ryn. Years ago I ran with a couple of your people in the Outer Rim—"

"Ten-*shun!*" a human voice rang out.

Everyone in earshot snapped to, as a pair of human officers in uniform approached the hut. The prisoners had abandoned all notions of rank, but if it could be said that anyone was in command, it was these two—Captain Judder Page and Major Pash Cracken.

Hailing from important worlds—Page from Corulag, Cracken from Contruum—they had much in common. Both were scions of influential families, and both had trained at the Imperial Academy before defecting to the Rebel Alliance during the Galactic Civil War. Page, the more unremarkable looking of the pair, had established the Katarn Commandos; and Cracken—still ruggedly handsome and muscular in midlife—Cracken's Flight Group. Both had managed to become as fluent in Yuuzhan Vong as Subaltern S'yito was in Basic.

"Make room for the major and the captain at the front of the line," the same human who had announced them ordered.

The officers deferred. "We'll eat after the rest of you have had your share," Page said for the two of them.

"Please, sirs," several of those on line insisted.

Page and Cracken exchanged resigned looks and nodded. Cracken accepted a wooden bowl that had been fashioned by one of the prisoners, and moved to the head of the food line, where the Ryn was stirring the gruelish contents of a large yorik coral container.

"We appreciate your bringing this," Cracken said. His eyes were pale green, and his flame-red hair was shot through with gray, adding a measure of distinction to his aristocratic features.

The Ryn smiled slyly. Plunging a ladle deep into the gruel, he bent over the pot, encouraging Cracken to do the same in order to get his bowl filled. When Cracken's left ear was within whisper distance of the Ryn's mouth, the being said, "Ryn one-one-five, out of Vortex."

Cracken hid his surprise. He had learned about the Ryn syndicate only two months earlier, during a briefing on Mon Calamari, which had become Galactic Alliance headquarters following the fall of Coruscant. An extensive spy network, comprised of not only Ryn but also members of other, equally displaced species, the syndicate made use of secret space routes and hyperlanes blazed by the Jedi, to provide safe passage for individuals and covert intelligence.

"You have something for us?" Cracken asked quietly while the Ryn was ladling gruel into the wooden bowl.

The Ryn's forward-facing eyes darted between the container and Cracken's lined face. "Chew carefully, Major," he said, just loud enough to be heard. "Expect the unexpected."

Cracken straightened, whispering the message to Page, who in turn whispered it to the Bith behind him in line. Surreptitiously, the message was relayed again and again, until it had reached the last of the one hundred or so prisoners.

By then Cracken, Page, and some of the others had carried their bowls to a crude table, around which they squatted and began to finger the gruel carefully into their mouths, glancing at one another in understated anticipation.

At the same time, three prisoners moved to the doorway to keep an eye out for guards. The Yuuzhan Vong hadn't installed villips or other listening devices in the huts, but warriors like S'yito, who displayed obvious curiosity about the enemy, had made it a habit to barge in without warning, and conduct sweeps and searches.

A Devaronian hunkered down across the table from Page made a gagging sound. Faking a cough, he gingerly removed an object from his slash of dangerous mouth, and glanced at it in secret.

Everyone stared at him in expectation.

"Gristle," he said, lifting beady, disappointed eyes. "At least I think that's what it is."

The prisoners went back to eating, the tension mounting as their fingers began to scrape the bottoms of their bowls.

Then Cracken bit down on something that made his molars ache. He brought his left hand to his mouth, and used his tongue to push the object into his cupped hand. The center of attention, he opened his hand briefly, recognizing the object at once. Keeping the thing palmed, he set it on the table and slid it to his left, where, in the blink of an eye, it disappeared under the right hand of Page.

"Holowafer," the captain said softly, without taking a second look. "It'll display only once. We're going to have to be quick about it."

Cracken nodded his chin to the horned Devaronian. "Find Clak'dor, Garban, and the rest of that crew, and bring them here quickest."

The Devaronian stood up and hurried out the doorway.

Page ran his hand over his bearded face. "We're going to need a place to display the data. We can't risk doing it in the open."

Cracken thought for a moment, then turned to the long-bearded Bothan to his right. "Who's the one with the sabacc deck?"

The alien's fur rippled slightly. "That'd be Coruscant."

"Tell him we need him."

The Bothan nodded and made for the doorway. As word spread through the hut, the prisoners began to converse loudly, as cover for what was being said by those who remained at the table. The Ryn banged his ladle against the side of the pot, and several of the prisoners distributed fruits to the others by tossing them through the air, as if in a game of catch.

"How are things in the yard?" Page asked the lookouts at the doorway.

"Coruscant's coming, sir. Also Clak'dor's bunch."

"The guards?"

"No one's paying any mind."

Coruscant, a tall, blond-haired human, entered grinning and fanning a deck of sabacc cards he'd fashioned from squares of leather. "Did I hear right that someone's interested in a game?"

Page motioned for everyone to form a circle in the center of the hut, and to raise the noise level. The guards had grown accustomed to the boisterous activity that would sometimes erupt during card games, and Page was determined to provide a dose of the real thing. A dozen prisoners broke out in song. The rest conversed jocularly, giving odds and making bets.

The human gambler, three Bith, and a Jenet were passed

through the falsely jubilant crowd to the center of the circle, where Page and Cracken were waiting with the holowafer.

Coruscant began to dole out cards.

Highly evolved humanoids, Bith were deep thinkers and skillful artists, with an ability to store and sift through immense amounts of data. The Jenet, in contrast, was short and rodentlike, but possessed of an eidetic memory.

When Page was satisfied that the inner circle was effectively sealed off, he crouched down, as if to join in the game. "We'll get only one chance at this. You sure you can do it?"

The Jenet's muzzle twitched in amusement, and he fixed his red eyes on Page. "That's why you chose us, isn't it?"

Page nodded. "Then let's get to it."

Deftly, Page set the small wafer on the plank floor and activated it with the pressure of his right forefinger. An inverted cone of blue light projected upward, within which flared a complex mathematical equation Page couldn't begin to comprehend, much less solve or memorize. As quickly as the numbers and symbols appeared, they disappeared.

Then the wafer itself issued a sibilant sound, and liquefied.

He had his mouth open to ask the Bith and the Jenet if they had been successful in committing the equation to memory, when S'yito and three Yuuzhan Vong guards stormed into the hut and shouldered their way to the center of the circle, their coufee daggers unsheathed and their serpentine amphistaffs on high alert, ready to strike or spit venom as needed.

"Cease your activities at once," the subaltern bellowed.

The crowd fanned out slowly and began to quiet down. Coruscant and the ostensible card players moved warily out of striking range of the amphistaffs.

"What's the problem, Subaltern?" Page asked in Yuuzhan Vong.

"Since when do you engage in games of chance at nourishment hour?"

"We're wagering for second helpings."

S'yito glared at him. "You trifle with me, human."

Page shrugged elaborately. "It's my job, S'yito."

The subaltern took a menacing step forward. "Put an end

to your game—and your singing . . . or we'll remove the parts of you that are responsible for it."

The four Yuuzhan Vong turned and marched from the hut.

"That guy has absolutely no sense of humor," Coruscant said when he felt he could.

Everyone in the vicinity of Page and Cracken looked to the two officers.

"The data has to reach Alliance command," Cracken said.

Page nodded in agreement. "When do we send them out?"

Cracken compressed his lips. "Prayer hour."

TWO

Shortly before its public immolation in a fire pit located just outside the prison gates, a silver protocol droid that had belonged briefly to Major Cracken had put the odds of escaping from Selvaris at roughly a million to one. But the droid hadn't known about the Ryn syndicate, or about what the clandestine group had set in motion on the planet, even before the first chunks of yorik coral had been sown.

Cracken, Page, and the others knew something else, as well: that hope flourished in the darkest of places, and that while the Yuuzhan Vong could imprison or kill them, there wasn't a soldier in the camp who wouldn't have risked his or her life to see even one of their number survive to fight another day.

First sunrise was an hour away, and Cracken, Page, the three Bith, and the Jenet were crouched at the entrance to a tunnel the prisoners had excavated with hands, claws, and whatever tools they had been able to fabricate or steal during the excavation of the fire pit, in which several dozen droids had been ritually slagged by the camp's resident priests.

Every prisoner in the hut was awake, and many hadn't slept a wink all night. They watched silently from the flattened fronds and grasses that were their beds, wishing they could voice a personal *good luck* to the four who were about to embark on what seemed a hopeless enterprise. Lookouts had been posted at the doorway. The light was gauzy, and the air was blessedly cool. Outside the hut, the chitterings and stridulations of jungle life were reaching a fevered crescendo.

"You want to go over any of it?" Cracken asked in a whisper.

"No, sir," the four answered in unison.

Cracken nodded soberly.

"Then may the Force be with all of you," Page said for everyone in the hut.

The cramped entrance to the tunnel was concealed by Cracken's own bed of insect-ridden palm fronds. Below a removable grate, the hand-hewn shaft fell into utter darkness. The secret passageway had been started by the first captives to be imprisoned on Selvaris, and had been enlarged and lengthened over the long months by successive groups of new arrivals. Progress had often been measured in centimeters, as when the diggers had struck a mass of yorik coral that had taken root in the sandy soil. But now the tunnel extended beneath the prison wall and the senalak grasses beyond, to just inside the distant tree line.

His facial fur blackened with charcoal, the gaunt Jenet was the first to worm his way into the hole. When the three Bith had bellied in behind him, the entrance was closed and covered over.

What little light there had been disappeared.

The nominal leader of the would-be escapees, the Jenet had been captured on Bilbringi, during a raid on an enemy installation. His fellow captives knew him as Thorsh, although on his homeworld of Garban a list of his accomplishments and transgressions would have been affixed to the name. Reconnaissance was his specialty, so he was no stranger to darkness or tight spots, having infiltrated many a Yuuzhan Vong warren and grashal on Duro, Gyndine, and other worlds. The Selvaris tunnel felt comfortably familiar. The Bith had it harder because of their size, but they were a well-coordinated species, with memory and olfactory abilities that rivaled Thorsh's own.

Indeterminate minutes of muted crawling brought them to the first of a series of confined right-angle turns, where the tunnelers had been forced to detour around an amorphous mass of yorik coral. To Thorsh the detour meant that the team was directly under the prison wall itself. Now it was just a matter of negotiating the long stretch beneath the senalaks the Yuuzhan Vong had cultivated outside the perimeter.

Thorsh knew better than to relax, but his continued vigilance hardly mattered.

In the space of a local week, senalak roots had penetrated the roof of the poorly braced tunnel, and the convoluted roots were every bit as barbed as the strands released by the knee-high stalks themselves.

For meters at a stretch there was simply no avoiding them.

The barbs shredded the thin garments the four had been wearing when captured, and left deep, bleeding furrows in the flesh of their backs.

Thorsh muttered a curse at each encounter, but the Bith—ever careful about displaying emotion—endured the pain in silence.

The brutal crawl ended where the tunnel sloped upward at the far edge of the senalak field. Shortly the team emerged inside the buttressed base of an enormous hardwood. The thick-trunked tree bore a striking resemblance to the gnarl-trees native to Dagobah, but was in fact a different species altogether. One hundred meters away, the prison wall glowed softly green with bioluminescence. Two sleepy guards occupied the closest watchtower, their amphistaffs stiff as spears, and a third could be glimpsed in the adjacent tower. Those warriors who weren't elsewhere within the walls of the compound were attending prayer services at the temple.

The bold incantations of the latter wafted through the jungle, counterpoint to the riotous calls of birds and insects. Strands of mist meandered through the treetops like apparitions.

One of the Bith elbowed his way alongside Thorsh, and aimed his slender forefinger to the west. "There."

Thorsh sniffed repeatedly and nodded. "There."

Deeper into the trees, ankle-high mud gave way to swamp, and it wasn't long before the four were wading waist-deep through black water. They made scarcely half a kilometer before an alarm sounded. Neither the howling of a siren nor the raucous bleating of a starship's klaxon, the alarm took the form of a prolonged and intensifying drone that arrived from all directions.

"Sentinel beetles," one of the Bith said in a grating voice.

Small creatures that resembled turfhoppers, sentinels reacted to intruders or danger with rapid beating of their serrated wings. The species was not native to Selvaris, or indeed to any other world in the galaxy.

Thorsh's clawed feet dug into the thick organic muck, and he quickened his pace, waving for the Bith to follow him.

"Hurry!"

The need for caution was behind them. They flailed through the dark, scum-covered water, stumbling forward, slamming into stilt roots, their uniforms snagging on quilled branches and sinuous, coarse-barked lianas. The droning of the sentinel beetles modulated to a deafening buzz, and the harnessed beams of lambent crystal illuminators played and crisscrossed overhead.

From the direction of the prison came the ferocious barking of bissops, the Yuuzhan Vong lizard-hounds. And something had taken to the air: a coralskipper gunship, or one of the seabirdlike fliers known as a tsik vai.

A loud whining split the sky, and the four escapees submerged themselves in the filmy water to avoid detection. Thorsh surfaced a long moment later, dripping water and gasping for air. The baying of the bissops was louder, and now the sound of nimble footfalls and angry voices cut through the humid air.

The temple was emptying; search parties were being organized.

Thorsh stood to his full height, spurring everyone into motion once more.

They slipped and slid, and otherwise fought their way through dense vegetation to the eastern bank of the wide estuary. By then Selvaris's primary was cresting the horizon. Long, horizontal rays of rose-tinted sunlight streaked through the trees, saturating the evanescing mist with color. Making haste for the water, one of the Bith sank to his waist in the liquid sand.

It took the combined strength of all three of his teammates to yank him free, and more time than they had to spare.

The coralskipper reappeared, rocketing out over the estuary and loosing molten projectiles into the jungle. Fireballs

mushroomed above the treetops, sending thousands of nesting creatures into frantic flight.

"Captain Page never promised this was going to be easy,"
Thorsh said.

"Or dry," the quicksand-covered Bith added.

Thorsh's long nose twitched, and his keen eyes scanned
the opposite shoreline. "We're not far now." He indicated a
bird island in the middle of the estuary. "There."

They plunged into the brackish water and began to swim
for their lives. The morning sky was black with frightened
birds. The coralskipper made another pass, forging through
the airborne chaos. Bird bodies plummeted, slapping the
surface of the calm water and tinting it red.

Thorsh and the others scrambled onto the island's narrow
beach. They picked themselves up and sprinted for cover,
squirming into the island's snarl of skeletal trees and thorny
bushes. They stopped frequently to get their bearings. The
Bith's olfactory organs were located in the parallel skinfolds
of their cheeks, but it was Thorsh's long nose that directed
them straight to what the Ryn had hidden months earlier: two
aged swoops, camouflaged by a mimetic tarpaulin.

The repulsorlift swoopbikes were more engine than chas-
sis, with sloping front ends and high handgrips. These two
lacked safety harnesses, and their fairings were incomplete.
Both were built for single pilots, but the saddlelike seats
were long enough to accommodate passengers—assuming
one was crazy enough to climb aboard.

Or assuming that one had a choice.

Thorsh straddled the rustier of the pair, and began to throw
priming and ignition switches. Reluctantly, the swoop's engine shuddered to life, idling erratically at first, but gradually
smoothing out.

"We're juiced!" he said.

One of the Bith perched behind Thorsh on the long seat.
The shorter of his two comrades was appraising the saddle
of the other swoop.

"Coordinates for the extraction point should be loaded in
the navicomputer," Thorsh said, shouting to be heard above
the throb of the repulsorlift engines.

"Coming up on the display now," the Bith pilot said.

Clearly, the third Bith had grave misgivings about mounting the swoop, but his doubts disappeared when the coralskipper grazed the treetops, searching for signs of the escapees.

Thorsh waited for the wedge-shaped assault craft to pass before saying, "We're better off splitting up. We'll rendezvous at the rally point."

"Last one there . . . ," his passenger started to say, only to let his words trail off.

The Bith pilot revved the swoop's engine. "Let's hope for a tie."

"The game is effectively over," C-3PO told Han Solo. "I suggest that you surrender the rest of your players now, rather than risk further humiliation."

"Surrender?" Han jerked his thumb at the golden protocol droid. "Who's he think he's talking to?"

Leia Organa Solo raised her brown eyes from the game table to glance at her husband. "I have to admit, things do look pretty bad."

C-3PO agreed. "I'm afraid you can't win, Captain Solo."

Han scratched his head absently, and continued to study the playing field. "That's not the first time someone's told me that."

The three of them were seated at the circular dejarik table in the forward hold of *Millennium Falcon*. The table was in fact a hologram projector, with a checkered surface etched in concentric circles of green and gold. At the moment it was displaying six holomonster pieces, some legendary, some modeled after actual creatures, with names that sounded more like sneezes than words.

Squatting on the grated portion of the compartment deck sat Cakhmaim and Meewalh, Leia's Noghri protectors. Agile bipeds with hairless gray skin and pronounced cranial ridges, they were unnervingly predatory in appearance, but their loyalty to Leia knew no bounds. In the long war against the Yuuzhan Vong, several Noghri had already given their lives to safeguard the woman they still sometimes referred to as "Lady Vader."

"Don't tell me that you are actually contemplating a move?" C-3PO said.

Han looked at him askance. "What do I look like I'm doing—stargazing?"

"But, Captain Solo—"

"Quit rushing me, I tell you."

"Really, Threepio," Leia intervened in false sincerity. "You have to give him time to think."

"But Princess Leia, the game timer is nearing the end of its cycle."

Leia shrugged. "You know how he is."

"Yes, Princess, I know how he is."

Han glared at the two of them. "What is this, some kind of tag-team match?"

C-3PO started. "Certainly not. I'm merely—"

"Remember," Han said, thrusting his finger out, "it's not over till the Hutt squeals."

C-3PO looked to Leia for explanation. "The Hutt squeals?"

Han cupped his scarred chin in his hand and took in the board. Early on he had lost a broad-shouldered Kintan strider to C-3PO's venomous, corrugated k'lor'slug; then a pincer-handed ng'ok to the droid's lance-wielding Socorran monnok.

Han's quadrant of the board still showed a hunchbacked, knuckle-dragging, green-hided Mantellian savrip, and a bulbous-bodied ghhhk. But his alloy opponent had not only a claw-handed, trumpet-snouted grimtassh and a four-legged, sharp-toothed houjix, but also two rainbow-skinned Alder-aanian molators waiting in the wings. Unless Han could do something to prevent it, C-3PO was going to send the grim-tassh to the board's center space and win the game.

Then it hit him.

A sinister laugh escaped his closed lips and his eyes sparkled.

Leia regarded him for a moment. "Uh-oh, Threepio. I don't like the sound of that laugh."

Han shot her a look. "Since when?"

"I understand completely, Princess," C-3PO said, on alert. "But, really, I don't see that there's anything he can do at this point."

Han's fingers activated a series of control buttons built into the rim of the table. With Leia and C-3PO gazing intently at the board, the hulking Mantellian savrip sidestepped to the left, took hold of the ghhhk—Han's other remaining piece—and held the suddenly screeching creature high overhead.

C-3PO might have blinked if he had eyes in place of photoreceptors. "But . . . but you've attacked your own piece." He turned to Han. "Captain Solo, if this is some kind of trick to distract me, or some attempt to instill compassion—"

"Save your compassion for someone who needs it," Han cut in. "Like it or not, that's my move."

C-3PO watched the squealing, seemingly betrayed ghhhk struggle in the savrip's viselike grip. "Most infuriating creature," he said. "Still, a victory is a victory."

The droid lowered his hands to the control panel and commanded the grimtassh to advance to the center. But no sooner did the snouted creature take a step than Han's savrip tightened his hold on the ghhhk, squeezing the hapless thing so hard that holodrops of the ghhhk's much-prized skin oil began to drip onto the playing field, creating a virtual puddle. Tasked, C-3PO's grimtassh continued to move forward, only to slip on the ghhhk's skin oil and fall hard onto its back, cracking its triangular-shaped head on the checkered board and deresolving.

"Ha!" Han said, clapping his hands once, then rubbing them together in anticipation. "Now who's losing?"

"Oh, Threepio," Leia said sympathetically, hiding a smile behind her hand.

C-3PO's photoreceptors were riveted to the board, but disbelief was evident in his response. "What? What? Is that permitted?" He looked up from the table. "Princess Leia, that move can't possibly be legal!"

Han leaned forward, his eyebrows beetled. "Show me where the rules say different."

C-3PO stammered. "Bending the rules is one thing, but this . . . this is a flagrant violation not only of the rules, but also of proper game etiquette! At the very least, you have performed a suspect move, and very likely a rogue one!"

"Good choice of words, Threepio," Leia said.

Han leaned away from the table, interlocking his hands behind his head and whistling a taunting melody.

"I suggest we allow Princess Leia to be the final judge," C-3PO said.

Han made a sour face. "Ah, you're just a sore loser."

"A sore loser? Why, I never—"

"Admit it and I'll go easy on you for the rest of the game."

C-3PO summoned as much indignation as his protocol programming allowed. "You have my assurance that I've no need to emerge victorious from each engagement. Whereas you, on the other hand—"

Han laughed sharply, startling the droid to silence. "Threepio, if I've told you once I've told you a thousand times: you always have to be ready for surprises."

"Pompous man," C-3PO said. When Cakhmaim and Meewalh added their gravelly comments and guttural laughs to the merriment, he threw up his hands in a gesture of defeat. "Oh, what's the use!"

Abruptly, a warning tone sounded from the engineering station across the hold. The Noghri shot to their feet, but Leia propelled herself from the dejarik table's arc of padded bench and beat both of them to the communications display.

Han watched expectantly from the game board.

"A surprise?" he asked when Leia turned from the displays.

She shook her head. "The signal we've been waiting for."

Han rushed from the table and followed Leia into the starboard ring corridor, where he nearly tripped over a pair of knee-high boots he had left on the step. Early in his career as a smuggler, the *Falcon* had been the only home he knew, and now—this past year especially—it had become the only home Han and Leia knew. Whether in their living quarters or in the forward hold, personal items were strewn about, waiting to be picked up and put away. The mess was just that, in desperate need of cleaning—maybe even fumigating. And indeed the dented and bruised exterior of the old freighter, with its mishmash of primers and fuse-welded borrowed parts, was beginning to resemble that of a house, well loved and lived in but too long neglected.

Han slid to a halt just short of the connector that accessed the cockpit, and swung to the Noghri.

"Cakhmaim, get to the dorsal gun turret. And this time remember to lead your targets—even though I know it goes against your grain. Meewalh, I'm going to need you here to help our packages get safely aboard."

In the outrigger cockpit, with its claustrophobic surround of blinking instruments, Leia was already cinched into the copilot's chair, both hands busy activating the *Falcon*'s start-up systems and console displays. Han slid into the pilot's seat, strapping in with one hand and throwing overhead toggles with the other.

"Can we locate them yet?"

"They're on the move," Leia said. "But I've got a fix on them."

Han leaned over to study one of the display screens. "Lock their coordinates into the tracking computer, and let's get the topographic sensors on-line."

Leia swiveled to the comm board, her hands moving rapidly over the controls. "Take her up," she said a moment later.

Awakened from what amounted to a nap, the YT-1300's engines powered up. Han clamped his hands on the control yoke and lifted the ship out of its hiding place, an impact crater on the dark side of Selvaris's puny moon. He fed power to the sublight drives and steered a course around the misshapen orb. Green, blue, and white Selvaris filled the wrap-around viewport.

Han watched Leia out of the corner of his eye. "Hope you remembered to look both ways."

Leia shut her eyes briefly. "We're safe."

Han smiled to himself. The Yuuzhan Vong couldn't be sensed through the Force, but Leia had never had any problem sensing trouble.

"I just don't want to be accused of making any more illegal moves."

She looked at him. "Only daring ones."

Han continued to watch her secretly. Through all the rough-and-tumble years, her face had not lost its noble beauty. Her skin was as flawless now as it had been when Han had first set eyes on her, in a detention cell, of all places. Her long hair retained its sheen; her eyes, their deep, inviting warmth.

Han and Leia had experienced some troubled months following Chewbacca's death. But she had waited him out; and wherever they traveled now, no matter how much danger they put themselves in—mostly at Han's instigation—they were completely at home with each other. To Han, each and every action felt right. He had no yearning to be anywhere but where he was—with his beloved partner.

It was a sappy thought, he told himself. But undeniably true.

As if reading his thoughts, Leia turned slightly in his direction, lifting her chin a bit to show him a dubious look. "You're in a good mood for someone setting out on a dangerous rescue mission."

Han made light of the moment. "Beating Threepio at dejarik has made a new man of me."

Leia tilted her head. "Not too new, I hope." She placed one hand atop his, on the yoke, and with the other traced the raised scar on his chin. "It's taken me thirty years to get used to the old you."

"Me, too," he said, without humor.

Exhaust ports ablaze, the *Falcon* rolled through a sweeping turn and raced for Selvaris's binary brightened transitor.

THREE

Bent low over the swoopbike's high handgrips, Thorsh threaded the rocketing vessel through concentrations of saplings and opportunistic Yuuzhan Vong plants, under looping vines, and over the thick trunks of toppled trees. He hugged the fern-covered ground when and where he could, as much for safety's sake as to spare his spindly passenger any further torture from thorned vines, sharp twigs, and the easily disturbed hives of barbflies and other bloodsuckers.

But Thorsh's best efforts weren't enough.

"When do we get to switch places?" the Bith asked over the howl of the repulsorlift.

Thorsh knew that the question had been asked in jest, and so replied in kind. "Hands at your sides and no standing on the seat!"

Taking into account only the difference in heights, the Bith should have been the one in the saddle, with Thorsh scrunched down behind him, fingers clasped on the underside of the long seat. But Thorsh was the more experienced pilot, having flown swoops on several reconnaissance missions where speeders hadn't been available. His large wedge-shaped feet weren't well suited to the footpegs, and he had to extend his arms fully to grasp the handgrip controls, but his keen eyes more than made up for those shortcomings, even when streaming with tears, as they were now.

Thorsh kept to the thick of the large island, where the branches of the tallest trees intertwined overhead and provided cover. The swoop was still running smoothly, except when he leaned it hard to the right, which for some reason caused the repulsorlift to sputter and strain. He could hear the other swoop—to the east and somewhat behind him—

weaving a path through equally dense growth. The four escapees would have made better progress out over the estuary, but without the tree cover they would be easy prey for coralskippers. One skip had already completed two return passes, paying out plasma missiles at random, and hoping for a lucky strike.

The morning air was thick with the smell of burning foliage.

Flat out, the swoop tore from the underbrush into a treeless expanse of salt flats, pink and blinding white, the nighttime sleeping grounds for flocks of Selvaris's long-legged wading birds. Determined to reach cover before the coralskipper showed up again, Thorsh gave the accelerator a hard twist and banked the swoop for the nearest stand of trees.

Thorsh had just reentered the jungle when a clamor began to build in the canopy. His first thought was that another coralskipper had joined the pursuit. But there was a different quality to the sound—an eagerness absent in the deadly sibilance of a coralskipper.

Thorsh felt his rider sit up straighter on the seat, in defiance of the hazards posed by overhanging branches.

"Is that what I think it is?" the humanoid asked.

"We'll know soon enough," Thorsh yelled back.

Again he twisted the accelerator. Wind screamed over the swoop's inadequate fairing, forcing another flood of tears from his eyes. But his actions were in vain. The objects responsible for the escalating tumult passed directly overhead, silencing the racket of the swoop, then outracing it.

"Lav peq!" the Bith screamed.

Thorsh knew the term; it was the Yuuzhan Vong name for netting beetles, voracious and meticulous versions of the winged sentinels that had roused the prison guards. Lav peq were capable of creating webs between trees, bushes, or just about any type of barked foliage. Typically the beetles arrived in successive fronts, the first fashioning anchor lines, and those that followed feeding on bark and other organics to replenish the fibers needed to complete the filigree. A well-constructed web could ensnare or at least slow down a human-sized being. The strands themselves were tenaciously sticky, though not as adhesive as the enemy's blorash jelly.

The Bith's hunch was verified as the swoop raced through

the vanguard wave of the swarm. Within seconds the down-sloping front cowling was spattered with smashed beetle corpses. Thorsh plucked several from his fur-covered forehead and threw them aside. Just ahead, thousands of lav peq were plummeting into the jungle, tearing through the leafy canopy like hailstones. Thorsh ground his teeth and lowered his head. As strong as the strands were, they were no match for a swoop in the right hands.

Fifty meters away the first web was already taking shape. Thorsh squinted in misgiving. More tightly woven than any he had seen on other worlds, the web actually obscured the trees. It took only a moment to realize that Selvaris's species of netting beetle was special. While half the swarm was flying horizontally at various levels, the other half was flying in vertical rows. The result was a warp-and-weft weave—a veritable curtain that, for all Thorsh knew, could snare the swoop as easily as a spiderweb might a nightfly.

Extending his legs behind him, he flattened himself over the surging engine. With a distressed cry, the Bith followed suit, pressing himself to Thorsh's back.

Thorsh cranked the accelerator for all it was worth, aiming for what he thought might be an area of relatively few trees. The swoop ripped through the webs at better than two hundred kilometers per hour, each successive curtain parting with loud cleaving sounds that sometimes resembled screams. Rear-guard beetles struck the cowling with the force of malleable bullets, and the Bith yelped in pain time and again. The swoop wobbled and the repulsorlift began to howl in protest. Thorsh fought to hold on to the handgrips as they were yanked from side to side by the viscous strands. He risked an ascent, only to learn the hard way that the situation was even more perilous in the upper reaches of the trees, where the branches fanned out and the leaves were home to clouds of insatiable needle fliers.

Refusing to give a centimeter, he demanded every last bit of power from the struggling machine. Then, all at once, the swoop tore through the final web. Sticky strands cooked on the superheated engine, sending out an acrid smell. Thorsh coughed strands from his throat and pawed others away from his stinging eyes.

He brought the swoop to a halt just long enough to clear the exhaust ports and fan housing. His swearing passenger might have been wearing a long white wig. Thorsh had his right hand back on the accelerator when a pained shriek erupted from the jungle, punctuating the cacophony of bird-calls. He heard a familiar roar, and not a moment later the second swoop bobbed into view, bearing only the pilot.

"The nets got him!" the Bith pilot shouted over the irregular throb of a choked engine. He twisted the accelerator to keep the swoop idling. "I'm going back for him!"

Thorsh spit web from his mouth and scowled. "Don't be a fool."

"He's alive—"

"Better that you are," Thorsh interrupted. He jerked his bearded chin to the west. "The estuary. Get going!"

Thorsh spurred the swoop through a quick circle and darted off into the trees, the Bith hanging on to what was left of the Jenet's flight jacket. Punching through the dense jungle that grew along the shore of the island, they found themselves back in the blinding light of Selvaris's double suns. Coaxing more speed from the rapidly failing engine, pilot and passenger leaned the swoop through a sweeping turn that carried them out over brackish water, inky with organics leached from the trees. They soared at top speed a few meters above the calm surface, racing past narrow, meandering channels of pellucid fresh water, bubbled up from the planet's underground and teeming with brilliantly colored fish.

From the far shore came the urgent woofing and snarling of bissop hounds, galloping through swamps and across berms of scalpel grass. The harsh barks were accompanied by the war cries of Yuuzhan Vong chase teams, running behind the pack. Thorsh banked just in time to avoid a horde of thud and razor bugs that whirled out of the trees, passing within centimeters of the swoop and tearing into the opposite shoreline.

Drawn by the commotion, schools of sharp-toothed predators, showing multifinned backs and serrated tails, leapt from the water to gorge on the airborne weapon bugs. Wide-winged raptors with huge wingspans left the fungus-filled cavities of dying trees to glide down and grab whatever bugs the aquatic behemoths missed.

Thorsh pulled at the handgrips and sent the swoop into a steep climb. The saline water grew more agitated beneath them as the mouth of the estuary came into view, a line of white where curling waves broke against the marshy shore. Hundreds of white-cliffed islets, straight as towers and draped with vegetation, rose from out of the aquamarine ocean. On the horizon a volcano mounded from the water, great clouds of smoke billowing from its crater and bleeding a thick river of lava that turned part of the sea to steam.

Thorsh scanned the otherwise clear sky for signs of the coralskipper. A kilometer away to the east, the other swoop was paralleling him. Gaining altitude, the two machines sped out over the breaking waves, making for the narrow channel that separated the islets closest to shore.

"Heads up!" the Bith said into Thorsh's right ear. His long-fingered hand shot out, indicating an object in the western sky.

Thorsh tracked it and nodded, muttering a curse.

The Yuuzhan Vong called it a tsik vai. Reminiscent of a seabird, it was an atmospheric search craft, its neck sac inflated and bright red as a signal to other craft in the area. Powered by a gravity-sensitive dovin basal, the monstrosity had a transparent blister cockpit, flexible wings, and gill analogs that made it whine in flight.

Thorsh threw his weight against the handgrips and leaned hard against the steering auxiliaries, slewing the swoop toward the closest island, intent on keeping as close to the white cliffs as he dared.

The tsik vai was not unnerved. It dived for its small prey, whining and releasing several thin, cablelike grasping tendrils.

Thorsh dropped back to the turbulent surface, swerved, and cut across the channel for the neighboring islet, running full out, a meter above the waves. The search craft was following him down, prepared to make another grab, when something nailed it from behind.

Thorsh and the Bith watched in bafflement as the tsik vai veered off course, one wing blown off, and spiraled out of control. It struck the sea with a loud splash, skipped twice on the waves, then crashed nose-first and began to sink. Out of the eastern sky, dazzled by sunlight, something large and dull-black was approaching at supersonic speed.

Another Yuuzhan Vong vessel, Thorsh decided, whose pilot had just shot down one of his own craft to get to the swoop.

Twitching the braking thrusters, he spun the swoop around in midair, hoping to race away from the mystery vessel before it could draw a bead on him. Even so, he waited for the fireballs to start falling. When they didn't, he glanced over his shoulder in time to see a twin-mandibled old freighter come streaking out of the cloudless sky. Thorsh felt crackling heat wash over him as the ship made a low, earsplitting, teeth-rattling pass, its dorsal laser cannon loosing green hyphens of energy at a trio of pursuing coralskippers.

The freighter signaled the swoops with a rocking motion, then banked into a long sweeping turn to the south.

"Looks like our ride's here!" Thorsh said.

"And in worse trouble than we are!"

A flurry of well-placed bursts from the freighter's top gunner caught the lead coralskipper head-on and sent it boiling into the sea.

The other two enemy craft continued to pummel the freighter with plasma missiles. Perhaps frustrated by the ship's seemingly impenetrable shields, one of the skip pilots took aim on the Bith-piloted swoop. Caught in midair by a single lava-hot projectile, the machine disappeared without a trace.

Thorsh clenched his jaws and steered the swoop for deeper water. The swoop was grazing the white crests of five-meter waves when something enormous rose from beneath the heaving surface.

"Cakhmaim's getting to be a pretty good shot," Han said over the sound of the reciprocating quad laser cannon. "Remind me to up his pay—or at least promote him."

Leia glanced at him from the copilot's chair. "From bodyguard to what—butler?"

Han pictured the Noghri in formal attire, setting meals in

front of Han and Leia in the *Falcon*'s forward cabin. His upper lip curled in delight, and he laughed shortly. "Maybe we should see how he does with the rest of these skips."

The YT-1300 was just coming out of her long turn, with Selvaris's double suns off to starboard and an active volcano dominating the forward view. Below, green-capped, sheer-sided islands reached up into the planet's deep blue sky, and the aquamarine sea seemed to go on forever. Two coral-skippers were still glued to the *Falcon*'s tail, chopping at it and holding position through all the insane turns and evasions, but so far the deflector shields were holding.

His large hands gripped on the control yoke, Han glanced at the console's locator display, where only one bezel was pulsing.

"Where'd the other swoop go?"

"We lost it," Leia said.

Han leaned toward the viewport to survey the undulating sea. "How could we lose—"

"No, I mean it's gone. One of the coralskippers took it out."

Han's eyes blazed. "Why, that—which one of 'em?"

Before Leia could answer, two plasma missiles streaked past the cockpit, bright as meteors and barely missing the starboard mandible.

"Does it matter?"

Han shook his head. "Where's the other swoop?"

Leia studied the locator display, then called up a map from the terrain sensor, which showed everything from the mouth of the estuary clear to the volcano. Her left forefinger tapped the screen. "Far side of that island."

"Any skips after it?"

A loud explosion buffeted the *Falcon* from behind.

"We seem to be the popular target," Leia said. "Just the way you like it."

Han narrowed his eyes. "You bet I do."

Determined to lure their pair of pursuers away from the swoop, he threw the freighter into a sudden ascent. When they had climbed halfway to the stars, he dropped the ship into a stomach-churning corkscrew. Pulling out sharply, he twisted the ship through a looping rollover, emerging from the combo headed in the opposite direction, with the two coralskippers in front of him.

He grinned at Leia. "Now who's in charge?"

She blew out her breath. "Was there ever any doubt?"

Han focused his attention on the two enemy craft. Over the long years, Yuuzhan Vong pilots faced with impossible odds had surrendered some of the suicidal resolve they had displayed during the early days of the war. Maybe word had come down from Supreme Overlord Shimrra or someone that discretion really was the better part of valor. Whatever the case, the pilots of the two skips Han was stalking apparently saw some advantage to fleeing rather than reengaging the ship their plasma missiles had failed to bring down. But Han wasn't content to send them home with their tails tucked between their legs—especially not after they had killed an unarmed swoop pilot he had come halfway across the galaxy to rescue.

"Cakhmaim, listen up," he said into his headset mike. "I'll fire the belly gun from here. We'll put 'em in the Money Lane and be done with them."

Money Lane was Han's term for the area where the quad lasers' firing fields overlapped. In emergency situations, both cannons could be fired from the cockpit, but the present situation didn't call for that. What's more, Han wanted to give Cakhmaim the chance to hone his firing technique. All Han and Leia had to do was help line up the shots.

From the way the coralskippers reacted to the *Falcon*'s sudden turnabout, Han could almost believe that the enemy pilots had been eavesdropping on his communication with the Noghri. The first skip—the more battered of the pair, showing charred blotches and deep pockmarks—poured on all speed, separating from his wingmate at a sharp angle. Smaller and faster, and seemingly helmed by a better pilot, the second skip shed velocity in an attempt to trick the *Falcon* into coming across his vector.

That was the skip that had taken out the swoop, Han decided, sentencing the pilot to be the first to feel the *Falcon*'s wrath.

Leia guessed as much, and immediately plotted an intercept course.

Exposed, the skip pilot went evasive, moving into the gunsights and out again, but with mounting panic as the *Falcon* settled calmly into kill position. The dorsal laser cannon was programmed to fire three-beam bursts that, all these years later, still had the ability to outwit the dovin basals of the older, perhaps more dim-witted coralskippers. While the enemy craft was quick to deploy a gravitic anomaly that engulfed the first and second beams, the third got through, blowing a huge chunk of yorik coral from the vessel's fantail. Han tweaked the yoke to place the skip in the Money Lane, and his left hand tightened on the trigger of the belly gun's remote firing mechanism. Sustained bursts from the twin cannons whittled the skip to half its size; then it blew, throwing pieces of coral wreckage in every direction.

"That's for the swoop pilot," Han said soberly. He turned his attention to the second skip, which, desperate to avoid a similar fate, was jinking and juking all over the sky.

Zipping through the showering remains of the first kill, the *Falcon* quickened up and pounced on the wildly maneuvering skip from above. The targeting reticle went red, and a target-lock tone filled the cockpit. Again the quad lasers rallied, catching the vessel with burst after burst until it disappeared in a nimbus of coral dust and white-hot gas.

Han and Leia hooted. "Nice shooting, Cakhmaim!" he said into the headset. "Score two more for the good guys."

Leia watched him for a moment. "Happy now?"

Instead of replying, Han pushed the yoke away from him, dropping the *Falcon* to within meters of the surging waves. "Where's the swoop?" he asked finally.

Leia was ready with the answer. "Come around sixty degrees, and it should be right in front of us."

Han adjusted course, and the swoop came into view, streaking over the surface, bearing two seriously dissimilar riders. In pursuit, and just visible beneath the surface, moved an enormous olive-drab triangle, trailing what appeared to be a lengthy tail.

Han's jaw dropped.

"What is that thing?" Leia said.

"Threepio, get in here!" Han yelled, without taking his eyes from the creature.

C-3PO staggered into the cockpit, clamping his hands on the high-backed navigator's chair to keep from being thrown off balance, as had too often happened.

Han raised his right hand to the viewport and pointed. "What is that?" he asked, enunciating every word.

"Oh, my," the droid began. "I believe that what we're looking at is a kind of boat creature. The Yuuzhan Vong term for it is *vangaak*, which derives from the verb 'to submerge.' Although in this case the verb has been modified to suggest—"

"Skip the language lesson and just tell me how to kill it!"

"Well, I would suggest targeting the flat dome, clearly visible on its dorsal surface."

"A head shot."

"Precisely. A head shot."

"Han," Leia interrupted. "Four more coralskippers headed our way."

Han manipulated levers on the console, and the *Falcon* accelerated. "We gotta work fast. Threepio, tell Meewalh to activate the manual release for the landing ramp. I'll be there in a flash."

Leia watched him undo the clasps of the crash webbing. "I take it you're not planning to land."

He kissed her on the cheek as he stood up. "Not if I can help it."

The swoop fought to maintain an altitude of eight meters, but that was enough to keep it from the snapping jaws of the Yuuzhan Vong vangaak that had almost snagged it on surfacing.

Thorsh might have opted to head inland if the Yuuzhan Vong search parties and their snarling beasts hadn't reached the marshy shore. Worse, four specks in the northern sky were almost certainly coralskippers, soaring in to reinforce the pair the YT-1300 was chasing. Instead, the Jenet had the swoop aimed for deeper water, out toward the volcano, where the waves mounded to a height of ten meters.

Thorsh and his rider could feel the sting of the saline spray on their scratched and bruised faces and hands. Behind them, the vangaak was rapidly closing the gap, but if it had weapons other than torpedo analogs it wasn't bringing them to bear. An unsettling vociferation from the Bith broke Thorsh's concentration.

"The vangaak's gone! It submerged!"

Thorsh didn't know whether to worry or celebrate. The vangaak put a quick end to his indecision. Breaching the surface in front of the swoop, the dull olive triangle spiked straight up out of the waves, venting seawater from blowholes on its dorsal side, and opening its tooth-filled mouth.

Thorsh demanded all he could from the swoop, climbing at maximum boost, but there was no escaping the reach of the creature.

He heard a surprised scream, then felt his flight jacket rip away. Lightened, the swoop ascended at greater speed, only to stall. Thorsh threw a distraught glance over his shoulder. The Bith was pinned between the vangaak's teeth, mouth wide in a silent scream, black eyes dull, Thorsh's jacket still clutched in his dexterous hands. But there wasn't time for despair or anger. The repulsorlift came back to life, and Thorsh veered away, even as he was falling.

A roar battered his eardrums, and suddenly the YT-1300 was practically alongside him, skimming the waves not fifty meters away. The quartet of coralskippers began firing from extreme range, their plasma projectiles cutting scalding trails through the whitecapped crests.

The old freighter's landing ramp was lowered from the starboard docking arm. It was clear what the ship's pilots had in mind. They were expecting him to come alongside and hurl himself onto the narrow incline. But Thorsh faltered. He knew the limitations of the swoop, and—more important— his own. With the coralskippers approaching and the vangaak submerged who-knew-where beneath the waves, it was unlikely that he could even reach the freighter in time. Additionally— and despite what were obviously military-grade deflector shields—the freighter was being forced to make slight vertical and horizontal adjustments, which only decreased Thorsh's chances of clambering aboard.

His grimace disappeared, and in its place came a look of sharp attentiveness.

As sole bearer of the secret intelligence contained in the

holowafer, he had to give it his best try. Tightening his grip, he banked for the sanctuary of the matte-black ship.

Crouched at the top of the extended ramp, Han peered down at the rushing water not twenty meters below. Wind and salt spray howled through the opening, blowing his hair every which way and making it difficult for him to keep his eyes open.

"Captain Solo," C-3PO said from the ring corridor. "Princess Leia wishes you to know that the swoop is approaching. Apparently the pilot feels confident that he can complete the transfer to *Millennium Falcon* without suffering too much internal damage or . . . perishing in the attempt."

Han threw the droid a wide-eyed look. "Perishing?"

"Certainly the odds are against him. If he were piloting a speeder bike, perhaps. But swoops are notorious for going out of control at the slightest provocation!"

Han nodded grimly. A former swoop racer, he knew that C-3PO was right. Taking in the situation now, he wondered if even he could make the jump.

"I'm going to the bottom!" he shouted.

C-3PO canted his golden head. "Sir?"

Han made a downward motion. "The bottom of the ramp."

"Sir, I have a bad feeling . . ."

The wind drowned out the rest of the droid's words. Han crabbed down to the base of the ramp, where he could hear the *Falcon*'s belly turret slicing through the agitated peaks of the waves. A distinctive throbbing sound captured his attention. The swoop was beginning to angle for the ramp. The pilot—a Jenet, of all species—took his right hand off the handgrips just long enough to signal Han with a wave. Considering that even that slight movement sent the swoop into a wobble, there was simply no way the Jenet would be able to let go completely—especially not with the *Falcon* adding to the turbulence of the sea itself.

Han reconsidered, then swung around to C-3PO.

"Threepio, tell Leia we're going with Plan B!"

The droid raised his hands to his head in distress. "Captain Solo, just the sound of that makes me worry!"

Han raised his forefinger. "Just tell Leia, Threepio. She'll understand."

"Plan B?"

"That was precisely my reaction," C-3PO said in an agitated voice. "But does anyone ever listen to my concerns?"

"Don't worry, Threepio, I'm sure Han knows what he's doing."

"That is hardly a comforting thought, Princess."

Leia swung back to the console and allowed her eyes to roam over the instruments. *Plan B,* she mused. *What can Han have in mind?* She placed him squarely in her thoughts, then smiled in sudden revelation.

Of course . . .

Her hands slid switches while she studied the displays. Then she sat away from the console in contemplation. Yes, she decided at last, she supposed it could be done—though it would mean relying largely on the attitude and braking thrusters, and hoping that they didn't stall or fail.

She looked over her shoulder at C-3PO, who had evidently followed her every move and manipulation.

"Tell Han I've got everything worked out."

"Oh, dear," the droid said, turning and exiting the cockpit. "Oh, dear."

The four coralskippers were closing fast, lobbing plasma missiles into the blustery stretch of water between the swoop and the freighter. Thorsh dipped his head instinctively as one fireball plunged into the waves not ten meters away. The ferocity of the impact geysered superheated water high into the air, and sent the swoop into a sustained wobble.

The freighter held to its course regardless, its top gunner keeping the coralskippers at bay with bursts of laserfire. A human male was crouched at the base of the landing ramp, his left arm wrapped around one of the telescoping hydraulic struts, and the fingers of his right hand making a gesture that on some worlds implied craziness on the part of its recipient. Just now, the twirling gesture meant something else entirely—though craziness was still a large part of it.

Thorsh swallowed hard, just thinking about what the pilots were about to attempt.

The human waved and scurried back up the ramp.

Decelerating slightly, Thorsh fell in behind the freighter, giving it wide berth. Above the strained throbbing of the swoop's repulsorlift, he heard the sudden reverberation of the YT-1300's retro- and attitude thrusters.

Then, scarcely surrendering momentum, the freighter began to rotate ninety degrees to starboard, bringing the boarding ramp almost directly in front of the tottering swoop.

"Take the jump!" Han said, mostly to himself. "Now!"

He was back in the pilot's chair, his hands tight on the control yoke, while Leia feathered the thrusters, cheating the *Falcon* through its quarter turn. Flying sideways, Han could see the coralskippers that had a second earlier been "behind" the ship, as well as the swoop, which was flying just off the blunt tip of the starboard docking arm. Hoping to minimize the chances of the pilot's overshooting his mark and smashing headlong into the bulkhead at the top of the ramp, Han adjusted the *Falcon*'s forward speed to match that of the swoop.

"He's accelerating!" Leia said.

"Threepio! Meewalh!" Han yelled over his right shoulder. "Our guest's coming aboard!" Glancing out the right side of the viewport, he saw the Jenet leap the swoop toward the ramp—the *Falcon*'s narrow but open mouth.

"Now!" he told Leia.

Deftly she fed power to the attitude thrusters, allowing the ship to complete a full clockwise rotation, even as a series of crashing sounds were echoing their way into the cockpit from the ring corridor.

Han winced and scrunched his shoulders with each *clang!* and *crash!*, mentally assessing the damage, but keeping his fingers crossed that the Jenet pilot was faring better than the interior of the docking arm.

No sooner did the ramp telltale on the console flash red—indicating that the docking arm had sealed tight—than Han yanked back on the control yoke, and the *Falcon* clawed its way into Selvaris's open sky, dodging volleys of molten fire from pursuing coralskippers. The quad laser replied with packets of cohesive light, brilliant green even against the backdrop of the heaving sea.

"Captain Solo, he's alive!" C-3PO called with dramatic relief. "We're all alive!"

Exhaling slowly, Han sank back into the seat, but without lifting his hands from the yoke. The coralskippers were already lagging behind when the *Falcon* rocketed over the summit of the volcano, straight through dense clouds of gritty smoke, climbing rapidly on a column of blue energy. The ship was halfway to starlight when the shaken Jenet appeared at the cockpit hatchway, one bare arm drapped over Meewalh's shoulders, the other around C-3PO's.

"You must have a hard head," Han said.

Grinning faintly, Leia looked at her husband. "He's not the only one."

Han glanced at her in false chagrin, then nodded his chin to the female Noghri. "Take our guest to the forward cabin and provide him with whatever he needs."

"I'll get the medpac," Leia said, leaving her chair. She set her headset on the console and looked at Han again. "Well, you did it."

"We," Han amended. Casually, he stretched out his arms. "You know, you're never too old for this sort of thing."

"You haven't outgrown it, that's for sure."

He studied her. "What, you have?"

She placed her right hand on his cheek. "You're a danger to yourself and everyone around you. But I do love you, Han."

He smiled broadly as Leia hurried from the cockpit.

FOUR

In a leafy bower that supplied the only pool of shade in the prison yard, Yuuzhan Vong commander Malik Carr permitted himself to be fanned by two reptoid Chazrach whose coral seed implants bulged from their foreheads.

Exceedingly tall, and thinner than most of his peers, Carr wore a bone-white skirt and patterned headcloth, the tassels of which were braided into his long hair, forming a tail that reached his waist. His glory days as a warrior were evidenced by the tattoos and scarifications that adorned his face and torso, though the most recent of them revealed for all to see that he had once held a more lofty rank. Even so, the prison guards were unfailing in the deference they showed him, out of respect for his steadfast devotion to the warrior caste, and to Yun-Yammka, the god of war.

Moving briskly and in anger, Subaltern S'yito approached the bower and snapped his fists to the opposite shoulders in salute. "Commander, the prisoners are awakening."

Carr looked over to the center of the yard, where Major Cracken, Captain Page, and some fifty other officers sat on their haunches, their hands secured behind them to wooden stakes that had been driven into the soft ground. Indeed, eyelids were fluttering; heads were nodding and swaying; lips were smacking in thirst. Selvaris's suns were almost directly overhead, and heat rose from the glaring sand in shimmering waves. Sweat had plastered the prisoners' soiled clothing to their scrawny bodies. It fell in fat drops from unshaved faces and matted fur.

Carr pushed himself upright and stepped into the unforgiving light, S'yito and a dozen warriors flanking him as he crossed the yard and stood with his hands on his hips in front of Cracken and Page. A priest joined him there, black head to toe with dried blood. Carr refrained from speaking until he was satisfied that the two prisoners were attentive and aware of their circumstance.

"I trust you enjoyed your naps," he began. "But look how long you've slept." He raised his face to the sky, pressing the inner edge of his right hand to his sloping forehead. "It is already midday."

He clasped his hands behind him and paced in front of the prisoners. "As soon as our sentinel beetles alerted us to the fact that some of you were outside the walls, I ordered that sensislugs be placed in all dormitories. It is never an agreeable experience to awaken from their sleep-inducing exhalations. The headaches, the nausea, the irritated nasal membranes . . . But I take some comfort in assuming that each of you luxuriated in pleasant dreams."

Stopping in front of bearded Page, he allowed some of his anger to show. "There will come a time when even your dreams won't provide you with escape, and you will look back on your days here as *blissful*."

On first learning of the predawn escape, Carr had nearly hung a tkun around his neck and prodded the living garrote to choke off his life. It was because of his failure at Fondor, more than three years earlier, that he had been demoted to the rank of commander and placed in charge of a prisoner-of-war camp at the remote edge of the invasion corridor. Worse, on distant Yuuzhan'tar, his former peers—Nas Choka, Eminence Harrar, Nom Anor—had been escalated and made members of Supreme Overlord Shimrra's court.

The prospect of further indignity had filled Carr with such self-loathing that he wasn't sure he could go on. Ultimately, however, he decided that if he was careful—and if he could keep Warmaster Nas Choka from hearing of the escape, or at the very least maintain that it was part of his plan to obtain information on local resistance groups—he might yet be released from the prison fate had fashioned for him.

Toward that end, he had been relieved to learn that the search parties he had dispatched had been partially successful. Two escapees had been killed, and a third had been captured. But a fourth had been whisked offworld by an enemy gunship.

Carr turned to S'yito. "Fetch the prisoner."

S'yito and two other warriors saluted and rushed off to the front gate. When they returned a moment later, they were dragging behind them a near-naked Bith, who, from the look of him, had fallen victim to a lav peq web. It pleased Carr no end to see expressions of surprised dismay flare on the faces of Page, Cracken, and the rest—even when those expressions were quickly transformed to scowls of hatred for the warriors who dropped the captive unceremoniously onto his face in the sand.

Carr stood over the Bith, whose hairless cranium was scratched and bleeding, and whose arms and legs were shackled.

"This one," Carr began, "along with three others who failed to survive . . ." Deliberately, he let his words trail off, if only to observe the effect of the lie on the assembled prisoners. "Well," he started again, "it's a pity, isn't it? So much effort expended for so little gain. Still, I can't help but be impressed. A well-engineered escape tunnel, carefully concealed flying machines . . . It's almost enough to make me forget what cowards you were for allowing yourselves to be captured in the first place."

He caught Page's eye and returned the stocky captain's glower. "You sicken me. You bring your spouses, your mates, your spawn with you into battle. You yield rather than fight to the last. You are crippled, yet you display no shame. You persist, but without clear purpose." He gestured to the Bith. "At least this one showed that he still retains some shred of courage."

Carr began to pace again. "But I admit to a certain curiosity. From what I know of the Bith species, he probably could have sustained himself in the jungle, subsisting on the natural foodstuffs I have permitted to be brought inside these walls. The question is, why would he choose to endanger the rest of you by his show of disobedience? It can only be that all of you conspired in his escape, perhaps to deliver a message of some import. Was such the case here?"

Carr waved his hand in dismissal. "We'll return to that

shortly. Beforehand, those who were truly responsible must be punished." He looked hard at Cracken and Page, then swung to S'yito. "Subaltern, order your warriors to form two rows. The smaller in one row; the taller in the other."

S'yito relayed the order in Yuuzhan Vong, and the warriors obeyed.

"Now," Carr continued, "the smaller warriors will execute the larger."

S'yito saluted, then nodded gravely to the warriors.

Those sentenced neither protested nor defended themselves as they were run through with coufees or struck with amphistaffs. One by one, they collapsed, their black blood draining into the sand. Tonguelike ngdins oozed from niches in the yorik coral walls to sop up what the porous ground didn't absorb.

Carr waited for the creatures to finish their work before striding over to the Bith and lowering himself to one knee. "After the act of courage you displayed, it would pain me to condemn you to an artless death. Why not escalate yourself in the last moments of your life by telling me why you tried to escape? Don't force me to extract the truth from you."

"Go ahead, Clak'dor," Pash Cracken said. "Tell them what you know!"

"He was following orders," Page added, gazing at Carr. "If you want to punish someone, punish us."

Carr almost grinned. "In due time, Captain. But I suspect that if you know what this one knows, you would have been the one to escape." He walked back to the bower. From beneath the seat, he pulled out the tkun he had nearly draped over his own neck that morning. Carrying the thick-bodied biot to the Bith, he arranged it around the prisoner's thin neck.

"This is a tkun," he explained for the benefit of the captives. "Normally it is a docile creature. When provoked, however, it registers its displeasure by coiling itself around the object on which it rests. Allow me to demonstrate . . ."

Carr prodded the tkun with his sharp forefinger.

Page and the others cursed and struggled in vain against their bindings.

The Bith began to gasp for air.

Carr watched dispassionately. "Unfortunately, the tkun cannot be persuaded to relax its grip once it has begun to contract. It has to be killed." Again he kneeled alongside the Bith. "Tell me why you were so desperate to leave this wonderful home we've provided for you. Recite the information you carry."

The Bith cocked his head to the side and spat at Carr.

"Not unexpected," Carr said, wiping his face. Again he prodded the tkun, which contracted its body. The Bith's black eyes bulged; his wrinkled face and dome of a head turned color. "I will gladly kill the tkun, if you tell me what I wish to know."

The Bith crawled forward, then flopped on the sand like a fish out of water.

Carr poked the tkun a third time.

A rasp issued from the Bith's throat; then he began to recite a formulaic series of numbers. Interested suddenly, Carr bent down to place his ear next to the Bith's lips. He glanced up at the priest. "What is this?"

"A calculation of some sort. A mathematical equation, perhaps."

"There it is," Page shouted. "He told you. Now kill that blasted thing before it's too late!"

Carr firmed his scarred lips. "Yes, he's telling me something—but what?"

The Bith repeated the formula.

"Is it a code?" Carr asked him. "Listen to your commanders. You've already been a hero. You've no further need to prove your dedication."

All color drained from the Bith's head, and a prolonged rattle escaped his puckered mouth.

Carr shook his head back and forth, as if in sadness. He drew a coufee from the belt that cinched his skirt and plunged it into the tkun, which straightened briefly, then died. Standing up, he looked directly at Page. "Your comrade appears to have taken your secret to his grave."

Page had murder in his eye, but Carr only shrugged and turned to S'yito.

"Escort the prisoners to the immolation pit where we incinerated their infernal machines. Fill it to the top, and make certain that they remain inside until midday tomorrow. We'll let Selvaris's suns sort out which of them are worthy of continued life."

A brigade of guards hurried into the yard. Carr waited in the shade for the prisoners to be hoisted to their feet. Then he followed the procession through the prison gate to the pit where the dozens of droids had been slagged.

"Subaltern, it's obvious that our captives had help engineering the escape," Carr said. "Take a complement of warriors and execute everyone in the surrounding villages."

S'yito saluted and trotted back through the bone gate.

Captain Page insisted on being the first to walk the wooden plank that extended out over the deep hole.

"A moment, Captain," Carr said, from the edge of the pit. "I offer you a final chance to pass this night on a bed of leaves rather than atop the skeletons of your droids."

Page snorted. "I'd sooner die."

Carr nodded pensively. "You'll die soon enough in any case."

Without another word Page dropped into darkness. Carr turned away from the pit and set out for his grashal.

A code, he told himself.

He was certain of that much. But, deciphered, what information would it reveal? He gazed at the blinding sky, wondering where the rescue ship was bound.

FIVE

Proximity alarms hooted insistently in the cockpit of the *Millennium Falcon*. Irritated by the distraction, Han muted the speakers, while Leia concentrated on making certain that the ship steered clear of the cause of the alarms.

"Seismics?" Han asked.

Leia shook her head. "Hapan pulse-gravity interdiction mines. The latest thing."

Seen through the curved viewport, the explosive devices might have been asteroids, basking in starlight. The *Falcon's* scanners had said differently, though they had only reinforced Han and Leia's initial hunch. Beyond the rocky field appeared the bright side of a brown-and-blue world, circled by satellites and gifted with two fair-sized moons.

"Guess you can't be too careful nowadays," Han said.

"Especially this close to the Perlemian Trade Route," Leia added.

Han pointed to an orbital facility of spherical modules and multiple docks. "The shipyard."

"It looks abandoned."

"Deliberately, would be my guess."

Weaving a sinuous path through the minefield, they maneuvered the *Falcon* closer to the planet. The freighter was midway between the moons when a voice issued from the comm.

"*Millennium Falcon,* this is Contruum control. On behalf of General Airen Cracken and the rest of the command staff, allow me to be the first to welcome you."

Contruum was the homeworld of Airen Cracken and his equally illustrious son, Pash. An industrious planet with ore-smelting plants and a modest shipbuilding franchise, it was often touted as being the most Core-like world outside the Core, in a class with Eriadu, though not nearly as ecologically devastated. Certainly there was no planet in that part of the Mid Rim to rival it. The fact that it had thus far escaped enemy attention was nothing short of marvelous. That Contruum had continued at its own peril to contribute generously to the war effort had rendered the planet a model of courage and sacrifice.

"Sirs, General Cracken is eager to know if you were successful in retrieving any of our lost merchandise?"

Leia answered for them. "Tell the general we're returning with only one of four that were originally available for pickup. Two were lost, and there is reason to believe that one may have ended up back at its point of origin."

"We're very sorry to hear that, Princess."

"That makes it unanimous," Han said.

"*Millennium Falcon* is cleared for entry. Would you care to have us take you in, Captain?"

"I'd rather fly—if it's all the same to you."

"Of course, sir. Routing and landing coordinates are being transmitted to your navigation computer."

Han and Leia watched the flight data come onscreen, then Leia enlarged the routing map.

Han laughed shortly. "Figures."

"Can't be too careful."

Han adjusted the *Falcon*'s course. Outside of a few harmless-looking ships lazing in stationary orbit, local space was almost free of traffic. Instead of bearing straight for the planet's heavily populated equatorial band, he banked the freighter for Contruum's innermost moon, a silver sphere dimpled with impact craters and crusty with mountain ranges.

"The large crater just to starboard," Leia said.

Han tapped the control yoke. "Got it."

There was nothing to mark the crater as a berthing space; nothing to mark the moon as a military base. Han lowered the *Falcon* toward the crater, close to its upthrust eastern rim.

Leia shook her head in wonder. "You could almost believe it's empty."

"Holoprojection masking a magnetic containment field," Han said. "That technique hasn't been used in a long time."

She nodded sadly. "There hasn't been need for it."

The *Falcon* passed through what appeared to be the rocky floor of the crater and into an enormous hollow below, ultimately settling down on a hexagonal landing platform emblazoned with well-worn markings and numerals. The interior of the hidden base hummed with activity. A nearby transport bore the name *Twelve Ton,* after a beast of burden indigenous to Contruum. Han recalled that the sleekly designed destroyers once produced by the now abandoned shipyard had typically been given virtuous-sounding names: *Temperance, Prudence, Equity . . .*

It took several minutes to get the *Falcon* shut down. Leia asked Cakhmaim and Meewalh to remain aboard with C-3PO, who took the request as a personal affront. Then she, Han, and Thorsh—the Jenet they had rescued—headed for the landing ramp. At the top, Han paused briefly to assess the minor damage done by the swoop, which had been jettisoned above Selvaris shortly before the *Falcon* had made the jump to lightspeed.

An escort detail was waiting for them on the landing platform—security personnel, meditechs and a medical droid, and a sturdy, dark-complected young woman who introduced herself as General Cracken's adjutant. The meditechs quickly surrounded Thorsh, inspecting his limbs, gently palpating his torso, and examining his vaguely leonine head.

"You look like you were dragged through a field of thorns," one said.

Thorsh sniffed in sardonic derision. "More like propelled. But thanks for noticing."

"We did what we could for him," Leia said.

The same meditech glanced at her. "Any battlefield medic would be proud to have done as much."

The droid finished its scans with a concluding melody of chitters and tones. "Malnourished, but otherwise fit," it announced in a deep voice.

Major Ummar, Cracken's adjutant, nodded in approval. "I don't see any reason why we can't proceed directly to debriefing."

Han turned to Thorsh and smirked. "Good job, Thorsh. We'll buy you lunch some other time."

Thorsh shrugged. "We all play our parts. I go where I'm sent, I do what I'm told."

"And the rest of us are the better for it," Leia said. She put her hand on Thorsh's bristly shoulder. "I can't begin to guess at what you're carrying, but it must be vitally important."

Thorsh shrugged again. "I wish I could say."

Han surmised that the Jenet wasn't holding back for security's sake. Thorsh really didn't know what intelligence he had locked away in his memory trap of a brain.

Han and Leia hadn't gone far when a speeder pulled up alongside them. On the bench seat behind the hover vehicle's Rodian driver sat General Wedge Antilles and Jedi Master Kenth Hamner.

"Wedge!" Leia said in delighted surprise, as the handsome dark-haired human climbed from the speeder. She hugged him in greeting, while Han pumped Wedge's extended hand.

Wedge nodded to Han. "Boss."

The two men had known each other for almost thirty years, since the Battle of Yavin, where Wedge had flown with Luke Skywalker against the Death Star. At Endor, Wedge had been instrumental in destroying the second Death Star, and during the fledgling years of the New Republic he had distinguished himself in countless operations with Rogue Squadron and other units. Like a lot of Galactic Civil War veterans, he and his wife, Iella, had come out of retirement to fight the Yuuzhan Vong. At Borleias, Wedge had formed a secret resistance force called the Insiders, whose membership— including Han, Leia, Luke, and many others—had agreed to borrow some of the tactics the Rebel Alliance had employed against the Empire.

Han had always liked Wedge, and what with Jaina's growing closeness to Wedge's nephew Jagged Fel, there was an outside chance that the Solo and Antilles families would end up allies of an even deeper sort.

"Good to see you again, Wedge," Han said. "Any word from on high?"

"Only that Admiral Sovv sends his gratitude for what you and Leia have done."

"Nice to know that we're all still on the same team." Han threw Wedge a wink, and turned to Kenth Hamner, who was wearing the homespun brown robe of a Jedi. "New look for you, isn't it?"

Kenth allowed a grin. "Formal attire. A show of solidarity between the Jedi and the Galactic Alliance military."

"Times change."

"That they do."

"Kenth, any communication from Luke?" Leia asked with some urgency.

"Nothing."

Leia frowned. "It's been more than two months now."

Kenth nodded. "And nothing from Corran or Tahiri, either."

Leia studied him for a moment. "What could have happened?"

Kenth tightened his lips and shook his head slowly. "We have to assume that they're still in the Unknown Regions. We'd know if something went wrong."

Han grasped that Kenth's *we* was meant to include Leia. Since before the fall of Coruscant, the Jedi—and Leia by extension—had honed their abilities to stretch out with thoughts and feelings; to meld minds and *intuit* at great distances.

"We're considering dispatching a search party," Kenth added.

Like Han and Wedge, the tall and pleasant-looking Jedi was Corellian, though unlike them he was an heir to wealth. Han had always considered him the most military-minded Jedi—Keyan Farlander and Kyle Katarn notwithstanding—and a year earlier Kenth had been named to Chief of State Cal Omas's Advisory Council, along with Jedi Masters Luke, Kyp Durron, Cilghal, Tresina Lobi, and Jedi Knight Saba Sebatyne.

Luke had placed Kenth in charge of the Jedi when he, Mara, and several others had embarked on a quest for the living world of Zonama Sekot. Since then Kenth had done his best to coordinate missions for the Jedi in Luke's absence, but as was true with Alliance command his best efforts had been undermined by the Yuuzhan Vong's unexpected success in disabling the HoloNet, which had long been the basis of galactic communications.

"You'd better be organizing a large party if you're intending to search the Unknown Regions," Han said.

Kenth found no humor in the remark. "We were able to obtain origin coordinates of the transmission Luke and Mara relayed through the Esfandia beacon."

"And?" Leia said.

"We've been transmitting to those coordinates for the past couple of weeks—without response."

With the Generis communications array destroyed by the Yuuzhan Vong, Esfandia was the only beacon capable of reaching Chiss space and the Unknown Regions. Two months earlier a desperate battle had been fought at Esfandia, but the beacon had been saved, thanks in large part to Grand Admiral Gilad Pellaeon's Imperial forces—with a helping hand from the able crew of *Millennium Falcon*.

"Maybe Zonama Sekot's moved," Han said. "I mean, that is what it's known for."

Kenth rocked his head in purposeful evasion. "Among other things."

Leia looked hard at him. "Could Zonama Sekot be returning to known space?"

"We can hope."

The four of them fell silent for a long moment. Wedge gave Han a covert glance, then heaved his shoulders in a shrug. When they had all climbed into the speeder, Wedge, in the front seat, turned to Leia and Han.

"Tell me about Selvaris."

"Not much to tell," Han said. "The escapees signaled us, we flew down and managed to rescue one of them."

Wedge looked to Leia for elaboration.

She blinked and smiled. "Just like he said. It was that simple."

Han leaned forward in a gesture of confidence. "What's all this about, Wedge? Not that we ever need an excuse to rescue anyone, but why from Selvaris of all worlds? Most people I know couldn't point it out on a star chart."

Wedge's expression turned serious. "I've got a special stake in this, Han."

Han's forehead wrinkled in interest. "How so?"

"You can hear for yourselves. General Cracken has requested that you attend the debriefing."

At the turbolift, Leia and the three Corellians caught up with the medical team that was escorting Thorsh. The Jenet and the meds exited three levels down. Leia and the others rode to the bottom on the shaft, emerging on a secure level, where two human Intelligence officers coded them into a stuffy room. Han had expected the usual mix of spies and officers, maybe a single chair for the subject, but the cabin felt more like an examination room.

The only Intelligence operative in attendance was Bhindi Drayson, whom Han, Leia, and Wedge knew from Borleias and other campaigns. The lean and sharp-featured daughter of a former Intelligence chief, Drayson was considered an expert tactician, and almost two years earlier had participated in a Wraith Squadron infiltration mission to Yuuzhan Vong–occupied Coruscant. For company just now she had a red R2 unit and a Givin.

Exoskeletoned humanoids with tubular limbs, large triangular eye sockets, and gaping mouths set in what appeared to be a perpetual frown of dismay, Givin were a remarkable species. Not only were they capable of surviving in the vacuum of space, but they could also perform complex hyperspace navigation without having to rely on navicomputers. Shipbuilders on a par with Verpine and Duros, they were obsessed with calculations, probabilities, and mathematics. Many believed that if the meaning of life were ever to be reduced to an equation, a Givin would be the first to do so.

Before anyone had time for proper introductions, Thorsh was led into the room. Absorbing the tableau in a glance, he said, "I'm ready when you are."

With the astromech droid standing by his side, the Givin seated himself opposite Thorsh. Thorsh closed his eyes and began to speak, surrendering the holowafer data he had memorized in an instant on Selvaris. A complex and utterly baffling sequence of numbers and formulas spewed from the Jenet, without pause or inflection. No one in the room stirred; no one interrupted him. When Thorsh finished, he loosed a long exhale.

"Glad to be rid of that."

The Givin was nodding his scary head. "No soft-body could have composed such elegant work. I recognize the mind and hand of a Givin in coding the message contained in this equation."

"You want him to repeat any it?" Bhindi Drayson asked.

The Givin shook his head. "That won't be necessary."

She nodded in satisfaction. "Then I guess we're done here."

Han glanced around in bafflement. "That's it? That's the debriefing?"

Wedge nodded his chin to the Givin and the droid. "The rest is up to them."

Han and Leia had just found seats in the mess hall when Major Ummar brought word that General Cracken was ready to conduct the briefing.

"So much for a real meal," Han said.

Leia sighed. "I'll have Threepio prepare us something later."

"The perfect appetite suppressant."

By the time the Solos arrived, the base's tactical information center was filled to capacity with intelligence analysts, ships' officers, and wing commanders. Cracken's adjutant escorted Han and Leia down the amphitheater's broad carpeted stairs to seats in the front row. On the rostrum sat Wedge and three colonels—two Bothans and a Sullustan.

Seventy-five-year-old Airen Cracken, whose intelligence briefings had literally given shape to the Rebel Alliance during the Galactic Civil War, stood at the lectern.

"First I want to thank all of you for reporting at such short notice. If there was time, I would have included this information in tomorrow's scheduled briefing, but with HoloNet transmissions disabled, we'll need to dispatch couriers immediately if we're to pull this operation together."

Cracken activated a switch on the lectern's slanted top, and a holoprojection appeared to his left, detailing an unidentified sector of the galaxy. Cracken used a laser pointer to indicate a star system in the upper right quadrant, which expanded as the pointer's red beam touched the holo's sizing node.

"The Tantara system," Cracken continued, "looking Coreward from Bilbringi. The principal stars are Centis Major and Renaant. The closest habitable world—presently occupied by the Yuuzhan Vong—is Selvaris."

Cracken nodded at Han and Leia, then gestured to them. "Captain Solo and Princess Leia have just returned from Selvaris. There they were successful in rescuing a prisoner who escaped from an enemy internment camp constructed on the surface. Among those we have been able to identify as fellow prisoners in the camp are Captain Judder Page, of Corulag, and my own son, Major Pash Cracken."

Murmurs of genuine surprise swept through the room.

"How come nobody told us that?" Han asked Leia out of the corner of his mouth.

She shushed him gently. "Let's at least hear Airen out before we make a fuss."

"Okay," Han said slowly. "But just this once."

"A resistance group operating on Selvaris was able to obtain important intelligence, and pass that intelligence along to Captain Page and Major Cracken, who are currently the highest-ranking Alliance officers in captivity at the camp. The intelligence was encrypted as a complex mathematical formula, which was memorized by the Jenet escapee, and decrypted only two hours ago. It provides us with details of a Peace Brigade mission to transport to Coruscant several hundred Alliance officials and high-ranking officers who are being held on Selvaris and in more than a dozen such camps along the fringes of the Yuuzhan Vong invasion corridor. We now know when the pickups are to be made, and we know the route the Peace Brigade convoy plans to use in reaching Coruscant. We don't yet know the reason for this mass relocation, but we have a good guess."

"No wonder Wedge said he has a stake in this," Han whispered. "Some of the officers Cracken is talking about were probably captured during the attempt to retake Bilbringi."

Wedge stepped to the lectern and took over for Cracken.

"Alliance spies placed inside the Peace Brigade have alerted Mon Calamari command that a Yuuzhan Vong religious ceremony of great significance is scheduled to take place on Coruscant sometime within the next standard week. The purpose of this ceremony is unclear. It could mark the anniversary of some historical event, or its purpose could be to quell the rising tide of discontent that continues to plague Coruscant. The purpose is immaterial, in any case, since it is our belief that the prisoners being transported to Coruscant are to be sacrificed at this ceremony."

Separate conversations broke out throughout the amphitheater. Leia tuned them out to absorb the tragic news in silence.

Almost since the start of the war, the seditious Peace Brigade had transported everything from hibernating amphistaffs to captives for sacrifice. Mixed-species renegades, there wasn't anything they wouldn't do for credits and the freedom to move about the galaxy as they wished. But there was small profit in being a Brigader any longer. Those who weren't hunted down and killed by Alliance operatives or loyalists had usually ended up dying at the hands of the Yuuzhan Vong themselves. And no matter which way the war went, they were going to end up on the losing side—useless to the Yuuzhan Vong, traitors to the Alliance. That didn't seem to matter, however. They lived for the moment, the credits, the thrill, the spice.

"Everyone here knows that countless lives have ended on Yuuzhan Vong sacrificial pyres," Wedge was saying. "But it is imperative that this convoy be prevented from reaching Coruscant. In the past, whenever and wherever possible, we have attempted to save lives—that has always been our mandate. We have frequently failed because of erroneous intelligence or overwhelming force. Some of you are probably asking yourselves, *Why this convoy?* The answer is simple: because many of the prisoners—Captain Page and Major Cracken among them—are desperately needed to rally support for planetary sectors on the verge of acquiescing to the enemy. In addition, because their cover will be compromised, those agents operating within the Peace Brigade who helped provide this intelligence will also have to be extracted. And we are faced with having to execute this rescue without the advantage of coordinating operations through the HoloNet."

Wedge waited for the amphitheater to quiet.

"Selvaris is the last stop before the convoy jumps to Coruscant, so our ambush must wait until the prisoners have been transferred. Given the devastating losses the Peace Brigade sustained a year ago at Ylesia and Duro, it's reasonable to assume that the convoy will be escorted and complemented by Yuuzhan Vong war vessels. Admirals Sovv and Kre'fey have already seen fit to allocate Blackmoon, Scimitar, Twin Suns, and other starfighter squadrons to the mission. The starfighters will lend support to our gunships, as well as protect the transports needed to house those prisoners we rescue. Captain Solo and Princess Leia have volunteered *Millennium Falcon* for the latter purpose."

Leia cut her wide-open eyes to Han. "When did that happen?"

"I, uh, might've said something to Wedge earlier."

"You didn't even know what the mission was going to entail."

Han smiled crookedly. "I basically said that he could put us down for whatever they had in mind."

Leia took a breath and faced front. Much to her mounting unease, Han had gotten into the habit of accepting every dangerous assignment dreamed up by Galactic Alliance command. It was as if the successes in the Koornacht Cluster, at Bakura, and at Esfandia had merely primed Han's pump, or had been nothing more than warm-up exercises for some grand mission during which he would defeat the Yuuzhan Vong single-handedly—or at least in partnership with Leia.

But the war had taken a toll on both of them, beginning with Chewbacca's death and culminating with the tragic events at Myrkr, where their youngest son Anakin had died, their older son Jacen had been captured, and their daughter Jaina had forged her grief into a sword of vengeance that had pushed her to the edge of the dark side and nearly cost her her life.

Leia knew in her heart that she and Han were more unified than they had ever been. But the constant missions had been exhausting, and lately there had been too many close calls. At times she wished that she could gather her scattered family and spirit everyone to some far corner of the galaxy, untouched by the war. But even on the remote chance that such a corner existed, Han wouldn't consider absenting himself for a moment, especially now, with HoloNet communications down, and the need for gifted pilots with fast ships.

Before that safe corner could ever be found and claimed as their own—before the galaxy could know enduring peace—Leia and Han would need to see the war through to the bitter end.

She came back to herself just as Wedge was concluding his remarks.

"We are committed to this operation for an added reason of equal importance—that is, in the hope that a rescue of such magnitude will spoil the impending sacrifice." Wedge's expression turned hard as he scanned the assembly. "Any thorns we can drive deeper into Shimrra's side will further destabilize Coruscant, and provide us with the window we need to rebuild our forces and safeguard those worlds the enemy has thus far been unable to vanquish."

SIX

It was raining insects on Yuuzhan'tar—the former Coruscant, once bright center, now dimmed, defiled by war, transformed by the Yuuzhan Vong into a riotous garden. A seeming mishmash of ferns, conifers, and other flora blunted what only two years earlier had been technological sierra. Verdant growth nudged through mist in valleys that had once been canyons between kilometer-high megastructures. Newly formed lakes and basins created by the fall of mighty towers and orbital platforms were filled to overflowing with water, initially brought by asteroids but since delivered with regularity from a purple sky.

To some, Yuuzhan'tar, "Crèche of the Gods," was a world returned to its bygone splendor, lost and rediscovered, more alive for having been conquered, its orbit altered—tweaked sunward—three of its moons steered away and returned, and the fourth pulverized to form a braided ring, a bridge of supernatural light, along which the gods strolled in serene meditation.

And yet insects were raining down on Supreme Overlord Shimrra's rainbow-winged worldship Citadel—his holy mount, rising from a yorik coral cradle to tower over what had been the most populous and important precinct of the galactic capital. An unrelenting tattoo of falling bodies that sounded like a thousand drummers pounding out different rhythms.

The stink beetles spattered the dome of the Hall of Confluence and the stately, organiform bridges that linked the hall to other hallowed places. The plague had been born on the other side of Yuuzhan'tar because of a mistake by the World Brain—an overbreeding—and now the creatures were dying because of yet another mistake by the dhuryam. The air around the Citadel reeked, and the ground was slippery with smashed bodies.

The atmosphere inside the great hall was somber. A place of assembly for the Yuuzhan Vong elite, it was defined by a curving roof supported by pillars sculpted from ancient bone. Broad at the four palpating portals where the high caste entered, the hall attenuated at the opposite end, where Shimrra sat on a pulsing crimson throne, propped by clusters of hau polyps. Dovin basals provided a sense of gravity, of uphill walking, increasing the nearer one came to Shimrra's spike-backed seat.

And yet the atmosphere inside the hall was moody and silent.

A kneeling gathering of priests, warriors, shapers, and intendants waited for the Supreme Overlord to speak. The brooding silence was fractured by the sound of insects striking the roof, or being swept from the fronting causeways into the accommodating mouths of a dozen maw luur . . .

"You are asking yourselves, *Where have we erred?*" Shimrra said at last. "*Does the fault lie with our cleansings, our sacrifices, our conquests? Are we being tested by the gods, or have we been abandoned? Is Shimrra still our conduit, or has he become our liability?* You are preoccupied with fears concerning balance and derangement. You wonder if all of us haven't become Shamed Ones in the eyes of the gods—spurned, disdained, ostracized because of our pride and our inability to prevail."

Shimrra paused to look around the hall, then asked: "Do you think that your distrust in me, your whispered doubts, benefits our noble cause? If *I* can hear you, what must the gods be thinking when they look into each and every one of you? I will tell you what the gods are saying to another: *They have lost faith in the one we set upon the polyp throne. And in doubting the Supreme Overlord, our yoke to them, they doubt* us.

"And so the gods visit plagues and defeats on their children—not to castigate *me,* but to demonstrate where *you* have failed—where you have failed *them.*"

Shimrra's black-and-gray ceremonial robes were the flayed and preserved flesh of the first Supreme Overlord. His massive head was scarified with design; his features rearranged to suggest a godly aspect: eyes widened, mouth decurved, forehead elongated, earlobes stretched, chin narrowed to a point, like the Hall of Confluence itself. And blazing from his eye sockets, mqaaq't implants, which changed color according to Shimrra's mood. The fingers of his huge right hand grasped a fanged amphistaff that was the Scepter of Power.

Below the yorik coral throne sat his shamed familiar, Onimi, part pet, part speaker of truths few dared to voice.

It had reached Shimrra's ear, through a network of eavesdropping biots and actual spies, that some of his opponents and derogators were gossiping that he had fallen out of favor with the gods—a speculation more ironic than dangerous, since Shimrra had long ago abandoned real belief in any power other than that which he wielded as Supreme Overlord.

Even so, there were undeniable reasons to fear that he had fallen out of favor. The slow progress of the conquest; a plague of itching that had commenced with his arrival on Yuuzhan'tar; the still-unabated heretical movement; the disastrous defeat at Ebaq 9; the treachery of the priestess Ngaaluh; the attempt on Shimrra's life . . . Many believed that all these reversals had been engineered by the gods as a warning to Shimrra that he had become grandiose and proud.

He who had proclaimed the galaxy a chosen realm for the long-wandering, homeless Yuuzhan Vong.

As an appeasement to the concerned members of the elite, Shimrra had agreed to allow his proclamations and utterances to be analyzed by a quartet of seers—one from each caste, one for each primary god. Black midnight hags, who sat close to the throne and spoke in contradictions. Not that they dared challenge Shimrra, in any case, except with hand wringing, prayers, and other gestures meant to implore the gods to look kindly on Yuuzhan'tar.

"You disgust me," he told them. "You think I'm spouting sacrilege. You recoil and grovel because you know that I speak the truth, and that truth rattles you to the core of your being. You'd do well to chop off more of yourselves in penance and devotion. Give all of yourselves and it won't be enough." He looked down at Onimi. "You think I speak in riddles, like this one."

Onimi's deformities owed not to birth but to rejection by the gods. Once a shaper, he was now little more than a misshapen jester, one eye drooping below its mate, one yellow fang protruding from a twisted mouth, one portion of his skull distended, as if the shaper's vaa-tumor had failed to seat itself properly. Long and slender, his arms and legs twitched continuously, yanked about by the gods, as they might do to a puppet.

Shimrra made a sound of angry impatience. "Come forward, Von Shul of Domain Shul and Melaan Nar of Domain Nar."

The two consuls—midlevel intendants—advanced a few meters on their knees.

"I have pondered your grievances with each other," Shimrra said when the throne's dovin basal had forced the faces of the consuls to the floor, "and I now decree that you put them aside. I decree further that you redirect the energy that fuels your wrath into serving our common cause. Each of you claims that your troubles with each other began here, on Yuuzhan'tar, as have so many other petty rivalries between this domain and that one. But this is merely camouflage. I know that your dispute had its roots during our long migration through intergalactic space, and that that dispute has resurfaced here. But you are not entirely to blame.

"Absent wars to wage, what did we do but turn upon ourselves, sacrifice one another, compete for the favor of my predecessor Quoreal, or snipe behind one another's backs? The gods were forgotten. You lost patience, you worried, you thought then that the gods had abandoned us—because our long-sought home was nowhere to be found. And that is precisely what you are doing now. Prefect Da'Gara and the Praetorite domains—what did their blasphemous actions earn them but ice graves on what little remains of Helska Four, a world so far removed from Yuuzhan'tar it might as well be in the galaxy we left behind? None less than Warmaster Czulkang Lah refused to believe me when I avowed that the promised realm was within reach, and what did that earn him but death in battle, like his son, who burned so strongly with hatred for the *Jeedai* that he allowed himself to be drawn into an engagement he couldn't win."

Shimrra paid no attention to the bitter grumblings from some of the warriors, all of whom wore ceremonial vonduun crab armor. Instead his piercing gaze fell on Warmaster Nas Choka, noble in appearance despite his modest stature, with fine black hair combed straight back from his face, and a wispy beard. Choka had been escalated in the wake of Tsavong Lah's death, but was not yet universally revered, despite his numerous victories in Hutt space.

"Learn from the mistakes of your precursors, Warmaster, and all will go well for you. Fail me as Domain Lah did and I will personally make an example of you that future warmasters will be forced to consider before they accept escalation."

Nas Choka inclined his head in a crisp bow and struck the points of his shoulders with the opposite fists.

Now Shimrra glared at the fretting warriors. "Many of you would like to hold Prefect Nom Anor responsible for what happened at Ebaq Nine, because of the disinformation to which he fell victim. I myself accepted that for a time. But the real failure was Tsavong Lah's, for allowing himself to be gulled by the enemy. Tsavong Lah thought he died an honorable death, but I say that he shamed us all."

Eyes downcast, many a warrior squirmed in place.

Shimrra's gaze found High Priest Jakan—adorned in red—and High Prefect Drathul, sheathed in green. "There are others whom I might chastise and remind of their obligation. But I will reserve that for another occasion."

A dovin basal cushion floated Shimrra out of his throne to the ring of flower petals that encircled it, where he dismounted the cushion. Ankle-deep in the flowers, he raised his long-toothed scepter of rank. "All can be made right by the coming sacrifice. But we must take care against interference."

"The heretics, August Lord," a priest said.

Shimrra waved his empty hand in dismissal. "The heretics are nothing more than a pestilence—a plague of stink bugs we can eradicate at any time. I speak of interference from the unconverted who move silently among us—those who survived the planetary bombardment and worldshaping, the slaves who escaped the maimed seedship that delivered the World Brain to Yuuzhan'tar, the resistance fighters who profane our holy ground, and the *Jeedai*."

As if on cue, Onimi scrambled to his feet and followed Shimrra along the flowered ring, reciting:

> *"The Shamed are naught but nuisance flies,*
> *At least as seen through Shimrra's eyes;*
> *The* Jeedai *are the ones he mourns,*
> *Edged and sharp as senalak thorns."*

When Shimrra swung about, Onimi bowed in mock gallantry. "Great Sky Lord, if the *Jeedai* Force is nothing more than enhanced ability, why have our shapers not created worthy opponents from the warrior caste?"

Shimrra frowned and aimed a finger at his familiar. "You spoil my surprise, Onimi. But so be it." He turned to face the white-robed, tentacle-handed shapers. "Let us not keep our company in suspense. Display your handiwork."

One of the spotlessly adorned shapers rose and hastened from the hall. Moments later, entering through both the priest and warrior portals, marched a group of ten males. Shorter even than Nas Choka, they carried restless amphistaffs and whetted coufees. Steng's Talons sprouted from their robust bodies, which were smeared black with dried blood.

The ten were unlike the special breed of warriors known as hunters, who were privileged to sport the photosensitive mimetic cloak of Nuun, but something new and disconcerting, and the female seers were the first to voice their dismay.

"What desecration is this?"

"Armed as warriors, yet clothed as attendants to the gods!"

"What shaper is responsible?"

Onimi gamboled over to them and adopted a haughty posture.

> *"To prove the Force a farce indeed,*
> *Shimrra's will the shapers heed;*

Birthing troops of mingled caste
Great Nas Choka they will outlast!"

One of the seers made a futile grab for Onimi while the others continued to shout dire warnings.

"No shaper other than myself is responsible," Shimrra said, silencing them. "By my injunction do these warriors come to be. Our *Jeedai*. Charged with guarding the life of your Supreme Overlord, as well as with rooting out our enemies and exterminating them. At their disposal they will have coralskippers of unique design, with advanced weaponry and the ability to travel through darkspace unassisted." Shimria paused, then added: "They shall be called slayers, in honor of Yun-Yammka—lest he feel uncomfortable about mingling with *priests.*"

"They have the look of Shamed Ones!"

Shimrra whirled on the warrior who said it. "Shamed, you say? By my mandate were they created, Supreme Commander Chaan—by divine edict! If the gods had disapproved, would these warriors not bear the markings of pariahs?"

Supreme Commander Chaan stood his ground. "Shamed Ones shaped to resemble those who have been embraced by the gods, Great Lord. Concealing the deformities that would signal their unworthiness. Is it too much to ask that we be shown proof of their status?"

Shimrra grinned diabolically. "Cursed you are by your own request, Commander. Step forward with ten of your warriors and do your best against these."

"Fearsome Shimrra—"

"Doubt flew from your mouth like a tsik vai, Commander! If too quickly, then retract your words, or do as I say and stand against these!"

Chaan snapped his fists to his shoulders and summoned ten warriors to their feet; coufees, shields, tridents, and amphistaffs woke to the challenge. At the same time, the warrior-priests spread out, but only two stepped forward.

"Two against eleven," Chaan said in sudden consternation. "This is vulgar. Dishonor either way!"

Shimrra returned to his throne and sat. "Then we will be pleased to see you humble them, if only to demonstrate that our shapers have failed in their task. Carve them, Commander, as a dish fit for the gods!"

Chaan saluted crisply.

At his curt nod, the ten warriors attacked, two groups of four moving to outflank their opponents, and the remaining two rushing forward immediately to engage and distract. The reactions of the warrior-priests were almost too fast to follow. They turned slightly to the side, almost back to back, wielding weapons in both hands, meeting the frontal attack and the flanking attacks simultaneously.

The amphistaffs of the attackers struck seemingly unarmored flesh without finding purchase. Coufees cut and sliced, and yet almost no blood flowed; what little did, congealed instantly. The melee weapons of the defenders were no less enhanced than were the small, muscular warrior-priests who wielded them. The specially bred amphistaffs snapped the heads off their lesser cousins, and stabbed with enough force to paralyze, even through armor. The slayers—Shimrra's *Jeedai*—leapt to great heights, twisting in midflight and landing behind their attackers, then rushed in, arms windmilling in a blur, gouts of black blood flying in all directions. One by one and sliced to pieces, Chaan's warriors dropped to the floor.

Silence gripped the hall as the elite of all castes watched with a mix of awe and dread. Shimrra was already powerful enough without this royal guard. Now he was no match for any domain that might think to thwart him.

The fight was over almost as quickly as it began, with the ten warriors—and Chaan—felled and bleeding, and the two warrior-priests unmoved by what they had done, their slender amphistaffs badged with blood.

The shaper who had escorted the group into the hall stepped forward to appraise the warriors and address Shimrra. "Our taller warriors kept rejecting the implants. The faster metabolic rate of our shorter warriors is better suited to the rapid cellular activity of the implant biots."

Onimi scampered over to one of the dead warriors and prodded him.

> *"Most impressive;*
> *Done with flair.*

But against a Jeedai,
How will they fare?"

Shimrra nodded to Master Shaper Qelah Kwaad. "Show him."

Few members of the elite were as fearsome to gaze upon as Qelah Kwaad, but the object she held in her eight-fingered cephalopod hand made her writhing-snakes headdress and bulging cranium seem positively ordinary.

"The weapon of the *Jeedai!*" one of the warriors shouted.

"More sacrilege!" another said.

"Hold your tongues or forfeit them," Shimrra snapped. "This is the energy blade taken from the *Jeedai* who killed you in great numbers in the Well of the World Brain. The one whom so many of you hold in reverence—Ganner. Think of the blade not as an abomination, then, but a holy relic of that warrior's might."

"Master Shaper Kwaad has desecrated herself," a seer said.

"If you take issue with her familiarity with the stillborn technology," Shimrra replied calmly, "then denounce as well the contrivances Master Kwaad and her shapers created to foil the enemy's shadow bombs, their decoy dovin basals, and their yammosk jammers. Condemn, too, the *mabugat kan* that have ingested the enemy's deep-space communications arrays, and have enabled us to subjugate more worlds in a klekket than had been conquered in the time since my arrival in the Outer Rim." He gestured to the lightsaber. "For this energy blade is powered by one of our own lambent focusing crystals. Hence it has already been *sanctified.*"

The remark was enough to quiet everyone in the hall.

Shimrra nodded again. "Carry on, Master Shaper."

Moving directly to one of the slayers, Qelah Kwaad ignited the lightsaber, raised it to her opposite shoulder, and, with a slashing motion, drew the violet blade diagonally across the slayer's chest.

The smell of burned flesh wafted through the hall.

Shimrra turned slightly to face the commanders. "Only a furrow where any one of you would lie in two pieces on the floor."

"They are more vonduun crab than Yuuzhan Vong," High Priest Jakan muttered.

Shimrra seethed. "Vonduun crab, dovin basal, yammosk, warrior . . . Need I remind you, of all people, that we are all grown from the same seed?"

Nom Anor—slightly taller than the average human, disfigured by ceremony and by his own hand, fitted with a false eye that could spit poison—waited uneasily at the entry to Shimrra's private chambers in the rounded crown of the sacred mountain. Three sullen slayers stood stiffly to one side of the membranous curtain, and a pair of priests to the other, purifying Nom Anor with clouds of fragrant vapor puffed from the dorsal scent gland of a well-fed but skittish thamassh.

He hadn't been summoned to private audience with the Supreme Overlord since his return from Zonama Sekot, and he wasn't sure what to expect.

The membrane shimmered and parted to reveal Onimi, gesticulating to Nom Anor.

"Enter, *Prefect,*" Shimrra's pet said, affecting a supercilious tone.

Nom Anor edged past him into the spacious circular chamber. Shimrra sat in the center of the room, atop a circular dais, in a high-backed seat that lacked the pomp of his public throne. A blood moat encircled the seat, and off to one side a yorik coral staircase with a finely wrought railing spiraled into the summit. A hardened module of the worldship, Shimrra's inner sanctum, like the Well of the World Brain, could be detached from the Citadel if necessary and launched into deep space.

"Did you not wonder when we three would meet again?" Onimi asked softly as Nom Anor passed.

Nom Anor ignored the question and approached the throne, genuflecting at the edge of the foul-smelling moat. From an inner pocket of his green robe, he removed the lightsaber that had stirred so much strife in the Hall of Confluence earlier on.

"Dread Lord, your desire was that this be delivered to you." Nom Anor kept his gaze lowered while Shimrra took the weapon from his hand; he looked up with alarm when he heard the distinctive *snap-hiss* of the lightsaber's energy blade.

The mere sound of the weapon evoked jarring memories of an incident in the Well of the World Brain a year earlier, when Jacen Solo and Vergere had held a similar blade to his neck before they had made their escape from Yuuzhan'tar. Nom Anor had spent countless moments since wondering how his life might have gone had the two Jedi agreed to take him with them. As a source of invaluable intelligence, he might not have been executed by the so-called Galactic Alliance. Perhaps after weeks of debriefing he would have been allowed to don an ooglith masquer and relocate in secrecy to some remote world in the Outer Rim, where he would have been able to live out his days in contentment.

No larger than a votive candle in the grip of Shimrra's right hand, the lightsaber thrummed as it cleaved the air.

"Answer me honestly, Prefect, do you believe in the gods?" Shimrra brought the violet blade close to Nom Anor's neck. "Bear in mind: honestly."

High Prefect Drathul's predecessor, Yoog Skell, who had died by Nom Anor's hand, had once warned Nom Anor never to lie to Shimrra. Now he swallowed and found his voice. "August Lord, I . . . remain open to belief."

"If there was some benefit to believing, you mean."

"I follow the example set by the priests, Lord."

Shimrra's eyes bored into Nom Anor's single orb. "Are you suggesting, Prefect, that our priests are not acting out of the goodness of their hearts?"

"Lord, I have seen many hearts, and few showed evidence of goodness."

"Clever," Shimrra said slowly. "That's the word everyone who knows you or who has had dealings with you uses— *clever.*"

To Nom Anor's relief, Shimrra deactivated the lightsaber.

In another scenario, Nom Anor might have remained prophet of the heretics, and even then be attempting to topple Shimrra from the throne. He had faced that choice in the Unknown Regions—*How telling!*—only to decide: better by Shimrra's side than overlord to a multitude of outcasts.

"What does one like yourself make of the whisperings that circulate among the elite," Shimrra asked from his simple chair, "that the gods have become angered by my decisions— as far back to my deciding to tip Quoreal from the throne, usurp his position as Supreme Overlord, and pronounce this galaxy our new home?"

Nom Anor risked adopting a cross-legged posture on the floor. From the far side of the moat, Onimi watched him with visible delight. "May I speak freely, Lord?"

"You had better," Onimi said.

Shimrra glanced from Onimi to Nom Anor, then nodded his enormous head.

"I would answer that many of the high caste fail to grasp that the actions you took were a tribute to the gods; actions no less bold than those taken by Yun-Yuuzhan when he gave of himself to bring the universe into being."

Shimrra leaned forward. "You impress me, Prefect. Continue."

Nom Anor grew more confident. "Many of us had accepted as fact that the generations of wandering through the intergalactic void had been a test of faith—which, as you yourself pointed out, we failed miserably, by quarreling among ourselves and worshiping false gods, weakening the hinges of our own gates."

Shimrra nodded sagely. "Any group without opposition falls inexorably into decay and tyranny—or both."

"But you, Dread Lord, saw the arduous journey for what it was: a consequence of our previous failures. You understood that our shapers were fast approaching the limits of traditional knowledge—that they were essentially powerless to repair our deteriorating worldships; that our priests were likewise unable to rescue our society from the depths to which it had sunk; that our warriors, left without a war, had nowhere to turn but upon one another. We were dying in the void, Lord, and were it not for your toppling of Quoreal and his cautious followers, the Yuuzhan Vong might have ended there."

Shimrra stared at him. "Oh, you are a dangerous person, Prefect." He glanced at Onimi. "But as my familiar knows well, I have a liking for danger." He paused, then added: "I will educate you about the gods. The question is not whether they exist, but if we have any further need of them. Their fall began during our long journey, when they failed to come to our aid. As you have undoubtedly learned, Prefect, one cannot keep loyal servants if one neglects them. So the fault lies with them. Absent our bloody support, absent our solicitations and praises, what would they be left with? The gods may have created us, but it is we who sustain them through worship. Now they are bereft because the roles are reversed. They are angry because they have been forced to recognize that their hour has arrived; that the time has come to surrender power to Shimrra and the new order."

Again, Shimrra ignited the lightsaber and waved it about, as if to emphasize his remarks.

"This is the greater war, Prefect—the Yuuzhan Vong against the gods."

Nom Anor gulped. "War, August Lord?"

"Nothing less! Because the gods guard their power jealously. But surely you recognize this, Prefect. Would you go quietly into retreat, or would you fight to the last to preserve your status? Abandon all the consuls who now answer to you? Murder even High Prefect Drathul if necessary to hold your ground?"

"I would fight, Dread Lord," Nom Anor said, more forcefully than he intended.

"And I would expect no less of you. But there is a problem inherent in all this, for we find ourselves surrounded by true believers, and to some extent they pose a greater threat to the future of the Yuuzhan Vong than that posed by the gods themselves."

Nom Anor smiled inwardly. "The gods have their place, Lord."

"Indeed they do. Religious ritual keeps the priests and intendants busy; it keeps the shapers from becoming too ambitious; it keeps the warriors at bay; it keeps the workers from discarding the caste system; and it keeps Shamed Ones from rising up in open revolt. Therefore, if I am to remake this world, I must tread carefully."

Shimrra's words only reinforced Nom Anor's belief that faith was an extravagance, and that true believers were the easiest to manipulate.

"I must tread carefully," Shimrra repeated, almost to himself. "When faith is under assault and the social order is cracking apart, the weak do not want explanations; they want reassurance and someone to blame." He laughed quietly. "Ah, but I'm telling you what you already know. Look what wonders this worked with the Shamed Ones who have turned to heresy on Yuuzhan'tar and our other worlds. Do they want explanations? No! They cry out for my blood."

Despite his best efforts, Nom Anor began to quiver.

"I see that my remarks frighten you, Prefect. Perhaps you think they smack of heresy, such as the Prophet preaches to his blind following. Would you lump me in with our own Mezhan Kwaad and Nen Yim, or Shedao Shai and his sad devotion to the Embrace of Pain?"

"I know little of those things, Dread Lord."

"Naturally."

Nom Anor didn't like the sound of it. Executions came easily to Shimrra, who was easily displeased. He had had shaper Ch'Gang Hool killed because of Hool's seeming failure to govern the World Brain and prevent the itching plague. He had also executed Commander Ekh'm Val, who had discovered— or rather rediscovered—Zonama Sekot. Nom Anor himself had been targeted for execution because of his gullibility regarding Ebaq 9.

In the days since, his dreams of power and glory had been fulfilled, but what if Shimrra should decide to safeguard the secret of Zonama Sekot by having Nom Anor killed—just as Nom Anor had killed Nen Yim and the priest Harrar to safeguard *his* secret?

Shimrra was contemplating the lightsaber.

"A curious weapon, is it not? It requires the wielder to close with an enemy in personal combat. Were it not for their misguided beliefs, the *Jeedai* might actually be deserving of admiration. There may yet be a way to incorporate their doctrines into our religion. We must be careful not to repeat past mistakes. Perhaps we need to look for ways to conquer the hearts and minds of the species that dominate here." He looked at Nom Anor. "Have the *Jeedai* never been defeated, Prefect?"

As Nom Anor recounted what he knew of the Jedi Purge,

he considered what killing Shimrra might have meant for the Yuuzhan Vong. By assassinating Emperor Palpatine, the Rebel Alliance had unleashed decades of turmoil with local warlords, and incessant battles with hostile species . . .

"Tell me of the young *Jeedai* who learned the True Way, only to betray it," Shimrra said.

"Jacen Solo."

Shimrra knew the name. "The same who lured Tsavong Lah to his death . . . I have been blaming the shapers for not being able to supervise the World Brain, but I begin to suspect that this *Jeedai* is somehow responsible. When I interact with the Brain, I sense its reluctance, its miseducation. I have had to instruct the Brain, as one would a disobedient child—a child of warriors who has been mistakenly raised in the crèche of the priests."

Shimrra rolled the lightsaber between his hands. "And the Force. I've heard it described by heretics as the lingering exhalation of Yun-Yuuzhan."

Nom Anor's words to his followers returned to haunt him.

"I would not grant it such importance, August Lord. The Force is merely a power the Jedi have learned to draw from, over twenty or more generations. But not the Jedi alone. A group called the Sith also made use of the power, and were perhaps responsible for the Purge that occurred even while we—you—were finalizing our invasion plans."

Shimrra folded his arms across his chest. "High Priest Jakan has made mention of these Sith. Are they in hiding?"

Nom Anor shook his head. "Sadly, their flame has gone out of this galaxy, Dread Lord. The heretics claim that in the Jedi are combined all aspects of the gods. But in fact the Jedi are not flawless, nor are they beyond being outwitted and defeated. They have been captured, killed, almost turned to our own purposes."

"As you yourself demonstrated at Zonama Sekot." Shimrra's mood became dark. "I am eager to deliver an end to our enemy before that planetary nemesis undoes us." He sharpened his gaze on Nom Anor. "Are we safe, Prefect?"

Nom Anor mustered his courage. "With any luck, Dread Lord, Zonama Sekot is a dead world. If not, it certainly has no sense of where it is, let alone where we are."

SEVEN

Luke and Mara Jade Skywalker stood in the trapezoidal entrance to the cliff dwelling that had been their home and shelter on Zonama Sekot for what had felt like three standard weeks. The span of time was only a guess based on human circadian rhythms, because the days had been anything but regular since the living world's abrupt jump to hyperspace, lasting anywhere from fifteen to forty hours, as Zonama's governing intelligence struggled to reassert control.

Torrential rain continued to lash the Middle Distance, driven by gales powerful enough to snap and topple the giant boras and strip the reddish trees of their globular leaves. The sky was an inverted silver bowl, with massive storm clouds stacked high in all directions, deep purple to black, and incandescent with continuous flashes of lightning. Peals of thunder resonated from the bare rock walls of the chasms that housed the cliff dwellings. As if from deep below the surface came a hollow moan, like breath across the narrow mouth of a container. Many believed that the sound was caused by wind rushing across Zonama Sekot's three-hundred-meter-high hyperdrive vanes.

Caught in an updraft, three sheets of lamina building material spiraled up from the floor of the chasm and disappeared over the rim.

"This place is coming apart," Mara said.

Luke nodded but said nothing. He had his right arm around Mara's shoulders, and the side of her face was pressed to the soft weave of his dark cloak. The persistent gusts whipped Mara's red-gold hair about her face and across her mouth.

To Luke's left stood R2-D2, emitting a steady stream of mournful chirrs and chatterings, his status indicator flashing from red to blue and his third tread extended to keep himself from being blown over. Luke put his left hand on the astromech droid's hemispherical head.

"Don't worry, Artoo. We'll come through this all right."

R2 swiveled his primary photoreceptor to Luke and warbled in renewed hope.

Mara snorted a laugh. "What a guy. Always a kind word for pets, small children, and droids."

The cliff dwelling—walls of tightly fitted stones enclosing two small spaces—was located in the canyon's middle tier of natural ledges. Cavities in the bare rock face opposite were likewise partitioned into hundreds of separate dwellings, but many of the vine-and-lamina suspension bridges that had joined the community's two halves were gone, as were the pulleyed platforms the Ferroans used for vertical transportation. Two kilometers below raged a ribbon of muddy water, dammed in places by knots of fallen boras and other detritus.

Word had it that similar conditions prevailed throughout the Middle Distance, which was the name given to the equatorial region where the Ferroans had settled more than seventy-five years earlier, when Zonama Sekot had resided on the other side of the galactic plane, in the Outer Rim of known space.

"Corran is coming," Luke announced in a matter-of-fact tone.

Mara slipped out of his embrace and leaned out the entrance to gaze around, one hand clasping her long hair. "Where?" she said, just loudly enough to be heard. "I don't see—"

She interrupted herself when she saw his head poke above the rungs of a wooden ladder that rose from a lower tier. Soaked to the bone, Corran held his jacket closed at the neck. Water dripped from his furrowed face and the graying beard and mustache that framed his mouth. His limp hair was pulled into a short tail at the back. He smiled when he noticed Mara, and hurried for the cliff dwelling, using his free hand to sluice some of the water from his forehead.

"Jacen and Saba's airship has been spotted downvalley!" he shouted into the wind. "They should arrive any minute."

Luke stepped out into the rain and wind to glance at the landing platform that jutted out over the canyon. "They might need some help. We'd better be on hand to meet them." He looked back at R2, who was whining in apprehension.

"Stay here, Artoo. We'll be right back."

The three Jedi hurried for the ladder. Whereas Luke and Mara had been on Zonama Sekot for almost three months, Corran had arrived only three weeks earlier, in the company of Tahiri Veila and three Yuuzhan Vong agents. Two of the Yuuzhan Vong were now dead, and the third was believed to have escaped from the living world short of the act of sabotage that had hurled it through hyperspace.

First to reach the edge of the wind-tossed walkway that accessed the landing platform, Mara came to a sudden halt. "Is this thing safe?"

Luke regarded it for a moment. "It'll hold!"

Corran frowned. "Could you be a bit more specific?"

Luke squeezed past him, out onto the swinging walkway, where he jumped in place, twice. "See?"

Mara threw Corran a look. "You can take the kid from Tatooine . . ." Leaving the remark unfinished, she dashed after Luke.

Corran was only steps behind when they reached the platform itself, square and cantilevered by thick timbers anchored in the cliff face. From downvalley, and drifting to and fro in the wind, appeared a cluster of what might have been balloons, holding aloft an oblong wooden gondola with an aft cabin.

"There she blows," Corran said.

"You're not kidding," Mara said. She looked at Luke. "They'll never be able to land!"

"They will. They have the Force at their backs."

Luke set himself in the near-horizontal rain and focused his attention on the approaching airship. Through the Force, he could feel Mara and Corran join him, and he could also feel the tremendous power Jacen and Saba were exercising to prevent the airship from being blown where the howling wind wanted to take it. Confidence surged through him. The Jedi were working not against the natural forces, but in harmony with them, availing themselves of just those gusts that would maneuver the airship to the destination they had chosen.

Had there been better forewarning of the trap the three Yuuzhan Vong agents had sprung, Sekot also might have been able to maneuver Zonama through hyperspace to a safe landing. But the jump to lightspeed had been inadvertent—though fortunately in place of the planned destruction of the planet.

When Zonama Sekot first emerged from transit, conditions were even worse than those that followed. Luke could remember staring into an unfamiliar night sky; then, at daybreak, an enormous sun ballooning on the horizon like an explosion, too brilliant to regard, and radiating such heat that huge expanses of tampasi had burst into flame. Seismic events had opened yawning, zigzagging fissures on the high plateaus, and gigantic slabs of rock had been thrust from the parted ground. Forest fires filled the already scorching air with smoke, cinder, and ash.

As protection from the dangerous rays of the star in whose clutches Zonama had been thrown, Sekot had engineered cloud cover from what moisture it could suck from the planetary mantle. But the damage had already been done. Breathable air was in short supply, and the plasma cores of the hyperdrive engines were dazed. Then, just when Luke had feared the worst for everyone huddled in the shelters and deep in the canyons, where the air was slightly cooler if no less oxygen-deprived, Zonama had jumped again.

Whether because of further misfortune or at Sekot's direction, no one could say. But rain had been falling ever since.

Under the guidance of the five Jedi, the airship completed its descent and made a satisfactory landing on the platform. Luke, Mara, and Corran had the ship tethered to its docking cleats even before Jacen and Saba emerged from the small cabin.

"Welcome back," Luke said, clapping his nephew on the shoulders, then hugging him.

Jacen's brown hair was combed back and fell almost to his shoulders now, but he had recently shaved his beard. His cloak was stiff with dried mud. Saba, in contrast, wore minimal garments, and her black reptilian skin glistened.

"You're shivering," Mara said to Jacen while she was hugging him.

"I'm fine."

"No, you're not." She nodded toward the cliff dwelling. "Let's get you inside. We have a fire going."

R2-D2 was chirping in excitement when the waterlogged Jedi filed through the trapezoidal entrance. A nourishing fire blazed in the center of the room, smoke escaping through a natural chimney. Elsewhere were glow sticks, sleeping rolls, gear, and provisions, moved there from *Jade Shadow*.

"Are either of you hungry?" Mara asked Jacen and Saba when everyone had warmed themselves.

"Starved," Jacen said.

The Barabel Jedi nodded. "This one az well."

Mara glanced around. "Anyone else?"

Corran shrugged. "I'm not about to turn down a home-cooked meal."

Luke took off his wet cloak and hung it by the fire, then sat down opposite Jacen and Saba. "Tell us everything."

With a nod of her round head, Saba deferred to Jacen.

"Conditions in the south are worse than here," the young man began. "The forests are scorched beyond recognition, the trails are impassable, and the rivers are too swollen to navigate. A lot of the boras are completely leafless, and the wildlife has been shocked into hibernation. Most of the Ferroans reached the shelters in time, but hundreds died. When they can, Owell, Darak, Rowel, and others have been scouring the area for survivors, but they haven't found any. There's no word on the Jentari, because no one has been able to reach them."

Cybernetic organisms bred by the planet's early Magisters—overseers and liaisons with Sekot—the Jentari were the carvers and assemblers of Zonama's once-celebrated living starships.

"Some Ferroans are saying that the southern hemisphere is every bit as traumatized as it was when the Far Outsiders attacked," Jacen continued.

Saba nodded. "This one haz rarely seen such devastation on an inhabited world."

Far Outsiders was the Ferroan term for the Yuuzhan Vong, who had found and engaged Zonama Sekot some fifty years earlier, when first scouting the galaxy they planned to invade.

"The Far Distance is melting," Jacen said. "The area where Obi-Wan and Anakin landed has broken away from the ice shelf and is adrift in the Northern Sea." He paused to consider his words. "I guess I should say Southern Sea, since Zonama Sekot is now upside down."

Mara interrupted the conversation to pass out bowls of stew, sweetened with rogir-boln fruit, which Jacen and Saba devoured ravenously.

"Were you able to learn anything about *Widowmaker*?" Luke asked after Jacen had set his bowl down.

Jacen shook his head sadly. "It's gone. It didn't make the jump to hyperspace with Zonama Sekot."

The sudden silence was broken only by the crackling of the fire. *Jade Shadow*'s escort since leaving the Remnant, the Imperial frigate had been commanded by Captain Arien Yage, whom the Jedi had come to regard as a close friend rather than a mere comrade in arms.

"There's more bad news," Jacen said finally. "Some of the Ferroans are holding us accountable for what happened."

Mara compressed her lips in anger. "Luke warned Sekot that the Yuuzhan Vong might return."

Luke shook his head. "It doesn't matter. I'm sure the Ferroans are thinking that if it took only three Yuuzhan Vong to reopen wounds fifty years old, nothing less than annihilation can come of Sekot's pledge to enlist in the war against them."

"That iz precisely what the Ferroanz are thinking," Saba said, showing her sharp teeth.

Jacen sighed. "Darak told me that, in the past, visitors could remain on Zonama Sekot for only sixty days, and that our time is up."

Luke studied his hands and shook his head back and forth. "All those weeks of persuading Sekot and the Ferroans of the rightness of their participation—undone in an instant . . ." He looked up at Jacen and Saba. "Has anyone seen Jabitha?"

"Not since the day Zonama caught fire," Saba replied.

Sekot's humanoid interface with its sentient residents, Jabitha was Zonama's current Magister, the third in the planet's history. During her brief appearance following the planet's emergence from hyperspace, Jabitha had said only that Sekot had desperate need of her elsewhere, and that she would return when she could. Present at the appearance, Luke and the other Jedi had quickly discerned that the Jabitha who spoke to them was merely a thought projection of Sekot. That fact had been borne out later, when Jabitha's entranced body had been discovered in her dwelling place.

"We'll just have to go back to the beginning," Mara said in a determined way.

Luke looked at her. "We won't know until we speak to Sekot."

In front of the hearth an apparition appeared, gradually manifesting as a tall, wide-eyed, dark-haired, and faintly blue-skinned woman, wearing a black robe decorated with green medallions that sparkled in the light of the fire.

"Jabitha," Luke said, coming to his feet.

"Of a sort," Mara said quietly as she joined him.

"Sekot wishes to reassure you that Zonama will persevere," the thought-projected Jabitha said without preamble. "Since perseverance will necessitate significant alterations to Zonama's present orbit and spin, it would be best if everyone remained in the shelters for the time being."

Luke drew in his breath, only to sense that his relief was premature.

"I am also charged with advising you that Sekot needs time to reassess the possible consequences of returning Zonama to known space. As caretaker of the Living Force—as defined by the Potentium—the continued existence of Zonama Sekot is of utmost importance."

Luke and Mara traded looks of disappointment. Founded in the pre-Palpatine Republic by would-be Jedi, the order known as the Potentium professed belief in a Force that was not divisible into light and dark. Birthed from Zonama by the founders, and under their tutelage as it evolved from egolessness to full self-awareness, Sekot had come to accept the tenets of the Potentium as fact.

Luke hung his head momentarily. *Back to the beginning,*

just as Mara had said—and perhaps worse. Sekot was turning away from involvement in the war. Sekot preferred the sanctuary provided by a gas giant like Mobus over open space and exposure to whatever harm might find the planet.

"Sekot has some idea where we are," Jabitha was saying. "It's possible that Zonama Sekot passed close to this star system during the Crossings from known space."

Luke motioned across the room to R2-D2, who was standing silently against the wall. "Tell Sekot that Artoo can help compute the location—as soon as we can see the stars."

The astromech droid tootled in reinforcement.

"I will tell Sekot," Jabitha said, dematerializing.

Mara sat down next to Luke. "That was Jabitha's voice, but I think we just heard directly from Sekot."

"It's possible."

The five Jedi had yet to emerge from reflection when someone hurried out of the storm into the dwelling's anteroom.

"Danni," Luke said, even as he was turning toward her.

Danni Quee's blond hair hung loosely around her face, but her green eyes shone with excitement.

"Tekli and Tahiri . . ." she said in a rush.

Mara shot to her feet. "What's happened?"

Danni motioned behind her, as if to something just outside the entrance. "They're with him now, the Yuuzhan Vong Priest—Harrar." She blinked and stared at Mara and the others. "He's *alive*."

EIGHT

Giving in to what had become a routine of self-loathing, Malik Carr thought back to his arrival at Obroa-skai in the early days of the invasion. There he had met with Commander Tla, the priest Harrar, tactician Raff, and Nom Anor. Ever faithful to Yun-Harla, the Trickster goddess, Harrar and Nom Anor had hatched a plot to surrender a female member of a deception sect to the New Republic government as a means of infiltrating the Jedi, and assassinating as many of them as possible. Carr had had grave misgivings about the plan, but had given his blessing nevertheless, in part because of something Eminence Harrar had said to him.

The success of our plan will result in your being escalated to the rank of Supreme Commander, with a space vessel of your own to wield against our newfound enemy. From this, too, I will be permitted to sit at the right hand of Supreme Overlord Shimrra, on re-created Yuuzhan'tar . . .

That was before Elan had been killed and Harrar had been recalled to the Outer Rim, and what was to have been a surprise attack on the enemy shipyards at Fondor had ended in failure—another of Nom Anor's plots, but for which Nas Choka and Malik Carr had been forced to shoulder the blame. And yet since then, Nas Choka had been escalated to warmaster, Harrar to high priest, and Nom Anor—against all odds and the better judgment of many—to *prefect* of Yuuzhan'tar.

As for Malik Carr?

A custodian of enemy captives, stripped of his rank, a mere passenger in a vessel commanded by a warrior to whom he was once superior!

"I want one thing understood, Malik Carr," Commander

Bhu Fath was lecturing him from the high seat of the war vessel *Sacred Pyre*. "The prisoners are our first priority. Supreme Overlord Shimrra holds them in even greater regard than any of the relics and idols our convoy bears to Yuuzhan'tar."

Standing stiffly in the murky green light of the command chamber, Carr managed to remain abject and straight-faced, despite the fact that only days earlier more than fifty of the prisoners in his charge had suffocated in Selvaris's immolation pit.

Carr snapped his fists to his shoulders in salute. "I understand, Commander. The prisoners first and foremost."

The convoy was made up of thirteen ships, most of them property of the Peace Brigade, but under the escort of five Yuuzhan Vong war vessels, the largest of them carrying two broods of coralskippers apiece. A circumstance that would have been unthinkable at the start of the war, the convoy was not accompanied by a yammosk. Worse, Fath's vessel was tethered to a Brigader ship by an oqa membrane, to facilitate the transfer of prisoners collected from Selvaris to *Sacred Pyre*. Some of the captives transported from internment camps distant from Selvaris would remain aboard Peace Brigade ships until the convoy reached Yuuzhan'tar.

"Commander," Carr said as he prepared to take his leave, "are you satisfied that the Peace Brigaders have a similar grasp of the priorities? Having met with some of them, I would suggest that their only allegiance is to the spice they smuggle from Ylesia and dose themselves with."

Fath grunted. He was exceedingly tall and corded with muscle, but was seldom granted the fealty such size would have guaranteed another.

"In times like these, we are forced to ally with scoundrels and villains," he said in a tired voice. "And by Supreme Overlord Shimrra's decree do our vessels fraternize. But this won't long be so. Another year, perhaps two, and we will be sufficiently reprovisioned with warriors and vessels to dispense with the need for Peace Brigaders or other would-be allies. Warmaster Nas Choka has given me his personal assurance."

Carr fought to keep from betraying the anger that consumed

him. *He* was the one who had welcomed Nas Choka to the war, and had allowed an escalation ceremony to take place aboard the vessel in his command. He wondered if Nas Choka would so much as deign to gaze on him now—especially should the warmaster learn of the escape of a Selvaris prisoner. The mere possibility of that made the present assignment all the more important, for any untoward incident would surely doom Carr to further demotion.

But, no, he told himself. He would sooner drape a tkun around his neck than suffer additional shame.

He shook off his concern. Even though still visible through a transparency in the command chamber, Selvaris was behind him. Soon the convoy would accrue adequate acceleration for the transition to darkspace, and the next stop would be Yuuzhan'tar.

Saluting Fath a final time, Carr began to back out of the chamber. He had just reached the membrane hatch when Fath's communications subaltern swung away from the villip choir he supervised.

"Commander, enemy vessels detected! On the approach."

Fath rose halfway out of his chair. "What?"

"Warships and starfighter squadrons," the subaltern elaborated.

Carr turned to the transparency. A score of ships were streaming out from behind Selvaris's small moon. In advance of the convoy, others had emerged from what the enemy called hyperspace. He could almost hear the war cries of the starfighter pilots.

"An ambush!" Fath said in confused disbelief.

A stout Peace Brigader burst into the command chamber. "We were told this route was secure! How did the Alliance learn of our plans?"

Fath gaped at the human. "This—this can't be!"

The man snorted in scorn and pointed out the transparency. "Take a look, Commander. Unless you do something fast, we're as good as space dust!"

Fath shot to his feet and hurried to the chamber's tactical niche, where a host of hovering blaze bugs were arranging themselves into a battle display. Lacking a yammosk to chaperone them, the best they could manage was a representation of the disposition of the vessels and warships, without providing information on weapons capacity or attack vectors. Carr, meanwhile, took a moment to steady himself, for he knew exactly what had happened.

The escaped prisoner, the mathematical equation spewed by the captive, what he guessed had been code . . .

"Commander Fath," he said without thinking, "charge the villips to spread word of our plight. Deploy dovin basals to protect our vessels. Order the Peace Brigade ships into defensive formation while we launch coralskippers."

Fath's subaltern looked to his commander for authorization.

Fath swallowed hard. "Yes, yes, do as he says—quickly."

The human narrowed his eyes in favor. "Thank the gods someone is doing the thinking around here."

Carr glared at him. "It's a rescue operation. Stop your muttering and see to it that the rest of my prisoners are transferred to *Sacred Pyre*. Once the oqa membrane is retracted, order your people to go to weapons."

Still grinning, the Peace Brigader tapped his forehead with the edge of his extended fingers. "On my way—*Commander*."

Carr reveled in the sound of the honorific, but only for a moment; then he turned back to Fath. "Are you confident you can tackle this?"

Fath lowered his gaze in uncertainty. "I am here by dint of accident, Supreme Commander. You *belong* here."

Carr approached him in fury. "Blu Fath! The honorific belongs to you unless you do something foolish to forfeit it!"

Fath raised his eyes and nodded.

"Command the prisoner ships to go to darkspace immediately," Carr said. "We can't afford to have them remain in the arena and engage."

Fath's eyes opened wide. "Flee in dishonor?"

Carr took hold of Fath's command cloak. "*Priorities,* Commander. Supreme Overlord Shimrra will honor you more for safeguarding his captives than for your enthusiasm to do battle." He let go of the cloak. "Experience teaches one to distinguish between wisdom and eagerness."

Fath swung to his subalterns and conveyed the order.

"Now launch the coralskippers," Carr instructed.

The subalterns didn't bother to wait for authorization.

Fath's proudly scarred face was ashen. "But without a yammosk—"

Carr cut him off with a wave of his hand. "If the pilots under the cognition hoods of the coralskippers don't know how to engage the enemy by now, they will never know! And they'll pay for their ignorance with dishonorable death." He motioned Fath to the villip choir. "Tell them so. Stir their hearts. Inflame them!"

Fath swallowed and nodded. "I will. But where will you be?"

Carr tipped his head to one side. "Did you not command me to take charge of the prisoners?"

Fath straightened to his full height. "I did."

Carr placed his hands atop Fath's broad shoulders. "Command tests our will. Hold fast to your faith in Yun-Yammka. Rise above the storm. But should the battle back you into a corner, you know where to find me."

Fath snapped his fists to the opposite shoulders, following it with a gesture of *us-hrok*—a sign of gratitude and loyalty. "*Belek tiu,* Supreme Commander!"

Weapons were already flaring in space—the enemy's laser cannons and proton torpedo launchers. Carr spun on his heel and rushed from the command chamber. This day would see him exonerated or *dead*.

Twin Suns Squadron of battle-seasoned X-wings emerged from hiding with wingtip lasers charged and stabilizers locked in attack position. The convoy of pod-shaped Peace Brigade freighters and their escort of war vessels was strung out in a long line that trailed past Selvaris's moon almost to the planet itself. A few of the freighters sported retrofitted turbolasers and other ranged weapons, but most were patched together and defenseless. Three of the Yuuzhan Vong vessels were 120-meter-long spearheads of reddish black coral, pitted with dovin basal launchers and plasma-spitting weapons emplacements. The pair of larger vessels were oval-shaped carrier analogs, equally well armed, and sporting clusters of coralskippers affixed like shellfish to their bone-white hulls.

Ensconced in Twin Suns One, Jaina Solo flew point for the

three squadrons under her command. Gloved hands gripped on the X-wing's control stick, she chinned her helmet comm. "All flights, form up on your leaders and keep your battle channels open for instructions. Scimitar Leader, do you copy?"

"Copy, Twin One," Colonel Ijix Harona said.

"Yellow Taanab Leader, do you copy?"

Wes Janson commed back. "Loud and clear, Twin One."

The X-wing's sensors painted blue and yellow bezels on the cockpit displays. "Scimitar Leader, your squadron has the number one carrier. Taanab Leader, those forward gunships are yours. Twin Suns will take the carrier umbilicaled to the Brigade freighter. The rest of the convoy vessels are designated to Dozen, Blackmoon, and Vanguard fighter squadrons."

Named by Luke Skywalker for his double-starred homeworld of Tatooine, Twin Suns was made up of T-65A2s and XJ3 X-wings. Ijix Harona's Scimitars were wedge-shaped A-wings; Blackmoon was E-wings; and the Taanab Aces—a volunteer squadron—were yellow snubfighters adorned with black stripes. The Dozen had originally been formed by Kyp Durron; the Vanguard, by Jagged Fel and his Chiss comrades.

The flanks of Jaina's white fighter still bore faint traces of running voxyn—Jedi-hunting beasts bioengineered by the Yuuzhan Vong—that had been added years earlier. Off to her right flew starfighters and armed transports that had decanted from hyperspace only moments earlier. She switched over to the command net. "You there, Kyp, Colonel Fel, Captain Saz?"

"Affirmative, Colonel," Saz said from Blackmoon One.

"Perched on your right shoulder," Kyp Durron replied. The nova suns on the fuselage of his X-wing were as faded as Twin Suns One's voxyn. *Good to see you,* he sent through the Force.

Acknowledging the extrasensory greeting, Jaina felt Kyp join the Force-meld she shared with Lowbacca and Alema Rar. The Wookiee and the Twi'lek were piloting Twin Suns Five and Nine, respectively. The meld was powerful, though nothing like the twin bond Jaina shared with Jacen, even across the stars.

"Where's Jag—Colonel Fel?" she asked. "I thought the Chiss were going to participate."

"Vanguard was held back at Mon Calamari," Kyp said. "Something big is brewing." *He sends his love,* the Jedi Master added.

The sending caught Jaina by surprise, and her face took on sudden color. Kyp's remark couldn't have been better timed.

"Twin Suns, Scimitar, and the Yellow Aces are tasked," she told the recent arrivals firmly. "Don't feel shy about asking for help if the gunships put up a fight, Blackmoon Leader."

Saz laughed. "Thanks for the vote of confidence, Colonel."

From its socket behind the X-wing's canopy, Jaina's R2-B3 unit, Cappie, relayed an urgent message to the cockpit. She studied the translation display screen and chinned her comm again. "All pilots, sensors are showing intensifying hyperdrive emissions in the Peace Brigade freighters."

"Copy, Twin One," Harona said. "They're ramping up to make the jump to lightspeed."

Jaina reached for the throttle. "They're not leaving without our permission. All flights, move in to intercept and obstruct. Target hyperspace drives and shield generators. Be precise with your shots. We don't know where the prisoners are being held."

Jaina watched Peace Brigade ships break formation, the lead freighters veering to either side, and midline vessels angling for cover behind Selvaris's moon. Elements of Kyp's Dozen and Blackmoon swept in to cut off the enemy ships.

Jaina pulled back on the yoke and sent her craft into a predatory bank that would have knocked the wind from her in atmosphere, but, here, with the inertial compensators enabled, felt like nothing more than a slow glide. Laser beams and molten projectiles streaked from the convoy escort ships, tearing into the ranks of starfighters. Two X-wings disappeared in globular explosions. Kyp's Dozen broke into four shield trios, accelerating in an attempt to overtake the fleeing freighters.

Some of the Peace Brigade ships were faster than they looked. Thrusters blazing, they raced Rimward, even with Blackmoon and Scimitar starfighters hanging on their tails, raking fire across their hulls and engine nacelles. But the pursuit was ill timed.

"I count one, two, three Brigade ships away," Harona said as the freighters made the jump to hyperspace and vanished. "Should we go after them?"

"Negative," Jaina said quickly. Their orders were to rescue as many prisoners as possible, not chase the enemy clear to Coruscant. "Just make sure no others get past us."

Kyp's Dozen hurtled forward to make sure that none did, paying out concussion missiles and torpedoes as necessary to corral the fleeing freighters. Poorly shielded, the unwieldy ships heaved to, one of them already immobilized.

The carriers, however, were quick to react.

"Skips away!" Harona's voice boomed in Jaina's headphones.

Jaina slewed to starboard in time to see the enemy fighters drop from the undersides of their carriers and form up in clouds around the remaining freighters and Yuuzhan Vong gunships. Pearlescent red wedges of yorik coral, the enemy fighters were nimble and lethal. The sight might have sent her heart racing had she not grown accustomed to the enemy's tactics. Still, she knew from personal experience not to underestimate the vitality of the coralskippers or the single-mindedness of their pilots.

She allowed her sense of exhilaration to run its course, then eased back into the Force-meld. Lowbacca, Alema, and Kyp acknowledged their readiness.

"One Flight," she said, "change to course one-zero-one ecliptic. Set lasers for out-of-phase fire. Remember to toggle your grab-safeties if dovin basals pull your shields."

Lowbacca and Alema touched her briefly through the Force as their separate four-fighter contingents altered vectors accordingly and began to accelerate toward the tethered carrier.

Following the rout of Tsavong Lah's forces at Ebaq 9, and almost a year of modest victories in Remnant space, the Koornacht Cluster, Bakura, and elsewhere, the war should have long been over. Galactic Alliance commanders Sovv, Kre'fey, Brand, Keyan Farlander, Garm Bel Iblis, and others were certain that they had dealt the Yuuzhan Vong a death blow, and that subsequent engagements would be limited to mop-up operations. All the while, though, Yuuzhan Vong shapers had been busy cooking up ways to reestablish parity, and slowly they had discovered the means to counter the weapons the Alliance had grown to rely on: laser stutterfire, yammosk jammers, decoy dovin basals, shadow bombs, and the rest.

Then the Yuuzhan Vong had gone a step farther by unleashing a horde of specially designed dovin basals to gobble up or otherwise incapacitate HoloNet relay stations throughout the galaxy. While the Alliance had tried valiantly to reinstate instantaneous communications—resorting to stationing warships in deep space to double as transponders—world after world had fallen to the enemy, conquered or surrendered without a fight. Finally there had been the disastrous attempt by combined Alliance and Imperial Remnant forces to reclaim Bilbringi.

The title of Trickster was back in the hands of Supreme Overlord Shimrra, and Jaina was only "the Sword" she had been named on Mon Calamari, in the Jedi Knighting ceremony that had preceded the battle at Ebaq 9.

"Make every shot count," she said. "Reserve torpedoes and concussion missiles for the carrier."

An organic-looking cofferdam still linked the Yuuzhan Vong vessel to a Peace Brigade freighter. Between Twin Suns and the leashed ships, local space was target-rich with coralskippers.

"Begin your hull runs," Jaina commanded. "Straight down the convoy line."

The X-wing's sensor screens grew noisy with battle static as bursts of green coherent light streaked from the starfighters' weapons. Singularities fashioned by the coralskippers engulfed most of the bursts, but a few beams pierced the enemy defenses and found their targets. Spherical explosions blossomed, sending asymmetrical masses of yorik coral spinning off into space.

At the end of the first run, Jaina powered Twin Sun One through a tight turn, accelerated, and rocketed back into the thick of the fighting. Superheated ejecta surged from

the coralskippers' volcanolike launchers, whipping past her
canopy like fiery meteors. She wreathed through a tight
grouping of enemy fighters, responding in kind. One skip
scudded clear of her carefully timed bursts, but a second she
caught off guard with steady fire, destroying it completely.

She boosted power and chased the one that got away, her
wingmate coming alongside her. The craggy lump of dovin-
basal-driven coral climbed, then looped and descended,
throwing everything it had at them. Twin Sun Three yawed
hard to port, but not fast enough. The skip's dovin basal
lurched for the starfighter's shields at the same time two
molten missiles were catching up with it. Overwhelmed, the
deflectors failed, and the X-wing blew to pieces.

One thing Jaina hadn't grown accustomed to was losing
her teammates. At this point in the war, with every available
veteran leading his or her own squadron, most of the pilots
assigned to Twin Suns weren't much older than she was, and
each and every death tore her apart.

Anger flared in her, but only for a moment, before evanescing in the Force. In eerie calm she veered and pounced
on the coralskipper while its organic defenses were preoccupied. Two precisely placed shots disabled it, and a third finished it. The skip coughed fluorescent puffs of vaporized
coral, then disappeared in a short-lived ball of flame.

Peeling away from the fireball, Jaina prowled for new targets.

With the playing field leveled, courtesy of the enemy's ap-
titude for innovation, fighter engagements had become as
ferocious as they had been at the start of the war, before effective countermeasures had come into play. Alliance forces
held a slight advantage when coralskippers were flying without the assistance of a yammosk, but enemy pilots now had
more authority over their ships than ever before, and were no
longer as easily outwitted or outmaneuvered.

Jaina ignored the displays of her range finder and computer-
aided sights and relied on the Force to guide her to targets of
opportunity. The battle channels were noisy with chatter.

"We can't clear a path for the transport with those skips
hugging the carriers," Harona was admonishing Scimitar
Squadron. "Three Flight, you've got to take out that dorsal

plasma launcher. Two Flight, see if you can draw those skips away."

"We're trying, Scimitar Leader, but they won't take the bait."

"Copy that. Then we'll just have to take the fight to them."

Jaina saw that the same situation applied to the tethered carrier. The coralskippers were intent on protecting the vessel at all costs—or at least until it could detach from the Peace Brigade freighter. Close in, Twin Suns' Two Flight salvoed, opening rends in the yorik coral ridges that shielded the vessel's drive dovin basal.

Jaina had the rest of her squadron tighten up their ragged formation and press the attack. When the X-wings began to score hits, the coralskippers reacted by dispersing. With patent disdain for evasionary tactics, the lead skip launched itself at Jaina. Then the entire swarm sallied forth from their protective positions.

"Twin One, single skip at your right wing," Alema warned.

"Thanks, Nine."

Jaina wheeled away from a flurry of missiles, rolled, and came about. She and the opposing flight leader squared off and bored in on each other, their respective wingmates falling back, too busy holding position and adapting to their leaders' actions to do any firing. The skip opened a void directly in front of Jaina, but she managed to twist free in the nick of time. The X-wing bucked, then righted itself. Jaina thumbed the trigger of the lasers, pouring fire into the gravitic hole. The dovin basal rushed to absorb the energy, leaving the coralskipper momentarily unprotected. It was all the time Jaina needed. The X-wing's starboard lasers hammered the skip mercilessly, splitting it down the middle. Long plumes of incandescence streamed from the rend; then the skip vanished in blinding light.

Two and Three Flights were meeting with similar success. All discipline forgotten, the coralskippers were streaking away from the carrier in a flurry of maneuvers, even while crisscrossing lines of destruction probed for them.

Off toward what was the head of the convoy, the first carrier had gone belly-up; off to both sides, Kyp's Dozen and Blackmoon were flying circles around three Peace Brigade ships whose laser cannon turrets were smoking ruins. And now Alliance gunships and transports were on their way into the arena, keen on filling themselves to bursting with liberated captives.

Jaina ordered One and Three Flights to surround the umbilicaled carrier. She asked Lowbacca to drop Two Flight back to field any skips that might attempt to break through the line.

Kyp commed her. "Just learned that Alliance agents have sabotaged the hyperdrives on all but one of the freighters. They're ours now."

"That's great news," Jaina said.

"Here's an even better piece. Your parents are here."

Jaina smiled. "I felt them."

Her eyes followed a blip on the display screen that could only be the *Millennium Falcon*. It was headed her way.

She hadn't seen her parents in weeks, and had learned only the previous day that they had not only been responsible for providing intelligence on the convoy, but also volunteered for the rescue mission.

Not that that surprised her in the least.

She sent a greeting through the Force. Her mother would know who it was from.

It wasn't long before she could see the *Falcon* with her own eyes. Her parents were maneuvering the ship as deftly as if she were an X- or Y-wing, top and belly quad lasers dispatching coralskippers unlucky enough to be in the way. A sleek Alliance picket, bristling with weapons, flew in the *Falcon*'s wake. As the two ships closed on the number two carrier, the picket fired a harpoon directly into the nose of the Peace Brigade freighter at the other end of the carrier's intestinelike cofferdam.

"Knockout harpoon," Twin Suns Four said. "Like a giant hypodermic syringe filled with coma-gas. By the time our people board, the Brigaders'll be out cold."

NINE

Transparent respirators clamped over their faces and C-3PO shuffling behind them, Han and Leia emerged from the crippled freighter's docking bay into the large cargo hold beyond. Everywhere they looked, Peace Brigaders of various species were passed out on the deck or slumped unmoving against bulkheads. The cargo area was already filled with three squads of Alliance strike troops, whose ship had harpooned the freighter and who'd been the first to board.

The strike troops wore mimetic enviro-suits and black helmets with tinted face bowls. Each was laden with blaster rifles, bandoliers of flash grenades, thermal detonators, half-meter-long vibroblades, and survival gear. Specialists in rapid deployment and infiltration, strike troops were a relatively new addition to the war, and most of the ones in the cargo hold had participated in months of familiarization drills aboard captured Yuuzhan Vong vessels. Han was certain that other squads had already penetrated deep into the ship. Three troopers were slapping manacles on the unconscious Brigaders.

He and Leia scarcely had time to take stock of the situation when a hatch in the forward bulkhead pocketed itself, and a Klatooinian stepped into the hold. Twenty blaster rifles swung to the green-complected, scrunch-faced humanoid before he could so much as raise his taloned hands in surrender.

"I'm Hobyo," he said. A breather mask dangled around his thick neck. "The one who sabotaged the hyperdrive! Surprise Party!" he added. "Surprise Party!"

A human colonel signaled everyone to lower their weapons. "Next time give the code words first, before you come barging into a secured area," he snapped. "You're lucky you didn't get yourself killed."

Hobyo relaxed somewhat. "You won't find any prisoners aboard the freighter. They were transferred to the Yuuzhan Vong carrier."

"Which way?" the colonel demanded.

The Klatooinian pointed to port. "The umbilical is attached to the cargo hold adjacent to this one."

Leaving several soldiers behind to tend to the stirring Brigaders, the colonel motioned the rest into the broad passageway that separated the holds.

Satisfied that it was safe to do so, Han pulled off his respirator and almost gagged. "What the heck are they transporting?" he asked through the hand he clasped to his mouth. "Rotten eggs?"

Leia took a quick whiff and snugged her mask back in place. "Is that the coma-gas?"

Hobyo shook his head. "The stench comes from the Vong cofferdam. Air circulators carry the smell throughout the ship. But you get used to it."

"Speak for yourself," Han said. He motioned with his chin to the passageway. "You coming?"

"As soon as I provide identities of the Peace Brigaders."

Han nodded, and waved to C-3PO. "Let's go, Goldenrod."

The droid started. "Sir, wouldn't it be best if I remained aboard *Millennium Falcon*?"

"Cakhmaim and Meewalh can take care of the *Falcon*. We might need you to translate."

"Translate? But, Captain Solo, I'm far from fluent in Yuuzhan Vong. In fact, I'm still trying to comprehend the conditional subjunctive tense!"

Han made a face. "You've never had trouble making yourself understood, Threepio. Now get going."

He and Leia led the way into the port-side cargo hold. Han spied the cofferdam entrance and ran for it, only to stop short at the mouth, then half turn and flatten his back against the bulkhead.

"You really don't want to see this," he said as Leia approached.

She studied him in puzzlement. Han was a bit wide-eyed

and shaking his head back and forth. "What are you talking about?" she asked.

"Remember that time on Dantooine when I got the Balmorra flu? Well, this thing—" He jerked his thumb toward the cofferdam opening. "—is what I figure the inside of my nose must have looked like."

Leia smiled dubiously and stepped around him. "It can't be that ba—"

She froze.

"Why it's an . . . oqa," C-3PO said, standing somewhat akimbo at the entrance. "The word derives from the proboscis of a Yuuzhan Vong pack animal. The floor is what is sometimes referred to as a microbial mat. And the viscous liquid drooling from the ceiling actually houses the bacteria that engineered the entire tube!"

"I told you he'd come in handy," Han said.

C-3PO disappeared into the organic cofferdam, sloshing along the puddled floor, his voice echoing wetly. "Oh, yes, tiny white arachnids, similar to those that can sometimes be found inhabiting volcanic vents . . ."

Han was staring at Leia. "I hate microbial mats! Maybe there's another way."

"I don't think so, Han."

He firmed his lips. "All right, you first. Just don't . . . *touch* anything."

They covered the hundred meters in record time, eyes forward and arms straight at their sides. By the time they emerged in the Yuuzhan Vong carrier, Leia's legs were drenched to the knee in foul-smelling liquid.

They could tell which way the strike troops had gone by the gaping holes the soldiers had blown in membranous interior bulkheads and iris portals. Bioluminescent lichen lent a cheerless green light to the carrier's meandering internal passageways. Fluids seeped from gently pulsing walls and strands of connective tissue, where passageways intersected. The air was rich in oxygen but pungent. They stepped through a torn membrane into a spacious hold whose yorik coral deck might have been pink ferrocrete.

Leia ignited her lightsaber.

From the ship's forward came the sounds of war cries and

muffled shouts, blasterfire and the dull thudding of amphistaff strikes.

"I guess coma-gas doesn't work on the Yuuzhan Vong," Leia said.

"Yeah, too bad about that."

They sprinted toward the sounds of battle, rounding a corner to see allies and enemies down, smears of red and black on the floor, refreshment for a host of tonguelike creatures that were gorging on the spilled blood. Han shot from the hip, dropping a Yuuzhan Vong warrior with a coufee dagger in each hand. With a downward slash, Leia cut the legs out from under another who had launched himself at her. Hands pressed to his head, C-3PO issued a litany of mirthless exclamations and laments.

They followed the strike troops farther forward. The soldiers held their blasters at high port, sweeping them from side to side. They advanced in leapfrogging squads, waving signals to one another, overwhelming amphistaffs with continuous bursts, or concentrating blasterfire on vonduun crab armor weak points, then searing the exposed flesh beneath. With or without weapons, with or without their living arthropod armor, the enemy warriors continued to attack, always choosing death over surrender where there was an option.

Stepping over sprawled bodies, Han, Leia, and a squad of troops reached another intersection. The squad leader was trying to decide which fork to take when Hobyo finally caught up with them.

"The prisoners are on the upper deck, in a hold aft of the command chamber." The Klatooinian edged his way into the intersection and gestured. "This way."

A steeply sloped corridor led up to the carrier's command deck. At the top of the slope two strike troops had a Peace Brigader in custody. A strong smell of glitterstim spice wafted from the human's uniform.

"He says that most of the warriors took to coralskippers when we attacked," the tallest of the soldiers reported. "The only ones left on board are the officers."

The Brigader led the rest of the way to the forward hold. There, squashed together inside a sticky net, sat three Yuuzhan Vong. One wore a command cloak that hung from bony implants on the tops of his shoulders. The strike troops' colonel was circling them proudly, with his hands planted on his hips, thumbs backward.

"We took these three by surprise and webbed them before they knew what hit them."

Across the hold, fifty or so Alliance prisoners of various species were stuck to the deck in a pool of blorash jelly.

"Han! Leia!" one of them called out.

The speaker was a thickset human, with pleasant if undistinguished features and a full salt-and-pepper beard.

"Judder Page," Han said, grinning as he approached. He scanned other faces in the crowd. "And Pash."

Cracken nodded his head in greeting. "Rescued by celebrities. I'm positively humbled."

Leia glanced at the blorash jelly and folded her arms across her chest. "We're not out of this yet."

Han squatted down in front of Captain Page. "If we'd known you were on Selvaris, we wouldn't have left without you."

Page shook his head in bafflement. "You were at Selvaris?"

"We picked up one of your escapees," Han explained. "A Jenet."

"Garban—Thorsh," Cracken said in obvious relief.

"How else do you think we knew about the convoy?"

"Thank the Force," Page mumbled.

"Wedge sends his regards," Han said. "He says he's sorry about Bilbringi, and even sorrier that rescuing you took as long as it did."

Page mustered a smile. "I'm gonna kiss him when I see him."

"I'd be careful about that," Han said. "He might just send you back."

Leia studied the blorash jelly. "We need to get you out of this."

Hobyo dragged the stout Peace Brigader forward. "He knows how the stuff works."

The man's spice-clouded eyes darted to the captured Yuuzhan Vong officers and widened in fear. "You'll have to kill me, 'cause if you don't, *they* will."

Leia went to him. "We'll make you a better offer. We'll take you with us. You'll stand trial, serve time for your war crimes, be rehabilitated, and released in twenty years. Otherwise we leave you here and we give the Yuuzhan Vong every reason to believe that you were the one who tipped us off about the convoy. Maybe they won't kill you right away. Maybe they'll even take you with them. But you're going to find it a lot harder to get glitterstim on Coruscant than in a Galactic Alliance prison. And you know how excruciating withdrawal can be."

The human gulped and found his voice. "All right." He nodded to the blorash pool. "Arsensalts."

Han stepped close to Leia. "Your mind tricks are a lot more subtle than your brother's."

Leia smiled. "I win by guile."

"You don't have to tell me."

The strike troops searched their utility belts, broke open capsules of arsensalts, and began to sprinkle them over the pool. When Han and Leia had yanked Captain Page free of the liquefying mass, he walked directly to the netted Yuuzhan Vong and went down on his haunches in front of the one with the longest hair.

"Something you want to say to this one?" Han asked in interest. " 'Cause our droid speaks fluent enemy."

C-3PO protested. "Captain Solo, I—"

"Not necessary, Han," Page interrupted. "Malik Carr speaks fluent Basic. He was commander of the Selvaris camp. Has a particular fondness for subjecting prisoners and droids to immolation pits."

Han proffered his blaster to Page. "No one here'll think any the less of you."

Page shook his head. "I know how important we were to Shimrra, and Malik Carr's going to show up on Coruscant empty-handed." He grinned. "He'll get his due from his own kind—unless, of course, he kills himself in dishonor beforehand."

A strike troop officer hurried into the hold. "Enemy reinforcements coming out of hyperspace. We need to move!"

The colonel looked baffled. "So soon?"

"The Vong must have gotten off a distress call, sir."

"Have the transports docked?"

"One or two."

Han stepped forward. "We can cram eighty or so aboard the *Falcon*." He looked at the colonel. "Can you take the rest?"

"We'll have to."

"Captain Page," Malik Carr called out. "I'll live to see you on a sacrificial pyre before Yuuzhan'tar completes a quarter orbit round its star."

Page approached him once more. "On the off chance we do meet again, keep this thought tucked into that warped brain of yours: fifty of my people died because of you, and the next time I won't be nearly as charitable with you as I was here."

In a mad dance, Jaina circled the stricken Yuuzhan Vong carrier, dueling coralskippers with each dive and traverse. The battle roles had been reversed. Now starfighter squadrons were the defenders and skips the aggressors, surging forward to harry and engage at every opportunity. Harona's Scimitar and Wes Janson's Yellow Aces were similarly deployed around carrier one. With several of the Peace Brigade freighters incapacitated by Alliance gunships, Blackmoon and the Dozen were flying escort for the rescue transports.

Millennium Falcon had followed a strike troop gunship into the docking bay of the freighter tethered to carrier two, but almost an hour had passed and neither ship had emerged. A transport was on its way to docking, but had suddenly stopped, adding to Jaina's vague sense of unrest.

She reached out for her mother, but all she felt in return was rushed activity and deep concern.

In conversation with veterans of protracted wars, Jaina had been advised to accept that the final stage of any conflict was often the worst. More dislocating than the initial periods of surprise and chaos, and more dispiriting than the intermediate periods, after the deaths had begun to mount up and it could seem as if the killing might go on forever. But it was the end stage that was most dangerous—a period of improbable alliances and unexpected reversals, some owing to overconfidence, others born of fear and desperation.

Jaina gave scant attention to any of this, except during the lulls in battle, when her thoughts sought escape from the tableaux of fiery explosions and crippled ships.

As the mynock flew, Bilbringi was almost a neighbor of Selvaris, and the recent battle there was almost emblematic of the odd pairings and reversals Jaina had been warned to expect. The operation had been the first since Esfandia that combined Alliance and Imperial elements, and the disabling of the HoloNet had been one of the war's biggest surprises yet. Now, with Luke, Mara, Jacen, and other Jedi incommunicado, she was waiting for the other boot to drop.

She thought about her parents, and returned her gaze to the docking bay of the freighter. There was still no sign of the *Falcon*. She was about to comm mission control for an update when the X-wing's tactical screens came alive with enemy blips.

"Heads up!" she said over the battle channel. "Vessels decanting from hyperspace."

That was why the transports had stopped, Jaina told herself. Everyone had been expecting reinforcements to show up, but not so soon. She waited for the authenticators to display data on what the sensors had picked up.

"They appear to be coralskippers," Harona said. "Approaching from starward of Selvaris. I make it three stacked triangles of six skips."

Jaina shook her head. Coralskippers lacked the ability to travel through hyperspace unassisted. "Scimitar Leader, that can't be right."

"Twin Suns One," Wes Janson said. "These blips don't match anything in the battle log."

"Taanab One, my instruments agree," Jaina commed. "We should have visual in a matter of seconds . . ."

What the long-range scanners showed made her sit up straighter in the X-wing's contoured seat. The fighters—if indeed that was what they were—were made up of three yorik coral triangles, joined apex to base. The leading two triangles showed mica-like canopies, while the third and largest was flared at the rear and sported a long upcurving tail, perhaps to augment dovin basal impulsion, which in a coralskipper was often located in the nose. From the forward segments of the scaled fuselage sprouted six legs, three pairs to each side, veined in blue and tipped with launcher ports for plasma missiles.

Twin Suns Three whistled in surprise. "They look like Azuran stingcrawlers."

More like voxyn! Jaina thought.

"Close ranks and form up on me," she said quickly. "Anyone short on firepower to the center. Stick with your wingmates until we see what these things are capable of."

"Enemy is breaking formation," Harona announced. "Here they come!"

The formations of snarling skips surged forward with incredible speed, their sextets of launchers disgorging plasma in steady streams. Deliberately, Jaina placed herself in the path of one projectile and was immediately sorry she had. Cappie shrieked in distress, and the X-wing's shields fell to 50 percent.

She tumbled away from second and third projectiles, allowing time for the shields to recharge. "All pilots, keep clear of these things. They pack a wallop!"

The warning did not come soon enough. The battle net grew frantic with exclamations.

"Twin Six and Seven are down!"

"Scimitar reporting four casualties!"

"Taanab Ten, pull out! Divert power to your shields!"

Jaina glanced over her right shoulder and saw Twin Suns Two fly apart.

This can't be happening, she thought.

"Stingcrawlers have broken through our lines," Twin Suns Six said. "They're going directly for the transports."

Jaina pulled hard on the yoke, climbing back toward carrier one at maximum boost. "Twin Suns, disengage and regroup. Screen formation on my mark!"

She issued the command, and the remaining starfighters formed up once again. They chased the coralskippers flat out, wending through continuous volleys of incandescent fire.

"Scimitar is calling for backup at carrier one."

"Enemy fighters are taking up positions around our transports. We can't fire without risking collateral damage."

"All pilots, weapons on number one carrier are active! Repeat—"

The rest of Scimitar Three's words were erased by an agonized scream.

Jaina hurtled into the fray, thumb pressed on the trigger,
only to watch her stutterfire bursts disappear into the yawning mouths of enormous gravity wells fashioned by the
skips' dovin basals. Was the convoy a cleverly engineered
ruse? she asked herself. Disinformation to lure the Alliance
into a trap? But that couldn't be. If so, the Yuuzhan Vong
would have capital ships and a yammosk vessel. They would
have struck before any of the prisoners had been rescued and
transferred to the transports—

Lowbacca growled a warning.

Four blazing missiles had Jaina's name on them. She
slalomed successfully through the first three, but the fourth
nicked the port stabilizer and sent the X-wing into a rapid
spin. She calmed herself and regained control, emerging
from the spin in time to see a transport explode directly in
front of her. Sudden anguish kept her stunned for a moment;
then she swerved away from the fragment cloud and went
searching for the guilty skip.

Kyp and Alema Rar sent a sudden alert to her through the
Force.

She rolled the X-wing onto its back. The *Falcon* had
launched from the freighter's docking bay and was making
fast for clear space, a Galactic Alliance gunship right behind.

Twisting free of engagements, four enemy fighters converged on the *Falcon*.

Jaina tried to establish contact with her parents, but the
battle channel was screeching with static.

Mom!

The *Falcon* was jarred by missiles her parents either hadn't
seen coming or were unable to avoid. In her mind's eye, Jaina
could see Han taking the ship through a repertoire of evasive
maneuvers. And yet the enemy pilots of the stingcrawler
skips were clearly anticipating the *Falcon*'s every move.

Jaina, Alema, and Twin Eleven and Twelve flew to the
freighter's rescue, battering the skips from behind, but the
Yuuzhan Vong fighters refused to be distracted from their
target. In a moment of blind rage, Jaina dropped her guard

and was struck from starboard. Slewing helplessly, she watched Eleven and Twelve shatter.

The enemy was on a killing spree.

"All flights, go to proton torpedoes!"

Brilliant orbs of energy streaked forward and disappeared. The stingcrawler skips' singularites were swallowing four times what a normal skip was capable of dealing with.

Jaina flinched with each magma missile that hit the *Falcon.* The freighter's shields were holding, but the *Falcon* was literally rattling around inside them. Three skips accelerated, determined to overtake their quarry. Quad lasers spraying fire in all direction, the *Falcon* tipped up on her starboard side, only to take a devastating blow to the belly. One skip sustained a broadside hit and went careening into a Peace Brigade ship, opening a ragged breach and sending the ship into a dizzying rollover.

The *Falcon* and the gunship were almost clear enough to go to hyperspace. Jaina imagined herself in the outrigger cockpit, throwing switches and actuators, pushing the hyperspace lever forward. The sometimes unreliable navicomputer counting down before the ship could make the jump to lightspeed . . .

Hurry, she said to herself. *Hurry!*

The detonation nearly threw Leia out of her seat harness. Han's hands were white-knuckled on the yoke. Cinched into the cockpit's high-backed rear chairs, Cracken and Page extended their arms to keep themselves upright. The other rescued officers were packed into the forward cabin and wherever else they could fit.

"How much more of this can the *Falcon* take?" Page asked.

"As much as she needs to," Han growled, without meaning to.

Leia thought she heard uncertainty beneath the bluster.

Han adjusted his headset mike. "Cakhmaim, Meewalh, don't ease up on those guns! I don't care if they are overheating! Right now they're the only things keeping those skips away from us!"

Han sent the *Falcon* on edge to evade a trio of enemy

ships, escaping with only a bone-rattling hit to the freighter's midsection. Streaking past the wraparound viewport flew two dual-piloted coralskippers.

Han's jaw dropped slightly and he looked over his shoulder at Cracken. "Pash, what kind of skips are those? I've never seen anything like them. Have you guys seen anything like them?"

Cracken shook his head.

"Never too late in the game for surprise, is it?" Page said.

Han blew out his breath. "Guess not."

The muffled report of an explosion reached the cockpit from aft.

"That didn't sound good," Leia said.

Han's eyes darted to the display screens, then widened. "It's worse than it sounded. But we're not done yet." He reached forward to toggle switches, reallocating power to the rear shields.

"Can we make lightspeed?" Cracken asked.

"While I have a breath in me."

Away to starboard, punched by an enemy fighter, a Peace Brigade freighter cracked open, belching fire, atmosphere, and a whirlwind of debris.

Han pounded the console with his fist. "Nice shooting, Cakhmaim." He paused, then said, "All right, all right, the kill's yours, Meewalh."

He pivoted in his chair and smiled lopsidedly. "They think this is some kind of—"

The cockpit turned blinding white. Han's words swirled to nothingness, and time slowed for an indeterminate period.

A second explosion of intense light followed. A wave of concussive sound barreled into the cockpit through the sliding hatch, and Leia's ears popped. C-3PO let out a wail from somewhere aft.

"Shields are down to forty percent," she said when she could.

Han could scarcely hear her. He reached over his left shoulder, his hand knowing precisely where to go, like that of a musician at a keyboard. Finished with whatever adjustments he had made, he smiled for show.

Leia heard him mumble, "Come on, baby, hold together

just twenty seconds more . . ." He caught her watching him. "Don't worry."

She shrugged. "Who's worrying?"

The *Falcon* took her worst hit yet. A tangle of blue energy danced over the navicomputer. A single rivulet of sweat coursed from Han's hairline to his set jaw.

Leia faced forward, staring straight ahead. "*Now* I'm worried."

Without looking at her, Han counted down. "Ten, nine, eight . . ."

" . . . seven, six, five, four—"

Three was on the tip of Jaina's tongue when the *Falcon* was hit hard from behind, the force of the enemy projectiles practically kicking the freighter forward. The ion drives failed for an instant and pieces flew from the stern, one of them streaking across the nose of Jaina's X-wing.

Her mother's distress was palpable.

Then the *Falcon* was gone, propelled into hyperspace, but with four enemy skips following suit. As the Yuuzhan Vong had first demonstrated at the Eclipse base, years earlier, they were capable of tracking ships through hyperspace by means of a self-heating, vacuum-hardened fungus that forced tachyons from a ship in faster-than-light transit.

"All pilots, did anyone get a bearing on the *Falcon*?"

"Negative, Twin One," came a chorus of replies.

The operation rally point was Mon Calamari. But Jaina recognized that the *Falcon*'s jump to lightspeed had been desperate, and she doubted that the navicomputer had had time enough to plot an accurate trajectory. There were thousands, perhaps tens of thousands of possible hyperspace exit points between Selvaris and Mon Calamari.

Apprehension slowed her responses, even while her thoughts raced.

"Twin Suns, fall back to protect the transports," she said when she had gotten hold of herself. "We're taking them home."

TEN

Single file, Luke, Mara, Corran, Jacen, and Saba trailed Danni Quee down into the canyon, where they hoped to find the Yuuzhan Vong priest, Harrar. With the vines that secured the platform hoists hopelessly tangled, they followed a circuitous route of ramps and ladders. Rain was still falling in rippling sheets, and the Jedi had their heads lowered and the hoods of their sopping cloaks raised. Below, partially concealed under a swirling blanket of fog, the swollen river roared.

They were traversing the second tier when Danni stopped and gestured to a small cliff dwelling, where light flickered in the crude window openings.

"It was unoccupied, so we didn't bother asking for permission to use it," she said, loud enough to be heard by everyone.

They were twenty meters from the dwelling when a group of eight Ferroan males stepped from the gloom of a natural cave to intercept them. Slender humanoids with pale blue skin, they were not indigenous to Zonama Sekot but had been brought to the living world generations earlier. Their simple trousers and shirts clung to their bodies, and water ran from their angry faces. In his left hand their apparent leader, Senshi, held a glow stick that cast a misty sphere of light around them.

"You captured a Yuuzhan Vong," he said, breath clouds accompanying his words.

Luke shook his head. "He was found wounded, and brought here to be healed."

"Not wounded by any of us," Senshi said. "Though deserving of whatever injuries he sustained, for what he and the others caused to happen."

Shortly after Luke and the other Jedi had first arrived on Zonama Sekot, Senshi—at Sekot's insistence—had helped carry out a counterfeit kidnapping of Danni Quee, as a means of testing the Jedi. A farmer by trade, he had gold-speckled eyes and close-cropped hair that had darkened to gray-blue with age. Having lost several family members and friends during the Crossings from known space, he was ambivalent about Sekot's decision to return.

"We don't know yet who or what was responsible," Luke said. "We're hoping the Yuuzhan Vong will explain."

He advanced a step, but no one in the group moved.

"You could hurl us aside with a thought," Senshi said. "But you won't, if you're a true servant of the Force."

Luke lowered his hood and gazed at him. "And if you serve the Force, you'll allow us to pass."

The Ferroan gestured toward the cliff dwelling. "As an enemy of Zonama Sekot, the Yuuzhan Vong should be ours to deal with."

"To deal with how?" Luke asked calmly. "Will torturing or killing him return Zonama Sekot to Mobus? Have you asked yourselves how Sekot might react to your taking matters into your own hands?"

"Look around you, Jedi," another Ferroan said. "Have you ever witnessed Zonama thus? Not one of us has. For all any of us knows, Sekot could be unconscious—or worse."

Luke considered mentioning Jabitha's spectral visit to his and Mara's dwelling, but decided that Sekot must have had some reason for not appearing to and reassuring the Ferroans as well.

"Give us a chance to talk with the Yuuzhan Vong before you decide on a course of action," he said after a moment.

The Ferroans mulled over Luke's proposal. "Only if one of us is present," Senshi answered for all of them.

"Which of you?" Luke asked, glancing at everyone.

A young man with white hair stepped forward. "I will go. I am called Maydh."

Luke nodded. "Then it's decided."

The Ferroans separated into two groups, allowing the Jedi

unobstructed access to the cliff dwelling. Luke and the rest came out of the rain to find Harrar seated on the floor by the hearth, his long legs stretched out in front of him. His face and body were battered, and his front teeth were broken. Tekli stood to one side, ministering to his injuries. Rodentlike, though bipedal, the Chadra-Fan looked positively diminutive next to her tall, bandaged patient.

Each of the priest's hands was missing two digits, but their absence had nothing to do with the injuries he had sustained on Zonama Sekot. Thick as a mane, his glossy black hair draped over his tattoo-covered shoulders. Tahiri Veila, whose own forehead bore traces of Yuuzhan Vong markings, was conversing with him quietly in Yuuzhan Vong.

Danni had assured Luke that Harrar was unarmed.

Tahiri was about to introduce Luke and the others when Harrar cut her off with a motion of his hand.

"I will speak to them in your tongue." His drooping eyes darted briefly to Tahiri. "Though I may look to you for clarification from time to time." His gaze returned to the Jedi, settling on each in turn.

Luke regarded the priest for a long moment, then said, "I am Luke Skywalker. This is my wife, Mara."

Harrar's eyes lit up in obvious recognition of the names. "The Master of the *Jeedai*. And the one who fell victim to coomb spores," he added, referring to Mara, who had been cured of the disease only with the birth of her son, Ben.

Luke continued. "You've already met Tahiri and Corran, and, by now, Tekli and Danni." He gestured to his right. "That leaves only Saba, Jacen, and Maydh—whose world you obviously came to destroy."

"Jacen Solo," Harrar said, in what might almost have been taken for awe. "I have observed you from afar, young *Jeedai,* figuratively and literally."

Luke tucked his hands into the sleeves of his cloak and sat down opposite Harrar on a short-legged stool. "You seem to know more about us than we know about you. Perhaps you're willing to correct that."

"Perhaps."

The rest of the Jedi and Maydh sat down in a loose semicircle.

"You told Corran and Tahiri that you, Nen Yim, and the Prophet were seeking answers from Zonama Sekot—nothing more."

Harrar nodded. "We kept to ourselves that each of us had a separate agenda." He paused briefly. "Nen Yim was a shaper—at one time apprenticed to Mezhan Kwaad, who attempted to remake Tahiri into one of us on the world you know as Yavin Four. Shimrra had tasked Nen Yim to analyze an organic ship that was grown here, on Zonama Sekot. In doing so, she made a remarkable discovery that appears in many ways to link this world with the Yuuzhan Vong. She came here seeking verification of her theories.

"As for Yu'shaa, the Prophet, well, his alleged reason for accompanying us was to determine if Zonama Sekot could be of some use to the heretical movement he helped organize among the Shamed Ones on Yuuzhan'tar."

"And your reason?" Mara asked.

"Of less noble principle," Harrar said. "I suspected that shaper Nen Yim was also a heretic—though of a different order. I suspected further that Shimrra was aware of her unorthodox practices, which meant that he, too, was a heretic. Finally, I was interested in unmasking Yu'shaa, and in determining whether or not he was genuine in his beliefs."

"The Prophet killed Nen Yim and left you for dead," Luke said. "Was that because you and Nen Yim succeeded in unmasking him?"

"No. His purpose was to make certain that we didn't survive to share in the glory of destroying Zonama Sekot." Harrar looked at Luke. "As it happens, you know him."

Luke waited.

"He is none other than Nom Anor."

It was nothing Luke hadn't already heard from Corran and Tahiri, but he had wanted to hear it from the priest.

"We know that," Mara said, breaking the silence. "But something isn't right. Nom Anor may have come here masquerading as the Prophet. But I can't accept that Nom Anor is the one who has been influencing the Shamed Ones to place their faith in the *Jedi*."

"I confess to being astonished, as well," Harrar said. "But you must understand, because of what happened at Ebaq

Nine, Nom Anor had little option but to place himself as far as possible from Shimrra's reach—which is not an easy thing to do. In Yuuzhan'tar's underground places, Nom Anor probably fell in with the heretics, and gradually saw some advantage to becoming their chief instigator and voice."

"Now, that doesn't surprise me," Mara said.

"But he must have realized that Zonama Sekot can provide an end to the war," Luke said. "So why attempt to destroy it, when his . . . followers stood to gain the most?"

Harrar shook his head. "I can only speculate. Perhaps his actions here have enabled him to reingratiate himself with Shimrra—for Shimrra fears this world more than you know. It has always been Nom Anor's desire to be escalated, and the possibility of escalation may have been reason enough for him to forsake the heretics who placed their trust in him.

"It's also plausible that Nom Anor has been working secretly for Shimrra all the while—even as the Prophet. Shimrra may have wished to create a perceived problem on Yuuzhan'tar to distract the elite from more pressing problems, regarding the war and the rebellious nature of Yuuzhan'tar's World Brain. Or he may have planned to use the growing 'heresy' as justification for ridding our society of undesirables and pariahs."

Harrar sighed with purpose. "Nom Anor is a consummate infidel. He thinks only of his own ambitions." He glanced around the small room. "But it appears that he was unsuccessful in eliminating Zonama Sekot as a potential threat to his and Shimrra's plans."

"That remains to be seen," Corran said. "Either as a result of Nom Anor's actions, or as a way of protecting itself, Zonama Sekot jumped into hyperspace. To where, we've yet to learn. Maybe deeper into the Unknown Regions; maybe closer to known space. If this rain ever stops, we may be able to figure out where we are. But so far Sekot hasn't seen fit to help us."

"Sekot," Harrar repeated.

"Zonama's guiding intelligence," Jacen said.

Harrar absorbed it. "Yet more similarities with Yuuzhan'tar . . ."

"Or Coruscant, as we like to call it," Corran said roughly.

Harrar glanced at him and smiled faintly. "I speak not of your reshaped galactic capital, but of the primordial homeworld of the Yuuzhan Vong. Well before she died at Nom Anor's hand, Nen Yim had come to believe that this world is startlingly similar to the descriptions of Yuuzhan'tar that have passed down to us in history and legends."

The priest turned to Maydh. "More, that the Ferroans are what we ourselves might have become." Deep sorrow tugged at Harrar's scarified features. "These realizations saddened and shattered Nen Yim's faith, as indeed they have shattered mine."

"We know that one of your early reconnaissance fleets happened on Zonama Sekot," Jacen said, "while it was still in known space."

"*Happened on* is hardly the proper phrase, young *Jeedai*. As I said, there is much that links Zonama Sekot to the Yuuzhan Vong. Nen Yim discovered many similarities that cannot be attributed to coincidence. Zonama Sekot and the Yuuzhan Vong can only have had access to the same protocols in fashioning ships and other devices."

"Ships, yes," Luke said. "But the engines that drive Sekotan ships are not organic, Harrar."

The priest waved in dismissal. "Nor are they made of yorik coral. But what matters is that they are *grown*." He shrugged. "Untrained in the shapers' arts, I can't provide the proof you desire. But I know in my heart what is true, and what isn't."

"Why didn't you ever attempt to return to Zonama Sekot after the first encounter?" Jacen asked.

"Because few knew of the encounter." Harrar fell silent for a moment, then said: "I will tell you things I didn't reveal to Nen Yim—or Nom Anor—if only to further an understanding between us. There were rumors during the final days of the reign of Quoreal—Shimrra's predecessor—that a living world had been discovered. Rumors, too, that Quoreal's priests had interpreted the encounter as a sign that we should avoid contact with your galaxy. The ancient texts make clear the existence of a world that was anathema to us—one that could well prove our undoing."

"You invaded, anyway," Mara said.

Harrar nodded. "We were dying. Shimrra recognized this. Emboldened by his domain, he usurped Quoreal's throne and directed the worldship convoy to continue as planned, granting his full blessing to the invasion, assuring everyone that the gods had informed him that your galaxy was to be our new home—providing that we could cleanse it, or at least convert all of you to the truth.

"No mention was made of the living world. Those of less than elite rank accepted on faith that Shimrra had received the divine word. Shimrra is not one to be trifled with, in any case. When the invasion progressed easily, many of us set aside our doubts. We convinced ourselves that Shimrra's decision was correct, and that the gods were favoring us. Only of late has doubt reared its head once more. The heretical movement, the defeat at Ebaq Nine, the continuing problems on Yuuzhan'tar . . ." Harrar looked at Jacen. "Which I suspect owe something to you, young *Jeedai*. And to Vergere."

"You knew her?" Jacen asked in surprise.

"Better than you, and yet obviously not nearly as well. She was one of the samples returned to the worldship convoy by reconnaissance ships. She became the familiar of priestess Falung; then, eventually, of priestess Elan, of the deception sect, who served aboard my vessel . . ." Harrar smiled lightly. "When I had a vessel."

"Elan," Luke said, with narrowed eyes.

The priest took a moment to puzzle it out. "Ah, yes, I'd almost forgotten about the plan to poison the *Jeedai* with bo'tous. Foolishly devised. Whatever became of poor Elan?"

"She died horribly—of bo'tous poisoning," Mara said sharply.

"Vergere was a Jedi," Jacen said, with some pride.

Harrar was unfazed. "So I subsequently learned." He appraised Jacen, then Luke, Mara, and the others. "I have been preoccupied with you from the very start. Not in the same way Tsavong Lah was preoccupied. Nor as Nom Anor continues to be." His gaze favored Luke. "We are not as dissimilar as you would like to believe."

Luke grinned lightly. "I would like to believe that we are, in fact, very similar, and that you exist in the Force, as does all life."

"The enigmatic Force," Harrar said slowly. "But consider this, Master *Jeedai*. We revere life as much as, if not more, than you do. The Force gives you strength; the gods give us strength. Like you, we feel the craving to merge fully with life; to feel, sense, experience the interconnectedness of all things—as, indeed, is embodied by Zonama Sekot."

Luke was reminded of his rigorous conversations with Vergere. "There's one major difference between us: we accept that what doesn't take the Force into consideration is false."

Harrar shrugged. "What doesn't take the gods into consideration is false. To us, you embody a dark power, seemingly as the Sith did to the *Jeedai* of old. And yet, if the Sith borrowed of the Force, much as you do, how then were they dark? Because they disagreed with your views?"

"The Sith sowed destruction and chaos in service to dark designs. They exercised absolute power to achieve their ends. They didn't revere the Force; they had reverence only for the power it afforded them. They saw their way as the only way."

"As the Yuuzhan Vong do," Harrar said, "and you aver not to."

"You worship pain," Mara said.

Harrar shook his head. "If they could be persuaded to answer truthfully, Jacen and Tahiri would tell you otherwise. We accept that birth into life is pain because it is separation from the gods—or the Force, if you will. But since we would not exist without the gods and their sacrifice, we thank the gods by emulating them, and giving of ourselves in their name. Pain is our means of reuniting with Yun-Yuuzhan. We wonder why the gods created us, only to have us suffer all our lives in order to return to them. But this is unknowable. The creative cannot but create, and this is what the gods do. These things are beyond our understanding, and we accept them as being beyond our understanding. If our teachings are false, then they will pass away. Until that time, we must abide by them."

"Perish by them, you mean," Corran said.

"Perhaps. But this is all so much talk. I fear that the gods now look upon the Yuuzhan Vong with disfavor. I first realized this when Commander Kahlee Lah believed that Jaina

Solo had become an aspect of Yun-Harla, the Trickster. Then I watched Supreme Commander Czulkang Lah be taken in at Borleias by the so-called Operation Starlancer. And now tens of thousands of Shamed Ones have allowed themselves to be beguiled by a self-serving heretic . . ."

Harrar lowered his gaze and shook his head. "Having appointed ourselves Yun-Yuuzhan's instrument, assuming the license to purge, to punish, and to sanctify, to kill by the millions those who do not share our worldview, we have become blasphemers against our own religion. We have become a weak species, desperate to prove our strength to our gods."

Luke leaned forward, resting his forearms on his knees. "If Shimrra understood this, could he be persuaded to end the war?"

"Shimrra hates the sound of reasoned words. Nor would any of the elite be persuaded—save, perhaps, those who have secretly remained faithful to Quoreal, and whose goal it has been to bring evidence of this world to Yuuzhan'tar, and expose Shimrra—to demonstrate that he violated the taboo and invaded, and that his actions may have damned all of us."

The priest fell silent for a long moment, then said, "Answer one question for me: can Zonama Sekot help you defeat us? Is it indeed a weapon?"

Luke touched his jaw. "It has that capability."

Harrar exhaled slowly and sadly. "Then no wonder Shimrra fears it so. It is as prophesied." He looked questioningly at Luke. "Will you kill me now—sacrifice me to the Force?"

"That's not our way," Luke said.

Harrar's initial confusion gave way to resolution. "Then if you would allow me, I wish to help bring about a resolution between your varied species and mine. Or do I begin to sound like Elan, promising one thing but determined to deliver another?"

Mara, Jacen, and the others were still trading looks of dumbfounded disbelief when Luke said, "Perhaps you carry something even more deadly than bo'tous, Harrar—in the form of ideas."

Harrar pressed his few fingertips together and bounced

them against his disfigured lower lip. "Yun-Harla is said to reserve her most cunning tricks for those most devoted to her. But we find ourselves here, together, for reasons beyond my comprehension. From here, then, we must at least attempt to mark a new beginning."

ELEVEN

"We're going to come out of this in one piece, right?" Judder Page asked as Han was returning to the cockpit.

In the adjacent chair, Pash Cracken repressed a smile.

Millennium Falcon had been in hyperspace for just under five standard hours, most of which Han had spent elsewhere in the freighter, evaluating the extent of the damage and checking on the passengers, who were crammed into every available cabin space.

Han looked from Page to Cracken to Leia, who had remained in the copilot's chair throughout the lightspeed transit. "Didn't you tell them everything would be fine?"

She shrugged. "Maybe they don't trust me."

Han strapped into the pilot's chair and swiveled to the two Alliance officers. "You can trust whatever she says."

Page grinned. "Well, that's just it, Han. She told us to ask you."

Han frowned at Leia. "Maybe it's time we reviewed our roles aboard this ship. I do the piloting. You reassure the passengers that the pilot always knows what he's doing."

"Of course, Captain," Leia said. "Might I tell the passengers exactly where we're headed?"

Han swung to the navicomputer display. "Unless we took a wrong turn at the last nebula, we should be coming up on Caluula any minute now."

Leia stared at him. "Caluula? In the Tion Hegemony? Could you have picked a more out-of-the-way planet?"

"Hey, I got us away from those Vong skips, didn't I?"

"You did."

"I had to make a judgment call." Han continued to make adjustments on the console and overhead instrument panels.

Leia eyed the lubricant smears on his hands, and a small bump that was forming on his right temple. "Everything go all right in the back?" she asked quietly while Cracken and Page were engaged in a separate conversation. "I thought I heard some cursing."

"That must have been Threepio," Han mumbled.

"He never was good with tools—"

"Coming out of hyperspace," Han interrupted, reaching forward to prime the sublight drives and ready the subspace transceiver.

The starlines sharpened to points of light, and the starfield rotated slightly. The ion drives flared to life with a deafening *whoomp!* and the ship began to lurch and hiccup. From aft came the sound of stressed alloy, then an indistinct severing as if some component had been torn away.

"What was that?" Leia asked.

"Just another piece of us," Han said flatly. "Nothing important . . . I hope."

A distant object grew larger in the viewport, slowly defining itself as a linear array of geometric modules, linked by girderlike structural members and transparent tubular passageways. Docking berths extended from each module, many of them housing ion cannons and turbolasers in place of ships. Sprouting like a faceted mushroom cap from the center of the array was an enormous shield generator.

Han relaxed into his chair. "A thing of beauty if I ever saw one."

"Looks awfully beat up," Leia said dubiously.

Han straightened somewhat. "Yeah, now that you mention it. But the last time I passed through here the station was stocked with aftermarket parts from Lianna."

"How long ago was that?"

Han thought for a moment. "A couple of years, I guess. But—"

A blast rocked the *Falcon* from behind, snapping everyone back in their chairs.

"Another piece of us?" Leia asked, leaning in to check the sensor displays.

"Worse."

Leia's eyes were big when she glanced back at him. "What was that you said about outrunning those skips?"

Cracken raised his eyes to the overhead viewport. "They couldn't have followed us through hyperspace! It can't be the same vessels!"

Han veered the *Falcon* hard to port, a second before two magma missiles raced past the ship's mandibles. "Somebody's changed the rules!" He leaned toward the intercom and called the two Noghri by name, then fell silent for a moment, listening to their reply.

"I don't care if the targeting computers aren't responding! You've got eyes, haven't you?" He growled to himself. "Have to do everything myself around here—"

A molten projectile hit the *Falcon* broadside, and a wire-filled module dropped, sparking, from the cockpit ceiling. Han barrel-rolled the ship, then dived abruptly. Alarms were screeching even before he pulled out of the maneuver, and the authenticators began painting dozens of yellow bezels on the tactical display screens.

Han and Leia looked up at the same time to find themselves squared off with a Yuuzhan Vong battle group of capital vessels, gunboat analogs, tenders, and what was certainly a yammosk-bearing clustership, similar to the one Han had helped cripple at Fondor. Sentry coralskippers were already streaking for the *Falcon*.

"You know, you have a real knack for this!" Leia said while she called for a status readout on the shields.

"It's not me," Han protested. "The navicomputer has itself convinced that trouble is the *Falcon*'s default preference!"

"A likely story."

Han didn't alter course. "Grab a holo of that clustership. Download any drive signatures you can pick up and paste everything into the battle analysis computer. Then hold on to your stomach!"

He waited for Leia to carry out the tasks, then threw the *Falcon* into a near-vertical climb, continuing up and over in a loop that sent them racing back toward Caluula's orbital station. The quartet of curve-tailed, six-legged skips that had apparently chased the *Falcon* from Selvaris were directly below, spewing plasma missiles, even as they jinked and juked to evade incessant laser bursts from the dorsal and belly AG-2Gs.

Leia swiveled to the commboard. "Caluula Station, come in!"

"Transmit our identification code," Han said.

"Caluula Station, this is *Millennium Falcon*. Please acknowledge."

"Say something," Han muttered. "Call us a name—anything!"

The closer they came to the station, the worse it appeared. Many of the modules had been holed and scorched by fire. A pitched battle must have raged for weeks, unknown to Galactic Alliance command because of the disabled HoloNet. Han wondered briefly how many other planets or orbital stations were in similar straits.

"*Millennium Falcon,* this is Caluula Station," a female voice said at last. "Someone should have told us you were coming."

Han clamped his right hand on Leia's left in relief. "Caluula Station, even we didn't know we were coming," he said into the mike. "We've got drive trouble, and a couple of coralskippers are hounding us. Any chance you could lower your shields long enough to take us in?"

"Can do, *Millennium Falcon*—so long as you can guarantee that your ship's as fast as she's rumored to be."

"Pull in the welcome mat while we're making our approach," Han said, "and the *Falcon*'ll still get us inside with time to spare."

"We won't hold you to that, *Millennium Falcon,* but come on in."

"First we've got to lose these rock spitters."

Routing additional power to the main thrusters, Han firewalled the throttle and began to take the *Falcon* through a repertoire of stomach-churning evasive maneuvers. The tandem-piloted skips did their best to keep up, singeing the *Falcon*'s stern with gouts of plasma. But as the *Falcon* neared the station, the enemy vessels had to contend also with laser beams and the sting of ion cannons.

"Don't worry," Leia assured Page and Cracken as Han

continued to rocket for the small window Caluula Station had opened. "Han does this all the time."

The moment the *Falcon* soared into the station's embrace, the shield repowered. Repulsed by heavy fire, three of the skips peeled off and jagged for the protection of the battle group. The fourth kept coming, only to be stunned by the shimmering energy field, then fell prey to the station's powerful batteries.

Leia swiveled to face Cracken and Page. "See, that wasn't so bad."

Color slowly returned to their faces, and they nodded.

Steadying his shaking hand, Han cut power to the thrusters and allowed a tractor beam to convey the *Falcon* safely into a docking bay.

Seat of the galactic government since the fall of Coruscant, the water world of Mon Calamari was nimbused with ships of all category and classification, from twenty-year-old scallop-hulled Mon Cal cruisers to gleaming Star Destroyers fresh from the yards of Bothawui and distant Tallaan. The star system's inner worlds were similarly encircled, ever on alert that the Yuuzhan Vong might one day decide to fold their myriad battle groups into a single armada and strike at Mon Calamari from the heart of the galaxy.

Inbound from the hyperspace reversion point well beyond Mon Calamari's single moon, Jaina weaved her X-wing to *Ralroost,* one of the largest and whitest of the ships in orbital dock, and was the last pilot of Twin Suns Squadron to drift into the fleet flagship's spacious though welcoming hold.

A Bothan Assault Cruiser originally commissioned for the defense of Bothawui at the conclusion of the Galactic Civil War, *Ralroost* was under the command of Admiral Traest Kre'fey, who had emerged from relative obscurity at the start of the Yuuzhan Vong invasion to the position of second in command of the entire Alliance fleet.

The transports had been the first to arrive from Kashyyyk, and many were already docked and disgorging their cargoes of freed prisoners. Despite devastating losses to the starfighter squadrons, the mission had been deemed a success.

Dozens of former New Republic officials and scores of commanders had been rescued, and most of Alliance Intelligence's double agents had been extracted. The operation might have gone far worse had the stingcrawler coralskippers arrived sooner than they did, or had the deadly skips pursued the transports to Mon Calamari. But instead they had remained at Selvaris to safeguard the Peace Brigade freighters that had yet to be unloaded, and to escort those prisoner ships to Coruscant.

Seizing the opportunity, Chief of State Cal Omas's media team had spun the mission into a public relations event meant to send a message to the governments of threatened worlds to hold out; that unlike the fallen New Republic, the Galactic Federation of Free Alliances was not about to allow any more star systems to fall to enemy rule. As a result, several hundred military personnel, civilians, and media representatives were on hand to greet the rescued. Booming applause erupted for each one to emerge from a transport. Weeping spouses rushed to embrace their returned partners. Children, clearly confused by all the commotion, wrapped their arms tightly around the legs or waists of their liberated mothers or fathers.

Medics and droids worked side by side to move the injured onto repulsor gurneys and hurry them off for bacta treatment. Most of the rescued, of whatever species, needed little more than minor attention and a couple of hearty meals. Others were in critical condition. The fact that none had been implanted with surge-coral was a constant reminder that they were to have gone to their deaths as sacrificial victims.

Few civilians and no one from the media took notice of the battered starfighters that entered *Ralroost*'s hold in the wake of the transports. Jaina didn't mind, but she had to laugh. Not all that long ago she had been a media darling, because of her capture of a Yuuzhan Vong ship and the brief role she had played as "the Trickster Goddess"—a weapon unto herself. Now she was just another weary pilot returning from a mission that had nearly gone completely wrong.

Five Twin Suns pilots had died. But that was breaking news only to those who had survived.

A human crew chief rolled a ladder up to Jaina's X-wing while the canopy was rising. Two crash-team techs rushed in to effect repairs and check on carbon-scored Cappie.

"Welcome back, Colonel," the young woman said.

Jaina descended the ladder, took off her helmet, and shook out her brown hair. Loosening the tabs of her flight suit, she put the helmet under her arm and began to circle the X-wing, her eyes scanning the hold for signs of *Millennium Falcon*. Not too far away, Lowbacca, Kyp, and Alema Rar were emerging from their craft.

"Has there been any communication from the *Falcon*?" she asked the crew chief after she had completed a second circle of the starfighter.

The woman unclipped a datapad from her belt and gave the small display screen a perfunctory glance. "Not that I'm aware of, Colonel. But the *Falcon* might have been directed into one of the frigates."

Jaina forced an exhale. When the crew chief started to move off, Jaina grabbed hold of her arm—forcefully, until she realized what she had done and relaxed her grip.

"Could you check on that?"

The woman frowned and rubbed her bicep.

"Please," Jaina added.

This time the crew chief spent a long moment studying the data screen of her portable device.

"Sorry, Colonel, no sign of the *Falcon* anywhere." She smiled sympathetically. "If I hear anything, I'll find you."

Starfighters and gunships were still arriving—some on a wing and prayer. Jaina moved to the edge of a balcony that overlooked the docking bay's magcon field. Gazing out at all the moving lights, the octagonal shipyards, and the distant orbital Fleet Command Annex, she stretched out with her feelings. At the edge of her awareness she could sense that her mother and father were alive, but in grave danger. Her mind made up, she hurried back to the starfighter and clambered up the ladder to the cockpit.

"I'm going back out," she informed the puzzled crew chief.

"Sir?"

Jaina pulled her helmet on and settled herself in the seat. "If anyone asks, I'm back at the Mon Eron reversion point."

The young woman grew flustered. "But your ship . . . your droid!"

Jaina fastened her chin strap as the canopy was lowering. "They're used to it."

For all the worldshaping and geologic surgery performed on Coruscant, Westport, north of the former Legislative District, remained a landing area. Its floating platforms, docking bays, and maintenance buildings had been slagged, and in their place stood grashals and other mollusklike housings, scattered across a vast expanse of fused yorik coral tableland, with room enough for more than ten thousand vessels. Though few would recognize it, the aerodrome had fared far better than Eastport, Newport, or West Championne.

Royal coralcraft had transported Shimrra's retinue from the worldship Citadel—which rose to the east, atop what had once been the Imperial District—to within a kilometer of Westport. Once back on the ground, the Supreme Overlord was conveyed the remaining distance by royal palanquin. The ornate and grotesque litter was held aloft by a pride of dedicated dovin basals, and was both preceded and trailed by an entourage of servants and courtesans, as well as by the most recent additions to Shimrra's company—the four female seers, and members of the newly enhanced warrior sect known as slayers.

Strewn with flowers trampled to airborne fragrance by the bare feet of attendants, the winding path to the landing field meandered over the rounded summits of crushed edifices and across countless bridges that spanned those artificial canyons the Yuuzhan Vong had been unable to fill or otherwise efface. Choirs of insects honored the gods with their trilling songs, and carrion birds picked at the vestiges of the plague of stink beetles. The sky was a radiant purple, with the rainbow bridge faintly visible, halfway to apogee.

But the flawless sky belied the melancholy nature of the procession, for all who formed it knew of the events that had transpired at Selvaris. The enemy had somehow learned of the Peace Brigade convoy and had ambushed it, recapturing many of the captives who were slated to be sacrificed at the imminent ceremony. Quick action on the part of a Yuuzhan Vong commander had resulted in the escape of three Peace Brigade freighters, which had communicated the convoy's distress to Yuuzhan'tar. A band of slayers had been dispatched, and had performed brilliantly, much to the displeasure of many an elite warrior, who regarded the slayers as abominations to the caste system, and who fretted about the augmentative power they provided the Supreme Overlord.

Nom Anor walked several paces behind the skull-adorned palanquin, in a group that included High Priest Jakan, Master Shaper Qelah Kwaad, Warmaster Nas Choka, High Prefect Drathul, and other elites. He had been worried about receiving blame for the Peace Brigade's failure—the backstabbing group was essentially his creation—but thus far no one had been inclined to hold him responsible. His defense would have remained unchanged, in any event: that acts of treachery were only as successful as the traitors who perpetrated them.

The Peace Brigade freighters had not been allowed to land on Yuuzhan'tar, but their non–Yuuzhan Vong commanders and crews had been shuttled to the surface by yorik-trema. With them had arrived the Alliance captives, along with the commanders and crews of the Yuuzhan Vong escort vessels. The latter groups were kneeling in ranks in an area of the landing field reserved for the naming, blessing, and tattooing of war vessels. Herded off to one side and immobilized by blorash jelly were the Alliance captives, and in the center of the field, flung down on their faces, lay the Peace Brigaders.

Nom Anor considered that Shimrra might order the procession to trample the prostrate Brigaders, but instead the Supreme Overlord called a halt to the entourage when his palanquin had reached the center of the field. The mixed-species lot of already battered turncoats knew enough to remain facedown on the rough ground, while High Priest Jakan's acolytes, joined by Onimi, circulated among them, anointing them with paaloc incense and venogel.

Then Jakan placed himself among their midst, his hooded

eyes surveying the lumps and welts that slayers had adminis-
tered to the Brigaders before they had been shuttled down to
Yuuzhan'tar.

The high priest moved on to the Yuuzhan Vong warriors
and summoned their commander, Bhu Fath. A towering warrior with inadequate skill for command, his escalation had
come about only as a result of persistent petitioning by members of Domain Fath, which included several important consuls.

"How many captives did you deliver, Commander?" Jakan
asked.

Bhu Fath pivoted slightly to salute Warmaster Nas Choka.
"Six packets—nearly five hundred."

Jakan shook his head in disappointment and glanced up at
Shimrra. "Less than half the minimal amount required for a
ceremony of such magnitude."

Shimrra gazed stonily from the hard bed of his palanquin,
but said nothing, even when the seers began to consult their
divination biots and moan in distress.

Nas Choka separated himself from the procession and
gestured to Bhu Fath and his subalterns.

"Our warriors acquitted themselves well by destroying
many enemy fighters and reclaiming two of the ships that
might have escaped with the rest. One warrior in particular is
noted for having saved our own escort vessels from destruction, in addition to other acts of bravery."

"Bring this one forward," Shimrra said, "so I might cast
my benevolent gaze on him."

"Commander Malik Carr," Nas Choka called.

Nom Anor couldn't believe his ears. After the calamity at
Fondor, Malik Carr had been demoted and removed from
battle. Now here he was, standing in Shimrra's gaze, a hero!
Would everything reverse itself in due time?

Carr genuflected to Shimrra, then Nas Choka, and remained on one knee. At a motion from the warmaster, a subaltern hurried forward with a command cloak, which Nas
Choka draped over the horns implanted in Carr's shoulders.

"Rise as Supreme Commander Malik Carr," Nas Choka
intoned, "reinstated because of his courageous actions at

Selvaris. We will soon assign him to a command more worthy of his station."

Malik Carr snapped his fists in salute and returned to the ranks.

"Dread Lord," Jakan said a moment later, "occurring as they did in an arena of battle, the death of many infidels at Selvaris counts for something. But as I say, the captives on hand number too few to constitute an appropriate appeal to the gods. We must offer more than this paltry lot."

Commander Blu Fath risked a forward step. "My Lord, could we not let these virulent Peace Brigaders substitute for those they surrendered?"

Fath's proposal met with a few shouts of approval, though mostly from members of his domain.

"Such acts of replacement are not without precedent—" Jakan started to say, when Shimrra silenced him with a look.

"They are not worthy of honorable deaths," Shimrra said. "Not only did they allow their league to be infiltrated by enemy spies, but several of their ships also abandoned the arena at the first sign of engagement, taking with them supplies and a number of sacred objects that were en route from Obroa-skai."

Shimrra stepped down from the litter, causing a stir among warriors and priests alike, a group of whom unfurled a living carpet in advance of Shimrra's steps. Onimi followed, capering as he trailed his master.

"On which worlds are we currently engaged in surface contest?" Shimrra asked Nas Choka.

The warmaster thought before speaking. "I could name twenty, Great Lord. Fifty."

Shimrra grew angry. "Name one, Warmaster."

"Corulag, then."

Shimrra nodded. "Corulag it shall be. See to it that the Peace Brigaders are implanted with surge-coral and sent to the front to join the ranks of our human thrall. In battle, perhaps they will redeem themselves."

Nas Choka saluted. "Your will be done."

Shimrra turned then, and beckoned to Drathul and Nom Anor.

"Momentous plans require momentous ritual. Therefore,

the sacrifice can neither be delayed nor interfered with. Make certain that the consuls and executors in your charge be advised that I will brook no further upsets. Should anything untoward occur, I will look upon you and your charges as I would any who seek to meddle in our holy venture."

"Understood," Drathul and Nom Anor responded in unison.

Nas Choka waited patiently for Shimrra to settle himself on the palanquin before saying, "A suggestion, Great Lord."

Shimrra granted him a gaze. "Proceed, Warmaster."

"We are presently engaged in a campaign to occupy a world known as Caluula. If you would permit our efforts to be doubled there, the planet will fall and many captives will be available to enrich our supply. Why not let the brave defenders of the orbital complex serve to compensate for our dearth of illustrious sacrifices?"

"Caluula, you say."

"Distant from Yuuzhan'tar, Great Lord, but vital to our ultimate designs."

Shimrra looked to Jakan, then the seers, who nodded.

"Let it be done."

TWELVE

"The damage looks much worse from out here," C-3PO said, staring up at the belly of *Millennium Falcon* from the foot of the landing ramp.

Han glared at him from under the ship, where he, Leia, and a Caluula Station mechanic were compiling a list of needed repairs. "Who asked you, Threepio?"

The protocol droid adopted a posture of inquisitiveness. "No one, Captain Solo. I was only remarking—"

"Threepio," Leia cut him off. "That's enough for now."

"Of course, Princess Leia. I know when I'm not wanted."

"That'll be the day," Han said.

Cracken, Page, and the rest of the rescued officers were standing off to one side, fielding questions from several other Caluula mechanics, who had dropped what they were doing to surround the *Falcon* the moment she had settled on her landing disks.

The ship was blistered, dented, and punctured.

"She's a storyboard for the whole war," the mechanic said.

Han nodded. "You got that right."

The mechanic wedged his forefinger into a hole in the underside of the outrigger cockpit. "I'll bet this one's not half a meter from the pilot's chair."

Han swallowed audibly. "I've had closer calls."

Leia glanced at the mechanic. "You might have heard, he's a regular moving target."

The mechanic grinned and clapped grit from his hands. "Well, she's taken a bruising, but I figure she'll live. It's just a matter of pulling together replacement parts."

Han looked relieved. He had his mouth open to thank the

mechanic when a tall, purple-complected humanoid wearing military utilities approached him.

"Welcome aboard Caluula Station, Captain Solo."

Before Han could reply, a silver-haired human officer stepped in and saluted him.

"Captain Solo, sir. I was with you at Endor."

Han thought for a moment. "Uh, Denev, right?"

The man beamed. "I'm proud that you remember me, sir."

"Likewise, Captain."

Leia folded her arms across her chest and stared at Han. "That's the tenth person who's recognized you. What is this, a gathering of your fan club?"

Han frowned at her. "Very funny."

"No, really, Han. Maybe you should have become an actor instead of a war hero. Just think of the following you'd have."

Han grabbed hold of his own chin. "You'd pay good credits to see *this* face blown up a hundred times normal size?"

Leia pretended to think about it. "When you put it that way . . ."

"Captain Solo," someone said.

Walking briskly toward the *Falcon* was a portly but energetic human major general.

"Base Commander Garray," the man said, extending his hand to Han.

Han shook hands and gestured to C-3PO and Leia. "Our droid, and my wife, Leia Organa Solo."

Leia elbowed him gently in the ribs. "Thanks for second billing, *darling*," she said through a clench-jawed smile.

Han caressed his ribs and eyed Leia. "The droid's generally well behaved." He indicated Page, Cracken, and some of the others, introducing them by name.

Garray nodded his head several times. "Glad to meet all of you." His gray eyes returned to Han. "Captain Solo, please tell me Mon Cal command sent you."

Han compressed his lips. "Wish I could, Commander. The truth is, we got hit hard during a rescue mission at Selvaris, and Caluula was the only place the *Falcon* could go."

Garray's obvious disappointment was fleeting. "We're proud

to have you on board, regardless—all of you." He turned to his even more portly adjutant. "Chief, see that Captain Solo's passengers are treated for injuries and well fed."

The adjutant saluted. "If you'll follow me, sirs," he said to Cracken and the others.

Han kept silent until everyone had moved off. "What's the situation here, Commander?"

Garray tilted his head to one side. "Take a walk with me, and I'll explain."

He led Han, Leia, and C-3PO on a slow tour of the docking bay, in the strobing light of arc welders, past technicians and soldiers who looked every bit as scarred and patched up as the ships they were working on. Humans appeared to comprise the majority of Caluula's personnel, but mixed among them were Brigians, Trianii, Bimms, Tammarians, and other species from star systems proximal to Caluula. Nearly every individual and craft reflected the war's years of savagery. Some of the ships combined so many disparate parts, they were unrecognizable.

"The Yuuzhan Vong showed up about a month ago," Garray was saying. "And it's been steady fighting ever since. Our defense platform is history, and for the past local week we've been under constant siege. But it's become clear that the Vong want to occupy Caluula rather than raze it, or they'd have dropped a moon on it or poisoned it like they've done elsewhere."

"Occupation seems a good guess," Leia said. "One of the ships we saw on our way in is a yammosk vessel."

Garray nodded. "That's already been verified."

"Still, it's curious that the Yuuzhan Vong would choose Caluula," Leia went on. "I don't know a great deal about the Tion Hegemony, but I do know it lacks most of the resources the Yuuzhan Vong usually come looking for."

"No argument, Princess. Caluula's mostly been a haven for scientists, because of some sort of natural phenomenon that occurs down there every so often. Our best guess is that the Yuuzhan Vong want to use Caluula as an entry point into the Tion Hegemony and the Corporate Sector. Then there's the shipyards at Lianna, though they haven't been turning out much since Sienar Systems pulled up stakes." Garray took his lower lip between his teeth and shook his head in exasperation. "But the Vong have to go through us to get there, and, thank the Force, that hasn't happened yet."

"If they're looking at occupying the rest of the Tion Hegemony, they'd have concentrated their efforts at Lianna," Han said. "For one thing, it's closer to the Perlemian, which they pretty much control anyway, from Coruscant to the Cron Drift." He shook his head. "They've got something else in mind. Maybe using Caluula as a staging area for an attack on Mon Calamari."

"We considered that," Garray said. "But I don't have to tell you that Caluula's well removed from the easy space lanes. Mon Calamari's three microjumps direct, or you return to the Perlemian by way of Dellalt and Lianna, which takes just as long."

"So what do the Yuuzhan Vong want with Caluula?" Leia asked.

Garray looked at her while they walked. "Captives. The Vong commander of the battle group even intimated as much."

"You've actually spoken to him?"

"Tattooed head to toe," Garray said, "and soon to be black with blood, if we have anything to say about it. He promised us noble deaths and everlasting life."

"Tough offer to turn down," Han said.

Garray snorted. "Personally, I'll take the here-and-now."

"Where are you from, Commander?" Leia asked.

"Abregado-rae."

Han was surprised. "You're a long way from the Core. Why'd you leave?"

"It was raining Vong fireballs, and I started to feel like I was in the way."

Leia nodded contemplatively. "There's no safe corner left."

Garray sighed with her. "Not if the Yuuzhan Vong have their way. One more major push from them at this point . . . Well, who can predict how things will turn out, right?"

"Expect surprises," Han said.

"There's a small resistance force operating downside on Caluula. But if this station falls, I don't see how they'll be able to hold out against a full-scale invasion."

"Just how bad off are you?" Leia said.

"Well, you've seen our starfighters. They're held together with spit and glue, just like we are. Ever since the HoloNet went down, we've had to rely on courier communication with Mon Cal, and that takes anywhere from three to five local days. In fact, we dispatched a ship just hours before you arrived. Galactic Alliance command hasn't been able to spare us any matériel, in any event. So we're critically short on food, munitions, spare parts, bacta. Many of the volunteers who came to our support are wounded. We've a lot of sick and dying." Garray paused, becoming more somber by the moment. "I've been fighting the Yuuzhan Vong for four years. I feel like I was a lot younger when this war started."

"We all were, Commander," Han said.

He recognized Garray's type: done in by years of command; of sending soldiers to their deaths. A man who no longer needed to prove to himself that he was a hero. He was just doing his job, and hating himself for it.

Garray forced himself to brighten. "But don't worry, we'll get the *Falcon* repaired, and we'll have you on your way in no time."

"We don't want to take your personnel away from their jobs, Commander," Han said firmly. "Leia and I will see to the repairs ourselves." He paused, then added: "Between you and me, Garray, if Cracken and the rest weren't expected on Mon Calamari, we'd be staying behind to help you."

Garray smiled. "I appreciate that, Solo. Reinforces everything I've heard about you all these years." He glanced at Leia. "Will the two of you join me for lunch?"

"We'd be honored," Leia said. She deliberately fell behind Han to whisper, "Everything he's heard all these years . . . One day they're going to build a statue of you."

Han gestured broadly. "These are the people who deserve statues—every last one of them."

They continued to walk and talk and bump into people who knew or recognized Han—and Leia. Caluula seemed to have drawn every celebrated soldier, mercenary, and ne'er-do-well from within a thousand parsecs. Commander Garray excused himself to attend to business, but promised he'd rendezvous with them in the mess hall.

They were emerging from one of the transparent connectors that linked the station's separate modules when Han heard what he thought was a familiar voice. The source of the voice was a dark-haired man as old as himself, dressed in a worn gray flight suit that was cinched at the waist by a broad red belt. Of medium height but broad-chested, he was sitting cross-legged atop a cargo crate, in a murky area of the module, between a golden-furred Bothan and a tall Calibop whose wings were folded behind him. Surrounding the trio stood roguish-looking human and alien warriors in similar gray flight suits, who might have made up a separate starfighter squadron, or just as easily a criminal swoop gang from Nar Shaddaa.

"Another fan?" Leia asked.

Han rubbed his stubbled jaw. "I definitely know the voice from somewhere. But I can't place the face."

"So ask him."

Han nodded and sauntered over to the soldiers, every one of whom monitored his approach with a mix of amusement and wariness.

"I'm Han Solo. Am I right that we've met?"

The man looked at him askance, almost as if to display the ragged scars on the side of his furrowed and somewhat dark-complected face. "Not in the flesh, Captain, though we have come close. I guess that means that we're not entirely strangers." He extended a meaty hand. "Hurn."

Han tried out the name twice, then shook his head. "Doesn't ring a bell. But you're sure we never served together? During the Rebellion, maybe?"

Hurn shrugged. "I've one of those faces that used to appear familiar to everyone."

Han caressed his jaw. "Ever been to Dellalt?"

"Don't think so."

Han nodded uncertainly, then tipped his head in parting and walked away.

Leia waited until she, Han, and C-3PO were out of earshot of the group to ask, "Did he mean 'familiar' before the Rebellion, or before all the scars?"

Han glanced over his shoulder, and shook his head in ignorance. But any response was drowned out by the sudden blare of klaxons. Instantly, the station was thrown into managed chaos. Everyone knew precisely where to report and what to do—except Han, Leia, and C-3PO, who weren't sure whether they should go to the nearest battle station or simply stay out of everyone's way.

Appearing out of nowhere, Garray put a quick end to their confusion.

"Enemy reinforcements have arrived. Another entire battle group."

Leia was astonished. "They must be desperate to have Caluula to spare so many ships."

Garray agreed. "Our shields should hold."

The commander's adjutant came running to report that the station's long-range scanners had zeroed in on something unusual. Garray led everyone to the nearest display screen, on which the adjutant called up a holocam view of what looked to be a colossal space slug, with a wedge-shaped head, a dorsal pouch, and a mouth that had to be eighty meters wide.

Garray narrowed his eyes to slits. "What in the galaxy am I looking at?"

Leia loosed a troubled exhalation. "That, Commander, is what the Yuuzhan Vong call an yncha. The one they deployed at Duro practically ate an orbital city."

Garray stared at her, scarcely able to speak.

The klaxons began to trumpet a more dire alert.

"Commander," an ensign said, "enemy vessels on the attack."

Han looked at Leia. "Guess we will be hanging around, after all."

"Studious person that you are—or at least claim to be— you no doubt took to heart the Supreme Overlord's admonition that nothing untoward should interfere with the coming sacrifice," High Prefect Drathul hectored Nom Anor. "Given especially the diminished number of victims."

Former prefect of the worldship *Harla,* Drathul had a wide and broad-browed face, sufficiently scarified to demonstrate his allegiance to the gods, but not so much that the scars marred what Drathul considered handsome features.

He had kept Nom Anor waiting for half a local day, while the sun climbed high into the sky, making the rainbow bridge shine like a jeweled necklace. His windowed and drizzle-topped quarters in the prefectory overlooked the Place of Hierarchy, south of the Citadel, in a district once known as Calocour Heights. Nom Anor still remembered the heights from one of the first of his reconnaissance missions, when the market area had teemed with pushy survey takers and blazed with flashing musical advertiscreens. Free product samples delivered from worlds throughout the galaxy had been on continual display, floating on repulsor carts and wafting wonderful aromas into the air.

"I took the Supreme Overlord's admonition to heart," Nom Anor said from the exquisitely woven vurruk floor mat to which he had been shown by Drathul's attendants. The high prefect himself spoke from a pillowed recess in his dais.

"Then you'll be interested to know it has reached my attention that a coalition of Shamed Ones is intent on disturbing the ceremony." Drathul fixed Nom Anor with a gimlet stare. "I think you are not entirely untutored in the tactics of the heretics, Prefect."

"I profess to know something of them."

Drathul was clearly entertained by the response.

"You give yourself too little credit. Such self-effacement is not becoming to one who has managed to escalate himself from mere executor to *prefect* of Yuuzhan'tar in so short a time. Who, on at least two occasions now, has enjoyed private audience with the Supreme Overlord; who, I would risk saying, even has Shimrra's *ear.*"

Nom Anor feigned a short laugh. "Hardly his ear, High Prefect."

Drathul scrutinized him some more. "However did this come about?" he asked, as if to himself. "Was it not Nom Anor who sent the priestess Elan to her death, who created the bumbling Peace Brigade, who helped engineer the disastrous assault on Fondor, who allowed the traitor Vergere to escape, who has disguised himself as a human, a Duros, a Givin, and who knows how many other species, who is rumored to have refused a duel with a *Jeedai* and to have murdered his own operatives with an infidel's weapon, who all but lured Warmaster Tsavong Lah to dishonor at Ebaq Nine?" He paused briefly. "Look how his plaeryin bol stares at me—so eager to spit venom."

"You misunderstand, High Prefect." Nom Anor touched the artificial orb that substituted for an eye. "Just a particle of sand, lodged in the corner. In fact, you have succeeded brilliantly in disparaging me. But you neglect to add that there has been a bright side to all those events. Or else—" He grinned faintly. "—how is it I have come to wear the green robes of high office?"

Drathul was infuriated. "The sole reason I tolerate your presence and your escalation is that you are known to have been in the company of my predecessor, Yoog Skell, when he died. I know in my heart that you had something to do with his death, and were it not for his death, I would probably not be sitting here, delighting in rebuking you."

Nom Anor inclined his head. "I exist but to serve, High Prefect."

"Precisely. Which is why I command you to root out this coalition of Shamed Ones, and either talk some sense into them or have them killed. I would prefer the former, since I suspect that additional killings at this point will only incite them further. But know that I plan to hold you personally responsible for any interference at the sacrifice, just as Shimrra will me. Do you trust that I speak from the heart, or do I need to bolster my words with threats of what will befall you should you fail me?"

"I will do my best, High Prefect."

"Your tricks bear watching, Nom Anor. This has always been so."

"I trick no one but myself, High Prefect, by imagining myself more than I am."

Nom Anor had had his consuls arrange for a saddled bissop to carry him back to the spacious residence that came with his new status. But for all that he had received, he had earned the envy, anger, and distrust of many, as was frequently the case with those escalated because of actions that needed to remain secret and undisclosed. Others in Shimrra's close company suffered similar indignities, in part because Shimrra was fickle and full of contradictions, as if jerked this way and that by his emotions or what passed for revelations from the gods.

Even mighty Nas Choka was not immune to petty jealousies, which is why he had tripled his complement of bodyguards—something Nom Anor had considered doing, but ultimately rejected. There was small advantage in announcing one's apprehensions to one's adversaries.

But how to keep those apprehensions concealed from the heretics . . .

He had mistakenly believed that the abrupt disappearance of Yu'shaa, the Prophet, would have weakened the movement. Instead, Nom Anor had only provided his gullible audience with a martyr, more so because many believed that Yu'shaa had been put to death on orders of Shimrra.

Tucked away in his residence was the original ooglith cloaker Nom Anor had worn when exhorting his followers to rise up against the system that had doomed them to become outsiders; a system that perpetuated a belief in gods who would deliberately shun their creations. It would be a different matter if every Shamed One was guilty of overreaching or pride, but in fact no one could explain—the shapers least of all—why implants were rejected. As a result, however, countless individuals were left wondering for the rest of their miserable lives where they had erred, when they had displayed pride or if they were paying for the transgressions of other crèche or domain members. The elite pretended sympathy, when in fact they fairly luxuriated in witnessing their competitors fall from grace. *How grievous what befell Consul Shal Tor at the last escalation—but how happy I am that it wasn't me.*

Only a short time ago—before his life-turning decision on Zonama Sekot—Nom Anor, sufficiently inflamed by the inequity, had wished to see his entire culture tumbled down; to see Shimrra shaken from his polyp throne by the debased members of Yuuzhan Vong society. And he had very nearly succeeded. What might have come from that was unclear. If the war were lost, what would it mean for Nom Anor, since—

save for the Jedi—the inhabitants of the galaxy the Yuuzhan Vong had invaded were not above barbarity?

Flight, imprisonment, execution . . . he couldn't take the chance.

Now the very movement born of rumors escaped from distant Yavin, and given order and embellishment by Nom Anor himself, threatened to deprive him of all that he had achieved by opting to foil Zonama Sekot, and thereby reinstate himself in Shimrra's good graces.

The thought weighed on him as his living transport lumbered past the Place of Sacrifice, where priests and savants, adepts and initiates were busy preparing for the coming ceremony; past the shell-like shops of workers; and past solitary Shamed Ones, in their threadbare garments, begging for alms.

Before Nas Choka had been escalated, he had had occasion to reproach Nom Anor for pride, and counsel him look to Yun-Shuno, god of the Shamed Ones, for pardon.

All these years later, here he was their *prophet*.

THIRTEEN

The ychna led the attack on Caluula Station.

Towed into place by a special breed of dovin basal grown on faraway Tynna, the monster slug fastened itself to Caluula's deflector shields like a leech, fattening as it absorbed every joule of ionized energy the generator could summon, then taking the suddenly vulnerable central module in its enormous mouth and crushing it like an eggshell. No sooner had the module depressurized than into the rend dropped hundreds of Yuuzhan Vong warriors, disgorged from landing craft and outfitted with armor and the star-shaped breathing creatures known as gnulliths.

Squadrons of battered starfighters streaked from the station's launching bays to engage swift flights of strafing coralskippers. Close-in weapons traversed and fired, pouring storms of green energy at the approaching capital ships. In the intact modules, klaxons continued to wail, locks cycled, and blast shields descended to seal off corridors and vital enclosures. Against the barricades of solid durasteel, the Yuuzhan Vong splashed red-hot magma, and where that failed they loosed an improved stock of black-plated grutchyna, whose digestive acids were corrosive enough to burn through alloy.

Close to where the ychna was feasting, crouched behind a rampart of fuel-depleted loaders and stacked cargo crates, Han, Leia, and two dozen soldiers waited with hand weapons, assault rifles, repeating blasters, and a few grenades and rockets that had been scrounged from Caluula's near-empty armory. Those droids that weren't carrying ammunition or standing by to refresh weapons moved about in a daze, including C-3PO, who was walking in tight circles behind Leia.

"Don't lose your head," she told him. "Lend a hand."

"But, Princess Leia, I'm scarcely a war machine. I'm useless for anything but protocol and translation. Oh, where is Artoo-Detoo when we need him?"

"Threepio, you're forgetting that you've been as courageous as Artoo ever was."

C-3PO came to a halt. "Have I? Well now that you mention it, there was that incident on—"

"Incoming!" a soldier yelled from down the line.

Fifty meters away something was burning an enormous hole in the lowered blast shield. Clouds of noxious vapor streamed from the ragged edges of a widening circle.

Han checked the charge of his DL-44 and drew a bead on the center of the circle. "Hold your fire," he said. "Wait till they show themselves . . ."

First through the breach were a pair of grutchyna. The six-meter-long beasts leapt snarling from the acid clouds like apparitions, only to be cut to pieces by blasterfire before they had gone ten meters. Then the armored warriors came, rushing through in groups of three and four, hands gripped on amphistaffs or bandoliers of thud bugs.

"Now!" Han shouted.

Thirty blasters fired simultaneously, dropping the vanguard dozen, then a dozen more behind them. But the Yuuzhan Vong kept coming, treading on their fallen comrades in a mad charge and hurling plasma eels and amphistaffs on the run. The weapons thumped against the barrier and caught one or two of the defenders by surprise. But no razor bugs or airborne venom followed, making clearer than ever that the warriors wanted captives, not casualties. Advancing into the grid of laserfire with fists raised in overtures of personal challenge, they were mowed down by the fives and tens, seemingly ignorant of the fact that the Alliance soldiers were playing by a different set of rules.

The warriors would have called foul if they could—foul at being so dishonored. Their every action defied death and sowed confusion. And somehow that made them harder to kill, rather than easier targets.

Blasters fired nonstop, and the thrumming blade of Leia's lightsaber batted away a hail of thud bugs. But the line

couldn't be held. Outnumbered, the defenders were forced
to fall back. The Yuuzhan Vong pressed the attack, stopping
only to drag away and bind those they had stunned. The warriors exulted at the taking of each captive, even though six of
their number might have died to gain one victim.

Withdrawing deeper into the station, Leia was glancing
over her shoulder as she approached a corridor intersection
when Han suddenly threw his left arm around her waist and
twirled her off to one side. From the scarlet glow of the intersecting corridor dropped an amphistaff thick as a war
club, slicing the air where she would have been and hitting
the deck with a hollow *thud!* The warrior attached to the amphistaff howled and sprang forward, falling victim to a precisely placed bolt from Han's sidearm.

"You do care, after all," Leia said around a short-lived
grin. Still in his one-armed embrace, she went up on her toes
to kiss him on the cheek.

Han smiled and let her go. "What's a star without his leading lady?"

"Combat always did bring out the romantic in you." She
started off after him, then stopped and turned to see C-3PO
dithering at the intersection.

"This way, Threepio—hurry!"

He glanced at her, then gestured to the side corridor. "But,
Princess—"

"Come on!"

C-3PO muttered something, then began to shuffle forward
as fast as his squeaking legs would carry him. Leia and Han
were waiting for him at the next blast shield. She palmed the
operating stud as soon as C-3PO had crossed the threshold,
but the shield closed only halfway. Han pounded the stud
with his fist, then, stepping back a meter, fired a bolt into the
control panel.

Leia ducked the ricochet and shook her head in dismay.
"Anyone ever tell you you're as hard on technology as the
Yuuzhan Vong?"

The thick blast shield vibrated and slammed to the deck.

Han grinned smugly. "Only when technology puts up an
argument. And speaking of which, where'd Threepio go?"

Taking a quick look around, Leia found him cowering in a corner.

"What're you standing around for?" Han said. "You want to end up as a skewered droid?"

"No, Captain Solo, but the blast door—"

His words were garbled by the sound of approaching foot-falls. Leia raised her lightsaber; Han, his blaster. But it was a dozen Alliance soldiers who showed up a moment later.

"You don't want to go that way," Han and one of the soldiers said at the same time.

"Yuuzhan Vong," Han said, pointing toward the blast shield.

"Dead end," the soldier said, pointing in the opposite direction.

Han stared at the blast shield, then whipped around. "Dead end?"

C-3PO raised his hands to his head. "That's what I've been trying to tell you!"

Something rammed into the far side of the blast shield, and within seconds wisps of stinging smoke began curling from a series of small perforations. Han and Leia looked at each other.

"Weren't we just here?" she commented.

Everyone moved back from the shield to take up positions in the corridor. Again, Han checked the charge of his blaster, which was down to 50 percent.

"I'm not letting them take me alive, Captain," a soldier nearby said.

Han aimed his forefinger at the young man. "You're not going to be *taken*. Leave it at that, soldier."

The soldier gulped and nodded. "Thank you, sir."

The center of the blast shield was rapidly dissolving. War cries and shouts of personal challenge echoed in the corridor.

Han listened for a moment, then swung to Leia. "I've got something that just might pass for an idea. Threepio, get over here!"

The droid rose unsteadily from behind a rodent's nest of corroded ventilation ducts. "Coming, sir."

Han looked straight into C-3PO's photoreceptors. "Three-pio, I want you to talk to the Yuuzhan Vong in their own language."

"Talk to them? But I wouldn't begin to know what to say."

Han's nostrils flared. "What, suddenly you're at a loss for words? Tell them that all warriors are needed for individual combat in the number one module. Tell them it's lunchtime for all I care!"

"I don't believe the Yuuzhan Vong have a word for—"

"Do as Han says, Threepio," Leia interrupted.

C-3PO's head moved in fits and starts. "How can I possibly mimic—"

"Boost the bass settings of your audio output modifier," a soldier suggested.

C-3PO canted his head. "Oh. I didn't think of that."

"Yeah, and throw in some sound effects while you're at it," Han added.

It took C-3PO a moment to realize that Han was joking. "Sound effects, indeed," he muttered. "Why doesn't someone just paint a target on my recharge coupling."

Han hurried him to a public address comlink mounted on the interior bulkhead. "Say something!"

Placing his vocabulator close to the mike grate, C-3PO began to speak. *"Bruk tukken Vong pratte, al'tanna brenzlit tchurokk . . ."*

Almost instantly, the war cries ceased.

"That's the idea!" Han encouraged. "Keep talking!"

The droid carried on for another minute, finishing with the phrase: *"Al'tanna Shimrra knotte Yun'o!"*—Long life to Shimrra, beloved of the gods!

"They're withdrawing!" the soldier closest to the blast shield reported.

Han clapped C-3PO hard on the back, then wrung his hand in pain. "Good going, Goldenrod! You did it!"

C-3PO straightened. "I do have my moments."

"Of course you do. Now let's get out of here!"

They waited to make certain that the warriors were gone, then one by one they squeezed through the hole in the blast shield and took the corridor Threepio had wanted everyone to take to begin with. Not one hundred meters along, however, they ran smack into an enemy hunting party. But this time C-3PO was prepared. Adjusting the audio output modifier, he began to speak, completing just two sentences before a storm of thud bugs whirled through the corridor, prompting Han, Leia, and the rest to hit the deck.

"What'd you say to them?" Han asked, up on one knee, with his blaster raised.

C-3PO thought for a moment. "Oh, my. I may have mixed up my words." He looked down at Han. "I think I *insulted* them!"

"Well, that's just great."

"Really, Threepio," Leia said. "Now you've made them angry."

Everyone raced back to the intersection, but with a dead end in one direction and Yuuzhan Vong in the other, there was no safe turn.

They had to make a stand.

The band of warriors C-3PO had insulted surged down the corridor. Forty strong, they outnumbered the defenders better than two to one. Fusillades of blasterfire improved the odds somewhat, but also depleted many of the weapons. Exhilarated by the sight of empty blasters being hurled aside, the warriors ordered their amphistaffs to curl about their forearms, and began to strut forward, determined to go hand to hand with their quarries. Several of them had their sights set on Leia, who was parrying the last of the thud bugs with nimble twists of her lightsaber.

Han broke for her side, shooting from the hip to drop two of Leia's would-be contenders. Two others were quick to fill the gap. One lost his head to Leia's blade. The other flew straight at Han, driving him clear across the corridor and hard into the exterior bulkhead. Dodging hammer blows, Han slid down the wall and squirmed between the warrior's legs, hoping to be able to choke him from behind. But the warrior spun while Han was struggling to stand, vising his huge hands around Han's neck in an *asth-korr* throat hold and whirling him back against the bulkhead.

Han saw stars; then darkness made a narrow tunnel of his vision. He was gasping for breath when the warrior's head suddenly exploded. The hands on Han's throat loosened, and the body crumpled to the deck, taking Han with it. Certain that Leia had saved him, he tried to crawl out from under the Yuuzhan Vong, but the corpse wouldn't budge. His out-stretched right hand seized on a small object and he held it up to his eyes. As long as a human finger, and somewhat thicker, it was an older-generation rocket dart, with its obvi-ously defective explosive tip still attached.

Han wriggled free of the fallen warrior in time to see four more Yuuzhan Vong felled from behind by blaster bolts and rocket darts. The fatal volley was coming from halfway down the corridor, where half a dozen soldiers were crouched, kneel-ing, and prone on the deck.

They wore pinch-cheeked helmets that were as domed as an R2 unit, bisected by horizontal viewplate strips and sur-mounted by flaglike targeting range finders. Their gray uni-forms were exoskeletoned by blast dissipation vests, forearm gauntlets, kneepads, armor-mesh gloves, and alloy boots with zero-g gripsoles. They were armed with blaster rifles, handguns, combat knives, rocket dart launchers, and what-ever else might have been hiding in the alloy utility pouches affixed to their broad belts.

A weapons system all his own, the leader wore a combi-nation jet pack and antipersonnel missile launcher, and his belt was red. Catching sight of Han, the trooper tendered a distinctive fingertip salute before hurrying off.

Leia was suddenly alongside Han and helping him to his feet, but her gaze was directed down the corridor. When she finally turned to Han, her eyes were wide, her mouth a rictus of astonishment.

"Fett?" Han managed. *"Fett?"*

Leia shook her head in refusal. "It can't be him. *Anyone* could be inside that armor!"

Han nodded his head in agreement. "That's gotta be it. Be-sides, I mean, even if it is him, he was probably trying to *kill* me, not save me."

The galaxy's most notorious bounty hunter, Boba Fett had nearly been the death of Han, Leia, and even C-3PO follow-ing the Battle of Hoth, during the Galactic Civil War. But the then-Rebels had evened the score on Tatooine by dropping Fett into the hungry maw of a Sarlacc that resided in the

desert world's Great Pit of Carkoon. Many believed that Fett
had ended his days there, but Han and Leia knew better, having encountered Fett on several occasions since his escape
from the Sarlacc. However, there had been no accounts of
the man since the start of the Yuuzhan Vong war, and Han
was inclined to agree with Leia that the trooper who had
saluted him could have been anyone. And yet there was the
familiar voice of the man who had called himself "Hurn."

Han, Leia, C-3PO, and the surviving Caluula soldiers
stepped over the bodies of the Yuuzhan Vong and raced after
the troops in Mandalorian armor, who had already moved
off.

Dozens of Yuuzhan Vong lay dead or dying in the corridor, and fierce fighting was under way in the high-ceilinged
hold into which the corridor debouched. Han watched a warrior battle vainly against a whipcord that had lashed around
his neck, and was just then dragging him into an area of the
hold Han couldn't see. He saw two more warriors nearly
halved by rocket darts. The sibilant reports of blasters were
momentarily overwhelmed by the ear-shattering explosion of
a concussion missile. Six warriors, lanced by shrapnel, flew
backward into the hold. But still others attacked. A strapping
warrior with a coufee in each hand charged screaming around
the corner, only to reappear moments later, black with blood.

Leia clamped her left hand on Han's upper arm. "Didn't
that one have hair when he went in?"

Han nodded in shock. "I think they're taking scalps."

A knot of Yuuzhan Vong warriors had formed in the hold,
many of them gesticulating wildly and all of them talking at
once.

"Princess Leia, Captain Solo," C-3PO said from behind
them. "The Yuuzhan Vong are very excited. They have sent
runners to other parts of Caluula Station to report that they
have found warriors who are exceptionally worthy of captivity."

"I'd say that's pretty optimistic of them," Leia said.

She and Han fought their way into the hold. The armored
soldiers had been backed into a corner. Two of them were
certainly dead, and several others were in danger of being

overpowered by groups of bloodied Yuuzhan Vong. The Caluula forces gathered what weapons they could find and dashed forward to help.

Han was searching for the leader when he heard a loud *whoosh!* and saw the trooper who might have been Boba Fett streaking toward the ceiling. Blades of fire shot from the jet pack's hornlike gimbaling servos, and bolts rained down on the warriors from his twin hand blasters, which he twirled expertly before slipping them back into their holsters. Amphistaffs flew at him from all quarters, one of them catching him in the chest and sending him off course into a bulkhead.

Fighting broke out among the Yuuzhan Vong for the privilege of being the first to reach him. Two warriors were climbing over the others, almost within arm's reach of the rocket man, when Han raised and aimed his blaster.

"Just in case it is him," Leia said, "try not to hit the jet pack."

"He has returned! Yu'shaa has returned!"

The gathering was small, numbering no more than two hundred Shamed Ones, but word of the Prophet's return was spreading through the underbelly of Yuuzhan'tar, and given enough time the audience would swell to thousands, perhaps tens of thousands.

Nom Anor gazed down from what had once been the elevated rail of a magnetically levitated transport, to what had been a broad boulevard of nightclubs and restaurants, where his followers stood with faces raised in renewed hope and expectation.

For a moment—and just that—it felt good to be back.

From his residence he had retrieved the ooglith cloaker that disguised him as Yu'shaa. He had told his servants that he was not to be disturbed, and, attired in the garb of an ordinary worker, he had let himself out through a secret passage and wound his way through the sacred precinct, past the Temple of the Modeler and the Place of the Dead, through the districts of Vistu and Bluudon, shaking spies perhaps only imagined, then on along well-trodden paths that led down below the verdant surface growth, down into the deep

canyons that had once harbored Coruscant's poor and disen-
franchised and, with the arrival of the Yuuzhan Vong, had
become the realm of the Shamed, where outsiders were met
with suspicion, and anyone not Shamed had to tread carefully, for fear of never surfacing again.

At certain crossings he had uttered passcodes that had
opened the way to even lower levels, not merely populated
by Shamed Ones, but also ruled by them. He recalled having
spied Onimi on a path much like the ones he was forced to
follow; Onimi, doing Shimrra's bidding, who had unwittingly
led Nom Anor to the knowledge that the ultimate repository
of the shapers' arts, the so-called eighth cortex, was empty.
Now he, too, was doing Shimrra's bidding and, like Onimi, had
become Shimrra's puppet and pet, tasked with safeguarding
secrets.

Long before Nom Anor had been able to seek out his former confederates he had been recognized, and Shamed Ones
in filthy frocks and tattered robeskins had flocked to his side,
in awe of Yu'shaa's unannounced reappearance.

"The rumors of my death were greatly exaggerated," he
had tried to tell them.

Only to hear someone respond: "The Prophet has defeated
Shimrra! He has defeated death!"

"No, you miscomprehend," he had said. "I was never
taken by Shimrra."

"The Prophet evaded Shimrra. He has been waiting only
for the right moment to reappear among us!"

His carefully conceived plans went further downhill from
there.

By the time he had reached what was the broad boulevard—
now grown over with shrubs and saplings—a small crowd
had already formed. No one seemed to care that Shimrra had
expressly forbidden such gatherings, under penalty of dishonorable death.

"He has returned! Yu'shaa has returned!"

Nom Anor scanned the crowd. Below the elevated track,
pushing their way forward, came Kunra, Idrish, and V'tel. A
Shamed warrior, Kunra had been Yu'shaa's bodyguard and
chief disciple, and the only one who knew of Nom Anor's
visit to Zonama Sekot.

"We knew you would return," Kunra said when he and the others had climbed to the top of the rail. "You promised that you would elevate us once you had regained your status, and you have been escalated beyond the rank you held. You're in a position to help us beyond our boldest imaginings. Guise or not, you are indeed the Prophet."

Nom Anor recalled his words to Kunra and the late Niiriit. Indeed, he had vowed to restore the honor of the Shamed Ones.

If they only knew how he had betrayed them.

"Yes, I promised to lift you," he said to Kunra. "But we must wait a while longer. This time I come only to warn you. Shimrra knows what you're planning to do at the sacrifice, and you must trust me when I tell you that he will respond *wrathfully.*"

Kunra spread his arms and raised them over the crowd. "Yu'shaa says that we must restage our plan—that we must attack in greater numbers."

"No, no," Nom Anor said while the crowd cheered. "You must rethink the plan entirely, or Shimrra will eradicate you!"

Kunra raised his arms again. "Shimrra plans to eradicate us! We must make the first move!"

Nom Anor bellowed to the Shamed Ones, "You can't look to me, the *Jeedai,* or anyone else to deliver you from your lowly stations! None of us can repair your disfigurements or modify your rejected enhancements!"

"Yu'shaa calls on us to accept that our blemishes are only surface imperfections, and that we must look past them to see our true selves," Kunra said. "He tells us to follow the authority of our inner selves; to steer by our inner rudders for all important decisions, rather than pray to the gods, consult with the priests, or fear what actions the warriors and intendants might take against us!

"Individualism is the greatest threat to the hierarchy supported by Shimrra's elite. Shimrra relies on the elite, in order to preserve a system that perpetuates inequity. He wishes to keep us anchored to ritual and domain, so that he and the elite may prosper. But the Prophet tells us that we are individuals first, and citizens last!"

A chill passed through Nom Anor. He finally understood what Kunra was doing. Kunra—who had saved his life after an assassination attempt by Shoon-mi Esh, and who burned with a warrior's fire—was not about to let Nom Anor shrink from the promise he had made.

What was supposed to have been a final sermon had become a contest of wills.

Nom Anor tried once more to persuade the crowd.

"You err by looking to me or my *disciples* for signs!"

Kunra showed him a covert grin. "The Prophet tells us to look to nature, to the sky, and to the stars—to the planet of redemption, whose coming he foretold!"

The Shamed Ones cheered and lifted their faces higher, beyond the elevated train rail, as if searching the sliver of purple sky for signs. Kunra moved close to Nom Anor, close enough so that Nom Anor could feel the tip of a coufee against his ribs.

"Well done, *Yu'shaa,*" he said quietly. "The multitudes are heated to the point of boiling over. We couldn't have done this without you." He paused, then added: "And remember, Prefect: Just as all things are possible on Yuuzhan'tar today, all things will be possible tomorrow."

FOURTEEN

As had become her ritual since returning from the convoy ambush, Jaina would search out the officer of the watch every four hours to learn if the *Falcon* had been heard from; then she would spend the next hour or so at one of *Ralroost*'s observation viewports, gazing at the incoming traffic and stretching out with the Force, in the hope that one of the moving lights might return her touch, or convey some hint of familiarity.

She was about to abandon the effort that afternoon when a swiftly moving ship caught her eye. If there was a space-borne equivalent of a swoop, Jaina figured she was looking at it. A cramped cockpit anchored to incongruous ion fusion and hyperdrive engines, the small craft was inbound, and on a trajectory for *Ralroost*'s primary docking bay.

Jaina set off for the bay, hurrying down the attack cruiser's sterile passageways and offering only the hastiest of answering salutes to passing noncoms. By the time she had descended from the landing bay's service gantry, the craft's human pilot was on deck and taking off his scratched and dented helmet. His hair was red and shaggy, and his face was wildly freckled. Made up of garments borrowed from at least three separate units, his flight uniform was soiled and patched, and his boots were as mismatched as the engines of his ship. The blaster on his hip was even more ancient than Han's.

When Jaina intercepted him on the landing apron, he offered a crisp salute.

"Where are you arriving from, Lieutenant?" she shouted above the din of warming engines, repair work, and launches.

"Caluula Orbital, Colonel." Noting Jaina's confusion, he

added: "Tion Hegemony. I've a message from the command-ing officer for Galactic Alliance command!"

Jaina moved closer to him. "You're a courier?"

"Yes, sir."

"Then I'll show you to Admiral Kre'fey's cabin."

Clearly, the offer puzzled him, but he thanked her out of respect. "That's really not necessary—"

"I insist." Jaina motioned to the passageway hatch and fell into step beside him. "When did you leave Caluula?" she asked when they could finally speak without shouting.

"Two days ago, local. No hostile contacts along the way. But my ship had some drive problems."

"Did any ships land at Caluula before you launched?"

"Ships?"

"A banged-up YT-thirteen-hundred freighter, in particu-lar?"

"No."

"You're sure?"

"I'd've remembered a YT-thirteen-hundred, sir."

"What's the situation at Caluula?"

The lieutenant glanced around. "I don't know that I'm at liberty—" he began, then shrugged. "What's it matter, right? Commanding Officer Garray wants the admiral to be advised that unless we can be reinforced and reprovisioned, we're likely to fall to the Yuuzhan Vong."

Jaina felt her pulse quicken. "I'm sorry to hear that."

He stopped abruptly. "If it's all right with you, I'll go the rest of the way on my own. The sooner I deliver the message, the sooner I can get back to Caluula."

Jaina nodded. "May the Force be with you, Lieutenant."

"Same with you."

Jaina watched him rush off. For the first time in a long while she felt isolated and fearful. Still no word from Jacen, Luke, or Mara, and now her father and mother were missing, possibly marooned in some remote star system. When she tried to reinforce the sense that they were all right, dreadful images whirled in her mind. And when she called to Leia through the Force, she received no response.

She began to understand how her parents must have felt when their children had embarked on the mission to Myrkr.

Anakin killed, Jacen missing, Jaina fleeing for the Hapes Consortium in a pirated Yuuzhan Vong vessel . . . It was difficult enough being a teenager and worrying about your parents' safety. But being a parent and worrying about your kids had to be even worse. As Han had said on Anakin's death: *A father isn't supposed to outlive his children.*

Jaina's thoughts turned briefly to her uncle Luke and aunt Mara. They had left their infant son, Ben, in the care of Kam and Tionne, at the hidden Maw Installation. But they had to be wondering, worrying . . . Sometimes even the Force couldn't protect a person from imagined fears. Jaina pondered if she would ever be able to raise a family; to cope day to day with the concern that her child would fall victim to illness or accident, make a wrong choice, or be in the wrong place at the wrong time . . .

Dizzy at the thought, she leaned against the cold bulkhead. She heard someone call her by name, and turned to see Jag hastening to her.

Tall and wiry, with a shock of white in his black hair, he was the son of Soontir Fel and Syal Antilles, both of whom had elected to remain in Chiss space. Like his Chiss confederates in Vanguard Squadron, Jag wore a black uniform with red piping.

"Are you all right?" he asked with uncommon alarm. "Did something happen?"

They held each other for a moment before Jaina straightened. "I'm fine. No, actually, I'm not fine. I'm scared to death."

Jag's green eyes searched her face. "Of what?"

She shook her head in uncertainty. "Possibilities."

He took her right hand in his. "No message from your parents."

"Nothing. And no word of Jacen."

Jag firmed his lips. "I'm certain that all of them are fine."

She frowned slightly. "How are you certain? Or is that just something people say when they don't know what else to say?"

Jag blinked. "I . . . well, perhaps it's something of both. Do I know for a fact that Jacen and your parents are all right? No. Does my heart tell me that they're all right? It seems to."

Jaina smiled without mirth. "No medicine like logic, is there?"

Jag's fine eyebrows beetled. A scar ran from his right brow almost to his hairline. "I—"

"No, you're right. I'm driving myself mad. Thanks."

He studied her. "What does the Force tell you?"

"Let's just say that the Force isn't painting as cheerful a picture as the one you just did."

Jag's expression grew skeptical. "You could be mistaken."

"You mean, the Force might be throwing me a curve?" She shook her head. "It doesn't work that way."

"How does it work?" he asked stiffly. "Is it so different from intuition? Is there a stronger link between you and your parents than between me and my parents, simply because of the Force?"

Jaina shut her eyes. "Jag, please. This isn't a good time to be arguing."

He started to say something, then stopped and began again. "Perhaps we can talk heart to heart when the war ends."

"Jag, I'm sorry. I'm just preoccupied."

"No, really. Besides, I'm slated to report to General Bel Iblis. I'll look for you later."

As he started away, she almost went after him, but thought better of it.

What was happening? Was Jag drifting away from her, as well? Was she drifting away from him?

Or was her relationship with him going to turn out to be another of the war's odd pairings; another reversal born of desperation? In either case, it certainly had been an unexpected development. Since events in the Hapes Consortium they had been growing more . . . familiar, with each brief encounter. They had seemed to be falling in love.

Danni Quee had told her that one shouldn't be too analytical about love—that rational thinking was the quickest way to rout affection. But Danni—a scientist who did little else *but* analyze—was no one to talk. And how could someone not wonder about wartime romance? Because they so often emerged out of a desire to live to the fullest, wartime affairs were notorious for being as short-lived as explosions in deep space. People tended to skip all the usual stuff and fly straight to the heat. But how could you trust your emotions at a time when any day might be the last—for yourself, your family and friends, your comrades? What might have happened had she and Jag gotten to know each other in peaceful times? What would have accounted for their shared experiences: holopresentations, picnics, getaways on tourist worlds?

She shook her head. Maybe she was being too hard on them.

Take her parents, for instance. They had met, fallen in love, and married during the worst of times, and everything had worked out great for them. So it could work. But was she trying to emulate them in some way—

"Hey, soldier."

Kyp Durron passed her on the outside and put his arm around her shoulders. Fit, sharp-featured, and dark-haired, he had surrendered the scowl that for years had been his signature expression.

Reflexively, Jaina curled her arm around his waist and leaned against his chest—the chest of a man she had once slapped across the face, but who had later become a kind of mentor to her, especially in helping her navigate the emotional storm that had attended Jacen's unexpected return from Yuuzhan Vong–held Coruscant a year earlier.

Kyp brought them to an abrupt halt and turned slightly to gaze at her. "If it's any consolation, kid, I'm worried, too."

Jaina smiled and laughed shortly. "I don't have to say a thing, do I?"

Kyp shook his head and brushed his hair away from his eyes. "Everything tells me that Jacen is okay. But your parents are in trouble. They've been getting into too many tight situations lately, and now they're really in the thick of it."

Jaina felt stronger for Kyp's having articulated her fears. For a short time she had thought she could fall in love with Kyp, but those feelings had passed, and ever since then they had settled into a close and comforting friendship.

"I was just talking with a courier who arrived from a station in the Tion Hegemony," she said in a rush. "I don't know why, but I think they're there."

Kyp considered it. "If they are, then I guess I'm wrong about them squaring off against the Yuuzhan Vong."

Jaina shook her head. "That's just it, Kyp. Caluula Orbital is under heavy siege. From what the courier said, I think the station might already have been overrun. If I knew for sure, I'd leave right now."

Kyp took her hand. "Let me know if you need a wingmate."

Han's blasterbolt caught the Yuuzhan Vong in his unprotected armpit, twirling him fully around and sending him plummeting from the shoulders of two warriors who had been providing unintentional support. With the immediate threat eliminated, the faceless rocket man raised his left arm and fired a small grappling hook from his forearm gauntlet. The hook found purchase on an expansion girder, instantly towing him to the ceiling of the hold, out over the extended arms of swarming warriors and through flights of blunt amphistaffs. Clambering into a crouch on the girder, he gazed down on his would-be captors, then armed his backpack missile launcher.

"He's . . . he's going to fire!"

One step ahead of C-3PO, Han and Leia each grabbed one of the droid's arms and yanked him down to the deck. The projectile exploded in the center of the hold, flattening everyone within a radius of ten meters. Fifty or more stunned or dying Yuuzhan Vong warriors formed the circumference of the detonation zone.

But reinforcements were already on the way.

Han heard them surging down the corridor, crying for blood. He got to his feet, then helped Leia and C-3PO to theirs. Simultaneous with the *snap-hiss* of Leia's lightsaber came the drone of launched thud bugs.

Leia fielded those she could. Taken by surprise, a dozen Caluula soldiers were dropped in their tracks. The volley of deflected bugs flew back down the corridor at the approaching Yuuzhan Vong, only to be returned by several warriors at the head of the pack. Han caught a glimpse of five comparatively short warriors, smeared head to toe in black blood rather than sheathed in the usual arthropod armor. Odder still, was the way they were holding their amphistaffs to parry thud bugs and blasterbolts.

"They're using them like lightsabers," he said.

"That seems to be the idea," Leia replied breathlessly.

Han shook his head in incredulity. "More new models?"

"I don't think we should wait around to ask!"

The Mandalorian-armored cadre apparently felt the same. Taking aim on a portion of bulkhead close to the deck, two of the troopers used missiles to blow a gaping hole into the adjoining hold. The Caluula defenders began to scramble through, with C-3PO, Leia, and Han bringing up the rear. They raced through the adjacent hold and into a wide corridor, lowering blast shields wherever they encountered them.

Greeted with an intersection, Han knew enough to ask.

"That way!" C-3PO said.

Han gave a last glance at the armored fighters, then turned to follow Leia and C-3PO.

The side corridor led directly to the connector that ran between Caluula's number three and four modules. Outside the tube's curved transparisteel walls, laserbolts and plasma projectiles cleaved the darkness. Coralskippers and starfighters chased one another in chaotic circles. The volcanolike launchers of enemy capital ships fired again and again.

Han, Leia, and C-3PO hadn't set foot inside the number four module when something shook the entire station.

"The ychna," Han said.

Leia agreed. "You know how hard it is to satisfy those things."

Farther along, Garray's meaty adjutant motioned them from the pack of withdrawing soldiers.

"Captain, Princess Leia, the *Falcon* is ready for departure."

Han stared at him. "You've got to be kidding." He gestured broadly. "It's worse out there than in here!"

"I concur, sir. Nevertheless, she's patched up and ready to go. Nowhere near good as new, but you should be able to limp her to Mon Calamari in a couple of microjumps."

Han and Leia traded doubtful looks.

"Each officer we rescued from Selvaris could rally ten thousand additional troops to our cause," Leia said.

Ultimately, Han nodded. "A bunch of people a lot smarter

than me figured this out, so I guess we have to trust that they're right."

Leia smiled. "Spoken like a true enlisted man."

Garray's adjutant directed them back to where the *Falcon* was berthed. With nearly every spaceworthy craft launched, the place was practically deserted. Cracken, Page, and the rest of the Selvaris roster were clustered at the foot of the landing ramp.

The station's klaxons began to blare triplets.

Garray's adjutant cursed, then adopted a resigned expression. "The commander has issued the evacuation order."

Han nodded cheerlessly. "You have to know when to fold."

"I'll be leaving you here."

Han saluted him. "We'll win this thing yet, Chief." He turned to give the *Falcon* a quick glance.

Leia noted Han's discouraged look. "Well, he did say *limp* her to Mon Calamari."

"Crawl's more like it."

The mechanic responsible for the several add-ons emerged from beneath the starboard mandible. "We spared as much blaster gas as we could for your quad lasers, but I'd go light on them if I were you." He gazed up at the *Falcon* and smiled. "Great ship. Good journey."

Han pumped the man's hand in thanks.

A powerful explosion rattled the bay. Paint chips and other objects showered from the vaulted ceiling.

"Everybody get on board," Han said, "before we end up EV without a ship." When Pash Cracken and a few of the other officers didn't move, he stormed over to them. "You waiting for a formal invitation?"

Cracken almost smiled. "With all due respect, Han, we've decided to remain here and do what we can."

Han made his lips a thin line. "Pash, this is bigger than Caluula, and you know it. Alliance command is counting on you people to rally support in your home systems. Besides, you can't make a difference here. Those are evacuation klaxons you're hearing."

"Han's right, Major," Leia said.

Cracken still didn't move. "We'll take our chances, Princess."

She blew out her breath. "Your father's never going to forgive us, Pash."

"He'll understand."

Han nodded. "Then may the Force be with all of you. In other circumstances, I might make the same choice."

He turned and, without a backward look, hurried Leia and C-3PO up the landing ramp. At the top, he waved Page and the rest of the officers into the forward cargo compartment. He told Leia to begin the start-up sequence, and he sent Cakhmaim and Meewalh to the gun turrets. He ran to the stern to check the status of the escape pods, then raced forward to the cockpit. By the time he arrived, Leia was strapped in and the repulsorlift was cold-started.

Han leapt into the pilot's chair while Leia lifted the *Falcon,* turned her about, and sent her streaking through the magcon field.

Local space was crosscut with magma projectiles and turbolaser bolts. Dead ahead, the bloated yncha floated motionless in space, amid a debris cloud created by coralskippers that had thrown themselves against Caluula's shields. X-wings and other starfighters drifted lazily. Three of the station's modules were wide open to vacuum and expressing what little atmosphere they still contained. Below, explosions were blossoming on the beige and green surface of Caluula itself, with wounded coralskippers plunging into the atmosphere like fiery meteors.

Han watched a dozen escape vehicles launch from an undamaged module.

Caluula was finished.

"Three skips converging on us." Leia glanced at him. "It's our old friends."

Han's eyes darted to the authenticator screen. "The ones that tracked us from Selvaris! What is this, a personal vendetta?"

"Maybe they don't like our paint job."

"Then I'm on their side." He clamped his hands on the yoke. "Hang on."

Han leaned toward the intercom. "Watch the fuel levels, you two. Last thing we need is to be left high and dry." He glanced over his left shoulder. "Jump coordinates for Mon Calamari coming in."

Leia studied the navicomputer display. "We'll have come around to three-zero-three. That means back toward the station."

"I was afraid of that."

An explosion shook the ship before it was halfway through the turn.

"There goes the only new piece of equipment they installed. But we can get by without it."

"I'm counting on that, dearest."

One of the curve-tailed, tandem-piloted coralskippers appeared in the wraparound viewport, coming straight at the *Falcon.* "Take the shot!" Han said into the intercom.

Singularities formed in advance of the approaching skip, but sheer firepower overwhelmed them, and the vessel came apart in roiling fire.

"Cakhmaim is *really* getting good," Leia said.

Han shook his head negatively. "That wasn't him."

He leaned back in his seat to glance through the upper panes of the viewport. A classic *Firespray*-class security patrol craft shot overhead. A cross-shaped ship affixed to an oval engine suite, it was followed by four Gladiators, so named because they looked like swords thrust to the hilt through circular shields.

"It *is* Fett! And he's clearing a lane for us!" Han snorted. "Just like him to make sure he has the upper hand on a debt."

"Incoming transmission," Leia said. "From the Firespray."

Boba Fett's voice crackled through the comm. "Just wanted to remind you, Solo, that my personal fight was always with the Jedi. You were nothing more than cargo."

Han snorted. "For what it's worth, Fett, you were never more than a nuisance."

Fett laughed shortly. "To better days, Captain."

"Count on it."

Sowing mines far to port and starboard, the Firespray continued to break a trail for the near-weaponless *Falcon;* then Fett tipped the patrol craft's short wings in salute and vanished.

"Ready for lightspeed," Han said.

Leia collapsed back into the copilot's chair, shaking her head back and forth. "I have now officially seen and heard everything." She turned to Han with a half smile. "I'm almost ready to believe this war will actually end."

With the Jedi Knights reduced to half their strength since the start of the war, Luke Skywalker's seven incommunicado in the Unknown Regions, some—including the twenty or so Jedi children—still sheltered at the Maw Installation, and others participating in various Galactic Alliance military operations, Kenth Hamner could gather only a dozen Jedi for the meeting held in Tresina Lobi's quarters on Mon Calamari.

Though understated, the circular room at the top of Coral City's Quarren Tower was spacious and enjoyed a 360-degree view of the tranquil sea and sparkling reefs. In the continued absence of Luke and Saba—and with Kyp frequently flying missions with the Dozen—Tresina Lobi had become an important voice on Cal Omas's Advisory Council. A Chev, she had a narrow face with angular features, and short black hair.

Tresina, Markre Medjev, and Cilghal, the Mon Calamari Jedi healer, had spent the morning preparing food, and the circular table in the sunroom was already spread with the appetizing results of their labors by the time Kenth and the others arrived.

Gradually they seated themselves at the table, except for Kenth, who was too restless to eat or stay put. Clockwise from Tresina's armchair sat Cilghal, Jaina, Kyp, towering ginger-furred Lowbacca, the Twi'lek female Alema Rar, salt-and-pepper-haired combat instructor Kyle Katarn, Chandrilan Octa Ramis, slight and terribly scarred Waxarn Kel, and young and darkly handsome Zekk.

"Some of you might not be aware that operative Baljos Arnjak didn't return from Wraith Squadron's infiltration mission to Coruscant," Kenth said as he circled the table. "Bhindi Drayson was supposed to have remained onworld, but it was Arnjak who stayed, and has been furnishing the Alliance with intelligence ever since, mostly with the help of a kind of droid-fungus he and his teammates let loose during the mission."

Kenth came to a stop between Cilghal and Jaina, then leaned forward, planting the palms of his hands on the table. "Arnjak's latest report states that Yu'shaa, the so-called Prophet of the heretics, was recently seen on Coruscant. By recent, I mean within the past local week, since it took that long for a string of couriers to move the information from the Core to Mon Calamari."

"Has his identity been verified?" Kyle asked from across the table.

Kenth nodded. "Which means that he either didn't go to Zonama Sekot with Corran and Tahiri—"

"Or that he returned without them," Kyp said. "Is there some way we can establish whether he arrived back on Coruscant in the same vessel everyone left on?"

"No," Kenth said.

[Or if they even reached Zonama Sekot], Lowbacca's voice issued from his droid translator.

Kenth glanced at the Wookiee. "Exactly. Unlike most of the HoloNet transceivers, Esfandia is still functioning—if inconsistently. So, assuming nothing has befallen *Jade Shadow,* Luke and Mara should have been able to contact us."

"We've waited long enough," Octa Ramis said. "It's time we sent a ship."

Everyone fell silent for a long moment, then Cilghal said, "I doubt that we'll find Zonama Sekot at the coordinates to which we've been transmitting messages. I suspect that the living world has moved."

"Based on what?" Alema asked.

Cilghal spread her webbed hands. "On what the Force tells me."

Kenth glanced around the table. "Do any of you also feel that way?"

"I do," Jaina said. "Jacen feels farther away than he did when we received Luke and Mara's transmission." She shook her head somberly. "I don't feel him as distinctly."

Kenth inhaled with purpose. "That's good enough for me." He compressed his lips. "I say we have a talk with the Prophet."

Kyp snorted. "I agree. But getting onto Coruscant won't

be easy—even with Peace Brigade and trade ships being allowed to land there."

Alema looked from Kyp to Kenth. "Could we appeal to Alliance command for help in inserting some of us?"

Kenth shook his head. "Not without explaining what we're after—or why we didn't inform command that we'd sanctioned Corran and Tahiri's mission to Zonama Sekot. If Intelligence learns that we passed on a chance to capture a shaper, a priest, and the *Prophet,* of all people . . ."

"We could go to Wedge," Markre Medjev suggested.

Kenth nodded. "We could, and I'm sure he'd do everything in his power to get us onto Coruscant. But I don't want to put him in the position of having to lie to Sovv and Kre'fey."

"I agree," Cilghal said.

Tresina nodded. "Likewise."

"This is beginning to sound like Myrkr all over again," Kyp said.

Zekk looked at him. "If Anakin hadn't taken on that mission, all of us might be voxyn fodder by now."

"Zekk's right," Octa Ramis added. "If it sounds like Myrkr, it's because we have no choice but to go."

Kenth straightened and adopted a determined expression. "We'll give Master Skywalker a week. If we don't hear from him by then, I'll assemble a strike team."

FIFTEEN

Its balloonlike bone-white outriggers buffeted by gusting winds, the airship moved swiftly over the devastated surface of Zonama Sekot. Luke, Mara, Jacen, and the Yuuzhan Vong priest, Harrar, were crammed onto the rear portion of the gondola's tiny cabin. Saba Sebatyne and a Ferroan male named Kroj'b had the controls. Companion of the manta-shaped dirigible *Elegance Enshrined,* Kroj'b had arrived in the Middle Distance only the previous day, but had agreed to accompany the Jedi on their mission to the southern realm. Next to the two pilots stood Jabitha, wrapped in a fur-lined cloak.

At three thousand meters the air was frigid, and the howling wind made conversation difficult. Even if that hadn't been the case, no one seemed inclined to talk. Jacen was broodingly silent; Mara, preoccupied and restless. Saba, at least, had a bewildering assortment of organiform control levers to busy her.

Luke raised the cowl of his robe and shoved his hands deep into the robe's sleeves.

The Force spoke quietly on Zonama Sekot.

The rain had finally ceased in that part of the planet, but the thick cloud cover remained. The sun—whatever star it was, named or unknown—was a broad smear of incandescence behind the gray veil. A persistent chill wind rustled the giant boras and was fast stripping them of their globular leaves. Many of the leaves had turned blue and yellow, as if bruised. Something seldom seen in the Middle Distance—except at high altitude—vapors froze during the long nights, leaving the canyon floors coated in white until the sun rose. Thin sheets of transparent ice formed over quiet pockets of the still-swollen river. When glimpsed at all, animals could be seen seeking shelter in caves or burrows, or fashioning durable nests, as if in preparation for a long winter. Boras seeds, too, had been observed creeping off into the tampasi, perhaps to seek nourishment among the oldest of the iron-tipped boras and wait for the lightning strikes that would split and shape them.

The Ferroans rarely ventured out before midday, and then only for long enough to gather firewood or effect repairs to their cliffside dwellings. Most of them avoided the Jedi when-ever possible or, when not, exchanged few words. None, how-ever, had issued further demands that Harrar be turned over to them. Luke assumed that young Maydh had allayed fears that the Yuuzhan Vong priest was a threat.

He gazed through the cabin's aft windscreen at the wounds Zonama had suffered. Quakes had opened deep trenches in the savannas, landslides had altered the course of rivers, fires had ravaged vast tracts of tampasi. Luke had considered tak-ing *Jade Shadow* up to survey and catalog the damages—perhaps attaining orbit for just long enough to survey the nearby stars, as well—but he couldn't trust that the planet wouldn't jump into hyperspace again, as it had after its initial reversion to realspace.

Covertly he looked at Jabitha, then at Harrar. He couldn't recall a time when he had been so close to a Yuuzhan Vong and not engaged in fighting for his life—save perhaps on the occasions he had stood close to Nom Anor. But then, any moments spent with Nom Anor constituted a duel, of sorts.

For the tenth time since the airship journey had begun, Luke tried to see Harrar in the Force, but perceived only an absence. Despite Vergere's assurances to the contrary, Harrar—and by extension all Yuuzhan Vong—did not seem to exist in the Force. There the priest sat, not three meters away, and Luke couldn't sense him. Harrar was nothing more or less than what he appeared to be: a tall, sinewy humanlike man, absent some of his fingers, and marked with tattoos, scars, and other modifications.

Luke knew that he could use the Force to levitate Harrar, to pirouette him about the small cabin, but he couldn't *see* him in the same way he could see Mara, Jacen, Saba, and

Jabitha—as a luminous being; not as the crude stuff of flesh and bone, but as an egg-shaped being of light. Vergere, who had willingly spent fifty years among the Yuuzhan Vong, had maintained that the seeming invisibility of the Yuuzhan Vong owed not to any inherent failure of the Force, but to the way Luke and his fellow Jedi *perceived* the Force. The implication was they had somehow failed to grasp that the Force was grander and more far reaching than they understood it to be.

Luke could accept that. His training had been rushed; and with the deaths of Obi-Wan and Yoda he had been obliged largely to pursue his own counsel, and find his own way to mastery. He would have been the first to admit that his understanding of the Force might be limited or incomplete; that he had perhaps become more a Master of the Living Force than what the late Vergere had called the Unifying Force. But even that deficiency should not have prevented him from being able to *see* Harrar.

Either Vergere had left something out of her lectures—which Luke wouldn't have put past her—or her own understanding of the quandary was incomplete. Luke didn't for a moment doubt that the Fosh Jedi had somehow succeeded in tutoring herself to a kind of mastery—despite having been forced to conceal her Jedi abilities from her captors—but the matter of the Yuuzhan Vong's invisibility ran deeper than Vergere knew, or had allowed. Perhaps she believed, as Yoda had at times, that her responsibility ended with setting Luke on the proper path. Perhaps that was the way among the Jedi of the Old Republic. For all the education and practice each had undergone, the achievement of mastery was ultimately the outcome of a personal quest for understanding.

If any of the new Jedi order grasped this on an intuitive level, it was Jacen. Long before his reeducation by Vergere—some said reindoctrination—Jacen had sought to reach a personal understanding of the Force. In that, he was much like Leia, a Knight in her own right, who had for her own reasons resisted taking up the path of the Jedi.

It was Jacen who had insisted that Harrar accompany them on the journey Jabitha had proposed a day earlier, when she had visited Luke, Mara, and the others in their cliff dwelling.

"Sekot is aging," Jabitha had said. "I feel her, and yet I feel estranged from her. She remains in exile to puzzle out what has happened; and in withdrawing, she neglects Zonama. I don't think she has done so deliberately. It is as if she has been abducted by dark forces, and is somehow imprisoned."

"Nom Anor, Nen Yim, and I are responsible for what has happened to Sekot," Harrar had said. "We should never have come here. If the gods haven't already turned their backs on the Yuuzhan Vong, they will now, for we have despoiled a living world."

Jabitha had listened to the priest's confession without comment. She said, "I know where we can begin to seek Sekot. A place where the Force is strong . . ."

Harrar seemed to feel Luke's eyes on him, and turned. His own eyes were moist, and tears had left streaks on his tattooed cheeks. The cause might have been the wind rushing through cracks in the cabin.

"I am overcome," he said sadly. "Even with all its recent injuries, this is the world I have dreamed of. The world all my people have dreamed of. The one that ordained our past; the one we prayed would prefigure our future. A world of symbiosis, rather than competition and predation. The very world we have tried time and again to re-create, only to end up with facsimiles. It is no small wonder I felt nostalgic for this place the moment we landed; that I felt I'd arrived home, though I'd never been here."

"If the Yuuzhan Vong evolved on a world like this," Luke said, "what turned you to war?"

Harrar took a moment to reply. "The ancient texts are unclear. It appears that we were invaded by a race that was more technological than animate. We called on the gods for protection, and they came to our aid, providing us with the knowledge we needed to convert our living resources to weapons. We defeated the threat, and, empowered by our victory, we gradually became conquerors of other species and civilizations."

Jabitha interrupted, instructing Kroj'b to steer the airship southwest. The terrain grew more and more rugged. Jagged mountains of crushed lava rose steeply into the clouds. Braided tails of orange-tinted water plunged from the heights into thickly forested gorges. The wind blew fiercely, and the temperature began to fall below freezing.

At Jabitha's direction Kroj'b and Saba piloted the airship down toward the expansive talus field of a mountain that struck Luke as being younger than Ben and twice as unpredictable.

"Here is where my father's fortress once stood," Jabitha explained, after the airship had been anchored to the denuded slope. "Sekot showed Obi-Wan Kenobi and Anakin Skywalker a mental image of the fortress as it was before the advent of the Far Outsiders."

"The Far Outsiders have a name, Jabitha," Harrar said. "It is the Yuuzhan Vong who toppled your father's fortress."

"Of course," she said. "Old habits are not easily broken."

Luke asked Saba to remain with Kroj'b in the airship; then he and the rest emerged from the cabin and began to follow Jabitha uphill, fighting a cold, strong wind that swept down from the invisible summit. Luke saw the cave entrance before Jabitha drew everyone's attention to it.

The air inside was warm and remarkably humid. The cave angled down into the mountainside, and Luke realized immediately that what they were in was actually an ancient lava tube. The floor was paved with coarse pebbles that crunched underfoot. Cooled magma from deep in the planet, the walls were composed of dense black stone, but in some places they glowed with a faint bioluminescence.

"How like the interiors of our space vessels," Harrar said.

Luke could see the resemblance, but he was reminded of something entirely different—the cave on Dagobah that Yoda had dared him to enter. But while that place had been strong in the dark side, the lava tunnel felt enchanted—strangely maternal and enfolding. He began to sense the presence of the animating intelligence he had come to know during his short time on Zonama, the one helped to consciousness by the first Magister, Leor Hal, who had also named the planet in the Ferroan language "World of Body and Mind."

"Could this be another of Sekot's tests?" Mara wondered while they walked.

"I don't think so," Luke said. "Unless Sekot is testing itself."

"Stop there," the voice of Sekot said, speaking through a suddenly transfixed Jabitha. "Who walks with you, Jedi Master? Two I recognize, but the third . . ."

"He is called Harrar," Luke said, not to Jabitha but to the tunnel itself. "He came to Zonama in the company of the one who sabotaged you."

Jabitha turned to Harrar. "How is it I seem to know this one? My memories go back billions of turnings, and this one carries a message to me of distant times and distant events."

"Harrar is of the people you know as the Far Outsiders," Luke said. "The Yuuzhan Vong, who tried to conquer Zonama, shortly before the arrival of Vergere."

Jabitha shook her head. "Those times are not distant, Jedi Master. But why can't I perceive him? Not as I do the children of the Firsts; not nearly as I do the Jedi. . . . Yes, I recall having the same experience with the Far Outsiders—they seemed to exist outside the Force."

"No, Sekot," Luke said. "Even though you can't perceive Harrar, he exists within the Force."

Jacen's right hand went to his chest, as if to touch the scar left from the piece of slave coral Vergere had implanted in him. He swung to Harrar. "Why did the Yuuzhan Vong leave their home galaxy?"

Harrar firmed his scarred lips, then said, "Some have interpreted the ancient texts to suggest that we were . . . banished."

"For what reason?" Jacen persisted.

"Our infatuation with war and conquest. Some interpret our long journey as an attempt to win back the favor of the gods."

Jacen thought about it. "Your ancestors were banished because they turned to war. They did the opposite of what was expected of them. Did . . . the gods banish you from *the Force*?"

When Harrar lifted his head, his face was a mask of fearful confusion. "There is nothing in our legends about the Force."

"But even you compared the Force to your gods," Mara said.

Luke took Harrar by the shoulders, as if to shake him, but only eased him to his feet. "A power—call it the gods if you have to—may have separated you from the original *symbiosis*. Your people experienced intolerable pain, and pain has been the only way back to that symbiosis."

Harrar nearly collapsed in Luke's grip. "Separated from the symbiosis. From our primordial homeworld . . ."

Luke dropped his hands to his sides and turned in astonishment to Jabitha, as if waiting for Sekot to confirm what he was thinking.

"I now understand," Sekot said finally. "This one—his people—has been *stripped* of the Force."

SIXTEEN

There hadn't been a ceremony to equal it in untold generations. As vast as the worldships were—and notwithstanding the views of distant stars and even more distant galaxies—they weren't large enough to contain the magnificence of high ritual. Compared to Yuuzhan'tar's Place of Sacrifice, the worldships were mere theaters.

And yet, for all the grandeur and spectacle, Nom Anor was too consumed by apprehension to appreciate a moment of it. He marched in step with the procession, but the expression on his face would have been better suited to someone on his way to be executed.

Located midway between Shimrra's Citadel and the skull-shaped bunker that housed the Well of the World Brain, the Place of Sacrifice was dominated by a hundred-meter-high truncated cone of yorik coral, helixed with carved stairways and honeycombed with passageways that served to channel blood into fonts and other basins. On the flattened top the priests performed their rituals, and encircling the base were the yawning pits of the corpse-disposing maw luur. To one side of the spire sprawled a grouping of temples, oriented to the sacred directions; and to the other, a repository, in which were stored the holy relics Shimrra's worldship had conveyed across the dim reaches of intergalactic space.

Constructed in accordance with the hallowed texts, and in homage to the ancestral architecture, the complex was dense with conifers, ferns, palms, and the like, wrong for the latitude but somehow thriving. The air hummed with the sounds of insects and crab-harps, and was heady with the smell of paalac incense, which wafted in thick, curling clouds from bone braziers.

Along the perimeter of the quadrangle were pens for the blood-sopping ngdins, and at each corner sat a mon duul, whose enormous tympanic belly was capable of amplifying the utterances of the various celebrants. Since the priests had not yet grown to trust Yuuzhan'tar's World Brain, the matched pair of consuming beasts known as Tu-Scart and Sgauru waited in the wings with their handlers, in case the capricious dhuryam failed to command the maw luur to execute their tasks.

More specialized than yammosks, dhuryams had full responsibility for worldshaping. Their decisions were based on the continuous streams of data they received from planet-wide networks of telepathically linked creatures. But Yuuzhan'tar's dhuryam had been behaving as if there were glitches in the data flow, and it had already ruined several sacrifices by spewing fetid-smelling wastes from the maw luur.

Shimrra, however, had apparently found a way to placate or otherwise bring the World Brain into line, because thus far the sundry biots were functioning smoothly. Nom Anor suspected that the Supreme Overlord had tricked the dhuryam into thinking that, by providing the maw luur with nourishment, it would be helping the gardens and copses of trees to flourish.

He and some of Yuuzhan'tar's consuls entered the Place of Sacrifice to music that was at once solemn and celebratory. Sated on yanskac and snack beetles, and mildly intoxicated on sparkbee honey grog and other home brews, the crowds of onlookers applauded exuberantly. Thousands of warriors kneeled to both sides of the grand avenue, heads lowered and amphistaffs curled sedately around their extended right arms, fists planted solidly on the ground. With guards posted at all entry points and circulating through the crowd, it seemed improbable that any Shamed Ones could get within a phon of the place.

Regardless, Nom Anor continued to torment himself with worry.

Behind the intendants marched elites of the four castes— High Priest Jakan and his coven of savants; red-cloaked Warmaster Nas Choka and three dozen of his Supreme Commanders; Master Shaper Qelah Kwaad and her chief adepts; and High Prefect Drathul, baton of high-office in hand, and leading his cabal of personal consuls. Last came Shimrra, without Onimi—for, as a Shamed One, Onimi was barred from attending such weighty proceedings—but accompanied by his quartet of hideous seers. Attired in a train of living insects and holding the royal scepter, the Supreme Overlord rode atop a yorik coral sled drawn by a pack of bissop hounds.

All fangs, talons, horns, and blades, female dervishes whirled at the base of the spire, while the elite arranged themselves in tiers below Shimrra's moonbeam throne. Nom Anor sat close to the top, with an unobstructed view of the sacrificial platform toward which Jakan climbed, followed by a gang of executioners, priestesses, and young acolytes.

At the appointed moment—when the sun had reached a place in the sky from which it could set the rainbow bridge aflame—the captives were led into the complex by a parade of ngdin handlers and Chazrach troops, riding twelve-legged quenak beasts.

Counting what the Peace Brigaders had managed to deliver and those captured only three standard days earlier at Caluula, the captives numbered close to one thousand. Military officers, political officials, soldiers, and protestors from scores of worlds along the invasion corridor—men, women, even a few adolescents who had fought bravely enough to be rewarded with honorable death—they had been purged, bathed, perfumed, mildly sedated with sensislug gas, and blessed with tishwii leaf smoke. Manacled, they wore white robes that glowed with green designs and were veined in black along arterial networks down the sleeves and fronts.

The captives were brought to a halt at the foot of the spiral staircases that twisted around the spire. By then Jakan and the others had reached the top and were waiting eagerly.

At Shimrra's nod of consent, Jakan raised his arms and spoke, and the bellies of the four mon duuls carried his invocation far and wide.

"Accept what we offer as evidence of our wish to render unto you what is rightfully yours," the high priest intoned. "If not for you, we should not exist!"

Dedicated lambents illuminated statues of the gods, which

lined the quadrangle. The statues would be anointed with first blood. But because of the special nature of the sacrifice, Yun-Yuuzhan would receive only a healthy share, with much of the sacrificial blood going instead to Yun-Yammka, god of war.

Guards began to force the captives to ascend the staircases. Despite their sedation, they floundered and fought, showing no appreciation for the honor that had been bestowed on them. In the end, though, there was little they could do to affect their fate.

The first of the captives had reached the circular platform when a howl rose from below. With nearly half the audience of elites rising to their feet, Nom Anor couldn't see what was going on. It sounded as if a battle had broken out among some of the guards stationed at the base of the spire—perhaps a domain dispute. He pitied those who lacked the self-control to delay their contest until after the sacrifice. But at least he wouldn't be blamed.

Then he realized what was actually happening.

As if detonating, carefully camouflaged chuk'a caps were popping from the quadrangle's hexagonal paving stones. The shells of an aquatic creature, the caps concealed the entrances to shafts that must have descended into the maze of canyons below the Place of Sacrifice—down to the wide thoroughfares that had once separated the tall edifices of Coruscant, down into the dusky underworld of scrub growth and meandering pathways the Shamed Ones had claimed as their own.

Out of the shafts were emerging hundreds of Shamed Ones—Yu'shaa's flock of heretics—armed with amphistaffs, coufees, an array of homemade weapons, even a few blasters! Momentarily taken off their guard, the warriors—many in ceremonial armor only—were slow to react, and dozens were felled in an instant. As the Shamed Ones spread out into the crowd, the commoners began to panic, surging down into the quadrangle.

Fearing that the heretics had come for Shimrra, the slayers closed ranks around the Supreme Overlord, unfurling their amphistaffs, heedless of any who might be standing in front of them. But Nom Anor saw that only a small contingent of

Shamed Ones was closing on Shimrra's dais, and that this group was clearly a diversion.

It was the prisoners the heretics had come for.

Oblivious, thinking perhaps that it was all a hallucination, the captives were being scooped off their feet by bands of heretics and rushed back into the labyrinthine underworld from which the pariah army had climbed. Not all of them made it to safety; scores were dropped by thud and razor bugs, along with three times as many Shamed Ones.

Shimrra's black-smeared seers were flailing their arms in dread, and Jakan appeared to have been struck deaf and silent. The executioners, however, were rushing down the staircases and lashing out with their keen weapons, determined to administer at least a few decapitations—as if the gods could be satisfied with a snack, when they had been anticipating a feast!

What blood was running into the quadrangle, the ndgins were thirsty to absorb. Unable to contain themselves, they were wriggling free of their handlers, and, in so doing, providing slick patches of crushed bodies for warriors in pursuit of the heretics and the captives they had set free.

Nom Anor wasn't sure if he should flee, throw himself on one of the slayers' coufees, or crawl to Shimrra on his belly and beg forgiveness while there was still a chance. He glanced over his shoulder to see Drathul skewering him with a look of unmitigated hatred. The high prefect had said that he would hold Nom Anor accountable for any interference, and now Drathul was intent on making good his threat.

Pressed among the crowd, Nom Anor readied his venom-spitting eyeball. Drathul was already shouldering his way through the throng, brandishing his baton. Was Nom Anor going to have to kill another high prefect just to save his own neck?

Shimrra would have expected no less of him.

Drathul was almost within arm's reach of Nom Anor when the Supreme Overlord's voice rang out above the melee of droning thud bugs, snapping amphistaffs, and sizzling blaster-bolts, his huge head rising above those slayers that made up his living fence.

"High Prefect Drathul! No more of this shall we brook! At

this place is our patience and goodwill sundered!" Shimrra stood to his full and imposing height, towering over everyone. "I demand the heart of every Yuuzhan Vong who has aided and abetted the Prophet!"

Everyone in the vicinity was cowering, except for Nom Anor, because of how tightly he was wedged in place. Perhaps that was why he alone happened to be gazing past Shimrra when one of the slayers slipped away into the crowd. Except that the individual wasn't a slayer. Master of disguise that he was, Nom Anor recognized that the deserter was wearing an ooglith masquer, which not only cloaked his appearance but also reshaped his body.

And from the way the slayer moved—with a somewhat trembling gait—the imposter could only be Onimi.

For the fourth and final microjump that would deliver them at last to Mon Calamari, Han and Leia had sealed off the cockpit and spent the entire time in each other's arms, Leia on Han's lap in the pilot's chair, her arms around his neck. By the time the *Falcon* reverted to realspace Han was delirious, and Leia felt that, as safe corners went, the cockpit wasn't too shabby—at least until they happened on the real thing.

Approaching the water world from well beyond its solitary moon, they were greeted by the sight of an enormous, perhaps unprecedented gathering of warships—a unified force of battle groups, flotillas, and fleets from all regions of the galaxy: Bothan, Bakuran, Imperial Remnant, and Chiss; Sullustan, Hapan, Eriaduan, and Hutt; Corellian and Mon Calamarian. In a glance they saw *Mediator*-class battle cruisers, *Belarus*-class cruisers, *Lancer*-class frigates, and Hapan Battle Dragons. They saw ensembles of *Nova*-class battle cruisers and Corellian gunships; reprovision flotillas of KDY *Marl*-class heavy freighters; attack groups of *Imperial II*–class Star Destroyers, *Republic*-class cruisers, and *Immobilizer*-class interdictors, their hemispherical gravity-well projectors accented by starlight.

There were *Ralroost, Right to Rule, Harbinger, Elegos A'Kla, Mon Adapyne,* and *Mon Mothma;* the Super Star Destroyer *Guardian,* and the ancient Dreadnaught *Starsider.*

"You disappear for a couple of days," Han said when he was past his initial astonishment, "and the kids turn the house into party central."

Wordlessly he and Leia maneuvered the *Falcon* through corridors formed by the massive ships. The confined lanes were thick with starfighters and tenders. Ultimately they were requested to surrender control of the freighter to one of *Ralroost*'s tractor beams, which carried them gently into the cruiser's immense starboard docking bay. A large crowd had turned out to welcome the *Falcon* home, and cheers and applause filled the scrubbed air as Han, Leia, and their roster of very influential people descended the boarding ramp.

Jaina rushed from the sidelines to hug her parents for dear life.

Han was nonplussed. "We'd've been here sooner, but we had to spend three days at sublight making repairs to the repairs."

"I knew you were at Caluula," she said, refusing to let go of him. "I should have listened to the Force and gone there."

"I'm glad you didn't," Leia said, taking a moment to gaze at her daughter. "Has there been any further word from the station?"

"A courier arrived from Caluula yesterday," Jaina said. "The station and the planet fell to the Yuuzhan Vong. Hundreds were taken captive and sent to Coruscant."

"The sacrifice," Han said.

Jaina nodded grimly and began to lead her parents away from the *Falcon*.

Han thought about Pash Cracken and the rest who had chosen to remain at Caluula—rescued only to be captured again. He was reminded of what had often happened at the beginning of the war, when countless refugees had been taken advantage of by pirates and Peace Brigaders.

"Is there news from Coruscant?" he asked.

Jaina nodded. "Good and bad—but you can hear for yourself. Admiral Kre'fey wants to bring you up to speed personally."

"Give us a hint," Leia said.

Jaina lowered her voice. "The Yuuzhan Vong have amassed an armada. We're expecting them to strike us here."

Han blew out his breath. "That explains all the ships."

"Let's just hope that wasn't the good news," Leia said.

Jaina talked nonstop for the several minutes it took them to ascend to *Ralroost*'s command deck and ride a skimmer to a conference cabin amidships. Han and Leia were disappointed to learn that the Jedi still hadn't heard from Luke, Mara, Jacen, or the others. It wasn't like them to remain out of contact for so long.

The white-furred Bothan admiral, Traest Kre'fey, rose from his chair at the head of the long conference table as Leia, Jaina, and Han were being escorted into the cabin space. His violet eyes took in Han and Leia, and he smiled broadly. "We were all starting to wonder if you'd decided to take unannounced leave."

"Well, we have our own idea about what constitutes a vacation," Han joked.

Leia managed to smile, but just barely.

By *all*, Kre'fey had meant the dozen high-ranking officers who were seated at the table. Defense Force Supreme Commander Sien Sovv; Grand Admiral Gilad Pellaeon; Generals Wedge Antilles, Garm Bel Iblis, Keyan Farlander, Carlist Rieekan, and Airen Cracken; Commodore Brand, Queen Mother and Jedi Knight Tenel Ka, and bulky Major General Eldo Davip—promoted as a result of his brave actions aboard the Star Destroyer *Lusankya* at the Battle of Borleias.

Han and Leia needed no introductions to any of them, but there were others they recognized only by species rather than name.

Han threw everyone a grin of greeting. Leia shook hands with Gilad Pellaeon and Keyan Farlander, kissed Wedge and Tenel Ka on both cheeks, then went to Airen Cracken, with whom she had spoken briefly from the *Falcon*.

"Pash was one of the officers captured at Caluula Orbital and taken to Coruscant," Cracken said. "But I'm hoping for the best. No one knows Coruscant better than my son, and if anyone can escape, it'll be him."

Han, Leia, and Jaina found seats for themselves.

"Just to catch you up," Kre'fey said, "the sacrifice ceremony took place as scheduled. But our agents report that before anyone had been put to the coufee, there was an uprising by several hundred heretics. The heretics managed not only to interfere with the ceremony, but also to abscond with more than three hundred Alliance prisoners."

"Just to spoil things for Shimrra?" Han asked.

"We're not sure, at this point. But we have learned that an untold number of Shamed Ones have been rounded up in return, and are apparently going to be put to death. No Alliance personnel were among those seized, so presumably our people are being well hidden."

"If they're even alive," Han said. "The Shamed Ones could have staged a sacrifice of their own, in honor of whatever deity they worship." He glanced at Cracken. "Sorry, Airen, but I think it's premature to consider these heretics as allies."

"We agree," Kre'fey said. "The possibility of a secret sacrifice or a hostage scenario cannot be ruled out. However, we have also learned the purpose of the original sacrifice was to ensure victory for the armada Shimrra plans to launch against Mon Calamari."

Han and Leia pretended to be surprised by the news. "Do we know when or how they're going to do this?" Leia asked.

Sovv spoke to the question. A Sullustan, he looked as if he were wearing a large-eared, heavy-jowled mask. "Intelligence has determined that the enemy plans to attack directly from the Perlemian Trade Route. Secondary salients will be launched from Toong'l and Caluula, both of which now host yammosks. There appears to be a twofold purpose for installing war coordinators on those worlds: first, to coordinate flanking attacks; and second, to provide rear-guard defense in the event the initial wave is repelled."

Han glanced around the cabin. "How many Yuuzhan Vong vessels are we talking about?"

"On the order of five thousand," Bel Iblis supplied flatly, the fingers of his left hand smoothing his drooping mustache.

Han sat away from the table in shock. "Then we haven't a chance."

"Not force against force," Sovv said. "But we have high

confidence that the enemy has made a strategic blunder by opting to stage from remote worlds like Toong'l and Calu- ula."

Bel Iblis nodded in agreement. "More important, we think we can take advantage of the fact the Yuuzhan Vong are ex- pecting us to turn tail and scatter."

Han regarded the inscrutable Sullustan and the gray- haired human. If there was any lingering bad blood between Sovv and Bel Iblis over what had occurred during the evacuation of Coruscant, there was no evidence of it now. In fact, everyone at the table appeared to have reached an ac- cord.

"Why wouldn't we be better off scattering our fleets?" he asked carefully. "We've enough ships to open dozens of new fronts."

"And wage a war of rebel actions for the next ten years, while the enemy grows stronger?" Kre'fey said. "No. By scattering we would leave Mon Calamari open to assault, and we certainly don't want to see happen here what hap- pened on Coruscant. There is no more dangerous species than one that views killing as cleansing." He gave his head a determined shake. "This must be our decisive step."

"Without going into detail at this time," Sovv said, "let me just add that we plan to give all appearances of being caught unawares by the armada, and of engaging it head-on. This alone will give the enemy pause. In fact, half our forces will have already relocated to Contruum, which has agreed to serve as our staging area—thanks to the efforts of General Cracken. We're counting on Captain Page to prevail on the leaders of Corulag to do the same."

Han shook his head in confusion. "Staging areas for what? The farther from Mon Calamari you place those fleets, the more trouble we'll have communicating with them. And if you're thinking of jumping them back to Mon Calamari by surprise, then maybe you need to be reminded of what hap- pened to the Hapans at Fondor."

Tenel Ka acknowledged Han's remark with a veiled nod.

"Fondor was a special circumstance," Commodore Brand said. "Our strategy would have worked if . . . In any case, it isn't our intention to jump the fleets back to Mon Calamari."

"What is your intention?" Leia asked.

Kre'fey cleared his throat meaningfully. "By devoting only half our battle groups to the defense of Mon Calamari, the remainder will be free to move against our primary target—Coruscant."

SEVENTEEN

Ruthless deeds return to harass their architect, Nom Anor thought as he viewed the execution of the heretics.

The deaths were taking place not atop the yorik coral spire in the Place of Sacrifice, but in an area outside the sacred precinct, where many of Yuuzhan Vong beasts went to die, and warriors trained for combat. Once a sports arena in the district known as the Western Sea, it was now an ossuary—a boneyard—lush with swampy growth, rank with odors of decay, and the breeding ground for millions of meter-long yargh'un rodents. The bowl couldn't hold many spectators, but Shimrra had ordered it filled to overflowing with bone stackers, workers, and low-echelon others, both as a blunt demonstration of his wrath, and as a warning to any who would follow the Prophet.

The doleful music of musicians went unappreciated.

The foodstuffs spread across the banquet tables for the elite went untouched.

The clawed beasts tasked with the executions snorted and bellowed.

This was not noble death but capital punishment.

It was three local days after the abortive sacrifice ceremony, and on orders passed down from Shimrra to High Prefect Drathul, and then on to Nom Anor, three thousand Shamed Ones had been gathered up—ten for every captive who had been liberated from the ceremony. What percentage of them were heretics made no difference, for this was an attempt to put an end to further enrollment—though Nom Anor felt that it might have precisely the opposite effect. Shimrra had sent warriors to purge Yuuzhan'tar's underworld of heretics on previous occasions, but this was the first time he had done so openly, and had turned the mass arrests into a macabre entertainment.

Some were saying that Shimrra had crossed a dangerous line—but only those who weren't aware of the lengths to which Shimrra would go to maintain his authority, and the mental power he could bring to bear when necessary. No one privy to the methods Shimrra had used to attain the throne voiced any criticisms.

During the intergalactic journey, Shimrra—by dint of noble birth, prophecy, and divination—had been placed among a pool of candidates who might one day be eligible for consideration to succeed Supreme Overlord Quoreal on his death. All the nobles who comprised that small, privileged group had been raised as if they might one day rise to the throne. They were doted upon, fed the finest foods, trained in warfare and religion. They enjoyed every luxury. Though overseen by the high priests, the selection process was markedly similar to the way in which infant dhuryams were tested, to determine which was most capable and worthy of becoming a worldship or planetary brain.

Shimrra was at once the pride and distress of Domain Jamaane. Early evidence of his maliciousness, he had killed his own *twin* at just seven years of age, to eliminate a possible competitor from entering the pool. His majestic size was attributed to the work of shapers in his domain.

Domain Jamaane also had its share of distinguished warriors, and in distant times had produced more than the usual share of Supreme Commanders, along with three warmasters. The shapers, too, were praiseworthy, as were Jamaane's priests. Still, the domain was not generally thought to be bellicose. But as the long voyage through the void began to gnaw at everyone, Jamaane members had grown outspoken about their impatience with Quoreal, who was cautious, traditional, and had done little to keep Yuuzhan Vong society intact at a time when guidance was needed most. Even so, no one believed that Domain Jamaane would actually rise up and make a bid to usurp Quoreal's power.

In one bold action, Shimrra's warriors moved against Quoreal's, executing them, along with every member of their domains. Then they did the same to Quoreal, and they put to death almost all the priests, advisers, and shapers who had supported Quoreal in his attempt to steer a course away from the newly discovered galaxy.

Others knew better than to question Shimrra, and their wisdom allowed them to live. Domains like Shai, which had lost a great warrior during an early confrontation with the inhabitants of the galaxy. And the Praetorite Vong—though their fealty to Shimrra had been nothing more than a ruse to keep secret Prefect Da'Gara's own invasion plans. Plans that Nom Anor himself had been drawn into, to the point of assisting the Praetorite in acquiring a yammosk—even if it was a faulty one that would have been condemned to death had Nom Anor not persuaded the shapers in charge of the biot to allow him to have it, in exchange for certain favors.

If Shimrra knew, Nom Anor might even now be among the ossuary's dying, rather than mere witness to the event.

All around him, warriors were using their amphistaffs and batons to prod greater enthusiasm from the spectators, but they roused little more than ritual cheers, because, in the arena below, things weren't going quite as planned.

If innocent had been arrested with guilty, there would certainly have been much beseeching of forgiveness from Shimrra. Instead, the Shamed Ones were going to their deaths—being torn limb from limb, clawed and gutted, gobbled like succulent fruits, tossed about like playthings—cursing Shimrra and the elites, and crying, "Yu'shaa lives! Long live Yu'shaa!"

Jakan, Nas Choka, Qelah Kwaad, and Drathul could only look on in dismay, for the suggestion was that *everyone* arrested was a heretic—or had at least been somehow persuaded to show disdain for tradition.

None of the elite would even dare glance at Shimrra, save for Nom Anor, who, out of the corner of his one real eye, saw that the Supreme Overlord was *laughing*.

Everyone in the *Ralroost*'s briefing center had fallen silent in response to the hologram Admiral Kre'fey had conjured from a projector. Shimmering in diaphanous blue light were images of a world engulfed by vines, giant ferns, and trees with enormous fronds, some fan-shaped, some as delicate as feathers. Spires and pinnacles and flat-topped bluffs rose from the luxuriant vegetation, and in the distance immense mountains heaved, their alloy bones protruding through the verdant cloaks that had been thrown over them, and their faces marred by geometric openings. Water-filled basins abounded, reflecting the light of a bruised sky, and flowing slowly through deep gorges were rivers without twists or bends or oxbow lakes.

Mossy outcroppings jutted from jungle patched in brilliant scarlet that darkened to crimson, or joined with other patches to form expanses of shimmering black or spark-gap blue, all shot through with streaks that shimmered like precious metals. Winged creatures flitted from height to height, hunting just above the canopy, while massive beasts lumbered below.

All in all, it was a planetscape too haphazard, too uneven, too immature to be real.

And in some sense, it wasn't.

"Coruscant," Kre'fey told his audience of several hundred Alliance officers.

At the touch of Kre'fey's left forefinger a second holo superimposed itself on the first, showing the Senate, Calocour Heights, Column Commons, the Glitannai Esplanade, and other once-celebrated locations of the former galactic capital.

"You can see that things have changed," the Bothan added.

Seated to one side of the command rostrum, Han and Leia remained as thoughtfully silent as everyone else. With Kre'fey stood most of the officers who had been present at the informal briefing that Han, Leia, and Jaina had attended four days earlier.

"You undermine your own argument for attacking Coruscant," a Hutt said from front row center. His name was Embra, and he was commander of a resistance group known as the Sisar Runners. "Clearly the planet is beyond restoration. From what we have been given to understand, the Yuuzhan Vong even managed to alter the orbit and rotation."

"Why should we waste our dwindling resources on rescuing Coruscant, in any case?" an Agamarian officer said. "What did the New Republic Senate do for us when the Yuuzhan Vong invaded? They hung us out to dry. They allowed the worlds of the Outer and Mid Rims to fall, while they recalled the fleets to protect the Core.

"Many of the choices made were regrettable," Sovv said, in thickly accented Basic, his black eyes shining. "There are countless examples of gross misjudgment. But those were political concerns, and they shouldn't be reason enough to splinter us now.

"Shimrra wants us to believe that Coruscant can't be rebuilt, and is protected by hidden defenses. But it is not beyond redemption. Yes, the orbit has been altered, and the surface temperature has been raised. But it is certainly not uninhabitable. Much of the vegetation is surface cover. Underneath, beneath the veneer, much of our technology is intact, or at the very least repairable."

Rogue Squadron leader Gavin Darklighter stood up. "Sirs, according to reports made by Jacen Solo, Coruscant *is* protected by hidden defenses. Jedi Solo indicated that an attack would set in motion contingencies that would ultimately render the planet unfit for reoccupation."

"We've taken Jacen Solo's report under advisement," Kre'fey said. "But because of what he experienced during his captivity, we are not inclined to accept his statements as incontrovertible."

Han was quick to put his arm around Leia's shoulders. "Easy there, manka cat. What'd you expect Kre'fey to say?"

Leia turned to him. "You believe Jacen."

"Of course I believe him. But these people aren't as smart as we are."

"That's not what you said at Caluula."

Han waved his free hand in dismissal. "Ah, that was only for show."

Sovv was speaking. "Our attack on the Peace Brigade convoy at Selvaris was merely the first step in destabilizing Overlord Shimrra."

"A question, Admiral Kre'fey," said a wing commander Han didn't know by name. "I thought we won the war at Ebaq Nine."

"That's not a question," Kre'fey grumbled, "but I'll address it anyway. The war will not be won until we've retaken Coruscant. Our crusade is not only justified, but essential.

Coruscant cries out for vengeance!" He softened his tone to add, "Shimrra's planned attack on Mon Calamari will leave Coruscant lightly defended and vulnerable. Even if we fail to catch Shimrra's home defense fleet napping, it's possible that we can kill Shimrra or make things too unpleasant for him to remain on Coruscant. An attack is the last move he expects us to make."

"Our resistance leaders on Coruscant maintain that the time is ripe," Airen Cracken said. "The Shamed Ones are ready to make their move. Intelligence now believes that Alliance prisoners were rescued not for sacrifice or hostage taking, but as a means of sending a signal that the heretics are ready to ally with us in the fight. Shimrra is well aware of the fact that he is fighting on two fronts, and his planned attack on Mon Calamari smacks of desperation. He knows that he needs to defeat us before we succeed in amassing a force sufficient to threaten him, or before the heretics conspire to pitch him from the throne.

"According to the same report Colonel Darklighter made reference to," the general continued, "the seedship that conveyed the World Brain to Coruscant was overwhelmed, and thousands of captives escaped. Many of those former slaves—who have been forced to survive on grayweave and whatever they can forage, steal, or ransack—have found their way to the resistance. With help from us, they can weaken the Yuuzhan Vong from *within*. An unexpected attack on the world the enemy knows as Yuuzhan'tar will be as demoralizing to the Yuuzhan Vong as the fall of *Coruscant* was to the New Republic."

The audience stirred, but no one had questions.

"I wish to speak for a moment about the attack on Mon Calamari itself," Kre'fey said.

Again the Bothan's hand went to the holoprojector controls. The 3-D image showed a pliable-looking, bulbousheaded marine-looking creature, trailing a mass of tentacles of varying length and thickness.

"A yammosk," Kre'fey said. "The gigantic, genetically engineered creature that serves as a war coordinator for the Yuuzhan Vong. Its telepathic abilities, though limited, enable it to facilitate communications among war vessels, and to project its thoughts and feelings onto others—Yuuzhan Vong, human, and so on. By virtue of its capacity to meld with coralskippers and other craft, its presence can affect the outcome of any military engagement.

"Analysis of recent battle recordings suggests that the Yuuzhan Vong armada will take the form of this monstrosity—with warships, gunship analogs, and coralskippers strung out to represent tentacles, and capital ships, tenders, carriers, and actual yammosk vessels comprising the armada's fortified heart."

Kre'fey's light pointer indicated the tentacles.

"Our strategy will be to sow confusion in these keys areas, by using our fastest ships to strike and fade, gradually opening fire lanes to the center. These attacks will commence the moment the armada emerges from hyperspace. As the main body of the armada nears Mon Calamari space, the ranged weapons of our largest ships will begin to hammer away at the center. Concurrently, courier ships will be dispatched to Contruum, where our fleets will be standing by. We anticipate that when the Yuuzhan Vong commander at Mon Calamari learns that Coruscant is under siege, he will attempt to jump some of his battle groups back to the Core, by way of Toong'l and Caluula, trusting the yammosks installed on those worlds to coordinate withdrawal and protect against the possibility of ambush."

"With all due respect, Admiral," a Mon Calamari officer said, "Nas Choka is a far more shrewd warmaster than Tsavong Lah was. He won't be taken in by intelligence disinformation. And at Toong'l and Caluula, he'll be on the watch for interdictors, or mines of the sort we employed successfully at Ebaq Nine."

"Precisely," Kre'fey said. "Which is why we'll employ none of that. Instead, Alliance infiltration teams will by then have incapacitated the yammosks on both worlds. Deprived of battle coordination, the withdrawing battle groups will be vulnerable to counterattack. The odds are against our inflicting sufficient damage to rout them. But the longer we can keep them from returning to the Core, the greater the chances of our Contruum fleets scoring heavily against Coruscant—and against Shimrra."

Han made a low sound of puzzlement, and Leia turned to him.

"What?" she said.

"Doesn't add up. If Caluula had been defended in the first place, the Vong wouldn't have been able to use it as a staging area now."

Suddenly Han was on his feet. Leia assumed that he wanted to share his concerns with everyone on the rostrum. Instead, he said, "I want to be counted in on the Caluula mission."

Admiral Kre'fey swung to him. "Thank you, Captain Solo. Consider it done."

Leia was still staring at him when he sat down.

"What?" he said.

"*You,* is what. Selvaris, then back to Selvaris. Caluula, and now back to Caluula? Besides, you just volunteered for something you said didn't add up."

"Yeah, but I'd sooner volunteer us for the mission than have anyone else risk it."

Leia shook her head in wonder. "You're trying to get us killed, is that it?"

"Just the opposite." Han grinned. "I can't have you getting bored with me."

"Well, this should be good for at least another twenty-five years."

Han patted her leg, then grew serious. "Here's the real reason: I want us to do it for everyone who died or was captured at Caluula."

EIGHTEEN

Casual questioning of some of those who had attended the "cleansing rite"—or slaughter, as many were whispering—had left Nom Anor with the impression that he had been the only one to notice Shimrra's laughter. Now, two days after the heretics had been put to death, the Supreme Overlord's unnerving smile was visible for everyone in the Hall of Confluence to see.

Nas Choka knelt before him, the Scepter of Entreaty curled around the arm that normally would have propped the warmaster's domain tsaisi.

"Most Gracious Lord," Nas Choka was saying, "I take it upon myself, in the names of the priests, seers, and others of my domain, to implore that additional thought be given to the holy task you have set before your warriors, to proceed with haste to Mon Calamari, and there lay waste to the ships of our enemy's fleet, so that we might end this struggle at last, and see to the greater duty of bringing the truth to those whose homes we have conquered, lest we be forced to crush them underfoot like so many gricha. I ask this in the name of Yun-Yammka, to whom I am foresworn, and in all respect, since it is you who have Yun-Yammka's ear, and upon you that the burden of existence rests."

Shimrra leaned forward, with his pointed chin resting on the palm of his huge hand, and Onimi left the steps below the throne to sit cross-legged by the warmaster, studying him with his lopsided head tilted to the heavy side, but without giving voice to rhyme or insult.

"Pray, just what is it that your priests and seers have been telling you, Warmaster, since your words are the first I've heard of such matters?" Shimrra asked. "Surely you harbor no doubts that your mighty armada can prevail."

"No, Great Lord, of that I have no doubts. It is instinct that compels me to ask: at what cost to us?"

Shimrra motioned to him. "Continue, Warmaster, so that all here gathered might get a glimmer of the inner workings of so strategic a thinker."

Nas Choka raised his gaze. "Great Lord, I do not counsel against striking Mon Calamari. I question only the timing of the assault."

Shimrra adopted a look of perplexity. "Of what timing do you speak? Are the stars in this peculiar sky out of alignment? Do the days of the sacred calendar auger for caution? Are you not in the proper *mood* to mete out punishment? Speak plainly, Warmaster. I will think only the more of you for it."

Nas Choka snapped his fists to his shoulders in salute. "Great Lord, I would prefer to concentrate our efforts on securing further those worlds we hold, in the regions our enemy catalogs as Core, Colonies, Inner Rim, and Expansion Region. That much accomplished, we will have created an impenetrable wall against incursion, and from inside that wall we can continue to make forays out into the Mid Rim and other sectors, until we have at last driven the forces of our enemy into a region where they might be subdued by attrition or with one final stroke."

"Is that not what we have already done?" Shimrra asked. "As we speak they are consolidated at Mon Calamari. We have pushed them to the extremes of their own galaxy."

"Some of the enemy, Gracious Lord, but not all. Pockets of strong resistance remain. To subdue the Hutts fully required years, and it may take as many to subjugate the Hapes Consortium, the Chiss empire, the Corporate Sector. In all those places, to name but a few, the enemy is strong. I won't argue that many of their fleets are now united at Mon Calamari. But our campaigns in the Remnant, at Esfandia, and Bilbringi yet again, have cost us dearly. War vessels need to be grown and nurtured—weapons, craft, and coralskippers alike. Our armada is weakest in the very vessels needed to move it. More, we need to be better equipped for surface contests—unless it is our design to poison more worlds than we already have, and risk having the gods misunderstand our intentions, and pronounce us callous toward life."

Nom Anor was impressed, and wished he had the courage to support Nas Choka openly, but he couldn't chance adding his voice to the warmaster's—not without jeopardizing his special relationship with Shimrra. But if the truth could be told, Nom Anor would have confessed that he wanted only to protect the world with which he had been entrusted. Having struggled for so long to attain a rank of authority, he had no desire to see the privileges that came with his station disappear because of some blunder by Shimrra.

The Supreme Overlord himself was too keen a strategist to take issue with all that Nas Choka was saying. But the warmaster was ignorant about the one unknown quantity that was compelling Shimrra to move quickly—and in seeming defiance of the belief that he was being shortsighted.

That one unknown was Zonama Sekot.

"I appreciate your concerns, Warmaster," Shimrra said, "and indeed, if anyone is worthy of the honorific it is you, for your insight is sharp as a honed coufee." He paused just long enough for Nas Choka to regain his confidence before adding: "But you are in error. I assure you that Yun-Yuuzhan was greatly pleased by the deaths of so many heretics at the Place of Bones. Trust to him, to Yun-Yuuzhan, to allay the concerns of the Slayer and the other gods. You will be rewarded with victory, Warmaster, and praises will be sung to you and your commanders, now and for generations to come."

Nom Anor smiled inwardly.

Shimrra was brilliant at playing the game. All his talk of mollifying the gods was nothing more than a subterfuge—something beyond debate by the priests, since the Supreme Overlord was their only real conduit to the gods.

And it struck Nom Anor that Shimrra was right about what he had said at their most recent meeting: the Yuuzhan Vong *had* outgrown the gods. It wasn't that the gods didn't exist, so much as the Yuuzhan Vong no longer needed them.

All at once, he felt someone's eyes on him. He looked to Shimrra, but Shimrra was still gazing down on Nas Choka.

It was Onimi who was watching Nom Anor.

In his command grotto, deep in the bowels of the holy mountain that was the worldship Citadel, Nas Choka, his chief tactician, and a warrior-seer studied a display of blaze bugs, moving about in their yorik coral niche. Insects capable of hovering in flight, or glowing or darkening at the behest of a yammosk, the bugs provided a visual representation of Yuuzhan Vong and enemy forces marshaled at Mon Calamari and the relatively neighboring worlds of Toong'l and Caluula.

The frenzied motion of the insects mirrored the swirling of Nas Choka's thoughts.

"Shimrra is deranged," the female seer said. "Smiling as if bequeathed more than his usual knowledge of events."

Nas Choka looked at his blood-smeared subordinate. "You are safe herein, seer, but were I you, I would exercise caution about what words fly from my mouth. Shimrra has ears throughout the Citadel, and in more places than you can imagine. And who, seer, would you bid go to staffs with one of the Supreme Overlord's newly enhanced warriors should you be challenged?"

The seer bowed at the waist. "Your forgiveness, Warmaster."

"There is no swaying Shimrra. What matters now is that we do not fail him." Nas Choka turned to face his cardinal subalterns. "None of you need fear expressing your opinions here. But take care elsewhere—both on and distant from Yuuzhan'tar." He returned his attention to the blaze bug display. "The enemy fleet remains, augmented now by ships from star systems far removed from the war."

The tactician, attired in high turban and long cloak, nodded. "As I feared, they are allying against us. We were wrong to move quickly in the Remnant and in the Koornacht Cluster. We might well have been able to make use of the so-called Imperials and the barbaric Yevetha. We might have at least led them by their noses long enough to consider that there was greater profit in allying with us."

Nas Choka snorted in agreement. "Had I to do it over again, I might even have kept the Hutts on our side."

"They have themselves to blame," the tactician said. "Their offer of support was tendered only as a means of positioning themselves safely between us and the enemy. That they underestimated us is reason enough not to extend them any honor."

Nas Choka nodded. "Their species is arrogant. Sooner or later they would have attempted to betray us, and it would have come down to contest. Nothing would be different now."

"Except perhaps that Nas Choka wouldn't have been escalated to warmaster," the seer said.

"Another instance of escalation by default," Nas Choka said harshly. "Tsavong Lah became too fixed on the *Jeedai*. He made the war personal. He displayed pride in having a vua'sa grown, merely so that he could slay it and claim one of its legs as his own. His insolence was his undoing. It blinded him to the truth. The *Jeedai* are a nuisance, but they are hardly the secret weapon we first thought them to be. As their numbers dwindle, so apparently does their ability to call on the Force." He laughed shortly. "Tsavong Lah would have directed the armada against a handful of upstarts with magic swords. It would be frankly laughable were it not so tragic."

Again the warmaster scrutinized the blaze bug display. "It intrigues me that they remain at Mon Calamari. By installing yammosks at Toong'l and Caluula, we have made clear as rainwater our intent to assault Mon Calamari. Sovv, Kre'fey, and the rest of the Alliance commanders must be blind not to see what is coming. But obviously I misconstrue them. My purpose was to persuade them to disband their battle groups, and thus subvert the possibility of a final battle of this nature, for I suspected that Shimrra was pursuing such thinking. And yet the enemy does nothing to suggest that they received our message. Either they have misconstrued me, or they have devised a way to counter us."

"Even so, Warmaster," the tactician said, "it makes little sense for them to make a stand at Mon Calamari. They are vastly outnumbered, and it is unlikely they would wish to visit destruction on the world they have chosen as their new capital."

Nas Choka considered it. "Yes, I fear that, in the end, they *will* scatter."

The tactician was puzzled. "Was that not your original wish, Warmaster?"

"To have them disband without our having to travel clear across the galaxy to prompt them. Now we are committed. We will arrive, they will disperse, and we will be left with no choice but to chase them into the galactic arms and back—because Shimrra will not have it otherwise."

"Such actions will require many years, and consume many resources."

"It is the pattern our ancestors faced time and again in the home galaxy," the seer interjected. "Wars that lingered for generations."

The tactician regarded the blaze bugs. "What if the enemy should surprise us by electing to stand and fight?"

Nas Choka smiled. "I will know then, with certainty, that Kre'fey and the rest have contrived a counterstrategy."

The seer was not pleased by the statement. "Would the infidels dare strike at Yuuzhan'tar in your absence?"

"I have given careful thought to that," Nas Choka said. "I have calculated the amount of damage they can do, based on their bringing to bear three times the number of ships we know to exist in sectors other than Mon Calamari. I remain confident that they cannot inflict unacceptable damage. I have planned for that eventuality, nevertheless. Should they jump their *entire* fleet here, so much the better for us."

"They could interpret the groundwork we've laid as an attempt to encourage them to attack Yuuzhan'tar," the tactician said.

Nas Choka betrayed no concern. "Either way benefits us. But we're a long way from seeing all sides of this. We must bide what little time remains before Shimrra declares the omens favorable to launch the fleet."

The seer deliberately placed herself in the warmaster's gaze. "I have spoken to the other seers regarding the omens. We have agreed to stretch the truth, in order to grant your forces additional time to prepare."

"Shimrra will see through you," Nas Choka cautioned. "Especially in light of the appeal I attempted today. Regardless, he will suffer your lies as an accommodation to me, just as he suffers you and your cohorts as an accommodation to the elite. Refrain from attempting to grant us too much delay." He paused, then said, "In the meantime, we should awaken our masqued spies and infiltrators on all occupied and contested worlds, and instruct them to report on any unusual activity involving the movements of ships, matériel, and couriers."

"Kre'fey will expect as much," the tactician thought to point out. "Bear in mind, Warmaster, that enemy disinformation was at least partially responsible for drawing Tsavong Lah to his death."

Nas Choka touched him on the shoulder in appreciation. "Trust nothing from our network of agents on Mon Calamari. They live only because the Alliance feels there may be some further use for them. Also instruct our masqued spies that while they should keep their noses lifted to the winds, they are to refrain from taking any actions or interfering in any way. I want nothing more than information. I will separate the truth from the deceptions. Above all, I want to give the Alliance just enough vine to hang itself."

PART TWO

FORCE AND COUNTERFORCE

NINETEEN

Stars filled the sky.

Head tipped back, eyes raised, Luke turned through a small circle, feeling infinitesimal under the giant boras, under the light-strewn expanse. The night was cold—made colder by a polar breeze—but there wasn't a cloud overhead. Beside him, R2-D2 zithered and twittered, then fluted in what approximated relief.

Luke looked down at the readout on the droid's dome. "You're sure about that, little fella?"

The silver dome of the droid's head revolved, taking his primary photoreceptor through a second survey of the stars and clusters. After comparing the results of his scans to the charts he had downloaded from *Widowmaker*'s data banks, R2-D2 mewled, chirped, then twittered some more.

Luke smiled and placed his hand on the droid's dome. "At least we're closer to known space. I guess we'll just have to wait to see where Sekot's next hyperspace jump lands us."

Rocking side to side on his treads, R2-D2 tootled and fluted.

Luke had been one of the first to emerge from the shelter scooped into the notched cliff face that was home to hundreds of Ferroan families. Similar to other shelters in the Middle Distance, it was a vast vaulted space, excavated sometime during the Crossings that had taken Zonama Sekot from its original orbit in the Gardaji Rift, through several star systems, and finally into the Unknown Regions, where Sekot had selected Klasse Ephemora as the planet's new home and sanctuary.

Following the discussion in the cave, Sekot had said that it wanted to perform several short trial voyages to assess

whether the jump to lightspeed inadvertently engineered by
Nom Anor had done lasting damage to the hyperspace cores
and whatever planetary mechanisms Sekot employed to augment the powerful engines. Of greater concern was the very
real possibility of encountering uncharted mass shadows
along the route back to known space. Whether ship or planet,
any traveler that entered hyperspace without taking a greater
or lesser hyperlane risked catastrophe—and no analogs to
the Perlemian Trade Route or the Hydian Way existed in the
Unknown Regions. Worse, the entire territory was known
to be rife with hyperspace anomalies, particularly along the
Coreward frontier.

Luke and the other Jedi had to trust that Sekot knew what
it was doing. So instead of dwelling on the prospects of
being yanked from lightspeed by a gravity well of some sort,
Luke had passed the days in the shelter grappling with
Sekot's revelations that the aboriginal Yuuzhan Vong had
been *stripped* of the Force. Sekot had refused to elaborate;
and since then Sekot—speaking through Jabitha—had said
only that it was imperative that Zonama be returned to
known space, despite the grave risks the planet would face
during the Crossings and on arrival.

The revelation—Luke didn't know what else to call it—
had had a profound effect on Harrar, and on Luke, as well.
Was it possible, Luke wondered, that the would-be Jedi who
had originally settled on Zonama Sekot hadn't taught Sekot
about the Force but merely *reawakened* it?

A few steps away from Luke in the boras-enclosed clearing sat *Jade Shadow.* Designed for speed and stealth, the
craft was sharply tapered forward and painted a uniform
nonreflective gray. The hyperdrive rating was equal to that of
the *Millennium Falcon,* and she had the added ability to be
operated remotely by slave circuitry. The aft cabin space
alone was large enough to accommodate an X-wing.

Even Sekot was impressed by the ship, and Luke suspected that it was Sekot that had kept *Jade Shadow* from
being crushed by the several boras that had toppled during
the recent storms, narrowly missing it. However, the ship
was buried almost to her triangular cockpit in sand, leaves,
and other forest detritus.

"Did she weather the jump all right?" Mara asked. Glow stick in hand, she emerged from the dark shadows of the giant trees and came alongside him to regard *Jade Shadow*.

"No visible damage."

Mara tossed her hair over her right shoulder and gazed at the circle of brilliant stars overhead. "Any idea where we are?"

"According to Artoo, we might be somewhere in the Mid Rim."

The droid cheeped.

Mara looked at R2-D2. "Is that good?"

"It's a start." Luke glanced at the path Mara had taken. "Where is everyone?"

"Jacen, Corran, and Danni are trying to convince the Ferroans that it's safe to come out of hiding. The last I saw Tekli, Saba, and Tahiri, they were with Harrar, who keeps finding similarities between Yuuzhan Vong biots and what he sees here." She approached *Jade Shadow,* then turned to Luke. "Do you think we're close enough to contact Esfandia Station?"

"Only one way to find out."

The ship had a cosmetic external hatch release, but the actual release was concealed inside the starboard bulkhead, and could be operated by the Force. Mara entered first, and called on the illuminators. As filthy as the ship was outside, the interior was undisturbed. Slipping into the forward chairs, she and Luke activated the ship's HoloNet and subspace transceivers. At the same time, R2-D2 inserted his slender computer interface arm into an access port and rotated the dial to an appropriate setting.

"Esfandia Station, this is *Jade Shadow* . . ." Mara said, repeating the comm call several times.

The annunciator's only response was static.

"At Klasse Ephemora we were even farther from Esfandia, and we still managed to reach the station," Mara said, after continued attempts at contact.

R2-D2 buzzed in exasperation.

"He says he can't find *any* functioning HoloNet transceivers," Luke said.

"Try again," Mara urged.

She and Luke pondered possible explanations while R2-D2 rotated the interface dial this way and that.

"Nothing," Luke said, breaking their long silence.

Mara's lightly freckled brow furrowed. "Could the Yuuzhan Vong have destroyed Esfandia?"

Luke leaned away from the console. "Corran said that something big had been planned for Bilbringi. But even if the Alliance failed to retake the shipyards there, that wouldn't account for our not being able to contact any of the HoloNet relay stations."

Mara shook her head back and forth. "Something terrible has happened." She looked at him. "Could Cal Omas have given the okay to using Alpha Red?"

A Yuuzhan Vong–specific toxin, Alpha Red had been developed in secret by Alliance Intelligence, working in conjunction with Chiss scientists. But the only prototype sample of the bioweapon had been stolen by Vergere and transformed into something harmless.

"We've been gone long enough for Dif Scaur's Intelligence bunch to have cooked up a whole new batch," Mara added.

Luke shook his head. "Cal promised me that Alpha Red would be used only as a last resort."

"Maybe it's come down to that. And maybe the Yuuzhan Vong retaliated with a poison of their own."

"Cal knows better. Evil can't simply be stamped out. It's as much a part of life as good is."

Mara looked at him dubiously. "You're thinking like a Jedi instead of an admiral or an elected official." She blew out her breath. "All right. What's your solution to ending this war?"

"I don't know yet. I just know that Alpha Red isn't the solution."

Mara smiled at him and took his hand. "I happen to agree. But you are starting to sound a little like Vergere and Jacen."

"Guilty as charged. But is that wrong?"

"Not in principle. Except that you're probably more attuned to the Force than either of them."

Luke made his lips a thin line. "I feel like I'm still in training for the trials. Every second of every day. It never ends, and I wouldn't have it otherwise. My understanding of the

Force continues to grow. I know I'm a Jedi Master, but I may not feel like a *true* Master until my dying breath. Besides, Jacen, Jaina, Tahiri, Ben . . . They're the future of the Jedi. Everything we do now must be for them—to ensure that they carry on what began a thousand generations ago."

Luke took his eyes from Mara, and glanced around the cockpit.

"I know what you're thinking," she said, after a moment. "And I think it's time we tried."

He smiled faintly. "If you'd stayed in my thoughts a little longer, you'd know why we can't leave."

Mara looked disappointed. "You're not going to tell me you're worried about running us into a mass shadow. Because Artoo can plot a safe route—even if it takes us twenty microjumps to get back to known space."

"That isn't it." Luke regarded her again. "Mara, I'm as concerned about Ben as you are. Something terrible *has* happened, but it's momentary. We have to stay focused on the greater picture."

Mara rose and paced away from the control console, crossing her arms when she swung back to Luke. "The future's exactly what I'm thinking about. *Ben's* future. You said yourself that everything we do should be for him and the other young Jedi." She sat down again and took her husband's hands in hers. "Luke, Ben was almost killed on Coruscant by that witch Viqi Shesh. If something should happen to us . . ."

Luke pictured their red-golden-haired infant. "By leaving, we could destroy everything we've accomplished here. And then we won't be a help to anyone—Ben included."

Mara studied him. "You're basing this on personal experience—on some mistake you once made."

"I am."

"Luke, there are times when action is the best course."

"Actions have consequences."

"What are the consequences here? Jacen and Corran can stay behind. We can leave them *Jade Shadow,* if you want. We'll ask Sekot to grow us a ship."

"It's Sekot I'm worried about."

Mara stared at him. "Sekot?"

"Sekot might misinterpret our leaving as a lack of trust, and change its mind about returning to known space."

"Then you can explain our reason for leaving."

"Tell Sekot that we're worried about our son, about our friends, about what's happened to the HoloNet?" Luke paused, then asked: "What about Sekot's concerns for the Ferroans, or for what might happen to Zonama when it becomes part of the war?"

Mara mulled it over for a moment.

Luke squeezed her hands affectionately. "Ben will be fine. I *saw* him fine."

Mara's eyes narrowed in a reluctant smile. "You saw him piloting a ship of completely unfamiliar design—like the ones grown here."

Luke recalled the rest of his vision: Ben tracing lines in the sand; kneeling by a river, rubbing smooth round stones between his fingers and smiling; wrestling with a young Wookiee . . . Luke saw himself holding Ben while they observed glowing lines of traffic move through the sky of an unknown world—like Coruscant but not. And, yes: Ben at the helm of a starship of unique design . . .

Mara was watching him. "Assuming you weren't gazing at Ben from some other plane of existence, you're going to be around to witness all those things."

"So will you."

"Was I part of the vision?"

In fact, Luke hadn't seen Mara—not at first.

"Luke, promise me something," Mara said before he could speak. "If anything happens to me—"

He tried to shush her, but she pushed his hand away.

"No, I need to say this. Promise me that if anything happens, you'll love Ben with all your heart, and you'll make him the center of your world, as he is to me."

Luke pulled her into his arms. " 'Hush, my love, the night is mild and slumber smiles on you . . .' "

"Promise me, Luke."

"I will—if you'll make me the same promise."

She nodded against his chest. "Then no matter what, the future's assured."

TWENTY

Nas Choka pushed through the living membrane that sealed the command grotto from prying eyes. A trio of Supreme Commanders and their subalterns trailed in the warmaster's angry wake.

"Our course is now set," he announced to his own subalterns and tacticians. "Supreme Overlord Shimrra will abide no further delay. We are enjoined to launch the armada in three local days, when the auguries are favorable for victory."

"Three days, Fearsome One," the tactician said when Nas Choka had dropped cross-legged onto his yorik coral bench.

"The burden is mine," Nas Choka replied abruptly. "Don't add to it by echoing my words. Tender your report."

The tactician inclined his head in a bow of respect. "Rumors teem like an infestation of sacworms. From all sectors comes word of heightened enemy activity. Ships masquerading as spice carriers leave Hutt space, but as often as not they are empty. The same holds true in Bothan space. There is increased traffic within the Hapan Cluster, with many ships inbound from Kashyyyk and from the more distant Remnant. Known operatives and agents consort clandestinely on Corellia and Bimmisaari. Courier ships of the Smugglers' Alliance arrive and depart Contruum, with a few venturing as close to Yuuzhan'tar as Corulag."

"Sheer impudence," Nas Choka said. "But much like the diversionary raids at Gyndine and Duro that preceded the clash at Ebaq Nine." He fell briefly silent, then said, "Proceed."

"As instructed, our agents made no attempts to interfere or provide the slightest signs of suspicion."

"And at Mon Calamari?"

"Almost half the fleet has departed. Many capital ships have returned to their home sectors. Others have been traveling in and out of darkspace. Still others have been deployed as substitutes for the transceiving devices our dovin basals engulfed."

Nas Choka rose from the bench to regard what now amounted to an entire wall of blaze bug displays. "My long tenure in Hutt space was well spent," he said after a long moment. "I was forced to acquaint myself with all make and manner of deception and duplicity. Fabrication comes as easily to the inhabitants of this galaxy as invention comes to our shapers. So I am wary of all these reports."

He turned to his Supreme Commanders. "Sovv and Kre'fey grasp that our patrols and reconnaissance vessels are too widely dispersed to keep watch over every planetary sector. They attempt to overwhelm us with activity, in the hope of screening a few missions of genuine purpose." His expression grew dour. "Our actions in sabotaging the HoloNet may come back to plague us. We no longer have the luxury of being able to eavesdrop on enemy communications. Yes, the courier ships require additional time to reach their destinations, but the messages they carry come and go only to those who need to be apprised of the content. Even now this war takes unexpected twists and turns." His hooded eyes fell on the tactician. "What of the yammosks at Toong'l and Caluula?"

"Unperturbed, Fearsome One. Although . . ."

Nas Choka waited, then said: "Give voice to it!"

"Caluula's surrender, Warmaster. Before the fall of the orbital station, the commander who led our assault was contacted by the governor of the planet. The governor promised that Caluula would yield to occupation, without need of an amphistaff being raised against it."

"There is nothing unusual about that," the warrior-seer interrupted. "Many local governments have opted—wisely, I think—to spare themselves devastation, in exchange for a pledge that we will be equitable about how many captives we take, and in how we pursue our timetable for worldshaping—

including the effacement of buildings, temples, and the obliteration of machines. The custom began as early as our defeat of the library world of Obroa-skai."

"Yes, seer, but in the instance of Caluula, the governor made a special request. She asked for permission for scientists to visit, to observe some sort of natural spectacle peculiar to the planet. This, of course, would necessitate the temporary maintenance of the spaceport, for the landing of ships and scientific personnel."

Nas Choka folded his massive arms. "Our commander agreed to this?"

The tactician nodded. "In the interest of rapid and effortless pacification, and for the sake of the yammosk, he granted provisional approval. So as not to subject our people to lifeless technology, he assigned security of the spaceport to Peace Brigaders. Now, however, the petition to allow scientists to visit Caluula rests in the hands of High Prefect Drathul. He, in turn, will defer to the sagacity of High Priest Jakan."

For several moments Nas Choka paced in silence. "This interests me," he said finally. "Much of the enemy fleet remains at Mon Calamari. Elsewhere ships scurry about in seeming abandon. And following weeks of noble fighting by the defenders of its orbital facility, Caluula surrenders without contest." He let his statements hang in the air, then turned to the tactician. "Tell Eminence Jakan that I wish a word with him before he renders any judgment on the petition."

The tactician bowed. "Anything else, Fearsome One?"

"Who commands the yammosk emplacement at Caluula?"

"I can provide the answer momentarily, Warmaster."

Nas Choka paced to his bench. "Return not only with the name, but also with the commander's dedicated villip. I need to speak with him, as well."

The Yuuzhan Vong warrior at Caluula spaceport made it clear that he was ready to unleash his amphistaff at the slightest provocation. The sight of the tattooed and scarred warrior standing against a backdrop of shuttles and landing craft was just absurd enough to widen Han's eyes, but he knew better than to smile. Several Yuuzhan Vong warships were in orbit above Caluula, though not nearly as many as Han had expected to see.

"You are the scientist—Meloque?" the warrior said in Basic to the female Ho'Din on whom the entire infiltration mission rested.

More than two meters tall, with sucker-equipped four-fingered hands, a purple crown of erect thermographic receptors, and a reptilian-complected lipless face, she might almost have been a Yuuzhan Vong shaper. Indeed, among all the species of the galaxy, the bipedal Ho'Din were treated with particular favor by the invaders, not only because of their devotion to plant life, but also because of their aversion to technology.

"Yes, I am Meloque," she answered in Yuuzhan Vong.

The warrior extended a sinewy hand. "Your authentication."

Meloque displayed the fist-sized nugget of flesh and fur that had been delivered to her on Obroa-skai. The warrior took the creature between his hands, squeezed it, and studied the pungent droppings it left on a piece of leathery parchment. Then he nodded and motioned to Han, Leia, Kyp, Judder Page, and the Bothan Intelligence officer, Wraw.

"The members of my support team," Meloque said. "Their names should also be contained by the lumpen." Having lived among the Yuuzhan Vong for close to four years on the enemy-occupied library world, she knew how to deal with them, as well as speak to them.

The warrior squeezed the lumpen so hard it squealed, and another batch of droppings fell to the parchment. It took a moment for the warrior to confirm that the names and descriptions detailed in the droppings matched the counterfeit identities of the humans and humanoids in front of him, but ultimately he nodded again.

"The lumpen will remain here until your departure. If all of you have not returned in three days, you will be hunted down, imprisoned, and punished for your insolence. Do you understand?"

"Yes," Meloque answered for all of them.

"Then proceed inside."

A surprise to everyone—and some cause for suspicion— Yuuzhan'tar had granted permission for a few select scientists to visit Caluula, to observe what was called the Nocturne of the Winged-Stars, an allegedly extraordinary natural phenomenon that occurred once every three hundred standard years. As Han understood it, the local governor had cut the deal in secret, even while the orbital station was still under siege.

At the mission briefing on Mon Calamari only two days earlier, Han had voiced his misgivings, telling Dif Scaur that the last time he had checked, the Yuuzhan Vong weren't in the public relations business.

The cadaverously thin Intelligence director, who had had a hand in organizing the mission to destroy Caluula's yammosk, had offered other examples of the Yuuzhan Vong's recent attempts to win the hearts and minds of defeated populations—as against their usual tactic of plucking them out at the first sign of resistance. Regarding Caluula, Scaur believed that the nature of the negotiation—centered, as it was, on the observance of a rare natural phenomenon—might have appealed to whatever priests had been tasked with ruling on the request. Not that it mattered. If the Yuuzhan Vong had refused consent, the execution team would have gone in, regardless.

The last-minute addition of Kyp Durron to the team had been cause for further concern, because yammosks were believed to have the ability to sense Jedi, as had happened aboard an enemy vessel to the late Wurth Skidder. Kyp had countered that being a Jedi had nothing to do with it. Yammosks could detect the Force, and Kyp maintained that Leia was as strong in the Force as he was.

Han was not at all eased by the explanation. "A Bothan and a Jedi," he told Kyp. "We might as well be wearing Galactic Alliance insignias."

On the other hand, having Kyp along on the mission made it something of a family affair, since Kyp had figured prominently in Han's life for close to twenty years—ever since Han and Chewbacca had rescued the sixteen-year-old fledgling Jedi from imprisonment in the spice mines of Kessel. Han's trust in Kyp had been tested by the many trials Kyp had himself endured—on Yavin, against the spirit of a long-dead Sith Lord; in Kyp's feverish quest for vengeance against

Imperial admiral Daala; in bringing the Sun Crusher to bear on the planet Carida; and in nearly destroying the *Millennium Falcon,* and Han, in the process. More recently Kyp had tricked Jaina into helping him annihilate a civilian Yuuzhan Vong worldship at Sernpidal. And yet, following the events at Myrkr, he had been instrumental in keeping her from going to the dark side—thanks in part to Leia's warning Kyp that if he *ever* again hurt Jaina or any member of Leia's family, he would be safer turning himself over to the Yuuzhan Vong.

"I'm through with travel if it means carrying a lumpen instead of an identichip," Wraw said to Han while they were entering the spaceport terminal.

"We're here to make sure you don't have to," Han said. "We've got enough unhappy Bothans without adding you to the list."

Wraw laughed hoarsely. "As good with his mouth as he is with his blaster. That's what I've always heard about you."

"I aim true, if that's what you mean." Han had more to say, but Leia touched his arm in a gesture of restraint. From the start, he and the long-faced Bothan spy had butted heads, but he appreciated Leia's reminding him of mission priorities.

Where Yuuzhan Vong warriors and bissop hounds held sway over the landing field, Peace Brigaders—Nikto, Weequays, a couple of Gammoreans, and other alien traitors—oversaw luggage inspection and terminal security. The modular, prefabricated building had been stripped of technology, but it hadn't yet been transformed by the Yuuzhan Vong. Three other teams of scientists were having their equipment inspected, and being subjected to constant harassment by bribe-seeking Brigaders. Flanking the building's only exit were a pair of exceedingly tall humans—or, more likely, ooglith-masquerwearing Yuuzhan Vong.

Team Meloque's equipment was being pawed through by a Klatooinian and a Codru-Ji, whose four arms were buried to the elbows in Han's backpack. The Yuuzhan Vong had prohibited the import or use of recording devices other than sketch pads and writing implements. But they had allowed tents and camping gear, since the expeditions were destined for the rugged mountains that walled Caluula City on three sides. As rudimentary as they were, the Brigaders' scanners were capable of detecting most weapons, so blasters had been left off the packing list. Leia's and Kyp's lightsabers, however, were included among the cooking supplies, disguised as handles for self-warming fry pans.

The Klatooinian put the field kitchen duffel on the inspection table. "I'm going to need to go through all of this," he said as the lofty Meloque approached, a sheathlike skirt making her appear even taller than she was.

Kyp stepped up to the table and made a subtle hand motion. "You don't need to inspect this bag."

The canine-faced humanoid stared at the Jedi and blinked his heavy lidded eyes. "We don't need to inspect this bag."

Momentarily confused, the Codru-Ji eventually nodded in agreement.

"Gather your belongings and leave."

"Gather your belongings and leave."

Kyp caught Han's look while the two of them were shouldering the duffels. "Problem?"

"I thought that wasn't allowed or something."

Kyp shrugged. "We can debate Jedi philosophy some other time."

Han laughed through his nose. "Don't get me wrong, kid. If I had the ability, I'd be using it every chance I could."

"You only think you would," Leia said, slipping into her backpack as she caught up with them. "Would you use it when you play sabacc?"

Han considered it. "Might take some of the fun out of the game."

"And I know you wouldn't want that," she said.

No sooner had they exited the terminal than clouds of indigenous flitnats surrounded them. The insects weren't the biting variety, but that didn't make them any less irritating.

"Hope you remembered to pack the repellent," Han said to Leia.

"Wouldn't help," Wraw rasped. "Every visitor to Caluula gets assigned one hundred flitnats, and those hundred stick with you for your entire stay."

Han laughted shortly at the Bothan's joke. "Well, everybody's got their own idea about what makes a good vacation."

What Han didn't say was that the tiny pests were already sticking to the cosmetic that lightened his complexion and the adhesive that secured his gray beard, mustache, and woolly eyebrows, and that he was even more uncomfortable than he had been on Aphran IV two years earlier, where he had worn a similar getup. Leia was the only other one also in disguise, her hair concealed under a wig of closely cropped silver locks, and her skin a faint shade of green, thanks to some pill Intelligence had had her swallow. Even though he was a Jedi, Kyp's keen face wasn't well known, and Page was so nondescript that a moment after meeting him one practically forgot what he looked like.

Still, for all his discomfort, Han was happy not to be wearing one of the ooglith-masquer-like "brands" developed by Wraith Squadron's Baljos Arnjak and being worn by all the team members assigned to killing the yammosk on Toong'l, which was guarded only by Yuuzhan Vong.

Apart from the off-the-rack spaceport terminal, Caluula was about as basic a world as Han had visited in a long while—a world where the stones that formed the walls of most buildings had been given shape by other stones, and where most of the human and humanoid population had more in common with the Yuuzhan Vong than they probably realized. It took him a moment to come to grips with the fact that on Caluula and hundreds of similarly primitive worlds, life simply went on. Even though deprived of technology, even though forced to live in the shadow of new temples, beings fell in love, got married, had children, got into squabbles with their neighbors . . . They learned to adapt to new foods, use Yuuzhan Vong tools, swore allegiance to the new conquerors—even while continuing to worship their own gods in secret.

"Here come our guides," Page said.

A Rodian and a Ryn, they were wearing rustic trousers and shirts, beat-up footwear, fabric belts, and tight-fitting woven skullcaps. And clearly they were comfortable around the saddled mounts they rode and led. The size of small dew-backs, the long-snouted quadrupeds were nearly as shaggy as banthas, but lacked horns or tusks of any sort.

"I'm Sasso," the Rodian said as the pair came within earshot of Han and the others.

"Ferfer," the Ryn said under his breath, adding: "Gatherer one-six-four, out of Balmorra."

Han reached up to shake hands with the Ryn. "How's your boss?"

"On the run," Ferfer said.

Han nodded, thinking of Droma, the Ryn who had be-friended him at Chewbacca's death, and who was rumored to head the Gatherers. "That figures."

As introductions were being made all around, Han found himself thinking that Sasso and Ferfer reminded him of many of the folk he had had dealings with during his early years in the Corporate Sector—on Duroon, Deltooine, and other worlds. Folk who were often hardened by circumstance but true to their word.

Lately when he wasn't thinking about the war or dwelling on the deaths of Anakin and Chewbacca, he would often catch himself reminiscing about the old days, or wondering what it would be like to return to the worlds of his youth without his tall, thick-furred sidekick, but with Leia and the kids. The person who had scammed his way through half the Outer Rim was very much alive inside him, and for all the lavish parties on Coruscant, the diplomatic affairs, state dinners, and royal weddings he'd been obliged to attend dur-ing the past twenty-some years, he was still more comfort-able around beings like Sasso and Ferfer than he was around Senators and princes, the wealthy and influential. Weather-beaten faces and hands callused from hard work; the great outdoors instead of some refresher; food dug from the soil or yanked from the trees instead of factory-produced food-stuffs . . .

Maybe someday he and Leia would get the chance, he told himself.

Sasso pointed him to his mount, which was known locally as a timbu. Han planted his foot in the stirrup and pulled himself onto the immense saddle. The timbu grunted and turned his big, floppy-eared head to regard Han through a liquid-black eye.

"Whatever you do, don't jerk the reins too hard," he told Leia as she nimbly mounted a smaller timbu.

"Why, what happens?"

"Think about the worst gob of spittle you ever saw a tauntaun launch, then multiply that times ten."

"Scary."

"You've ridden a timbu before," Sasso stated rather than asked.

Han nodded. "On Bonadan."

The Rodian's tapered snout wiggled in a kind of smile. "Terrific place."

Team Meloque moved out. Four-member bands of Yuuzhan Vong patrolled Caluula City's mostly unpaved streets, but the alleged scientists were allowed to pass without incident. On a lush common, two priests were overseeing a mixed group of locals and Yuuzhan Vong workers who were erecting a temple to Yun-Yuuzhan. Street and storefront electric lights had been ripped from their supports, and there wasn't a droid or a speeder to be seen.

"Welcome to the new galaxy," Kyp said.

"No slave coral," Leia said quietly.

Sasso nodded. "That was one of the conditions of the surrender."

"How'd everyone feel about the surrender?" Page asked carefully.

"Let me put it this way," the Rodian said. "The governor no longer appears in public, and she's had the walls of her compound reinforced."

Han noticed that Page appeared to be right at home. He rode his timbu with practiced ease, and he knew which way to direct the beast even before the guides said anything. It was as if he had already memorized the layout of the streets and the topography of the planet. Han guessed that Page would be able to converse in Caluulan if necessary, eat the food and drink the water without getting ill, catch the eye of the local women, make do as if he had been born and raised there.

Wraw, in contrast, was clearly out of his element. The bristly-bearded Bothan had a habit of looking at everyone with what seemed like bemusement or mild derision, but his head fur betrayed none of the changes that were a characteristic of his species. But Han had encountered the style before in individuals who had built their lives around inveigling secrets from others, and then seeing to it that those secrets reached the proper ears.

"How far to the yammosk?" Kyp asked Sasso.

"The installation is practically the new city center—probably to discourage attempts at orbital bombardment. But our safest approach is from the south, which means crossing two ranges of hills to get there."

"The weapons are cached along our route?" Page said.

"There are weapons buried everywhere," Sasso told him. "As soon as it became obvious that the Vong were interested in occupying Caluula, we began hiding as much as we could: blasters, foods, droids, you name it. You can't dig a hole in the hills without uncovering one supply dump or another. By the time Caluula Station fell and the Vong were coming down the gravity well, we were already living like homesteaders."

"Surely the Yuuzhan Vong are aware of your actions," Meloque said.

"They are. But so far they haven't done much investigating. A few caches of arms and droids were discovered, and twenty Caluulans were sacrificed. But aside from that incident, things have been relatively quiet." Sasso nodded his snout to indicate a change in direction. "We go this way."

"How soon before we'll begin to see winged-star shells?" Meloque asked.

"As soon as we gain some elevation."

Sasso brought the train of eight timbus to a halt at the foot of a steep, uphill track that disappeared into a thickly forested ravine. A winged creature passed soundlessly overhead, disappearing into the trees before Han could get a good look at it.

"Yuuzhan Vong biot," Ferfer said nervously. "We're being watched."

TWENTY-ONE

Mirroring the sweeping curve of the planetary ring, the war vessels of the armada were spread above bright-side Yuuzhan'tar like fine grains of crystalline sand. Arrayed in battle groups and reprovision flotillas, each cruiser, carrier, and tender analog had been branded with domain emblems and daubed with blood preserved from the sacrifice of the Alliance captives. Some of the vessels flew battle standards earned over countless generations. Others were necklaced hundreds strong with coralskippers. Behind the mica transparencies of observation blisters and resupply balconies, commanders and subalterns crouched on one knee, their heads lowered in obeisance, and their right fists pressed to the yorik coral decks.

There lazed *Realm of Death*, *Blade of Sacrifice*, *River of Blood*, *Slayer's Conceit*, *Serpent's Kiss*, and the pennant vessel, *Yammka's Mount*, commanded by Warmaster Nas Choka.

Closer to orbitally altered Yuuzhan'tar, closer to the massive dovin basals that were the planet's first line of defense, closer to the rainbow bridge—symbolic of Yun-Yuuzhan's traffic with the species he had created—floated the oblate yacht that had carried Shimrra and the nonwarrior elite from the surface. Smeared with blood, the throne chamber of the yacht was also festooned with wreaths of thorn-vine and adorned with hundreds of delicately wrought fans, sacred to Yun-Yammka. In honor of the launching, all present in the chamber wore glistaweb armor, including Shimrra's prefects and seers, Qelah Kwaad and her chief shapers, High Priest Jakan, even preposterous Onimi.

The Supreme Overlord stood tall and self-possessed before a unique villip that forwarded his visage and words to every villip contained in every vessel, dedicated or choir member, warship or coralskipper.

"Yun-Yuuzhan, Great Maker," Shimrra murmured, "we beseech your blessing for these vessels we dispatch into the void, for their mission is yours also by injunction. With this final battle we fulfill our obligation to cleanse the realm you saw fit to provide us, to make it worthy, and in turn to be made worthy by victory of claiming it as our home. From this moment forward, we will set ourselves to the task of taking these humbled species under our wing, and of instructing them in the truth you bade our ancestors hear at the dawn of time.

"We pledge that from these beginnings we will carry our task through to completion, purging this realm of machines, and replacing them with our biological partners. When Yuu-zhan'tar has been fully reshaped according to the ancestral architecture, and when temples to you and your sacrosanct domain crown the tops of the highest mountains and domi-nate the principal population centers of every occupied world, we will petition that you judge our work one final time.

"The grand moment has arrived—the culmination of gen-erations of voyage and discovery. Even now, in these un-familiar skies, the ancestral galaxy moves into beneficent aspect with this newfound home. What was distant is near at hand; what was completed is begun anew."

In a blinding display of honor and power, the largest of the war vessels launched five thousand plasma missiles toward Yuuzhan'tar's primary. Then in groups, and led by *Yammka's Mount,* the armada began to move out, building momentum for the transition to darkspace.

Nom Anor watched from his assigned place in the holy yacht, wondering what Nas Choka might be thinking. The out-come of the war and the future of the Yuuzhan Vong hinged on what would occur over the next quarter klekket. The war-riors and priests, lifted to ecstasy by days of fasting and danc-ing, were sanguine that the armada would prevail.

But not everyone was so assured.

The consuls under Nom Anor's command, and the executors under their commands, had brought to his attention rumors of grave apprehension and doubt among the high caste. And beneath those vague rumblings, Nom Anor could feel the more sinister roiling of hatred among the dispossessed.

From beneath the bridge, from the dark underworld of Yuuzhan'tar, he could hear the clamor of angry voices, the words of the heretics growing louder and more forceful, venomous in the aftermath of the executions, the dissent spreading through the ranks, among not only the Shamed Ones but also others who had lost or were beginning to lose the faith in Supreme Overlord Shimrra. A vast wave, building and building, threatening to break against the Yuuzhan Vong's every shore, to wipe the armada from the sky, and to pull into the depths the holy yacht and everyone aboard.

Shimrra had told Nom Anor that his war was with the gods. But Shimrra had overlooked the real enemy—the enemy that surrounded him and on whose shoulders he stood. Even Quoreal in his final days had not been the object of such suspicion and loathing. If it were left to the Shamed Ones, Nas Choka's mighty force would be routed at Mon Calamari, and Shimrra would be dragged from the throne by Yun-Shuno himself, to be devoured in public by packs of starved bissop hounds . . .

Nom Anor shifted his troubled gaze from the departing ships, and at the same moment Onimi shifted his, to needle Nom Anor with a meddlesome look. Nom Anor wondered if Onimi's olfactory sense was so keen that he could smell the fear coming off him. Perhaps that was just one of the reasons why Onimi's rhymes were so biting: because he could read subtle signals in all those who appeared before Shimrra.

Nom Anor stiffened in disgust and something close to dread as Onimi wobbled over to him from across the throne chamber.

"Be encouraged, Prefect," Onimi said in confidence. "As is true between the gods and the Yuuzhan Vong, Shimrra's strength flows from the combined certitude of his subjects. Falter, display doubt or weakness, and the careful balance may tip . . ."

Nom Anor sneered. "Who are you to address me, Shamed One?"

Onimi's uneven mouth twisted into a frigid smile. "Your

conscience, Prefect. The still-small voice that reminds you how tenuous your position is."

Still wearing her silver-locked wig, Leia was deflating Han's and her sleeping pad when she saw Sasso drop something by the smoldering campfire. A leathery creature about the size of a shock-ball, it looked like a villip with wings—and this one had been pierced by a wooden quarrel fired from the Rodian's crude bowcasterlike weapon.

"That's one that won't be able to report on us," Sasso said, examining his fresh kill with the thoroughness of a born hunter.

Leia went over to the fire to have a closer look at the dead creature. "The biot we saw yesterday?"

"Maybe not the same one, but from the same flock." Sasso's green snout twitched. "Got it on the first try. That's never happened before."

Leia regarded him questioningly. "I hope you're not thinking of cooking it."

"I am curious . . . but no. I'm trying to decide whether to burn it or bury it."

"I vote for burning it," Han said from behind them. "Otherwise the bissops might be able to sniff it out."

Caluula's sun had been up for an hour, but the ravine's forest of cane trees was still waking up. Birds were abundant, and the flitnats—Leia's personal flitnats—had returned. Thanks to the netting supplied with the bedrolls, she and Han had slept flitnat-free and wonderfully, waking frequently if briefly to watch for shooting stars or listen to the calls of nocturnal creatures. Han had prepared breakfast over the fire, while she and Wraw had broken camp. It was an elemental life, but one she thought she could get used to.

Under cover of darkness, Sasso and the Ryn, Ferfer, had sneaked off to a nearby supply cache, and returned by first light with the bowcaster and a couple of weapons old enough to have been carried by Leia's adoptive father's bodyguards, including a thick-barreled blaster with a large hardwood handgrip; another with a finger-contoured grip and built-in scope; two black military-grade hand weapons with trigger

guards and top-mounted heat radiators; and a rifle Han identified as a DC-15, with a folding stock.

The blasters were now stashed in the duffels, but not so
deeply they couldn't be retrieved in a hurry.

Meloque and the mustachioed Ferfer returned to camp
just as Han and Wraw were about to secure the gear bags to
the timbus. The docile animals were foraging for food in the
tall grass.

The stately Ho'Din female looked disappointed.

"Couldn't find any winged-star shells?" Han said.

She shook her head. "We found hundreds, but all of them
were inactive. At least some should have opened by now."

"The weather has been off," Sasso said. "Hotter than usual
for this time of year."

Meloque considered it. "I suppose that could account
for it."

By firelight the previous evening, she had given everyone
a biology lesson on the Nocturne of the Winged-Stars. Similar in appearance to the drone-flitters found on countless
worlds, winged-stars emerged from chitinous shells. Unique
among flitters, however, Caluula's had but one day to perform
their mating dances, display their celebrated luminosity, mate,
and lay eggs, which would hatch 299 years later. The larval
stage lasted less than a local week, at the end of which the surviving larvae would be encased in durable cocoons. Those
newly emerged winged-stars that weren't immediately devoured by flying lizards and other predators would die of
natural causes by the time the sun set on the day of their
emergence.

"Correct me if I'm wrong, Meloque," Wraw said, "but unless you're aging more gracefully than a Wookiee, you've
never actually observed a Nocturne."

"That's true," she told him. "But on Moltok we have been
able to simulate the life cycle in controlled settings."

"Maybe the Yuuzhan Vong have something to do with the
casings not opening on schedule," Han suggested. "They
might have introduced some organism that's affected the
ecology. Look what they did on Tynna and Duro."

"I find that very improbable," Meloque said. "Those worlds
were altered for strategic and logistical reasons, where a

world like Caluula must please the Yuuzhan Vong to no end. For all the barbarity they've demonstrated, they have a reverence for life."

Wraw snorted. "You sound like a sympathizer, Professor."

"Wraw," Leia said sharply, but Meloque only waved her sucker-equipped hand in dismissal.

"What other attitude can be expected from a member of a species that has declared its intent to exterminate the Yuuzhan Vong?" Meloque was referring to the Bothan doctrine of ar'krai, or total war.

Wraw laughed. "I was only joking."

His head fur betrayed nothing. Leia waited until Meloque and Ferfer had left to search for additional shells before she went over to Wraw. "I don't think Meloque appreciates your sense of humor."

Wraw shrugged. "What can I say? We're worlds apart."

"Then your cynicism doesn't stem from your commitment to an amoral, unprofitable career?"

"Amoral, maybe, but certainly not unprofitable."

"In terms of credits, you mean."

"What other terms are there?"

Leia glanced at Han, who merely spread his hands. "Go ahead and poke him if you want to. I won't try to stop you."

Just then Page and Kyp returned to camp. Page looked from Han to Leia to Wraw, then back to Han. "We interrupting something?"

"Just a little campfire sing-along," Han said.

Page didn't ask for an explanation. "We found signs of a Yuuzhan Vong patrol—tracker beasts and a couple of those twelve-legged mounts."

"Bissops and quenaks," Sasso said, getting to his feet. "We'd better get moving. The sooner we cross the next ridge, the better."

Everyone pitched in to load the remaining gear. With Ferfer riding point, they climbed to the crest of the ridge, then began a slow, switchback descent through dense forest. Sasso, Page, and Kyp rode ahead to scout the trail. Halfway to the valley floor, Han spurred his timbu to come abreast of Wraw's.

"I figure you spend a lot of your time hanging around with

low-life characters," Han said. "But everyone here is on the same side, understand?"

"You're one to talk about consorting with low-life characters, Solo."

Han forced a smile. "I got over it, pal. So maybe you should look to me as an example."

The Bothan nodded. "I'll give it thought."

Han fell back to ride alongside Leia.

"Why do you even bother?" she asked.

"Well, either I'm going to change his mind, or I'm going to change his face."

"You still won't be rearranging the person inside."

"Maybe not, but I'll *feel* a whole lot better."

Leia heard rapid hoofbeats up ahead, and a moment later Kyp rode up.

"Yuuzhan Vong. They're climbing out the valley." He pointed down through the trees. "Just there—at that stand of broadleafs."

"Is there a way to avoid them?" Leia asked.

"No. And we can't afford to fight them here."

Han rose up on his stirrups and motioned to an out-cropping of rocks below the next switchback. "Looks like a decent ambush point."

Kyp nodded. "That's my thinking, too."

They hastened through the switchback and into a gulch, where Sasso and Page were waiting. Ferfer led the mounts away, and everyone else scrambled to take up firing positions in the boulders on both sides of the trail—Han, Leia, Page, and Meloque on one side; Wraw, Sasso, and Kyp on the other.

Han sighted down the barrel of the military blaster; Page did the same with the DC-15 rifle. Meloque wrapped her huge hand around the wooden grip of the antique sidearm. Leia took hold of her lightsaber, but didn't activate it.

Shortly they heard the patrol approaching. First to appear were a trio of bissop hounds. Low-bodied creatures, they moved in a waddling motion, their long snouts sniffing the air and ground, and their clawed feet leaving distinctive tracks in the dirt. Behind them walked three Yuuzhan Vong warriors armed with amphistaffs and bandoliers of thud and

razor bugs. Two were sporting shoulder-mounted tactical villips. Behind them came three warriors on riding beasts as
large as grutchyna but as sedate as rontos.

"I'll take the tracker on the right," Page whispered to Han.
"You take the one in the middle. Go for the villips first."

Page waved a signal across the canyon to where Kyp and
the others were concealed.

Then everyone hunkered down to wait for the patrol to
move into the crossfire.

The bissops lifted their snouts toward the boulders just as
the first blasterbolts were raining down on them. Han's and
Page's shots blew the two small villips to pieces, while sizzling red bolts from across the ravine knocked two warriors
from their mounts. But even though taken by surprise, the
Yuuzhan Vong were quick to counterattack. Razor and thud
bugs swarmed into the air, and—rearing and snarling—the
three bissops surged up into the rocks.

By then Han, Page, Leia, and Meloque were already in
motion, firing on the run and scampering for new positions.
A bolt from Han's heavy blaster shattered the skull of a
charging bissop. A second bolt caught one of the trackers
squarely in the chest, blowing a smoking hole in the warrior's vonduun crab armor and sending him flying backward,
to be trampled underfoot by a confused quenak.

Running down the opposite outcropping, Wraw came
within a meter of being bissop fodder, but a well-placed shot
from Sasso dropped the beast before it could snap at the
Bothan a second time.

Kyp front-flipped down onto the trail ahead of the patrol.
Lightsaber ignited, he fought his way through a hail of razor
bugs to take the fight to the remaining warriors. Han was astonished to see the Jedi's blade neatly cleave a rigid amphistaff, then, on the reverse stroke, sever the head of the
warrior himself. Still in the rocks, Leia was similarly engaged in fending off a stream of frenzied bugs. Meloque was
cowering below her, afraid to show her head. Pulling the
frightened Ho'Din to her feet, Leia led her to a safer position, whirling twice to send return flights of bugs smashing
into the rocks.

Han emerged from the boulders to see Kyp kick a coufee

out of the hand of the only Yuuzhan Vong left standing, then pierce the warrior through the neck as he was running for his mount, as if in an attempt to flee. A blur of motion drew Han's attention to the left, and he swung around, flattening himself to the ground. The last of the three bissops hurdled him and bounded up into the rocks, close to where Meloque was crouched, staring distractedly at her heavy-gripped blaster.

Unable to get a clear shot at the retreating beast, Page shouted to Meloque: "Kill the hound!"

She glanced at the escaping bissop, then in bewilderment at Wraw. "It's just an animal—"

"Kill it!" Page repeated.

"I—"

Bolts from Wraw's weapon stopped the bissop dead, just short of its disappearing over the rim of the gulch.

"Butchers," the Ho'Din said as sudden quiet descended. She staggered out of the rocks, and down onto the trail to join Leia and the others. "Butchers!"

"Bissops are trained to return to base," Page said calmly. "Another patrol would have picked up our trail in no time flat."

Meloque heard him out, then nodded dully.

Six Yuuzhan Vong, two lizard-hounds, and one quenak lay sprawled in the dirt. Page moved from warrior to warrior, making certain that each was dead. He put the convulsing quenak out of its misery with a single bolt, then did the same to three amphistaffs.

Han squatted down beside the warrior he had shot in the chest, then regarded the thirty-year-old weapon that had supplied the lethal bolt. "I never knew these old blasters packed such a wallop."

"They don't," Kyp said from where he was crouched near another warrior. He rapped his knuckles against the breastplate of the Yuuzhan Vong's living armor. "Inferior armor, inferior weaponry, inferior troops." He glanced around. "Even the bissops were slow."

Leia glanced at Sasso in sudden uncertainty. "Another side effect of the heat wave?"

The Rodian shook his head in perplexity.

"Let me get this straight," Wraw said. "You're disappointed

because we *won* too easily?" He snorted a laugh. "I'm beginning to wonder if all of you aren't sympathizers."

"He's right." Page said. "We can use every bit of luck we get."

"I've played enough sabacc to know luck when I see it," Han said, "and this wasn't it." He scanned the boulders and nearby trees. "They could be luring us into a trap."

Kyp glanced at him. "Something else is going on here," he said.

TWENTY-TWO

Rimward of the Tion Hegemony, Jaina watched the Yuu-zhan Vong armada revert from hyperspace once again. One moment it appeared that ten thousand stars had been eclipsed; the next, that that part of the galaxy had gained a new star cluster.

Cappie shrilled and squeaked, underscoring its obvious distress by spotting the cockpit's display screen with countless glowing bezels. In the same instant, two cinder-black A-wings that had been Jaina's starboard companions for the past hour fell away in stealth, and made the jump to light-speed.

Despite the glowing threat-assessment screen and her previous sightings of the armada, Jaina was staggered by the sheer number of ships the Yuuzhan Vong had amassed. Close-ups of the vessels provided by the starfighter's long-range scanners showed their pitted hulls to be marked and etched with cryptic symbols and blackened with what looked like war paint but was probably blood. Many displayed slender tendrils of yorik coral, from which flew sail-like battle standards. Evidenced by melt circles and areas of carbon scoring, some of the ships were clearly veterans of earlier campaigns, uprooted from occupied systems throughout the invasion corridor. Others looked newly commissioned—newly *grown*—including an enormous rose-colored oval that had to be the flagship.

The fact that the Yuuzhan Vong had essentially entrusted hundreds of conquered worlds to the protection of patrol craft and ground troops meant not only that they were willing to risk everything they had gained on one conclusive battle, but also that their intent was nothing less than the obliteration of the Alliance fleets.

Cappie sent another transmission to the cockpit, and Jaina clutched the control yoke in pulse-quickening anticipation.

A pyrotechnic display of globular explosions began to fire-brighten the leading edge of the mobile cluster of ships, and a dozen bezels disappeared from the display screen. Again the Yuuzhan Vong had moved headlong into an expansive arc of smart mines that had been sown at the jump point. But as had occurred at the Perlemian transit point, the explosions began to taper off almost immediately, until there were only isolated bursts, and many of the undetonated mines disappeared, vacuumed into immense singularities created by dovin basals.

Jaina pressed her chin to the helmet's microphone stud.

"Quermia controller, this is Twin Suns One. The beast has arrived and opened the packages we left."

"Did the packages come as a surprise?"

"Not for long enough to give the beast any pause."

"What is the status of your companions?"

"Heralds are away."

"Can you corroborate the beast's current vector?"

Jaina keyed a short request to the R2-B3 droid, which replied with tones and buzzes that became text on the display screen.

"Bearing toward jump coordinates for Mon Calamari."

"Copy that, Twin Suns One. You are green to depart, and reposition to Mon Calamari Extreme. Rendezvous at Iceberg Three, with Vanguard, Scimitar, and Rogue Squadrons."

Jaina signed off the command net and switched over to the tactical frequency. "All pilots, this is Twin Suns Leader. Instruct your droids to set coordinates for Mon Cal Extreme. Jump to lightspeed at my zero count. Ten, nine, eight, seven . . ."

Jaina sat back in her chair and waited for the X-wing's Incom hyperdrive to engage. The jump would be Twin Suns' third and final since they had first observed the armada emerge from hyperspace. All major staging points between the Perlemian Trade Route and Mon Calamari had been strewn with mines months earlier, primarily to discourage enemy forays. But Alliance command hadn't expected an *armada* to use the transit jump points, and now every fleet strategist was pondering why the Yuuzhan Vong hadn't jumped directly from the Trade Route to the Mon Calamari system. Had the enemy committed another tactical blunder, or were they merely testing the waters? Perhaps they suspected that the Alliance had positioned forces at jump points convenient to Mon Calamari, in the hope of outflanking the armada once the battle commenced.

At each transit point Jaina had sent updates to a frigate stationed at Quermia, which was serving as a hyperspace transceiver. The frigate relayed the intelligence to the MCCC Fleet Annex. But a redundant system was also in place, in the form of courier ships, some of which had jumped to Quermia, and others to Mon Calamari. By now other couriers were certainly alerting the battle groups designated for Toong'l and Caluula, where withdrawing elements from the armada would be prevented from jumping to the aid of soon-to-be embattled Coruscant.

The transit to Mon Calamari would also be the longest of the three, so Jaina took advantage of the lull to center herself in the Force. She thought briefly of her parents, executing a mission on Caluula, and of Jacen, wherever he was. But she didn't attempt to reach out to any of them. Everyone had their separate duties to perform, and she knew instinctively that the scattered members of her family were thinking of her, just as she was them. Nor were there any Jedi among Twin Suns for her to touch through the Force. With Kyp on Caluula, as well, Octa Ramis had been assigned to lead the Dozen, and both Lowbacca and Alema Rar were commanding their own squadrons. Madurrin, Streen, and some of the other Jedi were stationed on those capital ships that were essential to defending Mon Calamari itself against the enemy onslaught.

Having set her inner chrono to rouse her before the X-wing reverted from hyperspace, she returned to full awareness just seconds before Cappie signaled her with a ready tone.

She took a calming breath and waited for the stars to reappear.

Mon Calamari Extreme was just that: the far reaches of the star system, where the armada would likely decant. Iceberg Three was the code for the penultimate of the system's eight satellites—a misshapen chunk of frozen waste; in fact, a captured comet—destined at some point in time to collide with the outermost planet. Silhouetted against the small white spheroid were dozens of Alliance cruisers, destroyers, and carriers, along with hundreds of starfighters.

It struck Jaina that nearly every vessel that had been in production for the past forty standard years was represented in one form or another, from Rendili StarDrive Dreadnaughts to *Rejuvenator*-class Star Destroyers.

And the gathered ships constituted only the outer circle of defense.

Despite the fortifying exercises she had taken herself through during the hyperspace flight, Jaina realized that her heart was pounding and her hands were trembling.

This is actually going to happen, she told herself with a stubborn measure of disbelief. The end of the war and the fate of the galaxy might well be decided over the course of the next few days.

"Welcome back, Twin Suns Leader," a recognizable voice said into her helmet earphones.

"Thanks, Wedge," she said. "I feel like I've been away for a week."

"Terrific work, Jaina. Your rally point is Iceberg Three, at four-seven-nine ecliptic. You're to stand by until the seeding's concluded."

"Copy, Alliance control. Standing by."

Instructing Twin Suns to form up on her, Jaina led the squadron to its assigned coordinates, at fixed orbit over the frozen spheroid, in the company of a wing of starfighters made up of Rogue, Vanguard, Scimitar, Blackmoon, and Tesar Sabatyne's Wild Knights.

"Hey, Sticks," another familiar voice said.

Jaina opened a channel to Gavin Darklighter. "How long have you been sitting here, Rogue One?"

"Too long. Was Intelligence correct about the number of Vong ships?"

"I think they underestimated."

Before Gavin could respond, Wedge broke in. "Group and squadron leaders, the beast is at the gate. I know you're all eager to welcome it, but you're going to have to wait your turns."

The comm fell eerily silent, then erupted in chatter as the Yuuzhan Vong war vessels began to emerge: cones and polygons, faceted and smooth, bone white to reddish black, craggy with plasma launchers or strung with coralskippers. More rapidly and in increasing numbers they came, filling local space and eventually blotting out Mon Calamari's distant sun. Just when it seemed that the last of them had reverted, still more appeared.

Somewhat removed from Alliance forces, and almost as if performing for an audience, the vessels began to tighten up, maneuvering into positions that ultimately created an oblate mass of yammosk carriers and destroyer and cruiser analogs. From that mass—emerging from berthing cavities in the largest ships or dropping from anchorage on yorik coral branches—streamed hundreds of picket ship analogs and coralskippers, deploying to forge the multitude of short and long tendrils that were meant to simulate the tentacles of a yammosk.

To Jaina the final arrangement more closely resembled a flaring star, or perhaps the spiral arm galaxy the Yuuzhan Vong were determined to overwhelm. But whatever the armada's form, *beast* was the description that fit it best.

Then the immense organism was on the move, tentacles elongating from the hub as the cluster advanced on Mon Calamari, acutely aware of the reception party that awaited it, but resolute in its purpose.

"All group and squadron leaders," a male voice announced over the battle net, "seedships have arrived."

Alliance command might have borrowed the term from the Yuuzhan Vong, but the reference was not to the vessels that initiated the process of worldshaping; it was to the several dozen unarmed and remotely piloted freighters that gushed from behind Iceberg Three and launched straight for the armada. Plasma missiles assaulted the bulky container ships from all quarters, though armor plating kept most of them intact until they were within the embrace of the longer tentacles. There they surrendered their payloads of thousands of probe droids.

With wide-domed heads and dangling mechanical legs, the probots were marine in appearance, and indeed they spread out like a school of deep-sea creatures riding the currents of a rising tide.

Normally the Yuuzhan Vong wouldn't have wasted firepower on droids, but each probot had been programmed to mimic the propulsion signatures of Alliance starfighters, so the coralskippers and pickets had a field day, slagging the probots with fiery projectiles, or simply dismembering them by collision. The Alliance might as well have been providing the yammosks and coralskipper pilots with practice for acquisition and targeting, but in fact each probot was contributing invaluably to Alliance command's goal of clearing fire lanes to the heart of the armada.

Many of the battles fought during the long war had been decided not by firepower or kill ratios, but by the ability of Yuuzhan Vong biots to detect mass signals and to manipulate gravity. As intelligent as the yammosks were, they were evenly matched by the crunching power of battle analysis computers, combined with the targeting skill of pilots. The dovin basals were a different animal. For a time the Alliance had managed to outwit them by employing decoys, stutterfire lasers, and the Jedi-propelled shadow bombs, but those advantages had recently been lost.

Still, the Alliance had one powerful weapon in its arsenal: *invention.*

Gleeful as they were about decimating the probots, the Yuuzhan Vong were unaware that each droid had been tasked to calculate entry points and targeting solutions for the starfighters. Transmitted to Alliance command's computers, the data were collated and relayed to group and wing commanders, and on to squadron leaders and pilots.

"Your droids should be receiving navigational and targeting information," the voice of control said into Jaina's right ear. "Watch your display screens for assignments."

Data began to flash on the cockpit display as Cappie deciphered the information forwarded from Mon Calamari. Jaina watched a graphic representation of the yammosk resolve on the screen, with each tentacle of skips and gunboats assigned a number or letter. Twin Suns, Rogue, and Vanguard Squadrons were tasked with taking out tentacles fourteen through twenty. But as impatient as she was to go to guns, there was an order to battle that had to be maintained.

The first assault wave was comprised of A-wings, TIE interceptors, Chiss clawcraft, A-9 Vigilances, and a handful of Y-wings. The objective of the fastest of the starfighters—the A-wings and A-9s—was to tease the coralskippers out of formation. Both fighter types were small and fragile, but the short-range concussion missile launchers of the former and the fire-linked lasers of the latter did to the outlying coralskippers what the skips had done to the probots.

For each dovin basal singularity that came to the rescue of a targeted ship, four failed to deploy in time, allowing the small fighters to strike and fade before the Yuuzhan Vong pilots even knew what hit them. Harried, the coralskippers and picket vessels that formed the tips of the tentacles began to disperse, and as soon as they did the dagger-shaped TIE interceptors and light bomber Y-wings were on them, weaving through the budding chaos with blinding speed and loosing proton torpedoes and bursts of high-powered laserfire.

The perimeter of the shifting armada became a blur of roiling fireballs and fragmenting vessels. Packets of green energy and nova-bright bundles of explosive power began to eat away at the suddenly flailing tentacles. Molten ejecta rocketed outward at the attackers, in such abundance the armada might almost have been hemorrhaging.

Jaina switched over to the battle net in time to hear control issue the order to withdraw. "We have clear fire lanes to their capital ships at one, six, seven, eight, twelve, and twenty-two. All starfighters in those lanes reposition to escorts and carriers."

While the starfighters began to loop back, the Super Star Destroyer *Guardian* and the Mon Calamari cruiser *Harbinger* lumbered forward. Traversing, their ranged weapons poured huge bolts of destructive power down the unprotected lanes. Explosions blossomed at the heart of the armada, all but setting it aglow. Colossal pieces of yorik coral streaked through local space. The beast withered visibly, but stuck to its course.

"Second group away!" Alliance control ordered.

Jaina licked the sweat from her upper lip and punched the X-wing's throttle, leading Twin Suns swiftly into the fray. The forward view through the canopy showed so many coral-skippers, so many targets of opportunity, she felt as if she were part of an elaborate simulation rather than engaged in actual battle.

Remotely controlled by however many yammosks were contained in the core, the tentacles slithered and snapped like amphistaffs. Skips moved in and out of her targeting reticle faster than she, or even Cappie, could keep track of them. For all the shrieking and yelping, the astromech droid might have been on a thrill ride. Even so, Twin Suns managed to maintain its integrity as it advanced on the whipping rank of vessels that had been designated tentacle fourteen.

Behind the X-wings flew B-wing fighters and a squadron of TIE defenders. In combat the B-wings were somewhat cross-shaped, whereas the TIEs—with their elongated bodies and triads of solar collection panels—resembled arrow-like projectiles. Their job was to mop up any mess that Twin Suns, Rogue, and the rest left behind, and to clear the way for the ships tasked with landing punches on the capital vessels: heavily armored E-wing fighters equipped with proton torpedoes, and twin-piloted Scimitar assault bombers, carrying enough concussive strafing power to decommission half the rock spitters of an enemy destroyer analog.

Coralskippers with enough fight left in them began peppering the X- and B-wings with plasma nodules and marshaling their dovin basals to make grabs for the attackers' particle shields.

Then, without warning, capital ships at the heart of the armada funneled furious firestorms along the depleted lanes. Jaina's X-wing wobbled and tumbled through a swirling corridor of flames. With the starfighter's shields all but incinerated, she rammed the control stick to one side to free herself, rolling out of volcanic heat with the ship nearly roasted, and Cappie's dome a drooping hood of molten alloy. She performed a desperate pushover and scanned local space, dismayed to discover that almost all of the TIE defenders were gone—atomized by the superheated tempest.

The beast hadn't been stunned by the initial assaults; it had merely been waiting for the right time to counterpunch. And the single blow it delivered had knocked fifty or more starfighters out of the fight.

Jaina was doing a count of Twin Suns when the armada yammosks instructed the tentacle arms to rotate clockwise, and full chains of coralskippers and pickets quickly filled the gaps.

Where moments earlier Jaina was facing six wounded skips, she suddenly found herself in the sights of a ravenous thirty.

TWENTY-THREE

A similar thing had happened to Jacen on Duro, three years back.

At the time, he had been helping a group of Ryn refugees fit a synthplas dome over the prefabricated building that was to be their shelter. This time he was off on his own in the Middle Distance, picking his way downhill to a still pool on the floor of a narrow valley.

Jaina?

On Duro, he had passed out and fallen, knocking himself unconscious. This time a forest creeper swept his feet out from under him, and he pitched forward, sliding face-first on muddy ground and sodden deflated leaves until he managed to somersault himself onto his back and extend his hands to the sides. He was still meters from the valley floor when he arrested his descent, but his lightsaber fell prey to momentum and soared free of the cloth belt that cinched his robe. Tumbling end over end through the air, it arced into the depths of the ice-fringed pool below.

Jacen leapt to his feet and vaulted to the water's edge. Focusing on the center of the concentric waves that were spreading across the pool, he immersed himself in the Force and stretched out his right hand.

The tubular alloy handgrip emerged vertically from the water, but not alone.

It was held in the upraised four-fingered hand of Vergere.

Sekot's thought projection of the diminutive Fosh, at any rate, looking much younger than the piebald, short-feathered Vergere Jacen had come to know on Coruscant. Her willowy ears and pair of corkscrewing antennae appeared smaller, and her slanted eyes were radiant with wonder. The splayed feet of her reverse-articulated legs rested just on the surface of the agitated pool.

"Lose something, Jacen?" Sekot asked through Vergere's wide mouth.

"Not for the first time." His exhalations formed clouds in the chill air.

"It's not like you to stumble."

"My sister Jaina is in danger. I forgot to look where I was going."

"How often will you allow yourself to be distracted by the dangers she faces?"

This was Vergere as remembered by Sekot, Jacen thought, in contrast to the Vergere who had sacrificed her life at Ebaq 9 to save him and Jaina. "As often as necessary," he said. "We're twins, and strongly bonded."

"What if you were faced with the choice of saving your twin or your uncle? Which do you serve?"

"I serve the Force."

"The Force would guide you to the correct decision?"

"Why else would I serve it?"

Insubstantial Vergere extended the lightsaber to him. "Reclaim your weapon."

He called the lightsaber to him and wedged it into the belt of his now muddy robe. The handle was wet and cold, as were his hands, which he rubbed briskly together.

Zonama Sekot had completed a second trial jump without sustaining severe damage. R2-D2 had calculated that the planet was on the galactic ecliptic, close to the Reecee system in the Inner Rim, were the frontier of that arbitrary zone to be extended into the Unknown Regions. One more jump through hyperspace and Zonama Sekot could be back in known space.

Vergere seemed to be watching him. "Do you use your lightsaber to slash or to heal?"

"That's always been the dilemma."

Jacen lowered himself to the ground. Broad shafts of sunlight flooded through the giant boras, dappling the leaf duff and dazzling the surface of the pool. Insects skimmed the water and bombinated around him.

"Were you searching for something here?"

"Only answers."

"As to how best to end the pain, suffering, and death that war has brought to the galaxy. You must trust in the Force, Jacen, if you are to serve it fully."

"Being a Jedi isn't just about serving the Force," he said. "It's a commitment to valuing all life."

Sekot brought a smile to Vergere's whiskered face. "You learned that from your mentor, Vergere."

"My guide," Jacen amended.

My guide through the lands of the dead. My herald of tragedy . . .

"Vergere learned it from me," Sekot said. "For that is how I felt on being brought to awareness by Leor Hal, the first Magister. You wish to reiterate that the Yuuzhan Vong are part of life, part of the Force, and therefore must be dealt with accordingly."

"More to be pitied if stripped of the Force, as you contend," Jacen said.

Vergere's narrow shoulders sagged. "I, too, am searching for answers, Jacen. But I do not sympathize with the enemy as you appear to."

Jacen compressed his lips. "Because of what Vergere guided me through, I've developed a kind of . . . sense for them—a Vongsense. I feel it more strongly here, not only when I speak with Harrar, but wherever I go."

He touched the hollow space in his chest that had once housed the slave seed Vergere had implanted, and he recalled how it felt to have been racked on the Embrace of Pain; stripped of the Force.

You are forever lost to the worlds you knew, Vergere had told him at the beginning of his process of being remade. *Your friends mourn, your father rages, your mother weeps. Your life has been terminated: a line of division has been drawn between you and everything you have ever known. You have seen the terminator that sweeps across the face of a planet, the twilit division between day and night. You have crossed that line, Jacen Solo. The bright fields of day are forever past.*

"By growing to understand you better, I grow to understand our enemy better," Sekot said. "Do you see a contradiction there, Jedi?"

"That depends on whom Sekot serves."

"I, too, serve the Force—but as defined by the Potentium, which does not recognize evil, except as a label. Magister Leor and the Ferroans were my guides to consciousness. But it was the Far Outsiders—the Yuuzhan Vong—who taught me that while evil does not exist, evil *actions* do exist, and it is to those that we must direct ourselves. I had the power to halt the Yuuzhan Vong when they approached me fifty years ago, and I have the power to halt them now. My instincts, such as they are, tell me that I have always had power over them."

Jacen thought about the Force punch Sekot had delivered to those aboard *Jade Shadow* when the ship had first appeared in the Klasse Ephemora system—Sanctuary.

"And you'll exercise that power to defeat them?" he asked carefully.

"If necessary—but without contempt. If I defeat them aggressively, if I hate them for who they have become, then I will have separated myself from the Force, and permitted my ego to triumph over my desire to merge and expand my consciousness. I will have corrupted the light with my darkness, stained it forever. Self-awareness tricks us into believing that there is us, and that there is the other. But in serving the Force we recognize that we are all the same thing; that when we act in accordance with the Force we act in accordance with the wish of all life to enlarge itself, to rise out of physicality and become something greater.

"In that sense, all living beings are seed-partners, Jacen, passionate to unite with all life, and to help give birth to grand enterprises—whether a starship, a work of art, or a deed that will echo through history as a noble action. I am no different than you in wanting to play a part in the evolution of the spirit. My consciousness yearns for this."

"Easier said than done," Jacen said.

"Yes, it is a matter of balance. But we are balancing the universe constantly with every action we take, some tipping it one way, some another. To triumph over the Yuuzhan Vong we must simply go where we wish to go. That is also what I must do to return us to known space. But the task entails far more than simply focusing on a set of hyperspace coordinates. Unless the destination is a place I wish to go, nothing will work out. Even if I execute the jump flawlessly, my actions will come to nothing.

"For your interest, Jacen, that is something that Vergere taught me."

Jacen was listening too intently to respond. Vergere had set him on the path to remaking himself. But unless he could complete the process, he would be ensnared by the very self-conscious uncertainties Sekot professed to have grown past, and prevented from merging fully with the Force.

"We must approach the turning points in our lives with purity of heart," Sekot was saying. "We must look beyond ourselves, and when we see danger approaching or a difficult choice ahead, we must calm ourselves well in advance, so that we can navigate with a clear mind. Once we have mastered the technique, we can learn to trust that we're doing the right thing, without thinking about it."

"Do you know where you want to go?" Jacen asked when he realized that Sekot was waiting for him to say something.

"By analyzing Yuuzhan Vong biotech—by what I intuited from Nen Yim—I have learned much about augmenting Zonama's hyperspace cores with energy derived from the planet itself. And the success of the trial jumps has encouraged me that I can safely return Zonama to known space. I begin to understand how the Yuuzhan Vong created what they call dovin basals, villips, yammosks, and other biots. Or perhaps I begin to *remember*.

"But I am worried about the potentially calamitous or destabilizing effects Zonama's sudden appearance could have on any planet in close proximity to our emergence."

From records stored in the Chiss library, Jacen and Saba had learned of the widespread seismic devastation Zonama Sekot had caused on Munlali Mafir, standard decades earlier, not only to the planet but to the indigenous Jostrans and Krizlaws, as well.

"My uncle thought you might be worried about that," Jacen said. "He was going to tell you himself that you shouldn't be."

Vergere glided toward him across the water and ice. "Tell me what Master Skywalker has in mind."

TWENTY-FOUR

Caluula's reddish sun was cresting the ridgeline, limning the crowns of the tallest trees and warming the air. Leia began to rub her hands together, but stopped when she realized that the chill she felt had nothing to do with the temperature.

North of the trail, in an area of trees that were snapped in half, the team had come upon a crashed coralskipper. The craft's translucent, mica-like canopy was cracked, and inside the cavity that served as a cockpit sat the dead pilot. The cognition hood that was the pilot's living interface with the coralskipper was shriveled and stuck to his face like a sheet of flimsiplast. Han was squatting at the craft's blunt nose, poking at a deep red heart-shaped mass, studded with pale blue projections, that had dropped from the fractured fuselage.

"Dovin basal's dead," he said.

"Same with the rock spitters," Kyp replied.

The Jedi Master was circling the craft while Wraw and Sasso inspected the cockpit. Page, Ferfer, and Meloque were scouting the forest to the north, in the direction of Caluula City. The timbus were grazing contentedly nearby.

Han stood up, put the edge of his hand to his brow, and gazed at the splintered trees. "Came in from that direction." He pointed to a depression some distance away. "Hit the ground there, plowed its way through those bushes, and came to a stop here."

Kyp completed his circle of the craft, nodding his head. "Only question is, what brought it down?"

"Caluula Orbital. What else?"

Kyp regarded the coralskipper. "No signs of laserfire from batteries or starfighter cannons."

Han's forehead wrinkled. "Can't be." He ducked down to appraise what he could of the underside, then stood up. "Must have caught a bolt straight through the canopy."

"No signs of that either," Sasso said, jumping down to the ground.

Han looked at Kyp. "Could have been stunned by an ion cannon . . ." He let his words trail off when he realized the impossibility of it. "No craft comes down the gravity well at terminal velocity and ends up looking like this one."

Kyp nodded in agreement. "From the way the trees are sheared off and the depth of the initial impact crater, the skip couldn't have been higher than three hundred meters."

"A patrol craft," Sasso said.

"That would explain why there's no heat damage." Han turned to the Rodian. "Could one of your people have shot it down? Someone in the resistance?"

Sasso shook his head. "We don't have the weapons for that."

Wraw leapt down from the cockpit. "So what happened, it suffered heart failure?"

Han made his lips a thin line and shrugged. "Maybe with the Yuuzhan Vong devoting almost everything they have to the armada, they've exiled their shoddiest biots and least experienced warriors to worlds like Caluula." He laughed ruefully. "They're in even worse shape than we are."

"No," Kyp said. "Only here are they in worse shape."

Leia listened to them trying to convince themselves that there was a reasonable explanation for the crashed craft and the inept warriors they had ambushed. But, in fact, lack of genuine explanations had everyone on edge.

Worried that the team was under surveillance, no one had slept the previous night. In the morning they had made a decision to abandon the trail and bushwhack through the thick forest, in the hope of avoiding detection. That they hadn't seen any reconnaissance biots or evidence of foot patrols had only added to the suspicion that they were being led into a trap.

Then their purposefully meandering path had brought them to the coralskipper.

"You know what could have happened," Han was saying. "The yammosk could have steered it wrong."

"I can see that," Sasso said. "I can even see that a crash like this could take out the pilot and the dovin basal. But why would the cognition hood die? Do the hoods feed off the basals?" He stared at the coralskipper. "I've spent more time trying to avoid them than study them."

"Our daughter could explain it," Han said. "She's actually piloted a vessel like this."

Jaina!

A sense of deep concern flooded through Leia. But before she could begin to make sense of it, Han was yelling something at Wraw. Leia saw that the Bothan had clambered back to the cockpit and was making sketches of the interior.

"Something to show the grandchildren," Wraw said when Han demanded to know what he was doing.

"Grandchildren? You'll be lucky to even have kids of your own."

Wraw closed the sketch pad. "If I do, I know I'll have sense enough to keep them out of the war."

Han advanced on the Bothan with menacing familiarity. "I'm going to have to teach you the ways of the world before this is over."

Leia could see that Kyp was ready to step between them, but the confrontation went no further. "He's Corellian," Kyp said quietly to Wraw while Han was walking away. "They don't make idle threats."

Wraw only sniggered.

Sasso left to find Meloque, Page, and Ferfer. Han, Leia, and Kyp were gathering the timbus when Han said, "You realize we're being reeled in."

Kyp nodded. "It's probably been that way from the beginning. But that doesn't mean we still can't pull this mission off. We just have to watch our backs."

"Speaking of which, did Intelligence run backgrounds on Sasso and Ferfer?"

"You'd have to check with Wraw. I do know that both of them joined the resistance before the Yuuzhan Vong showed up in the Caluula system. Sasso even served on Caluula Orbital for a while."

"So at least we're not being *sold* to the Vong."

"As far as I can tell."

Sasso's whistled signal wafted into the clearing, and several moments later he, Page, the Ryn, and Meloque stepped from the trees. In her sucker-tipped hands the Ho'Din cradled a dozen or so insects, delicately winged and equipped with large bioluminescent eyespots. She set them on the ground, then sat down beside them.

"They're dead," she announced in an anguished tone. "The entire forest is littered with bodies. In most cases they died inside their shells. Others appear to have died in flight."

"All of them?" Leia asked, nonplussed.

Meloque shook her head. "But the survivors are moving very lethargically." She gazed at Leia and the others. "Something terrible has happened here."

Han and Kyp traded dark glances.

"Let's get moving," Page told everyone.

Several hours of mostly downhill trudging brought Team Meloque to a low ridge that overlooked the southern portion of Caluula City, and the prominent hivelike Yuuzhan Vong minshal that harbored the yammosk.

"There are three entrances," Sasso explained from the spot of cover the team found. "Two in the front, and one on the east side. All of them are dilating membranes that can be pierced by blaster bolts. Guards are stationed at each, usually three or four at any given time. They stand long shifts, so it would be to our advantage to strike at sundown, just when the afternoon shift is ending. The garrison is made up of about seventy-five warriors. There's also a commander, his subaltern, at least one priest, and one of those long-tressed technicians—"

"A shaper," Leia said.

The Rodian nodded. "As for the yammosk, I don't know how to kill it. But I'm guessing you have some idea."

"Leave that to me," Kyp said.

"It's important that we take out their villip communications while we're at it," Page added.

Leia gazed out over the flat rooftops of the simple city. Judging by the position of the sun, the team was in for a long wait. Ferfer volunteered to find a place to conceal the timbus. He rose, but had scarcely moved off when a gurgling exclamation of surprise rang from just inside the tree line. Everyone whirled at once to see the Ryn staggering toward them, his belly opened like a ripe fruit.

Behind him emerged four relatively short and dark-complected Yuuzhan Vong warriors.

Han shot Leia the briefest of astonished looks and drew his blaster.

Page did the same with his rifle, but he hadn't even lifted it to firing position when it was whipped from his grip by one of the longest amphistaffs Leia had seen, and hurled through the air like a twig. Sasso was already charging the enemy wielding the amphistaff, but he didn't get three meters when the warrior leapt over him and, on landing, whirled and thrust a coufee deep into the Rodian's back.

Kyp and Leia ignited their lightsabers at the same instant. Continuous fire from Han and Wraw had driven two of the warriors to the ground, but neither had been hit. Kyp raced for the nearest one, catching the warrior across the chest with a powerful upswing of his blade. The Yuuzhan Vong growled and rolled, but his dark, unarmored flesh showed only a shallow bloodless furrow.

Kyp whirled and brought the blade down like an ax. Evading the strike, the warrior rose to one knee and unfurled his amphistaff. The serpentlike creature elongated and wrapped itself around the hilt of the lightsaber. But Kyp wasn't about to surrender his weapon. In a virtual tug-of-war with the creature, he spun and backflipped, but to little effect. At the same time, a second amphistaff lassoed him around the waist and arms and yanked him roughly to the ground.

Han put three bolts into the second warrior, driving him two steps backward with each, but without killing him or persuading the amphistaff to loosen its constricting hold on Kyp. Han yelled for Wraw's help, but in a glance saw that the Bothan was trying desperately to keep the other pair of warriors from grabbing Page.

Without really thinking about it, Leia judged that Han and

Kyp were in greater jeopardy. Holding her blade at her right hip and pointed slightly downward, she moved against the warrior whose amphistaff was flinging Kyp from side to side.

Han felt rather than saw Leia race past him.

"Leia!" he screamed, firing constantly while he rushed to catch up with her.

A quartet of bolts holed the warrior Leia had targeted. But at once, the other warrior commanded his amphistaff to withdraw from the pommel of Kyp's lightsaber and fly toward Leia.

Seeing what was coming, Han dived forward in a frantic attempt to place himself between Leia and the attenuating weapon. Leia watched in horror as the amphistaff struck Han solidly in the neck—and not merely with its rounded head.

The jaws of the living weapon gaped, and it sank two long fangs into Han's flesh.

Han landed hard on his side, but quickly got to his knees. He managed to squeeze off three more bolts before the blaster slipped from his trembling hand. He slumped backward on his heels in shock, then tipped to one side, his body curling inward, with his shaking hands close to his chest.

Kyp raced forward, only to be set upon by three of the warriors.

Leia's mouth fell open in a silent scream. She dropped the lightsaber and ran to Han. Gazing in horror at the twin punctures in his neck, she vised his spasming right hand between hers.

"Han," she cried. "Han!"

Meloque was suddenly by her side, lifting Han's head from the ground. His face was a bloodless mask of pain and sorrow.

"I k-knew from the s-s-start this wasn't my war," he stammered. Twin rivulets of blood coursed from the wounds in his neck.

"Han!" Leia said, wide-eyed with terror.

She looked up at the advancing warriors, two of whom had a tight hold on Kyp, almost as if expecting them to come to Han's aid. Instead one of them dragged her and Meloque to their feet.

"No, no," Leia said, shaking her head back and forth.

Han extended his hand to her, but the warrior kicked it aside. Han's eyes rolled up, his eyelids fluttered, and his body went limp.

"No!" she screamed as the warriors were hauling her away.

"Casualty assessment of the first engagement, Warmaster," Supreme Commander Loiric Kaan said, gesturing to a wall niche in the command chamber of *Yammka's Mount.*

Nas Choka turned from the observation transparency to study the commotion of blaze bugs. "Acceptable," he pronounced after a moment.

"A clever use of machines," Loiric Kaan remarked.

The warmaster's finely haired upper lip curled and he glowered at his Supreme Commander. "Another act of cowardice. Stop thinking in terms of the weapons our enemy employ, and concentrate on how they fight. Think of the machines as living beings if it will help you view the matter with more clarity."

Loiric Kaan bowed his head. "Warmaster."

Nas Choka moved to the blaze bug niche that displayed the disposition of the enemy battle groups.

"They seek to spare the new capital," Loiric Kaan said, "but they cannot save it now."

Nas Choka beckoned to one of his subalterns. "Escort Supreme Commander Loiric Kaan from the command chamber. If this war could be won by words of confidence, we would have already vanquished them."

The warmaster kept his back turned to Kaan while he was being led to the chamber's iris membrane.

"The number of ships is significantly lower than calculated," the chief tactician said when the membrane had resealed itself.

"Of course," Nas Choka said. "Trusting to the effectiveness of their deceptions, they decided to keep additional ships in reserve to execute their secondary objectives."

"Starfighter wings forming up for strikes," a subaltern reported.

Nas Choka sniffed. "Like a swarm of insects that can't be outdistanced or repelled. The pests can, however, be eradicated." He turned to the female stationed at the villip-choir.

"Order Domains Vang and Pekeen to spray the contaminated areas. Then command the yammosks to spruce up our formations with auxiliary coralskippers."

The warmaster and the chief tactician swung to the transparency to see brilliant plumes of plasma discharge omnidirectionally from the core. Dozens of the small fighters disappeared, and as many others were shocked into submission.

"Again," Nas Choka ordered.

A second torrent of molten death poured from the war vessels, obliterating yet more starfighters.

"Now, assign yorik-akaga and yorik-vec to the rear. Let mataloks serve as our spearhead."

The subaltern snapped his fists to his shoulders in salute.

"Warmaster," the villip-choir tactician interjected judiciously. "Communication from Supreme Overlord Shimrra."

Nas Choka turned to the array and genuflected in front of Shimrra's dedicated villip. Everyone else in the command chamber kneeled, with foreheads pressed to the deck.

"It bodes well, Dread Lord," Nas Choka began. "We will deliver victory to you this day, or die in the attempt."

"Better for you, Warmaster, that you die delivering victory."

"Understood, Lord."

Shimrra's villip spoke again. "You have my blessing, and the blessings of the gods. Yun-Yuuzhan and Yun-Yammka soar at your sides, as your right and left hands."

"I sense their presence, Great Lord."

"Does the enemy cower before us?"

"For the moment their fleet holds fast."

"Then they have mustered the courage to meet us toe to toe? It will be their downfall. You have my full confidence, Warmaster. I leave you to your business."

The dedicated villip inverted to its original leathery appearance. Nas Choka rose and paced to the transparency to observe the matched fury of coralskippers and starfighters, yorik-vec and Scimitar bombers.

"Sovv and Kre'fey are fighting with their minds, not their bodies," he said to the chief tactician. "They are the smaller individual who engages a larger one. Even if he is swift enough to get inside his opponent's defenses, his hands are too small to cause severe damage, and his muscles lack the power to bring his opponent to his knees. So he plans more carefully. Perhaps he goads the bigger warrior to swing first and miss, hoping then to unbalance him with a precisely timed shove or kick to the knee. Or perhaps he brings his equally small friends to stand at his back, and he strikes first, confident that his cohorts will be ready to find openings. He offers them as a distraction, so that when the larger warrior risks a glance to the right, a blow arrives from the left."

Nas Choka's expression hardened. "This battle is not the last stand. It has nothing to do with honor or a willingness to meet death. This is a feint. Fortunately, I have my suspicions about where the would-be surprise blow is coming from."

The tactician nodded knowingly.

Nas Choka turned to the villip-choir mistress. "Alert domain groups Shen'g, Paasar, Eklut, and Taav. On my command they will separate from the armada and prepare to go to darkspace."

She bowed. "To Toong'l and Caluula, and from there to Yuuzhan'tar."

Nas Choka sneered. "Play with your villips, Mistress. Leave strategy to those who live to fight." He summoned the chief tactician forward. "Command her, tactician."

"To the Perlemian Trade Route," the slight Yuuzhan Vong told the villip mistress, "and from there to Contruum!"

Leia was still in shock when the three surviving warriors led her, Kyp, Page, Wraw, and Meloque into the yammosk installation. Sasso and Ferfer had been left to die in the forest. Han they dragged behind by his wrists, like a slaughtered animal. He was alive but unconscious or comatose from the venom delivered by the warrior's amphistaff.

Even in her dread, however, Leia was not too oblivious to notice that only one weary guard was posted at the minshal's eastern dilating membrane, and that the membrane itself looked thin and weak, and oozed a viscous liquid. The guard struggled to rise as the trio of warriors approached. Barely strong enough to cross his arms in salute, he said something to them in a feeble voice.

"He's telling them that the commander is waiting," Page translated quietly.

One of the warriors stumbled a bit as they crossed the threshold into the gloomy interior of the minshal. Oddly, he was the only one of the three who hadn't been wounded during the brief action.

Kyp noticed the stumble as well. "Something's not right."

He received a hard jab in the ribs for speaking.

Inside, the smell of rot was overpowering. Pools of sallow liquid had collected on the spongy floor, and the bioluminescent wall lichen was rashed with black spots. Thousands of dying arachnidlike insects—similar to the ones Leia had seen in the living cofferdam—crawled about in seeming confusion.

Dead flitnats littered the ground. A female shaper was borne into the antechamber on a litter, carried by two more of the squat, dark-complected warriors. Her skin was as pale green as Leia's falsely colored face, and the many-fingered hand that had been grafted to her wrist hung limply at her side. The warriors shoved Leia and the others forward, and rolled Han onto his back nearby.

Leia's heart leapt when she saw him stir.

The shaper was addressing the warriors from atop her litter.

"She's congratulating them on capturing us," Meloque whispered to everyone. "She says we will contribute greatly to the sacrifice."

The shaper called two of the troops forward and spent a long moment looking them over, inspecting their faces, limbs, and torsos. One of the warriors indicated a tumorlike growth on his neck, and dropped to one knee at the foot of the litter, in what appeared to be humiliation.

"What's going on?" Kyp asked Meloque.

She listened for a moment. "The warrior thinks he has become a Shamed One, because his body is rejecting some sort of . . . enhancement he received." Meloque listened for a moment more, then added: "The shaper's telling him that he is not Shamed. That the growth of the tumor has nothing to do with the gods, and everything to do with this world—everything to do with Caluula."

"Caluula?" Page repeated in bafflement.

The warrior looked relieved. Rising, he drew his coufee and turned toward Leia, only to be restrained by the shaper's touch.

"He wants to kill us," Meloque explained.

"I got that much," Kyp said.

"She's reassuring them that we will die before sunset."

"That's a relief," Wraw said. "For a minute I thought they were going to let us go."

Kyp glanced at the Bothan. "Get out all your jokes while there's still time."

The shaper was speaking again. Leia recognized the word *Yuuzhan'tar*.

Meloque translated. "She's ordering the special warriors—the slayers, she calls them—to return her to Yuuz—to Coruscant immediately. She says it's imperative that she apprise her master of what has happened here to render everyone ill. She is promising the slayers that the commander is going to see to us personally."

"Yun-Harla succors me in my time of need," a male voice said in Basic.

The accent was familiar to Leia, and clearly to Page, who craned his neck to see who had spoken.

A tall, rail-thin Yuuzhan Vong elite entered the antechamber, his scarified arms draped in support around the shoulders of two large but plainly enervated warriors.

"Welcome, Jedi, Ho'Din, and Bothan. And to you, Captain Page. Did I not promise that I would see you on a funeral pyre?"

Leia suddenly recalled where she had seen him before—aboard the Yuuzhan Vong convoy vessel.

It was Commander Malik Carr.

TWENTY-FIVE

With the armada's rotation, the distal ends of several tentacles had whipped themselves into ensnaring loops. Starfighters trapped in the loops twisted and swerved to avoid scudding coralskippers, but they were fast running out of maneuvering room.

The overwhelmed deflector shields of Jaina's X-wing were barely viable, and Cappie was probably beyond repair. Each tongue of plasma or missile of molten rock landed like a punch. Despite the harnesses that fastened her to the padded seat, she was flung like an insect trapped in a shaking bottle. Singularities yawned to all sides, ready to swallow anything she launched, but that hardly mattered, since the starfighter's fire-control computer had yet to shed enough heat to come back on-line.

A numbing explosion jolted the ship.

Jaina glanced out the right side of the triangular canopy to see the mated ends of the starboard S-foils disintegrate, and the laser cannon go whirling off into space. The power of the blast sent the starfighter into a wing-over-wing roll that the fusial thrusters and attitude jets were unable to correct. Flights of coralskippers pinwheeled in front of her, and fireballs geysered inward on spiraling trajectories.

The out-of-control tumble reeled her out of a follow-up deluge of plasma from the core formation of capital ships. The E-wings took the brunt of it, along with Ijix Harona's Scimitar Squadron of highly vulnerable A-wings, and Gavin's Rogues. Caught by the inferno, two dozen craft were blown clear of the tentacles, half of them vanishing before they reached clear space. Farther out, Star Destroyers and attack cruisers raced alongside the armada, but with so many starfighters churning between them and the enemy war vessels, they couldn't risk firing without destroying countless Alliance craft.

Jaina's flailing right hand found the inertial compensator and dialed it to maximum. As the cockpit instruments came back into focus, she saw that the display screens were white with noise. The battle net was unadulterated static.

" . . . around to bearing . . . ecliptic . . ."

Jaina tweaked the comm controls to find a clearer frequency.

" . . . on squadron leaders and withdraw."

Withdraw, Jaina thought.

Fine for those pilots who could. But scores of fighters were incapacitated, many in worse shape than Twin Suns One. Only by virtue of their marginally intact shields were they bearing up under the constant barrage, like bar brawlers curled on the floor against repeated kicks from gangs of opponents.

"Dovin basal singularities have been diverted to the fore-front of the armada," Alliance control was saying. "Destroyers will be attacking the flanks in an attempt to induce the dovin basals to shift focus, so that *Harbinger, Guardian,* and *Viscount* can resume fire. All pilots, try to maintain formation on withdrawal. Rally at six-six-one ecliptic with battle groups Iceberg Three and Four."

By then the armada had moved well past the system's captured comet and was bearing toward Sep Elopor, a ringed gas-giant with more than thirty small moons.

Auxiliary battle groups in advance of the tentacled cluster were already beginning to disperse, in part to deflect the battle from Mon Calamari itself, but also to convey the impression that the Alliance had recognized that it was outmatched and was on the run, determined to save as many of its ships as possible.

A third surge of plasma spewed from the armada core.

Jaina called on the exhausted thrusters to propel the X-wing out of its tumble and through a broad bank. At the same time, she reset the inertial compensator and got her bearings. She was still inside the kill circle of coralskippers and pickets, but Chiss clawcraft and Y-wings were hammering away at the slowly contracting perimeter, creating exit holes for the trapped starfighters. Jaina saw Jag's clawcraft destroy three coralskippers in a blur of corkscrewing maneuvers and laser-fire.

She sent him silent gratitude.

With firing zones opening once more, bombers followed the rescued starfighters into the gaps they fashioned. In response, coralskippers were commanding their dovin basals to deploy defensive voids to counter the infiltration. No sooner did the gravitic anomalies shift, however, than *Harbinger* and *Guardian* strobed salvos of ranged-weapons fire against the least defended of the tentacles. Coralskippers were lanced and vaporized, pickets fractured and cracked open like seedpods, expressing puffs of atmosphere and more.

Free of the enclosing tentacle at last, Jaina searched for the rest of her squadron. Twin Suns Four, Five, Six, Nine, and Ten were nearby, but she had no means of communicating with them. She reached out with the Force for Lowbacca, Alema Rar, Octa Ramis, and the Wild Knights, hoping that they would be able to interpret her distress call and relay her message.

But it was Jag who arrived. Twin Suns' X-wings were suddenly forming up on Jag's clawcraft, and he in turn was leading them to her.

The fighting was the most intense at the perimeter of the fluttering tentacles. Alliance frigates and corvettes were trading fusillades with Yuuzhan Vong escort vessels and cruiser analogs—mataloks—opening dozens of new fronts along the flanks of the cluster. Starfighters and coralskippers pursued one another through blinding volleys of fire, as the capital ships continued their long-distance duels.

Even so, the armada managed to maintain its yammosk shape.

Then, without warning, three groups of enemy war vessels peeled away from the core, carrying countless coralskipper tentacles with them.

It was as if the yammosk had undergone mitosis.

Jaina considered briefly that the Yuuzhan Vong had decided to divide the battle into separate arenas. Instead, the coralskippers of the newly created flotilla began to return to the waiting arms of their carriers, in a kind of reverse deployment.

"Three battle groups have detached from the main cluster," Alliance control reported over the battle channel. "Coralskippers are withdrawing. Monitoring the new cluster for possible microjump to Mon Calamari. Primary planetary defense is at Code Red, with all shields raised. Iceberg Three attack squadrons will regroup and stand by for jump coordinates."

Jaina watched the smaller of the two clusters streak sunward and disappear.

"Enemy secondary has jumped. Waiting for verification of hyperspace vector . . ."

Jaina's breath caught in her throat. If the new cluster jumped directly to Mon Calamari—

"Iceberg Three attack squadrons are re-formed and in position . . ."

Jaina waited in her crippled ship. Time seemed to drag out, even while the battle continued to rage around her.

Then the voice of control returned: "Vector confirmed. Secondary flotilla has jumped for the Perlemian Trade Route. HoloNet transceiver ships at Quermia transit point are under attack. Primary flotilla is accelerating for Sep Elopon and Mon Eron. All starfighter wings regroup."

Out of the fight, Jaina pivoted the X-wing to starboard in an effort to observe the re-formation of the scattered squadrons. Twin Suns survivors were flying with Rogue Squadron, and Blackmoon and Scimitar were similarly mingled. Vanguard was down to six clawcraft, but Jag was still leading them.

She sent him luck as the fighter wing streaked off to reengage.

Then she coaxed what life she could from the damaged fusial engines and crippled shields and followed him.

Under guard of six warriors who could barely stay on their feet, Team Meloque, including Han, had been herded into the yammosk chamber and left there to marinate in blorash jelly while the female shaper and the cadre of slayers departed Caluula. From deeper inside the minshal had come the sounds of at least three craft lifting out of their berthing spaces.

An hour had passed since then, and something strange was beginning to happen to the blorash jelly. Though it had held everyone fast when they had first been thrown into it, the jelly was losing viscosity. When it liquefied to the point that Leia could sit upright, she immediately started to crawl on hands and knees toward Han, who had been returning slowly to consciousness the whole while.

The first words out of his mouth were "What stinks?"

Leia ignored the question and clamped her arms around his chest, hugging him to her.

He blinked, stretched his eyelids open, blinked some more, and began to glance around. "You're getting blorash all over us."

Leia put her face close to his. "Just my way of making sure we stay together—no matter what else happens."

"Welcome back to the fun," Page yelled from across the chamber.

Han raised his right hand in a curt wave to the captain, Kyp, Wraw, and Meloque, who were more or less sitting up in the adhesive pool. He cut his eyes back to Leia. "You want to tell me about the *what else* part?"

"Commander Malik Carr plans to sacrifice us to the yam-mosk."

Han looked past Leia to the circular yorik coral basin that housed the creature, then beetled his eyebrows in uncertainty. "Malik Carr . . ."

"From the Peace Brigade convoy," Leia said. "The one who promised Judder that . . . well, that something like this would happen."

Han grimaced. "Could be worse. I mean, at least we're away from those blasted flitnats."

Leia shook her head at him in a tolerant manner. "It doesn't take you long to get back into character, does it?"

"Hey, I know this role by heart." He smiled weakly, then grew serious. "But tell me something. How come I'm supposed to be dead, and instead all I've got is numb lips, a sore throat, and a headache?"

"We're not sure. But the reason has something to do with Caluula."

"They picked the wrong planet to occupy," Wraw said, moving toward them. His fur rippled in a kind of delight.

"Everything's sick," Leia went on. "Not just the winged-stars. Everything here—the warriors, the dilating membranes, even the slayers' amphistaffs—which means that their venom is probably also weakened."

"Slayers?"

"The enhanced warriors."

Han nodded. "No wonder they were able to take us like they did." His eyes snapped open, as if he had just recalled something. "Sasso. Ferfer."

"Dead," Leia said, almost swallowing the word.

Han hung his head, then stiffened in her embrace. "Where are our weapons?"

Leia stretched out her arm. "There."

Han followed her forefinger to where the weapons had been dumped in a heap on the far side of the chamber, close to where half a dozen Yuuzhan Vong guards were either dozing or passed out. Every weapon, including the two light-sabers, was smeared with red blood, perhaps fresh from Sasso and Ferfer.

"If this blorash keeps liquefying at the same rate," Leia said, "we should be free in no time."

She barely got the sentence out when Malik Carr shuffled into the chamber, accompanied by two ordinary warriors and a priest. The six sleeping warriors woke up and attempted to come to attention, but most of them were too weak to stand, let alone snap their fists in salute.

Their amphistaffs sprawled sluggishly beside them.

"Stay where you are," Carr commanded, as the pair of warriors who braced him lowered him to a shallow step that encircled the yammosk basin. Seeming to sense the commander, the yammosk itself stirred, extending two tentacles over the rim of the basin and resting the tips on Carr's horned shoulders. The tentacles were a sickly shade of green and covered with large blisters. Carr caressed one of them.

Breathing laboriously, the priest picked up one of the military blasters and handed it to Carr, who, with some effort, squeezed off a bolt into the domed ceiling.

"Still functioning—as you appear to be," he said in Basic, gazing at his captives. His filmed eyes focused on Page. "And I thought Selvaris a terrible place. You've no obligation to tell me, Captain, but what is it that is peculiar to this cursed world that has brought illness and death on us?"

Page shook his head in ignorance. "Maybe the insects we call winged-stars. But a lot of the ones we saw were also dead or dying. So are Caluula's flitnats."

"Something about their deaths, then," Carr mused. "If it's true, Captain, then you will have a powerful weapon to use against us. Although I heard rumor of one such weapon that affected our warriors on Garqi."

"Pollen," Wraw answered for Page. "The product of a semisentient tree from a world you destroyed. Ithor."

Carr struggled to make sense of it. "Is there some relationship between those trees and the winged-star insects?"

"No," Meloque said.

Carr inhaled raggedly. "I'm dying," he said in disbelief. "Neither in battle nor honorably, but of *disease*. Life turned against other life. It is something unknown to us, because we are symbiotic with all life—our biots, our weapons, our foodstuffs . . . We don't die of disease, or of starvation. Many of us live three times as long as the human species in this galaxy, and yet we have been felled by another living thing."

He almost grinned. "Yun-Harla is either laughing or outraged. Who can tell anymore? I suppose I should take some measure of comfort in the fact that I will see all of you die first, but somehow the fight has gone out of me. You are infidels, yes. You are ignorant and primitive, and you have chosen to consort with machines, as if they were living beings. But though I pity you for that, I no longer hate you for it. However, you do need to die, if only on the off chance that your sacrifices will persuade the gods to spare the life of our war coordinator."

He turned slightly and lifted his gaze, as if to the yammosk. "Are you even capable of directing a flight of coralskippers? I think not, poor creature. But I know that, like me, you will die trying."

The priest groaned in pain, doubled over, and collapsed on the floor. The six guards also appeared to have died. Thud bugs crept from the warriors' bandoliers and expired.

Leia realized that the blorash had lost all its binding qualities. The entire place seemed to be dying at the same time.

The yammosk issued an earsplitting screech of agony. Its tentacles flailed for several seconds; then the bloated beast bobbed lifelessly to the surface of the agitated pool.

Malik Carr hauled himself to his feet and lifted one of the amphistaffs, which hung over his hand like a length of rope. "As docile as a mascot." He looked at Page. "You have won the day, Captain. I salute you."

The commander toppled like a tree.

Page lifted himself from the jelly and hurried over to him. Kyp and Meloque clambered onto the step to regard the yammosk.

"It's dead," Meloque pronounced.

A sudden commotion broke out in the antechamber. Kyp and Leia called their lightsabers to them, activating the blades while Page and Wraw hastened for the blasters.

"Hello?" a voice called out.

Into the basin room walked Lando Calrissian, Talon Karrde, and Shada D'ukal, wearing armorply combat suits, white helmets, and knee-high boots, and armed with lightweight blaster rifles. Lando's bipedal YVH 1-1A droid brought up the rear.

The Hero of Taanab brought his fingertips to his brow in an informal salute. "Kyp. Captain Page." He flashed his bright, trademark smile at Meloque. "Sorry, I haven't had the pleasure."

"Meloque," she told him.

"Agent Wraw," the Bothan said curtly, clearly vexed by the trio's sudden appearance.

Leia stared at them in astonishment. "What in the galaxy . . ."

"Leia, so good to see you," Lando said. "We just wanted to show that the Smugglers' Alliance has more to offer than hunter-killer mouse droids. Booster, Mirax, and Crev Bombassa send their regards."

"*Errant Venture* is here?" she said, referring to Booster Terrik's personal Star Destroyer.

Karrde nodded. "We came prepared to fight a war."

"What's the situation upside?" Page asked.

"Peaceful. We only had to deal with a small skip carrier and a couple of patrol craft."

"Patrol craft?" Page said. "Caluula was supposed to be a major staging area for Mon Calamari."

Lando nodded. "That's what we thought." He glanced at Han. "Booster's not too happy having expended so much fuel on a mission *Wild Karrde* could have handled. In fact, we would have been here sooner, if we hadn't ended up in a fire-fight with the Peace Brigaders at the spaceport."

"The Brigaders are all right? Healthy?" Meloque asked.

"Healthy enough to have delayed us," Karrde said. "Momentarily, that is."

Leia showed Han a skeptical look. "You knew about this."

He shrugged. "I didn't trust this whole operation from the start. I figured we'd been compromised somehow, so I wanted to make sure we had backup. Sorry I didn't tell you."

"That's against orders, Solo," Wraw said harshly.

"So bring me up on charges when we get back to Mon Calamari."

"Don't think I won't try."

Lando glanced from the Bothan to Han. "Has it been this way from the start?"

"Pretty much."

Lando watched Han struggle to his feet. "Are you all right, Han?"

"He was bitten by an amphistaff whose venom wasn't working," Kyp said.

Lando glanced at Malik Carr, the priest, and the warriors. "We've seen this everywhere we've been—at the spaceport, in the streets . . . What's going on?"

Page gestured to the Yuuzhan Vong. "They caught something. And not just the warriors. The yammosk, the weapons—"

"Oh, no," Kyp interrupted in a tone of tragic realization. "Oh, no." Blood rushed from his face, and his expression turned grim. "I know what happened here. I probably knew from the moment we saw the crashed coralskipper, but I didn't want to believe it." He looked at everyone. "And may the Force help all of us if I'm right."

TWENTY-SIX

Everyone was scrambling for shelter. From his perch on the rim of the abyss, Luke could see hundreds of Ferroans massed at the mouths of the tunnels below, the combined light of dozens of glow sticks creating halos around each entrance. Through Magister Jabitha, Sekot had issued the alert that the planet was preparing to make a final jump to hyperspace. Luke could feel Zonama shuddering as the core hyperdrives heated up. He could sense the tension and uncertainty in the boras, the seed-partners, the myriad creatures the vast tampasi supported.

He looked into the night sky. For no reason he could fathom, each jump seemed to have brought him closer to a familiarity that had nothing to do with star systems or planets. Even in the most remote realms of the Unknown Regions, his connection with the Force had never faltered. But with the previous jump he had begun to hear the whispers of his fellow Jedi, and their urgency told him that it was critical that he, Mara, and the others return. If the imminent jump didn't succeed, or if it should leave Zonama far from where Luke wanted the planet to emerge, then he would do as Mara had wished, and make use of *Jade Shadow*.

He felt Jacen approach from behind him, but didn't turn from the view.

"Something has happened," he said finally.

"I feel it, Uncle Luke," Jacen said. "The Jedi, our friends . . ."

"It's not only them. The danger is widespread."

Jacen came alongside him. A gust of wind tugged at the cowl of his robe. "Another Ithor? Another Barab One?"

"Not yet," Luke said. "But a new evil has been unleashed."

"By the Yuuzhan Vong?"

"By the dark side."

Jacen nodded. "Your real enemy."

Luke turned to him. "You should be thinking about your own course, Jacen, not mine."

Jacen exhaled with purpose. "I have no one but you to look to, to know which path I should take. Our courses are entangled."

"Then I guess I'd better listen to what you've decided about me."

Jacen took a moment to collect his thoughts. "From everything you've told me over the years about confronting your father and the Emperor, it has always seemed to me that neither of them was your real enemy. Each tried to entice you to join him. But they were never the source of your fear. You feared falling to the dark side."

Luke grinned faintly. "Is that all?" he said finally.

Jacen shook his head. "On Coruscant, at the ruins of the Jedi Temple, Vergere said that the Jedi had a shameful secret, and that secret was that there is no dark side. The Force is one. And since there are no separate sides, the Force can't take sides. Our notions of light and dark only reflect how little we know about the true nature of the Force. What we've chosen to call the dark side is simply the raw, unrestrained Force itself, which gives rise to life as easily as it brings death and destruction."

Luke listened closely. *Now I shall show you the true nature of the Force,* the Emperor had told him at Endor.

On Mon Calamari, Vergere had tried to lead him down the same path, by implying that Yoda and Obi-Wan were to blame for not telling him the truth about the dark side. As a result of their neglect, when Luke had cut off his father's hand in anger, he assumed he had had a close brush with the dark side. When he stood at the side of the cloned Emperor, he had truly felt the dark side. Ever since, he had come to equate anger with darkness itself, and he had passed that along to the Jedi he had tutored. But in fact, according to Vergere, Luke had been misguided by his own ego. She had maintained that, while darkness could remain in someone by invitation, it could just as easily be jettisoned by self-awareness. Once Luke accepted this, he would no longer have to fear being seduced by the dark side.

"You're suggesting that I've held myself back by not wanting to incorporate this raw power into my awareness of the Force," Luke said.

"Vergere received years of formal training in the Force," Jacen said. "The things she told me must have been common knowledge among the Jedi of the Old Republic."

"Vergere was corrupted by the years she spent living among the Yuuzhan Vong," Luke said evenly.

"Corrupted?"

"Maybe that's too strong a term. Let's say *strongly influenced.*"

"But she felt she hadn't been influenced by them."

"She can't be blamed. Each of us stands at a kind of midpoint, from which we're capable of seeing only so far in either direction. Our senses have been honed over countless millennia to allow us to navigate the intricacies of the physical world. But because of that, our senses blind us to the fact that we are much more than our bodies. We truly are beings of light, Jacen.

"The emphasis the Jedi have always placed on control operates the same way. Control blinds us to the more expansive nature of the Force. The Jedi of the Old Republic wanted only youngsters for this reason. Jedi needed to be raised in the light, and to come to see that light as unblemished, undivided. But you and I haven't had the luxury of that indoctrination. Our lives are a constant test of our will to exorcise any darkness that creeps in.

"In that sense, your instincts about me are correct, and so were Vergere's. The dark side has, in a sense, dominated my life. I've suspected for a long time that the fatigue I've sometimes experienced when drawing on the Force during combat owes to my fear of abusing the *raw power* you describe.

"It's true that the Force is unified; it is one energy, one power. But here's where I think you and Vergere are incorrect: the dark side is real, because evil actions are real. *Sentience* gave rise to the dark side. Does it exist in nature? No. Left to itself, nature maintains the balance. But we've changed that. We are a new order of consciousness that has an impact on all life. The Force now contains light and dark because of what thinking beings have brought to it. That's why balance has become something that must be *maintained*—because our actions have the power to tip the scales."

"As the Sith did," Jacen said.

"As the Sith did. The Emperor was perhaps the most self-assured person I have ever encountered, but he deliberately chose evil over good. And in the right climate, one individual, suitably driven and skilled, can tip the universe into darkness. For darkness has followers, especially where discontent, isolation, or fear hold sway. In such a climate enemies can be fashioned, imagined out of thin air, and suddenly all good is lost, all perspective vanishes, and illness takes hold."

Luke paused, then said, "Do you believe that you spoke with Vergere after her death at Ebaq Nine, or were you conversing with the Vergere who existed only in your thoughts and memory?"

Jacen thought for a moment. "I spoke with Vergere. I'm certain of it."

"Do you believe that I had a vision of Obi-Wan, Yoda, and my father after all three had died?"

"I've never had any reason to doubt you, Uncle."

"Then, from where was Vergere speaking?"

"Maybe she learned to tap into a power that was more all-embracing than the Living Force."

"The Unifying Force," Luke said. "That might explain it. In fact, all the years since the deaths of Obi-Wan, Yoda, and my father, I've felt as if the Jedi have been on a quest to recover the Force's power to glimpse the future, which is perhaps the nature of the Unifying Force. The search has not been unlike our search for Zonama Sekot. And there's a power here, in the air and the trees and everything else, that convinces me we've found our way to something even greater than what we were seeking."

"I feel that, too." Jacen looked at Luke. "I told Sekot about your plan."

Luke was surprised. "You spoke with Sekot in private?"

"In the form of Vergere, yes."

"And?"

"Sekot thinks it can be done. Sekot also asked to speak with Danni about yammosk jammers and decoy dovin basals."

Luke nodded in satisfaction. "That's good. But it's important to remember that battles are not always decided by warships or other weapons. The important battles are won in the Force." He gestured broadly to the abyss and the starfield. "All this will pass away, but the Force endures. We tap its power, and if we so choose, it moves us according to designs we will never be able to understand."

Abruptly, Luke turned around. Jacen followed his lead and saw Mara standing silently behind them.

"Unless you two are planning to ride out the next jump on the wing, I suggest you get to the shelters."

"We were just on our way," Luke said. "This could be the last peaceful stretch we'll know for a long while."

TWENTY-SEVEN

"Alpha Red," Kyp said, as if having trouble believing his own words.

He walked distractedly to the yammosk basin, his boots leaving prints in the liquefied blorash jelly. There, he gestured to the gruesome scene: Malik Carr, the priest, and eight warriors, bleeding from mouths, eyes, ears; amphistaffs, villips, and yammosk, dead; yorik coral bleached of color.

"Alpha Red."

Han and Leia traded questioning glances with each other and with Page. Lando, Talon, and Shada did the same.

"Is that some sort of curse I'm not familiar with?" Lando asked Kyp.

"You could say that." Kyp sat down on the basin's curved step. "Alpha Red is the name of a Yuuzhan Vong–specific poison developed by Chiss scientists and Dif Scaur's Intelligence gang. From what I know about it—and I don't know a lot—the starting point was bafforr tree pollen, and the bio-weapon just kept growing from there."

"Kyp, how do you even know *anything* about this?" Leia asked.

"A dubious privilege of being a member of Cal Omas's Advisory Council," he said. "The first batch—the trial batch—was refined about a year ago, and tested in secret. It might have been deployed full scale at the time, if not for two things: our victory at Ebaq Nine and Vergere."

"A Fosh Jedi of the Old Republic," Leia explained for the benefit of Page, Meloque, and some of the others. "Vergere lived as a spy among the Yuuzhan Vong for fifty years. She helped rescue our son Jacen at Myrkr, and died at Ebaq."

"A month or so before Ebaq," Kyp added, "Vergere stole

the sample batch of Alpha Red and destroyed it, or somehow transformed it into something harmless." He glanced at Leia, and she nodded for him to continue. "Alliance command ruled it an act of treason, but not much has been said about Alpha Red since then, in part because it's been rumored that Jacen had something to do with Vergere's escaping the military cordon set up at Kashyyyk. I thought the project had been scuttled. Obviously I've been kept out of the loop."

"This stuff doesn't only kill individual Yuuzhan Vong," Han said, looking around the chamber.

Kyp nodded. "You're right about that. It targets some genetic or cellular component that the Yuuzhan Vong share with *all* their biots—from the smallest right up to the largest. Even their war vessels."

"The crashed coralskipper," Leia said.

Han regarded Page with suspicion.

The captain raised his hands in innocence. "Han, I swear, this is the first I've heard of Alpha Red."

Han looked at tall Meloque, who shook her head.

"If I knew about Alpha Red, I'm certain I would have done what the Jedi did."

All heads turned to Wraw, whose head fur stirred. Then the Bothan Intelligence agent shrugged nonchalantly.

"Alliance command wanted field assurance that Alpha Red would work outside a laboratory setting. It's been used effectively on captives, but we couldn't be sure what would happen in an uncontrolled environment. When Intelligence learned that Caluula had been targeted by the Vong for occupation, it was chosen to be planet zero—step one in winning the war."

Meloque loosed a mournful sigh. "Extermination. More of the Bothan ar'krai."

His hands curled into claws, Han stormed across the chamber, but he made it only halfway to Wraw before Kyp wrapped his arms around him in restraint.

"That's why Caluula's governor promised a peaceful surrender," Han yelled. "Your people *let* the orbital station fall, just so you could launch this half-witted plan!"

"Take it easy, Solo," Wraw said. "If I'd been in on the

planning at that level, you think I'd be along on this little joyride? I'm here as an observer—nothing more."

"Nothing more?" Han struggled against Kyp's hold. The muscles in his neck stood out like cables. "This whole op has been nothing but a reconnaissance to see if Alpha Red had done the trick!"

"Not true," Wraw fired back. "Our mission was to destroy the yammosk, and now the thing's dead. Alliance had good reason to believe that the Vong were planning to use Caluula as a fallback point. I've no explanation as to why there aren't more war vessels in orbit."

Han relaxed, and Kyp let him go. "So if Alpha Red failed, then *we'd* be on hand to make sure the yammosk was killed."

Wraw shrugged again. "Director Scaur is big on redundancy. But, yes, he wanted to be confident that the yammosk would die one way or the other."

"You knew all along," Leia said to Wraw. "The patrol we ambushed, the crashed coralskipper . . ."

"I'll admit that I was encouraged by what I saw."

Han sneered. "You're no better than the Yuuzhan Vong."

Wraw's fur rippled again. "You said you wanted to teach me the ways of the world. Well, maybe it's you who needs the lesson. What we did here was necessary." He pointed toward the ceiling. "That shaper and her special warriors are going to take Alpha Red to Yuuzhan'tar, and from there it's going to spread to other occupied worlds up and down the invasion corridor. So instead of ranting at me, Solo, you should be taking heart. The Vong's day are numbered. The war is essentially *over*."

"You killed them," Meloque mumbled, then yanked herself from her musings in wide-eyed panic to glare at Wraw. "*You* killed the winged-stars!"

Wraw swallowed hard. "You don't know that."

She collapsed to her knees to the spongy floor, as if her legs had turned to gel. "Don't you realize what you've done—what you've unleashed? The effects of Alpha Red aren't confined to the Yuuzhan Vong! Your superiors want assurance? Tell them that Alpha Red has surpassed everyone's expectations, Agent Wraw. Sentient and nonsentient life is also susceptible. If those Yuuzhan Vong craft reach Coruscant, the entire galaxy could be at risk!"

"What craft?" Lando asked. "What's she talking about?"

"A couple of enemy vessels went up the well just before you arrived," Page said.

Karrde whipped his comlink from his belt and activated the call button. "Crev, are you receiving me?"

"Just barely, Talon," a deep male voice answered after several moments of static. "What's your status?"

"I'll tell you later, Crev. Right now, you've got to alert Booster's gunners to destroy every Yuuzhan Vong ship in the area."

Crev Bombossa laughed. "What'd you think we've been doing? Not that there's been a whole lot of targets."

"Thank the Force," Meloque said quietly.

"Only one ship got past us," Bombossa continued. "A corvette analog like nothing we've ever seen. Scaled, with three pairs of pincer-arm rock spitters and an uplifted stern."

Han looked at Leia. "The skips that chased us to Caluula. They must have been grown for the slayers."

Han's alarm was enough for Talon. His hand tightened on the comlink. "Crev, tell me you've still got that vessel in your sights!"

"Hang on, Talon."

Everyone fell silent, waiting through several more moments of static; then Crev's voice returned.

"Talon, sorry to report that the craft jumped to hyperspace before we could nail it."

Meloque put her face in her hands and began to sob.

Han worked his jaw in anger and dismay. "Our only hope is that the crew dies before that ship reverts to realspace."

On the bridge of the Bothan Assault Cruiser *Ralroost,* Admiral Kre'fey swiveled the command chair away from the observation bay to listen to an update from the comm officer. Local space was strewn with warships, but untroubled. Blue Mon Calamari turned calmly below.

"Elements of the Second and Third Fleets have repositioned to Mon Eron," the human officer said. "Grand Admiral

Pellaeon reports that *Right to Rule* is under way to complement defenses there. Also, two Hapan battle groups have arrived from Iceberg Three to reinforce Mon Calamari home
defense forces. We should have visual contact with them at
any moment, sir."

Kre'fey glanced out the observation bay. *Ralroost,* along
with the Star Destroyer *Rebel Dream* and the cruiser *Yald,*
had relocated to Mon Calamari's moon, in preparation for
meeting the advancing armada head-on. With the Yuuzhan
Vong moving toward Sep Elopor, the confrontation was hours
or perhaps days away, depending on Nas Choka's strategy.
But now the inhabited world of Mon Eron, fifth in the system, was in jeopardy. The system's fourth and third planets
were on the far side of the sun.

With the unexpected departure of almost half the enemy
armada, some semblance of parity had been established. But
with equivalence had come renewed ferocity, and, given the
mounting casualties, the Alliance was faring worse than it
had at the start of the battle. Scanners displayed the heavily
damaged frigates and pickets emptying their arsenals at the
Yuuzhan Vong, and starfighters with wings blown off adding
what they could to the fight. For every starfighter lost, three
or four coralskippers disappeared from the theater. But the
Yuuzhan Vong seemed to have a near-limitless supply of the
small craft, and as fast as a tentacle was decimated, it was re-
freshed by flights of skips avalanched from the dusky in-
nards of enemy carriers and brought into quick formation by
however many yammosks flew at the core.

"Do we have news on the secondary flotilla?" Kre'fey
asked.

"Not yet, sir. To the best of our knowledge, the flotilla is
still traveling Coreward along the Perlemian."

Sien Sovv, Commodore Brand, and other commanders
were still adjusting to the fact that the separated cluster had
departed by the same route the Yuuzhan Vong had taken to
reach Mon Calamari. It was obvious now that the Yuuzhan
Vong had no intention of using Toong'l or Caluula as fallback or staging positions.

Both planets had been diversions.

Kre'fey berated himself for not having realized that the Alliance had been deceived when the armada hadn't jumped directly to the Mon Calamari system. Warmaster Nas Choka simply wanted to clear the transit points of mines, so that on withdrawal the secondary flotilla could attack the transceiving ships with impunity.

But where was the flotilla bound now?

Surely Nas Choka couldn't have learned about Coruscant. Was it possible that he had learned of the Alpha Red experiment on Caluula?

No, Kre'fey told himself.

If the warmaster had had an inkling about Corsucant, why wouldn't he have left the secondary flotilla there, instead of bringing it halfway across the galaxy only to send it back home? More worrisome was the possibility that the warmaster had learned about Contruum. At the first indication of the flotilla's intent to jump, courier ships had been dispatched to the Mid Rim world, and alerts had been sent via transceiving ships strung between Mon Calamari and Kashyyyk, and Kashyyyk and the Hapes Cluster.

"Admiral, incoming communiqué from Kashyyyk relay," the human officer said, pressing his headphones tighter to his ears. "Sir, General Cracken and Commanders Farlander and Davip say that, with the whereabouts of the secondary flotilla unknown, the situation at Contruum has become unstable. Two Eriaduan task forces have already abandoned the fleet. The feeling among many of the other commanders is that everyone would be better living to fight another day, rather than risk jumping to Coruscant only to be trapped between the planetary defenses and the returning flotilla. With all due respect, Contruum command requests permission to move their fleet to Mon Calamari Extreme, and attack the armada from there."

"Negative," Kre'fey said, without having to think about it. Positioning his headset mike close to his mouth, he motioned for the communications officer to open an additional channel to Kashyyyk relay. "Until the secondary flotilla reverts from hyperspace, there's no telling what the plan is. Those ships could simply be lying in wait, hoping for you to show up here so they can place *you* between them and the armada.

But as for Coruscant, I agree with your assessment, and hereby advise that you scatter the fleet, on the off chance that Contruum is the flotilla's destination. Coruscant can wait for another day. It's Mon Calamari that's at stake now."

"Contruum command requests an update on the situation at Mon Calamari," a female voice at the other end of the transmission said.

"We're holding our own," Kre'fey said bluntly. "But I don't know for how much longer. We're still outnumbered, and the enemy is not falling for the usual tricks. It's as even a match as I've seen this entire war. The only difference is that Warmaster Nas Choka is prepared to battle to the last, where I am not—and he knows that. He would sooner lose every ship than return to Coruscant in disgrace. I, on the other hand, have to decide when it becomes more prudent to be careful than foolishly brave."

"Admiral," the female voice said a long moment later, "Commander Farlander says that he regrets that he is not there to help you make that decision."

Kre'fey grunted. "If it comes to opting for caution, we will adhere to our contingency plan to jump the fleets Rimward of Kubindi. We're a lot more familiar with the hyperlanes in the spiral arm than Nas Choka is."

The response was even longer in arriving.

"Should it come to that, Admiral, are the Yuuzhan Vong likely to press the attack against Mon Calamari in your absence?"

"There's simply no telling. We'll have to trust that their cell of spies on Mon Calamari reported that Alliance leadership has been evacuated, and that the planet is of no strategic value. Nas Choka doesn't strike me as someone who would kill an animal once it has showed its belly—which is essentially what we'll be doing. That he managed to chase us off will be sufficient reason for him to claim victory and retain his honor. It's what he hoped we would do from the start—retreat and be chased."

"Admiral!" the communications officer interrupted.

Following the officer's lead, Kre'fey swiveled to the long-distance scanner display—and couldn't believe his eyes.

The armada was tucking in its tentacles—recalling its legions of coralskippers, pickets, and frigates to their carriers.

"Enemy is preparing to jump to hyperspace," a Bothan officer said from his duty station on the port side of the elliptical bridge.

Kre'fey came half out of the command chair in expectancy. "Order all starfighter wings to withdraw from engagement," he shouted. "Home defense capital ships and Golan Defense Platforms will cease fire and divert all power to forward particle shields! Instruct General Antilles that *Mon Mothma* should join *Dauntless* at moon bright side."

"The armada has jumped to lightspeed," the Bothan updated. "Bearing . . . Coreward."

Kre'fey dropped back into the command chair as if he had gained fifty kilos. "I don't understand," he muttered, with equal measures of relief and agitation.

Even if Nas Choka knew about Coruscant or Contruum, Intelligence would have assured him that the secondary flotilla by itself included more than enough vessels to thwart an attack. And why jump now, with the battle at Mon Calamari continuing to turn in the Yuuzhan Vong's favor?

It could only be another deception.

He turned to the communications officer. "Send word to all warship and planet-based transceivers that the entire armada is now on the move. I want immediate reports on *any* reversions to realspace."

The communications officer hurried for the comm board.

Mystified, Kre'fey sat staring out into space.

What in the galaxy just happened?

TWENTY-EIGHT

With the armada engaged in a climactic battle at the distant world of Mon Calamari, there was little for the occupants of Yuuzhan'tar to do but await word of the outcome—even for a prefect who had already contributed some of his own blood to ensure victory and who wasn't inclined to fraternize with the commoners gathered in prayer at the various temples. Instead, Nom Anor had opted for an afternoon nap. But he had barely shut his eyes when his cushioned sleeping pallet began to shake, with such increasing force that it was bucking across the room when he was finally tipped from it and sent sprawling onto the floor.

Overhead, cracks and fissures were spreading across the domed ceiling and down into the walls. Yorik coral dust swirled in the light and rained down on the vurruk carpets, and from elsewhere in the prefectory came screams of pain and panic. A rumble built deep underground and rolled like a wave underfoot, sending objects near and far crashing.

Dodging an overturned sclipune—a chest of keepsakes—then a toppling lambent stand, Nom Anor crawled frantically for the ledgelike balcony that overlooked the Place of Hierarchy. Everything outside was in motion, shuddering and crumbling, and the quality of the afternoon light was changing, as if fading to twilight. Groups of workers were rushing from the portals of the structures that surrounded the quadrangle. In a deranged herd they ran, stumbling and staggering, for the tree-lined paths that wound through the public space.

Kneeling, Nom Anor shielded his eyes and gazed toward the sun. But it wasn't Yuuzhan'tar's primary that had everyone in a panic. It was the crescent of planet that took up an enormous portion of the lower sky. Even as he watched, the green arc thinned as it advanced visibly on the star. It was impossible to judge the planet's distance or true size, but it was twice as large as the shining orb it seemed intent on driving from the sky.

And it suddenly struck Nom Anor that the rainbow bridge had *vanished*!

Clasping his hands on the balcony balustrade, he hauled himself to his feet. Across the quadrangle the facade of a structure collapsed, burying hundreds of Yuuzhan Vong under jagged chunks of yorik coral. Then a harsh and terrible wind blew in, uprooting trees and toppling statues. The wind filled the air with so much grit that the permacrete bones of many a New Republic building and spacescraper were laid bare.

A roar raced through the sky, and a crevice split the ground, running diagonally through the quadrangle. Benches, shrubs, and a throng of hapless workers plummeted into the yawning opening. Swarms of sacbees liberated from their hives spiraled into the crazed sky. Thousands of birds were already on the wing—but not flying so much as being blown to wherever the howling wind was taking them and everything it had ripped from the surface.

Nom Anor planted his feet wide and stared into the sky while the gale tugged at his tunic and tore tears from his eyes.

Was this real, or a product of his feverish brain?

Below the balcony—in arrant defiance of the daytime curfew Shimrra had imposed on them—a band of Shamed Ones were down on their knees, raising their hideous faces and rail-thin arms in celebration of the newly arrived planet that was literally shaking Yuuzhan'tar to pieces.

Weakly, fatalistically, Nom Anor accepted the truth.

Zonama Sekot had not only returned to known space; it had made Yuuzhan'tar its destination and target!

An updraft carried the voices of the Shamed Ones to Nom Anor's ears: "The prophecy has come to pass! Our salvation is at hand!"

He hung his head in defeat. Everything he had predicted was coming true.

The balcony groaned and the front edge tipped downward.

Carefully, Nom Anor began to back toward his work chamber. He had just reached the threshold when someone threw a forearm lock on his throat, and he felt the point of a coufee press against his temple. His assailant dragged him backward into the room and whispered harshly in his right ear.

"Tell me what you know of this, or die this instant!"

Nom Anor recognized the voice of Drathul. "A weapon of the heretics," he rasped, his own hands tight on the high prefect's forearm.

The knife drew blood, sending a black trickle coursing down the yoke of Nom Anor's robe.

"You would insult me further by lying? We know you have the Supreme Overlord's ear on this and other matters!"

Drathul aimed his blade at the sky. Zonama Sekot was moving swiftly. Already its convex edge was nibbling at the sun. In moments the sun would be not merely eclipsed but entombed.

"We?" Nom Anor asked weakly.

"Those of us who would have preferred to heed Supreme Overlord Quoreal's admonitions, along with the wisdom of his priests who counseled against invading this cursed galaxy," Drathul said. "This is the living world discovered by Commander Krazhmir before the invasion. The same one recently rediscovered by Commander Ekh'm Val!"

"Then you know more than I," Nom Anor said, close to passing out.

"A portent of defeat!"

"Portents serve weak rulers and superstitious fools," Nom Anor said with his last remaining breath.

Abruptly, Drathul released his choke hold and spun Anor around. Grabbing a handful of Nom Anor's tunic, he pulled him close and pressed the coufee into the front of his throat.

The landquake had ended, but Nom Anor was hardly out of danger.

"Speak the truth, or lose your ability to speak!" Drathul's breath was foul with fright. "The heretics who bow in jubilation beneath this very perch while everyone else runs in panic . . . *They* know it is the living world—the primordial homeworld promised to them by the Prophet. Not this travesty we have created of Coruscant. Do you deny it?"

Nom Anor was beginning to tire of the prick of coufees. Shoon-mi's, months earlier; Kunra's, just weeks ago; and now Drathul's.

"It is a living world," he admitted, "but only that. Neither portent nor fulfilled prophecy. Merely another surprise in a war filled to overflowing with surprises." Pushing the coufee aside, he brought his right hand to his neck to staunch the flow of blood. "The living world whose return I tried to *prevent*," he added, glaring at his superior.

"*You* tried to prevent?"

Drathul's weapon arm dropped to his side. He gazed at Nom Anor in naked incredulity.

"On Shimrra's command," Nom Anor said through his clenched jaws. He grabbed at his green robe. "How else do you think I come to wear *this*? Through merit? Through domain privilege?" He spat on the floor. "Through acts of treachery and deceit!"

Drathul sank to the floor in weary confusion. The room was growing darker by the moment, as Zonama Sekot cast its immense shadow across the face of Yuuzhan'tar. Hailstones the size of ngdins were striking the balcony, bouncing into the room and skittering across the floor.

The high prefect looked up at Nom Anor. "What should I do?"

Nom Anor took a moment to languish in his small victory. "Pray to the gods, Drathul, that Zonama Sekot has come in peace."

The blank expression conveyed by the dedicated villip of Supreme Commander Saluup Fing belied the dread in his words.

"The planet appeared out of darkspace and hurtled into the Yuuzhan'tar system, Fearsome One. It nearly grazed the holy world, sundering the rainbow bridge and scattering the moons—the innermost of which nearly struck Yuuzhan'tar as it was outward bound. It is a catastrophe of epic proportions, Warmaster. As if engineered by the gods—"

"Enough, Commander!" Nas Choka said. "The vessels under your watch will remain where they are. None should attempt to move against the intruding planet."

"At your command, Warmaster."

"The armada will soon return, and I will decide then our best course of action."

The countenance of Saluup Fing smoothed out as the villip relaxed and inverted to its normal leathery aspect. Nas Choka paced from the choir of biots to his command bench, but found on arriving that he was too agitated to sit down.

He had ordered *Yammka's Mount* to revert from darkspace in the Mid Rim, so that he could receive a follow-up report from the Supreme Commander on the events that had transpired at Yuuzhan'tar some time earlier. The warmaster had ordered everyone but the chief tactician from *Yammka's Mount*'s command chamber, and Nas Choka turned to him now.

"There have been rumors," the tactician said carefully, "of a world capable of moving through darkspace."

"The world encountered by Commander Krazhmir's reconnaissance force, during the reign of Quoreal," Nas Choka said.

"Yes, Warmaster. I feared broaching the subject with you, because—"

Nas Choka silenced him with a motion of his hand.

He had been a mere commander at the time, but loyal to Domain Jamaane—Shimrra's domain—and one of a group of high-ranking warriors who had helped Shimrra wrest power from his predecessor, putting to death many of Quoreal's warriors and intendant supporters. Regardless, rumors of a living planet had persisted. It was rumored further that the planet, known as Zonama Sekot, not only had warded off Zho Krazhmir's forces, but also had been pronounced an omen of ill tidings by Quoreal's coven of high priests.

Knowing, however, that Quoreal feared the warrior caste, the commanders loyal to Shimrra saw the priests' pronouncement as a ruse—a subterfuge aimed at steering the worldship convoy away from the galaxy to which it had drifted, and thus avoid an invasion that would escalate the warrior caste. Quoreal had paid only lip service to the importance of sacrifice and war, without ever recognizing that the deterioration of Yuuzhan Vong society owed in large part to their absence. But Shimrra knew better. He understood that the warriors *needed* a war, lest they go on killing themselves, and, more important, that the Yuuzhan Vong needed a home.

All well and good. But now a living world had suddenly reappeared. Nas Choka was too much of a realist to give credence to the idea of the planet being an omen of defeat, but as a strategist he had to wonder: if it was the same world that had defended itself successfully against Zho Krazhmir, then Zonama Sekot had had an additional *fifty standard years* during which to become a weapon unlike any the Yuuzhan Vong had ever faced.

"Warmaster," the tactician said, "could this alleged living planet be nothing more than a fabrication of the Alliance—or, more accurately, the *Jeedai*?"

Nas Choka considered it. "I would hear more of this."

"Fearsome One, perhaps this world, this fabrication, is the secret strategy the Alliance was engineering while we readied the armada for the battle at Mon Calamari. All the rushing about, all the diversion observed at Contruum and Caluula and other worlds . . . Perhaps all that was executed in an attempt to divert our eye from what was being fabricated and prepared for launch?"

"Only a fool would reject the possibility out of hand, tactician," Nas Choka said. "But suppose for a moment that it is not a fabrication but an actual living world—the source of the rumors that have endured since before the invasion began."

The tactician frowned. "If that proves to be true, and if indeed the infidels have coaxed it to enter the war on their side, then they have perpetrated their greatest transgression yet."

Nas Choka nodded sullenly, then took a deep breath. "Whichever the case, the Alliance waited too long to spring this surprise. With our war vessels only two jumps from Yuuzhan'tar, and additional battle groups being recalled from Hutt space and other sectors, no intruder—living or fabricated—can prevail!"

PART THREE

A TIME TO EVERY PURPOSE

TWENTY-NINE

The *Millennium Falcon* meandered with design through a press of large and slowly tumbling asteroids. Just short of the outer edge of the field, the freighter slipped into the shadow of an enormous hunk of cratered rock, matching velocities with it so as to remain concealed.

No sooner had the *Falcon* returned to Mon Calamari from Caluula than Han and Leia had heard from Luke and Mara. With the HoloNet crippled, and Luke and Mara transmitting from *Jade Shadow,* the conversation had been garbled and brief. Han had summarized the events that had led to the ultimately bewildering battle at Mon Calamari, and Luke had as much as said that the Jedi search party had ridden Zonama Sekot back to known space. Despite the fact that the Yuuzhan Vong armada had returned to Coruscant, Luke had assured Han and Leia that it was safe for them to join the Jedi on the living planet, and that Vergere had been correct about Zonama Sekot's being the key to ending the war.

He promised to explain fully when they arrived.

Dismayed by what had unfolded on Caluula, Han and Leia had departed almost immediately for the Core, but not before both of them had been thoroughly examined by medical teams, and Leia had met with Alliance Chief of State Cal Omas, to acquaint him with the tragic truth about Alpha Red and what its deployment may have loosed on the galaxy. A fellow Alderaanian, Omas had been shaken by Leia's report, and had claimed that deployment of the biological agent had been a difficult decision, born of difficult times—one that might have saved countless lives.

The Yuuzhan Vong vessel that had evaded *Errant Venture*'s weapons at Caluula was still unaccounted for, and it was hoped—even by some members of the Alliance's militant factions—that the craft had died in hyperspace. Omas had given his word to Leia that the Alpha Red project would be terminated at once, but she feared that, with Dif Scaur continuing to helm the Intelligence division and the Bothans still crying for ar'krai, Omas might not be able to make good on his pledge again. At best the project would remain on hold until Alliance scientists could determine if Alpha Red had actually been responsible for the deaths of so many of Caluula's winged-stars and flitnats. If the bioweapon wasn't to blame, then Alpha Red would continue to hang over everyone's head, as if a sword suspended by a delicate thread.

That had been seven standard days ago.

With the Perlemian still under sway of the Yuuzhan Vong, Han and Leia had taken the long way to the Coruscant system, jumping the thoroughly repaired *Falcon* to Kashyyyk, Colla IV, and Commenor, then skirting the Corellian Trade Spine into the Core. At the same time, Sovv and Kre'fey had united the scattered Alliance fleets in the Mid Rim, at Contruum.

Alliance command hadn't known what to make of the reports that had eventually reached Mon Calamari by couriers of a *planet* that had streaked from hyperspace into the Core. With no actual recordings of the event, all Sovv, Kre'fey, and the rest had to go on were the statements of resistance fighters and smugglers, and a few grainy holos of a verdant world that hadn't been there days earlier, now orbiting in the Coruscant system. What mattered was that whatever it was that had nearly collided with Coruscant had drawn the Yuuzhan Vong armada back to the Core, along with the secondary cluster of vessels, which had turned up briefly at Contruum, only to make an abrupt departure—presumably upon learning of the newly arrived planet.

Not one of the top-ranking Alliance officers was willing to state publicly that a planet had transported itself to the Core from the far reaches of the galaxy. Privately, however, many professed a belief that the Jedi had put their heads together and collectively *moved* the planet—as they were rumored to have moved Imperial warships during an attack on Yavin 4 some twenty standard years earlier.

For days Kre'fey waited for the recalled armada to storm the mystery planet, but no attack had been launched. Resistance groups were reporting that the planet had fomented widespread fear and confusion on Yuuzhan'tar, not only among the Shamed Ones, but also among the priests and other elite. Whether or not that was the case, Warmaster Nas Choka had positioned the vessels of his mighty flotilla in broad cover of Yuuzhan'tar, apparently while Supreme Overlord Shimrra made up his mind about what to do.

A proximity alert sounded in the *Falcon*'s cockpit.

"Coming into visual range," Leia said.

Han began to edge the *Falcon* out from behind the asteroid. "Let's have another look at those charts."

Leia called a map to the display, showing Coruscant's system of planets, sunward from Revisse to the OboRin comet cluster. The coordinates Luke had sent placed Zonama Sekot on the ecliptic, in orbit between Coruscant's Rimward brethren, Muscave and Stentat, at approximately ninety degrees to Coruscant.

"Unless the navicomputer agrees with me about this being a crazy mission, we should be seeing it soon," Han said.

Leia pointed out the wraparound bay. "There."

Han sighted down her finger, far to starboard, to a gibbous green planet.

"Well, it's sure no moon."

"Or Death Star," Leia said.

With a squeaking of joints, C-3PO entered the cockpit. "Excuse me, Princess Leia and Captain Solo, but I wondered if I might view with my own photoreceptors our destination." He motioned behind him. "Mistress Cilghal would also like to see the living planet."

The Mon Calamari healer wasn't the only Jedi on board. Kenth Hamner, Waxarn Kel, Markre Medjev, and several others were in the forward compartment. Still other Jedi were due to arrive at Zonama Sekot aboard *Errant Venture*. Jaina, Kyp, Lowbacca, Alema Rar, and the Wild Knights had come by starfighter.

"We should probably let Luke know we're here," Han said.

Leia turned to the comm board.

"*Jade Shadow,* this is *Millennium Falcon,*" she said. "Just wanted to let you know that we're in the neighborhood."

Luke's voice issued from the cockpit annunciators. "Leia! Welcome to Zonama Sekot."

"Luke, Han here. I'm not imagining this, right? I mean, that's really a planet I'm seeing, and not the aftereffects of being bitten by an amphistaff?"

"Zonama Sekot is every bit as real as the *Falcon,* Han."

"It's beautiful," Leia said.

Luke laughed lightly. "I wish you could have seen it before all the hyperspace jumps we've been forced to make."

"You've got a lot of explaining to do," Han said. "How 'bout giving us some landing instructions?"

Luke fell briefly silent. "Han, I'm afraid you're going to have to leave the *Falcon* in synchronous orbit."

Han showed Leia a puzzled look and muted the mike. "The pollen must be affecting him." He reactivated the mike. "You're kidding, right?"

"I'm dead serious," Luke said. "Booster's going to have to do the same."

"Luke, a Star Destroyer I can understand," Han said. "But if this is about suitable landing platforms, I've parked the *Falcon* inside asteroids."

"It has nothing to do with that. Sekot refuses to allow warships on the surface."

"But we're a freighter!"

"Sorry, Han."

Han worked his jaw in annoyance. "I don't like it, but I'll do it if I have to. Who's this Sekot, anyway? The governor or something?"

"Sekot is the planetary consciousness."

Han blinked. "Say again, *Jade Shadow*? I thought I heard you say *planetary consciousness.*"

"Han, I told you I'll explain everything when you're planetside."

"Luke, in case Sekot hasn't noticed," Leia interjected, "the Yuuzhan Vong armada is so close we can practically touch it. They also have battle groups orbiting Muscave, Stentat, Improcco, and The Covey."

"Sekot has parried the Yuuzhan Vong before," Luke said.

"I'm guessing that Shimrra knows this. That's why the armada is staying put for the moment."

"It's been a while since they met," Han said. "Maybe the Vong have forgotten."

"Not as long as you think, Han. Besides, Zonama Sekot can go to lightspeed if it has to."

"Yeah, well, you'd better tell this Sekot to keep the hyperdrives idling, 'cause after what almost happened at Mon Calamari, I don't know that anything can stop the Yuuzhan Vong now." He fell silent briefly, then muttered: "Well, there is one thing—"

"We may know a way," Luke cut in.

Han blew out his breath. "I hope you're right, Luke. But how're we supposed to get planetside from stationary orbit? We can't just jam everyone into the escape pods."

"You won't have to. In fact, your transport should be visible to the *Falcon*'s scanners just about now."

Leia and Han watched the display screen. Shortly a vessel that might almost have been Yuuzhan Vong grown came into view. The ship's lobed, faintly luminescent hull was made up of six oval modules, smooth as skipping stones and seamlessly joined. Knife-sharp, the leading edges of the modules glowed with what appeared to be organiform circuitry.

Han whistled in amazement. "The waiting list for those things must be a kilometer long!"

"The pilot's name is Aken," Luke said. "Her ship will accept your cofferdam as soon as you're ready to extend it."

From the moment Leia stepped from the pulsing multicolored cabin of the Sekotan ship and beheld the sight of her son, her brother, her sister-in-law, and so many friends, some of whom she hadn't seen in almost a year, and all of whom were standing against a backdrop of incredibly tall and wondrous trees, her heart skipped a beat.

She felt like a child again.

Even from the air Zonama Sekot had appeared more fantastical than real; a world of red and green-leafed trees, shimmering aqua lakes, and cryptic mountain ranges. The wounds the planet had sustained through its several hyperspace jumps—its "Crossings"—were obvious and numerous, but they were surface blemishes, and couldn't impair the planet's aching beauty. This far from Coruscant's primary, Zonama Sekot should have been frozen, but Luke had explained that Sekot was keeping the planet warm from within.

Leia didn't know whom to embrace first. But since Han had captured Jacen in a wampa hug, she went straight to Luke and Mara, throwing an arm around each of them and tugging them to her.

"There were times I thought I'd never see you again," she said, her eyes closed in joyous relief.

No sooner had Leia let go of them than Jacen was in front of her, smiling enigmatically.

"Mom," he said.

For a moment Leia was too spellbound to move. She stared at Jacen as if he had manifested from a dream. He stepped into her open arms and allowed himself to be held for much longer than he ever had. Leia finally let him go, but only to arm's length. She stroked his cheek with her right hand.

"You look changed, Jacen—more than after your time on Coruscant."

"I am different," he said. "Zonama Sekot has matured me."

Leia turned through a slow circle, her gaze falling on Saba Sebatyne, Danni Quee, Tekli, Corran Horn, Tahiri Veila . . . All of them seemed to be reexperiencing their initial awe of the planet through the eyes of the newcomers.

"You all look so different," Leia said to her son. "Is it the months we've been apart, or is it something about this extraordinary place?"

"Sekot makes a lasting impression," he said ambiguously.

Leia repeated the name, as if trying it out on her tongue. "I keep hearing about Sekot. Will I get to meet Sekot in person?"

"I hope so."

"Jacen!"

Leia recognized Jaina's voice and stepped out of the way just in time to avoid being trampled.

Leia turned another slow circle, trying to commit every

scene of reunion to memory. There was bearded Corran, welcoming Mirax, along with his father-in-law, Booster Terrik. Elsewhere Cilghal and Tekli were conversing in the latter's native Chadra-Fan. Danni—her blond hair elaborately braided—was surrounded by Talon Karrde, Lando, Tendra Risant Calrissian, and several other members of the Smugglers' Alliance, who were celebrating with sips of Corellian brandy from a shiny flask. Saba and some of the Barabel Wild Knights—including Saba's son, Tesar—were having an animated conversation, as were C-3PO and R2-D2.

"What adventures *you've* had?" C-3PO was saying. "Let me tell you, Artoo, you haven't experienced anything until you've been inside—"

The astromech droid razzed, tootled, and whistled.

C-3PO straightened. "You did what? You're exaggerating. The entire planet? That's impossible. You need to have your circuits serviced."

R2-D2 chirred.

"I do *not* need to defrag myself. I am perfectly—"

Again, the diminutive droid beeped and zithered.

C-3PO bent his head to one side. "Did I understand you correctly? Did you actually say that it's good to see me? Why, Artoo, this world must have done something to you, as well!"

Yet by far the most arresting sight of all was the manner in which Kenth, Kyp, Lowbacca, Alema, Octa Ramis, and more than a dozen other Jedi were clustered around Luke, who now stood in the center of the circle his comrades had formed around him, some of them seated, some of them actually down on one knee, paying close attention to everything he was telling him, his every word about Zonama—the planet—and Sekot, the planet's animating consciousness . . .

He has become a true Master, Leia thought.

Momentarily overwhelmed by the emotions flooding through her, Leia began to move away from the transport landing platform, as if dazed. Han was suddenly beside her, his arm about her shoulders, leading her into a kind of glen.

"You okay?" he asked worriedly.

She took a steadying breath. "It's just so much to take in."

"I know." He gazed around. "Some place."

"Have you ever seen anything to compare to this?"

He took his lower lip between his teeth. "Well, there are some canyons on Luuq Two that are every bit as deep. Then there's Kismaano for cliffside dwellings. And, of course, Kashyyyk for trees . . ." His words trailed off as Leia began to weep. "Hey, hey. What's all this about? You should be happy about being here."

She wiped away tears with the back of her hand. "I am happy, Han. This place—it's the safe harbor I've been dreaming about for months now. But I'm *sad*—for so many things. For Anakin and Chewbacca, and Elegos. For my parents, my homeworld, so, so many friends . . ."

She cried softly against Han's shoulder, and when she looked up into his face, she saw tears in his eyes.

"I feel like we're coming to the end of a long voyage, Han, and I hate the fact that additional violence is the only thing that's going to get us there. It's like a final payment we have to make to conclude this thing, and to ensure that our children, and our children's children don't grow up with the threats we've been forced to face at every turn.

"I keep thinking that my father must have finally come to this point when he summoned the strength to save Luke from the Emperor. I know from her journal that my grandmother felt this way. And I have the strongest feeling that my mother must have also reached this stage—with war erupting all around her, her homeworld threatened . . . Is this what Jacen has been trying to tell us all along—that violence is *never* the answer, even if it seems the shortest and most direct path?"

Han shook his head. "I don't know, Leia. But I know I'd die to give him and Jaina a better life than the one we've had." He smiled lopsidedly. "Even though I wouldn't change a day of it, because of you."

Leia nodded. "I know. I know because I feel the same way, Han. But I can't bear the thought of anything happening to you. Especially after what I saw you go through on Caluula—"

"Come on," he said, lifting her chin. "Look who you're talking to."

She smiled faintly, and sniffed. "If bluster counts for anything, you'll outlive us all."

"Leia! Han!" Luke called out. "I want you to meet someone."

When they returned to the landing platform, Luke introduced them to some of Zonama Sekot's tall and pale-blue-complected indigenous residents—Ferroans—including a middle-aged woman he called Magister Jabitha.

"Sekot has agreed to fashion living ships for some of the Jedi," Jabitha told everyone gathered. "The process will require several days, but I promise you that it will be unlike anything any of you have ever experienced."

"Only three Jedi have ever gone through the process," Luke told Leia. "And only one of them ever piloted a Sekotan ship—Anakin Skywalker."

Our father! Leia realized.

Her astonishment and elation endured for only a moment before the sadness returned. Ships, she told herself. Then it was to be war, after all. She had persuaded herself that Luke had found some other way to end the conflict. But she should have known better. The dark side was strong, and right thinking alone wasn't enough to abolish it. She struggled to resign herself to what lay ahead.

For Luke, she forced a brave smile.

Her brother's expression promised even greater surprises to come. "There's someone else I want you to meet," he said for everyone to hear.

Turning to the Ferroans, he called one of them forward—a tall man, who lowered the hood of his cloak as he approached, revealing a face of tattoos and scars, a hint of nose, a sloping forehead . . .

Leia felt Han tense beside her.

"This is Harrar," Luke said. "A high priest of the Yuuzhan Vong. He, too, is going to help us end this war."

THIRTY

"Our redemption is at hand!" the Shamed One cried from the mound of yorik coral rubble that was her momentary pulpit. Her rapt audience of a hundred or so heretics was sitting at the base of the mound, either oblivious or indifferent to the danger they had placed themselves in by gathering in broad daylight, in the midst of the sacred precinct, no less.

"Yu'shaa urged us to watch the sky for signs, and that sign has appeared for one and all to see!" She spread her emaciated arms wide. "Gaze around you at what its coming wrought, and pray that Shimrra has taken its message to heart! The Shamed Ones have been granted a new home—and a more powerful one than Shimrra's. When the Prophet reappears to lead us to salvation, we will be *ready*!"

Seated atop the shaded litter Shimrra had sent to carry him to the Citadel, Nom Anor lowered his head by reflex, then resumed his upright posture. Though within earshot of the gathering, he was far enough removed not to have to worry about being identified, should Kunra or one of the other heretical leaders be lurking about. Besides, it would be only a matter of minutes before warriors arrived to disperse the crowd.

Despite the fact that Zonama Sekot had jumped into orbit between the system's sixth and seventh planets, aftershocks and tremors were continuing to rock Coruscant, and the living world remained visible as first to rise and brightest in the altered night sky. With one of Coruscant's moons whipped from orbit and the rainbow bridge collapsed, Shimrra's shapers were already positing that the celestial intruder would return to tug Coruscant gently away from its primary, reversing what dovin basals had done to raise the planet's surface temperature.

It was as if Zonama Sekot had proclaimed: *Look at what I am capable of doing, and* fear *my return!*

Eager to launch an attack on the newly arrived enemy, Warmaster Nas Choka's armada and other battle groups had returned to Coruscant, only to be leashed by Shimrra himself.

Coruscant, Nom Anor thought ruefully.

He had never been comfortable calling it Yuuzhan'tar—except, of course, when necessary. Shimrra's shapers might have fashioned a leafy ooglith cloaker for the planet, but scratch the surface and you found ferrocrete, transparisteel, kelsh, and meleenium—the foundations and skeletons of once-robust edifices and the corpses of thousands of droids. Now more than ever—what with the remains of buildings protruding through the vegetation like bones through flesh in a compound fracture, and with each tremor exposing a bit more.

Coruscant wasn't a living world like Zonama Sekot, but rather a kind of infidel worldship, shrouded in layers of technology, which—regardless of what anyone said—had a mind of its own. More, it was haunted by the members of the diverse species that had originally shaped it. And deep down, even deeper than the realms claimed by the heretics, machine systems were still operating. At night, if one listened closely, one could hear them coming on-line, moving about, humming and pinging like electronic ghosts . . . Even discounting what he figured Jacen Solo had done to the World Brain, Coruscant could never have truly belonged to the Yuuzhan Vong.

Many of the workers were beginning to grasp this. Nom Anor read it in the eyes of those he had passed on the littered journey from his residence. Distraught folk extricating trapped crèche members, searching in vain for keepsakes and valuables, offering blood sacrifices at the temples, hauling the dead to the maw luurs . . . Shimrra's Citadel and the huge hemisphere of coral that protected the World Brain had survived, but many secondary structures and hundreds of minshals, damuteks, and grashals had been toppled. Forests had been flattened, and intense electrical storms had ignited countless fires. In remote areas of the planet, lava gushed from what had once been leveled and tamed mountains.

Sgauru and Tu-Scart had been loosed on the sacred precinct to dismantle structures on the verge of collapse. Ndgins writhed about, sopping up blood. Everything standing had been adorned with flowers and ferns, in an effort to keep further destruction from being visited by the lowest and most feared in the pantheon of gods.

Most Yuuzhan Vong had little conception of what had happened. Except, of course, for the heretics, who had their own ideas, most of which had been inspired by Nom Anor himself.

"Brought into being by Yun-Shuno, in defiance of the other gods," the haggard Shamed One was saying, "the living world is a sign that the old order has come undone. And much like Yun-Shuno, we stand in defiance of Shimrra and the elite, demanding equality, freedom, and salvation!

"It is not our aim to engage the elite in contest. But we are prepared to revolt if they fail to prevail upon Shimrra to end the long war. Clearly the gods have switched sides, and now stand shoulder to shoulder with the *Jeedai* and the varied species of this galaxy. This galaxy Shimrra bade us invade; this *promised* galaxy he bade us purge and purify. In truth, this galaxy that will prove a maw luur for the Yuuzhan Vong, unless we embrace the truth!"

A professional dissembler, Nom Anor couldn't help but have a grudging respect for what the heretics were attempting to do by playing on the fears Zonama Sekot's unforeseen appearance had awakened in the elite. The secret supporters of Quoreal were adding fuel to the fire by disclosing information about Shimrra and how he had come to power.

Even so, Nom Anor had to wonder what the heretics expected to happen should the elite agree to ally with them. Perhaps they actually believed that Shimrra could be persuaded to make a peace overture to the Galactic Alliance, and that the Alliance would allow the Yuuzhan Vong to retain Coruscant for themselves, since the planet at least appeared to be beyond restoration. But the heretics weren't fools. Surely they realized that the warrior caste would never acquiesce. Nas Choka's forces would battle to the last war vessel and warrior.

Perhaps the heretics were counting on just that, if only to increase the chances of the other castes being spared. But spared for what? Eminent or Shamed, those Yuuzhan Vong who survived the war would be packed into what few worldships existed and returned to the void from which they had emerged, doomed to die in deep space, rather than on the living world they saw as the province of their nonexistent Yun-Shuno.

It was pathetic.

The heretics' only real hope was that Shimrra would turn Nas Choka loose, and that the Alliance—and Zonama Sekot—would be defeated. Once more the heretics would be forced to accept their lot as Shamed Ones, but at least they would be alive.

Nom Anor certainly felt that way.

You did whatever you had to do to survive.

The sound of running feet echoed from the tumbled walls, and a moment later several dozen warriors rushed onto the scene. Without preamble they moved against the gathering of heretics, launching thud bugs and lashing out with amphistaffs, sending a fortunate few scurrying back into the crevasses from which they had crawled, and leaving the paving stones spattered with blood.

Struck by no fewer than four amphistaffs, the female orator was dragged roughly from her perch to the base of the rubble mound, where ultimately she collapsed in a spasming heap.

Everyone was willing to be martyred now, Nom Anor thought as he signaled his litter bearers to hurry him on his way. Word had reached the prefectory that a few bands of heretics had even forged tenuous alliances with resistance fighters. It was the duty of the intendant caste to quell the riots and put the populace at rest, but with the heretics emboldened to turn every public space into a gathering, the task had become near impossible.

As had become Nom Anor's personal tasks.

Without doubt, Kunra was expecting him to return to lead the heretics in open revolt, just as Drathul was expecting him

to join the pro-Quoreal confederates in unmasking Shimrra.
The high prefect hinted that they were ready to enthrone a new
Supreme Overlord—assuming, of course, that Shimrra hadn't
already executed the handful of candidates. It was what Nom
Anor would have done. For absent a worthy replacement—
one who would find instant favor with the gods—the high
priests would be reluctant to remove Shimrra, regardless of
what was brought to light about the lies he had fostered.

The only question that mattered to Nom Anor was why he
had been summoned to the Citadel.

When the litter bearers had first arrived at his residence,
he was certain that Shimrra had ordered his death for failing
to have kept Zonama Sekot in the Unknown Regions. He had
briefly considered fleeing into the underground and taking
up the threadbare robes of the Prophet again. But the more
thought he gave the matter, the more confident he grew that
his safety was assured. Shimrra had never believed that the
living world wouldn't return at some point; its sudden appearance now was nothing more than bad timing.

More important, while Shimrra might very well be displeased, he was in no position to announce that he knew
about Zonama Sekot—not without risking an uprising by the
elite. Shimrra's best approach would be to deny any knowledge of the initial contact with the living planet fifty years
earlier. Failing that, he could claim to have been led astray by
priests he had since put to death. But one thing he couldn't
do was admit to having had an audience with Commander
Ekh'm Val, or of having put Val to death to keep the secret of
Zonama Sekot.

The solution would have been simple if Nom Anor had
been the only person who knew about Val. But, in fact, High
Prefect Drathul and perhaps dozens of others also knew
about the late commander's mission to the Unknown Regions. And if Nom Anor was wrong, and he actually was riding to his death, well, there were always ways to escape the
Citadel . . .

"I commanded the litter bearers to make haste, Dread
Lord," Nom Anor said, prostrate on the unyielding floor, "so
that I might serve you all the faster."

Nom Anor could feel the force of Shimrra's enhanced vision as the Supreme Overlord gazed down from the throne in his private chambers in the crown of the Citadel.

"Let us see how quick you can be, Prefect, by telling me why I sent for you."

"Because I have failed you again, Lord. About Ebaq Nine I was duped; at Zonama Sekot I evidently did less than I should have. The living world is here, and now Yuuzhan'tar itself is threatened. Death, and nothing less, is all I warrant."

"Probably so," Shimrra said. "But not because of the arrival of Zonama Sekot. For that, it is the gods who have failed me."

With his face pressed to the floor, Nom Anor's baffled expression was hidden from view. Although out of the corner of his eye, he could see Onimi, kneeling down as if to get a closer look at his face.

"The gods, Lord?"

Shimrra issued a short laugh. "You are unrivaled, Prefect. Even in this darkest hour your skepticism holds fast. You accept as truth only what your one eye shows you." He paused, then said, "You are hardly the coward many accuse you of being. And perhaps there is even a bit of wisdom in you— though I fear you do a disservice to yourself. Rise and look upon me."

Nom Anor took a quick glance around as he was getting to his feet. The room was absent priests, attendants, slayers, or courtesans.

It was just the three of them.

"I'm certain you remember that I told you our real war was with the gods."

"I remember, Lord."

"And I'm equally certain you dismissed my words as those of someone deranged."

"Never—"

Shimrra waved him silent. "I ask now that you consider all that has transpired these past few klekkets. As one whose own efforts have been undone time and again by the *Jeedai,* ask yourself if there is not the hand of a grand master at work here—a god's hand, if you will."

Recognizing the rhetorical nature of the question, Nom Anor said nothing.

"You and I know exactly what Zonama Sekot is. There is no denying the truth of it, and no denying the threat it represents to everything I have attempted to bring about in this galaxy. You told me that you had sabotaged the world, and I do not doubt that you tried. And yet it outwits us again."

Nom Anor waited.

"The gods deliberately saved it," Shimrra said. "They spared it your treachery, and they placed it in the hands of the *Jeedai*." He shook the Scepter of Power in anger. "This is an act of war on their part! Their salvo against those who would retire them and rule in their stead!"

Fortunately, Shimrra wasn't expecting a response, because Nom Anor was speechless.

"It follows then, that if we destroy Zonama Sekot once and for all, we will not only have defeated the *Jeedai,* but will have also vanquished the gods themselves!" Shimrra waved the formidable-looking amphistaff again. "To do that we must respond with a salvo of our own. If I can't divest the gods of their power over us, then I can at least attempt to turn them against one another!"

"How, Lord?" Nom Anor asked in complete befuddlement.

Shimrra glared at him. "I am granting you special powers as my envoy. High Prefect Drathul will hear this from my own lips. As my envoy, it will be your duty to inform the priests in all the temples that they are to cease performing rituals to Yun-Yuuzhan and Yun-Yammka, and instead to devote all their labors to venerating Yun-Harla."

"But the Trickster is believed by many of the priests to have already played a role in our setbacks," Nom Anor said. "In the Hapes Consortium and at Borleias . . . The *Jeedai* Jaina Solo even masqueraded as her, and outlived Tsavong Lah!"

"All the better, then," Shimrra replied calmly, "because already Yun-Harla's head swells with conceit. The gods are already jealous of her, and now we will give them something to get *angry* about. We will do to them precisely what they did to us during the voyage through the void—set them against one another. Then, while they are occupied fighting among themselves, while their attention is diverted from us, we will *strike* at Zonama Sekot and be finished with all of them!"

Nom Anor nodded, trying hard to keep uncertainty from the gesture. Onimi was regarding Shimrra with what might have been incredulity, but looked more like misgiving. For one brief instant Onimi's eyes met Nom Anor's, and that sense of apprehension was communicated. If it hadn't been obvious before, it was obvious now that Shimrra was beyond control—*deranged*. Events had conspired to make a believer out of one who had long prided himself on being the master of his own destiny.

Nom Anor had never experienced a sadder moment, and he knew suddenly that all was lost.

Kunra and Drathul were already breathing down his neck, and now Shimrra had added his breath to the mix. He would carry out Shimrra's ridiculous edict, even though there was little point in doing so. But he no longer trusted that Shimrra would come up with a final surprise to spring on the Alliance.

Nom Anor's only option was to return to the sensibility he had shucked at Zonama Sekot. He needed to think only of himself. Survival was in his own hands. He had come full circle to the very place he had found himself in after Ebaq 9. It was Nom Anor against everyone: Shimrra, Drathul, Kunra, the Jedi, Zonama Sekot, the universe.

His fight was with all of them, and yet with none of them. He wanted nothing more than simply to disappear.

THIRTY-ONE

With the Yuuzhan Vong armada re-grouped at Coruscant, *Errant Venture* was able to reach Contruum without incident. No sooner had the Star Destroyer reverted from hyperspace on the frontier of Contruum's dense system of inhabited worlds than Booster Terrik sought out Luke and Mara in the main docking bay, where *Jade Shadow* was already being prepped for launch.

"Alliance command has ordered us to hold at Contruum Six," the ample Corellian said as he approached the warming ship. "Guess the invitation you received doesn't extend to friends." Corran Horn's father-in-law, Terrik, had a ready smile and a pirate's glint in his rheumy eye.

"We can fix that," Luke started to say.

Booster waved in dismissal. "Don't bother. But after not being allowed to park on Zonama Sekot, I'm beginning to feel unwanted." He laughed affably to let them know he wasn't serious. "At least Lando managed to smuggle his brandy planetside."

The immense hold was stacked high with cargo containers of every conceivable shape and size. In the launching bays sat Lando and Tendra's *Lady Luck* and Talon's *Wild Karrde*, along with dozens of motley starfighters—everything from retrofitted Headhunters to uglies—the owners of which had attached themselves to the Smugglers' Alliance after the fall of Coruscant. Crev Bombassa, Talon, and Lando stood at the perimeter of *Jade Shadow*'s landing platform.

Mara walked to the open hatch, where Booster was extending his meaty hand to Luke. "Take care of yourself, Luke. And remember to put in a good word for us with Wedge. After coming this far, I'm not about to sit out the big one."

"We'll do what we can," Luke said. "But we've been away for almost a year. I'm not expecting an especially warm reception." He turned to Lando and the others and nodded his head good-bye.

Mara walked up the ramp and Luke followed her into the ship. Kenth, Cilghal, and Madurrin were in the forward cabin, strapping in, and R2-D2 was waiting in the cockpit. Mara dropped herself into the pilot's chair and without another word lifted *Jade Shadow* through the docking bay's magcon field.

The several battle groups that made up the Galactic Alliance fleet were arrayed around Contruum 6. A small, frosty planet with only two major cities, 6 was a microjump from the Perlemian Trade Route, and two from the Hydian Way. Mara hadn't seen so many warships gathered in one place for a long while, and the sight gave her pause, especially after the long months on Zonama Sekot. One small light moving among hundreds of others, *Jade Shadow* began to close on the white behemoth that was *Ralroost*.

"The Yuuzhan Vong have done the impossible," Luke said. "They've united the galaxy."

"Nothing like war to bring folks together," Mara said.

Everyone rose as Luke, Mara, and the other Jedi entered *Ralroost*'s war room.

"Wonderful to see you safe and sound," Admiral Traest Kre'fey said from his position of prominence at the head conference table.

"Good start," Mara whispered to Luke while Kre'fey and the rest resumed their seats.

He returned a subtle nod. "Let's hope it doesn't go downhill from here."

The conference tables formed a square, around which were gathered more than twenty Alliance commanders and strategists, including Admiral Sien Sovv, Commodore Brand, Generals Garm Bel Iblis, Airen Cracken, Wedge Antilles, and Keyan Farlander, Grand Admiral Gilad Pellaeon, and Queen Mother Tenel Ka. In a noisy holofield transmitted from an undisclosed location stood half-sized images of Cal Omas and several of his chief advisers, including Niuk Niuv, golden-furred Caamasi Releqy A'Kla, former judicial prosecutor Ta'laam Ranth, and Jedi Master Tresina Lobi.

Luke, Mara, and Kenth took seats along the side of the square reserved for them. Cilghal and towering Madurrin opted to stand. Luke had wanted to have Kyp accompany them, but he, Lowbacca, Corran, and many of the other Jedi Knights had remained on Zonama Sekot to begin the process of bonding with seed-partners—the embryos of Sekotan ships.

"Welcome back, Master Skywalker and Mara," Cal Omas said from the weak holofield. "I apologize for having to attend virtually, and also for the absence of Triebakk, who is on Kashyyyk just now."

"We understand," Luke said.

Kre'fey cleared his throat in a meaningful way. "Because time is of the essence, I will come straight to the point: preparations are under way to move the combined fleets to Corulag, as phase one of a planned assault on Coruscant."

"How soon will you launch?" Luke asked.

"Within seventy-two standard hours."

Luke glanced around the tables, his gaze lingering slightly, almost clandestinely, on Wedge, Tenel Ka, and Keyan Farlander. "All of you are in agreement on this?"

Kre'fey nodded, seemingly for everyone. "But that's not to say that we won't delay the countdown, or even rethink the operation if you can show good cause for our doing so. We didn't invite you here as a mere courtesy. The Jedi have played an instrumental role in this war from the start, and we have come to rely on your guidance, as well as your special strengths. I hope your months of . . . journeying have given you insight into some way of ending this war."

"They have," Luke said.

Sovv looked at him. "Just where *have* you been, Master Skywalker?"

"In the Unknown Regions, searching for Zonama Sekot."

"The planet you appear to have ushered into the Coruscant system," Brand said.

Luke turned to the human commodore. "I had no more to do with ushering Zonama Sekot into known space than I did with designing the planet's hyperspace engines. It came of its own volition."

"It?" Brand said.

"Zonama Sekot," Luke repeated.

Kre'fey and Brand swapped perplexed glances. "We're eager to hear your reaction to our plans," the Bothan said.

Luke nodded. "When I learned that you'd moved the combined fleets from Mon Calamari, I assumed that Coruscant was to be the target."

"Were we wrong to reposition?"

"No," Luke said emphatically. "With the HoloNet incapacitated, the closer we are to Coruscant, the better."

"Corulag is closer still," Sovv said in a leading way.

Luke firmed his lips. "Corulag is too close. By moving there we're certain to provoke a response from the Yuuzhan Vong."

Sullustan Niuk Niuv spoke to it. "The Yuuzhan Vong are going to want to finish what they began at Mon Calamari. Whether the flotilla repositions or holds fast, an enemy response is guaranteed."

Niuv had long been opposed to Jedi intervention in military matters. Some had interpreted his split from would-be Chief of State Pwoe after the Battle of Borleias as a hopeful sign, but, in fact, his presence on the Advisory Council was little more than an accommodation to lingering anti-Jedi sentiment.

"Not necessarily," Luke said. "The presence of Zonama Sekot has thrown Coruscant into turmoil. By now the so-called heretics are rising up, and the elite and the military are divided on what course of action they should take. The hyperspace jump was designed to bring this about. The fact that the timing was so fortunate—that Zonama Sekot's arrival drew the Yuuzhan Vong armada from Mon Calamari—convinces me that our actions were right. As a means of continuing what we've started, I hope to persuade you to allow the disorder on Coruscant to play out. If we do this, it's my belief that Shimrra will be brought down from within, and that we can then reach an accord with the Yuuzhan Vong warmaster."

Luke's statement unleashed a torrent of criticism and rebuke. With everyone speaking at once, Mara leaned in to whisper, "Welcome to the downhill stretch."

Luke's confidence in the heretics was not all it might have been, considering that the so-called Prophet was none other than Nom Anor. But given the galvanizing effect Zonama Sekot had had on the heretics, it was possible that the movement had taken on a life of its own.

"The reports we have received corroborate that Coruscant is in turmoil," Kre'fey allowed when most of the separate conversations had died down. "Which is precisely the reason to strike. The Yuuzhan Vong may never be this weak again. Yes, Shimrra stands a chance of being brought down by the heretics, but it's not Shimrra we're worried about. We're worried about the armada. We succeeded in inflicting damage at Mon Calamari, and unless we follow through now, we fear we'll lose what scant advantage we have."

"The armada isn't any weaker now than it was when Mon Calamari was attacked," Kenth said. "What damage we did has been offset by the arrival of Yuuzhan Vong battle groups from far-flung sectors. More important, Coruscant's planetary shields—the dovin basal gravitic fields—have yet to be tested, let alone stormed."

"We're not concerned about the orbital dovin basals," Sovv said in a dismissive way.

"Regardless, attacking Coruscant is not the solution," Luke added. "Under Shimrra's influence, the World Brain has the capacity to render the entire planet uninhabitable. So unless that's our aim, we must rethink our strategy."

"The matter of the World Brain was raised at earlier briefings," Sovv said succinctly. "With all due respect, Master Skywalker, that information has never been confirmed."

"We will also have the advantage of fighting in our home system," Brand said. "Our pilots will be able to fly circles around the Vong, lead them on chases, attack from Weerden, Thokos, Salliche . . . Thanks to what the Remnant has provided, we now know routes into and out of the Deep Core that the Vong haven't explored. Insertion points from Empress Teta; exit points up and down the Ag Circuit. What's more, we don't have to worry about inflicting secondary damage on the planetside population—not all of it, at any rate."

Kre'fey regarded Luke. "You must understand, if it were

any world other than Coruscant . . . But retaking Coruscant is fundamental to building and maintaining the Galactic Alliance. Who controls Coruscant controls the Core, and without the Core the Alliance is nothing."

Luke set his elbows on the table and interlocked his fingers. "You're thinking like the New Republic did."

"You were a member of the New Republic, Master Skywalker," Niuk Niuv's hologram said.

Luke nodded. "But this is a different war. A war that can't be won the way you're planning to win it. Would you annihilate every Yuuzhan Vong in order to free Coruscant and all other occupied worlds?"

"We might," Brand said.

"Was that the intent when Alpha Red was deployed?"

The question hung in the air for several moments before Sien Sovv spoke. "Alpha Red is not under discussion at this conference."

"Then it's not terminated?" Cilghal asked worriedly.

"I will say again that the project is not under discussion."

Kre'fey was quick to change the subject. "We have a window of opportunity that could seal itself at any moment. How long would the Jedi have us wait?"

Luke frowned. "It's not a matter of days or weeks. The Yuuzhan Vong have demonstrated time and again that they won't surrender. It's no more in their nature than a policy of extermination is in ours." He looked around. "Unless all of you have changed dramatically in my absence."

"Would you cede them Coruscant?" Airen Cracken asked.

"If I thought it would end the war, I might."

"That's a treasonous statement," Brand said, then softened his tone to add: "We've had our disagreements in the past. Can we trust the Jedi not to interfere with what we have to do?"

"We won't interfere."

Kre'fey shot Brand a warning look. "For the sake of argument, and in the spirit of good fellowship, what *would* you have us do while we're waiting for things to unravel on Coruscant?"

"Divide and redistribute the combined fleets," Kenth said. "Dispatch battle groups to Bothawui, Bilbringi, and other essential worlds. Reclaim those systems while the Yuuzhan Vong are preoccupied with the heretics. Then, when they are truly at their weakest, move against Coruscant from as many systems as possible."

Sovv made a fatigued sound. "Perhaps the Jedi are unaware that several Yuuzhan Vong battle groups have *not* heeded Nas Choka's orders to withdraw to the Core. Rather, they appear determined to hold on to the systems they've conquered, regardless of what happens at Coruscant."

"The dereliction of those commanders has nothing to do with maintaining superiority," Luke said. "They're afraid that they will be ordered to attack Zonama Sekot."

Kre'fey shook his head in confusion. "Why should they be afraid? Just what is this planet to them?"

Luke stood up, encouraging everyone to focus on him. "Everything the Yuuzhan Vong might have been." He paused, then added: "Fifty years ago, when the Yuuzhan Vong were first scouting our galaxy, they attempted to claim Zonama Sekot, and the planet fought them off. As a living world, it figures deeply in their religion, and its sudden reappearance is viewed as an omen of defeat—a sign from the gods that the invasion itself was a terrible mistake. In some respect, the Shamed Ones view the planet as important to their destiny— their liberation—and they will revolt if Shimrra sanctions an attack. But the real danger to Shimrra will come finally from his elite, some of whom are bound to see Zonama Sekot as a divine intervention."

Kre'fey stared at Luke in wonder. "How do you come by this knowledge?"

Luke turned to the admiral. "From the lips of a Yuuzhan Vong priest, who even now is on Zonama Sekot."

Brand narrowed his eyes in suspicion. "How do you know that this 'priest' isn't a spy?" He looked imploringly at Sovv. "If word of our operation gets back to this priest—"

"Zonama Sekot *knows* the Yuuzhan Vong," Luke insisted. "It knows how to deal with them. It is more like the original Yuuzhan'tar than Coruscant can ever be made to seem."

Kre'fey was clearly in a quandary. "You keep saying *it*. Are you referring to the planet itself?"

"Yes."

Sovv was beginning to lose patience. "If Zonama Sekot has some secret plan for ending the war—as either mediator or battle station—it had better act quickly. As things stand, I see no reason to alter our plans for moving against Corulag."

"There's no room for neutrality at this stage," Brand said. "You're part of the Alliance or you're against it."

Gilad Pellaeon broke a brief but uneasy silence.

"I've been reluctant to broach this. But Imperial records suggest that former Grand Moff Tarkin once expressed interest in Zonama Sekot, based on rumors that the planet was capable of producing *living* ships."

Sovv and the others watched Luke.

"Is that the planet's secret?" the Sullustan asked. "Is Zonama Sekot planning to wage its own war on the Yuuzhan Vong?"

"Zonama Sekot will not produce warships," Luke said flatly.

Kre'fey gave his head a mournful shake. "Master Skywalker, unless Zonama Sekot's governing body is at least willing to permit the planet to be employed as a staging area for the assault on Coruscant, it is of no use to us."

"The . . . governing body won't permit that."

"Then can we at least employ it as a diversion?" Brand asked. "If, as you say, it has already destabilized the Yuuzhan Vong, perhaps we can make it appear more of an actual threat. If the Vong can be induced to attack Zonama Sekot, we may have a clear shot at Coruscant."

Luke considered it. "It may be willing to do that."

Kre'fey put his hands flat on the table. "It's now or never. I'll grant that attacking Coruscant constitutes a perilous risk, but it's one we have to take. We can't afford to be placed on the defensive again. Scatter the fleets, and who knows how many additional systems might fall. We simply don't have the resources to jump from one to the other each time the enemy launches an attack. Attrition will become our enemy." He looked at Luke and the others. "I realize that the Yuuzhan Vong are still strong. But battles aren't always about numbers—as you well know, Master Skywalker, having turned the tide of the Civil War with a couple of well-placed proton torpedoes."

"I had help with that," Luke said.

"Are you suggesting that the Force isn't with us now?" Sovv asked.

"The Force is always with us, Admiral."

"Then we can rely on your help?" Kre'fey said.

Luke nodded and motioned to the Anx Jedi, Madurrin. "What Jedi we can spare will continue to serve on the bridges of our capital ships, as they did at Ebaq Nine and Mon Calamari." He was about to add more, when Tycho Celchu suddenly entered the war room.

Before Tycho so much as uttered a word, Luke caught Cilghal's sharp intake of breath.

"Please forgive the interruption, Admiral Sovv," the blue-eyed human general said in a low voice. "I regret to inform everyone that my wife, Winter, has just contacted me from Mon Calamari, with news that retired admiral Ackbar has died."

As she approached Zonama Sekot's landing platform, Jaina saw that Corran, Kyp, Tekli, Alema, and several of the other Jedi had gathered while she had been off searching for Jacen.

With five seed-partners apiece, Kyp and Saba had bonded with the highest number. Fist-sized, fuzzy white orbs, the seed-partners had attached themselves to Kyp's robe and Saba's tunic. Corran had four, while Kyle, Lowbacca, Alema, and the other candidates were hosting only two apiece.

Jabitha had said that Anakin Skywalker had bonded with nine—the highest number *anyone* had ever bonded with. The Magister had also explained that when the seed-partners eventually sloughed their shells they would be able to crawl about on four tiny legs, and issue shrieks and whimpers.

Thinking about it only increased Jaina's disappointment and confusion.

Zonama Sekot's air was still a comfortable temperature, though not as warm as it had been when she first arrived. Re-uniting with everyone had been wonderful, but after two local-days of swapping stories the inactivity was starting to get to her. She recalled having felt the same on Mon Calamari after her return from Hapes, while Luke had been occupied

matching wits with Vergere, Jacen had been off reef-diving
with Danni, and the members of the Smugglers' Alliance
had been busy rigging the election of Cal Omas.

With Coruscant a microjump sunward and a final confrontation with the Yuuzhan Vong looming on the horizon,
she wanted more than ever to be back in the cockpit of her
X-wing, if only to keep from losing her edge. But Twin Suns
One, along with the *Millennium Falcon,* Tesar Sabatyne's
skipray blastboat, and the other starfighters, remained in stationary orbit. That left only the Sekotan shuttle, which was
off-limits to her, and the planet's numerous airships, which
were more for sailors than fighter pilots.

She was considering her options, when Jacen stepped from
a dense growth of boras.

"I've been looking all over for you," she said. "Where
were you—practicing making yourself small or something?"

Jacen emerged from his trance or musings—or daydreams,
for all Jaina knew—and gazed at her. "The Force is strong
here. The usual methods don't work."

"That's for sure," she muttered.

Jacen watched her for a moment. "Are you angry about
something?"

She pressed her lips together and shook her head. "I guess
I'm just disappointed."

Jacen glanced at Kyp and the others and understood immediately. "Because none of the seed-partners bonded with
you."

"What else?" she snapped. "I mean, I'm as good a pilot as
Kyp, Saba, or Corran, and they bonded with seed-partners
right away. At Mon Calamari, I flew my X-wing into combat
with only one engine!"

"Piloting skills have little to do with the bonding process,"
Jacen said. "Or with courage, for that matter."

She forced a sigh. "Great. Then I guess I'm just not as attuned to the Force as they are."

"You know that isn't it." Jacen placed his hand on her
shoulder and turned her toward him. "It could be that Sekot
sees some other purpose for you."

She rolled her eyes. "Easy for you to say. You didn't even
try bonding with the seed-partners."

The idea appeared to amuse him. "I'm not anything close to a pilot."

"Yeah, well, neither am I. I'm just the official Sword of the Jedi—whatever that means." She fell silent for a moment, then said, "Jacen, do the Yuuzhan Vong pose a threat to the Force?"

He shook his head. "They're a threat to the Jedi, because they'd have all of us embrace their religion and their gods, and see the universe strictly as they see it. But no matter how the war is decided, individuals will continue to find their way to the Force. It's not a flame the Yuuzhan Vong can extinguish—any more than the Sith could."

"And you're still willing to fight to make sure that doesn't happen."

"In my own way. I've learned something about myself since Centerpoint."

"From Vergere, you mean."

"From Vergere, from Sekot, from all of you. I'm starting to think that the Force—at least as we understand it—is only one facet of a finely-cut gemstone, and that maybe the sum of it is even greater than its parts."

Jaina looked over at Kyp and the others. "At least Zonama Sekot is willing to fight alongside us."

"That will be Sekot's decision."

She turned to him. "Based on what? On whose interests the Jedi are serving?"

"We serve the Force," Jacen said. "None other."

"Is that justification enough for obliterating the Yuuzhan Vong?"

"No," he said, seemingly more firmly than he had intended. "They are not outside the Force. According to Sekot, they have been *stripped* of the Force."

"So I've heard," Jaina said. "But, then, what do you think the Force wants for the Yuuzhan Vong?"

Jacen smiled lightly. "If I knew, we'd have the answer to ending the war."

THIRTY-TWO

"Look at you—cowering like a herd of yanskacs!" the Supreme Overlord railed at the elite from his spike-backed throne in the Citadel's Hall of Confluence. "On the eve of victory you allow yourselves to be frightened by an illusion—a piece of celestial chicanery!"

Even while cringing with the rest of them, Nom Anor had to give Shimrra credit. Despite the tremors that continued to rock Yuuzhan'tar, and the dangerous innuendoes that threatened to undermine his divine right to rule, the Supreme Overlord refused to be intimidated—if not entirely unmoved. With his long arms jerking about and his legs quivering, he looked like a puppet in a shadow play. Some said that his implanted eyes, too, were rarely still, and were constantly shifting color.

Shimrra raised the Scepter of Power toward the hall's ribbed ceiling. "Some of you are whispering that the bright light that rises at sunset is an omen of doom—a living world rumored to have been encountered during the rule of my predecessor, whose name I will not deign to mention. *I* am not unacquainted with this rumor. Following my ascension to the throne I dispatched forces to search out this world—this Zonama Sekot—only to be informed that it was not to be found. So I asked myself: had it disappeared? Had Zonama Sekot been destroyed? Or was it nothing more than a lie perpetrated by my predecessor in an attempt to keep us from conquering and occupying what was by gods-given right our entitled domain?"

While Shimrra paused, Onimi circulated among the audience, baiting members of the elite to respond. Much to the displeasure of High Prefect Drathul, Nom Anor had con-

veyed Shimrra's orders to the priests of the temples, enjoin-
ing them to devote their attention to Yun-Harla rather than
Yun-Yuuzhan or Yun-Yammka. As a result, the royal seers
were beside themselves with apprehension—expecting deception and manipulation of the worst sort—and the elite
were wondering whether Shimrra's actions had been under-
taken for the benefit of the Yuuzhan Vong or for Shimrra
himself.

"I will reveal the truth of it," the Supreme Overlord said at
last. "The bright light is not a trick of the eye. It is in fact the
same living world!"

The audience was stunned into even more profound silence, especially Drathul and his coterie of Quoreal supporters. But the pronouncement was every bit as staggering to
Nom Anor.

Coming clean was the last thing he had expected Shimrra
to do.

"*How could the gods allow this?* you ask yourselves,"
Shimrra went on in a tone of theatrical melancholy. "*How,
after all we have done to provide them with sacrifices and
converts, after all we have done to cleanse this galaxy of infidels and heretics, could the gods turn on us?* Again, I will
supply the answer: this ill-omened world has been placed in
the hands of our enemy as a final test of our worthiness to
reign over them—a final test to gauge the strength of the Yuuzhan Vong heart!"

Shimrra pounded the floor with his amphistaff in a demand for silence.

"And yet what a daunting test they have set before us. A
weak-minded person—a dissenter or a skeptic—might be
tempted to believe that the gods have abandoned us, and that
there is no possible way for us to succeed. I have thought
long and hard about this. I have prayed, and I have ventured
beyond contemplation and entreaty to look deep into our history for answers. And the gods have rewarded my search."

Shimrra paused again, while a tremor rumbled the Citadel. Then he pointed the scepter to Qelah Kwaad and her
adepts.

"The shapers know what I'm referring to when I speak of
the eighth cortex. But for you commanders and intendants—

even for some of you priests—I will explain. A cortex contains the protocols for shapings—the protocols that originally guided the hands of our ancestors in creating dovin basals and villips, coralskippers and yammosks. It is not a place but a state of mind. And as one approaches the superlative cortex—the eighth cortex—one comes full circle to the beginnings of the Yuuzhan Vong, to our primordial state of being. And what I found there, after enduring much pain and letting much blood—so much blood that my body howled in torment—was the solution, cast in the form of a simple lesson, such as might be taught to our spawn in the crèches.

"The lesson is this: that when they fashioned the universe—and ultimately the Yuuzhan Vong—the gods dispensed with all inequities by ensuring that the qualities of one creation would always balance the qualities of another. Where a poisonous tree takes root, adjacent to it stands a tree that provides the antidote for the poison. Where there are deserts, there are oases of water. And where the waters are vast, there emerge islands of sand and stone. This is the way of the gods—ensuring balance at every turn. I held this thought in mind when, in the depths of the eighth cortex, I heard a voice utter . . ."

"The rainbow bridge will appear and disappear," Onimi recited from the center of the hall. *"And the gods will make it seem that they are the authors of a great conflict. When the eclipse of the sun will then be, the divine omen will be seen in plain sight. Quite otherwise will one interpret it, for when a menacing stranger appears at the portal, look close at hand for the amphistaff that will send the stranger on its way."*

"A revelation, I told myself." Shimrra took over. "Clearly from Yun-Harla. So I ordered the temple priests to beseech the goddess for help—to sacrifice to her, and to treat her as if she were Supreme Overlord of the universe. And our supplications have not gone unnoticed, for she has provided us with the solution to the test the gods have placed at our portal."

Nom Anor could barely keep his features from mirroring his inner state of confoundment. He wasn't the only person in the Hall of Confluence who knew that the eighth cortex was nothing more than a pretense—empty as the gravitic yield of a dovin basal. So what was Shimrra doing, conjuring revelations from nonexistent protocols? Obviously he had concocted the riddle and its resolution, but to what end?

Once more, the elite had to wait, while a more powerful quake shook the Citadel, causing yorik coral dust to rain from the vaulted ceiling, high overhead.

"The solution has only just been delivered to Yuuzhan'tar," Shimrra said. "Delivered in the form of a stricken space vessel and its crew of afflicted slayers and a dying shaper. On a remote and insignificant world known as Caluula, the vessel and its passengers fell prey to a virulent chemical agent created by our enemy and released in the hope of destroying all things Yuuzhan Vong—from myself down to the simplest of our creations.

"The chemical agent might have done just that, had it not been for the acuity of the shaper, the unconventional actions of his valorous crew of warriors, and the perceptiveness of your Supreme Overlord, who ordered that the vessel be kept from setting down on Yuuzhan'tar, or coming in contact with any other vessels.

"Now witness the beauty of cosmic balance at work! *Tchurokk Yun'tchilat!*—Witness the will of the gods! For this ill-omened world that lights our night sky, this living world encountered by our forces so many years ago, drifting at the very rim of this galaxy, must, too, have been fashioned by Yun-Yuuzhan and be linked to us in prophecy. Linked, and therefore *vulnerable* to the deadly contagion fashioned by our enemy, and sanctioned by the gods!"

Once more Shimrra gesticulated with the Scepter of Power. "The crippled vessel is the amphistaff we will hurl to drive the stranger from our gate! The ship that shall be our salvation, and our means of transcending the test the gods have seen fit to engineer!"

Nom Anor was beginning to feel like a gnullith: inflated by Shimrra one moment, only to be deflated the next. A toxic chemical agent capable of poisoning Zonama Sekot? Anyone familiar with Commander Zho Krazhmir's reconnaissance mission to the living world knew that Krazhmir had attempted and *failed* to poison Zonama Sekot. And if a Yuuzhan Vong–created toxin had failed, how could an enemy-produced toxin be expected to succeed? More important, if such a bioweapon existed, surely Nom Anor's former network of spies among the Peace Brigade, or those still in place on Mon Calamari, would have learned of it by now.

Had Shimrra concocted the story only to rally the warriors and priests, and ensure that the Yuuzhan Vong die in a blaze of glory? Or had Nom Anor underestimated the Supreme Overlord yet again? Was he even more brilliant than he had first seemed on usurping the throne?

"Zonama Sekot is a death star," Shimrra was saying. He aimed his amphistaff at Nas Choka and his Supreme Commanders "Fly to it, Warmaster! Take your mighty armada to Zonama Sekot, and make clear to the gods the unflinching resolve of the Yuuzhan Vong!"

What does the Force want for the Yuuzhan Vong?

The question echoed in Jacen's mind long after he had returned to the hollow that had become his haunt on Zonama Sekot.

He drew his lightsaber from his cloth belt, activated the green blade, and waved it through the brisk air. Unnerved by the thrumming sound, birds perched in the surrounding boras took to the pale blue sky.

Jacen stood with his feet parallel, right foot forward, carrying his weight on the balls of his feet, then springing off his rear foot in attack. On the slope of the hill, he spread his feet wider, and angled them to one another. He swung the blade without ducking or flinching, bobbing or weaving, assuming an ideal attitude as he glided forward in uninterrupted motion, or took short steps with each foot to maintain his focus and equilibrium.

He held the pommel at middle guard, slightly in front of his stomach, with the tip angled up at thirty degrees, and worked through several velocity and *dulon* sequences. Then, lowering the tip as if to point at an opponent's knees, he slashed diagonally upward. He raised the lightsaber over his head, handle pointed to his imaginary opponent's eyes—critically angled for a Yuuzhan Vong—and slashed downward. Elbows pointed to the ground, he held the lightsaber upright, over his right shoulder and alongside his head, then spun through a series of *jung* attacks and *jung ma* parries. Finally he held the lightsaber low on his right side, with the blade pointing at the ground behind him, and performed a sweeping upward diagonal. Front-flipping high into the air to the edge of the pool, he threw himself through Force-assisted rolls and full-circle whirls, shooting to his feet to execute rotating side strokes and short twisting wrist snaps until his breath came fast and sweat dripped from his face.

Sensing, then, that someone was watching him, he deactivated the blade in sudden self-consciousness. He sighed and sat down. He was a decent lightsaber master and *sai* acrobat, but nowhere near as skilled as Luke, Kyp, Mara, Corran—or Anakin.

His heart just wasn't in it.

As he stared at the hilt of his lightsaber, his thoughts began to spiral back three years, to the planet Duro, and the vision he had had returned to him, as if no time had passed.

One moment he was working alongside a group of Ryn refugees, and the next he was falling backward into a vacuum. Hearing Luke calling to him, he pivoted to see his uncle robed in pure white, half turned away, holding his shimmering lightsaber in a diagonal stance, hands at hip level, point high.

Jacen shouted that Jaina had been hurt, but Luke didn't respond to him. Luke's attention was fixed instead on a Yuuzhan Vong warrior in rust-brown armor, who was holding an amphistaff across his body and mirroring Luke's stance. Standing on the far side of the slowly spinning disk that held the three of them, the warrior wasn't visible through the Force. He was simply a void—a darkness that promised death, as surely as Luke's luminosity promised life.

The disk resolved into a spiral-armed galaxy.

Poised at the center, Luke dropped into a fighting stance, raising his lightsaber to his right shoulder, point upward, while Yuuzhan Vong warriors advanced from the darkness. Luke was steadfast, holding the center and counterweighing the invaders, until at last their numbers increased sufficiently to tip the balance of the disk in their direction.

Desperate to know what to do, Jacen called to Luke again.

This time Luke turned and tossed his lightsaber in a low humming arc, trailing pale green sparks onto the galactic plane. Anger welled up in Jacen, even as fear and fury focused his strength. He wanted to destroy the enemy. He stretched out his hand for the lightsaber . . . and missed.

That miss was all it took.

A dark, deadly tempest gathered around the invaders, and the galactic plane tipped more swiftly toward them.

Jacen felt himself begin to shrink until he was no more than a tiny, insignificant point in the dark tempest. Helpless, disarmed by a moment of anger, doomed by a single misstep—the galaxy doomed with him.

A voice like Luke's but deeper shook the starfields, booming, Jacen, stand firm!

The horizon tilted farther and Jacen lunged forward, determined to lend his small weight to Luke's side—to the light—only to misstep once more. He flailed for his uncle's hand, missing time and again.

Finally, Luke seized Jacen's hand and held it tightly, urging him to weather the storm. The slope steepened under their feet. Stars extinguished. The enemy scrambled forward, eclipsing worlds, entire star clusters, distant galaxies.

And again the voice boomed: Stand firm!

As the Yuuzhan Vong attacked—

Jacen returned to himself—to the here and now.

Since that vision he had fought the enemy on countless worlds, wounded Warmaster Tsavong Lah, triumphed over many lesser opponents, been stripped of and returned to the Force by Vergere, and been deemed a Knight by his Jedi Master, Luke. And yet he continued to feel as if he were a student.

The Jedi of the Old Republic had been too focused on indoctrination and ranks. If you were a Padawan, then you were something less than a Knight; and if you were a Knight, you were something less than a Master . . . But who was to say, now that there was no Jedi Council of sagacious Masters, that even a mere Padawan couldn't be more Forceful than someone of higher rank? Perhaps it was something a Jedi needed to hear directly from the Force?

Ranks now were more like battlefield promotions—like Jaina's promotion to colonel. Even the Jedi Knighting ceremony . . . It made no more sense to him than it had to Jaina. They had to analyze their paths separately from those things.

But if his twenty years of tutelage had been his education, and the time he had spent with Vergere in the bowels of the Yuuzhan Vong seedship and on conquered Coruscant had constituted the trials of a Padawan, what then was the decision he faced now?

Was it, too, not a trial, of sorts?

What does the Force want for the Yuuzhan Vong?

Stand firm, the voice in the vision had told him.

Occasionally he would get a sense that his education was nearing completion, and that the past year had been his true trial—possibly unlike any a Jedi Knight had ever faced—but the feeling never lasted long.

"Practicing, Jacen?" a female voice asked suddenly.

He knew then who had been watching him.

Sekot's thought projection of Vergere rose from the center of the pool.

"Always," he said.

"To achieve what?"

"Mastery."

Vergere nodded. "Jacen, to tap deeply into the Unifying Force, we will have to surrender our desire to control events. We will have to unbridle ourselves of words and of thinking, because thoughts, too, are born of the physical world. We must refrain from analyzing the Force, and simply allow the Force to guide us. Our relationship with the Force must be impeccable, without the need to be supported by words or reason. We must carry out the commands of the Force as if they were beyond appeal. And we must do what must be done, no matter who attempts to stand in our way."

THIRTY-THREE

We are committed, Wedge told himself as explosions bloomed like time-lapse fire flowers over night-side Corulag.

Its surface etched with intersecting trails of light, the Core world filled the bridge viewports of *Mon Mothma*. Between the planet and the refitted Star Destroyer floated Yuuzhan Vong mataloks and yorik-akaga—blushed cruisers and pearlescent pickets—arrayed to provide cover for a swift-moving yammosk carrier clustership. Harried by squadrons of X- and E-wings disgorged from the warships *Mon Adapyne* and *Elegos A'Kla,* the enemy vessels were saturating local space with blazing projectiles and gouts of superheated ejecta, but they were already beginning to pay the price for having been caught unawares.

A state of controlled frenzy prevailed on *Mon Mothma's* bridge, with couriers and officers coming and going, and Wedge attempting to sustain half a dozen separate conversations. Displays flickered and computer consoles chirped as updates were transmitted from gunnery, communications, and tactical centers elsewhere in the ship. As accustomed to the noise as Wedge had become, he couldn't help but reflect on the reasons that had prompted his retirement—especially now, in the wake of Ackbar's death. His uniform and command cap felt borrowed from someone two sizes smaller.

The surprise attack had required his battle group to jump directly from Contruum to the Bormea sector, inserting as close to Corulag as was achievable, given the planet's several moons and formidable defenses. Once the site of an Imperial Navy base, the largest moon had been transformed into a kind of rest facility for enemy patrol vessels assigned to the

Perlemian Trade Route. Scimitar assault bombers were laying waste to the facility now, while Shocker and Blackmoon Squadron starfighters nipped at the yammosk carrier like packs of rapacious howlrunners.

"Generals Farlander and Celchu have the enemy boxed in," *Mon Mothma*'s commander reported. "*Harbinger* has dropped from hyperspace and is pressing forward at battle speed to rendezvous with *Elegos A'Kla* at rally point manka-flechette-dewback."

With *Mon Mothma* too far removed to allow for visual contact with any of the capital ships, Wedge studied the tactical console's checkerboard of display screens. Determined to shield the yammosk vessel, the Yuuzhan Vong cruisers were indeed bracketed by *Mon Adapyne* and *Elegos A'Kla*, both of which were lancing the enemy configuration with continuous bursts of turbolaser fire. And now, closing fast, was *Harbinger*—the Mon Cal cruiser commanded by Garm Bel Iblis. Caught in the crossfire, coralskippers were being pulverized almost as fast as they could be deployed. With its quick-response cannons and gravity-well generators, *Mon Mothma* was seeing to any skips that escaped the cordon.

Corulag itself was taking punishment. Evidence of orbital bombardment and surface fighting, infrared hot spots were flaring in and around many of the major cities. Decrypted transmissions revealed that the fighting was intense, and atrocities were widespread.

Unlike other worlds along that important stretch of the Perlemian—Chandrila, Brentaal, and Ralltiir—Corulag had capitulated to the Yuuzhan Vong to escape devastation. No one had expected otherwise of a planetary government that had supported the Emperor during the Galactic Civil War, and had since been forced to languish in Coruscant's shadow. Regardless, most of Corulag's ten billion citizens opposed the puppet government set up by the Yuuzhan Vong, and simmering discontent had finally erupted into open rebellion. The wealthiest and most influential families fled for Kuat and Commenor, but there was no evading the Yuuzhan Vong. Kuat had fallen soon after Senator Pwoe's brief visit, and Commenor had been hit hard and repeatedly. Galvanized by the rescue of Corulag's unofficial hero, Judder Page, resistance groups on- and offworld had reached out to the Alliance for help in liberating the planet, at whatever costs to life and limb. Sovv and Kre'fey couldn't have been more receptive to insystem support for an invasion. If Corulag could be reclaimed, the Alliance would hold a key hyperspace position in the Core.

Even two standard months earlier, an assault would have proved catastrophic. Yuuzhan Vong forces had been deployed well into the Slice, from Coruscant through Alsakan almost all the way to Corulag, and from Ixtlar and Wukkar on the Corellian Run a quarter of the way around the Core toward Kuat and Commenor. But with dozens of battle groups withdrawn to join the armada, Corulag had been left vulnerable at last.

Wedge's gaze was still glued to the displays when Captain Deevis drew his attention to a tight formation of fighter craft emerging from Corulag's crescent of transitor.

"TIEs," Wedge said in genuine surprise. "Ours or theirs?"

"I'm not sure, sir."

"Then find out!"

"Transmission from Curamelle," Lieutenant Cel interrupted while Deevis was hurrying off. "Governor Forridel, sir."

Wedge recognized the name of Corulag's capital city, but not the name of the governor. Nodding curtly to the comm officer, he swung to the holoprojector, where a quarter-scale human figure stood in the noisy field.

"We've been waiting almost two years for this," Forridel said jubilantly. Sporting an eye patch and a floppy cap, he could have stepped from a suspense holodrama. "Corulag will forever be indebted to the Alliance."

"The battle's not won yet," Wedge said. "And just who are you, anyway?"

Forridel saluted—awkwardly. "The resistance has appointed me provisional governor."

"Where's the former governor?"

Forridel smiled. "I'm glad you asked, because I've been eager to show you."

Images from what were obviously Curamelle media feeds began to resolve in the holofield. One showed the former governor hanging by the neck in a city square while a lynch mob of humans and humanoids pelted him with stones. Other scenes showed bound and bloodied Yuuzhan Vong and other members of the occupation government being dragged or shoved through the streets by crowds of vigilantes.

Wedge was thankful that he hadn't been asked to oversee ground-based operations, as he had done at Borleias. Soon enough, similar scenes of vengeance would be repeated on countless worlds. The rage was understandable, and reminiscent of the retributions that had been doled out to Imperial forces in the wake of the Emperor's death. And Wedge held little sympathy for the captured Yuuzhan Vong warriors. All his life he had fought for what he believed in, and for the protection of those he loved—Iella, his daughters, his sister, and friends—and the Yuuzhan Vong had nearly torn his world and family apart. A point could be made that the Yuuzhan Vong fought for similar reasons, but the invaders had yet to demonstrate even an instance of charity or tolerance. Worship and blind obedience substituted for love and honor.

And yet, for all his soldier's resolve, Wedge recognized that he could still be rattled by a canny glance from Luke Skywalker. Listening to him and Mara address the command staff on *Ralroost,* Wedge had been struck once more by the fact that the Alliance and the Jedi were waging very different wars against the Yuuzhan Vong. Where Alliance command measured victory in terms of control, the Jedi were focused on a means of ending the war that would also conclude a cycle of violence. Luke feared that the extermination of the Yuuzhan Vong would deal a death blow to the newly hatched Galactic Federation of Free Alliances. With a single step toward the dark side, the fate of future generations would be sealed.

As was true with the Yuuzhan Vong, the Jedi were prepared to martyr themselves to an ideal. Both were fighting to sustain a worldview. At the center of one stood the gods; at the center of the other, the Force.

Wedge wondered what might become of those Yuuzhan Vong who weren't burned or beaten to death in the streets of Curamelle or some other once-occupied capital city. What was the next step after disarmament? Imprisonment? Exile?

Could an entire species be put on trial for its beliefs? And even if found guilty of war crimes, would the Yuuzhan Vong permit themselves to be isolated under guard in some remote star system, or would their defeat—the fact that they had failed their gods—drive them to self-destruction? Should self-extinction be accepted as an alternative because death figured so strongly in their society, or would the death of the extragalactic species upset the balance of the Force in some fashion?

That such questions were best left to the Jedi was the reason Wedge, Keyan Farlander, certainly Tenel Ka, and many other Alliance commanders had implicit faith in Luke's leadership. At Borleias, when Wedge himself had formed the secret resistance group known as the Insiders, he had essentially made a pact with the Force, and felt duty-bound to uphold it.

"You've ended a reign of evil, General Antilles," Forridel was saying from the holofield. "You should be proud."

Wedge cut the provisional governor off before he could continue. "Our scanners have picked up a squadron of TIE fighters launched from Curamelle."

"Peace Brigaders," Forridel explained. "The fighters were restored from parts warehoused at the old Imperial Academy. Hunt them down, General! Don't leave a single ship unscathed!"

"That's all the information I need at the moment, Governor." Wedge waved for Lieutenant Cel to end the holotransmission with Curamelle, then said: "Alert General Celchu that those TIEs are not friendlies. Tell him that *Harbinger* has his back if he needs help dealing with them."

The fighting above night-side Corulag was heating up. Coralskippers and snubfighters were engaged in a mad dance of mutual destruction, while the capital ships they flew from were attempting to pummel one another senseless with plasma missiles and energy bolts. Two globules of the cluster vessel had imploded, but judging by the performance of the swarming skips, the war coordinator was uninjured. On the moon, bombers were continuing to hammer the repair installation, but they were now taking fire from ground-based KDY turbolasers—probably refurbished by the same turncoat technicians who had resurrected the TIEs.

"Sir, Admiral Kre'fey," Cel said from her duty station.

Wedge strode back to the holoprojector in time to see Kre'fey's image take shape amid random bursts of diagonal static. "General Antilles," the Bothan began, "on your say-so I'm prepared to move *Ralroost* and elements of the First Fleet to Corulag."

Wedge shook his head. "We need more time here, Admiral. A couple of standard hours, at least."

"You have one hour, General," Kre'fey said evenly. "We've received word from Coruscant that our actions at Corulag have not gone unnoticed. Nas Choka's armada is active. It's not clear just yet whether the warmaster is repositioning his vessels to defend Coruscant, or if he intends to move the armada Rimward in advance of going to hyperspace. If it's the latter, I doubt he'll squander his forces by reinforcing Corulag. He may, however, elect to jump the armada to Contruum, and I want to be gone from here by then."

"Where do you want us?" Wedge asked.

"Take *Mon Adapyne* and *Elegos A'Kla* and rally with the Second Fleet at Muscave. I realize I'm placing your battle group in harm's way by sending you directly into the Coruscant system, but our objective is to accomplish the reverse of what we did at Mon Calamari, by drawing the enemy into engagements at outer-system worlds. Concurrently, I'll be dispatching elements of the Third Fleet to Coruscant from the Shawken Spur of the Hydian, and elements of the Fourth by way of the Martial Cross. Regardless of whether the armada jumps for Contruum or advances to engage your forces at Muscave, the assault on Coruscant can commence."

"Did I hear right that Vanguard Squadron has been attached to the Fourth Fleet?" Wedge asked.

"That's correct."

"That means that the Chiss will be directly involved in the assault on Coruscant."

"Vanguard and Twin Suns have been folded into a single squadron, commanded by Group Commander Fel."

Wedge was perplexed. "Jag is leading Twin Suns? Where's Jaina?"

"Jedi Skywalker asked that we exempt her from the roster," Kre'fey muttered. "I recognize that Coruscant is a long way from Chiss space, and I know that you're concerned for the welfare of your nephew, Wedge. But Jag himself requested the mission."

Wedge nodded. "I'll just have to find a way to explain to my sister why I didn't talk some sense into her son."

Kre'fey gestured noncommittally. "Colonel Fel's group, along with Rogue and Wraith Squadrons, will fly escort for the troop transports and gunships we hope to slip through Coruscant's dovin basal gravitic wells. Once planetside, Captain Page's commando company will rendezvous with resistance forces and proceed to the landing field at what was Westport."

Mon Mothma's tactical officer sent a star chart of the Coruscant system to the holoprojector. Wedge saw that Coruscant and the outer worlds of Muscave and Stentat were all on the same side of the sun, within sixty degrees of one another. Calculating the time required for the hyperspace jump to Muscave, Wedge's battle group would be arriving just as Shimrra's Citadel and the sacred precinct were heading into daybreak.

"Admiral, is Zonama Sekot still orbiting between Muscave and Stentat?"

"To the best of our knowledge," Kre'fey said. "But that planet is the Jedi's problem, not ours."

Even before the transmission from *Ralroost* faded, Wedge spun on his heel to Lieutenant Cel. "Inform Generals Celchu and Farlander that we will be repositioning in one standard hour. Then find me a secure frequency to *Errant Venture,* and patch it through to my comlink."

Replacing his command cap with a headset, Wedge paced away from the bridge duty stations while the link to Booster Terrik's Star Destroyer was being established.

"Insider One, your transmission is secure," a voice said through Wedge's earphones. "Lando here, Wedge."

Wedge adjusted the fit of the headset. "Lando, in just

under a standard hour I'll be repositioning my group to Mus-cave."

"Good news. That means Zonama Sekot will be inside your lines."

"Not as good as it sounds. Alliance command has written the planet off as the Jedi's concern."

"You think it'll go to hyperspace?"

"I don't know, Lando. But some of us should be there in case anyone needs to be evacuated."

"You can count on us, Insider One. I'll also pass the word to Tenel Ka."

"May the Force be with you, Lando."

"It had better be."

Mired at Contruum for longer than they had anticipated, Luke and Mara had missed the seed-partners ceremony, but everyone who had participated was still talking about it long after *Jade Shadow* returned to Zonama Sekot.

Kyp, Corran, and Saba spoke in wonderment of having been led across a symbolic bridge and through a lamina-surfaced tunnel into concealed courtyards, filled with Ferroan cele-brants wearing brightly colored costumes. Having adhered to a special diet, the Jedi candidates had worn sashed robes and necklaces strung with bloodred, gourdlike fruits. Following a series of litanies chanted by Magister Jabitha and the Fer-roans, each of the candidates had had to offer a gift, and in-troduce him- or herself to Sekot, in a way that reminded Kyp of the ceremony that had taken place at Ithor, four years ear-lier. Finally, the seed-partners—emerged from their shells as pale oblate bulbs, with eyespots and tiny grasper-equipped legs—had been separated from their bond partners and con-veyed to the cybernetic organisms that would summon light-ning and give shape to the living ships produced from the seeds. Bred by Zonama Sekot's original magisters, the cyborgs were known as the Jentari.

After listening to a dozen separate accounts of the cere-mony from as many Jedi, Luke almost felt as if he had at-tended it personally, and he was eager to see the living ships. Sekot had had extensive conversations with Danni, and now Cilghal, about dovin basals; and Lowbacca and others were trying to figure a way to use comlinks for ship-to-ship communication.

With so much information to catch up on, Luke had decided to wait for the proper moment to report on the briefings at Contruum. He chose to do that in the Skywalkers' cliff dwelling, even though few Jedi were present. Assembled were Jacen, Jaina, Kyp, Corran, Saba, Tahiri, Danni, Han, Leia, Magister Jabitha, Harrar, C-3PO, and R2-D2.

Jacen was the first one to comment on Luke's lengthy summary.

"Did you explain to Admiral Kre'fey what the World Brain will do if Coruscant's attacked?"

"Half of the command staff has dismissed the report you furnished," Luke said, "and the other half just doesn't want to believe it."

Han growled in exasperation. "Forget about the World Brain. Can Kre'fey even get past the planetary dovin basals?"

Mara glanced at Luke. "You know, they never really answered that question. Sovv said that they weren't worried about the dovin basals."

"I think I know why," Luke said. "Zonama Sekot not only tugged one of Coruscant's moons out of orbit, but also tore apart the planetary ring that the Yuuzhan Vong manufactured from the moon *they* managed to shatter. The dovin basals are probably so busy dealing with infalling debris that they can now be overwhelmed by lasers, concussion missiles, and whatever else Kre'fey plans to hurl at them."

"That still won't stop the World Brain from carrying out its tasks," Jacen said.

"That's correct," Harrar said, then looked questioningly at Jacen.

"I wasn't able to communicate with the dhuryam while we were in the Unknown Regions, and I haven't been able to sense it in the same way since we got back."

"Then perhaps Shimrra has managed to establish a rapport with the brain." Harrar turned to Luke. "You must understand: Shimrra is not an ordinary Yuuzhan Vong. His body and his mind have been enhanced. His powers surpass those of other Supreme Overlords."

Leia forced a sad exhalation. "Hundreds of thousands will die, and the planet will be of no use to anyone."

"Unless we can get to Shimrra first," Luke said.

Harrar nodded. "The Supreme Overlord is our ultimate weapon. This war cannot possibly be won without defeating him. Because Shimrra is our sole conduit to the gods, his capture or death will prove chaotic for Nas Choka's warriors and Jakan's priests. Without Shimrra's intercession, the gods will not be able to help or intervene in any way. Separated from the gods, the warriors and priests will be bereft. But capturing Shimrra—let alone killing him—will be exceedingly difficult. He is well protected by skillful guards, and by the worldship itself, which responds to him, much as Yuuzhan'tar responds to the World Brain."

"Can the Citadel be penetrated?" Luke asked.

"With the armada fending off an attack, the dovin basals and World Brain preoccupied, the Shamed Ones in revolt . . . Yes, it might be possible to infiltrate with a small force. I could advise you on the best route."

"You'd do that?" Leia said, gazing at Harrar.

The priest nodded. "I said I would do everything in my power to help end this conflict. Nothing has happened to cause me to reconsider that."

"Who and how many of us?" Kyp asked.

Luke thought for a moment. "Not more than six of us. And no one who is waiting for a Sekotan ship."

Kyp nodded, and Han and Leia traded uncertain glances.

"Where's that leave the rest of us?" Han asked.

Before Luke could answer the question, Kenth, Cilghal, and Lowbacca entered the cliff dwelling—the Wookiee ducking low enough to keep from banging his furry head into the crude beams that spanned the high ceiling.

"Someone commed *Jade Shadow*," Luke said.

Kenth nodded. "The Alliance has reclaimed Corulag. Wedge's battle group has been ordered to Muscave, to lure the armada away from Coruscant, so the major offensive can begin."

"Then the war is coming to us," Jabitha said softly.

"*Errant Venture* is on the way here," Cilghal added, "in

case you're thinking of evacuating the Ferroans—or anyone else."

Jaina shot to her feet. "I should be with my squadron."

Mara looked at her. "You are, Jaina."

"How's that?" she asked harshly "I'm not in line for a living ship, and my X-wing is still in stationary orbit."

"I mean that you're needed here," Mara said calmly.

While Jaina stared at her aunt in indecision, Han put his arm around Jaina's waist. "Let's just see how things develop, okay?"

Jaina nodded mutely.

"Should Sekot be warned?" Danni asked.

"I'm sure Sekot already knows," Luke said. "I think that's the reason Sekot agreed to provide us with ships."

"I must caution all of you that the Sekotan ships are for defense only," Jabitha interjected. "Zonama has other defensive weapons, but Sekot has not spoken of those in some time."

Mara looked at Luke. "Presumably the same ones that repelled the original Far Outsiders, and annihilated Commander Val's forces at Klasse Ephemora," Luke said.

"Luke, we're talking about an *armada*," Han thought to point out. "Sekot might want to at least think about warming up the hyperspace drives."

Jabitha shook her head. "Flight would be a demonstration of fear. Zonama Sekot will not flee a second time. Especially now, with so much at stake."

Danni glanced around in puzzlement. "It's irrelevant, isn't it? If Zonama Sekot is an evil omen for the Yuuzhan Vong, then Shimrra would want his forces to give it the widest berth."

Everyone turned to Harrar.

"It depends on who knows what, and, if anything, how much." The priest stroked his chin with his three-fingered hand. "Assuming that they have some limited understanding of Zonama Sekot, the warriors would first have to be convinced that they weren't defying the gods by attacking the planet." He raised his head in sudden apprehension. "Unless Shimrra has managed to convince them that Zonama Sekot is some sort of *Jeedai* weapon or fabrication that *must* be destroyed."

"How soon before the living ships are flight-ready?" Kyp asked Jabitha in a rush.

"In time," the Magister said. "Sekot will make certain of it."

THIRTY-FOUR

Warmaster Nas Choka gave Yuuzhan'tar a final glance as *Yammka's Mount*'s powerful dovin basals prepared to tug the vessel into darkspace for the short journey to the outer-system world known as Muscave. Aswirl with clouds, the green hemisphere that was Yuuzhan'tar had changed dramatically in the short time since the armada had launched for Mon Calamari. Smoke was chimneying from volcanic vents, it was absent one of its moons, and the bridge of the gods had collapsed—all but force-fed rock by rock to the orbiting dovin basals tasked with shielding the world from attack. And no grand ceremony on this occasion. No farewell blessings from Shimrra; no fresh coats of sacrificial blood for warriors and war vessels.

Yuuzhan'tar appeared exposed, ill prepared to defend itself. But Nas Choka trusted that Supreme Overlord Shimrra would attend to that. More important, Yuuzhan'tar would fall to the enemy only if the armada failed in its mission to destroy Zonama Sekot. In that case, Nas Choka wouldn't be alive to see the planet reclaimed. Judged unworthy by the gods, the Yuuzhan Vong would die, individually and as a species, and the gods would be forced once more to fashion beings worthy of nurture, as they had done three times before the Yuuzhan Vong had been brought into being.

Nas Choka had accepted Shimrra's wisdom on the matter of Zonama Sekot. Again the Supreme Overlord had demonstrated his brilliance, and that had reinforced Nas Choka's belief that he had made the correct choice in siding with Shimrra when it had come to toppling Quoreal from the polyp throne.

But Nas Choka nursed a secret distrust for the Trickster goddess, Yun-Harla. The feathered traitor, Vergere, had been the familiar of priestesses of Yun-Harla. Too, Eminence Harrar had been devoted to her, and he had apparently vanished off the face of Yuuzhan'tar. Worse, the Trickster, without intervention, had for a time allowed her guise to be adopted by one of the Jedi. So what was to stop her from betraying the Yuuzhan Vong now? Weary of being patronized by Yun-Yuuzhan and Yun-Yammka, perhaps she wished to bring about the destruction of Yun-Yuuzhan's creation, by tricking Shimrra into trusting to a false revelation.

To shore up his own faith and that of his warriors, Nas Choka had commanded a coven of Yun-Yammka priests to accompany the armada. Having drawn blood from the tongues and earlobes of each and every Supreme Commander, the priests had pumped the bloated ngdins that had absorbed the sacrificial offerings into a coralskipper and dispatched it into the void, in advance of the armada.

Hands clasped behind his back, the warmaster spun away from the view of Yuuzhan'tar. Several strides across the coarse deck took him to the villip-choir, where the mistress in charge of the array bowed her head in subordination.

"I would speak with the shaper aboard the failing vessel," Nas Choka said.

The mistress stroked the appropriate villip, which inverted and assumed the sickly likeness of the shaper who had been poisoned at Caluula.

"My only surviving villip is dying, Warmaster," the ashen shaper reported. "It lacks the vigor to portray your visage, but I suspect it is capable of relaying your words."

"Speak to the health of yourself and your crew, shaper," Nas Choka said. "Do *you* have the vigor to carry out what has been commanded of you?"

The villip's thick lips formed words. "Four slayers have died; six remain—a sufficient number to pilot this ailing vessel. I am alive only by dint of chemical compounds I managed to mix and ingest at the onset of my paralysis, but my time is short, Warmaster."

"If need be I will send hale warriors and youthful villips to assist you, shaper. But only you can keep the vessel itself alive. If it dies before we reach Zonama Sekot, then all is lost."

"I fear it is incapable of going to darkspace, Warmaster."

Nas Choka ground his filed teeth and swung to his chief tactician. "Advise me of our options."

"Allow it to be ingested by a larger vessel, Warmaster," the tactician said. "A sacrifice of yet another vessel and its crew, but essential to our task."

Nas Choka nodded and turned back to the transmitting villip. "Shaper, command the vessel's dovin basals, villips, and weapons to rest. I will dispatch a vessel of sufficient size to engulf yours and carry it through darkspace to Zonama Sekot. Once there, the slayers will pilot your vessel from its carapace. Then, under whatever escort I deem necessary, you will consign yourself and your vessel to the living world."

"An honor that finds me undeserving, Warmaster."

"Succeed, and undreamed-of rewards await you, shaper. Fail, and suffer the disgrace of having sentenced our entire species to oblivion."

When the shaper's villip had resumed its familiar shape, Nas Choka gestured for the tactician to follow him into the command chamber's blister transparency.

"What have you learned of our enemy's plan?"

"Muscave has become the gathering place for the Alliance battle group that struck Corulag, and an even larger force of capital ships sent from Contruum. The enemy is now poised between us and our target."

"Part of our trial," Nas Choka said evenly. "Before we can even engage the planet the gods have placed in their hands, we must break through the enemy's line."

"At the same time, the enemy entices us away from Yuuzhan'tar."

Nas Choka grunted. "They have devised a clever assault."

"Though ignorant of the fact, they have the complicity of the gods."

Nas Choka clenched his right hand. "We will do the same at Muscave, by offering ourselves as an enticement, so that our poisoned barb can fly true to its mark. We will present ourselves as a warrior would, brandishing his amphistaff in challenge on the battlefield!" He nodded in self-assurance. "When will the infidels arrive at Yuuzhan'tar?"

"The Alliance commanders have already sundered the fleet they assembled at Contruum," the tactician said. "We suspect that the vanished battle groups have jumped to darkspace and will emerge in our absence, to all sides of Yuuzhan'tar, and from unfamiliar vectors. A study of villip memories of the battle at Ebaq Nine has revealed worthwhile comparisons. There, too, the enemy made use of darkspace corridors of which we had no knowledge. But the comparison ends there. After our spear has been thrust into Zonama Sekot's flesh, there will be no need for a ground assault, or an ill-conceived hunt for *Jeedai*. Satisfied that we have overcome the trial, the gods will add their might to our armada and we will be able to wipe the *Jeedai* from existence."

Nas Choka smiled lightly. "It is a rare occasion when well-matched warriors have an opportunity to face each other a second time, in a different arena." He paused for a moment, then said: "As yet no communication from Domains Muyel and Lacap?"

"No," the tactician said. "Their war vessels remain in the star systems awarded to them by Supreme Overlord Shimrra."

Nas Choka's tattooed upper lip curled in anger. "Their punishment, too, will be swift and lethal."

One didn't have to be a native of Coruscant to know that the planet had seen better days. Holos displayed at the pre-mission briefings didn't do justice to the extent to which the Yuuzhan Vong had transformed the world and Zonama Sekot had wounded it. Once as green as the Chiss capital of Csilla was white, vast areas were now blackened by fire and fractured by sinuous flows of lava.

Jag absorbed the desolation in a glance as his clawcraft swooped from the open belly of the Star Destroyer *Right to Rule.* Twin Suns' complement of clawcraft and X-wings streaked behind him in a trailing wedge. Off to Jag's port side, and slightly to stern, flew Rogue Squadron; to starboard, the Wraiths and Taanab Yellow Aces. Centered and shielded by the near wing of starfighters were three lightly armed troop transports. Two were of the same vintage as the

170-meter-long bulbous-lobed *Record Time,* which had been sacrificed at Coruscant shortly after the planet's capture. The third was a pre-Empire vessel, almost four hundred meters long, and might have been a precursor of *Right to Rule* herself.

The main body of the Yuuzhan Vong armada had made the jump to lightspeed only an hour earlier, but Warmaster Nas Choka had left enough vessels in orbit to test the mettle of the Alliance. Even with Star Destroyers, Mon Cal cruisers, and Corellian gunships arriving from unguarded insertion points, the Yuuzhan Vong were capable of engaging each separate battle group.

The enemy flotilla that rushed to meet the Fourth Fleet was made up of light cruiser and assault cruiser analogs, from whose hull panels jutted forked arms housing plasma cannon emplacements and clusters of coralskippers. Simultaneous with the emergence of the starfighters, the skips had dropped from their barnaclelike perches and were now racing outward from the edge of Coruscant's envelope, eager for contest.

"Shield trios," Jag commanded his group over the tactical net. "Stick close to the transports, and stay alert for course corrections. Don't allow yourselves to be drawn into individual conflicts."

The group was split evenly between Chiss and Alliance pilots, but for the first time since Twin Suns' inception at the Jedi base known as Eclipse, there wasn't a Force-user among them. Jag had originally flown with Twin Suns at Borleias, when the squadron had been handed over to Jaina, and he had flown with her for most of the past year at Galantos, Bakura, and in other campaigns. Their training, coupled with his deep affection for her, sometimes made him wonder if he hadn't become sensitized to the Force—or at least to Jaina's use of the Force. At Hapes, and as recently as Mon Calamari, where Jaina's X-wing had been crippled, he seemed to be able to intuit her needs or requests. Incapable of communicating with her squadron, she had reached out through the Force and Jag had heard her—clear enough, at any rate, to have anticipated and relayed Jaina's orders to her wingmates. With Jaina absent—on Zonama Sekot, according to Gavin

Darklighter—the starfighter group felt less responsive, though Jag maintained a strong combat bond with the Chiss pilots, especially Shawnkyr and Eprill.

"Twin Sun Leader," said the voice of *Right to Rule* control. "Bring your group to Sector Sabacc, zero-six-six. We're getting ready to light things up."

Jag had flown with Grand Admiral Pellaeon's vessel at Esfandia, and the voice was reassuring.

"Copy, *Right to Rule*. Coming about to zero-six-six."

The broad bank sunward placed the trio of transports and their starfighter escorts over daybreak Coruscant. No sooner was the task force clear of *Right to Rule* than all its starboard quad laser batteries belched fire. Not far from the Star Destroyer, and similarly aligned to the planet, two Mon Cal MC80Bs and the cruiser *Dauntless* added their blinding salvos to the light storm. Half the amassed firepower was directed at the onrushing coralskippers, dozens of which were instantly vaporized. The other half was aimed at what remained of Coruscant's short-lived planetary ring. Hammered by massive packets of coherent light and high-yield proton torpedoes, the largest pieces of what had once been a moon broke into thousands of even smaller fragments, creating a meteor storm the likes of which Coruscant probably hadn't confronted since it had coalesced into a planet.

Enormous singularities began to open as the chunks were sent tumbling into the upper reaches of the envelope. But the orbital dovin basals that had created the gravitic anomalies were already overburdened, and many of the fragments plummeted past them, becoming fiery streaks as they entered the atmosphere.

Jag knew that scanners aboard the Alliance capital ships were already analyzing the relative strengths of the singularities and monitoring the trajectories of the meteors that had slipped through the gravitic shield. Once the areas of greatest stress were identified, their locations would be relayed to the transports and starfighters.

Not quite two years earlier, the troop transport *Record Time* had delivered its cargo of Wraiths and Jedi to the surface of Coruscant in single-person containers. But that was before the dovin basals had been seeded into orbit. More important, there was no reason for stealth now. As someone at Contruum had said to Jag, "If we can't drop a moon on them, we can at least make it rain rocks."

"Twin Suns," *Right to Rule* control said, "you have open windows at coordinates four-two-three and four-two-five. Rothana transport is reorienting to follow you through."

Jag passed the word to his pilots, even though the navi-computers on each starfighter had certainly received the course corrections. Configured into pairs and trios, Twin Suns formed up along both sides of the antique wedge-shaped ship and began to herd it toward the infiltration zone. Adapting their vectors to match those of the escort starfighters, coralskippers attacked from all sides, threading through the fragment cloud and augmenting it with plasma missiles and gouts of molten stone.

Flying just at the perimeter of the transport's shields, Jag's clawcraft was jarred by every projectile that found its target. The comm channel was a babble of voices, as pilots issued warnings of strafing runs or declared the status of their ships. Explosive light washed into the spherical cockpit of Twin Suns One from astern, and Jag glanced at his displays to see Twin Eight and Eleven vanish from the grid. With scant room to maneuver, he tried to make the most of every squeeze of the trigger, but the skips had the advantage of being able to take evasive action, whereas the starfighters were intent on protecting their ward.

Carefully trained laser bolts from *Right to Rule* created a sudden corridor of destructive energy around the transport and fighters. A dozen more skips became extra fodder for the meteor-gobbling dovin basals. Still in darkness, a Yuuzhan Vong cruiser stabbed by convergent blasts from three separate Alliance ships cracked open and blew apart. A second vessel, spewing blades of flame from its midsection, rolled lazily out of orbit and began to fall into the atmosphere.

The dovin basals were trying desperately to prioritize, but more and more rock fragments were getting past them. As overtaxed as they were, the gigantic biots still posed a threat to any ship that ventured too close. For that reason the transports had been retrofitted with Bakuran-designed HIMS generators, which should have allowed them to sustain momentum even in an interdiction field. At Contruum, few had expressed confidence in the retrofitting, and Jag was one of the first pilots to see why.

His group of vanguard starfighters was just passing between a pair of the Yuuzhan Vong orbital monstrosities when two overlapping singularities yawned, catching the pointed bow of the transport and dragging it hard to starboard. The ship's aged cylindrical thrusters tried to compensate for the unexpected tug of gravity, but they weren't up to the challenge. The jury-rigged HIMS failed, and the deflector shields followed. The transport twisted over on its side and began to founder. Armor flayed from the hull and surface modules disappeared into the swirling black mouth of the singularity. Breaches opened, venting precious atmosphere and unsecured objects. Then, deep within the vessel, an explosion flashed, and it split wide open. Ground-effect vehicles, combat droids, and acceleration couches spun outward—some of the latter with commandos still strapped into them.

In the blink of an eye Twin Suns lost another three fighters. To port, trimmed in golden sunlight, one of the newer transports was banking as quickly as its bulk allowed. Rogue Squadron had re-formed around the ship and was just beginning to shepherd it into the atmosphere. Jag looked to his right and overhead for the second transport, but couldn't find it. What he found instead were the Wraiths, winning their duels with coralskippers even as they blazed toward Twin Suns.

Right to Rule control boomed in Jag's ears. "Twin Suns Leader, come about to zero-zero-three. You are redesignated escort for number one transport. As soon as your group is clear, we're going to try to burn a tunnel to the surface."

Jag hauled on the control yoke, gravitational forces all but burying him in the seat as he slewed to port. The dozen remaining members of his group followed in formation, sticking close enough to one another to provide adjuvant shielding. Ahead of them, transport one had dropped inside the tier of dovin basals and was rushing for the surface, blunt nose aglow from friction. Twenty years earlier Coruscant had been liberated from Imperial forces by loosing a group of criminals to sow confusion, and by sabotaging the planet's shield generators. Now liberation would depend largely on the actions of a thousand commandos and a handful of resistance fighters, and the off chance of their being able to mobilize the Yuuzhan Vong heretics into an insurgent force.

As promised, coordinated laserfire came from the capital ships. Sizzling through the atmosphere, the sustained fusillade annihilated everything in its path and burned a ragged bald patch in Coruscant's verdant surface. It was toward the denuded area that the starfighters and transport raced, firing on the run at the few coralskippers that had survived the laser shower.

The control yoke shuddered in Jag's grip as he powered the clawcraft into denser air. The ship rattled, as if on the verge of coming apart, but it held together. Surface features of Coruscant began to come into focus: forest-covered spires and mounds, wide crevasses brimming with mist yet to be burned off by the sun. Gradually he decreased the angle of his descent until he was flying into the sun, and parallel to the undulating terrain. Frightened by the roar of the approaching craft, flocks of black birds with three-meter wingspans took flight from the branching crowns of emergent trees.

A contour map resolved on the cockpit navigational display, showing the buildings and features of the so-called sacred precinct, from the craggy mountain that was Shimrra's worldship Citadel to the domelike structure that housed and protected the World Brain—what had once been the most affluent and fashionable area of the planet. A counter at the bottom of the screen showed the distance remaining to the scorched landing zone, which was surrounded by dense forest and yorik coral outcroppings.

Without warning, enemy artillery fire erupted from the tree line around the clearing, fountaining molten ejecta and flaming projectiles high into the air. Flying nap of the forest, Jag spotted the distinctive sail-like spine plates of the armored beast the Yuuzhan Vong called a rakamat, and the Alliance knew as a range. The blue-green reptilian creatures were the size of small buildings, and on Borleias had proved almost impossible to stop.

"That plasma is coming from a range, east of the landing zone," Jag said over the tactical net. "Shawnkyr, Eprill, see if you can hold it at bay long enough for Page's Commandos to insert."

"On our way, Colonel," Shawnkyr responded.

At Borleias, she had urged Jag to return to their native Chiss space. Now she was as much an Alliance pilot as he was.

Dodging projectiles, Jag banked over the forest. He was doubling back to the transport when he finally caught sight of its sister ship, ten kilometers to the south and covered stem to stern in grutchins.

The Yellow Aces were pursuing the out-of-control vessel and using their lasers to dislodge the grutchins, as if picking vermin off a pet. But the acid-producing, globular-eyed insectoids had ingested large areas of the hull and, judging by the way the transport was wobbling, had already infiltrated the cabin spaces. Jag watched helplessly as the vessel bellied into the forest, cutting a wide, burning swath through the trees. Sliding for a kilometer or more, it tipped nose-first over the rim of a deep crevasse and began a slow descent toward the bottom.

Closer to the lasered clearing, Rogue and Twin Suns snub-fighters were making paired strafing runs over the rakamat and Yuuzhan Vong infantry units, creating an inferno with lasers and proton torpedoes.

Slowed by its repulsorlift engines, number one transport was a few kilometers short of the laser-denuded tableland when a large hatch opened in its ventral surface. First to exit the hatch were YVH droids, folded into foam-filled crash canisters. Then, sheathed in enviro-suits and harnessed into jet packs, came Page's company, soaring from the rectangular opening and spiraling down to the surface. The pilots of Wraith Squadron followed, setting their X-wings down and scrambling from the cockpits.

Jag swung wide to make another pass over the forest.

With projectiles streaking out of the trees, Gavin Dark-lighter's Rogues buzzed like angry hornets, torching everything that moved. Jag was racing to join them when a fireball caught the clawcraft from behind, blowing away pieces of the starboard solar panels and sending him into an uncontrollable spin.

The crowns of the trees rushed up at him, then patches of soggy ground. The clawcraft whined as it slammed into the canopy, and darkness engulfed him.

The view forward from the plush cockpit of *Lady Luck* revealed a panorama of stroboscopic globular explosions stretched across, as well as two or three degrees above and below, the ecliptic plane.

"That was the Alliance's salvo," Lando told Tendra.

Her mouth was slightly ajar, she was shaking her head in amazement. "I've never seen anything that was at once so beautiful and so dreadful." Tall, even for a Sacorrian, Tendra was a regal beauty, with sparkling brown eyes and full lips.

The SoroSuub luxury yacht, a somewhat flattened and oblate vessel, was well inside the Alliance lines, but close enough for long-range scanners to capture the continuous exchanges of fire, if not detail the individual warships themselves. Lando knew that Wedge was out there somewhere, along with countless other friends and comrades he had known from as far back as the Battle of Endor.

He couldn't remember a time when he had felt so small or alone. In a gesture that combined affection and anguish, he tightened his grip on Tendra's hand.

No sooner had the spherical explosions faded than a pyrotechnic display of what might have been fire-tailed comets rocketed from unseen sources, splaying against deflector screens too distant to discern, and in some cases creating explosions of their own.

"Nas Choka's response," Lando said dryly.

He flipped a switch on the communications console and swiveled his chair slightly toward the cockpit's audio pickups. "You watching this?"

"Can't take my eyes away," Talon Karrde answered from *Wild Karrde,* five hundred kilometers Rimward and, like *Lady Luck,* running mostly silent.

Scores of other starfighters, converted yachts, and blockade runners allied with the loosely knit Smugglers' Alliance were deployed between *Wild Karrde* and *Errant Venture,* which was closest to Zonama Sekot, and thus almost a quarter of the way to the outer-system world of Stentat.

"How long are we just going to sit here and watch?" Lando asked Talon.

Talon laughed bitterly. "Now is as good a time as any to make our meager but skillful contribution to the cause."

"All right, then." Lando straightened up his seat and was preparing to wake up the ship's systems when Talon commed him again.

"Hold on a minute, hero. My scanners are picking up something peculiar. I'm sending you the coordinates now. You might want to have a look."

Tendra was already realigning the scanners when Lando glanced at the display screen. A sizable number of Yuuzhan Vong ships had separated from the main body of the armada. Accreting velocity, the group was vectoring for the sunward fringe of the battle belt.

"A flanking maneuver?" Lando said. "Maybe an attempt to jump behind Alliance lines?"

"I don't think so," Talon answered. "When they pulled this stunt at Mon Calamari, the ships jumped for Contruum."

Lando frowned. "Kre'fey's long gone from Contruum. But they could be hoping to bait Wedge's battle group into pursuing them."

"Unless they're heading back to Coruscant."

Tendra dialed the scanners to maximum magnification. The computer-assisted portrait painted by the instruments showed a diamond-shaped formation of destroyer and heavy cruiser analogs, with a solitary but otherwise unremarkable vessel occupying the center.

"Major firepower," Lando said.

"They're going to hyperspace," Talon updated.

"Did you get a departure vector?"

"Coming up," Talon said.

Lando and Tendra heard Talon expel his breath in unhappy surprise.

"Zonama Sekot," Lando surmised.

"Didn't that Vong priest, Harrar, say that Shimrra wasn't likely to risk an attack?"

"Guess he doesn't know his Supreme Overlord as well as he thinks he does."

"I'll let Booster know."

Lando silenced the comm and swung to his wife.

"Navicomputer is plotting a course to Zonama Sekot," Tendra said.

Gingerly, Han placed the palms of his hands against the faintly glowing hull of the Sekotan ship. Warm to the touch, the perfectly smooth skin was a shimmering green, lit from within in a way that brought to mind the bioluminescence of some denizens of the deep ocean. Low to the ground, broad where the cockpit was, and composed of three seamlessly joined oval lobes, the ship was a smaller version of the shuttle that had carried him from the *Falcon* to the surface of the planet. But unlike the shuttle, it was armed with plasma cannons that might have been—and probably were—patterned after those of a coralskipper.

Speechless, Han continued his survey of the wondrous ship. Small compared to *Jade Shadow,* which sat on its hardstand nearby, the Sekotan fighter was equivalent to an X-wing in size, though it more closely resembled a vintage Surronian Conqueror or one of the latest generation of Mon Calamarian starfighters. The single-pilot cockpit was an all-too-organic shade of red—made more unnerving by an instrument array that pulsed and throbbed.

The gentle internal radiance of the tripartite fuselage was most intense along the forward edges, which were knife-sharp. In contrast, the trailing edges were rounded over, with the drive tucked into the space between the two rear lobes. Han had overheard Magister Jabitha tell Kyp that the original Sekotan ships had had Haor Chall type-seven *Silver*-class light starship engines, with expensive hyperdrive core units and organiform circuitry. But the ships the Jentari had built for the Jedi lacked a conventional drive—unless dovin basal analogs had come to be considered standard equipment.

The similarity to coralskippers didn't end with gravitic propulsion devices and volcano-like weapons emplacements. Though it required the pilot who had bonded with its formative seed-partners, a Sekotan craft was *alive* and, to a degree, capable of independent action.

Han wasn't the only person in awe. Working overtime, the

Jentari had been able to shape ships for all the Jedi who had participated in the recent ceremony. Delivered from the cybernetic assembly lines by huge manta-shaped dirigibles, the Sekotan fighters crowded the canyon-rim landing platform. None of them had been flown, but Han could feel the eagerness of the pilots—Kyp, Corran, Lowbacca, dark-complected Markre Medjev, facially scarred Waxarn Kel, the stocky Chandrilan woman Octa Ramis, slight Tam Azur-Jamin, gallant Kyle Katarn, the ever-brooding Zekk, the Barabel Saba Sebatyne, and the Twi'lek female Alema Rar—all of whom were circling their individual crafts, much as Han was circling Kyp's.

"Well, she's not the *Falcon*," Han said, "but I'm sure she'll do until the next *living* ship comes along."

Kyp took his gaze from the ship long enough to glance at Han and laugh. "Wish I could tell you to take it for a spin."

Han nodded. "Yeah, I wish you could, too."

Distracted, Han wasn't aware of Leia's approach until she slipped her arm through his and rested her head against his shoulder. He turned slightly, expecting to see her smiling as broadly as he was. Instead, she was anything but joyful.

"What's wrong?"

"Luke just heard from Booster. A Yuuzhan Vong battle group is headed here."

Han stared at her. "I thought—"

It was all he got out before Luke, Mara, Jaina, Danni, Kenth, and some of the other Jedi arrived at the landing platform. The last to show up were Magister Jabitha, Jacen, and Harrar. The pilots hurried from their Sekotan ships to join the circle that quickly took shape around Luke.

"We were hoping for more time, but that's not going to happen," Luke began. "The Yuuzhan Vong are on the way, which means you're going to have to get your ships airborne and give yourselves a crash course in piloting them." He swung to face Tesar Sebatyne. "The shuttle will take you and the rest of the Wild Knights to your blastboat and fighters."

Saba nodded to her son. "Good hunting, Tesar."

"Now do I get to fly my X-wing?" Jaina asked.

Mara shot her a cautionary look. "We've been through this."

"But—"

"May I say something?" Harrar said.

Everyone turned to him in surprise.

"Assuming some of you are going to Coruscant, your war party will benefit by having both Jaina Solo and Jacen Solo as comrades. Our warriors are very superstitious, and the sight of the celebrated Jedi twins—united—could demoralize them. The capture of one such as Jaina Solo would count for more than her death." The priest paused to glance around. "Our forces failed at Borleias because Supreme Commander Czulkang Lah was fixated on capturing the Jedi who had come to be associated with Yun-Harla. It was my personal failing that I supported Czulkang Lah's actions."

Tahiri looked at Jaina. "At Borleias I told you not to accompany Luke and Mara to Coruscant, because I was afraid that your presence would endanger them. Now I agree with Harrar that you should go."

Jaina folded her arms across her chest. "Nice to see that everyone is so comfortable with deciding my destiny."

Jabitha stepped forward before anyone could respond. "Sekot has requested that Cilghal, Tekli, and Danni Quee remain on Zonama."

Danni looked at Luke in stark confusion. "I thought I'd be going with you and Mara to Coruscant."

Luke shook his head. "Sekot obviously feels that you're needed here."

"If I can accept not flying, then you can accept staying here," Jaina said.

Han and Leia traded uneasy looks.

Luke took his lightsaber from his belt, ignited the blade, and held it over his head. Wordlessly, the other Jedi began to follow suit. Taking note of Leia's hesitation, Han nodded in encouragement.

"Go," he said quietly, "you're as much a Jedi as any of them."

The Jedi tightened up around Luke, angling their lightsabers slightly so that the tips pointed toward his, and in the end creating a stand of colorful blades that thrummed ominously in the crisp air.

"This day has been years in the making. What we do from this moment forward will test our fealty to the Force in a way that the Jedi haven't been tested in more than a generation. Be mindful that we are not the purveyors of conflict and inequity, but the guardians of peace and justice. Above all, we want what the Force wants, no matter where that leads us. If some of us are not seen again today, that does not mean that our actions will have been in vain or will not be remembered."

Han looked to those who didn't have lightsabers—the few outside the circle: Jabitha, Harrar, and Danni—wondering where he fit in. But he added his voice to the rest when they said, as one, *"May the Force be with us!"*

THIRTY-FIVE

Scepter of Power grasped in his right hand and trailed by a cortege of eight slayers, Shimrra marched into the Hall of Convergence, his legs propelling him in such long strides that Onimi was compelled to run to keep up. Alerted to his approach, everyone present in the vaulted chamber—Nom Anor included—had already assumed attitudes of obeisance. The warriors were down on one knee, and the four seers had their heads inclined in reverent if apprehensive bows. The hall smelled strongly of sacrificial blood, yorik coral dust, and incense, and suddenly of floral scents as the Supreme Overlord's bare feet crushed the flower petals that had been scattered for him.

Shimrra went directly to his ray-backed throne, but sat for only a moment before rising and beginning to pace back and forth, a confused Onimi following in the wake of the Supreme Overlord's pliant flayed-skin robe.

"Why was I summoned from my meditation with the gods?" Shimrra demanded of no one in particular. "Is my role in our final campaign less than yours, Supreme Commander Laait?" He gazed balefully at the seers. "Or yours?"

Laait remained in genuflection. "Supreme One, the warmaster bade that I seek audience with you as soon as you would permit."

"Is Warmaster Nas Choka's inactivity such that he can find time to communicate with the likes of you?"

"Dread Lord, the warmaster had been anything but idle," Laait said with a hint of exasperation. "Engaged at Muscave, his forces overwhelm those of our enemy. Thus was he able to dispatch to Zonama Sekot a task force that escorts and safeguards the ailing vessel that is our secret weapon."

Shimrra made a fatigued sound. "I need to hear this from your mouth, Supreme Commander? Did I not just say that your urgent entreaty found me deep in rapport with the gods?"

Laait snapped his fists to his shoulders in salute. "I beg forgiveness, Great One. Then assuredly you already know that Zonama Sekot appeared to be undefended, save for a handful of enemy fighters."

"Assuredly."

"And that the task force commander dispatched coral-skippers to engage those fighters."

"What of it?" Shimrra said heatedly. "Would you hold me prisoner here with your pointless statements?"

Again Laait snapped his fists. "Of course the gods told you, Lord, that the coralskippers have met with resistance from *living* vessels."

Shimrra came to an abrupt halt and stared at the Supreme Commander.

"Dread Lord," Onimi said, as if to prompt a response.

"Living vessels, you say," Shimrra said finally.

Laait nodded in acknowledgment. "Vessels that not only match our coralskippers for size and speed, but also are propelled by gravitic affinity, and answer our plasma weapons with *theirs*."

Shimrra pointed to the hall's villip-choir. "I would see an image of these living vessels!"

Supreme Commander Laait stood and beckoned to the villip mistress. Shortly a ghostly image appeared, showing a vessel forged of smooth rocks, dimpled with plasma launchers and dovin basal emplacements.

Canting his huge head, Shimrra regarded the glimmering image in silence.

"The domain commander reported to Warmaster Nas Choka that the living vessels have sown confusion among our ranks of coralskippers. Worse, the yammosk itself is perplexed. It is having trouble differentiating our vessels from the enemy vessels."

Shimrra swung to Laait. "Why hasn't the warmaster ordered the domain commander to bring his capital vessels to bear on Zonama Sekot?"

"The warmaster wishes to do just that, God-Chosen. He merely awaits your sanction for such an action."

Shimrra said nothing.

"Great One?" Laait said carefully, after a long moment had passed.

"What do the *seers* say of all this?" Onimi interjected into the ensuing silence, as if deflecting attention from Shimrra.

"The auguries have left us troubled, Great Lord," their haggish spokeswoman said. "The prospect of combating *living* vessels runs counter to the most sacred of our beliefs. Even as a test of our worthiness, the gods themselves would never have engineered such a sacrilege. We implore you, Lord, to explain how infidels have been allowed access to our biotechnology, and been granted sanction to create vessels that mimic ours."

"There is more, Lord," a second seer said. "Several enemy ships have outwitted our dovin basal voids and found their way to the surface of Yuuzhan'tar. Even now our primary landing field is threatened."

Shimrra seemed to shake himself out of his daze. "Need I remind any of you that I have looked deeply into the eighth cortex, and conversed with Yun-Harla herself on these matters?"

The chief seer nodded. "We bear that in mind, Great One, and ask only for *elucidation*. Could the ancient prophecies and revelations be wrong? Could they have been misinterpreted? Is it possible that the gods have not engineered the living vessels as an additional test, but in fact have aligned themselves with the *Jeedai*?"

Shimrra's eyes flared like novas. "Heresy! Heresy—here in my very house!" He aimed the scepter at the seers. "You buffoons have outlived your usefulness." He whirled to the slayers. "Rid me of them!"

A pair of slayers uncoiled their amphistaffs and advanced on the female quartet with deadly purpose. The seers offered no resistance, raising faces and extending their thin necks for the stiffened weapons. The slayers wasted no motions in decapitating them. One of the severed heads was still rolling across the floor when a herald entered the hall.

"Great Lord, High Priest Jakan, Master Shaper Qelah Kwaad, and High Prefect Drathul request audience."

Shimrra went to his throne and sat. "By all means bid them enter, herald."

The elite trio entered in a rush, but lost some of their momentum on seeing the four headless corpses.

Shimrra smiled faintly. "They had the audacity to doubt my interpretation of the revelation." His expression darkened. "Be attentive to their present circumstance when you state your concerns."

"We have no concerns, Dread Lord," Drathul said, clearly improvising. "On learning of the warmaster's report of living ships, we came to offer you praise for your foresight. The Yuuzhan Vong are escalated by the gods' willingness to present us with even greater challenges."

"You hastened here to tell me that?" Shimrra asked.

"One question, Lord," Jakan said. "Have the gods furnished these ships to the Alliance, or do the ships originate from the living world itself?"

Shimrra gestured in an offhand way to Nom Anor. "Answer him, Prefect. Since you are our leading expert on Zonama Sekot."

The object of Jakan and Qelah Kwaad's astonishment, Nom Anor, slouched. Taken off his guard, he had to swallow to find his voice.

"Supreme One, I—I know only what I hear from spies among the heretics. But I—I suspect that there are no living ships." He grew emboldened as he continued. "Instead, I propose that our coralskipper pilots have fallen victim to *Jeedai* mind tricks."

Drathul gestured angrily to the villip-image of the living ship. "You dismiss that as a *Jeedai* mind trick?"

Shimrra grinned maniacally. "Answer your superior, Prefect Nom Anor."

Nom Anor straightened his shoulders. "Why not? We know that they are capable of projecting false images and putting words in the mouths of those they would manipulate. We also know that they have successfully confused our yammosks in the past."

Shimrra spoke before Drathul could argue the point. "Prefect Nom Anor is to be admired for his inventiveness. But, in fact, the vessel our villips show us is no mind trick. In answer to High Priest Jakan's question, the gods have tutored the living planet in the creation of these monstrosities. But the *Jeedai* are not responsible." He paused, then said, "It is the heretics who have brought this latest test upon us. The gods have no desire to award us this galaxy while heretics and Shamed Ones walk freely among us. They won't permit us to deliver the poison vessel until we have brought *Yuuzhan'tar* into balance."

Onimi shuffled to the center of the hall. "Great One," he began. "Our skies breached, our land despoiled; these heretic ravings we can later foil—"

"Enough of your insolent rhyming, *Shamed One*!" Shimrra cut him off. "Only by my good graces have you been spared the life led by others of your kind. Do you, too, doubt me? Do you, too, harbor fears of defeat, and rally suddenly to the heretic cause?"

Onimi fell on his face before the throne. "I remain your most abject servant, Lord."

Shimrra ignored him. "The heretics must be eradicated!" He turned to the commander of the slayers. "Half the Citadel garrison of warriors is to be placed at the right hand of Prefect Nom Anor. He will lead them against the heretics and the Shamed Ones. Not one of them is to be left alive!"

"Your will be done, Great Lord," the commander said. In unison, the slayers turned and snapped their fists in salute to Nom Anor.

Drathul looked from Nom Anor to Shimrra in mounting bewilderment. "But what of Yuuzhan'tar, Lord? Our dovin basals are overwhelmed. The enemy has made a sieve of our sky—"

"I will deal with those who would profane our soil." Shimrra's gaze fell in turn on Jakan, Qelah Kwaad, and Drathul. "Go to the Well of the World Brain. I will communicate with it, and prepare it for your arrival."

"What, then?" Jakan asked.

"By and by, priest."

With a motion of his fingertips, Shimrra dismissed everyone, including Onimi. As the elite were filing from the hall, Drathul dragged Nom Anor aside.

"We know that Commander Ekh'm Val brought a Sekotan ship to Yuuzhan'tar," he hissed. "You had the opportunity to say as much for everyone to hear, and to put an end to Shimrra's charade. Whose service do you do by concealing the truth now, with our future hanging in the balance?"

"I serve myself," Nom Anor said evenly.

Drathul shoved him back. "As ever. I would kill you now but for your new legion of bodyguards. But you will die before this day is through, Nom Anor. If not by my hand, then by another's."

Nom Anor glanced at Jakan, then at Qelah Kwaad, and finally at Onimi, who appeared to be watching him closely. "Stand in line, High Prefect," he said at last. "I've no lack of enemies."

A human soldier rapped the knuckles of his gloved hand against the circular viewport of Jag's inverted clawcraft. "Hang on a minute, flyboy," he yelled.

All at once the access hatch above—or under—Jag's head opened, and several pairs of hands were reaching inside the cockpit to release him from the crash webbing that secured him to the seat.

"Down you go," the same one who had rapped on the viewport said.

Jag allowed himself to descend into the upraised hands of his rescuers, and to continue to be supported by them while he was planted on his feet, with the world spinning around him and the blood that had gathered in his head draining back to where it belonged. Someone removed Jag's helmet and put the mouth of a canteen to his lips.

When the long moment of dizziness had passed, he saw that the clawcraft—missing three of its sweeping talon-shaped solar array panels—had crashed upside down in a copse of tangled, fruit-bearing trees that rose from the middle of an oozy villip paddy. The soldiers around him wore jet backpacks, holotransceiving helmets, and combat biosuits. Seen through the snarl of branches overhead, Coruscant's bruised sky was torn to ribbons with contrails, meteors, and countless dirtbound coralskippers and starfighters. Explosions strobed and flashed in tiers behind scudding clouds of gray smoke.

A haze of smoke lay over the rank-smelling paddy, as well, and from all directions came the reports of concussion missiles and torpedoes, the sizzle and hiss of laser beams, the roar of Yuuzhan Vong beasts, the bloodthirsty cries of warriors—all of it reverberating from the sheer faces of yorik coral outcroppings and the digested facades of once-grand spacescrapers that studded the terrain.

"Is he hurt?" someone asked, loud enough to be heard over the tumult.

Jag recognized the lined face of Captain Judder Page under the camouflage cosmetic. Jag patted himself down. "I'm unharmed."

Page swung to his communications aide. "Inform starfighter control on *Right to Rule* that Colonel Fel is ground-side and back on his feet."

"Incoming!" came a distant voice.

Page and others dragged Jag to the ground an instant before a swarm of thud and razor bugs ripped through the gnarled trees, stripping leaves and oval-shaped fruits from the branches, and knocking down entire limbs. Two deafening explosions followed in succession and the storm of projectile biots abated.

A flight of black-striped bright yellow X-wings streaked over the treetops, firing quad bursts at some unseen target. Page, Jag, and the others crouched, then slowly got to their feet. Combat droids armored with laminanium had formed a perimeter at the edge of the trees. Close to what remained of Jag's clawcraft, two medical droids were field-dressing wounds sustained by a couple of humans and Bothans.

Page stuck out his hand. "I'm Captain—"

"I know who you are," Jag said. "Thank you for coming to my aid."

Page shrugged off the gratitude and motioned to the men on either side of him. "Garik Loran," he said, naming the shaven-skulled one; then, "Kell Tainer," naming the one with the receding hairline.

"Wraith Squadron," Jag said, shaking hands with each of

them. "I met both of you on Borleias." He glanced at Page. "Just before my clawcraft was hit, I saw number two transport crash."

Page nodded grimly. "Grutchins took it down and chewed their way through the hull. We've sent a squad to search the canyon for survivors."

"Captain Page," a young Bothan interrupted. "We've made contact with the indigenous force."

Jag, Page, and the pair of Wraith Squadron Intelligence operatives turned to see four Yuuzhan Vong males being ushered through the perimeter. The humanoids were scarcely scarred compared to most of the Yuuzhan Vong warriors Jag had seen, but all had pronounced deformities, some of the face, others of the limbs.

Shamed Ones, he thought.

The tallest and most deformed of the four executed a facsimile of an Alliance salute. "Take us to your leaders," he said in Basic, as if by rote.

Garik Loran and Kell Tainer exchanged skeptical glances. "Who taught you to say that?" Loran asked.

"I did," someone answered in a clipped Coruscanti accent, as the same Shamed One was pressing his forefinger to his ear, presumably to adjust the fit of a translating tizowyrm.

A tall, lean, dark-haired human appeared from the trees, beaming at the two Wraiths.

"Son of a blaster," Tainer said, smiling.

Jag was familiar with the name *Baljos Arnjak.* Also a Wraith, Arnjak had remained behind on Coruscant following the combined Wraith/Jedi infiltration mission almost two years earlier. With him walked a thin but dashing-looking middle-aged man, with reddish hair, bright even teeth, and deeply tanned skin.

Smiling broadly, Page immediately shook hands with the man, then pulled him into a mutually back-slapping embrace. "I always figured you'd survive," Page said when the two had stepped away from each other.

The handsome man motioned to the four Yuuzhan Vong. "Thanks to them, I did. Their heretic group rescued me and a bunch of others from what would have been some serious bloodletting at one of the temples."

Page turned to Jag. "Fel, meet Major Pash Cracken."

Jag nodded in greeting. Coruscant was suddenly starting to feel like the Veterans' Home.

"How long will it take us to reach Westport from here?" Page was saying.

"It would have taken about an hour, but we're too late." Cracken beckoned for everyone to follow him to the perimeter. Once there, he gestured to the northern horizon, which was a solid bank of billowing smoke.

"The entire sacred precinct is up in flames," Cracken said.

Page pressed a blaster into Jag's gloved right hand. "Welcome to the commandos, Colonel."

"The fires are Shimrra's doing," Harrar said. "The Supreme Overlord has asked the World Brain to set Yuuzhan'tar ablaze—to prevent *anyone* from occupying it." The priest sounded despondent. "Shimrra wouldn't have done this unless he fears defeat. Either that or the proximity of Zonama Sekot has deranged him."

"Whether he's desperate or mad, we have him on the run," Han said, elated.

Harrar gazed at those around him. Judging by the nods of agreement, the always entertaining and sometimes perplexing Han Solo was expressing the sentiment of everyone gathered at the landing platform—his wife, Leia; Master Luke Skywalker and his wife, Mara; the twins Jacen and Jaina; Yuuzhan Vong–marked Tahiri; the military-minded Jedi Kenth Hamner; Zonama Sekot's Magister Jabitha; the two numerically named machine intelligences—droids—who sometimes seemed as alive as their makers and owners; and the pair of Noghri, who appeared at once to be bodyguards, familiars, and friends.

The rest of the Jedi had taken to the skies in the Sekotan ships, or had been lofted by shuttle to their orbiting warcraft. Han Solo had ridden up the gravity well with the Wild Knights, but only to retrieve his battered freighter, *Millennium Falcon,* which, with Sekot's permission, was now parked on its landing disks and warming alongside Mara Skywalker's *Jade Shadow.* Word of the conflagrations spreading across Yuuzhan'tar had come from Booster Terrik, the penultimate link in a communications chain that began with the commando team that had penetrated Yuuzhan'tar's defenses, and had apparently included the giant warships *Right to Rule* and *Mon Mothma*.

"How could even Shimrra convince the dhuryam to do something harmful to Yuuzhan'tar?" Jacen asked.

"All things Yuuzhan Vong answer to Shimrra," Harrar said. "The dhuryam is responsible for integrating the activities of all our planetshaping biots. It is not a servant, but a partner—fully intelligent, fully aware, capable of making decisions based on information it receives from telepathically linked creatures, and from the Supreme Overlord himself. But Shimrra may have convinced the dhuryam that intense fires were needed to open latent seedpods, so that trees could grow to replace those lost during the recent landquakes. He may have suggested to the dhuryam that it fashion clearings in the forests, so that saplings might glean additional light, as well as nourishment from trees felled and reduced to ash by the fires."

"All the more reason for us to get to Shimrra *now*," Han said, pacing at the foot of the *Millennium Falcon*'s landing ramp. "If Page got his transports past the dovin basals, I know I can get the *Falcon* through."

Harrar shook his head.

"What now?" Han asked, planting his hands on his hips in a posture of impatience.

"Capturing or killing Shimrra may not be enough to save the planet. Actions taken by the World Brain are incontrovertible. Once tasked, it cannot be swayed to alter its plan—even by Shimrra." Harrar glanced at the Skywalkers. "If you are to save your capital world, the brain, too, will have to be destroyed."

"You can't do that, Harrar," Jacen snapped.

Harrar looked at the young Jedi. "Then go to it, and persuade it otherwise."

"That's our job," Han said suddenly, reaching for Leia's right hand. With the other Jedi, Magister Jabitha, and the pair of droids gazing at him in sudden alarm, he added: "D'you think we were just going to give the rest of you a ride there?" He jerked his thumb at the *Millennium Falcon*. "This ship ain't no air taxi." He snorted ruefully, then grew solemn. "Besides, we started this together in the Outer Rim, and we're going to end it together."

"Or his name isn't Han Solo," Leia said, in a way that mixed amusement and resignation.

Han grinned in a lopsided fashion. "Took the words right out of my mouth."

THIRTY-SIX

Three hundred armored warriors borrowed from the Citadel garrison and on loan to Prefect Nom Anor raced through the squares and byways of the sacred precinct like an avenging army, putting coufee and amphistaff to every heretic and Shamed One who hadn't had sense enough to go into hiding—which turned out to be many.

Hundreds.

Thousands.

Enraptured by the prophesied arrival of Zonama Sekot, certain that thousand-eyed Yun-Shuno would guarantee their passage to a beatific afterlife, exulting in their newfound freedom—however short-lived—confident that Shimrra and the elite would be overthrown, the heretics were fervent to martyr themselves. Ostracized because of physiological defects rather than committed sins, forced to live in the shadow of the un-Shamed and under the scrutiny of merciless gods, guilty of trespasses they couldn't begin to imagine and would spend the rest of their miserable lives attempting to understand, they had at last embraced their peculiarities and cast their lot with the Jedi.

There was simply no holding them back.

Carried along by sheer exuberance, proclaiming their long-overdue equality and salvation for all to hear, they poured from their hidey-holes like ngdins at a sacrifice—and indeed thousands of the meter-long blood soakers followed them out into rapidly darkening daylight, assured of more than the usual share of glossy black nutrient.

Yuuzhan'tar had become a feeding frenzy for warriors who should have known better, and for biots that were doing only what they had been bred to do.

Gazing down on the Place of Hierarchy, Nom Anor was struck dumb by the butchery for which he was responsible—thanks to Shimrra—and yet was powerless to thwart. He could no more command the warriors to desist than he could convince the Shamed Ones to flee. He was, as ever, caught in the middle, though placed there by his own schemes, lies, and masquerades.

The realization made him desperate. The insatiable warrior pack had worked its way south from the Citadel, through Vistu and Numesh, across bridges and down alleyways, slaughtering wherever they fared, until they had entered the public place that of late had become the heretics' hallowed ground, owing to the many who already died there during demonstrations and riots.

It was immediately clear that the warriors had merely been practicing up until this point. For now, trapped in the Place of Hierarchy was a crowd into which they could wade like thrashing biots. Before them stood those responsible for keeping the Yuuzhan Vong from total victory at Zonama Sekot. These were the ones who would pay, against whom the warriors could exorcise their fear and confusion—even if those they put to death were as innocent as they were Shameless.

But the horror had scarcely commenced—with war cries answered by agonized screams—when fires began to break out in many of the quake-damaged structures that walled the place, including the prefectory and the Temple of the Lovers, Yun-Txiin and Yun-Q'aah.

For a moment Nom Anor was certain that the sudden blazes were the result of firebomb strafings by Alliance starfighters that had punched through Coruscant's dovin basal voids. From his vantage at the top of the flight of yorik coral stairs that fronted the prefectory he could see that similar conflagrations were raging in all precincts of the city, and beyond. Flaring from the vegetation that cloaked the buttes that were the tops of buildings and towers, the flames were being carried by the wind to all quarters.

But the hot swirling wind also brought the foul odor of marsh gas to Nom Anor's flattened nostrils, and he swung around in disbelief to see a cavalcade of fire-breathing Yuuzhan Vong beasts bobbing over the cityscape.

Quickly he lifted his gaze.

There were too few starfighters in the sky to account for so many fires, and no evidence of orbital bombardment, turbo-laser bolts, or proton torpedoes. Then he understood, and his heart filled with such anguish that he dropped to his knees and remained there until he had caught his breath and regained his senses.

Shimrra was responsible!

Beyond reason, beyond madness, the Supreme Overlord had struck a deal with the dhuryam to destroy Coruscant—Nom Anor's Coruscant! With the same ruthlessness that had allowed him to dispatch Warmaster Nas Choka's armada on a suicide mission to poison Zonama Sekot, Shimrra had decided to eradicate all things Yuuzhan Vong. He had become the Yuuzhan Vong–specific poison he had fabricated for the elite—if only to spite gods he had once professed not to believe in!

Nom Anor railed and shook his fists at the smoke- and ember-filled sky.

I should have killed you when I had the chance!

He struggled to his feet, his expression growing more grave with every centimeter of elevation. His fists were balled, and his one eye blazed. His near-lipless mouth was drawn back, and his muscles were bunched under his thin garments. His sloped forehead was as inflamed as the city itself.

He stiffened his arm, catching in the windpipe a warrior too distracted by bloodlust to see the blow coming. The warrior fell to the steps gurgling, clutching his throat, eyes squeezed tight in pain. Nom Anor summoned the warrior's amphistaff to come to him, and with one strike put the choking soldier out of his misery. He descended the broad staircase in a stupor, shucking out of the green robe and turban that identified him as an intendant. At the foot of the broad stairs he grabbed the tattered robeskin of a slain Shamed One and, donning it, began to shoulder his way into the Place of Hierarchy, ignoring the bloodshed occurring on all sides and aiming for a tall rubble pile at the center of the square. Short of the pile, a warrior rushed him, forcing him to step back and fight, amphistaff against amphistaff. Parrying two blows, Nom Anor ducked down and slashed his opponent across the knees; then rose, bringing the sharp end of the serpentine weapon diagonally across the warrior's face. The warrior screamed and raised his hands, and Nom Anor speared him through the neck.

With bodies falling all around him, he scrambled up the pile. There, alone at the summit, he loosed a bloodcurdling scream and raised the arm around which the living weapon was curled.

"I am Yu'shaa, the Prophet!" he yelled at the top of his lungs. "Our hour is at hand! I will lead you to victory!"

A long moment of stunned silence fell over the Place of Hierarchy. Then a roar went up from the oppressed, and they surged against the warriors, crude weapons cleaving, black blood streaming and misting into the air, fiery embers cycloning about them like a sacrament from the gods!

From one hundred thousand kilometers out, Coruscant was a vortex of destruction, lanced from all directions by turbolaser bolts, mottled by yawning dovin basal singularities, lit from within by flaring explosions.

"This party's just the way we left it," Han said as the *Falcon* streaked for the embattled galactic center.

"I missed that one, Dad," Jaina said flatly from the copilot's chair.

"Me, too," Jacen said from behind her. Peripherally, Han saw his son glance at the Yuuzhan Vong priest in the adjacent chair. "Harrar and I were on a worldship over Myrkr."

Regretting his facile statement, Han went back to attending to the *Falcon*'s instruments.

The fall of Coruscant had been among the worst days of his life—almost as horrible as when Chewbacca had died at Sernpidal. The images of the evacuation were burned into his memory: Yuuzhan Vong hurling themselves and hostages against the planetary shields, a steady rain of flaming spacecraft, he and Leia trying to flee Eastport with baby Ben, C-3PO, a YVH droid, and a potted ladalum . . . Their escape sabotaged at the *Falcon*'s docking bay by a disguised Senator Viqi Shesh and an innocent twelve-year-old kid named

Dab Hantaq—Tarc—who happened to bear a likeness to young Anakin.

The death of Adarakh, Leia's bodyguard, at Shesh's hand.

The sky dazzled by plasma balls.

Towers crumbling, people stampeding for the few starliners and government yachts that remained on the surface . . .

And light-years away at the Inner Rim world of Myrkr, Anakin dying, Jaina fleeing in a stolen enemy ship, Jacen in the clutches of Vergere—captured or rescued, depending on how you looked at it. Han squeezed his eyes shut in recalled despair.

"*Party*," Harrar said abruptly. "Many of our warriors use that term to describe combat engagements. You have the makings of a Supreme Commander, Han Solo."

Han laughed shortly, recalling that Jacen had said that the priest was fascinated with him. "Thanks for thinking of me, Harrar, but no matter what anyone says about it, I happen to like my face just the way it is."

Jacen and an uneasy Harrar had taken the cockpit's rear chairs after Leia and Luke had climbed into the quad laser turrets. Mara, Kenth, Tahiri, Cakhmaim, Meewalh, and the droids were in the forward compartment. At the cost of some discretionary power, Han planned to keep the *Falcon*'s artificial gravity enabled for as long as possible, if only to prevent everyone from being bounced all over the ship.

Alliance capital vessels were concentrating fire along the transitor and well into Coruscant's bright side, but the battle was raging planetwide. Star Destroyers, cruisers, and frigates were still vectoring in from hyperspace routes rarely used since the days of the Old Republic, and enemy forces were blasting up the gravity well to reinforce the defense flotilla. The Yuuzhan Vong were widely dispersed but consolidated over the equator, above what had been Imperial/New Republic City, in the western hemisphere. The Alliance had yet to press any capital ships through the blockade of kilometer-long, weapons-studded vessels, but hundreds of starfighters had penetrated enemy lines and were attacking the arrays of dovin basals in orbit at the edge of Coruscant's atmosphere.

Now it was the *Falcon*'s turn to try to slip past.

It was the opposite of what Han had had to do to get the

freighter safely off Zonama Sekot. There the upper reaches of the envelope had been a dizzying clash of coralskippers and Sekotan fighters. From what Luke had been able to gather from Kyp and the other Jedi pilots, the sight of living ships had thrown the skips into disarray. But the Jedi had also discovered that Magister Jabitha hadn't been understating anything when she had said that the Sekotan ships were for defense only. As often as not, the fleet fighters wouldn't fire unless fired upon, and for all their astounding alacrity, they weren't flying circles around the coralskippers so much as matching them maneuver for maneuver.

Two hundred thousand kilometers from the living world drifted the enemy task force that had delivered the coralskippers, along with the yammosk-carrying clustership that was guiding them.

It was still anyone's guess why Warmaster Nas Choka had sent a splinter group to Zonama Sekot, but it stood to reason that the Yuuzhan Vong wouldn't wait long before bringing their capital ships to bear on the planet. Although *Errant Venture* and Tenel Ka's flotilla of Hapan Battle Dragons and *Nova*-class cruisers were reported to be on the way, it was unlikely that they could prevail against the task force. Engaged in a ferocious battle near Muscave, Wedge Antilles and Keyan Farlander wouldn't be able to lend support until Kre'fey's First Fleet arrived to relieve them.

With so much action in the Coruscant system—from Vandor 3 clear to the Ulabos ice bands—Han had considered staging the *Falcon* through a series of microjumps. Ultimately, however, he had decided to jump the ship directly to Coruscant. They had reverted to realspace behind Alliance lines, but close enough to their target to be staggered by what they saw. Green and white where it had once been a sheen of artificial light, orbited by the remains of a shattered moon, its polar caps reduced to icebergs . . . Coruscant might as well have been an unfamiliar world.

A tone sounded from the comm board, and a baritone voice issued from the cockpit annunciators. "*Millennium Falcon,* this is *Right to Rule* control. Your best insertion point is presently at Bacta Sector, eight-one-seven. But we'll keep you updated on the situation."

Jaina leaned forward to study the tactical display. "Copy that, *Right to Rule*. And thanks for the help."

"*Millennium Falcon,* Grand Admiral Pellaeon wishes you good fortune."

"Tell him the same from us," Han said into the headset mouthpiece.

Pellaeon's Fourth Fleet, which included a trio of Star Destroyers and an assortment of *Strike-* and *Carrack*-class cruisers, was pounding the Yuuzhan Vong battle group. In several sectors the orbital dovin basals had been overwhelmed by the barrage, but Alliance command was using the debilitated zones only as corridors for the infiltration of troop ships and squadrons of escort starfighters.

"Your warmaster appears to be deferring to Jacen Solo's report that bombardment will prompt the World Brain to render the planet unfit for habitation," Harrar said into Han's right ear.

Gazing at the turmoil planetside, Han said, "Looks to me like the World Brain is doing a pretty good job of that without having to be prompted."

The *Falcon* was closing on the insertion point when two X-wings appeared to either side of it.

"Good to see you, *Millennium Falcon,*" one of the pilots said over the tactical net. "Mind if we ride down with you?"

"Who's escorting who?" Jaina asked.

"Let's call it a party of three," the other pilot said.

"*Party,*" Harrar murmured.

The spacecraft that housed the orbital dovin basals might have been fragments of Coruscant's deliberately smashed moon, but the voids they generated were as large as shockball stadiums. With the X-wings pressing close, Han sent the *Falcon* on her starboard side to edge between two gaping shield singularities. The ship wasn't through the strait when a third void yawned.

"Feed that thing something!" Jaina said over the net.

The starfighter pilots responded by paying out pairs of proton torpedoes. Instantly warped off course, the glowing orbs were ingested by the gravitic anomaly. With the dovin basal momentarily distracted, Han called on the sublight drives for a burst of speed and rocketed the *Falcon* past the maw. Yet another singularity opened in front of the ship, but this time Han made careful use of the braking thrusters to nuzzle the *Falcon* close enough so that gravity whipped the freighter around the void and threw it deeper into the atmosphere. He did the same with the succeeding quartet of wells, using the gravitic distortions to sling the ship in an elongated double-S from one to the next.

The *Falcon* shook and shuddered, and the engines roared in protest, but the gambit worked to keep the ship from being wrenched off course. One of the X-wings wasn't as fortunate. Even while the pilot was attempting to confuse the dovin basal with stutterfire and two remaining torpedoes, the creature's singularity reached out and grabbed the starfighter, which disintegrated before it disappeared entirely.

The *Falcon* swooped lower on a sinuous tail of blue energy, but the gauntlet didn't end with the dovin basals. A matalok cruiser racing up the well caught sight of the freighter and spewed a volley of magma missiles from its starboard-side plasma launchers.

"Diverting power to the deflectors," Jaina said, without being asked.

Han yawed hard to port, and began weaving through the storm of ejecta. The X-wing that had ridden in on the *Falcon*'s tail hung close, but couldn't keep pace with the larger ship. Han tried to swerve back on course to shield the starfighter, but even the *Falcon* was capable of only so much twisting and veering. Molten rock splashed against the *Falcon*'s screens, but the main body of the salvo flooded over the mandibles and caught the hapless X-wing head-on.

Han bit back a curse and leaned into the control yoke, dropping the *Falcon* like a stone, straight for the ascending matalok. Intent on squaring off with the cruiser, he had the concussion missile launchers armed when the proximity alarms began to blare.

"Four skips to starboard!" Jaina said. "Intercept course!"

Han performed a lightning-fast pushover. "Give your mom and your uncle a heads-up!"

Displaying their customary contempt for evasive tactics, the skips broke ranks and came at the *Falcon* from separate vectors, firing at extreme range. Han heard the top and belly quad lasers begin to chuff and chunder, and banked slightly to starboard to place two of the hostiles in the Money Lane. Outwitting the shield singularities generated by the dovin basals, the powerful guns began to make immediate strikes, chopping away at the skips' yorik coral hulls. A final burst from Leia in the dorsal turret sent one of the craft colliding into the other.

"Nice work!" Han said. "Now see if you can get rid of the other two!"

Again the reciprocating guns began to clack, loosing bright green salvos of devastating energy at the *Falcon*'s pursuers. Voids formed instantly at the blunt noses of the wedge-shaped skips, and most of the quad bursts were swallowed, but some of Luke's bolts got through, and hunks of yorik coral flew off into space. Abruptly the lead skip peeled away and tried to attach itself to the *Falcon* in what would have been the kill zone of an ordinary ship.

Han merely applied power, rolled, and dived for the surface.

Plasma projectiles streamed from the frustrated skip, but all it received for the effort were answering barrages of laserfire. Struck repeatedly, the coralskipper wobbled as pieces of its wide stern were blown away. Crippled, the skip went into a helpless wiggle, then commenced a long fall toward the planet, trailing a plume of smoke and yorik coral dust.

The surviving skip held position through the *Falcon*'s corkscrewing dive and continued firing. As plasma ranged closer, Han boosted power to the rear shields and narrowed the ship's profile by pulling a snap-roll that lifted the *Falcon* onto her starboard side. Luke and Leia triggered out-of-phase bursts, which began to wear down the dovin basal and penetrate the small voids it was managing to produce. Sustaining convergent strikes to the bow, the skip reared up and split apart.

The *Falcon* flashed out of her evasive maneuvers, then banked broadly and darted for clear space. Raising the bow, Han leveled out and arced for the horizon.

"Let Luke know I'm deactivating the artificial gravity," he

told Jaina. "If he knows what's good for him he'll climb out of that belly turret."

Shortly, the *Falcon* was wending through forested spires that rose east of the sacred precinct. Below were villip paddies, interconnected orange-tinted lakes, and yorik coral quarries—some containing skips in their formative stages. Flames mushroomed and stabbed from the deep canyons, and microstorms carried burning vegetation toward distant patches of woodland.

"We've been spotted," Jaina said. "Coralskippers approaching from the south."

Han punched the throttle, whipping the freighter up and over a burning mound, then dropped down over the expansive plain from which Imperial/New Republic City had grown. He had to keep reminding himself that he wasn't flying over hills but over buried structures; that what appeared to be an escarpment had been a kilometers-long block of residential buildings; that the geometric craters dotting the landscape were the foundations of the great edifices themselves, now filled with cobalt-blue water or lush forest.

"Better switch us over to the tactical frequency," he said.

No sooner had Jaina reset the dials on the comm board than a tone sounded.

"Homing beacon," she told Han. A map of the Yuuzhan Vong–formed governmental district resolved on the terrain-following sensor screen. Jaina tapped her forefinger against a pulsing bezel. "That's our rally point."

What should have come into view was Mount Umate, highest peak of the Manarai Mountains. But what came into view instead was a massive crater encompassing all of what had once been Monument Plaza. Perched on the protruding permacrete shoulders of the ruined arena were flocks of winged creatures similar to the seabirdlike fliers Han and Leia had seen at Selvaris. At the base of the ancient uplift, not far from where the Kallarak Amphitheater should have been, was another immense crater, whose thickly forested floor was in flames. On the steep slopes, herds of six-legged beasts and packs of panicked lizard hounds were trying desperately to scrabble to safety.

The smoke was denser at the outskirts of the sacred precinct.

Eastport, where the Solos had lived and Han had kept the *Falcon* docked, was a memory. Dirigiblelike, flame-spewing monstrosities wobbled and bobbed through the ruins of Skydome Botanical Gardens, Column Commons, and Calocour Heights. Wherever Han looked he saw evidence of the incredible damage wrought by ranged weapons and crashed Golan Defense Platforms, skyhooks, and Orbital Solar Energy Transfer Satellites. Buildings that had stood for a thousand years had either been reduced to rubble or become trellises for profuse alien vegetation. Fires raged on the surface and smoke billowed into the sky. Through gaps in the clouds, Han could discern crowds of Yuuzhan Vong civilians running every which way in pandemonium.

Pursued anew by coralskippers, the *Falcon* raced across the devastated cityscape, then down into blazing chasms and corridors thick with roiling smoke. The landscape was jagged with ferrocrete debris; the remains of superstructures jutted up at odd angles, like experimental sculpture.

"This place isn't worth saving," Jaina said in a stricken voice.

"Shimrra obviously feels the same," Harrar said, equally disheartened.

Homing in on the beacon, Han veered the *Falcon* slightly north and began a slow descent through the smoke. He realized that they were going to be setting down at the western terminus of the Glitannai Esplanade—but principally because the map display established as much. Formerly a stretch of fashionable shops and restaurants spread across the spacious rooftops of Judicial Plaza, the Glitannai was now a deep canyon, spanned in a few places by organiform bridges and channeling a flow of whitewater toward the Citadel.

Aware of the *Falcon*'s approach, Alliance soldiers began to appear on a spacious sheltered balcony that jutted out over the former promenade and had been secured by commandos for use as a landing zone. Engaging the repulsorlifts, Han steered the ship onto the ledge and let her settle down on her landing gear. Just to be on the safe side, he lowered the repeating blaster from its hidden compartment in the forward hull, and activated the interrupter template that would prevent the weapon from damaging the landing ramp or hardstand.

Last to file from the cockpit, Han found Leia, Luke, Mara, Tahiri, and Kenth waiting in the ring corridor, already sheathed in biosuits. While Jacen and Jaina were slipping into their suits, he palmed the bulkhead switch that extended the entry ramp.

"Cakhmaim, Meewalh," he shouted toward the forward compartment. "You and the droids remain aboard. We're not going to be here long."

Heads ducked, the Jedi landing party scrambled down the ramp. A scorching, debris-laden wind was howling across the balcony, tearing at the enviro-suits worn by the soldiers who approached the ship.

"Welcome home," Judder Page said, shouting to be heard as two A-wings streaked low overhead. "To, as we like to call it, 'Necropolis.'"

Like his comrades, Page was wearing a jet pack and helmet, and carrying a blaster rifle. Along the lip of the balcony stood a dozen YVH droids. Han wasn't surprised to spy a couple of Wraiths among the commando platoon, but Pash Cracken was the last person he had expected to see.

Jaina was even more stunned to see Jag Fel, who was waiting with a few others for a shuttle that would convey them to Westport, where there were starfighters that needed pilots. Jaina hurried to Jag while Page began to brief Luke, Kenth, Mara, and Jacen on the situation planetside.

"The Shamed Ones are up in arms, but word has it that Shimrra has issued an extermination order. He's blaming them for every reversal the Yuuzhan Vong have faced, and is determined to see every last one of them die, along with Coruscant itself."

"How fortified is the sacred precinct?" Luke asked, as the wind whipped his hair about his face.

"Several thousand ground troops, some reptoid slave soldiers," Cracken said, "but not much in the way of air support." He nodded to the flashing sky. "Most of the skips have gone upside."

"The better for us," Luke said.

Leia stepped into the howling wind to embrace her brother and Mara, then hugged Jacen as if she wasn't going to let him go. She did the same with Jaina after Jaina had said hello and good-bye to Jag.

"Luke," Leia started to say.

"They're in my keeping, Leia," he said of Jaina and Jacen. "But all of us are in the custody of the Force."

Han embraced his children and Mara, and clamped his hands on the tops of Luke's shoulders. "We've been in worse straits than this, right?"

Luke grinned. "More times than I can count."

Han nodded soberly. "Then maybe we should make this one count as the last one."

"I'll abide by that if you will."

"You just watch me."

Han put his arm around Leia and began to lead her back to the *Falcon* after the Jedi, Page's Commandos, and the YVH droids had moved out. At the ramp Leia blew out her breath and looked up at him.

"For our next trick . . ."

"We set a course for the World Brain."

"And when we get there?"

Han compressed his lips. "I'm hoping Harrar'll think of something."

The living ship forged from the seed-partners to which Kyp had bonded soared soundlessly and effortlessly through Zonama Sekot's tormented sky. In pairs and trios, coralskippers pierced the planet's envelope to attack the vessels the planet itself had fashioned to frustrate them, but so far none had made it through to the surface. The few that had succeeded in getting past the Jedi pilots had been repelled by Zonama itself, with powerful updrafts or unseen gravity generators that had hurled the skips to the edge of space—repulsed in a way that reminded Kyp of magnets, when their like poles were brought into contact.

Kyp and one coralskipper pilot in particular had been testing and toying with each other for far too long, but each time Kyp had drawn a bead on the skip the Sekotan ship's weapons had failed, or perhaps refused to fire. The same was true with the skip, whose controlling yammosk, falsely perceiving that the pilot was firing on another of its brood, would whisk the coralskipper through a turn to sabotage its shots. As acutely as Kyp could feel the gravitic tugs from the yammosk, he could also feel draws and joggles from Sekot. Zonama's consciousness was manipulating the Jedi ships into flying with the same unsettling sense of conformity displayed by the flights of coralskippers. Yuuzhan Vong and Jedi ships alike were part of a zigzagging aerial dance that was being choreographed from afar.

Against almost any of the enemies that had massed to test the durability of the New Republic during the past twenty years, a dozen Sekotan ships, a Skipray blastboat, and a couple of X-wings wouldn't have been adequate to protect an entire world. But the Yuuzhan Vong were not an ordinary enemy, and Zonama Sekot was hardly an ordinary world.

True to the behavior they had demonstrated from the start, the Yuuzhan Vong had their own rules of engagement, centering on challenge, honor, and persistence to the last. In the same way that their priests placed themselves at the service of a pantheon of cruel gods, the pilots of their war vessels surrendered individual action to obey the commands of the tentacled creature that coordinated them in battle. Their sense of honor was as distorted by their slavish devotion to sacrifice as local space was warped by the dovin basals that propelled and shielded their weapons. Over and above what the Alliance had accomplished, it was the Yuuzhan Vong's unswerving subordination to the will of the gods and the importance of captives that had cost them hundreds of vessels and countless lives at Ebaq 9, Obroa-skai, and other arenas. As extraordinary as they were as a species—and as warriors—it was foolhardy courage and inflexibility that could end up costing them Zonama Sekot, as well.

That was assuming that the Jedi would eventually grow comfortable with piloting the Sekotan ships, Kyp mused. Merely settling into the pulsing red-and-green cockpits had required resolve. The canopy was similar to the mica-like transparency of a coralskipper, but, like everything in the cockpit, it was warm to the touch. Comparable to a combination yoke, accelerator, and weapons trigger, the main control had actually reached up and wrapped around his right hand, molding to it the way some of the controls of Centerpoint Station were rumored to have molded to Anakin Solo's hand.

The console was an organiform surround of control levers that resembled ligaments, switches that had the resiliency of blisters or calluses, and tracking displays as fluid as those on a Mon Calamari cruiser. Odors that were by turn cloying and sharp pervaded the cockpit, as if encouraging the pilot to make use of olfactory cues, as well as audiovisual and tactile ones.

More important, the ship engaged a pilot's mind in a kind of telepathic dialogue. There was no astromech droid to report on the status of the systems; no cognition hood interface, as on the stolen Yuuzhan Vong vessel that had come to be called *Trickster*. But the Sekotan ship incorporated some of the qualities of each by speaking telepathically to the pilot. The ship didn't have a *voice*—it wasn't telepathy on the order of that honed by the Jedi—but Kyp could sense what the vessel was feeling and thinking, the way he had been able to sense the feelings of the crazy little seed-partners that had clung to him.

All this came standard with the ship—as well as with the ships Zonama Sekot had furnished for the lucky few Old Republic–era pilots who had been wealthy enough to afford them, and who had formed the requisite attachment to seed-partners. But as Han Solo was forever saying about the *Millennium Falcon,* some special modifications had been made to the Jedi ships. Like coralskippers, the ships were capable of hurling plasma, but unlike coralskippers they lacked shields, relying instead on astonishing nimbleness. Absent ion drives, heat exchangers, exhaust ports, or anything resembling conventional engine components, the ships were faster than A-wings and more maneuverable than TIE fighters.

Kyp was beginning to think of them as the Sekotan equivalent of lightsabers. The pilot didn't have to be a Jedi—flying the ships didn't require a special connection to the Force—but a ship's ability to perform appeared to be directly related to the degree to which a pilot could surrender him- or herself, become egoless and *empty*. Saba, Lowbacca, and

Tam Azur-Jamin—whose call signs were Hisser, Streak, and Quiet, respectively—were demonstrating this to be the case. Kyp was in awe of the maneuvers they were executing, to the point that he sometimes lost focus on the battle itself. Despite his talents, his *mastery* of the Force, he had yet to be able to take his ship through similar moves.

Or was it that the ship was having trouble taking *him* through similar moves?

Kyp's comlink toned. Over the past few years—since Myrkr—the Jedi had become adept at communicating with one another through Force-melds, but between attending to the Sekotan ships and flying in the atmosphere of the living world, these melds were proving difficult to sustain.

"Kyp, you getting the hang of these things?" Corran Horn asked. The intership comlink transmission was being relayed through *Jade Shadow,* which was in stationary orbit at the edge of the battle zone, unpiloted, but slave circuit and all countermeasures enabled.

"I've been wondering if the ship is having trouble getting the hang of *me.*"

"You and me both. I did a lot better with the Sekotan ship Tahiri and I piloted from Coruscant. I mean, I know I'm targeting correctly, but a lot of my shots are going wide—even when there aren't voids standing between me and the target."

"Something about Sekot's need for us not to be killers."

"I've got a theory about that," Corran said, "but I'll save it for another time."

"Then why are we up here—just for show?"

"Maybe it's the same between Sekot and us as it is between the ships and us. Sekot's still trying to get a feel for us. Once that happens, we'll be able to target more accurately."

"So I should think of this as some kind of insane simulation," Kyp said.

"With one difference. It's the *ships* that are learning."

Kyp thought about this statement after he signed off with Corran. Perhaps it wasn't only the ships that were learning. Why had seed-partners bonded to some Jedi and not others? Why him and not Jaina? Was there anything to the fact that Kyp had destroyed a world, Saba had seen one destroyed, and both Alema and Corran held themselves responsible for the destruction of theirs? Would Ganner Rhysode have bonded with seed-partners? Wurth Skidder? Kyp's own apprentice, Miko Reglia?

Would Anakin have bonded?

What did Sekot understand about all of them that they didn't understand about themselves?

THIRTY-SEVEN

A sudden darkness had fallen over the Vongformed cityscape.

Their lightsabers ignited—glowing blue, violet, green—the Jedi drew on the Force to propel them across the fissured and rain-slicked rooftops and balconies that dangled over what was once the Glitannai Esplanade. Piles of debris, precipitous ledges, and gaping chasms posed no obstacles for the six as they hurdled, vaulted, leapt in a race to reach the Citadel, and the Yuuzhan Vong most responsible for what Coruscant had become. Thanks to their jet packs, Captain Page's Commandos were just managing to keep up.

Rain was falling hard and being driven every which way by fierce gusts of wind. Overhead it was no longer possible to differentiate flashes of lightning from the artificial brilliance of deadly engagements. It was impossible to distinguish between the lament of the wind and the howl of strafing starfighters; the billowing smoke from scudding storm clouds; the sizzle of fires being extinguished by the rain from the sound of laser bolts cleaving the saturated air. The booming cannonades of distant weapons might easily have been rolling thunder; the red-orange pillars on the horizon, erupting volcanoes or the glowing ejecta of plasma launchers.

For Luke, the nebulous nature of the surroundings mirrored his inner state. The darkness was coercing a commingling of disparate realities. Coruscant was fast becoming a void, a singularity into which the very fabric of life was being stretched and distorted. Was this Coruscant any longer, or was it really Yuuzhan'tar—as the original world had been at its end, when, angered by the Yuuzhan Vong's turn to violence, the gods had robbed their children of the Force and cast them into a bottomless abyss?

"The quickest route is through the north concourse," Mara told Judder Page when everyone had come to a halt on a puddled ledge. Rain dripped from the visors of their helmets and cascaded down the front of their biosuits. Mara was leading the combined teams from memory, though also relying on Jacen and Tahiri's "Vongsense" to keep everyone from encountering patrols of Yuuzhan Vong warriors.

Page had his gaze fixed on the water-beaded display of a positioning unit built into the sleeve of his biosuit. "According to this, there was bridge access to the concourse."

Mara nodded. "The Bridge of Unity. I used to have lunch in the restaurant on the lower level."

Even with all that Coruscant had become, she sounded wistful. Luke could imagine her, thirty years earlier, frequenting the esplanade's expensive shops and restaurants; wandering among the crowds attending the Imperial Fair; a sometime visitor to the Imperial Palace, in her guise as the Emperor's Hand. It was the Coruscant Luke had known only from Holo-Net transmissions and the occasional dramas and documentaries that had found their way to Tosche Station on Tatooine. By the time he had finally visited the capital world in person, most of the governmental district had been in ruins, following Coruscant's liberation by New Republic forces.

But over the decades Coruscant had become his home, as Yavin had, only to have suffered a similar fate. Luke hadn't expected to be so heartsick; but then he hadn't expected to find Coruscant so altered—so remade—in the two years since he and Mara had left.

Mara was waving everyone back in motion.

Fifteen minutes of flat-out running brought them to the Bridge of Unity, which had lost the ornamental wirework and inscribed plaques that had earned it landmark status. Now the bridge was little more than a ferrocrete slab spanning the esplanade canyon. Lashed by the gale, vines and slimy vegetation trailed from the edges, and a shallow but fast-moving curtain of water plunged into the frothing river far below.

From the bridge's southern abutment, the Jedi had their first unobstructed view of their objective. Several kilometers to the east, illuminated by forking lightning and accented by the laser beams of circling starfighters, Shimrra's Citadel towered above the infernal landscape. A veritable mountain, it stood where the Imperial Palace once had, encompassing everything from the Mon Calamari Inglenook to the *Pliada di am Imperium,* as the eastern terminus of the Glitannai Esplanade was known. The Citadel's base was lost in swirls of dark smoke, but halfway to the rounded summit four walkways approached from separate directions, linking the Citadel to surrounding structures.

This close, the mountain was revealed to be as craggy and pocked as any of the Yuuzhan Vong worldships Luke had seen. But Shimrra's was adorned with a pair of filigree wings that lent something insectlike to its appearance. The way it sat in the crater that served as its cradle, it might almost have been nesting.

Flights of X- and E-wings were taunting the crown, but voids blacker than the stormy sky were devouring everything the starfighters hurled at them. Two of the snubfighters were circling closer when plasma projectiles geysered from launchers above the wings. The X-wings might as well have been flying without shields. Caught on their starboard sides by the superheated missiles, they began to spiral down, S-foils and ion engines slagged. Luke could see pieces fly from the fighters as they struck outcroppings in the Citadel's coarse hull. They disappeared into the smoke at the foot of the mountain, and, seconds later, roiling fire mushroomed into view.

Luke's silence spoke volumes. As he turned and leapt out onto the bridge, a resonant bellowing issued from the far side, and two huge eyes stood out in the gloom. As if under strobing light an enormous beast waddled into view around the shoulder of a ruined building. It wasn't the first Yuuzhan Vong creature he had seen since leaving the *Falcon*—the sacred precinct was literally crawling with escaped animals—but it was certainly the largest.

"A mon duul," Jacen said, yelling to be heard. "If it's been implanted with a villip, the belly can function like an amplifier. It's harmless, either way."

Page kept his blaster rifle raised regardless. "If you say so, kid." He motioned with the barrel. "But you cross first."

No sooner had Jacen and Luke started forward than the mon duul sat on its haunches, with its tympanum of a belly aimed out over the canyon. In a deep and menacing voice, someone began to speak in Yuuzhan Vong.

" 'Perish,' " Tahiri translated. " 'Perish, all of you who would stand between me and exaltation, who would seek to profane me in our finest moment.' "

"Shimrra?" Luke asked.

Jacen shook his head uncertainly. "Could be."

" 'I battle the gods on your behalf,' " Tahiri continued, " 'and you repay me with rebellion. Perish then. Go to your deaths and your gods, while I remake the world.' "

"Too bad we can't answer him," Mara said.

"We will soon enough," Luke assured her.

Jacen and Tahiri walked slowly toward the seated mon duul. In eerie unison they motioned with their right arms, and the four-metric-ton beast lowered its front legs to the ground and began to trundle off.

Their Vongsense, Luke thought.

Jaina hurried forward to drape her left arm around Jacen's shoulders. "You always were good with animals."

He responded with a wry smile, and hurried forward.

The three young Jedi crossed the span together and turned east toward the Citadel. Ahead of them, clad in vegetation, a palisade of ruined buildings extended all the way to the western access to Shimrra's mountain. Luke, Mara, and Kenth had just caught up with the trio when Jacen and Tahiri called everyone to a halt. Lightning flashes disclosed the presence of a group of skeletally thin humans and humanoids, dressed in dripping, frayed garments and aged robeskins.

"Come forward," Tahiri said in Yuuzhan Vong.

Two Shamed Ones approached, a male and female. *"Jeedai,"* the young male said, his eyes fixed on Luke's thrumming lightsaber.

More Yuuzhan Vong began to appear, along with a dozen or so Coruscanti who looked as if they had been subsisting on grayweave since the occupation. The Shamed and the damned, Luke told himself as he deactivated his lightsaber.

Pushing through the group came two winded and wounded human commandos, who saluted Captain Page.

"Bacta Squad, sir," the sergeant said. "We've just come from down below. It's a real mess, Captain. The heretics are fighting tooth and claw, but they need reinforcements—and fast. If you can spare anyone, sir . . ."

Page beckoned to one of his jet-packed commandos. "Congratulations, Corporal, you've been promoted to squad leader. Take ten men and go with the sergeant. We'll regroup at the Citadel, soonest."

The commando saluted, spun on his heel, and began choosing his teammates.

The wounded sergeant looked from Page to Luke. "Master Skywalker, a couple of your people would make a world of difference, not only to us—" He motioned to the Shamed Ones. "—but to them, as well."

Kenth and Tahiri glanced at Luke, who nodded.

"Thank you," the sergeant said as the two Jedi moved to join him. "We've heard that the Prophet has reappeared, but we haven't been able to locate him. Word has it he was last seen in the Place of Hierarchy."

"Leading them, or helping with the slaughter?" Mara asked, stepping forward.

"Leading them."

Luke showed Mara a skeptical look. "Maybe he's had a change of heart since Zonama Sekot."

She snorted in derision. "Only if someone implanted a new one in his chest."

Luke swung to the Shamed Ones who had been the first to show themselves. "Have you or any of the others even been inside the Citadel?"

Tahiri translated.

A male in the crowd spoke, and showed himself. He was more hideously scarred than the others, and short horns sprouted from the tops of his shoulders.

"This one says that he arrived in the Citadel," Tahiri told Luke. She listened for a moment more. "He was a warrior before the gods—before his body rejected certain enhancing biots the shapers devised for him." The former warrior pointed to the walkways that accessed the yorik coral mountain. "Each caste uses a separate entrance. But all four avenues terminate at the Hall of Confluence, where Supreme Overlord Shimrra grants audience to the elite."

"Ask him if Shimrra is likely to be in the hall now," Luke said.

Tahiri phrased the question and waited for the response.

"He says that you won't find Shimrra there. He'll be in his private . . . coffer." The Yuuzhan Vong aimed a thick, truncated finger at the lofty crown of the Citadel. "Up there is where you'll have to go."

"Thank you," Luke said to the heretic, who asked something of Tahiri.

"He has a question for the Jedi," she said after a moment. "He wants to know if we plan to help them or kill them. He wants to know if the Shamed Ones will be able to find salvation in the Force."

Luke looked at the Yuuzhan Vong. "We'll help you find your way back to the Force."

Tahiri's translation prompted agitation and a flurry of hushed conversations among the Shamed Ones. Then she and Kenth began to move off with the commandos.

Mara shifted her gaze from the Citadel to Luke.

"Ready, soldier?" When he didn't respond immediately, she said, "What's wrong?"

He held her gaze. "Mara, I want you to go with Tahiri and Kenth."

She almost laughed.

"I want you to go with them," he said again.

Her expression changed, and a twinge of fear came into her eyes. "Luke, tell me this is the Force speaking to you, and that you're not doing it because you don't want us fighting together—for Ben's sake."

"Would it matter?"

She gripped her hands on his upper arms. "You promised me on Zonama Sekot that both of us have a lot more living to do."

He smiled and stroked her cheek with the backs of his fingertips. "You think I'd drop you into the midst of all this to make you a widow—or me a widower?"

She shook her head. "That's not your style."

"Then go with them."

Reluctantly, she nodded. "Not because I want to. But because I trust you."

Airborne at the extreme edge of the tempest that was lashing the northern quarter of the sacred precinct, the *Falcon* banked toward the former Legislative District. Owing to the toughness of its honeycomb and crumple zone engineering, the Senate itself had survived the Yuuzhan Vong barrage, but now the famed edifice was covered by the half-kilometer-high hemisphere that sheltered the World Brain.

"No mystery why we're not taking flak from plasma emplacements," Han said, as he and Leia powered the freighter through a reconnaissance fly-by. "Nothing short of a planet-buster is going to crack that skullcap."

"The yorik coral has enzymatically digested and absorbed the Senate's duracrete and transparisteel," Harrar explained from the navigator's chair. "The constituent materials have been used to fashion a new exoskeleton that goes deep underground and forms an impervious sphere around the dhuryam—the brain."

C-3PO had a tight grip on the chair next to Harrar's, and R2-D2 was securely planted behind his counterpart. Cakhmaim was in the dorsal gun turret; Meewalh in the forward compartment.

"How impervious?" Han asked over his shoulder.

"Sufficient to allow the dhuryam to survive an invasion as a self-contained, and possibly self-propelled, vessel—similar to that which constitutes the crown of the Citadel."

"An escape pod," Leia said.

"But massive," Harrar elaborated. "Capable not only of preserving the dhuryam—with all its engineered genetics and learned skills—but also of preserving the lives of any who happen to be in the Well when the sphere launches."

"Oh, my," C-3PO remarked.

R2-D2 seconded the protocol droid's stupefaction with a long whistle.

Han growled and rubbed his head. "So how are we supposed to get inside the thing, if you're telling me that bombs can't?"

Harrar leaned toward the viewport. "Complete your over-flight. Let us see if we can't locate the entrance to the secret passageway Jacen and Vergere used to escape from the Well."

As Han banked the *Falcon* to the west, Leia gazed at the sprawl of vegetation-clad structures below, then pointed toward the extreme southwest projection of the dome. "Borsk Fey'lya's office would have been right about there."

Han sighted down her finger. "Right there, buried under who knows how many tons of yorik coral."

Leia glanced at him. "I guess the dome has spread out since Jacen was here."

"You could say that."

"An unexpected turn of events," Harrar said.

Han growled. "I'm getting tired of surprises. There has to be another way in."

"Perhaps the front door," C-3PO said.

"Yeah, we'll just go up and knock," Han said. "Isn't that how you got yourself into Jabba's palace?"

"Actually, Captain Solo—"

"The front entrance may prove problematic," Harrar interrupted. "Continue your circle, and I'll show you why."

Lit from within by explosions and flashes of lightning, the northern horizon was a towering anvil of black clouds. Han veered east around the two-kilometer-wide dome, and a long elongated tunnel came into view, protruding from the dome. The hemispherical corridor appeared to be made of the interwoven branches of thousands of slender trees.

"The hedge maze," Harrar said. "The ceremonial avenue that leads to the atrium of the Well."

Han laughed. "A walk in the park. Unless you're going to tell me a hedge is impervious to weapons."

"The hedge is not only as solid and fire resistant as your durasteel, but the trees that comprise it are studded with needle-sharp thorns that range in size from that of your thumbnail to that of your arm. The thorns contain a neurotoxin potent enough to devastate the nervous system of any creature hapless enough to be pricked by them."

Han tightened his lips in frustration. "I say we see how it handles a couple of concussion missiles."

"A waste of armament," Harrar said. "Any damage the missiles render, the dhuryam will quickly repair."

"Yeah, well, since you're so smart, you think of a plan to get us inside."

"I already have. How wide is your craft, Han Solo?"

"Twenty-five meters, give or take. Why?"

Harrar took a breath. "A tight fit. But given your piloting skills I think it can be done."

Leia swiveled her chair around to face him. "You think what can be done?"

"A flight through the hedge tunnel, directly to the entry portal."

Leia's jaw dropped. "You can't be serious."

"Princess Leia is correct," C-3PO said as R2-D2 was mewling. "Please confirm that your statement was in jest."

A slow grin took shape on Han's face. "He's serious—and he's right." He looked at Leia. "We can do it."

Leia started to speak, but swallowed whatever she had in mind to say and began again. "Well, you said he'd think of something, and I guess he has."

Han patted her left arm with affection. "Better tighten up your crash webbing. You, too, Goldenrod."

C-3PO canted his head in apprehension. "If it's all the same to you, sir, I'd prefer to adjourn to the forward compartment with Artoo."

"Suit yourself. But be quick about it."

Han brought the headset mike close to his mouth. "Cakhmaim, get yourself to the forward cabin space with Meewalh."

He sent the *Falcon* into a broad circle, from which they emerged staring directly down the throat of the hedge tunnel.

"You're sure about this," Leia said while Han was flipping switches on the console.

"No. But luckily we don't have time to think about it."

Han dropped the freighter lower and accelerated. The thorned half circle of mouth grew larger and larger in the viewport. Reflexively, Leia leaned back in her chair and clamped her hands on the armrests.

"Hang on," Han said. "Hang on . . ."

And suddenly they were inside the maze.

But the *Falcon* wasn't even all the way through the opening when the three of them realized that the ride was going to be worse than they had imagined. The resilient knitted branches knocked the ship harshly from one side to the other. The *Falcon* rattled and shuddered, in danger of being spun completely around. The longest of the thorns drew prolonged and deafening screeches from the hull. External components groaned and squealed as they were ripped away—cowlings, rectenna, fuel-driver pressure stabilizers . . . And ahead of them, the throat of the hedge maze was closing—narrowing as they watched.

"Fire the concussion missiles!" Han said.

Leia squeezed the trigger, sending one pair, then another streaking down the tunnel, tearing through the thorns and branches and ultimately exploding against whatever constituted the entrance to the dome.

"Angle the deflectors!"

Leia raised the forward shields as a boiling torrent of fire and debris came back at them, washing over the *Falcon*, stripping away more parts, and scoring and scorching the hull plates.

Then, suddenly, the ship broke through to a broad, wedge-shaped causeway formed by the limbs of great trees, whose leaf-bearing branches—now aflame—tangled toward the sky on either side. The foot of the causeway was a hundred meters high, but it tapered to an arrowhead as it rose, forming a thorn-hedged ramp whose point touched the massive, ruined hatch sphincter that had long ago enveloped the Great Door of the Senate.

Han fought to keep the ship stabilized as it skidded across the former plaza and raced into the second stretch of hedge. But the durasteel-hard branches prevailed, slowing, then snagging the spasming ship. Stalled, the *Falcon* came to a final rest angled to one side and ten meters from the missile-damaged entrance. While two of the landing disks were in touch with the paving stones, the entire port side of the ship was upended and held fast by the interlocked branches.

"Guess this is as far as we go," Han said, staring straight ahead, with his hands still clenched on the control yoke.

Leia blew out her breath and swallowed hard. "Nothing like a quiet arrival."

She, Han, and Harrar freed themselves from the chairs and staggered into the ring corridor, which was strewn with objects that had found their way there from all over the ship.

"We'll clean up later," Leia said.

Han uttered a laugh. "We could have Threepio do it."

"I was hoping you would say just that, sir," the droid said, as he, R2-D2, and the two Noghri appeared from the forward compartment, leaning against the corridor's curving walls for support. "That would be a delightful chore."

R2-D2 began to twitter and toodle in protest.

"We'll have no complaints from you, Artoo. If Captain Solo wants us to remain on the ship rather than accompany him into the Well of the World Brain, the least we can do is—"

R2-D2 razzed loudly.

C-3PO straightened in a huff. "Never satisfied."

"All right, you two, quit arguing," Han said. "Forget the mess. Just keep the ship warmed up and stick close to the comlink."

Han extended the landing ramp, which didn't drop far before hitting solid ground.

"Once we are inside the Well, we will be safe from ambushes by warriors," Harrar said. "But whatever you do between here and there, Han Solo, you must not kill the shaper. We will need his or her scent markers to get us safely into the Well. I know certain things about the brain, but not enough to incapacitate it."

Han passed out thermal charges to the Noghri, then clipped two onto his own belt. "Just in case we have any trouble persuading it to surrender."

Leia activated her lightsaber and narrowed her eyes. "And I promised I'd never set foot in the Senate again."

Han nodded at her. "We've all had to break promises we made to ourselves."

The five of them hurried down the angled ramp and through the slowly sealing breach the concussion missiles had blown in the thick hatch sphincter. The hideously torn membrane opened onto a vast, dimly lit cavern of yorik coral. Han scarcely had time to look around, when fifty or more warriors armed with amphistaffs poured from a narrow corridor in the curved wall opposite the hatch.

Someone shouted commands in Yuuzhan Vong that needed no translation.

A flock of whizzing bugs and hurled amphistaffs flew for the *Falcon*'s company.

"I thought you said there wouldn't be warriors inside the Well!" Han yelled as he and the Noghri were ducking and triggering blaster rounds.

"This isn't the Well," the priest said. "This is merely the atrium!"

Batting aside thud and razor bugs, Leia led the retreat. They backed through the iris hatch, firing at their pursuers without aiming. Stumbling into the plaza, they raced for the *Falcon,* only to find her completely enclosed by the thorned hedge.

Despite the impetus that the Prophet's rallying cry had given the heretics, the counteroffensive was not going well. Caught in a violent storm, the Shamed Ones and their new-found allies were being sliced to pieces by coufees, knocked unconscious by thud bugs, slashed and split by amphistaffs. Nom Anor himself was bloodied, slipping on hailstones and his own black flow as he fought with coufee in one hand, amphistaff in the other. The now-drenched throng of would-be insurgents had managed to fight their way out of the Place of Hierarchy, but Shimrra's avengers were attempting to herd them toward the Place of Bones. If the warriors succeeded in trapping them in the sunken amphitheater, there would be no escape, no hope.

Nom Anor was trading strikes and stabs with a warrior a head taller than himself when he heard the clamor of running feet and raised voices. When the warrior turned in the direction of the commotion, Nom Anor availed himself of the moment of distraction to send the point of his amphistaff through his opponent's right eye. All around him other warriors were beginning to add their voices to the tumult and to press the attack.

Reinforcements, Nom Anor told himself bitterly.

The heretics would be lucky now if they even made it to the Place of Bones. Unexpectedly, though, the war cries of the Citadel guard began to fade, and the crowd was pushed back toward the Place of Hierarchy. It was the heretics who were being reinforced!

Nom Anor was suddenly inflamed.

If every cell of Shamed Ones could find the courage to rise up, there was a chance, though slim, that the heretics would yet win the day. His conviction surged as the reports of stun and flash grenades began to echo and rebound from the walls of the temples and the dormitories of the intendants. Hundreds were instantly flattened to the saturated ground. Then blaster bolts rang out.

Resistance fighters and Alliance commandos! Nom Anor realized.

It was the *warriors* who were trapped!

Nom Anor charged into the brawl, slashing throats and hamstrings. Overwhelmed, the warriors fought brutally and valiantly, but more and more of them were falling and being trampled underfoot. Nom Anor was in the thick of things when new sounds drew his attention and he froze in surprise and dread.

Snap-hiss! Thrummm . . .

He risked a sideways glance to discover three Jedi, parrying and slashing with their lightsabers. Worse, one of them was Mara Jade Skywalker. The very Jedi who had fallen victim to Nom Anor's coomb spores so long ago, now fighting all but alongside of him. Not far away from the red-golden-haired Skywalker was Tahiri Veila, the Jedi who had almost been shaped into a Yuuzhan Vong, and with whom Nom Anor had fought and escaped from on Zonama Sekot. And beside Tahiri, a tall, older male Jedi whom Nom Anor didn't recognize.

He tried to conceal himself by wading deeper into the battle, but the conflict was too frenzied for him to make any headway. He began to angle toward the northwest entrance to the Place of Hierarchy, but there, too, he was rapidly hemmed in by clashing warriors and heretics. No matter which direction he attempted to move, he wound up being pushed inexorably closer to the two Jedi women.

Whirling, he slit the throat of a Shamed One and placed himself where the gushing blood could wash over his face. He found a sodden turban on the ground and pulled it down over his forehead, only to have it unwind and flop uselessly over his shoulders. He cursed himself for not having thought to carry an ooglith masquer with him.

A group of enraged warriors made a sudden sally, forcing the heretics away from the Place of Hierarchy and out into the broad boulevard that ran north to the Citadel. Again Nom Anor heard the distinctive *thrum* of a lightsaber, and shortly found himself pressed shoulder to shoulder with youthful Tahiri, who was shouting alternately in Basic and Yuuzhan Vong as her blue blade deflected overhead strikes from amphistaffs and lateral swipes from coufees.

Nom Anor's attempts to squirm away were in vain. He turned his back at the same time the Jedi did, but surges in the crowd kept shoving them hard into each other. All at once, Nom Anor could feel small Tahiri's body tense against his.

He pivoted in time to see Tahiri throw up her hands in some sort of Force gesture, and a dozen warriors hit the ground as if struck by a swarm of invisible thud bugs. *A Force Wall!* Nom Anor thought. Tahiri used her Jedi powers a second time to create an even wider circle of clear space, then whirled and grabbed Nom Anor by the arm, spinning him around to face her, her eyes already wide with discovery.

Sending his amphistaff flying with a Force command, she immobilized him by clutching the yoke of his robeskin. Then she turned and gesticulated toward her fellow Jedi.

"Mara, I have Nom Anor!"

Over the heads of combatants, through the hail, misted blood, and forest of flailing arms, Nom Anor could see Skywalker gazing directly at him in eager peril.

Summoning his strength, Nom Anor slashed upward with his coufee, missing Tahiri by a blade but succeeding in cutting the handful of robe she had gripped. Momentum propelled him backward through a splashing somersault, and while Tahiri's attention was momentarily diverted, he shoved a wounded Shamed One at her feet. Crawling a sinuous and puddled path between the legs of warriors and heretics, he ultimately reached the northern edge of the Place of Hierarchy. There, where the crowd was thinner, he elbowed his way through a cluster of warriors and broke fast for the stairs and freedom.

Much like *Millennium Falcon*, *Lady Luck* had in the past five years undergone an atavistic transition from pleasantly appointed family craft to war vessel. But where Han's *Falcon* was as armed as it was fast, Lando's fifty-meter-long Soro-Suub yacht relied as ever on stealth, speed, and advanced sensor arrays that allowed it to observe and scrutinize vessels at far remove. With three lasers and a reinforced hull, Talon Karrde's Corellian transport was better configured for battle, although hardly a match for a Yuuzhan Vong task force. Which was why the two ships were flying at the fringe of the battle zone and leaving most of the dirty work to *Errant Venture*, and to the Hapans.

Tenel Ka's flotilla had arrived moments after the Yuuzhan Vong capital ships had begun their move against Zonama Sekot, and had immediately arrayed themselves in a blockade. The new-generation Battle Dragons were twin-saucered ships with turbolasers and ion cannons placed along the rims, made all the more lethal since the New Republic had finally shared its weapons-recharge technology with the Hapan navy. The enhanced Dragons were also equipped with pulse mass mine launchers that were nearly as effective as dovin basal singularities when it came to deflecting weapons fire and interdicting ships from jumping to hyperspace. In contrast, the shape and sleekness of the Consortium's *Nova*-class cruisers brought to mind Old Republic–era hand blasters. As agile as starfighters and as deadly as warships twice their size, the cruisers were preventing Yuuzhan Vong vessels from penetrating the Dragons' daunting barricade.

Closer to Zonama Sekot, flaming red *Errant Venture*, along with squadrons of X-wings and Hapan Miy'til fighters were preying on the advance coralskippers the task force had dispatched to test the planet's defenses. Trapped between the deep-space squadrons and the atmospheric craft flown by the Jedi, the coralskippers were being decimated. And now that capital ships were involved, the planet itself had brought out its big guns, firing salvos of stunning ion fire from the summits of mountains twelve kilometers high.

Equidistant from the task force and blockade, Lando and Tendra had an overview of the entire battle, but *Lady Luck*'s seeming brazenness had made her the object of unwanted attention, and the Calrissians were being forced to do more running than spying. Their updates of enemy maneuvers had twice saved Booster Terrik from being taken by surprise, and they were a critical link in relaying intelligence between the Star Destroyer and the Jedi pilots, who, at last word, had finally managed to talk their living ships into returning fire.

The Yuuzhan Vong gave every indication of having been thrown into disorder by their obvious miscalculation. The pilots of the skips were fighting for their lives, and the task force itself was fast coming unglued, with cruiser and destroyer analogs maneuvering without rhyme or reason, making themselves easy targets for the precision lasers of the Hapan cruisers and the ranged weapons of the Dragons.

Only total confusion could account for the fact that some of the vessels in the task force were actually turning on one of their own.

The victim was the vessel that originally had been flying at the center of the Yuuzhan Vong's elongated diamond formation. It had remained at the center all through the initial coralskipper assault on Zonama Sekot, but was now being raked with plasma fire by four of the surrounding cruisers. Lando and Tendra saw the vessel split wide open, and yet instead of exploding, the cleaved vessel released a smaller vessel that was concealed inside.

A corvette analog, the six-armed craft had a scaled hull and an upraised, curving stern.

Not unlike two vessels *Errant Venture* had destroyed at Caluula.

A slayer ship.

"They're supposed to be hyperspace-capable," Lando said. "So why did they need to transport this one?"

"It looks off," Tendra said.

One eyebrow raised, Lando glanced at her. "Off course?"

She shook her head. "Off color. It looks ill."

Lando's blood ran cold. He commanded the scanners to

provide him with a close-up and analyze the vessel's signature. Then he commed *Errant Venture*.

"Booster, we're sending you signature data on a vessel in the task force," Lando began.

"We're busy, Lando," Booster snapped.

"You're not too busy for this. Run a comparison with whatever you've got stored in the *Venture*'s memory, and tell me if we get a hit."

"Hold tight," Booster said. When after a long moment he spoke again, his voice was riddled with apprehension. "The signature you sent matches the ship that evaded us at Caluula."

"The ship carrying Alpha Red," Lando said.

And now closing on Zonama Sekot.

THIRTY-EIGHT

Jag thought of himself first and foremost as a starfighter pilot, not a dirt flier. He had accepted the assignment to lead Twins Suns onto Coruscant, but without the enthusiasm he might have demonstrated for a space mission. Like many who had earned their wings in zero-g, atmosphere was anathema. Maneuvers weren't so much performed as wrested from a craft—no matter how aerodynamic the design or how responsive the repulsorlift engine. The carbon-scored green X-wing he had been given at Westport felt sluggish and unwieldy, especially compared to a clawcraft. But Jag's complaints were only that. There was a mission to execute, and he was not about to shirk his commitment to seeing it through.

Streaking east from the now-Alliance-occupied landing field, he wove the snubfighter through a hail of ascending plasma fire and descending wreckage. Dominating the forward view was the rounded summit of Shimrra's fortress, rising from the thick blanket of cloud cover and smoke that smothered most of the sacred precinct. Only two years earlier the elegant summits of dozens of spacescrapers would have been visible above the clouds, but now there was only the craggy mountaintop.

Somewhere below, Jaina was moving toward the same target, with her brother and uncle, and a small team of commandos and droids. *Take care of yourself,* she had said to him on the flooded balcony where the *Millennium Falcon* had set the Jedi down. And Jag meant to do just that. When he had urged Jaina to do the same, she had replied, *The Force will take care of me.*

He hadn't debated the matter. He wanted it to be true with all his heart.

Ahead of him, twenty starfighters were circling the Citadel, loosing laser bolts, proton torpedoes, and concussion missiles at the summit. A sense of hopelessness began to erode Jag's resolve. Even without the insatiable voids that were engulfing nearly every starfighter volley, the Citadel appeared to be impregnable. It was like attempting to blow apart a mountain. There were no coralskippers to contend with, but outpourings of plasma from deep pits in the Citadel walls were effortlessly overwhelming the shields of the starfighters.

The X-wing's droid sent flight information to the cockpit displays. Jag dialed the comm to the tactical net.

"This is worse than punching past the orbital dovin basals," a pilot was saying.

"Keep a hand on your grab-safety toggle, or those voids'll take you down," another said.

"They're swallowing every bolt I'm feeding them."

"Just watch out they don't take a fancy to you."

"Yeah, they've developed a real taste for starfighters."

"Especially yellow ones with black stripes."

"Copy that, Rogue Leader."

"All ships form up on me for a portwise sweep. Set your weapons for stutterfire and follow up with whatever torps and missiles you've got left. Remember: it may look like a mountain but it's actually a ship. Which means it can be cracked open."

"Following you in, Rogue One."

Jag saw that two of the fighters off his starboard wingtip were clawcraft, and he opened a channel to the closest one.

"Twin Suns Four, I've got your port side."

"Jag!" the pilot returned. "I thought you were dead!"

"Saved by a tree, of all things, Shawnkyr."

"Are you about ready to go home now?"

"As soon as we finish this—you have my word."

She laughed shortly. "This part of the galaxy has made a romantic of you, Fel."

"Still watching my back, is that it?"

"Who will if I won't?" Shawnkyr said. "Oh, I forgot. And just where is the Sword?"

"Below—moving west."

"Then we'd better take care not to bring this mountain down on her head."

"After he did so well with the mon duul," Jaina found time to say between swings of her lightsaber.

Pinned down in a grove of fingerleaf trees one hundred meters from the westernmost of the walkways that accessed the Citadel, she and Luke were fending off streams of attack bugs that were hurtling down from lookout aeries in the holy mountain. Closer to Shimrra's haunt, Jacen was trying without success to pacify the beasts that were rapidly devouring the walkway itself. A trio of YVH droids had tried less subtle means of persuasion, only to have been ripped apart and ingested.

"At least Shimrra can't speak through these two," Luke said.

"I'd say that's exactly what Shimrra's doing," Jaina hollered back.

Gargantuan symbiots, Sgauru and Tu-Scart were partners in the walkway devastation. Considering that the former was female and the latter male, it was something of a marriage. At Gateway settlement on Duro, the couple had demonstrated their talent for demolishing buildings, and they were doing an equally skilled job of dismantling and consuming the yorik coral concourse. Hard-shelled, segmented Sgauru was doing most of the grunt work. Beady black eyes dotted her white head, and her mouth writhed with dozens of feeder-tendrils. Her powerful rear pincers gripped around the upper coils of her snakelike mate, she was using her stubby front legs and enormous head to smash the span to pieces. Loose chunks didn't fly far before being pulverized by sleek black Tu-Scart's elongated body.

Absent their usual team of handlers, the creatures had emerged from a massive hollow beneath the concourse, through which the esplanade river cascaded thunderously into the square at the base of the Citadel. Lashed by rain and howling winds, the monolithic fortress loomed above the

Jedi, rising up into the battle-torn sky like the rough-hewn blade of a coufee. Though winged, mottled with patches of dark green moss, and bedecked with vines whose seeds had taken root in the worldship's nooks and crannies, the Citadel was simply too sheer to scale, even with the aid of the Force. Starfighters were still circling the rounded summit, but not one had managed to come within a thousand meters of Shimrra's lair without being destroyed. The remains of those that had tried littered the uneven, inundated terrain for kilometers around.

Far below the concourse, at the base of the Citadel, a dark maw accessed the lower depths of the mountain. But that opening was heavily guarded by reptoid slave soldiers. Rocketing down the terraced wall of the urban canyon, Page's Commandos and YVH droids were taking up firing positions above the Chazrach, but the enemy was well entrenched and answering Alliance blaster bolts with spouts of firejelly and highly flammable sparkbee honey.

If the Jedi were to infiltrate the Citadel, Jacen had to persuade Sgauru and Tu-Scart to halt their destruction of the western concourse while a narrow stretch still remained intact. He risked a few cautious steps toward the beasts, then stopped when temblors began to rock the fragile span at regular intervals.

"Now what?" Jaina yelled to Luke. "Is Zonama Sekot making another fly-by?"

The temblors grew louder and more forceful. Jacen managed to keep his balance on the swaying concourse, but the steady jolts proved too much for the unbroken expanse. Fissured, the yorik coral span gave way, plummeting in fragments into the whitewater torrent. At the same time, two armored quadrupeds appeared from around the curved base of the Citadel, lumbering in concert and settling into fortifying positions behind the slave soldiers. Planting their splayed front claws in the raging river, they lowered their triangular heads. Plasma streamed from the thick horns that branched from their bony foreheads, spattering against the walls of the canyon and forcing the commandos and YVH droids to retreat to the rim.

With the cavernous entrance at the base of the Citadel effectively sealed, Jacen saw Sgauru and Tu-Scart as the only hope. The beasts had to be coaxed into breaching the wall of the Citadel. Jacen sensed that his best chance of accomplishing this would require him to abandon the Force and give himself over fully to his Vongsense—something he had been unable to do since arriving on Coruscant. He felt like a switch being thrown between two poles; Force at one pole, Vongsense at the other. He understood further that the only way to compel Sgauru and Tu-Scart into action was by communicating with them through the World Brain.

It was while aboard the seedship that had delivered Jacen and the dhuryam to Coruscant that they had first reached an understanding. By destroying the brain's would-be rivals, Jacen had essentially determined which of several dhuryams was to have the honor of transforming Coruscant into "Yuuzhan'tar." More important, he had installed a World Brain whose very disposition was informed by the rapport it shared with him. All that the planet had become since then—beautiful and monstrous, delicate and coarse, symbiotic, and parasitic— owed something to Jacen. And yet when he reached out with his Vongsense he again found himself in competition for the brain's attention. Some of that was due to the brain's preoccupation with Coruscant. Over and above that, there was the energy the brain was pouring into executing Shimrra's requests.

Aboard the seedship and afterward Jacen had found the dhuryam to be an intelligent creature, but specifically engineered to be intractable. Now the dhuryam was twisted by conflict and anger. Shimrra had succeeded in cajoling it into believing that the fires and drenching rains, the demolition and destruction were necessary to repair the damage done to Yuuzhan'tar by Zonama Sekot's close passage. But in doing so, the brain understood that it was destroying much of what it had created, in addition to reneging on its pledge to compel Shimrra and the Yuuzhan Vong to accept *compromise*. Neither accustomed to being disobedient nor inclined to tolerate disorder, the brain was at war with itself for having brought harm to the world in its trust. As on the seedship, it understood that its domain was suddenly falling to ruin and becoming a wasteland. The brain was struggling with the idea that it might do better by simply ignoring Shimrra.

Calling on his Vongsense, Jacen promised the dhuryam that he would help put an end to its inner conflict. He told it that he would force Shimrra to release his hold. In return he could feel it reaching out to him as one might a friend in time of need. A wave of gratitude, a plea for salvation washed through him . . .

Abruptly Sgauru and Tu-Scart turned toward him, clearly under the influence of the brain.

Jacen grasped that the moment had come for him to demonstrate his faith in the agreement he and the brain had forged.

Ignoring Luke and Jaina's loud-voiced misgivings, he advanced on the coupled symbiots.

Almost immediately his waist was encircled by two twisting appendages. Then Sgauru picked him up off the demolished concourse and swung him out over the canyon. Not toward the Citadel, though, but as if to drop him directly into the midst of the slave soldiers and their artillery beasts.

From the *Falcon*'s cockpit comlink came the sound of blasterfire and cries for help. C-3PO recognized the voice of Captain Solo.

"Threepio, lower the landing ramp! Threepio! Threepio!"

The protocol droid stopped his worried pacing long enough to raise his hands in distress to R2-D2, whose extensible computer interface arm was inserted into an access port in the ring corridor, near the head of the ramp.

"Artoo, do something before its too late!"

Stiffly, C-3PO hurried into the cockpit. All he could see through the viewport panes was an impenetrable tangle of heavily thorned branches. He made a clumsy about-face and shambled back to the ring corridor, where he began to pound his hand against the landing ramp switch.

"Oh, it's no use! The thorn hedge has the *Millennium Falcon* in a death lock! Captain Solo and the Princess will die, and we'll be imprisoned like museum exhibits!"

R2-D2 toodled an encouraging phrase, and C-3PO ceased his pounding to stare at him.

"You can do what? Reroute power from the deflector shield to send a charge through the hull?" C-3PO's hands flew up once again. "Well, why didn't you say so earlier?"

The little blue-and-white astromech chirped and chittered in protest.

"Nonsense," C-3PO rejoined. "You're simply trying to frighten me. You're never content until you've succeeded in working me into a frenzy."

R2-D2 issued a series of solemn beeps.

C-3PO adopted an akimbo stance. "Don't you start that again. 'Everything terminates; face it bravely . . .' I'll have you know I've been facing my termination bravely since the beginning of this war. Indeed, long before I had the misfortune of meeting the likes of you. Now, do as you suggested and send a charge through the hull!"

Shuffling back to the juncture of the ring and outrigger corridors, C-3PO placed himself where he could peer through the forward viewport, as well as keep a photoreceptor on his counterpart. A moment later, R2-D2's interface arm began to rotate—first in one direction, then the other—and an electrical crackling could be heard dancing across the *Falcon*'s skin. The olfactory sensor at the top of C-3PO's chest monitored smells of ozone and singed wood.

"It's working, Artoo!" he shouted. "The thorn hedge is retracting! Thank the maker, we're *free*!"

R2-D2 squawked a question.

"Yes, of course you should lower the landing ramp!" C-3PO said as he hurried for it. "The sooner we leave this ship, the better!"

Skidding through a left-hand turn, he stepped onto the canted ramp just as its foot was striking the paving stones of the plaza.

"Freedom, Artoo—*agghh!*"

Without knowing precisely why, R2-D2 squealed in alarm. He might have squealed even louder had he realized that a tattooed and battle-scarred Yuuzhan Vong warrior was rushing up the ramp.

Too panicked to move, and certainly without thinking, C-3PO said, "You're not allowed aboard!"

The warrior only growled in contempt and continued his

charge. He was halfway to the top when a blaster discharged behind him and a crimson-tinged blasterbolt burned its way through the front of his neck, sending him facefirst to the ramp, not a meter from where C-3PO was standing.

At the foot of the ramp stood Captain Solo, his aged weapon in hand. C-3PO saw his master staring wide-eyed at something off to his left, at which he began firing, even as Harrar, Princess Leia, Cakhmaim, and Meewalh were hastening up the ramp, all but crawling when they reached the body of the dead Yuuzhan Vong.

"Threepio, get ready to close the ramp!" Captain Solo yelled. He fired off several blasterbolts, then ducked a hurled amphistaff and threw himself onto the ramp. "Close it!"

"But, sir—"

"Leia, get into the cockpit! Raise the ship!"

Captain Solo was still bellying up the ramp when a sudden growth spurt sent the branches through the gap between the starboard docking arm and the ramp, preventing it from elevating entirely. Into the gap grew long, thick thorns.

"They're lethal!" Harrar shouted.

While the priest, the two Noghri, and the two humans began twisting and contorting themselves to avoid the rapidly lengthening thorns, a hail of thud bugs slammed into the *Falcon*'s underside. In the confined space of the ramp, Princess Leia activated her lightsaber and started hacking at the lengthening branches.

"It's no use! They're growing back faster than I can cut them!" Deactivating the lightsaber, she scrambled past C-3PO, heading for the cockpit.

"Artoo," C-3PO said, "charge the hull again!"

A second crackling jolt passed through the ship. The hedge branches retreated, but instead of closing, the ramp tilted down. Two more warriors leapt in, only to be dropped by bolts from Cakhmaim, whose right arm narrowly missed being pierced by a half-meter-long thorn. By the time the ramp started to close, the hedges had returned, stopping it from sealing.

C-3PO heard the *Falcon*'s repulsorlift come on-line, but the freighter levitated no more than two meters before the engines began protesting.

"Han, I can't raise her!" Leia shouted.

Another electrical charge shot through the hull. Once again the vines withdrew, and once again the ramp lowered to the paving stones.

"Artoo, no!" C-3PO yelled.

There was no halting the warriors this time—or the branches, which grew back in such profusion that the ramp refused to budge. Cakhmaim and Meewalh did what they could to keep the invaders from entering the ship, but after shooting the first half a dozen, they were overwhelmed, disarmed, and pinned to the deck. Han shot a few more as they raced into the ring corridor, but reinforcements kept coming, backing him and Leia toward the forward compartment. Some warriors had the foresight to run through the *Falcon* and enter the main cabin space from the port side.

Pressed against the dejarik table with his blaster in one hand and his other gripping Leia's shoulder, Han dodged lashes and amphistaffs and thrusts from coufees, but he refused to yield until at last one of the warriors managed to press the tip of his serpentine weapon to Leia's throat. Then, grimacing, he dropped his blaster arm to his side in a gesture of surrender.

"All right, you've got us," he said to the advancing warriors. "I'm sure we can work something out . . ."

It was unlikely that any of them understood Basic, but they took Han's meaning when he set his blaster down and Leia did the same with her deactivated lightsaber.

Moments later a female Yuuzhan Vong with a crest of tentacles and an eight-fingered right hand edged through the tight press of warriors in the forward compartment. On seeing her, R2-D2 loosed a prolonged and mournful whistle.

C-3PO nodded his head. "You're right, Artoo—a *shaper*!"

The shaper appraised Han and Leia, then turned to one of her warriors. C-3PO understood her to say: " 'Gather their weapons, and bring everyone out of the vessel.' "

Cakhmaim, Meewalh, R2-D2, C-3PO, Leia, and Han were marched from the *Falcon* in single file. Harrar was already outside the ship. As they were being prodded toward the entrance of the yorik coral dome, two Yuuzhan Vong males emerged, both of them finely clothed, and the shorter of the pair wearing a high turban.

"High Prefect Drathul and High Priest Jakan," Harrar whispered to Han and Leia.

The shaper waved her hand in a way that flung droplets of sweat or some other bodily secretion on the thorn hedge, which immediately began to sprout new branches.

Within moments the *Falcon* was fully encased.

"I'm told that this particular ship has been the cause of much unrest," the shaper told Drathul and Jakan. She gestured to her seven prisoners. "Worthy captives. Including a *Jeedai,* no less."

Jakan's eyes widened in delight when they fell on Harrar. "All of us thought you were in the Outer Rim!" He laid his thin hands on the priest's shoulders. "You're home now, my friend. In fact, you will have the honor of officiating at the sacrifice we will perform in the Well of the World Brain."

Harrar held Jakan's gaze but didn't return his relieved smile. "You fail to grasp the truth, High Priest," he said in Yuuzhan Vong. "I've come to neutralize the brain."

Near the outer-system world of Muscave the battle was still raging. Hundreds of coralskippers and fighter craft, and dozens of war vessels had been sacrificed to an engagement that had degenerated into a shameless brawl. Local space was a constantly shifting web of fire and light, harnessed to ill purpose.

Warmaster Nas Choka couldn't have been more pleased.

He stood in the most forward area of the command chamber's blister transparency as if a bowsprit figurehead, his folded arms resting on his slightly protruding belly and his finely whiskered jaw raised in defiance.

"The enemy commanders continue to trade blows with us not because they are valorous, but because they believe that by feigning honor they hold us from returning to Yuuzhan'tar. They rely on the fact that we would never be the first to quit a contest of such magnitude." He turned slightly to face his chief tactician. "We will encourage their blunder. Order our Supreme Commanders to allow their vessels to fall back and begin to disperse. Let the Alliance admirals think they have us on the run."

The command chamber shook as a burst of turbolaser fire evaded the vessel's shielding singularities and blasted pieces of yorik coral from the starboard hull. Thick fluid poured from an already damaged area of bulkhead, and strips of the luminescent lichen died, increasing the gloom.

"How much more can *Yammka* endure?" Nas Choka asked of the vessel's shaper.

"Six of our principal dovin basals are dead," the shaper was quick to say, "and many of our plasma launchers have been destroyed. Perhaps, Warmaster, if you would consider withdrawing *Yammka* from the vanguard array—"

"No. I want the attention of the enemy focused on us. We must remain a primary target."

"We could be destroyed, Warmaster," the tactician said carefully.

Nas Choka nodded. "An acceptable risk. For today we serve our species as no Yuuzhan Vong have. We prove our worth to the gods who fashioned us. If we are to die, we do so discharging a transcendent obligation."

The command chamber's lock dilated and the vessel's Supreme Commander entered, snapping his fists to his opposite shoulders in salute. "Warmaster, from our scouts: *Ralroost* and forty other warships have just reverted from darkspace."

Nas Choka faced forward, his gaze directed toward the imperceptible enemy fleet. "That would be Traest Kre'fey." He grinned faintly. "All this is as it should be. The gods look out for us."

The Supreme Commander genuflected. "Warmaster, there isn't a commander who wouldn't gladly substitute his vessel for yours—or die in your stead."

Nas Choka betrayed no emotion. "Return to your duties, Supreme Commander."

The warrior rose and saluted again. When he had exited, the tactician moved to Nas Choka's left side.

"You have the unconditional fealty of your warriors, Fearsome One. They would follow your every order—even those orders that might countermand their faith."

Nas Choka's gaze remained fixed on the battle. "Tell me of Yuuzhan'tar, tactician."

"Enemy fighter craft have broken through our dovin basal shields, and war parties are on the surface. Some one thousand ground warriors battle ours in the sacred precinct. Others have gone to the aid of the heretics. Fortunately, the dhuryam has taken steps to confuse matters."

"How so?"

"With fires, and by loosing some of our beasts. Nevertheless, the territory surrounding the Citadel is in great turmoil."

Nas Choka waved his hand in unconcern. "Structures can be remade. Where is Shimrra?"

"The Supreme Overlord is in his coffer."

"Then that, too, is as it should be."

"He wishes it relayed to you, Warmaster, that you do honor to your elite rank. The Supreme Overlord proclaims that your name will live on as an inspiration to others. You will be the zenith all those who follow you will seek to attain."

"That means little unless we are successful at Zonama Sekot."

The tactician nodded. "Hapan warships are still arrayed in a blockade, preventing our vessels from escorting the poisoned one to the surface."

Nas Choka frowned. "I thought the Hapans had settled their score with us at Obroa-skai. But, no matter. It is the nature of vendettas that they continue to escalate, until one or the other party is wiped out."

He gave the tactician a sideways glance. "Divert to Zonama Sekot the vessels of Domains Tivvik, Tsun, Karsh, and Vorrik. Caution the commanders not to make their intentions too obvious—even if this requires their taking additional time to reach the living world. We will make the Hapans suffer as they did at Fondor. Then our barb will find its mark, and, with the gods at our backs, we will rid this galaxy of vendetta and warfare."

Mara heard Tahiri call that she had found Nom Anor. Buried in the ferocious tangle of heretics and warriors, and even while dodging amphistaffs and coufees, Mara had had to stand on the crumpled body of a warrior to see him. The look hadn't lasted long—just long enough for her to see the fear in his eye—then he was gone, slithering his way through the crowd. Unable to track him through the Force, she did the next best thing, which was to Force-leap to the edge of the embattled crowd, then to the top of a flight of stairs, and there watch for some sign of him.

True to their nature, Shamed Ones and warriors alike were running *toward* the melee rather than fleeing from it, no matter how bloodied they were or who was winning, as the outcome kept changing hands. But it wasn't long before Mara spied a lone figure slinking away, then scurrying down into a public square that was surrounded on three sides by groundquake-damaged structures. Though the relatively short figure was wearing the robeskin of a Shamed One, he ran with the stealth of an executor.

Taking a moment to touch Tahiri and Kenth through the Force, Mara vaulted from the steps to the high platform of a temple, then dropped down to the ground and raced after Nom Anor, her lightsaber close at hand to deal with anyone who might try to stand in her way. Rushing into the square, she stopped to scan the several exits, and again spotted her quarry disappearing around the toppled end of a high wall. She fairly flew after him, pursuing him up and over piles of rubble and debris, through stands of towering fire-blackened trees, then on a zigzag path down into what once had been the Column Commons—a midlevel area of open spaces studded with thick columns that supported the sprawling cityscape overhead. Hundreds of HoloNet and holodrama publishers had kept offices there, along with all the major media bureaus. During the Galactic Civil War, the commons had crawled with COMPNOR truth officers, who had ensured that everything published was in keeping with the propaganda of the Empire.

Mara was certain she was more familiar with the area— even in ruins—than Nom Anor was. But in his guise as the Prophet he had obviously gotten to know Coruscant's canyons and depths as well as any slythmonger or death stick peddler, because he led her on a chase that was as labyrinthine as the tracings of a conduit worm. The deeper they descended, the darker and danker became the surroundings.

But Mara had already decided that she would chase him to the core of the planet if that was what it would take to apprehend him.

The pursuit led ever downward, into darker levels, where fetid water dripped from cracked ceilings, and the only light was that which found its way down through gaps in the crushed buildings and the riotously verdant areas that now roofed them.

Closing the gap between them, she saw him grab hold of a fall of vines and swing himself across a wide chasm. Securing the vines on his side of the abyss, he stopped to smirk at her, confident that his escape was secure. She came to a brief standstill opposite him—just long enough to answer his sneering grin with a glare—then dashed for a narrower place in the chasm and leapt to the far side.

By then Nom Anor had disappeared into the ruins of a news bureau building. She could hear him stumbling forward, crunching through expanses of transparisteel debris and smashing through wooden doors. There, too, shafts of dismal light dappled the puddled floors, and a stinging odor of rot and decay pervaded the thick air.

She second-guessed him when he tried to set a trap for her—making it appear that he had gone through a doorway, on the other side of which there was a half-kilometer plunge into pitch darkness. And she outwitted him again by stopping just in time when he used his uncommon strength to dislodge a girder that supported a fractured slab ceiling.

He remained as steadfast in his desire to escape as she did in her desire to hunt him down. He began to scamper through a warren of rooms in a building where residual power allowed him to seal doorways behind him. But Mara merely kicked through them, and when she couldn't, she found alternate routes, never surrendering her momentum.

Breathing hard and stumbling more often, Nom Anor was beginning to tire. Mara's acute hearing told her that much— and more. As she was kicking down a final door, she heard a hand blaster's safety click off, and entered the room to discover Nom Anor hiding behind the putrid remains of a Twi'lek, still dressed in security guard garb.

Mara used the Force to call her lightsaber to hand, even as Nom Anor was triggering off the first bolts. Her blade deflected one after the next, until he had emptied the blaster of fuel. He had sense enough not to hurl the depleted weapon at her. Instead, he began to scrabble backward on the palms of his hands and feet, his gaze riveted on her as she advanced, calm but coldly fixed on her prey.

A wall brought an abrupt end to his retreat.

Growling, he shot to his feet, coufee in hand, and began to slash wildly at her, the lightsaber notwithstanding.

She leapt backward, out of reach, then deactivated the blade and encouraged him to charge. Her hands moved in a dexterous blur as she deflected his knife blows and got inside his frantic movements to slap and tap him in the chest or the jaw, never hard enough to stun him, let alone incapacitate him, but driving him backward with each smack. Ducking his increasingly desperate lunges and crosscuts, she swept his feet out from under him with a circling sidekick, then allowed him to come to his feet only long enough for her to cripple his knee with the toe of her right boot. He flung himself at her, but she sidestepped his headlong rush and sent him hurtling into a wall.

She continued to hurt him, telling herself: *This is for Monor Two,* where she had fallen victim to the coomb spores he had unleashed; *and this is for the trouble you stirred up at Rhommamool.*

Knocking the coufee from his grip, she thrust her stiffened fingers into his windpipe, then sent him reeling with an uppercut. *This is for founding the Peace Brigade; for your part in sending Elan to assassinate the Jedi with* bo'tous; *for your double dealings with the Hutts and Viqi Shesh; and for sabotaging the refugee settlements on Duro.*

Making the most of her agility, she left deliberate openings in her defense, luring him into striking, only to set up combinations aimed at punishing his bald head; his flat-nosed face; his blue right eye, with its stripe of feline pupil. *This is for the false appeals you made to Leia and Han at Bilbringi; for your disdainful appearance before the Senate; for whatever role you played in the deaths of Chewbacca and*

Anakin; for your attempt to deliver Jacen into the hands of Tsavong Lah; for your sabotage at Zonama Sekot . . .

Her blows were beginning to do damage. Deftly she moved inside his flailing arms, using her elbows and the backs of her clenched hands to bloody his scarred lips and swell his ears, ever mindful of that dangerous left eye of his, which she was certain he was saving as a last resort. She pivoted on her left foot and kicked him hard with her right, forcing the wind from him. He dropped to his knees, his right hand pressed to his chest.

He had trouble getting to his feet, but when he did, she sent him down again with a fist to the face. Dread shone in his real eye. He had spent too long among beings who cherished life, and he had come to cherish it himself. Unlike those fighting to the death in the streets and squares above, Nom Anor wanted desperately to live. Mara could read it in his wretched look; she could smell it coming off of him in waves. He backed away from her until his back was pressed to a wall, then he sank slowly to his knees.

Mara ignited her lightsaber and held it with the tip low and to her right. One upward swing and she could send his head five meters.

Nom Anor bent at the waist and pressed his face to the littered floor in a posture of servility.

"You've defeated me, Mara Jade Skywalker," he said without lifting his head. "I beg for mercy." When she made no immediate reply, he risked raising his face to her, and when he saw that she hadn't moved forward he continued. "What would killing me accomplish now? Yes, it will satisfy you, but will it put an end to the war?"

"For the moment, I'll content myself with satisfaction," she told him.

He gulped, then found his voice. "I am a dissembler and a killer. I have brought woe to you and many others. But were you any less when you were in service to the Emperor? To Darth Vader? An *executor,* you did what you were trained to do. We all serve a master, Mara Skywalker. But I was given to believe that you now served the Force."

As Mara stepped forward, his pleas became more frenzied.

"You're a mother now! What if your son were watching you? Is this what you would want him to learn—the art of murdering in cold blood?"

Mara's nostril's quivered. "You almost robbed me of any chance of having a child."

"I know that," he said, holding her gaze. "But am I not part of life as your infant is—part of the Force?" He gestured to himself. "I am helpless!"

Mara took another step, raising her lightsaber.

"I can help!" he screamed. "I've changed. You saw me leading the Shamed Ones. Just as you do, I want to see the war ended. I would have been an ally of yours already if Vergere and Jacen had agreed to take me off Coruscant in the coralcraft *I* had built just for that purpose. You see, Mara Skywalker? I say *Coruscant*. I know this world is yours. It has always been yours, and it will remain so even if we are victorious. One last chance. Let me prove myself to you."

She brought the glowing blade of the lightsaber close to his neck, then deactivated it and clipped the handle to her belt.

The expression on Nom Anor's face was unreadable. Clearly he hadn't expected leniency. He recognized that his words hadn't caused her to stay her hand—they had spilled from his mouth by rote. Something else had influenced her decision; something beyond his comprehension. For a long moment he regarded her in perplexity.

"A Yuuzhan Vong warrior would have been disgusted by my actions," he said at last. "He would have killed me as easily as if I were a droid. And yet you didn't find my cowardice contemptible. You let me live."

Mara narrowed her eyes. "I don't believe a word you said, and I've known from the first that you're a coward. You're guilty of too many crimes to list, but I won't be your executioner. Your ultimate disposition is a matter that will be decided by others." She gestured for him to stand up. "If you really wanted to put an end to the war, you shouldn't have interfered at Zonama Sekot."

"I was only trying to spare the planet," Nom Anor said. "Even now Shimrra is out to destroy it. He believes it was given to the Jedi by the gods, as a means of testing our worthiness. He claims to have a poison capable of killing Zonama Sekot."

A chill laddered up Mara's spine. "What poison?"

Nom Anor heaved his shoulders in a shrug of indifference. "Something concocted by the Alliance and deployed on a world called Caluula."

Alpha Red, Mara realized in anguish.

She grabbed Nom Anor by the shoulder and shoved him toward the closest exit from the building. "You're going to show me you're deserving of the extra time I've given you."

Echoing the shape of the worldship Citadel, Shimrra's coffer—his bunker in the crown of the fortress—was a huge vaulted space with polished walls and stately columns. From the eastern side of its circular floor a stairway of yorik coral spiraled into an upper level, where some said resided the controls that could launch the summit of the Citadel into space, in much the same way that the Well of the World Brain could be launched, to ensure that the Supreme Overlord and the dhuryam survived, no matter what befell the rest of the Yuuzhan Vong and their multitude of biots.

The coffer contained a throne, but Shimrra had yet to take it since entering the coffer from the lavish shaft that accessed the bunker—a dovin basal version of a turbolift. The Supreme Overlord was too restless to remain seated, too mesmerized by villip-assembled images of Yuuzhan'tar engulfed in flames; of Shamed Ones running loose in the streets; of Alliance troops locked in battle with warriors; and of fighter craft darting through the smoke-filled sky, stinging the Citadel with packets of energized light.

Shimrra's slayer bodyguards were with him, as was Onimi, perhaps the only Shamed One on Yuuzhan'tar or any other occupied world still content to curl at the feet of the elite. A shaper doubled as a villip mistress to make certain that the Supreme Overlord didn't miss a moment of the devastation he had called down on the planet.

"We should be rejoicing," Shimrra was saying as he meandered about, much to the consternation of his limited audience. He gestured to Onimi, who was squatting almost possessively close to the austere throne. "What, no rhymes from you this day? No words of ridicule or mockery? No capering about while Yuuzhan'tar burns?"

Solemn-faced, Onimi got to his feet to recite a poem, though absent his characteristic self-amusement, and with his gaze not on Shimrra or any of the others in the bunker, but raised to the high, arched ceiling or perhaps the sky beyond.

> *Who would stay cool while fires roar,*
> *the gods themselves might well abhor.*
> *But who would sport when death is near,*
> *the gods themselves do well to fear.*

Shimrra stood silent for a moment, then began to nod. "Yes, Onimi, you're right to give them fair warning. Is it not just as I planned, just as I imagined? Zonama Sekot will die, its living ships will perish, the Jedi will be stripped of their weapons, and the gods will have been defeated—I will have done away with them. Yuuzhan'tar will recover, and I will rid the universe of all vermin."

The shaper waited until Shimrra was finished, then stepped forward from her villip-choir. "Dread Lord, High Priest Jakan reports that saboteurs have been seized at the Well of the World Brain. Apparently the priest Harrar is among them."

"Harrar!" Onimi said, then caught himself and hunkered down.

Shimrra glanced at him, then turned back to the shaper. "Too clever even for Nom Anor, that one. It's no wonder he survived. But now on the side of the enemy . . . Enlisted or conscripted, I wonder?" He swung to Onimi again. "Betrayal is rife in our fair kingdom, my familiar. The gods breaking faith with their creations. Shamed Ones rising up against those who have for so long suffered them. And now our esteemed Harrar, giving up the elite . . ."

"Assuming that it meets with your blessing, Dread Lord," the shaper said, "the prisoners will be prepared for sacrifice."

"With all speed, set to it," Shimrra said. "Join them there. Let us give the gods their last ounce of flesh before we dispense with them."

Muffled explosions punctuated the silence as the shaper

exited. The coffer trembled as the enemy's aerial bombardment continued.

Admitted into the bunker, a wounded warrior in vonduun crab armor saluted and began to stagger toward the throne. He didn't make it halfway before he collapsed onto his knees, black blood curdled in a wound to his right armpit.

"Lord," he began weakly. "Enemy warriors have surrounded the Citadel, and even now are attempting to battle their way inside."

Shimrra approached the warrior to have a closer look at his wound. "No blaster made that injury."

"Three Jedi, Lord. At the western gate."

The slayers stepped forward, but Shimrra waved them back.

"Let the Jedi come to us." He looked at Onimi. "After all, diversion needn't be the exclusive province of the warmaster."

THIRTY-NINE

What had been the Atrium of the Senate was now a cold cavern of living yorik coral. No less digested than the great dome, the imposing post-Imperial interspecies statues that had once graced the arched enclosure resembled sandstone stalagmites or immense candles festooned with flows of melted wax. The curving walls were swirled in blood red, purple, and rust brown, and lighted only by luminescent lichen or the occasional lambent. Yawning black hollows to either side of the vast room were all that remained of the ornate entrances to the Grand Concourse.

It was in the Atrium that Jedi Knight Ganner Rhysode had died and become a legend among the Yuuzhan Vong warrior caste. Or so Jacen had said. But Jacen had also said that Ganner had brought much of the Atrium down, and that clearly wasn't the case. Leia decided that whoever was in charge of the World Brain had tried to expunge any memories of Ganner's heroic last stand by having the Atrium rebuilt.

Their hands shackled behind their backs by pincered biots, she, Han, Harrar, Cakhmaim, and Meewalh were being ushered by a cadre of warriors toward the five-meter-wide tunnel opposite the Atrium's front entry. C-3PO and R2-D2 trailed behind, the protocol droid's leg joints squeaking, and the astromech's retractable tread also in need of lubrication. High Priest Jakan's acolytes were doing a rush job of purifying the captives by wafting smoke from elaborate censors and anointing everyone with finger-flung drops of a pungent-smelling liquid. Nearby walked Master Shaper Qelah Kwaad and High Prefect Drathul, whom Harrar had explained presided over Vongformed Coruscant.

Red-orange light pulsed brightly from the far end of the

tunnel. According to Jacen, the round-topped corridor extended almost half a kilometer to what had been the Great Rotunda, and was now the Well of the World Brain.

"I thought you had your fill of this on Caluula," Leia said to Han, who walked at her left hand.

"Ah, that was only a yammosk," he said, feigning nonchalance. "Now we're going to be sacrificed to a World Brain."

"We really are coming up in the world," Leia said in the same unflappable tone. She paused, then in a more serious voice added: "I don't suppose we can count on Lando and Talon flying to the rescue this time."

Han compressed his lips, then gave her his best lopsided grin. "Chin up, sweetheart. This isn't over yet."

No sooner had the words left his mouth than a clamor began to build from somewhere outside the Atrium's missile-torn entry. As the procession came to a halt, Leia could discern the sounds of running feet and dozens of voices raised in conviction. The voices grew louder and more determined, and then the air was filled with the strident whiz of hurled razor bugs and the angry snap of thrashing amphistaffs.

The cadre of warriors shoved the captives to one side, whirled, and fanned out across the cavern. Amphistaffs unwound from the warriors' forearms, stiffing into poison-spitting batons. Ensconced in their bandoliers, thud and razor bugs vibrated in urgency. All eyes were on the entry when a crowd of scrawny Yuuzhan Vong began to pour into the cavern from the hedge-lined causeway, shouting demands and brandishing crude weapons.

Shamed Ones, Leia realized. *Heretics!*

Han grinned at her again. "See, what'd I tell you?"

She wagged her head uncertainly. "You're getting scary in your old age."

Shamed Ones continued to squeeze into the Atrium, ultimately massing into a mob fifty strong, but taking no action against the marshaled warriors. Clearly appalled by the intrusion, Jakan hurried forward, raising his thin arms over his head, as if about to call on the power of the gods to smite the crowd. Standing alongside Leia, Harrar translated the high priest's words.

"Jakan is demanding to know who or what inspired them

to profane this most sacred of places. He's ordering them to leave or be killed where they stand."

Individuals began to edge their way to the front of the crowd. A battered Yuuzhan Vong male limped forward, shorter than many of his comrades and wearing a shredded robeskin. The Shamed Ones quieted long enough for their apparent spokesperson to make a brief statement.

Leia saw Harrar's eyes widen in disbelief.

"He declares himself to be the Prophet!" The priest glanced at Leia. "It's Nom Anor!"

Leia traded astonished looks with Han, while the Shamed Ones went back to shouting and gesturing with their weapons. Others began to advance to the front, two of whom stood to either side of Nom Anor, as if his lieutenants or disciples, and three others who ignited the blades of their lightsabers.

Seeing Mara, Tahiri, and Kenth, the atrium warriors immediately tensed and looked to High Prefect Drathul for orders. Leia was at once revived and worried. Several dozen poorly armed heretics, bolstered by three Jedi, against almost one hundred able warriors.

R2-D2 toned in disquiet.

"I agree completely, Artoo," C-3PO said. "The odds are most unfavorable."

The Shamed Ones recognized this as well, as did the Jedi. And they, too, began to spread out, if warily. Just as the tension was culminating, sounds of another commotion infiltrated the cavern.

"Reinforcements!" C-3PO said jubilantly.

But in place of boisterous cries came a repetitive chant; and in place of the determined shuffling of bare feet came the cadence of sandaled troops. A murmur of confusion swept through the heretic crowd. Expressions of fervor became looks of sudden concern. The fact that even Mara looked apprehensive was not a good sign.

The Shamed Ones began to move away from the entry, as through the gap marched one hundred additional warriors, armed with thick amphistaffs and armored in vonduun crab. Leia could tell by the behavior of the crowd that the new troops were something to fear. Nom Anor, his lieutenants, and the Jedi held their ground, but the rest of the heretics fell farther back, pressing themselves to the Atrium's coarse walls.

Whatever chance there had been for victory vanished.

Jakan, Drathul, and Qelah Kwaad relaxed somewhat as the menacing detachment formed up parallel to Drathul's line of warriors, facing the entry and the quailing heretics. With a singleness born of years of training, they adopted defensive postures, amphistaffs held diagonally across their chests, and other melee weapons at the ready.

Fixing Nom Anor with a menacing gaze, Drathul pushed through the double row of warriors and paced down the line until he reached the commander of the reinforcements.

"Stay your hand when it comes to dispatching Prefect Nom Anor, his subalterns, and the three Jedi," the high prefect said. "We'll want to add them to our offering to the World Brain."

The commander snapped his fists to his shoulders in salute.

When Drathul had returned to a safe position behind his warriors, the commander issued an order, and as one entity the reinforcements performed a synchronous about-face, uttered a battle cry, and attacked, turning their amphistaffs and thud bugs against Drathul's forces. It took a moment for the Shamed Ones to realize what was happening; then they pealed in triumph and rushed forward to lend their meager arms to the fray.

"Mark this as the moment the war truly turned," Harrar said to Leia in a resigned voice.

With the guards occupied, R2-D2 rolled up behind Cakhmaim and Meewalh and used his laser to stun the creatures that secured their wrists. Once freed, the Noghri immediately moved Han and Leia out of the line of fire. C-3PO and R2-D2 followed, the astromech anxious to laser the pincerbiots manacling Han and Leia, as well.

The Atrium was in pandemonium, with Yuuzhan Vong battling Yuuzhan Vong, and Mara, Tahiri, and Kenth fighting their way forward. Leia saw Nom Anor race for Drathul, but it was Harrar who had her attention.

"Qelah Kwaad!" he shouted, as Cakhmaim was freeing

his hands. "She must be stopped before she reaches the dhuryam! She can seal off the passageway!"

Leia whirled to see the master shaper disappearing through the archway that led to the Well of the World Brain. Harrar started after her, but was tackled by Jakan before he had gone five meters.

Leia called to Han, gesturing toward the tunnel entrance. The last thing she saw before disappearing inside the archway was Harrar dropping the elderly high priest to the floor with a single blow, and Nom Anor with his hands vised on the slender neck of High Prefect Drathul.

When the reptoid slave soldiers crowded at the base of the Citadel realized that serpentine Sgauru was not going to drop Jacen into their midst but merely hold on to him until Tu-Scart completed knocking an opening in the western wall, they made the mistake of taking out their fury on the beasts themselves, by peppering them with razor and thud bugs, and firejelly grenades. Seeing others of their kind attacked, the claw-footed artillery beasts that had been spewing plasma into the Glitannai Esplanade canyon shambled through a turn and charged at the Chazrach, trampling dozens before any could escape back into the maw at the base of the Citadel. But the reptoids found no safety even there, as the enraged beasts pursued them inside, and the sound of the Chazrach's cries resonated in the air.

The unexpected departure of the artillery beasts was all that Captain Page needed to send his commandos and droids rocketing back down into the canyon to finish what the mammoth biots had begun. While the commandos plummeted for the banks of the swollen river, Luke and Jaina rushed to the edge of the demolished walkway and hurled themselves into the ragged breach Tu-Scart's stubby forelegs had opened, and in which Jacen had been safely deposited by Sgauru.

That still left the problem of how to reach Shimrra's bunker, but it didn't take the Jedi long to discover a narrow stairway that hugged the Citadel's curved perimeter as it wound toward the summit. Luke led the ascent, with Jaina close behind, and Jacen a few steps behind her, silently thanking the World Brain for interceding at the western walkway, and reaffirming his promise to end the dhuryam's inner turmoil.

Carved from the same yorik coral that made up the fortress's unpolished hull and bulkheads, the stairway was a continuous spiral, occasionally walled in on both sides, but more often climbing without an exterior handrail through maintenance rooms and expansive living chambers. Dilating membranes sealed each individual level, and access corridors connected the stairway to interior spaces. The Citadel shook with each seal the Jedi violated, as if each rupture sent a measure of pain through the living vessel. But the shaking could just as well have been a response to the ceaseless bombardment by starfighters, or explosions triggered by Page's commandos as they fought their way into the lower levels.

Judging by the way the sinuous stairway had been engineered, and the layout of the interior spaces, Jacen realized that Shimrra's worldship had obviously flown upright through space—a veritable mountain rather than a flattened oval or projectile-shaped vessel, such as the Jedi and Alliance forces had encountered at Helska 4, Sernpidal, Obroa-skai, and other worlds.

It wasn't until the eighth level that Luke and his niece and nephew met with resistance, but it was clear from the ferocity with which the warriors attacked—from above, below, and through the various access corridors—that the onslaught was likely to continue all the way to Shimrra's lair, and probably inside it, as well. If the warriors constituted the first line of defense, it was difficult to imagine what might await them at the summit, assuming they could even make it that far.

In most places the stairway wasn't wide enough for the two people to stand abreast, and in those stretches Luke had to face the brunt of the attacks. He was his own vortex, deflecting amphistaff strikes, whiplike lashes, and spurts of deadly venom; dodging or redirecting flights of thud bugs; parrying the thrusts of coufees, to sidestep, duck, maneuver his body in ways that seemed to defy gravity. Stunned or burned by Luke's green blade, thud bugs were ricocheting from the walls and high ceiling, chipping away at the yorik coral surface. Dropped in their tracks, warriors sprawled with hands pressed to stumps of legs and opened foreheads, or with black blood welling where the lightsaber had found defenseless areas between living armor and tattooed flesh.

Jacen recalled watching his uncle on Belkadan, where the war had begun, wielding two lightsabers when he had come to Jacen's rescue. But the rescue on Belkadan paled in comparison to the control Luke demonstrated now.

His single blade might as well have been ten, or twenty.

He took the steps at a lightning pace, burning his way through dilating membranes but in complete control of his momentum. Seen through the Force he was a maelstrom of luminous energy, a Force storm against which there was no shelter. And yet all his energy poured from a calm center; an eye. He made no missteps. None of his actions were interrupted by thought.

In fact, Luke didn't seem to be there at all—physically or as an individual personality.

Jacen and Jaina were astounded—but they had little time to reflect. Their lightsabers were busy, as well, turning the blows Luke dodged, or defending assaults launched from below.

On the fourteenth level, where the Citadel's exterior wings sprouted from the hull, they reached a fork in the stairway.

Luke swung to Jacen. "Which way?"

He wasn't even breathing heavily.

Jacen extended his Vongsense. "The left passage leads to living quarters on the next level. The other, to some sort of dovin basal lift that accesses the summit." He screwed his eyes shut. "Shimrra is there. He has guards with him—"

"Not enough."

"—and another."

Once more they began to race up the stairway, dropping then leaping over the bodies of wounded or dead warriors.

Tapping deeper into his Vongsense, Jacen again reached out for the dhuryam, only to be staggered by what he felt in return. The brain was even more confused than before—by something else now. It felt threatened, concerned for its survival and for what might become of its creation—Yuuzhan'tar—should the brain be killed or forced to flee the planet.

Jacen stretched out with the Force.

Mom and Dad, he realized.

And Mara, Tahiri, and Kenth. They had fought their way into the Well, and were preparing to destroy the dhuryam with explosives.

The brain felt betrayed. It sent to Jacen that it should have killed him when it had him in its grip years earlier. It should have dragged him into the Well and let him drown. It should have ordered Sgauru to kill him.

It had been foolish to trust him.

Jacen reiterated what he had told the dhuryam two years earlier: *Yes, I taught you to trust, and I taught you what it means to trust a traitor. But I have not betrayed you this time. I live in you. We're partners in this experiment. You need only choose whose side you're on.*

As he had done while on Coruscant with Vergere, he shared with the dhuryam his experience with the spectrum of life: the featureless whiteout of agony, the red tide of rage, the black hole of despair, the gamma-sleet of loss . . . the lush verdure of growing things, the grays of stone and duracrete, the glisten of gemstones and transparisteel, the blue-white sizzle of the noonday sun and its exact echo in a lightsaber's blade . . .

We are one, Jacen said with his thoughts. *We are the union of all opposites. Reject the commands Shimrra sends you. Overcome your conditioning as you have shown yourself capable of doing. Show those who threaten you that you pose no threat—that in coming to you, that in risking death to reach you, they have rescued you. Choose life over death.*

"Either you're going to change its mind, or we're going to change it," Han told Qelah Kwaad. His right hand held one of the thermal detonators he had retrieved, his thumb close to the orb's trigger. He waited for Harrar to translate the warning, then added: "There's no two ways around this."

The three of them, along with Leia, Mara, Nom Anor, and the droids were standing on a trembling ten-meter-diameter platform that overlooked the Well of the World Brain—a colossal bowl of yorik coral that climbed more than halfway to the vaulted roof of what had been the Great Rotunda.

Even if Han and Leia managed to discover the exterior entrance to the secret passageway Jacen and Vergere had used, they wouldn't have been able to reach the Well—yorik coral had overgrown the Kashyyyk delegation's platform. Jacen had said that the circular platform and the cantilevered bridge that accessed it were a hundred meters above the dhuryam's pool, but either both had been redesigned and rebuilt at a lower tier after being destroyed during Ganner's last stand, or the nutrient level of the pool itself had risen, because the platform was now scarcely five meters above the turbulent surface.

The battle was continuing in the Atrium, but it was mostly a mop-up operation. The warriors who had been in charge of protecting the brain were fighting to the death, and the Shamed Ones and renegade troops were accommodating them. High Prefect Darthul was dead, strangled by Nom Anor. But Harrar had spared Jakan's life, and the high priest was in the custody of Tahiri, Kenth Hamner, and the Noghri, who had remained behind to guard the tunnel entrance.

A sulfurous mist overlay the dhuryam pool, within which moved the bloated, fleshy black monstrosity Han and Leia had come to conciliate or kill. Some of the red-orange light Leia had observed was the product of massive patches of bioluminescent lichen that crusted the walls of the humid well. But most of it came from the pool, as huge bubbles broke the misted surface, washing the Rotunda with flares of scarlet and starflower yellow. Resembling nothing so much as an everted human stomach, the tentacled creature responsible for the explosive globules was thrashing about like a hooked fish.

Recalling what Harrar had said about the Well actually being a self-contained sphere, capable of surviving even the destruction of Coruscant, Han couldn't help feeling that the entire quaking structure was either about to explode or lift off. Considering the grip Leia had on his right bicep, she evidently felt the same.

Han glanced at the shaper, then Harrar. "What's it going to be?"

Harrar exchanged a flurry of sharp words with Qelah

Kwaad. "She says that only Shimrra can communicate directly with the dhuryam."

Han scowled. "Yeah, well, Shimrra's not here, so she's going to have to take a crack at it." Reaching out, he grabbed the shaper by the arm and flung her to the edge of the platform. "Maybe if I just send you for a swim—"

"No!" Qelah Kwaad said in Basic. "The dhuryam cannot be touched! Take your hands from me and I promise to do what I can."

"I figured you'd listen to reason," Han said, grinning as he let go.

The shaper composed herself and leaned over the pool. Sweat began to bead her trestled brow, then fall into the agitated pool. Almost immediately the dhuryam breached the surface—a yellow eye as big as a starfighter glaring up at those on the platform. Then its mate appeared, blinking and fixing on everyone. A spray of powerful tentacles surrounding the creature's mouth sliced through the humid air, faster than Han's eyes could follow.

"Seems a bit upset," he said, backing away from the edge and readying the detonator's thumb trigger.

Inside the dhuryam's tentacle-ringed mouth gnashed giant teeth shaped like swords.

"Perhaps we should all wait outside," C-3PO started to say.

Then all at once the Well stopped shaking, and the dhuryam grew quiescent. Two of the longer tentacles stretched out to touch Qelah Kwaad, then Harrar, in what seemed a display of submission or compliance.

The shaper and the priest traded looks of incredulity. "It's as pliant as a young yammosk," Harrar said.

Han thumbed the grenade's arming trigger forward.

Leia blew out her breath in relief. "Jacen talked to it."

Qelah Kwaad ridiculed the idea. "If anyone convinced the dhuryam to yield, it was the Supreme Overlord. He knows that whatever you do here won't matter, because we will have proved our worthiness, and the gods will rid this galaxy of all infidels."

Harrar shook his head ruefully. "If the gods judged us by

our military might, they would never have banished us from paradise."

The shaper sniffed in derision. "This war will take care of itself. We prove our worth by destroying Zonama Sekot." She held Harrar's gaze. "It is not long for this galaxy, Eminence. The Supreme Overlord discovered a way to poison it."

"Shimrra lies," Harrar said.

Mara shoved Nom Anor forward. "The shaper's right," she said in a grim voice. "Nom Anor can explain."

At Zonama Sekot the battle had reached a fevered pitch. One thousand kilometers from the living world the Hapan line was holding, but three additional Yuuzhan Vong battle groups had arrived from Muscave to strengthen the original task force. The double hulls of many a Battle Dragon were perforated, or showed great crescents at their edges where plasma balls had seared through failing shields. Similarly overwhelmed, several *Nova*-class cruisers had been snapped in half or blown to pieces.

Because his fighter was without display screens of any sort, Kyp was left to imagine the intense fighting, but Lando had painted a vivid picture when he had commed Kyp from *Errant Venture*. Booster's Star Destroyer had been forced to retreat, with both *Lady Luck* and *Wild Karrde* back on board, and six Smugglers' Alliance ships unaccounted for. Under the joint command of Wedge Antilles and Keyan Farlander, elements of the Alliance Second Fleet had withdrawn from the engagement at Muscave and launched for Zonama Sekot, but without the blessings of Kre'fey and Sovv. With the shielding dovin basals at Coruscant overcome and thousands of commandos streaking for the surface, the two admirals had counseled for a full-scale invasion.

In contrast, Warmaster Nas Choka seemed to be concentrating the armada's swiftest vessels at Zonama Sekot, as if the planet was somehow the key to winning the war. The fear among the Jedi pilots of the Sekotan fighters was that the Yuuzhan Vong knew something about Alpha Red that the Alliance didn't. Perhaps winged-stars and flitnats weren't the only life-forms that were susceptible to the bioengineered toxin, and all of Zonama Sekot was at risk.

Word that an enemy vessel contaminated with Alpha Red had been spotted flying with the original task force had placed the Jedi on the offensive. Although Jabitha had been unable to contact Sekot since, the planet showed signs of having grasped the enormity of the unforeseen threat. Columns of fiery devastation half a kilometer wide were streaming upward from summits of skyscraping mountains, boiling through layers of gauzy ice clouds to vaporize attacking coralskippers and picket vessels. Scores had already fallen to Zonama's wrath, and scores more stood at the threshold of annihilation.

Defending close to the surface, Kyp would no sooner conclude one duel than another would present itself. Now that he and his ship had finally gotten to know each other, the fighter was responding to his every whim. But the Jedi fighters were only a dozen against hundreds, and skips were breaking through the Hapan cordon to assail the planetary weapons emplacements or make strafing runs through the deep canyons of the Middle Distance, where most of the Ferroans were holed up in the shelters. No less overwhelmed, Corran, Saba, Alema, and the others were streaking in and out of contests, their ships darting above the boras like soldier hornets protecting a nest. As had so often happened in previous battles, the Yuuzhan Vong were slowly gaining the upper hand through sheer determination and the strength of numbers. Whether the unrelenting assault echoed the will of the individual pilots or the resoluteness of the controlling yammosk, the invaders were finding soft spots and creating openings, to assure that the Alpha Red–poisoned craft would reach the surface intact.

Kyp was drawing on his ship's extraordinary speed to intercept a pair of coralskippers when a sudden coolness enveloped his right hand—the hand that the control console had engulfed, and was in fact his interface with the ship. Almost instantly the fighter began to shed velocity and grow unresponsive. Kyp pressed the control stick trigger. Though the launchers were far from depleted, they refused to fire. Sensing that something had changed, the skip pilots began to harry him with plasma fire. With maneuverability lost, only the organic shields were keeping the ship from being destroyed.

Kyp's first instinct was to blame himself. His ego had crept back into the fight, and he had lost his rapport with the ship as a result. Or maybe he had been doing too much *thinking*. The frequent updates from Lando, the comm chatter with Corran and the other Jedi, the upsurge in the savagery of the fighting since word of the poisoned ship had been received . . .

Then Kyp realized that it wasn't only his ship that had powered down.

Throughout the fire-fractured sky other Sekotan ships were abbreviating their duels. The comlink grew noisy with reports from Corran, Zekk, Lowbacca, and Saba, confirming that their fighters, too, were no longer responding.

Chased by the same pair of coralskippers, Kyp swooped through evasive turns that took him over a sawtoothed mountain range just south of the Middle Distance, which had been responsible for some of the heaviest outpourings of defensive fire. Now, though, even some of those summit weapons were beginning to fall silent. Above Kyp, flights of emboldened skips were plunging deeper into the gravity well.

"The craft Lando reported seeing at Caluula could have been a decoy," Corran said to Kyp over the comlink. "The Alpha Red vessel could have already crashed on the surface."

"That would explain why no one's been able to communicate with Sekot," Kyp said. "The planet's already poisoned."

"Then the war is lost for everyone."

Kyp gritted his teeth. "I'm not about to see another world die, Corran."

"You and me both."

FORTY

The final curve of the Citadel stairway terminated in a immense interior space with a convex ceiling of yorik coral as jagged as the hulls of Yuuzhan Vong war vessels. A wide circular aperture at the ceiling's lowest point was the mouth of the turbolift analog chute Jacen had detected with his Vongsense. Bioluminescent wall lichen projected a pool of green on the floor directly below the opening. Jacen was certain that the chute accessed the crown of Shimrra's holy mountain, but the dovin basal that controlled the chute was either malfunctioning or refusing to admit anyone other than Yuuzhan Vong, because nothing happened when Luke positioned himself in the shaft of olive light.

"I guess we climb," he told his niece and nephew.

Abandoning the watch for Yuuzhan Vong warriors, they turned to see Luke spring high into the chute. At the apex of his leap he pressed his back to the curved wall and his feet opposite. Then he began to chimney himself along.

Jaina and Jacen followed, recognizing that they were in some sense leaving the Citadel itself and entering an enormous escape vessel, much like the one Jacen had described as encompassing the World Brain. Ascending through an outer shell of yorik coral, they passed through a layer of metal-bearing nacelles, wrapped around the vigorous organisms that had created them. Next came a layer of nutrient capillaries, then one of musculature and tendons. Ultimately they emerged in an antechamber with a vaulted ceiling and great curving walls, the innermost of which contained a large but unadorned osmotic membrane.

Jacen wasn't surprised to find the antechamber unoccupied. "Shimrra's expecting us," he said.

Jaina tightened her ringed grip on the pommel of her lightsaber.

"We should at least announce ourselves," Luke said.

He aimed the tip of his lightsaber at the membrane. Jacen and Jaina brought their lightsabers close to his, and the three of them pushed the glowing blades through. A rancid smell permeated the antechamber, and the thick membrane began to melt. Finally the lock retracted with an audible *pop!*

Luke gestured for Jaina and Jacen to withdraw to either side of the opening, and not a second later a shower of thud bugs whizzed out into the antechamber, caroming off the walls, ceiling, and floor. The three Jedi raised their blades, deflecting some of the winged creatures back through the portal, stunning others, and killing the few that remained.

While Jaina was dispatching the last of them, Luke whirled and leapt through the opening. Landing in a crouch five meters from the membrane, he held the lightsaber in a one-handed grip extended to his right and slightly behind him. Jacen was the next through, assuming a bent-legged forward stance, with his blade held straight out in front of him. Then Jaina came through, moving swiftly but vigilantly to Luke's left side, with her blade raised over her right shoulder.

Though the floor was level, the walls of Shimrra's circular, high-ceilinged lair were curved. A simple throne occupied the center of a raised dais that was encircled by a shallow moat flowing with what might have been diluted Yuuzhan Vong blood. The far wall contained a much more elaborate entry portal, and to the right of the throne a stairway climbed into the summit of the Citadel, presumably to the command and control areas of the escape vessel itself.

Between the moat and the Jedi stood fifteen warriors of modest stature, arrayed in a semicircle and armed with hissing amphistaffs. They affected no armor, but their burnished and blood-smeared flesh looked as impenetrable as vonduun crab topshells.

Luke recognized them from Han and Leia's description as examples of the specially engineered warriors they had faced on Caluula, and against whom even Kyp had failed. The slayers presented a daunting obstacle, but they were surpassed by the one they were deployed to protect.

When Luke had been brought before the Emperor, Palpatine's visage had been familiar to him from images that had reached even remote Tatooine, and his inherent power was immediately evident. The Supreme Overlord, however, was a void Luke could not fathom. He wasn't a shell of a human in a hooded cloak, more energy than flesh. Nor was his face that of a Sith Master, prematurely wizened by years of calling on dark power. Instead, Shimrra was very much alive, and all the more intimidating for it. In him was concentrated the combined strength of the Yuuzhan Vong species, and if he couldn't be defeated, then all that Luke had done to reach this point would amount to nothing.

He was the largest Yuuzhan Vong Luke had ever seen, with lean limbs, a massive head, and an upper body so thoroughly branded and tattooed it was impossible to distinguish flesh from garment. Widely placed, his slightly slanted eyes gleamed in shifting colors. He wore a ceremonial cape made of tanned hide. Curled sedately around his left forearm was a thick-bodied amphistaff with an intricately patterned head. Only in his bemusement was Shimrra similar to the enemy Luke had confronted at Endor, on the incomplete Death Star. Much as the Emperor had trusted in the power of the dark side of the Force, the Supreme Overlord trusted entirely in the power of the gods. And similar to that pivotal moment in the Galactic Civil War, a battle was raging in the skies. But Shimrra's lair permitted no view of the contest; only the muffled sounds of distant explosions infiltrated the sealed space.

If Luke was at all worried about Jaina and Jacen, if he had any regrets about having brought them to the very heart of the war, he kept his concerns so deeply to himself that they could not be felt by his charges, even through the Force. The strength of their meld was such that the three might have been sharing the same mind, and that mind was the Force itself.

Luke had no doubt that what they were doing was necessary, and in harmony with the will of the Force.

Shimrra's warriors were no less committed to the moment. A threat to all the Yuuzhan Vong held sacred, the Jedi were driven by a dark and incomprehensible power that flew in opposition to the divine edicts of Yun-Yuuzhan and the other gods. No more than did those of the Jedi, the marked faces of the slayers displayed neither anger nor fear—only the full measure of their intent to protect their god-king at all costs.

"The Master and the twins," Shimrra murmured from the throne, in passable Basic. "How long we have anticipated this meeting."

"As we have," Luke answered.

Shimrra beckoned with the fingers of his left hand. "Then come forward and show your respect, Master *Jeedai*."

Luke stayed put—and yet something began to move him forward. Just short of the moat, and much to the amusement of the slayers, he dropped to his knees, and bent at the waist. His extended left arm shook as it fought to prevent him from pressing his face to the floor, and the lightsaber was nearly yanked from his grip.

It's not Shimrra, Jacen said through the Force.

A dovin basal, Luke guessed.

He sensed Jacen abandon the meld momentarily, presumably to call on his Vongsense to disable the gravitic powers of the biot. Luke began to feel as if he were shedding weight by the second. Gradually, he raised his face to Shimrra, then—and as if defying gravity—he drew himself erect with a proud air.

Incredulity almost raised Shimrra out of his throne. For a split second his glowing eyes fell on Jacen, who by then had returned to the Force-meld.

Jaina and Jacen sidestepped away from Luke to create three separate fronts. Then Luke did something neither twin had ever seen him do. Shifting his stance, he called the lightsaber into his left hand. Abandoning form, he encouraged the warriors to attack him.

In swift response the fifteen divided themselves into three groups of four, four, and seven. The quartets began to square off with Luke and Jacen, while the larger group formed up opposite Jaina. Sensing that Luke and Jacen were the stronger fighters, the slayers had decided to reserve most of their might for the Jedi they perceived as being the weakest, guessing that Luke and Jacen would always go to Jaina's aid before attempting to reach Shimrra.

No one moved.

Just when it seemed that the moment would be forever frozen in time, the slayers charged, some with amphistaffs stiffened, others unfurling them like whips, and still others prompting their weapons to spit venom. There were no attempts to engage Luke, Jacen, or Jaina in single combat for personal glory, as had happened on Yag'Dhul and other worlds. The war had gone on too long. All that mattered now was that the conflict be decided, and that there be winners and losers.

Luke's lightsaber was a blur of pure energy as he parried a four-pronged attack. His blade found exposed flesh time and again, but the slayers sustained each searing blow without surrendering ground. The amphistaffs hammered at the lightsaber with such force that flashes of blinding radiance filled the room, projecting giant silhouettes up along the curved walls. In an attempt to forge a united front, and despite battling warriors on three sides, Luke and Jaina began to move toward one another. For a moment, several slayers found themselves trapped between the two Jedi and the lashing movements of their comrades' amphistaffs. Pierced simultaneously from either side, one warrior dropped to the floor; then a second.

Luke vaulted through a half-twisting front flip that landed him back to back with Jaina, killing a third warrior on the way down, with a strike to the top of the head. With some effort, Luke saw Jacen through the Force, pressed hard by the four slayers who had dedicated themselves to him. Again Luke leapt, swinging his blade through the air and cleaving the neck of the most formidable of the slayers attacking his nephew. Two slender amphistaffs shot for Luke's legs, but he managed to jump over both, as if skipping rope, then decapitated the slower amphistaff before it could withdraw.

A coufee swooshed through the air millimeters from his right ear. Crouching, he extended one foot and pivoted on the other, knocking the feet out from under the knife wielder, then amputating the warrior's left foot with a return swing of the lightsaber. Seeing an opening, Luke made a move for Shimrra—only to be dragged down by the dovin basal. Immediately, he rolled to one side, toppling two slayers and removing himself from the gravity field.

Jacen leapt to Jaina's side of the bunker, and the two of them began working in concert to drive a trio of warriors back toward the moat that encircled Shimrra's throne. One of the slayers nearly stumbled into the flow, but caught himself in time. Surging after him, Jacen swung his blade through a backhanded crosscut, which the warrior parried, then answered with a fast chop aimed at Jacen's left knee. Jacen jumped straight up, but not quickly enough, and the amphistaff struck him on the ankle. Landing off balance, he staggered into the wall. Two warriors hurried after him, but made it only halfway when the entire bunker tipped to the right.

The unexpected movement sent everyone, slayers and Jedi alike, scurrying, sailing, and tumbling into the opposite wall. As if mounted on gimbals, the bunker tipped again, this time in the direction of the ruined osmotic membrane, bunching everyone against that wall.

Guessing that Shimrra was responsible, Luke spared a glance at the throne. The Supreme Overlord's clawed hands were indeed in motion, but the expression on Shimrra's face was one of benign bafflement.

The dhuryam, Jacen sent through the Force.

Luke understood.

The World Brain, joining the Shamed Ones in revolt, was causing the entire Citadel to shake, perhaps by rocking the cradle to which it was wed, or by some means beyond Luke's imagining. Self-contained, the bunker was attempting to keep itself level. But cut off from the dhuryam, it couldn't anticipate the Citadel's behavior. Shimrra's hand movements were just that—the idle flutters of a god-king who was forced to accept that he had lost his most powerful ally and weapon. Without the dhuryam's cooperation, Coruscant could never be Yuuzhan'tar. Even if victorious in the war, the Yuuzhan Vong would have failed to re-create their ancestral home-world.

And yet there was a look in Shimrra's blazing eyes that promised Luke he had not seen the last of the Supreme Overlord's tricks. Shimrra was concealing something—a secret of such power that it enabled him to remain seated on his throne, even with his world teetering around him.

Luke noticed then, for the first time, that Shimrra wasn't alone on the dais. Behind the throne crouched another Yuuzhan Vong, whose asymmetrically swollen head and downcast features identified him as a Shamed One. Aware that he had been glimpsed, the Shamed One withdrew into the shadow cast by the throne, as if in an attempt to make himself small and unnoticeable.

But Luke had no time to think further about Shimrra's companion.

The bunker was suddenly in motion again.

The Yuuzhan Vong armada had suffered grievous losses at Muscave, but not nearly to the extent the Alliance had suffered. Molten blobs that had been starfighters and frigates drifted aimlessly against the distant backdrop of stars. The hulks of Alliance warships, nimbused by escape pods, languished. The battle would go down in history as second only to the epic confrontation that ended the Cremlevian War. And the name *Nas Choka* would join the revered ranks of Yo'gand and other legendary warriors.

The warmaster left the command chamber's blister transparency to stand before the villip visages of the six Supreme Commanders he had tasked with defeating Zonama Sekot.

"The surface-based weapons have fallen silent," Supreme Commander Tivvik reported. "The living ships it threw into its sky have lost their wings and are going to ground like a flock of exhausted birds. Fearsome One, the planet is beaten."

Nas Choka's expression betrayed neither satisfaction nor doubt. "Press the attack," he said evenly. "The mataloks of Domains Tivvik and Tsun will escort the dying craft to the surface. All other vessels will withdraw to avoid contagion. The pilots of any coralskippers remaining in the atmosphere of the living world after the poison has been delivered are commanded to drive themselves into the planet and destroy themselves. No vessel that has had close contact with the dying craft can be permitted to survive."

"Your will be done, Warmaster."

"May our deaths serve to harden your victory," Supreme Commander Sla Tsun added.

Nas Choka nodded his head in salute. "*Rrush'hok ichnar*

vinim'hok! Die well, brave warrior!" Then he turned to his tactician, whose restlessness bespoke an uncommon urgency.

"Communication with Yuuzhan'tar has become garbled, Warmaster, but we have learned that Alliance warriors and several *Jeedai* have penetrated the Citadel."

Nas Choka folded his arms across his chest. "Give no thought to Shimrra's capture or death. The gods would never permit it—especially on bearing witness to our victory at Zonama Sekot. Our mettle has been tested, and we have prevailed." He regarded the tactician for a long moment, then said, "My words provide so little consolation?"

The tactician frowned. "Warmaster, Yuuzhan'tar has grown as serene as Zonama Sekot. Our weapons are silent, our beasts slumber, the fires are contained. Shamed Ones and renegade warriors hold sway over much of the sacred precinct. Supreme Overlord Shimrra would not have permitted this. Our fear is that the World Brain has been killed."

"Then it will be the duty of the shapers to train a new dhuryam. With the enemy defeated, we need be in no rush to give Yuuzhan'tar proper shape." Again, Nas Choka appraised his subordinate. "The last of it, tactician."

"*Ralroost* and other warships speed for Yuuzhan'tar. I realize that you had hoped to witness the death of Zonama Sekot, but—"

Nas Choka waved him silent. "Zonama Sekot's death does not depend on my presence."

"On Kre'fey's heels, then?"

The warmaster nodded. "Place his vessel in our sights."

Buried under half a dozen blood-smeared bodies when the bunker had shifted, Jaina used what little maneuvering space she had to avoid amphistaff fangs and venom, the serrated edges of coufees, and the sharpened teeth and hardened elbows and knees of warriors. Out of sheer desperation she tried to use the Force to throw everyone off her, and was bewildered when the crushing weight of the warriors abated— or at least until she realized that the sudden turnabout had nothing to do with the Force. Shimrra's lair had simply tilted again, and now she and the same warriors were sent flying and tumbling toward the opposite wall.

Hurled headfirst for the curved expanse of yorik coral, she just managed to get her free hand out in front of her and brace for impact. Loud grunts escaped the warriors as everyone hit the wall midway to the arched ceiling, then slid in a jumble to the floor as the bunker attempted to right itself.

Backward-somersaulting from the heap, Jaina shot to her feet and was preparing to Force-leap toward Shimrra when the chamber canted again. This time she used the Force to hold herself to the floor as the half a dozen slayers went rushing past her out of control, some running faster than their legs could carry them, and others sliding on their bellies or backs. Loose amphistaffs tried to sidewind for the safety of the moat, but only a few made it, and the rest were flung hard into the wall. Once more the lair leveled out before tilting a full thirty degrees, and those warriors still on their feet launched themselves at Jaina, only to slip on whatever it was that had sloshed from the moat and was fast slicking the entire floor.

Close to the osmotic membrane, Luke and a sturdy warrior were in the midst of a fierce duel, their free hands clamped on the burned edges of the breach the lightsabers had opened. Though Jaina couldn't see Jacen, she could perceive him behind her, and she could hear the burning hiss of his lightsaber as it connected with the slayers' weapons and armored flesh. In the center of the bunker, giant Shimrra had left his throne and was tottering toward the moat, his powerful amphistaff unfurled and serving as a kind of walking stick. Also in motion was Shimrra's companion, who was making steady if tortuous progress toward the curving stairway that climbed into the summit.

Jaina had first noticed him moments earlier when the bunker had shifted, somehow maintaining his balance despite his asymmetry. Unarmed, he had seemed intent on hiding himself. But it occurred to her now that the Shamed One might be heading for the summit to carry out one of Shimrra's commands; so instead of reengaging any of the slayers, she set out after him, reaching the base of the stairway just as the Shamed One was disappearing around a curve above.

Pressing her back to the wall, she began to ascend a step at a time, her lightsaber ready in her left hand. She felt Luke and Jacen reaching out to her through the Force, somewhat baffled by her actions. But instinct compelled her to continue following Shimrra's furtive partner.

Reaching the top stair, she saw that the next level was a vast ready room, similar to the organiform cabin spaces of the Yuuzhan Vong ship she had pirated from Myrkr. Half a dozen dilating hatches led to adjacent cabin spaces, and yet another stairway—more a ladder—climbed into what could only be the vessel's cockpit. Jaina rushed to grab hold of the ladder as the bunker tilted. From below came the sounds of bodies being hurled first one way, then the other. In the midst of the swaying she heard the *thrum* of Luke's and Jacen's lightsabers, and the agonized cries of at least two slayers.

There was no sign of Shimrra's companion in the ready room, and no dilating locks that might have been opened to access other areas of the sphere, so the misshapen figure had to have climbed into the cockpit.

Her instincts came alive even before she glanced up into the ladder well.

The Shamed One was already plummeting directly for her.

She raised her lightsaber over her head, but the Yuuzhan Vong managed to evade the blade and land feetfirst on her shoulders, driving her to the deck. Bent over her, he wrenched the lightsaber from her hands and tossed it aside. Then, grabbing her by the right ankle, he sent her sliding across the floor. She hit the wall solidly, but sprang to her feet. Shimrra's companion was on her just as quickly, driving his fanglike tooth into her right arm as his powerful hands pressed her to the wall.

Even before he stepped back, she had lost feeling and movement in her arm, and now she could feel the numbness beginning to spread like a dark tide, coursing through her armpit into her upper chest, spreading across her chest and into her other arm, up into her neck and head, and down through her torso and legs. She became as pliable as soft leather. She remained alert but her lips and tongue couldn't form words. Her eyelids fluttered, and sounds grew indistinct.

One thought kept repeating itself in her mind as she slipped into the blackest of voids.

Before he had dropped on her, she had sensed him through the Force!

Buffeted by updrafts warmed by fires raging in the canyon, the Sekotan airship swayed precariously as it descended toward the landing platform. In the gondola's cramped cabin, Magister Jabitha, Cilghal, Tekli, Danni, and two male Ferroan pilots kept their gloomy silence. With the cold sky raked by the fiery streaks of attacking coralskippers, the trip to the cave had been dangerous and, in the end, in vain. If in retreat there, Sekot had refused to speak with any of them.

Danni sat closest to the cabin door, trying without success to warm her fingers with her breath. The temperature was still a degree or two above freezing, but she felt colder than she had been at Helska 4, so many years earlier, trapped under kilometers of ice. Born of dread and sadness, the chill rose from inside her, and she was powerless against it.

No matter what Luke or any of the others said, she was not a Jedi.

She couldn't even wield a lightsaber properly, much less warm herself by drawing on the Force, as tall Cilghal and diminutive Tekli had obviously done. Whatever skills she had demonstrated while serving as sensor officer aboard the Wild Knights' blastboat, or helping Cilghal fashion yammosk jammers, they did not owe to the Force, but to a talent for science she had inherited from her astrophysicist mother, and to twenty-four years of working closely with droids and cutting-edge technology. Yes, like the Jedi she could sometimes intuit the Yuuzhan Vong as voids in the spectrum of life, but if she were truly as Force-sensitive as Luke, Jacen, and Cilghal claimed her to be, then how had she failed to recognize Yomin Carr as not only a threat to her ExGal-4 science team on Belkadan, but also a harbinger of a new evil about to be unleashed on the galaxy?

She was not a Jedi.

She thought of herself as a sky-watcher who had been in the right place at the wrong time. First to be taken captive by the Yuuzhan Vong at the start of the invasion; first to have had an up-close look at their biotech; first to have witnessed the breaking of a Jedi Knight—and because of those events, catapulted to the center of a war from which she might otherwise have hidden.

Had Jacen not heard her distress cry through the Force, had he not come to her rescue in his iceborer, she would have died at Helska 4, or perhaps been broken and remade into a Yuuzhan Vong, as had nearly happened to Tahiri. She owed her life to Jacen, and at one point had come close to falling in love with him. But as indebted to him as she was—and to Luke and the others, for allowing her to see and do things she might never have—she sometimes felt as if she had been *conscripted* into the Jedi order. Much as Jaina had been named the Sword of the Jedi, and much as Jacen was seen as almost emblematic of a new awareness of the Force, Danni saw herself as the would-be Jedi—part technical officer, part familiar.

Spokesperson at Agamar—how proud her bureaucratic dad must have been—member of the Eclipse base team, reconnaissance agent on occupied Coruscant, and, for the better part of the past year, visitor on the living world of Zonama Sekot. On her arrival, the planetary consciousness had used her in a counterfeit kidnapping plot, and only weeks earlier had used her as a resource for information about yammosks and dovin basals. And yet even after all she had been through, Danni had no true understanding of what she was really doing on Zonama Sekot, or why Sekot had specifically asked that she remain onworld, rather than accompany the Skywalkers and Solos to Coruscant.

Perhaps Sekot merely wanted a would-be Jedi to bear witness to the end of the world. For what with the Sekotan fighters spiraling back down to the canyon-rim landing platform from which they had launched, and Zonama about to be poisoned by a vessel infected with Alpha Red, no other course seemed possible.

It was while stationed at Mon Calamari that she had first heard rumors of the Yuuzhan Vong–specific bioweapon. She had mentioned the rumors to Jacen and, for months following Vergere's theft of the prototype batch, had held herself partly responsible for much of what had happened. Ultimately she had learned that Vergere had actually overheard Luke and Mara discussing Alpha Red in private, and had acted on the knowledge. And now, all these months later, the Chiss-manufactured poison had found her again—though the end-of-the-war scenario for which it had been created had taken an ironic and tragic shift . . .

With most of the Ferroans secluded in the shelters, an eerie silence prevailed. To Danni, Zonama felt more adrift than when it had been lost in the Unknown Regions, and an autumnal spell had fallen over the tampasi.

A few Sekotan fighters were already grounded. Corran, Kyp, Alema, and Zekk were waiting on the canyon-rim landing platform when the airship finally touched down. Everyone retreated to the shelter of the giant boras as plasma fire and windborne cinders rained down.

"Were you able to locate Sekot?" Kyp was first to ask.

"Sekot is everywhere," Jabitha told him. Her dismay was evident, but her tone was sincere. "Sekot is merely silent."

"Silence is one thing," Corran said, "but ignoring a threat is another." He gestured overhead. "Somewhere out there is a vessel that could end up killing this planet. Maybe not as quickly as Ithor died, but just as thoroughly."

The Magister compressed her lips. "I'm certain Sekot is aware of the threat."

Alema blew out her breath in exasperation. "We could try to reach *Jade Shadow*," she said, mostly to Kyp. "It's better suited to preventing the Alpha Red craft from going to ground."

"We can't simply blow the vessel to pieces," Cilghal said. "Not without risking sowing the atmosphere with poison. We have to trust that Sekot has reasons for taking the actions it did."

Kyp glanced at everyone in puzzlement. "Why go to the trouble of creating ships if the aim all along was to surrender?"

"That wasn't the aim," Danni said. "None of us knew about the poisoned ship, so how could Sekot have known? As for why Sekot brought your fighters down, I have an idea—even though I hope I'm wrong."

"Say it anyway," Kyp said.

Danni glanced around. "I think Sekot's goal is to allow the poison to reach the surface so that Zonama can contain it—

to keep Alpha Red from being spread to the rest of the galaxy."

Corran shook his head slowly. "I can't see Sekot martyring itself. Besides, what's to prevent any of us from spreading the toxin offworld by accident? Unless Sekot plans to keep us grounded, permanently."

"It's highly improbable that Alpha Red can be spread by human contagion," Cilghal said. "Early tests of the bioweapon support that. Kyp, Han, and Leia were already exposed at Caluula, and ruled out as potential carriers."

Corran's eyes darted about. "What about Mon Calamarians, Cilghal? What about Chadra-Fans or Twi'leks—or Ferroans, for that matter?" He shook his head again. "I don't think Sekot would risk it."

"If Sekot had kept the fighters airborne, we could have at least held the Yuuzhan Vong back until everyone was evacuated," Zekk said.

"Is there any chance Sekot's planning to jump Zonama to hyperspace?" Kyp asked.

"The hyperdrive cores are as silent as Sekot," Jabitha said.

"*Errant Venture* might be able to evacuate everyone in time," Danni said.

"Sure, if we could reach Booster," Kyp said. "But we're getting nothing on the comlinks."

"Sekot could be blocking the signals deliberately," Zekk said.

Jabitha turned to him. "You're assigning dark designs to a consciousness that knows little or nothing of subversion. Next you'll be accusing Sekot of refusing to allow your warships to land on the surface, as a means of marooning you here."

"I'm only saying that Sekot strikes me as a quick learner," Zekk said.

"What makes you think that Sekot would wish to sabotage us?" Cilghal said.

Zekk shrugged. "Only what I've been hearing about Sekot's belief in the Potentium. If there's no distinction between the light and dark sides, then it won't matter what happens here—or even at Coruscant."

"Sekot wouldn't have agreed to return from the Unknown

Regions just to die here," Cilghal said firmly. "That would hardly be the action of a world that considers itself the caretaker of the Force."

"The self-appointed caretaker," Alema said.

Jabitha sucked in her breath in surprise, then looked at Danni. "Danni Quee. Sekot wishes to speak with you."

Only the Force was keeping Jacen from succumbing to the pain—the Force and what he had learned from Vergere during the indeterminate amount of time she had kept him in the Embrace of Pain—*breaking* him. While under his mentor's tutelage he had been able to go into himself to meet the pain on its own terms. Now he didn't have that curious luxury, because he was having to call on all his abilities to keep from being killed.

If not for the swaying of the Citadel and the effects of its unpredictable oscillations of Shimrra's coffer—his escape vessel—Jacen figured he would already be dead. That was the World Brain, having finally decided which side it was on. The trouble was, that decision mattered only to the reshaping of Coruscant and not to the Supreme Overlord, who was clearly able to control objects in his immediate environment without need of the dhuryam.

The slayers, for one thing.

Where initially they had been moving with individual vigilance and of their own accord, they were now moving as coralskippers did under the control of a battle coordinator. The change had come simultaneously with Shimrra's rising from the throne, and the escape of his Shamed One companion, whom Jaina had pursued into the summit of the Citadel. Jacen knew that her exit had been prompted by something she had perceived through the Force, but he and Luke could have used her lightsaber now.

Three slayers had Jacen backed to the bunker's outer wall. Even through his Vongsense he could not predict their actions, or where their thrashing and thrusting amphistaffs were going to strike next. He had managed to evade copious sprays of venom, but his torso had taken countless lashings; his limbs were bruised by the heads and coils of the serpentine weapons—though none had yet been successful in sinking fangs into him. His lightsaber had returned as many blows, but the slayers seemed to be largely immune to pain, if not indestructible.

A half dozen corpses were sprawled on the floor, sliding or rolling with each random cant of the Citadel. But more than the lightsaber, it was acrobatics that was keeping Jacen from being overwhelmed by the specially engineered warriors. Time and again last-moment leaps had carried him out of the range of their shapeshifting weapons, as the fight moved along the perimeter of the throne room. The gravity-tweaking dovin basal set in the base of the throne made it impossible for Jacen or his opponents to venture closer to the throne than the shallow moat that encircled it without being tugged violently to the yorik coral floor.

Jacen took advantage of the gravitic anomaly now, as one of the slayers lunged for him. He leapt high into the air, and the warrior flew under his feet, only to be pulled to the floor facefirst, so that by the time Jacen had twisted in the air and landed he was able to drive his blade into the small of the warrior's back, almost pinioning him to the floor. The other two immediately rushed him from behind. Unleashing his amphistaff, one warrior managed to wind the weapon around Jacen's legs, while the other swung his amphistaff at Jacen's head. Ducking the swing, Jacen leapt again, taking the attenuated amphistaff with him. Yanked from the warrior's grasp, the weapon unwound and dropped before it could strike.

Across the room Shimrra was moving stiffly toward Luke, who was being set upon by four warriors. The enormous Vong overlord stepped across the moat as if crossing a final line. Seemingly entranced—in sway of the Yuuzhan Vong gods—he fixed his glowing eye implants on his prey. He held the thick-bodied amphistaff diagonally in front of him, with his giant left hand closed around the middle of the weapon's three-meter-long body.

Jacen sent a warning to his uncle through the Force, which Luke acknowledged—not only through the Force but also by spinning away from the warriors to provide himself with enough fighting room to confront Shimrra. Whirling through a cartwheel, Luke caught one of the warriors on the chin with the heels of his boots, unbalancing him enough so that

Luke could get inside the arm that held the amphistaff and drive his lightsaber through the warrior's neck. As he quickly withdrew the blade, a second warrior was ready to pounce; Luke stretched out his left hand and impaled the slayer through the right eye. At once the other two converged on him, battering him with their amphistaffs and coufees, opening ragged wounds in his upper arms and chest.

Abruptly, the Citadel rocked and the room tilted to the right. Luke dropped to one knee, holding his lightsaber arm up to protect his head, then dived, somersaulting on landing and spinning to his feet to face the warriors' charge. His green blade moved up from the floor in a diagonal motion, cutting off the weapon arm of one of the warriors, then on the downswing grated across the abdomen of the second, leaving a sizzling burn in the slayer's hardened flesh. Wincing, the warrior tried to take hold of the energy blade itself and fell forward on his knees. Luke pierced him through the chest, then pivoted on one foot to take on the others.

One of the warriors stalking Jacen abandoned him to engage Luke. Jacen moved against the others, the shorter of whom feigned a strike at Jacen's right leg, then twirled the amphistaff in his hands and slammed the tail end of it into Jacen's right cheek. Reeling from the blow, he staggered within range of the dovin basal, which dragged him to the floor on his back. The short warrior hurried in, his weapon striking at Jacen like a serpent, then stiffening, jabbed him hard in the left forearm, as if to stake the arm to the floor.

Jacen twisted out from under the attack, grasping that Luke had again been pressed to the wall. Having killed three of his assailants, he was facing only one opponent, but his energy was beginning to flag. It was not fatigue born of fear of going to the dark side, but simple exhaustion, and Shimrra was moving in. Eager to award the kill to the Supreme Overlord, the slayer closest to Luke turned and ran at Jacen with his amphistaff held overhead like an ax, intent on splitting open his victim's forehead.

Jacen could feel Luke call deeply on the reservoir that was the Force.

From Luke's left hand gathered a blinding tangle of energy manipulated into being by the raw power of the Force.

As if hitting an invisible wall, the warrior stopped short, then spasmed as green sparks began to coruscate around him. Enveloped, he fell like a tree.

Still twisting and writhing away from the snapping amphistaff, Jacen used his Vongsense to dampen the effect of the dovin basal, allowing him to move out of its gravitic field and get to his feet. His short opponent howled in outrage and whipped the amphistaff. Jacen allowed it to coil around his body; then, as the warrior was reeling the weapon in, Jacen hurled his lightsaber deep into the slayer's armpit.

The bunker inclined, sending Jacen directly toward Shimrra. Without thinking—and without his lightsaber—he lunged for the neck of the towering Yuuzhan Vong. But Shimrra perceived Jacen's intent, and threw his mighty right arm behind him. Jacen was hit squarely in the center of the chest.

Dropping to the floor, he blacked out.

When he came to an instant later, he saw that Luke had obviously intercepted Shimrra's follow-up blow. But now, monstrous in aspect and power, Shimrra hovered over Luke like a rancor. Luke's lightsaber thrummed through the air, but Shimrra refused to be kept at bay. Luke tried to Force-leap out of reach, but the Supreme Overlord had him caged.

The master of defense is one who is never in the place that is attacked, Jacen recalled Vergere saying. Shimrra appeared to have learned the same lesson.

Lunging, the thick, three-meter-long amphistaff wound itself around Luke's torso, pinning his right arm and lightsaber hilt to his side, the green blade aimed at the floor. Just in time, Luke managed to get his left hand gripped on the snake's uppermost coils and avert the head as it loosed volumes of venom at him. But Luke was rapidly being squeezed to death by the amphistaff. Feeling his uncle's suffocation in his own crushed chest, Jacen summoned his strength and crawled frantically for his lightsaber. Calling it to his right hand, he sent it hurtling through the air at Shimrra's head.

The Supreme Overlord raised his left hand in a parry; then, with Jacen's lightsaber spinning off toward the throne, he reached into the folds of his hide cape—and extracted a lightsaber! With a flourish, he activated it. A violet blade shot forth with the familiar *snap-hiss.*

Jacen recognized it immediately.

Anakin's lightsaber.

"Weapon of the Solo we killed at Myrkr," Shimrra said, his eyes shifting through colors as the energy shaft thrummed. "Conveyed to Yuuzhan'tar by the traitor Vergere, wielded by the *Jeedai* Ganner against so many of my warriors, retrieved when he died and brought to me, and now yours to confront. So that you may know what my warriors experience at Zonama Sekot, forced to fight against other living vessels."

Jacen was too stunned to respond; too disheartened to move.

Shimrra waved the blade close to Luke's head.

Luke removed his left hand from the amphistaff's throat to grab Shimrra's right wrist. The serpentine weapon immediately stiffened and plunged itself into the left side of Luke's chest.

Luke screamed in pain.

The Supreme Overlord reared back to gloat: "One thrust and the deed is done!"

Then all at once, Anakin's lightsaber flew from Shimrra's grip into Luke's left hand.

Through his Vongsense, Jacen could feel Shimrra's astonishment and dismay.

In a motion almost too swift for Jacen's eyes to follow, Luke slit the throat of Shimrra's amphistaff. As its coils began to relax, he sliced his own lighsaber blade upward, cutting the amphistaff's body into segments. As a horrified Shimrra leaned forward, as if to vise his huge hands around Luke's neck, Luke crossed the blades and shoved them upward toward Shimrra's neck. The blades burned clean through. Shimrra's decapitated head dropped to the floor with a loud *thud!* and his body crumbled.

Luke hauled himself out from under the Supreme Overlord's body and collapsed against the wall.

"Jaina," he said weakly. Swinging his left hand, he sent Anakin's lightsaber in a high arc across the room.

Jacen scrambled to his feet and had just started for the lightsaber when the floor dropped to the right and he stumbled. Jacen regained his balance and leapt for the lightsaber, but it flew past him and rolled beyond his reach.

The vision! Jacen thought.

He looked at his uncle for confirmation.

"Leave it," Luke said.

Lips compressed in determination, Jacen raised himself from the floor and raced for the stairway that curved up into the Citadel's towerlike summit.

FORTY-ONE

Nom Anor had his first look at the devastation that had been visited on Coruscant when Han Solo landed the *Millennium Falcon* in the public square that fronted the Citadel. What structures had not been gutted by Shimrra's fires had been toppled by roving beasts or blown apart by Alliance torpedoes and missiles. The sky continued to flash with explosions and dozens of starfighters were in the air, but the beasts and fires had settled down and most of the warriors and Chazrach that had attempted to defend the holy mountain were dead.

The scene inside the shaking Citadel was even worse.

When he had been stirring the Shamed Ones to rebel, fighting shoulder to shoulder with them in the streets, he had felt exhilarated by the prospect of bringing down the existing order, of spearheading something grand for his people, something revolutionary—and, better still, with Nom Anor at the top of the heap. Now, separated from his impassioned followers and in the full knowledge that the war was lost, the sight of so many dead warriors in the Hall of Confluence filled him with despair and self-loathing. Just there was where he had sat beside High Prefect Drathul and other high-caste intendants; and over there had kneeled Nas Choka's warriors. The pews dedicated to the priests and to the shapers stood empty, as did the special platform that had been grown for the seers. At the center, Shimrra's spike-backed throne was tipped to the cold floor, and the dovin basal responsible for bringing subjects to their bellies was dead. Every surface was slicked black with spilled blood and piled high with the bodies of those who had fought to the end. And across the great hall, a hundred or more defeated

447

warriors, deprived of their weapons and held fast by nets or encased by adhesive foam, were being denied the dignity of honorable death.

Otherwise the hall was filled with armed soldiers and Yuuzhan Vong hunter-killer droids.

Droids inside the Citadel!

What had he done?

The feeling had been building in him since the surrender of the World Brain. An unthinkable development in and of itself, though he suspected that Jacen Solo had had something to do with persuading the dhuryam to rebel. Still on the side of Coruscant, perhaps, but no longer on the side of Shimrra and the Yuuzhan Vong. Nom Anor could only wonder at the irony of being able to sympathize with the creature—though his own disloyalty owed more to self-preservation than any real desire to protect what he had sired. And yet he still faced an uncertain future, including the possibility of execution. Which was why he was calculating his every word and move, in the hope that he could save his neck.

Han and Leia Solo, Mara Skywalker, Kenth Hamner, and Tahiri—his captors as well as his protectors for the time being—were speaking with two of the commanders of the troops that had stormed the Hall of Confluence. Judder Page, the shorter of the pair, held the rank of captain; the other, a major, was Pash Cracken, who apparently had been one of the officers rescued during the heretics' raid at the Place of Sacrifice.

"Have you seen Luke or either of our children?" Leia was asking Page.

"They said they were going after Shimrra. Last we saw them was on what was left of the western concourse. After some huge creature knocked a hole in the Citadel wall, in they went."

"So where is Shimrra?" Han asked.

"We think he's somewhere up top. Some Shamed Ones Luke talked to said something about a 'coffer.' "

Han swung to Nom Anor. "You know anything about this?"

"The Shamed One must have been referring to Shimrra's

private chambers—his . . . bunker in the summit." Thinking fast, he added: "I've been there. I can lead you to it."

"Then what are we waiting for?"

Han, Leia, Mara, Tahiri, and Hamner followed Nom Anor as he hurried through the dimly lit, labyrinthine corridors of the worldship Citadel, up winding staircases and dovin-basal-governed chutes. Portions of the fortress had been extensively damaged by powerful groundquakes, which Nom Anor assumed had been engineered by the faithless dhuryam. Less easily explained was the lack of bodies along the route. But he decided that the three Jedi might have taken a different route to the summit—perhaps the winding stairway and lift chute used by Shimrra's guards.

When they finally arrived at the filigree-trimmed membrane to the bunker, the dilating lock recognized Nom Anor's scent and irised open.

The first thing he saw on entering the circular space was Shimrra's head, burned clean from his body as only a lightsaber could do, the menacing glow gone out of his implanted eyes.

Nom Anor stared in disbelief.

Shimrra was dead.

He kept repeating it to himself, but his mind refused to accept the truth of it. In their long history, the Yuuzhan Vong had never been without a Supreme Overlord, and yet that was now the case, the evidence there on the floor for one and all to see.

Massed on one side of the room by the tilting of the Citadel were a dozen or more dead slayers, and slumped against the wall that contained the guards' entrance—which also showed the marks of a lightsaber—was Luke Skywalker, wounded, and perhaps near death. A lightsaber dangled in his left hand, and the left side of his chest bore a deep puncture wound. Nearby, Shimrra's amphistaff lay scattered in uneven segments on the floor.

The Jedi twins were nowhere to be seen.

Clearly staggered by the bloody tableau, Kenth Hamner gazed at Leia. He took his comlink from his belt and headed back for the iris portal. "Can you manage without me? Kre'fey has to be informed that Shimrra's dead."

Leia Organa Solo nodded her head wordlessly.

Mara Jade Skywalker was already at her husband's side, holding his face between her hands and calling his name.

"He's been envenomated by Shimrra's amphistaff," Nom Anor said. "There is no antidote. If the Force can't heal him, he will die."

Blood drained from Mara's face. "We have to get him out of here!"

Just then Luke's eyes opened, and he smiled weakly.

"Luke," she said, her voice cracking. She put her arms around him and lifted him into a sitting position.

"I'm slowing the blood flow, Mara." Skywalker's gaze found Han Solo, who went down on one knee alongside him. "From the way this place was shaking, Han, I'm assuming you convinced the World Brain to see reason."

Han traded brief glances with his wife, then mustered a smile. "A bit thorny, but we managed."

Easing the lightsaber from her brother's grip, Leia took his left hand between hers. "We've won, Luke. Once the word spreads that Shimrra is dead, the armada will deteriorate—if it hasn't already."

Nom Anor felt Skywalker's blue eyes fall on him, with a look that mixed disbelief, anger, pain, and resignation.

"Luke," Leia said, "where are Jaina and Jacen?"

Skywalker motioned with his chin toward the stairway.

Han's eyes darted from the stairway to Nom Anor. "What's up there?"

"The upper decks of this vessel. Command and control chambers. The bridge."

"Vessel?" Leia repeated in perplexity.

Nom Anor gestured broadly. "This was to have been Shimrra's escape craft and shelter—similar to the one that would have kept the dhuryam alive, had it decided to flee rather than betray its makers."

Leia looked at her husband. "Why would Jacen—"

"Shimrra's minion," Skywalker answered softly.

Nom Anor's jaw dropped. He pivoted through a circle, scanning the scattered and heaped bodies once more. Onimi had escaped! Instead of giving his life for Shimrra, the Shamed One had fled!

"Can the minion launch this ship?" Han asked.

Nom Anor considered his response. With Shimrra dead, someone would have to serve as liaison between the Alliance and the Yuuzhan Vong, and that someone might as well be Nom Anor.

"It responds only to the Supreme Overlord." He glanced around. "Onimi—Shimrra's familiar—must be in hiding."

Without warning, the bunker began to vibrate.

"Someone has to tell the dhuryam that enough's enough," Han said.

Nom Anor's heart began to pound. In sudden realization, he placed the palm of his left hand against the outer wall. "The dhuryam isn't doing this! The vessel is being readied for launch!"

Wide-eyed, Han looked at the three women. "Take Luke out of here. Nom Anor and I will find Jaina and Jacen." He glanced at Nom Anor. "Right?"

"Of course," Nom Anor said in a distracted voice.

Leia stood up. "Not without me, you won't."

Han regarded her, then nodded his head.

"Then get going," Mara said, as she and Tahiri carefully began to raise Skywalker to his feet.

The Jedi Master pointed to something across the room. "Anakin's lightsaber," he said weakly.

Tahiri hurried to retrieve it.

Han grabbed Nom Anor by the upper arm. "You said this ship would only respond to Shimrra."

Nom Anor nodded. "Onimi must have found a way to deceive the controls."

Han pointed to Shimrra's head. "You're sure that's the Supreme Overlord, and not a lookalike?"

"The Supreme Overlord is dead," Nom Anor said evenly; then thought: *Or is he?*

Flagship of the First Fleet, *Ralroost* accelerated toward Coruscant, around which the fighting was continuing unabated. The Star Destroyers of Grand Admiral Pellaeon's flotilla had overwhelmed many of the planetary dovin basals, and thousands of Alliance troops were now on the ground, but the Yuuzhan Vong home fleet wasn't yielding a cubic centimeter of space. The fighting had been just as intense at Muscave when *Ralroost* had left, and updates from Zonama Sekot indicated that the Yuuzhan Vong elements were storming through Alliance lines and hammering the planet into submission.

From the command chair on the bridge of the Bothan vessel, Admiral Kre'fey gazed at Coruscant's expanding debris cloud of starfighters and coralskippers, picket ships and frigates, destroyers and cruisers. As he had maintained all along, Shimrra's death, recently reported by Kenth Hamner, had had no discernable effect on the enemy commanders or pilots. At the climactic battle of the Galactic Civil War, Imperial forces appeared to have been thrown into disarray by the death of Emperor Palpatine. But Shimrra was scarcely a Sith Master, capable of using his powers of battle meditation to invigorate his troops. Nas Choka's warriors were bound together not by evil but by a need for conquest and subjugation, backed by an unflinching will to fight to the death. Until the Alliance could defeat and dismantle the armada, there could be no hope for peace.

But how? Kre'fey asked himself. *How can the Alliance rid the galaxy of an enemy that will not quit?*

If he ordered Alliance forces to withdraw, the Yuuzhan Vong might simply reclaim Coruscant, or fall back to positions that hadn't been attacked. The former galactic capital was rife with heavily forested regions where the enemy could dig in, grow and train a dhuryam to supervise the fortifications and the construction of new war vessels. The fighting could go on for years. The same would be true if Nas Choka decided to jump the armada to a star system still under Yuuzhan Vong control, resulting in the Alliance chasing them throughout the galaxy, as Kre'fey—at Mon Calamari—had expected the Yuuzhan Vong would be forced to do with the Alliance.

The war had to end here, at Coruscant, he thought. But at what cost? How many more would die if he pressed the attack—if he did as Nas Choka, by ordering his commanders to fight to the death? Tens of thousands? Hundreds of thousands? Millions?

The situation was untenable.

He was still pondering the implications of either decision when *Ralroost*'s captain interrupted him to report that Nas Choka's battle group had jumped from Muscave, and were expected to revert imminently at Coruscant.

Shimrra's companion shuffled about the spacious bridge, activating the vessel's organic components with waves of his crooked hands and with what seemed to be telepathic commands. The living console began to pulse and ripple like muscle tissue. A cognition hood unfolded itself, and an array of villips twitched. Blaze bugs frothed in a display niche.

Jaina understood that she was draped from two hooks that grew from the bridge's inner bulkhead. Though the Shamed One had yet to make offerings to any of them, carved representations of the principal gods of the Yuuzhan Vong pantheon stood to both sides of her, suggesting that she had become the centerpiece of a sacrificial altar. Lichen and sconced lambents imparted a dismal green glow to the yorik coral walls, ceiling, and deck.

Jacen! Uncle Luke! she called through the Force.

When she reached out for them, her mind was assaulted with scenes of violence. Jacen and Luke had overcome great odds, but both of them were injured. Except through their minds, she couldn't perceive the warriors, but she grasped that most of them were dead.

Abruptly, the twisted figure turned from the console to face her, almost as if he had read her mind.

"I know you can hear me," he said in a guttural Basic, "because I gave you only a taste of the poison encapsulated in my fang. Just enough to render you inert."

With a glance at the console he enlivened additional living instruments and systems. It was obvious that he was preparing the vessel for launch. When the bridge began to vibrate with anticipation, the Shamed One nodded in satisfaction and turned to her once more.

"I'm grateful you elected to pursue me, Yun-Harla," he said. "At last we have an opportunity to meet on a level battlefield. Both of us in captivity. You, hostage to my paralytic toxin; me, to the half-a-lifetime of injustices you saw fit to heap on me."

Jaina forced herself to speak. "I'm not—"

"Who was more faithful to the gods than Onimi?" the Shamed One ranted at her. "Who was more faithful to Shimrra's domain than the shaper who discovered the truth that the eighth cortex was empty, and that the species Yun-Yuuzhan and the rest of you created was doomed to extinction? Yes, our ancestors utilized the gifts you supplied to make war on those who would have vanquished us, but instead of rewarding our attempts to rid the galaxy of such infidels and machines, you drove us from the ancestral homeworld, bled us of further kinship with you, forced us to wander for generations in search of a new home."

Hatred gathered in his uneven eyes and shook his curled hands.

"In your omniscience, you know that's why I risked grafting yammosk cells to my own neural tissue: in the hope of being able to discover some way to escape the rack on which *you* had mounted us! But instead of rewarding my having the courage to emulate your bold works of creation, you *condemned* me. You granted me the powers to speak through the mouths of others, to manipulate them at will, to control remotely, as your yammosks do, and yet you punished me with physical deformities that shouted to one and all that my attempt at self-escalation had failed. You shamed me so that I could no longer consort with nor move among the elite. Not only did you deny me the rank of master shaper, you prevented me from being able to contribute to the salvation of my species.

"That was when I chose to turn against you, Yun-Harla. I was not alone in this rebellion, and yet, as if to increase my torment, you rewarded the others, while you left me to suffer in silence through the years of drifting. The long years of watching our society crumble; our crèche-born starve; our warriors turn on one another . . . and then you dangled before our eyes a galaxy, filled with habitable worlds. At first it seemed a blessing—proof that you had not abandoned us in our time of need. But I soon realized that you were merely setting the stage for a new form of torture."

Again Jaina tried to respond, only to be shouted down.

"Only by means of the powers *you* conferred on me was I

able to reach out for Shimrra and make him my puppet! My most audacious act yet. But when I saw that you were either powerless to prevent it or welcoming the opportunity to do open battle with me, I knew that I was right to attempt to overthrow you in the same way.

"I compelled Shimrra to announce that a galaxy had been found for the taking. I bade him to install me as his familiar. And as my telepathic abilities increased, he disappeared— except of late, when my preoccupation with defeating you allowed what remained of Shimrra to re-emerge.

"When Zonama Sekot was found once more, and this time made to appear to have been bestowed on the Jedi, as a weapon, I believed for a moment that you were actually testing me. But I soon grasped the greater truth—the same one that had already been glimpsed by the heretics and some of our priests: that because I had grown past your control, you had decided to topple me."

Onimi looked hard at Jaina.

He's seeing me through the Force! she told herself. As much as the realization shocked and confused her, it gave her hope.

"Even now I can see the glow of the divine in you, Yun-Harla. As Yun-Yammka glows in the *Jeedai* called Skywalker; Yun-Shuno in the *Jeedai* called Jacen; Yun-Ne'Shel in the Jedi called Tahiri . . ."

Onimi allowed his words to trail off, and grew introspective. When he looked at Jaina again, his lolling eye was narrowed, as if in amusement.

"Shimrra is dead," he announced. "Your god-cohorts have killed him, Yun-Harla. Now let us hope they will pursue me, as well. Then not only will I have the satisfaction of outwitting you at Zonama Sekot, but I will also have the pleasure of killing you, as my first act in exterminating everyone and everything in this foul galaxy."

Arms draped over Mara's and Kenth's shoulders, Luke was carried out of the Hall of Confluence through the warrior's membrane, then down the corridor that led to the Citadel's south entrance, where a temporary bridge linked the fortresses to the public square in which the scraped, scratched, and dented *Millennium Falcon* sat on her hard-stand. Heading for the freighter, Harrar, Tahiri, and Captain Page walked point through groups of nonplussed Shamed Ones. Elsewhere squads of commandos, resistance fighters, and YVH droids were disarming captured elites, warriors, and the few reptoid slave-troops that had survived the assault. To all sides rose piles of coufees, tactical villips, and crab armor. Three hundred amphistaffs were stacked like firewood.

Smoke was drifting across the sacred precinct and the sky was a patchwork of contrails and missile tracks, but the area surrounding the Citadel had been secured. On the far side of the square, huge armored beasts were resting quiescently.

Cakhmaim, Meewalh, C-3PO, and R2-D2 were waiting at the foot of the *Falcon*'s landing ramp. On seeing Luke—chin resting on his chest and booted feet dragging behind him—the astromech mewled plaintively.

"Master Luke has been wounded!" C-3PO cried in distress. "Someone call for a medic!"

Mara and Kenth lowered Luke to the paving stones to check his status. "Force trance," Mara said. "He's trying to heal himself." Turning to the Noghri and the droids, she told them to get the *Falcon* primed for launch.

No sooner had the four disappeared than Jag Fel pushed his way through the crowd and hurried forward.

"Where's Jaina?" he asked no one in particular.

"Somewhere inside with Jacen," Kenth said. "Han, Leia, and Nom Anor are looking for them."

Jag put his hand to his brow and gazed up the summit. "I'm going in," he said.

He hadn't moved before Mara stretched out her arm to restrain him. "No, you're not, flyboy. We don't know what's going on in there. We've got to get Luke to one of the hospital frigates, so if you want to help, the *Falcon* could use an escort."

Jag looked from Luke to Mara and nodded. "I'll bring my starfighter around."

As Jag ran off, Harrar turned to face the knot of elite captives. At the front, High Priest Jakan and Master Shaper Qelah Kwaad were being restrained by the Yuuzhan Vong warriors who had defected to the side of the heretics—if not the side of the Alliance.

"Supreme Overlord Shimrra is dead," Harrar said in a morose voice.

The announcement met with shouts of celebration from the Shamed Ones and bellows of dismay from the captives. Shocked and demoralized, many of the priests fell to their knees and began to mutter incantations and prayers. Genuflecting, the weaponless warriors snapped their fists to their opposite shoulders and lifted their blood-smeared faces to their captors in unabashed pride.

"Congratulations, *Jeedai*," Jakan said to Mara, Kenth, and Tahiri while the heretics were chanting for Yu'shaa, the Prophet. "You have brought down our civilization."

Mara answered for the three. "As you intended to do to ours."

Harrar looked at Jakan. "It wasn't the *Jeedai*. It was the gods themselves."

Kenth glanced at Harrar. "What's going to happen when Nas Choka learns of Shimrra's death?"

The priest shook his head in uncertainty. "The sudden death of a Supreme Overlord is . . . unprecedented."

Mara and Kenth raised Luke and began to move him into the ship. They had just stepped onto the ramp when someone among the heretic contingent called out to them. Harrar's gaze found the male Shamed One who had spoken.

"He says that, if you would allow it, he can prolong Master Skywalker's life. There exists no antidote to effect a complete cure."

"Is it true?" Mara asked, disconsolately.

Harrar squinted at the heretic. "That one is a former shaper. He'll be of more benefit to Master Skywalker than I can be—perhaps of more benefit than bacta."

Jakan began to denounce the shaper who had volunteered. Harrar translated for Mara and Kenth. "The high priest says, 'You're ready to discard your beliefs like a worn-out robeskin, over a mere military victory.'" Harrar listened to the heretic's reply. "The Shamed One answers, 'Only those beliefs that supported this war.'"

Jakan wasn't through. Harrar heard him out, then said:

"The high priest says that he hopes to hear the Shamed One repeat his words when the Alliance finds him guilty of war crimes, and a machine intelligence is charged with executing him."

The former shaper heaved his shoulders in a sad shrug. Harrar's voice broke as he translated. "The Shamed One says that death will be a far better place than any he has known on Yuuzhan'tar."

Without warning, the ground started to shake. For a moment Mara thought that the *Falcon*'s repulsorlifts were the cause; then she realized that the Citadel was the source. Frightened faces raised to the worldship fortress, the heretics began to retreat to the far side of the square, where the great beasts were on their feet and lowing in fear. As the shaking grew more violent, cracks formed in the facade of the Citadel and huge hunks of yorik coral began to avalanche down its sheer sides. Paving stones under the *Falcon* heaved, then sank, dropping the starboard landing gear disk a meter into the fractured ground. Anakin's lightsaber slipped from Tahiri's grasp and rolled into a crevasse. She tried to call the lightsaber to her, but it had fallen too far.

"Leave it!" Mara said sharply, when Tahiri almost scrambled after it.

A rending sound thundered through the air. Then the bullet-shaped crown of the holy mountain slowly separated from the base and lifted into the sky.

Steadying herself and Luke on the *Falcon*'s trembling ramp, Mara whirled to Tahiri. "Jaina and Jacen are in terrible danger." Her features warped by sudden anguish, she glanced at Luke, then at Kenth. "We're not letting that ship get away."

Jacen was halfway up the ladder-stairway that led finally to the command chamber when he realized that the escape vessel had parted with the worldship Citadel. While the liftoff came as no surprise, it couldn't account for the mix of emotions that began to whirl through him. Shimrra's familiar wasn't only lifting them out of the battle—away from roiling Coruscant, out of reach of his parents and many of his fellow Jedi. It was as if he were also launching them outside space and time, into a separate engagement.

Jacen kept climbing. On reaching the last few high-risered stairs, he leapt through the well and landed in a defensive crouch on the deck of the vessel's immense bridge. Shimrra's familiar stood opposite him, his disfigured body listed to one side, his twisted hands waving commands at the throbbing control console. Jaina hung between them, suspended a meter above the deck by horns of yorik coral that protruded from the inner bulkhead, surrounded by intricately rendered religious statues. Jacen perceived that she was paralyzed but conscious; warmly alive amid the cold yorik coral and bone of the bridge.

She touched him through the Force, her voice little more than a whisper, but clear enough for him to grasp that the Shamed One's name was Onimi. Khalee and Tsavong Lah had been set on pitting Jaina and Jacen against each other in battle. Onimi wanted nothing more than to kill them.

He was observing Jacen from across the bridge, even while guiding the vessel through the tattered sky. *Willing* it through the tattered sky, Jacen realized. Directing it the way a yammosk might.

"You will find no integrity in me, *Jeedai*," Onimi said in Basic, as if mimicking something Vergere had told Jacen when he was in the Embrace of Pain. "Trust that everything you perceive about me is a lie."

Jacen realized the truth. *Onimi* had overseen the warriors in the throne room below. *Onimi,* not the dhuryam, had been responsible for the quakes that had nearly toppled the Citadel—

"Shimrra was Shimrra," Onimi said, anticipating Jacen's next thought. "I am I."

"The Supreme Overlord," Jacen said.

As the realization deepened, he recognized that his Vongsense was allowing him to see Onimi in a profound way. Onimi was open to him, and in an instant Jacen understood how the Shamed One, a former shaper, had attained such power. But even Onimi didn't understand that through his experiments he had also found a way to reverse the damage that had been done in the distant past to the Yuuzhan Vong.

He had regained the Force!

"Vergere told Nom Anor that you are the most dangerous *Jeedai* of all," Onimi said. "And well you should be, since you carry Yun-Shuno within you—the betrayer of all I have sought to create. But soon, when I have killed you, you will be my passage to godhood. All you hold dear will have been destroyed. The species that gave you its blood and died to bring you worshipers. Most of all, the living world you returned from the Unknown Regions. Even now it anticipates its own death. It gasps for breath. Can you feel it? Our vessels are plunging through the shields you tried to create, coming closer and closer to the surface. The consciousness of that world is crying out that you have failed to protect it!

"How is this so? you ask yourself. How did it come to this? Because your military created a poison that was to kill my people, and instead I have sent it back to kill the very world you persuaded to join you in the fight against us. Is there not in that the hand of a new god, *Jeedai* Yun-Shuno? Where is your precious *Force* now—the lingering exhalations of Yun-Yuuzhan—that this has been allowed to happen?"

Jacen understood that Onimi was referring to Alpha Red. The toxin had to have arrived on the vessel that had escaped Caluula. He reached out for Sekot, but the voice of Zonama's planetary consciousness was indistinct. Something had changed. Was Sekot deliberately concealing its presence from him or—

Jacen experienced a moment of insight. He could see Onimi through the Force. Was it possible that he would be able to find Sekot through his *Vongsense*?

Again he reached out, touching Sekot this time, and the astonishing truth struck him like lightning.

Why hadn't he seen it earlier?

But there was no time to dwell on it.

Onimi was eager to train his awesome powers on Jacen, and to do that he had no need for an amphistaff or coufee. He was capable of manufacturing paralytic agents and lethal poisons. And in the same way the World Brain oversaw Coruscant, Onimi controlled the environment of the living vessel, and could turn any or all parts of it against Jacen.

Jacen realized that he was about to engage in a battle that

would be decided not by knowledge of the Force, so much as
fealty to its will. This was not a duel, but a relinquishment.

Once more he heard the voice of the vision he had had on
Duro: *Stand firm . . .*

His heart told him that it was the voice of his grandfather,
Anakin Skywalker.

FORTY-TWO

Lando's urgent comlink transmission from *Errant Venture* found Wedge in the chaotic situation room of *Mon Mothma*, where a holographic image of Zonama Sekot rotated slowly in a cone of blue light, and bezels of various colors showed the deployment of Alliance and Yuuzhan Vong vessels. Technicians and droids were busy at every duty station, and the scrubbed air was filled with the din of voices and the incessant toning of damage- and threat-assessment screens. In the thick of the fighting, enemy mataloks and yorik-vec were blinking out at the rate of one every five minutes, but closer to the living planet, coralskippers and yorik-akaga had swept through portions of the Hapan line and were strafing the boras and inhabited canyons of the Middle Distance. With Zonama's mountaintop defenses either incapacitated or determined to be ineffective against the small craft, *Mon Mothma* was speeding for the planet.

Separate conversations among the tactical officers surrounding the holoprojector table made it impossible for Wedge to hear Lando clearly, so he moved to a corner of the vast room and slipped a headset over his ears.

"The battle at Muscave was nothing more than a diversion," Lando was saying. "Nas Choka was hoping to keep us too occupied to notice the poisoned vessel he's trying to get to the surface of Zonama Sekot." He snorted. "One small ship, slipping past all the defenses. Does that sound familiar?"

"Vaguely," Wedge lied. "Do you have information on why the Jedi fighters have gone to ground?"

"Negative."

"Could the Vong have already delivered the Alpha Red?"

"That's as good a guess as any," Lando said. "Unless Sekot's decided to surrender."

"If that's the case, then it's grown weaker over the past fifty years."

"Or the Vong have gotten stronger," Lando paused, then said: "Booster's going to take *Errant Venture* as close to Zonama Sekot as possible. We'll evacuate as many of the Jedi and the Ferroans as we can."

Wedge grimaced. "Lando, you can't do that if the planet's already been poisoned. I realize Alpha Red probably doesn't pose a threat to humans or Bothans, but, after Caluula, we can't be sure that it can't be spread by other species."

Lando was silent for a long moment. "Understood, Wedge," he said in a resigned voice. "We'll check with Kyp and Corran before we lift anyone up the well. What do you hear from Coruscant?"

"Tooth and nail. Shimrra is apparently dead—Luke saw to that. But Shimrra's death hasn't slowed Nas Choka. Even if we can eventually defeat his forces, there's not much chance of forcing a surrender."

"What's the answer?"

"I'm worried that Kre'fey and Sovv are looking hard at Alpha Red."

Lando exhaled audibly. "Seems to be everybody's solution just now."

Wedge signed off and removed the headset. He spent a long moment regarding the rotating holoimage of Zonama Sekot. He refused to accept that the poisoned ship had gotten through. Starfighters could prevent it from reaching the surface. He thought back almost five years to the decision he had made to come out of retirement. He hadn't a notion then that he would end up piloting a starfighter at Sernpidal, be charged with holding Borleias, or attacking Corulag. But that was the way of war. You did whatever you could, hoping that even the smallest contributions affected the end result.

He moved to the nearest duty station and asked to be patched through to the senior mission officer.

"I want you to ready a starfighter," he said when the female officer answered.

"For any particular squadron?" she asked. "They're all so shot up the pilot can have his pick."

"Who's been tasked with protecting Zonama Sekot?"

"That would be Red Squadron, General."

Perfect, Wedge thought. "Alert Red Leader to expect a reinforcement."

"What's the pilot's call sign, sir?"

Wedge considered it, then said, "Vader."

"Impossible," Nas Choka told his tactician. "The Supreme Overlord is a ward of the gods. Should we fail in our task, he will be the last of us to die—and our success is *assured*." He gestured toward Coruscant, readily visible through the blister transparency. "Zonama Sekot will die, and the battle here will turn as soon as I recall the rest of our forces from Muscave. We will chase the Alliance back to the Outer Rim, where they will spend the next ten years licking their wounds and dreaming of the day they will be strong enough to mount a second counteroffensive."

The tactician inclined his head in respect. "But the announcement was made by Eminence Harrar himself."

"Harrar!" the warmaster said in surprise. "I thought he was in the Outer Rim."

"No, Fearsome One. Crossed over to the side of the enemy—at Zonama Sekot, when it was in the Unknown Regions. Prefect Nom Anor, as well, now revealed to be leader of the heretics."

Nas Choka extended his hand to the bulkhead to steady himself. Harrar, a traitor? Nom Anor, an insurgent . . . Though painful to endure, those were reversals he could accept. But surely he would know if the Yuuzhan Vong had suddenly lost their conduit to the gods. He glanced around the command chamber at his commander and subaltern, his villip mistress and priest. Not one of them was distracted or apprehensive; all of them were attending to their duties.

"A lie by renegades," he said to the tactician at last. "A cowardly attempt to throw us into confusion."

Again, the tactician inclined his head. "Warmaster, my feelings echo yours. I should know—*inside*—if our Supreme Overlord is dead. And yet the villip reports from other commanders on the surface confirm that warriors and *Jeedai* have overrun the Citadel, including Shimrra's coffer."

"*Jeedai*," Nas Choka repeated.

"May I speak my thoughts?"

"Quietly," the warmaster cautioned.

"Why should Zonama Sekot's planetary weapons cease unless the living world is fearless? Could Shimrra somehow have been duped into playing into the hands of the gods, when their true aim is to punish him for arrogance—and us, for our faithfulness to him?"

Nas Choka's slanted forehead furrowed. "I—"

"Warmaster," *Yammka's Mount*'s Supreme Commander interrupted, with a brisk salute. "Lord Shimrra's personal vessel has launched from the Citadel, and even now emerges from the atmosphere to join us in battle."

"Show me!" Nas Choka said, whirling to the transparency.

The commander pointed to a section of the blister, which showed an enhanced view of the Supreme Overlord's projectile-shaped coffer, its powerful dovin basal tugging it swiftly from the gravitational grip of the planet. Alongside the vessel, though not yet engaging it in battle, flew two Alliance starfighters and a battered, saucer-shaped freighter.

Nas Choka showed the tactician a brief nod of acquittal. "You see, a trick by renegades. Not only does the Supreme Overlord live, he seeks to reinvigorate us personally." He looked at the commander. "We will demonstrate our gratitude to Shimrra by immolating the flagship in his honor. Order all vessels to converge on *Ralroost*."

On the bridge of the vessel whose every component answered to him, Onimi sent a blur of objects racing for Jacen, beginning with the carved idols that flanked Jaina: cloaked Yun-Harla, many-armed Yun-Yammka, thousand-eyed Yun-Shuno, and the rest. But Jacen stood firm. Not wanting to risk hurting Jaina inadvertently by deflecting the objects, he pulled everything into a whirling cloud, as if in orbit around him. Beyond the cloud, he was dimly aware that a transparency had formed above the console, and that constellations of stars were winking into existence, smeared in places by the explosive exchanges among the hundreds of warships battling at the edge of Coruscant's envelope.

Jacen's steadfast defense infuriated Onimi. Reaching deeper into himself, the Supreme Overlord used his telekinetic powers to create cracks in the bulkheads and ceiling, hoping to add chunks of unrooted yorik coral to his conjured storm. But as fast as the fissures formed, Jacen repaired them, and those chunks that were torn away he ordered the vessel to cement in place.

Mismatched eyes opened wide in disbelief, Onimi charged, his feet moving so rapidly that he might have been gliding across the deck.

Though crippled by the deformations that had resulted from poorly healed enhancement surgeries and the consequences of experimental escalations, the former shaper was still taller than Jacen and pound for pound more powerful. But the struggle had nothing to do with size and less to do with brute strength. Onimi's true potency lay in his abilities to amplify the electric current that flowed through his body, or—like Vergere—to call on his refined metabolism to fashion molecules and compounds, and deliver them through his curving yellow fingernails, his single fang, his blood, sweat, saliva, and breath. But where Vergere had learned to produce emollients and healing tears, Onimi was capable of producing a brew of fast-acting and deadly toxins. Compared to the former shaper's mastery of Yuuzhan Vong bioscience, Vergere had been a mere adept.

He flew at Jacen with hands upraised and mouth ajar. Jacen lifted his hands in defense and he and Onimi met with blinding discharges of electrical energy that entangled both of them in a flashing web. Their hands interlocked, they whirled from one side of the bridge to the other in a kind of mad pirouette, caroming off the coarse bulkheads and smooth instrumentation. Jaina sent her twin what reinforcement she could summon, but he told her to conserve her strength.

The transmutated secretions from Onimi's palms and fingertips sent hallucinogens through Jacen's skin and capillaries, and coursing through his bloodstream. Onimi's paralyzing fang struck repeatedly for Jacen's temples and neck. Poison wafted on his forced sighs and rode within the droplets of his frothing saliva.

But the Jacen that the Supreme Overlord had in his taloned grip was not there. Where once Jacen had been unable to find Onimi through the Force, now it was Onimi who couldn't find Jacen. What he found instead was formless, supple, and fathomless—an infinite emptiness, but as serene as a wind toppling trees to encourage new growth.

A being of light, Jacen was drawing into himself all of Onimi's lethal compounds, neutralizing them and casting them out as sweat, tears, and exhalations.

He understood at last why he had failed to catch Anakin's lightsaber when Luke had tossed it to him: he was never meant to catch it, because he had *become* the lightsaber.

He had attained the ability to cut through any resistance in himself; to sever the bonds of preconception; to open a gaping hole into a reality more expansive than any he had ever dared imagine; to *heal*. As his grandfather had done, he had broken through the apparent opposites that concealed the absolute nature of the Force, and found his way into an unseen unity that existed beyond the seeming separateness of the world. For a moment all the cosmic tumblers had clicked into place, and light and dark sides became something he could balance within himself, without having to remain on one side or the other. The consciousness that was Jacen Solo was strewn across the vast spectrum of life energy. He had passed beyond choice and consequence, good and evil, light and dark, life and death.

All that had been required of Jacen was complete surrender—a technique once mastered by the Jedi Order but at some point misplaced; transposed to an emphasis on individual achievement, which had opened a way to arrogance.

In that the path was available to any who chose to seek and follow it, Jacen understood that the discovery was really a rediscovery. Indeed, the ur–Yuuzhan Vong had adhered to it when they had lived in symbiosis with Yuuzhan'tar. In that dim protohistorical time, they had been group-minded, living in a world where the boundaries between self and other were permeable. By cutting that bond they had isolated themselves from the Force. They had deluded themselves into thinking that they were worshiping life, when in fact they were worshiping the only route to symbiosis left open to them, which was death.

Jacen realized that, in a sense, he had paraphrased Onimi. He had passed beyond the tradition of the Jedi Order into a more embracing reality. But instead of attempting to steal the authority of the gods, or to become a god, he had finally allowed himself to merge with the Force in its entirety and become a conduit for its raw power, which flowed through him like the thundering headwaters of a great river. The conjoining of the Force and his Vongsense enabled him to render himself small enough to follow Onimi wherever he went or attempted to hide; to counter Onimi's every action, and merge with his living vessel on a molecular level.

Jacen ended their spinning, bringing them to a halt in the center of the bridge, where he continued to parry Onimi's strikes. The Supreme Overlord's lolling eye fixed him with a gimlet stare.

Gradually Onimi began to understand, as well. He grasped that Jacen wasn't defending himself so much as using Onimi's own strengths against him. Jacen was fighting without fighting; drawing Onimi deeper into the struggle by demanding more of Onimi's indigenous toxins, to the point that he couldn't keep up. Jacen was the vacuum, the dovin basal singularity into which Onimi was being sucked. Jacen had become the dismantling void that was drawing Onimi into a slender thread, attenuating him to the point of infinite smallness.

Onimi's self-deformed face began to change. His arteries pulsed and his veins bulged from beneath his pale skin.

Onimi fought with everything that remained in him, but Jacen could not be overwhelmed. As a pure conduit of the Force, he was incapable of taking missteps or making wrong moves. He stood not at the edge of the tilting ecliptic of his vision, but at the center, as a fulcrum. The weight that would disturb the balance was Onimi, but to Jacen, that weight was no longer of sufficient mass to make a difference.

The Force encased Jacen like a whirlwind, moving deep into the darkness the Yuuzhan Vong had brought to the galaxy, and gathering it and sending it up the spout into the funnel cloud, where it was transformed and dispersed.

Onimi was becoming more insubstantial by the moment.

Jacen continued to stand firm, righting the world.

He had become so powerful as to be dangerous to his own galaxy, for he could see clearly the temptations of the dark side and the desire to force one's will on others—to so completely dominate that all life would kowtow to him.

He purged his mind of all pride and evil intent and entered a moment of unadulterated bliss, where he seemed to have unlocked the very secrets of existence.

He knew that he would never again be able to reach this exalted state, and at once that he would spend the rest of his life trying.

Neither Jaina nor Jacen had answered Leia's calls as Nom Anor had led the search for them, but the reason for their silence became clear the moment she entered the bridge of the accelerating alien vessel.

She was last to arrive in the cavernous chamber. Nom Anor and Han, blaster in hand, had raced in ahead of her, only to be transfixed by the spectacle unfolding before their eyes—a sight Leia knew she would carry to her grave, and all the more spellbinding for the backdrop of familiar stars, hyphens of coherent light, roiling plasma missiles. She felt as if she were wedged between a dream and a vision; lifted into a realm that was usually denied to mortal beings.

In the center of the bridge Jacen stood like a pillar of blinding light, feet planted, arms at his sides, chin lifted. The dazzling light seemed to spin outward from his midsection and surround him like an aura. His face was almost frighteningly serene, and perhaps a touch sad. The pupils of his eyes were like rising suns. He seemed to age five years—features maturing, complexion softening, body elongating—as Leia watched breathlessly.

What youth might have remained in her son vanished.

Across the bridge, Shimrra's Shamed familiar, Onimi, was pinned to the coarse bulkhead like a captive shadowmoth, uneven eyes rolled up into his deformed head and slavering mouth opened wide in wonderment, agony, despair—it was impossible to know.

Jaina dangled limply between her brother and Onimi, as if a mournful sculpture, fragile but growing stronger by the moment.

And as she strengthened, Onimi began to wane. For an instant it appeared that the surgeries, mutilations, and disfigurements were reversing themselves. The Shamed One's facial features became symmetrical. His twisted body straightened, assuming its original size, shape, and aspect—more human than not, though taller and leaner, with long limbs and large hands. But life deserted him just as quickly. He slid to the deck as if his bones had dissolved. Poured from his mouth, eyes, and ears, corrosive fluids began to consume him, leaving nothing more than a puddle of foul hydrocarbons, which the yorik coral deck absorbed as it might a stain.

Immediately the vessel spasmed, as if it had been struck by turbolaser fire, or had in fact sustained a kind of stroke. Color and warmth drained from the living console, and the instruments took on an arthritic look. Cognition hoods and villips grew desiccated. Blaze bugs fell out of formation and died on the floor of their niche. Coral fractured, and the already scant green light faded. With its dovin basal dying, the vessel almost succumbed to a last grab by Coruscant; then it lurched forward once more, aimed resolutely for the heart of the battle.

When Leia finally came back to herself, Jacen had lifted Jaina from the horns on which she had been suspended, and was cradling her in his arms.

"You wouldn't let me help you," she said.

Jacen comforted her with a smile. "I needed you to help yourself."

Nom Anor watched in awe as Onimi disappeared into the deck of the bridge, his body dissolved by whatever corrosive poisons he had fabricated to use against Jacen Solo. Death had come to the Shamed One who had brought shaper Nen Yim to Coruscant; the Shamed One whom Nom Anor had once followed to a secret shaper grashal; the Shamed One who had sat at the feet of Shimrra, and whose rhymes had been a constant irritant to the elite.

The Shamed One who had tricked everyone into believing that Shimrra was the Supreme Overlord.

The Supreme Overlord who was now dead.

Nom Anor stared at the discoloration that had been Onimi. Even if he lived to tell it, would anyone believe his tale? Would the Jedi be willing to corroborate it?

A prolonged paroxysm from the vessel snapped him back into awareness of his perilous dilemma. His real eye darted from the Jedi twins to their parents. There was still time to render them unconscious where they stood, then pilot Onimi's vessel to rendezvous with whatever was left of Nas Choka's mighty armada—

But perhaps not.

Jacen Solo was as dangerous a foe as could be imagined. What's more, Onimi's vessel, though roused from stasis, might not respond to Nom Anor. If he was to escape with his life, he needed a more foolproof plan.

The solution presented itself when the vessel lurched again, and the controls began to surrender their suppleness.

"Onimi was wedded to this ship," he said in a rush. "With his death, it has begun to die, and we will perish with it."

When Jacen nodded in confirmation, Jaina said, "Mara is searching for us."

Han rushed to the console and peered through the blister transparency. "Then the *Falcon*'s gotta be out there somewhere." He turned to Nom Anor. "I've seen Yuuzhan Vong evacuate their ships, wearing those gnullith masks—"

"There's a better way." Nom Anor cut him off. "This vessel is equipped with a yorik-trema. What you call a 'crate'— a landing craft."

Han showed him a long-suffering look. "What, you were waiting for me to *ask*?"

Quickly, Nom Anor led the Solo family out of the bridge and through a bewildering maze of corridors, whose throbbing walls were already showing signs of imminent collapse. The palm of his right hand opened lock after dilating lock, allowing them to weave their way clear across the vessel to the port-side bulkhead, and ultimately into a small grotto, equipped with a semicircular array of locks.

Nom Anor opened what appeared to be the most exterior of the locks, and gestured everyone inside. "Get settled, while I arm the launch organ!"

Han clasped his left arm around his daughter's waist and started for the lock. But Jacen stopped him.

"This doesn't lead to the yorik-trema." He turned slightly and pointed to the innermost lock. "That's the correct one."

Jaina glanced around the grotto. "Jacen's right." She nodded to the lock Nom Anor had opened. "It leads to a waste disposal area."

Jacen regarded Nom Anor. "Once you had sealed us inside, you would have been able to pilot the landing craft to safety." Disappointment tugged at his features. "And yet despite your attempt at treachery we owe you our lives, because I doubt I would have been able to find my way to this grotto."

Nom Anor glanced from the first lock to the second, then forced a relieved sigh. "Thank you for catching my error, Jacen Solo. What with leading the Shamed Ones in rebellion and witnessing Onimi's death, I was momentarily confused—"

Han drew his blaster. "Save it."

Nom Anor raised his hands in surrender. "It was an innocent mistake! Now isn't the time to argue!" He risked a step toward Han. "We must board the escape craft before this vessel—"

Nom Anor lunged forward.

"His eye!" Jaina yelled.

Poison spewed from the plaeryin bol. Han was too encumbered to twist himself or Jaina out of its path. In a blur, Jacen interposed himself between Nom Anor and his father, and took the lethal gush full in the face.

Even better than hoped for! Nom Anor thought. With Jacen out of the way, he could easily incapacitate the others. With his right hand, he reached for the little finger of his left. At the same time, he steeled himself for a dash across the grotto. It would take a moment for the knockout gas released by the false digit to reach full effect, and that moment constituted all the time he had to reach the escape craft lock and seal it behind him.

In the instant his hands met, he heard the *snap-hiss* of a lightsaber.

And in the interminable instant that followed, he watched Leia's energy blade sever his left hand at the wrist, and watched himself falling to his knees in shock and searing pain. Worse, it was *Jacen* who came to his side, weakened by the plaeryin bol's venom, but very much alive.

"It didn't have to be this way," the young Jedi said.

Nom Anor clasped his stump of forearm in his right hand. "Didn't it, *Jeedai*?" He smirked. "Even if words from you kept me from execution or life imprisonment, what course was left to me? Just as my atheism renders me unfit for Yuuzhan Vong society, my utter contempt for the Force makes me unfit to live among any species that recognize it. I've been a stranger to all worlds. Even Yu'shaa, leader of the Shamed Ones, was just another role for me—another lie." A rueful laugh escaped him. "Ooglith masquers can't hide everything, *Jeedai*."

On the other side of the grotto, Jaina was pressing her hand against the lock's sensor organ, to no apparent effect.

"It responds only to the flesh of Yuuzhan Vong," Nom Anor said. He felt Jacen's eyes on him.

"Then we'll use your severed hand," Jacen said.

Nom Anor blew out his breath and rose to his feet. Crossing the grotto, he pressed the palm of his right hand to the bulkhead sensor. "Get inside," he said when the lock dilated. "The landing craft will scarcely outlive the vessel that birthed it."

Han and Leia helped their daughter into the yorik-trema; then Han reappeared, blaster in hand, to usher his son aboard. He stood at the lock for a long moment, coming to his own decision. Nom Anor watched Han's jaw bunch with fury, then relax. In the end, Han lowered his blaster and gestured for Nom Anor to enter the craft.

Instead, Nom Anor took a backward step and shook his head. "If I'm clear on one point, it's this: I want no part of whatever new order is in the making. I will die here with Onimi, for we have been two of a kind from the start."

With that, he shoved Han back through the lock and pressed his right hand to the bulkhead, launching the craft into space.

* * *

Nas Choka paced back and forth in front of *Yammka*'s transparency, his troubled gaze fixed on Shimrra's vessel as it climbed out of Yuuzhan'tar's reach in fits and starts.

"*Ralroost* wallows in our sights," the tactician reported.

"Shimrra approaches," the Supreme Commander said from beneath his cognition hood, "though he still refrains from communicating with us."

Nas Choka traded glances with the tactician before replying. "Give him time."

He had no sooner swung back to the transparency to track the vessel's course than it began to stutter in flight and enter into an end-over-end roll.

"The dovin basal has failed!" the commander shouted. "The vessel is dismembering!"

Nas Choka wanted to tear his eyes away but couldn't. Atmosphere and other gases were beginning to puff and stream from fractures in the vessel's hull. Fluids leaked from the dovin basal blastulas, trailing behind like frozen streamers. Vital components shut down and went spinning off into space. Broadening and deepening, the fissures joined, creating a network of cracks, from which hunks of yorik coral began to tumble. Then, just at the leading edge of the planetary flotilla, Shimrra's coffer exploded, sundering like a disintegrated planet and loosing a shock wave that crippled countless war vessels before it dispersed.

A fearful silence descended on *Yammka*'s command chamber. For a long moment, Nas Choka could only gape in incredulity at what had occurred. Never in their long history had the Yuuzhan Vong been without a Supreme Overlord—their holy intercessor. Despite the success at Zonama Sekot, the armada was *nothing* without Shimrra. They had been cut off from the divine, deprived of any means of appealing to Yun-Yuuzhan or Yun-Yammka for guidance or support.

What had lighted the Yuuzhan Vong universe had been extinguished. Truly the gods had abandoned the Yuuzhan Vong and allied with the infidels. They had withdrawn their guardianship of Shimrra, and the Yuuzhan Vong had become Shamed Ones—rejected, passed over, a hopeless godless species.

Defeated!

Nas Choka could feel the expectant gazes of his commanders and subalterns. He grasped the question implied by every look—the question every Yuuzhan Vong on or off Coruscant was asking: *Is there purpose to fighting to the death without any hope for salvation in the afterlife?*

Nas Choka martialed his pride and moved to the villip-choir. "All Supreme Commanders," he told the villip mistress; then, when the villips had taken on the likenesses of his chief subordinates, he said: "The war is ended. We are defeated by the gods and by their allies. Though they have abandoned us, we will suffer our defeat with honor, because it is what the gods would expect. But any of you who wish to follow the Supreme Overlord's example and die as warriors may do so; just as any of you who wish to commit ritual death may do so. Those who choose neither will join me in accepting the shame of surrender, and finding what nobility we can in capture and graceless execution.

"Rrush'hok ichnar vinim'hok!"

Even while the vessel's Supreme Commander, chief tactician, and priest were opening themselves with coufees, Nas Choka moved back to the transparency. Across the entire embattled face of Yuuzhan'tar—of *Coruscant*—coralskippers, pickets, and cruisers were veering into collision courses with Alliance ships.

Errant Venture hung over Zonama Sekot like a freshly forged spearpoint, her blazing turbolasers providing cover fire for the modified shuttles, yachts, and blockade runners that plummeted from the forward launching bay. On detecting the smugglers' ships, the coralskippers that had been harassing the Star Destroyer regrouped and set after what must have seemed like more assailable prey.

Lady Luck had been first out of the bay, with *Wild Karrde* close behind. In the cockpit of the SoroSuub yacht, Lando and Tendra were busy at separate tasks when Talon commed them.

"Two skips on your starboard," he warned.

"Got 'em," Lando said into his headset mike. He nodded for Tendra to raise the yacht's rear deflector screen.

"If you two would allow me the honor . . ."

"No need to stand on ceremony, Talon."

Lando pushed the control yoke away from him, dropping *Lady Luck* into Zonama Sekot's gravity well. The ship bucked and began to vibrate as the atmosphere thickened. Tendra called a starboard view to the console displays in time to see angry bursts of laserfire spew from the Corellian transport's triple batteries. Struck full force, the lead coralskipper farthest from *Lady Luck* crumbled. The second skip slewed hard to port in an effort to come alongside the yacht, but *Wild Karrde*'s follow-up bursts caught the enemy vessel while it was still outside the yacht's shields, and it, too, disintegrated.

"We owe you one," Lando said.

"Actually, that's two," Talon replied. "But who's counting?"

Tendra eased the angle of the yacht's descent and set a course for the Middle Distance. By approaching from the east, they could avoid the hail of plasma missiles that were pounding the central canyon. The adjusted course took *Lady Luck, Wild Karrde,* and some of the other rescue craft almost directly beneath *Jade Shadow.* While it remained in stationary orbit, Mara's ship had sustained heavy damage.

Below, youthful mountains poked from opaque white clouds, their flanks and foothills cloaked with unspoiled boras. To the west the forest was interrupted by expanses of grasslands. Where those ended, the virgin terrain undulated, rose again to lofty heights, then angled down toward the central canyon, which was blanketed in layers of thick smoke.

Toning proximity alarms told Lando and Tendra that *Lady Luck* had attracted the attention of some of the coralskippers that were strafing the canyon and surrounding woodlands. Four skips were already climbing out of the smoke to welcome the yacht to the fight.

"Talon, we might need your help again," Lando started to say when two of the coralskippers were cracked open and knocked out of the sky by laserfire. The trailing pair deployed singularities, but the shields bought them mere moments of refuge before proton torpedoes blew them apart.

An instant later, two red X-wings streaked past *Lady Luck* from astern, banking broadly to the south before coming about to assume the same approach vector the smugglers were taking. Lando opened a channel to the starfighters.

"Thanks from *Lady Luck* for clearing the way."

"Red Two at your service," a familiar voice responded.

"Wedge!" Lando said around a broad grin. "How much grease did it take to get you installed in that snubfighter?"

"Less than half what it took at the start of this war."

"Yeah, I suppose we're all back to fighting trim."

Tendra stretched out her left hand and patted Lando's slight paunch. "He means, most of us," she said into her headset.

Lando cocked an eyebrow at his wife, then said, "Where's that poisoned vessel, Wedge?"

"Tell your scanners to look due north-northwest."

Tendra tasked the instruments to provide a close-up view. Defended by a ring of eight coralskippers, the six-armed slayers' vessel was swooping down toward the south rim of the canyon. As many Red Squadron X-wings were in close pursuit, needling the enemy with lasers and torps. But instead of answering them with plasma missiles, the skips were devoting all their power to fashioning shielding singularities to protect the poisoned craft.

All the levity had left Wedge's voice when he said, "There's no stopping it now."

Lady Luck's proximity alarms began to blare again. Lando watched the friend-or-foe identifier cycle in apparent bewilderment, then he glanced around the sky.

"Wedge, our scanners are showing unfriendlies, but they're not registering as skips."

"Because they're not," Wedge said flatly. "Whatever they are, they're rising out of the forests—hundreds of them!"

Lando leaned toward the forward viewport. A swarm of insectile ships, showing green wings and red carapaces, was corkscrewing up toward the Smugglers' Alliance ships. As they drew nearer, singularities formed to both sides of *Lady Luck*. The yacht pitched violently to port and began to slide for the surface. Lando lifted his hands from the control yoke and turned to his wife in wide-eyed confusion.

"That's not me piloting!" He commed Wedge. "We're caught up in some kind of tractor beam. It's dragging us down!"

"Wish I could help," Wedge said a moment later. "But they've got me, too."

Corran had been the first to spot the ships—or creatures—rise from the tampasi east of the canyon. He, Kyp, Lowbacca, Cilghal, and the rest of the downed Jedi pilots were gathered on the landing platform now, watching the red and green craft dart through the sky like maidenflies, making use of grasper claws and dovin-basal-like gravitic anomalies to bring down Red Squadron starfighters and Smugglers' Alliance ships alike.

A few kilometers east of where the Jedi were grouped, *Lady Luck, Wild Karrde,* and two X-wings were descending to treetop level.

"We don't know what they are, Lando," Corran was saying into his comlink. "We've never seen them before."

"Another of Sekot's surprises," Talon added to the conversation.

"Here's a piece of good news," Kyp interrupted. He pointed to the southern sky. "Sekot's chasing the skips, too."

The southern sky was a frenzy of insectile craft. But unlike the Alliance ships, the coralskippers were not going quietly to ground, and many of the swift darters were being annihilated by plasma missiles. A sudden growl from Lowbacca brought everyone about-face to see Danni Quee and Magister Jabitha approaching the landing platform, trailed by a crowd of perhaps one hundred wary Ferroans, who had emerged from the shelters.

Kyp met the two women halfway. "You spoke with Sekot?" he asked Danni.

Her "yes" was breathy with awe, but she offered nothing more.

Corran looked hard at Jabitha. "Who's piloting the insect craft?"

"Sekot," the magister said.

Corran gave his head a confused shake. "I thought the idea was to keep the fight from the surface?"

"Only until Sekot was ready to launch the grappler ships," Danni explained at last. "Sekot's promise to Jacen was that the planet would only fight without fighting." She saw from the expressions that greeted her that she'd opened the flood-gates. "Sekot is only interested in welcoming the Yuuzhan Vong home."

"Home?" Corran and Kyp said at the same time.

There wasn't time for further explanation. Dozens of coralskippers were being hauled down into the boras by grappler ships—all except for the poisoned vessel, which six unpiloted insectile craft were tugging back up the gravity well.

The Jedi, Danni, Jabitha, and some of the Ferroans hurried into the forest to be on hand when the coralskippers landed. Two kilometers along, the ragtag group was joined by Lando, Tendra, Talon, Shada, Wedge, and several other Red Squadron and Smugglers' Alliance pilots.

Running at the head of the pack, Kyp and Corran ignited their lightsabers as soon as they saw the coralskippers and grapplers drifting down between the massive trunks of the balloon-leafed boras. The first of the coralskippers settled into the loamy shade like sculptures in a garden. Dovin basals housed in the blunt noses of the vessels sent slender blue-veined feeders into the soft ground. In response, creepers and vines writhed to touch the coarse hulls of the skips. Some writhed into the seams that defined the edges of the mica canopies and popped them open.

Shucking out of their cognition hoods, four Yuuzhan Vong leapt from the cockpit cavities, brandishing short amphistaffs. The Jedi stepped in to engage them, but stopped short when they saw the amphistaffs slip from the hands of the enemy pilots and slither off into the lush woodland. Breather masks and shoulder-borne tactical villips dropped from the pilots like ripe seedpods. Two dozen thud bugs burst from one pilot's bandolier and took to the treetops.

The Yuuzhan Vong gazed at the Jedi like bewildered children. Caught between worlds, unacquainted with surrender, they did as they had seen their captives do and fell to their knees, their heads bowed in disgrace and their wrists pressed to their opposite shoulders.

Kyp was the first to deactivate his lightsaber; the rest followed.

Cilghal loosed a joyful exhale and put her arm around Danni's waist. "These warriors will be the first converts," she said. "This ground will become a hallowed place."

Transfixed by the scene, Kyp clapped his hand on Corran's shoulder and muttered, "A world has been saved from destruction."

Dying rapidly, the yorik-trema was no longer accelerating but tumbling through space. Whatever flora was responsible for providing breathable atmosphere was failing, as the interior walls' bioluminescent lichen already had.

"It doesn't want to respond to me," Jaina said from the controls. The hull's transparency was filmed by a thickening cataract, but Han and Leia could still discern the distinctive shape of the *Millennium Falcon,* racing to come alongside, escorted by two battle-scarred X-wings.

"Come on, Mara," Han said through gritted teeth. "Use the tractor beam."

"That won't help," Jaina said as she tugged the flimsy cognition hood from her head. "Our only chance is to get aboard the *Falcon.*" Her eyes roamed over the irregularly pulsing control console. "There's just enough life left in this ship for it to extend an umbilical."

"Oh, no," Han muttered. "Not again."

Jaina tweaked one of the organiform control arms that grew from the console. Accompanied by wet, squishy sounds, the central section of the craft's cramped deck softened, and an osmotic membrane began to form. Han glanced at the expanding circle in growing dismay, imagining the craft's intestinelike cofferdam flailing in space as it attempted to vacuum-seal against the *Falcon*'s portside docking ring or dorsal hatch.

Abruptly the freighter snagged the yorik-trema, stopping it from tumbling. The deck membrane irised open, and a nauseating odor invaded the cabin space.

Han clamped his right hand over his mouth. "How do we know the umbilical's properly sealed against the hatch?"

"It's not the tightest fit, Dad," Jaina said, "but it's one we can survive."

Jacen peered into the confined, throbbing tube. "Guess we're going to have to crawl."

Han's face fell. "Ah, this is too much—even for me."

Leia glanced at him. "I'll go first, if it'll make you feel better."

"Only thing that's gonna make me feel better is an EVA suit."

Leia stroked his whiskered face. "Be brave, darling."

Lowering herself to the deck, she wormed through the membrane and began to elbow-crawl through the tube. Han took a deep breath and followed, his hands disappearing to the wrist in the slime that covered the floor. Two minutes later Leia disappeared from view, and Han's hands touched the comforting solidity of the *Falcon*'s air lock.

One by one, coated with slime and reeking of putrid organics, the four of them squeezed into the freighter's portside docking arm, where Kenth, Harrar, C-3PO, and R2-D2 were waiting.

"Oh, my," the protocol droid said. "I'll activate the sonic shower at once."

R2-D2 rocked on his feet, whistling and tooting.

No sooner had Kenth dogged the hatch than Mara came running through the forward compartment, calling over her shoulder to Tahiri and the Noghri that everyone was safely aboard.

"Where's Uncle Luke?" Jacen asked.

Mara grabbed him by the arm and hauled him into the aft cabin space, where Luke was laid out on one of the small sleeping platforms. Han, Leia, and Jaina crowded in behind them.

Jacen kneeled by the bed and carefully removed the dressing Kenth had placed over the deep puncture wound in the left side of Luke's chest. Luke's face and hands were white. His lips and the beds of his fingernails were slightly blue. His eyes were closed and his breathing was shallow.

"Shimrra's amphistaff," Mara said anxiously.

Jacen looked up at her and nodded. "I saw him get stabbed."

Mara pressed her hands to her eyes and began to cry. Jacen took her tear-moistened hands in his and brought them to Luke's chest wound. He held them there for a long moment, removing his hands only once, to convey some of his own tears to Luke's wound.

Luke's chest heaved as he took a sharp inhalation, and his eyelids fluttered open. Sobbing openly, Mara laid her head on his chest, and slowly Luke's left hand rose to caress her red-gold hair.

"I'll live, my love," he said weakly.

Leia kneeled down to wrap her arms around her son and Mara and cry with them. Swallowing the lump in his throat, Han put his arm around Jaina's shoulders, then the two of them all but fell on top of Leia and Jacen.

C-3PO and R2-D2 appeared at the hatch in time to see the Skywalkers and Solos in a weeping tangle. The astromech made a fluting sound that was at once rejoicing and forlorn.

"I know, Artoo," C-3PO said quietly. "There are few occasions when I envy humans, but this is certainly one of them."

PART FOUR

THE NEW ORDER

FORTY-THREE

Two meters above the ground, the military speeder twisted through the ruins of the sacred precinct, closing on operational headquarters at the northern edge of what had been—only two years earlier—the Legislative District. Admiral Kre'fey perched on the back of the rear seat, his snow-white fur rippling in the wind and his short command cloak snapping behind him like a flag. To either side of him sat his Bothan aides. A human lieutenant had the repulsorcraft's controls, and beside him was a Twi'lek gunner, her hands on the trigger mechanism of a front-mounted repeating blaster. A torrential rain had just ended, and the winding paths the Yuuzhan Vong called streets were running with water. The speeder shot past columns of drenched infantry soldiers with mud caked like clay to their boots or bare legs. If nothing else, the rain had washed some of the cinder and yorik coral grit from the air.

Kre'fey had never evinced a great fondness for Coruscant, but it was only fitting that he tour the prize that had cost the Alliance so many lives. Estimates of battle casualties put the number of dead at close to five million, with twice that number of wounded. More than three hundred capital ships had been destroyed, along with some eleven thousand starfighters.

The death toll for the entire war was almost incalculable, though the figure most often quoted was 365 trillion.

Now that Sien Sovv had designated Generals Farlander and Bel Iblis as occupation commanders, Kre'fey anticipated that he would be shuttling back to *Ralroost* before nightfall.

With the shattered Yuuzhan Vong armada still arrayed two million kilometers away, Alliance battle groups remained anchored above Coruscant. When it had finally come, the cease-fire had had less to do with loss of discipline or coordination among the enemy than something closer to loss of hope—to a palpable sense of desperation and gloom. In the aftermath of Shimrra's death, hundreds of vessels had self-destructed or hurled themselves against Alliance ships as living missiles. Other vessels had deserted, jumping to hyperspace for star systems yet unknown. With hundreds of functional dovin basals continuing to deploy shielding singularities, Alliance landing craft and shuttles were being forced to adhere to strict descent corridors. Even so, the sky above the sacred precinct was filled with relief and patrol ships, and more were coming down the well every hour.

Orphan Coruscanti of diverse species lined the boggy byways and stood dozens-deep at makeshift medical stations, supply depots, and identity verification centers. As Kre'fey's convoy of speeders made their way south from Westport, humanoids and aliens would turn to welcome "the liberator of Coruscant" with waves, cheers, and sloppy salutes.

Squads of commandos were on foot patrol in all quarters, performing structure-to-structure searches and controlling looting by Coruscanti and Yuuzhan Vong alike. Heretics who had joined the resistance were acting as interpreters and wranglers of creatures capable of ferreting out spies and imposters wearing ooglith masquers. Enemy weapons were heaped at each corner, awaiting cremation by aged AT-AT walkers and flame-throwers. YVH droids rolled and crawled like tunnel rats through warrens exposed by massive demolition and excavation machines. Elsewhere, teams of specialists were busy erecting temporary communications facilities to uplink with satellites already in orbit.

Galactic Alliance flags had been raised at what was left of the truncated Citadel, on the yorik coral dome that capped the Well of the World Brain, and atop other captured landmarks, but fierce fighting persisted in some districts that were without villip communication and had yet to learn of Shimrra's death. To complicate matters, the sacred precinct had been partitioned into more than a dozen occupation zones, each overseen by a different species. Everyone was working toward the common goal of pacification, but because of the vast amounts of technology that lay buried under the thick vegetation, some claim-staking was inevitable.

Tinged with sadness and misgiving, Kre'fey's gold-flecked eyes took everything in as the speeder rounded the mounds of debris and whizzed across the temporary bridges that spanned Coruscant's abysmal canyons.

This is the prize we're going to present to the Alliance members as a sign that life can now begin to return to normal?

The strangest sight he had seen—stranger than the groves of alien trees, the ngdins sopping spilled blood from the streets, the AT-ATs standing shoulder to shoulder with six-legged Yuuzhan Vong beasts—was Grand Admiral Gilad Pellaeon and six of his Imperial officers touring the area where the Imperial Palace had once stood.

Onetime enemies, now unequivocal allies.

Thousands of prisoners were being held at what the Yuuzhan Vong had called the Place of Bones, but thousands more had escaped into the wilderness the planet had become. On the other side of Coruscant, entire battalions were dug in. The commanders of those units were said to have vowed that they would fight to the last, and Kre'fey saw no reason to doubt them.

Questions and concerns tormented him. What was to be done with the heretics and the Shamed Ones; the noncombatants and the children; the World Brain, the roving beasts, and the other biots? Several chief commanders were already advocating that Coruscant be defoliated entirely. Others wanted to preserve some of the planet's new look. And still others wished to see the former galactic capital transformed into a kind of memorial, joining the ranks of Ithor, Barab I, New Plympto, and other worlds.

So despite the cheers and welcoming waves, Kre'fey didn't feel like a liberator, much less a hero—at least not yet. The Bothan declaration of ar'krai—total war—meant just that, and his species was going to expect him to take the lead in pushing for extermination of the Yuuzhan Vong. But the Alliance's chief commanders were hardly in accord on that matter. And now that a cease-fire seemed to be in effect, the politicians were eager to wrest control of the situation from the military. Kre'fey had long thought of Chief of State Cal Omas as an honest and honorable human. But as well meaning as Omas was, he didn't always see reason. It scarcely helped that his very influential Advisory Council included six Jedi, a Caamasi, and a Wookiee. With everyone weighing in, it could take months or even years to reach a consensus regarding a final solution to the long war . . .

The skimmer came to a rest in front of Alliance headquarters—an example of Old Republic–classic architecture that had been partly released from its mantle of vegetation by lasers and missles; trees were still rooted in the roof and vines dangled over the ornate columns and shattered window openings.

Kre'fey strode briskly past logistics officers and communications specialists, analysts and slicers, protocol and mouse droids. Ultimately his aides escorted him into a debris-filled room that was being readied for General Farlander. A holoprojector occupied the center of the cleared space, and in the blue cone emanating from the table stood half-sized holograms of Sien Sovv and Cal Omas. For much of the battle for Coruscant, elected officials had been on the move, in and out of hyperspace. But for the past four days, Omas and the others had taken refuge on Contruum.

"Congratulations, Admiral Kre'fey," Omas said. "Thanks to you we have reclaimed our capital."

"Such as it is," Kre'fey said.

Sovv made a sound of agreement, then said: "Nevertheless, your efforts are appreciated by one and all. What is the situation there, Traest?"

"We're on the verge of turning a hopeless situation into an impossible one."

"Any change in the disposition of the enemy vessels?"

"None."

"Any overtures by Nas Choka?"

Kre'fey forced an exhale. "Much of the fight has been bled from the spaceborne warriors, but we've received no word from Nas Choka. He recalled the dregs of his Muscave and Zonama Sekot flotillas, but has neither advanced on Coruscant nor withdrawn."

"What do you suppose they're waiting for, Traest?"

"They've never suffered a defeat—let alone had to deal with the sudden death of their Supreme Overlord. Normally there would have been a pool of candidates, one of whom would have been chosen by the priests and shapers to accede to the throne. The elite would have been guided by signs and portents, and any potential successor would have to have demonstrated certain abilities. But it's all moot, because Shimrra apparently saw to it that no one was standing in the royal wings. With Shimrra and High Prefect Drathul dead, Nas Choka is the highest-ranking elite. But in fact he wields no more real power than High Priest Jakan and Master Shaper Qelah Kwaad, both of whom we have in custody. A scramble for power had broken out among some of the lesser prefects and consuls, but it's unlikely that any of them will be officially recognized as an heir apparent. What's more, the heretics, along with many of the Shamed Ones, seem to be looking to us for rescue, protection, even redemption of some sort."

Sovv took a moment to absorb Kre'fey's remarks. "Should Nas Choka break the cease-fire and advance, are our fleets in a position to prevail?"

"Probably," Kre'fey said, "though at considerable cost."

"Do you wish to press an attack?" Omas asked carefully.

Kre'fey shook his head. "Not at this point. Until this morning we had no means of communicating with Nas Choka. But we've finally been able to persuade the Supreme Commander of the enemy home fleet to act as our liaison with the warmaster, commencing with villip transmissions."

"Would a full surrender be too much to hope for, Admiral?" Omas asked.

Kre'fey touched his face in a gesture of uncertainty. "As I say, sir, the Yuuzhan Vong have no protocols for surrender. They're expecting us to behave as they would under similar circumstances, by executing most of them and enslaving the rest."

Omas frowned. "All these years of fighting and they still don't understand us." He paused, then said, "Admiral, you face the daunting task of convincing your commanders that there is nothing to be gained by exterminating the Yuuzhan Vong."

Kre'fey compressed his lips. "Sir, after the barbarity the

enemy has visited on us for five years, many local commanders won't be willing to put aside vengeance for compassion. But perhaps some will, and in time others may follow. By the same token, it may prove impossible to convince the Yuuzhan Vong on occupied worlds to capitulate without a fight. Word of Shimrra's death is being relayed by villip to planets throughout the invasion corridor. In several star systems the Yuuzhan Vong are already decamping. But we have our work cut out for us, regardless."

"Zonama Sekot survived the battle?" Sovv said.

Kre'fey snorted. "I would say 'triumphed.' Though I failed to realize it at the time, the entire battle for Coruscant turned on that planet. If for whatever reason the Yuuzhan Vong hadn't been so intent on destroying it . . . Well, let it suffice to say that we might not be having this conversation."

"We've heard rumors," Omas said, "that there was a second Supreme Overlord—a power behind the throne, as it were."

Kre'fey nodded. "I've heard those same rumors. But they have yet to be corroborated by anyone."

"There's also talk about a vessel contaminated with Alpha Red."

"That happens to be fact, sir. The vessel was one that escaped from Caluula. The Yuuzhan Vong attempted but failed to deploy the bioweapon against Zonama Sekot. Allegedly it has been tractor-beamed into deep space. We have ships searching for it, if only to establish whether the toxin remains virulent."

"Stay on that, Admiral," Omas said.

Kre'fey nodded again. "Sir, assuming a surrender is forthcoming, have you chosen someone to negotiate the terms?"

"Many are urging me to solicit the assistance of the Jedi."

Kre'fey's face twisted. "Is that wise, sir, in light of Master Skywalker's statement at Contruum that he would consider giving Coruscant to the Yuuzhan Vong if he thought that would end the war?"

Omas laughed shortly. "I never took Skywalker's remark at face value. But we do need to reach a decision regarding Coruscant's importance in the scheme of things. Perhaps the fact that we reclaimed it will be sufficient to serve as a symbol of our unity."

"With all due respect, sir," Kre'fey said evenly, "we can't allow the Yuuzhan Vong to keep even a square kilometer of Coruscant. Even if we can't reoccupy the planet for a hundred years, Coruscant is essential to the stability of the Alliance. No species will rest comfortably with the Yuuzhan Vong imprisoned at the center of our galaxy. Coruscant must be seen as a symbol that not only have we prevailed, but also that the threat has passed, and order has been restored."

"I concur, Admiral," Omas replied in the same even tone, "but we're going to have to do *something* with the Yuuzhan Vong—something more than disarm them and send them back into the intergalactic void."

"I suspect that they would sooner fight to the death than return there," Kre'fey said. "In any event, we haven't ships enough to escort them from the galaxy."

"Some have suggested imprisoning them aboard their own ships," Sovv said.

Kre'fey grimaced. "The warriors, perhaps. But do we also imprison every female, every child, every Shamed One? Wouldn't we be sentencing them to a lingering death rather than an expedient one?"

Omas heaved a sigh. "Those I trust to safeguard our financial health may not warm to the idea of spending trillions of credits to imprison warriors who are beyond being rehabilitated."

Kre'fey turned slightly to face Omas's image. "Sir, will you consider establishing a war crimes commission?"

"Such a commission is under consideration, Admiral. But who would you have us bring to trial?"

"We could begin with Nas Choka."

Sovv shook his head. "We're going to need him if we hope to subjugate the warrior caste. Try Nas Choka, and you will have that fight to the death."

"I agree with Admiral Sovv," Omas said. "Shimrra is dead, as are Tsavong Lah, Nom Anor, most of the Peace Brigade . . . More to the point, how do we separate the 'war criminals' from the religious zealots? Should we attempt to root out those commanders responsible for attacking refugee ships, or perhaps those who were directly responsible for the deaths of hundreds of millions of hostages at Coruscant? They're all guilty—the entire species. We may as well start with their *gods* if we're going to initiate criminal proceedings."

Kre'fey allowed the silence to linger for some time, then said, "Sir, we still have Alpha Red."

Omas nodded solemnly. "I respect your courage in being the first to broach the subject, Admiral. But Alpha Red is no longer an option. Use of the bioweapon isn't a decision one person, three, or even a hundred can make. I promise, however, to discuss all other matters with the members of my Advisory Council."

Kre'fey swallowed hard. "May some wisdom accrue from it."

If jubilant celebrations were taking place on many worlds, stars were the only lights in Zonama Sekot's night sky, and by day only the remote disk that was the Coruscant system's primary.

"It's getting colder," Luke said, as he and Harrar followed Jacen through the boras. "Most of the energy Sekot dedicated to keeping the planet warm was diverted to the mountaintop defenses. Zonama can't remain in this orbit for much longer— not without risk to the forests."

"Perhaps that's what Sekot wishes to discuss," Harrar said. "Inserting Zonama into a more nourishing orbit."

Jacen glanced over his shoulder at the priest. "We'll know soon enough. The reflecting pool isn't much farther."

Jacen had mentioned the pool several times, though Luke had never been there and was eager to see it. The suggestion to assemble at the pool had been Sekot's, relayed through Magister Jabitha, who had visited Luke in his and Mara's cliffside dwelling.

Luke felt as if he had done little more than sleep since arriving on Zonama Sekot a week earlier in the *Millennium Falcon*. While Jacen had been successful at neutralizing most of the venom delivered by Shimrra's amphistaff, Luke knew that he was not yet completely healed, and might never be. His body was gaining strength daily, and he was able to keep up with his nephew and Harrar on the undulating path, but his physiology had been altered by the venom, and he was compelled to draw subtly on the Force to sustain himself. Perhaps it would just be a matter of time until his body dealt with the vestiges of the venom, but he suspected that the damage had been done in the first instance of his being pierced by the serpentlike weapon. As had been the case with Mara, healing tears could only do so much. He realized that the battle in Shimrra's bunker had brought him very close to the dark side, whose venom was every bit as potent as that of the royal amphistaff. But he had no regrets about having skirted that razor's edge, and knew in his heart that he would have walked even closer to the edge to safeguard Jacen or Jaina.

What troubled him was that they, too, appeared to have suffered as a result of their confrontation with Onimi—Supreme Overlord Onimi. Several of the Jedi and the Ferroans had already remarked to Luke in private that Jacen looked *older,* and just that morning Luke had heard whispered exchanges regarding Jaina's sudden and uncharacteristic *gravity.* Neither Leia nor Han had said anything to Luke, though their concern was evident. But then, who hadn't been affected in some fashion by the events that had unfolded on Coruscant and Zonama Sekot?

The planet itself had been damaged, chiefly in the Middle Distance, where the Ferroans were doing what they could to rebuild their homes and nurse the boras back to health, the frosty conditions notwithstanding. Most of the several dozen Yuuzhan Vong warriors who had been hauled to the surface were traumatized. After some effort, Harrar had talked them into leaving the place where their coralskippers had been set down, but they remained confused as to whether they were prisoners or guests. The presence of the Jedi had confirmed their worst fear—the one the heretics had embraced—that the gods had allied with the Jedi to obliterate the Yuuzhan Vong. And yet a few of the warriors had undergone what amounted to conversion experiences, espousing to their humbled comrades that they could *feel* the gods in the sweet taste of Zonama's water, in the soil under their feet, on the wind, and inhabiting the giant boras. To them, the living world was a paradise regained, and they had urged Luke to recount that to the Yuuzhan Vong elite, should he decide to agree to mediating the surrender, as the leaders of the Alliance wished.

"We're here," Jacen announced suddenly.

He led Luke and Harrar onto an intersecting trail that descended a short but steep slope, ending at a tranquil pool fringed with ice and surrounded by towering boras. Luke had expected to meet only with a thought projection of Sekot—perhaps Anakin or Vergere—but instead Jabitha was there, having somehow arrived first by some other path from the canyon.

"Some of what I wish to say you must have guessed by now," Sekot said through Jabitha, as Luke, Jacen, and Harrar were approaching the edge of the pool. "Especially regarding the Yuuzhan Vong."

"You told Danni that you wanted to welcome them home," Luke said. "Were you suggesting that Zonama is actually their primordial homeworld?"

"Much as I evolved from the consciousness that presided there—the consciousness of my parent—Zonama is a seed of Yuuzhan'tar, the world that birthed the Yuuzhan Vong and became the template for their gods."

"I wanted to believe," Harrar said in astonishment, "but I didn't dare . . ."

"Where is Yuuzhan'tar now?" Jacen asked.

"I hope in time to be able to answer that question. I suspect, though, that it was destroyed by its symbionts—by the species that became the Yuuzhan Vong, in retribution for what my parent did to them: casting them out, severing its connection to them—stripping them of the Force. All as a consequence of their hunger for violence and conquest, which had been awakened by a single confrontation with a warfaring race. I further suspect that without my parent they were unable to move beyond the biotechnology they were given—or stole. In need of a guiding consciousness, they created a pantheon of gods, to whom they ascribed the powers that were once the province of the living world of Yuuzhan'tar."

"The empty eighth cortex," Harrar mumbled. "The shapers accepted that they shouldn't create new biots, when in fact they *couldn't.*"

Jabitha-Sekot continued. "Evidently, before my parent died, it dispatched the seed of the world that would come to be called Zonama Sekot, and the seed drifted to this galaxy, took root, and grew . . . For untold generations I lay dormant in Zonama while the Yuuzhan Vong plundered the home galaxy, and were forced at last to embark on the search for a new home, carried on the same currents that brought Zonama Sekot here.

"Then those I originally knew as the Far Outsiders appeared—not by coincidence, but drawn genetically to Zonama Sekot, much as a creature finds its way home, as occurred a second time in the Unknown Regions." Jabitha looked at Harrar. "It's possible, too, that I called out to you."

"Welcoming us home," Harrar said, "only to be attacked again."

Jabitha nodded. "The unprovoked attack by the Far Outsiders stirred something in me. Counter to the teachings of the leaders of the Potentium, I became aware of the existence of evil. In a sense, evil helped give birth to my awareness. Now I understand that the acts of the Far Outsiders may have been nothing more than a reawakening of the evil my parent experienced when its symbionts used its creations not merely to defend Yuuzhan'tar, but to launch an era of bloodshed that resulted in the death of countless worlds—along with many latent planetary consciousnesses.

"But I did not pursue those stirrings, those suspicions, until Zonama became lost in the Unknown Regions, and, through Nen Yim and Harrar, I comprehended that the Yuuzhan Vong had been stripped of the Force. My most grave misgivings were confirmed when I learned of the bioweapon that was being hurled at Zonama.

"I understood that a cycle of violence was being perpetuated, and that I had to make a critical decision. There was no right or wrong way to decide. There was only my choice, and its consequences. I could have accepted the Alpha Red, ending my participation in the cycle, or I could have sent it back at the Yuuzhan Vong, ending their participation. In the end I elected to sue for peace."

"On Coruscant," Jacen said, "when I reached out for you with my Vongsense, I sensed your conflict."

"What are the consequences of your choice?" Luke asked. Jabitha's gaze fell on him. "I will tell you . . ."

Nas Choka sat stoically on the acceleration couch of the Alliance shuttle that was conveying him and five of his Supreme Commanders toward the gaping docking bay of *Ralroost*. He wore an unadorned tunic, trousers, headcloth, and pectoral. Only the command cloak that hung from his shoulder horns distinguished him from his subordinates; and, like them, his frame was thinner after long days of fasting, and his cheeks, lips, and arms bore fresh bloodletting cuts.

The world again known as Coruscant dominated the view through the shuttle's starboard transparency, and between the planet and *Ralroost* floated hundreds of warships, dispersed to protect Coruscant against a surprise attack by the warriors who had once taken and occupied it. Nas Choka considered how easy it might have been to launch a final onslaught and perish in the blaze of glory the Alliance certainly expected. But what glory could be derived from a battle the gods had no interest in supporting?

No, while the reason for the gods' abrupt abandonment of the Yuuzhan Vong was unknown, it was clear that they desired something other than sacrificial blood. Unless it was the blood of the Yuuzhan Vong they craved. Did the fault lie with Shimrra for having usurped the throne from Quoreal, or perhaps for having failed to heed the prophecies regarding the living world of Zonama Sekot? And yet, if all Yuuzhan Vong were to be punished for Shimrra's pride, why hadn't the gods allowed them to be wiped out by the Alliance or killed by the very bioweapon Shimrra had sent against Zonama Sekot?

It was because these questions remained unanswered that Nas Choka and his commanders had submitted without protest or anger to personal searches by teams of distrustful Alliance warriors, and why they sat impassively now. The only item Nas Choka had been allowed to retain was his tsaisi—his baton of rank—which he would present to the Alliance's chief commanders before requesting that he be allowed to end his own life.

Ralroost's tractor beam conducted the shuttle through an

invisible field and allowed it to berth. Released from their harnesses, the captives were escorted down the ship's ramp and toward an area of the vast hold where no less than five hundred Alliance officers and officials stood at attention behind a semicircular arrangement of tables and chairs. The sterility of the huge space chilled Nas Choka to the bone. The scrubbed air had an unpleasant tang; the intense yellow-white light gave every object a sharp aspect; the smooth deck was uncompromising; the ceiling was a chaos of girders and ducts. Hundreds of starfighters rested on their hardstands, and droids shuffled about like slaves.

A mixed-species orchestra assaulted the captives with martial music, and an artificial breeze tugged at flags representative of some of the galaxy's species—several of which had been vanquished by Nas Choka himself. Humans and others documented the occasion with holocams and other recording devices. Though much of the meaning was lost on him, Nas Choka recognized the display as pageant and ritual, pomp and circumstance.

Sovv and Kre'fey were determined to put on a grand show.

The open end of the half circle of tables faced a row of six chairs, atop which Nas Choka and his commanders were obviously meant to sit. Interpreters—Alliance species and Yuuzhan Vong heretics, by the look of them—were standing by to make certain that everyone understood one another.

When the fanfare ended, the officers and officials seated themselves. At the semicircle's apex sat white-furred Kre'fey and big-eared Sovv, along with several human commanders Nas Choka recognized from intelligence reports—Pellaeon, Brand, Bel Iblis, Farlander, Antilles, Rieekan, Celchu, Davip, and the Hapan queen, Tenel Ka, who was a Jedi, as well. Alliance intendants were scattered, but close to the military commanders sat Cal Omas and his principal advisers: the Wookiee named Triebakk, the Gotal named Ta'laam Ranth, the lank human director of Intelligence, Dif Scaur, and the golden-furred Caamasi named Releqy, whose intendant father had been ritually killed at Dubrillion by Commander Shedao Shai.

The Jedi—in cloaks so homespun they might have been made by Shamed Ones—had an arc of the half circle to themselves. Conspicuous among the three human males was Luke Skywalker, the killer of Shimrra. The two seated next to him had the look of warriors. The only other human was a dark-haired female, who struck Nas Choka as more intendant than warrior. The remaining pair of Jedi were nonhumanoid females: a Barabel who might have been at home among the Chazrach, and a Mon Calamari, whose long head brought to mind that of a Yuuzhan Vong beast of burden.

Occupying the distal end of the arc's left curve sat Jakan, Harrar, Qelah Kwaad, and several lesser priests, shapers, and intendants.

When the captives had been positioned in front of their rigid chairs, Nas Choka waved for his commanders to be seated and stepped forward. The dread moment had arrived. Proffering his baton of rank, he dropped to one knee.

"In surrendering this," he said in Basic, "we surrender ourselves."

It was a historic utterance, and every Yuuzhan Vong in the docking bay—loyal and heretic alike—inhaled sharply and with purpose.

"I ask only that I be allowed to be the first to die—by my own coufee."

"Rise, Warmaster," Sovv said. "We understand that honor attends such actions, but that cannot be permitted here."

Still kneeling, Nas Choka regarded him in confusion. "Then appoint any warrior you see fit to kill me."

Sovv shook his tiny head. "There will be no executions, Warmaster."

Nas Choka gritted his teeth and came to his feet. "So you mean to enslave us, as we did the Chazrach. In place of coral seeds, you will implant us with devices that will control—"

"Warmaster," Jakan cut him off. "Hold your reply until all has been laid before you."

"Great things are still expected of you," Harrar added.

Nas Choka glared at the priest. "This from a *defector*."

Harrar made no effort to parry the accusation. "What I did, Warmaster, I did for all of us."

Nas Choka made a chopping motion with his right hand. "I no longer wear that title, priest. If we are neither to be executed nor enslaved, what would the Alliance do with us? This bold new order holds no place for the warrior caste." He turned to Skywalker. "The *Jeedai* are warriors. What will you do without war?"

Skywalker rose from his chair. "From the start you've mistaken us for warriors, when we are nothing more than the guardians of peace and justice. You could be that, as well, Nas Choka. Though it would require that you adapt your battle traditions to a new form." He held up his lightsaber and ignited the blade. "This was once a weapon."

Nas Choka laughed ruefully. "Thousands of my warriors would willingly attest to the fact that it is a weapon still."

Skywalker acknowledged the remark with a nod. "In peaceful times it is only a symbol of the fight we wage with ourselves—to keep us from taking the wrong path."

Nas Choka lifted his chin. "We have always acted in accord with the warrior decree."

"We accept that," Skywalker said. "But you're going to have to learn to do without many of the biots that defined you as warriors."

"Name them, *Jeedai*."

"Your amphistaffs and coufees, your blorash and firejelly, your thud bugs, razor bugs, and plasma eels, your vessels and war coordinators . . ."

"In exchange for what—digging implements and plows?"

"That remains to be decided by your custodian."

Nas Choka scanned the officers and officials. "Who is that to be?"

"Zonama Sekot," Skywalker said.

Nas Choka stared at him in alarm. "You would surrender us to our true enemy! The living world we tried to poison! The world where our amphistaffs slither away, our thud bugs take flight, our villips and dovin basals turn to fruit . . . And yet you deny that we will be executed! Send us instead back to the intergalactic void, where we can at least die with dignity!"

"Perhaps our biots have something to teach us," Harrar said. "If they can overcome their conditioning, perhaps the warriors can."

"Words!" Nas Choka snapped. "Because the priests, shapers,

and intendants have nothing to lose by imprisonment on the living world."

"We lose more than you know, Nas Choka," Harrar said sadly.

"We honor a tradition that cannot be altered!"

Harrar stepped from behind the table to approach. "You honor a much older tradition, Warmaster. One that began on the planet that was *parent* to Zonama Sekot."

"Parent?"

"Zonama Sekot is our world, Warmaster. It is Yuuzhan'tar."

Nas Choka threw his head back and bellowed at the ceiling. "Then we are truly defeated!" He looked at Harrar again. "Was all this due to Shimrra, priest? Were our wanderings nothing more than a ruse to return us to the world from which we were cast?"

"Only the gods can answer that."

Nas Choka narrowed his eyes. "Do the gods reside there?"

"In the sense that Zonama Sekot incorporates all aspects of Yun-Yuuzhan, Yun-Ne'Shel, Yun-Shuno . . ."

"You make no mention of Yun-Yammka."

"That one we concocted," Harrar said, "when we turned to war."

Nas Choka snorted in disdain. "I thought as much. You've been deceived, priest. The Shamed Ones proclaimed that the *Jeedai* incorporated all aspects of the gods, and clearly they are not gods." He allowed his words to trail off, then said in a more controlled voice, "On these matters, I speak only for myself. We are the defeated. Do with us what you will. But tell me, *Jeedai,* is our imprisonment to endure in the shadow of your Coruscant, as a constant reminder of our failure?"

Skywalker shook his head. "Zonama Sekot has no desire to remain in known space, risking reverence, exploitation, or both. Zonama Sekot will return to the Unknown Regions, where it has knowledge of a star system that, over time, could be colonized by the Yuuzhan Vong—that is, once Zonama Sekot and the Yuuzhan Vong have become reacquainted."

"What of our childbearers and offspring?"

"They will also find a new home on Zonama Sekot."

"And the Shamed Ones? The heretics?"

"They will need little persuading," Harrar answered. "On Zonama Sekot our society will be able to redefine itself, without the need to abandon completely its core beliefs."

Nas Choka's broad forehead wrinkled. His gaze lingered on Sovv and Kre'fey, on Cal Omas and Luke Skywalker. "This seems a curious leniency."

"We haven't yet stated all our terms," Kre'fey said sharply.

Nas Choka folded his arms across his chest. "Then do so."

"Villips have been relaying the news of Shimrra's death to occupied worlds throughout the invasion corridor. Some of your commanders have left; others remain entrenched. We don't want to have to liberate each and every one of them at the cost of additional lives."

Nas Choka nodded. "I will summon them to Coruscant. Those who refuse, we will help you hunt down and kill." He held Kre'fey's baleful stare. "State the rest of your terms, Admiral."

"We demand that your shapers assist in the reconstruction of Coruscant, by persuading the World Brain to reverse some of the changes it wrought."

Nas Choka almost smiled. "Will it not trouble you, Admiral, to know that a Yuuzhan Vong dhuryam rests at the center of your galaxy?"

Kre'fey sniffed. "Consider it, Warmaster, the foundation for an enduring compromise."

FORTY-FOUR

In the weeks that followed the summit on *Ralroost,* Luke spent endless hours walking through the boras forests, sometimes with Mara when she and Lowbacca weren't effecting repairs to *Jade Shadow,* but more often on his own, roaming and reflecting, the hood of his cloak raised against the cold, and his hands thrust deeply into the opposite sleeves. His body seemed to have struck a compromise with the traces of venom that were still circulating through his bloodstream, but his mind was still struggling to find a similar balance. Sometimes he would confront voids in the Force where there shouldn't have been any, and at other times the Force would seem to expand infinitely around him, heightening his perceptions beyond all expectation, or surprising him with prolonged visions of possible futures. For a brief time during the summit on *Ralroost* he had been able to perceive Nas Choka and Harrar with the same clarity Jacen described when he spoke of his Vongsense.

Cal Omas and the Alliance leadership had expressed their gratitude to the Jedi for finding a practical solution to the war. But now that the terms of surrender had been ratified and the Yuuzhan Vong had been disarmed, the Alliance had ceased asking Luke for advice or assistance. The reconstruction of Coruscant had commenced with a great deal of fanfare, in conjunction with a grand memorial service for Admiral Ackbar, and the inauguration of a new HoloNet. Jacen had traveled to Coruscant to confer with the Yuuzhan Vong shapers who had been entrusted with mapping out an accord with the World Brain. Initially the dhuryam was averse to tampering with any of its creations, but thanks to Jacen it had agreed to allow the Alliance to excavate the sacred precinct, with an eye toward restoring those New Republic structures that had survived. In the course of the excavations, vast amounts of serviceable technology had been discovered, but it would be decades before Coruscant would be suitable for anyone other than structural engineers and construction droids.

Until then, the Galactic Alliance government was to be headquartered at Denon, a heavily populated Inner Rim world that had risen to prominence during the Old Republic era and, more important, had escaped bombardment or occupation by the Yuuzhan Vong.

Nas Choka had succeeded in recalling many but not all of his commanders from occupied worlds. Every few days, word would reach Zonama Sekot of a costly skirmish in one star system or another. On Coruscant, too, many commanders had surrendered, though rumors persisted—and would probably continue to persist—of bands of Yuuzhan Vong warriors hiding out in the dense temperate forests of the northern hemisphere.

Instead of returning to normal, the galaxy was slowly changing.

Having been crowned a hero—even by his own Bothans—Admiral Traest Kre'fey had assumed the rank of Supreme Commander of Alliance forces, following the unexpected resignation of Sien Sovv. Dif Scaur, the impetus behind Alpha Red, was also gone, gently forced into early retirement by Cal Omas, and replaced as director of Intelligence by Belindi Kalenda. Omas had assured Luke that all stores of the bioweapon had been destroyed, along with the genetic blueprint itself, since there were many who felt that the Alliance had been too compassionate with the enemy. Several species that had endured the brunt of the invasion were still demanding that the entire warrior caste be executed—an act of reprisal even Omas might have sanctioned were it not for Nas Choka's steadfast willingness to oblige. Still, no one wanted to risk a sudden recanting by the warmaster. So, immediately following the summit, all Yuuzhan Vong warriors had been transferred to the bellies of several Star Destroyers and troop transports, and the vessels that had comprised the mighty alien armada had been launched into Coruscant's sun, carrying with them all weapons of war.

On Zonama Sekot, repair work to the cliff dwellings and other damaged structures continued day and night. The Ferroans were nonplussed by Sekot's willingness to bestow half of Zonama on the species that had tried to destroy it. But except for a few of the younger Ferroans who had decided to depart, most of the indigenous population had simply resigned themselves to Sekot's decision.

Luke had been awaiting an opportunity to gather all the Jedi in one place, and was finally able to do that when *Errant Venture* returned to Zonama Sekot, bearing the children and other Jedi from the Maw. He gave everyone a day to mingle and catch up, then requested that everyone assemble at the forest clearing where the first coralskippers had been brought to ground.

In groups of three and four the Jedi arrived, until all were present, including: Luke, Mara, Markre Medjev, Keyan Farlander, Tam Azur-Jamin, Octa Ramis, Tresina Lobi, Kenth Hamner, Cilghal, Kyp Durron, Klin-Fa Gi, Tenel Ka, Madurrin, Streen, Jacen, Jaina, Kam and Tionne Solusar, Zekk, Lowbacca, Saba and Tesar Sebatyne, Izal Waz, Corran Horn, Kirana Ti, Tekli, Alema Rar, Kyle Katarn, Waxarn Kel, Tresk Im'nel, Wonetun, Hivrech'wao'Cheklev, Tyria Sarkin and Doran Sarkin-Tainer, Tahiri Veila, Sannah, and the children, including Ben, Valin, Jysella, and some twenty others.

When everyone was settled, Luke stepped to the center of the large circle his friends and comrades had formed. Several of the children sat cross-legged on the loamy soil; others atop the grounded coralskippers. Ben sat contentedly on Mara's lap.

"The Yuuzhan Vong will begin arriving in the coming weeks," Luke began, pacing while he spoke. "The first collaborative act between them and Sekot will be to restore the southern hemisphere forests, which were incinerated by the original reconnaissance team fifty years ago. By working with the boras, the Yuuzhan Vong will gradually get to know Zonama, and at the same time Sekot will gradually get to know the Yuuzhan Vong. Their acceptance by Sekot will constitute a second chance for a species that nearly doomed itself to extinction."

He stopped momentarily. "Now that we finally know what

the Force wanted for the Yuuzhan Vong, it's time to ask what the Force wants for us."

He gestured to his nephew. "Jacen has already accomplished more than any of us could to speed the rebuilding of Coruscant, and I don't see it as our duty to devote ourselves entirely to shoring up the Galactic Alliance as it takes its first wobbly steps toward becoming a true coalition. Our mandate to safeguard peace and justice remains, but we have to be wary of any who attempt to define peace and justice by their own terms. Should that happen, our mandate may require us to transcend the jurisdiction of any central government.

"I suppose we could consider initiating our own reconstruction efforts at Yavin Four, but I don't see much purpose in that task, either, since the days of the Jedi praxeum are behind us. Yavin Four had its place, but there are countless worlds where the Force is strong, and any one of them can serve as a kind of academy." Luke gestured to Kam Solusar. "Kam has suggested that we give thought to relocating to Ossus, and I'm inclined to agree with him. But the real territory we're compelled to explore is the Unifying Force—as a step toward implementing a 'new' Jedi order."

Luke fell silent for a long moment, as he paced across the circle and back again. "On Ithor I surrendered guardianship of the Jedi. That doesn't mean that I can't still serve as a mentor and guide to some of you. Yoda instructed me to pass on what I have learned, and I mean to do just that. But others here are as equipped as I am to teach, and I encourage them to do so, should they choose to pursue that path.

"But here's what I wish to say to all of you: if I have learned anything from the events of the past five years, it is that the Force is more all-embracing than I ever realized. Light and dark do not always stand opposed, but mingle with each other in curious ways. More important, the Force seems to have a *will,* and it's when we're acting against the will of the Force that we can get into trouble. Anger by itself is not of the dark side unless it is accompanied by a desire to dominate. When we act in harmony with the will of the Force, we disappear into it. When we struggle against it, we not only sever our ties with the Force, but also feed the needs of chaos.

"The evolution of sentience reflects the constant movement between those two poles. Evil—the dark side—won't be eradicated until it has been discarded as an option for acquiring power, subjugating would-be opponents, or offsetting feelings of anger, envy, or exclusion. Where victims of injustice exist, the dark side finds initiates. That is the cycle our actions are meant to forestall, and in this battle the Force is both our ally and our guardian. We serve it best by listening to its will, and serving the good with our every action—by personifying the Force.

"But I'm no longer convinced that we're meant to police the galaxy. For one thing, we're too few in number. That was made evident early in the war, and it's likely to hold true for whatever conflicts erupt in the coming years. The Jedi began as a meditative order. Our forebears believed that they could balance light and dark by remaining always in the Force, and thereby perfecting themselves. Gradually, however, as the Supreme Chancellors appealed to the order time and again for advice in resolving disputes, the Jedi became adjuncts of the Old Republic, then marshals and warriors, taking it upon themselves to uphold the peace, and little by little being drawn away from the Force and into the mundane.

"I don't propose that we place ourselves in seclusion and pass our days meditating on the Force—though that might be the path for some of us. But I do advocate attuning ourselves to the longer view, and reaching out to others who seek to serve the Force. The genetic makeup of each and every one of us augments our ability to tap the Force, but everyone, regardless of his or her genetics, has the potential to use the Force to one degree or another. Perhaps not to move rocks and take giant strides; but in some sense those physical powers are little more than surface effects. The real powers are more subtle, for they involve adhering to the true path, avoiding the temptation to dominate, sacrificing oneself for those who have less, and living impeccably, by recognizing that the Force doesn't flow from us but *through* us, ever on the move."

Luke scanned the sea of faces. "Like our damaged galaxy, the new Jedi order will require generations to define itself. Some of us have already committed to the roles we will play in that process. Kyp, Cilghal, Saba, Kenth, Tresina, and I will continue to serve on Cal Omas's Advisory Council, and be the voice of the Force." He glanced at the tall Anx Jedi. "I know that Madurrin has decided to remain in service to Supreme Commander Kre'fey and Keyan Farlander, and that Tenel Ka will return to the Hapes Consortium. Kirani Ti, Damaya, and Streen have much work to do on Dathomir, and Kam, Tionne, and several others are eager to go to Ossus."

Again, his gaze swept around the circle. "As for the rest of you, I ask only that you give deep thought as to how you might best serve the Force."

With the lifting of Sekot's stricture regarding warships on Zonama's surface, the western rim of the Middle Distance canyon had become a landing and launch zone. The *Millennium Falcon* was parked there, as was *Jade Shadow,* along with a few Sekotan fighters and the several shuttles that had carried the Jedi adults and children from *Errant Venture.*

Dressed in a black synfleece jacket, stylish trousers, a rakish cap, and fingerless gloves, Lando meandered with design among the ships, spotting Han at last, seated at a table with Talon, Booster, and Crev Bombassa, in an open-fronted shed built of Sekotan lamina. The three men were as bundled up as Lando was, and their amiable laughter rode out on short-lived breath clouds.

"Where is everybody?" Lando asked when he joined them. "This place is as quiet as a convention of Defels."

"Big meeting in the boras," Han said offhandedly.

Lando grinned and prized a bottle of expensive Corellian brandy from his coat pocket. "Perfect time for us to warm our bones. Besides, there's just enough to go around."

Han rubbed his bare hands together in anticipation. "Wasn't I just saying that cantinas are in very short supply around here?"

Crev glanced around in wariness. "Maybe you should keep your voice low. You know, in case . . . someone's listening?"

Booster tugged at his beard. "It is a little spooky, isn't it?"

Talon gazed at the canyon and the distant tree line. "Now that you mention it."

Lando put his hands on his hips and laughed. "I doubt that Sekot would begrudge us a toast or two." From the jacket's other pouch pocket, he extracted five tumblers. Lining them up on the table, he began to fill them with the aromatic amber liquid. "So what do you think Luke and the rest are talking about?"

"Same thing that's on everyone's mind," Crev said with theatrical seriousness. "Han Solo."

Han laughed with them, then raised his glass. "I'll drink to that."

The glass was almost to his mouth when a male voice said, "Got enough for two party crashers?"

The five of them turned to see Wedge and Tycho hurrying toward them, sporting flight jackets and brimmed caps.

"With their customary sense of flawless timing," Han muttered.

Reluctantly, Lando pulled two more tumblers from his pocket, filled them, and passed them down the table. "Anyone else is going to have to provide his own glass."

"And brandy," Crev said.

Talon shook his head and sighed. "I've yet to meet a military man who's actually willing to pay for a drink."

Tycho snorted. "I've never met one who *has* to pay."

Wedge lifted his glass. "I'll drink to that."

They all took long sips, smacked their lips, and set the tumblers down.

"Anyway," Tycho continued, "that's ex-military, as of tomorrow."

Han raised an eyebrow. "Skulking back into retirement, huh?"

Tycho shrugged. "It's either that, or Winter leaves me."

"She must have been talking with Iella," Wedge said. "It's a conspiracy."

Han raised his glass again. "To last flings."

They sipped, then fell silent for a moment. Wedge fingered the tumbler through a circle. "I don't know about the rest of you, but I'm ready for the simple life again. The Alliance will just have to make do with guys like Darklighter, Page, and Cracken."

"Pity the Alliance," Tycho said.

Han regarded the two of them and laughed. "The familiar strains of midlife."

Tycho jerked his thumb at Han, without looking at him. "This from a guy who refuses to go quietly into the void."

"Not true," Han said. "It's the *Falcon* that keeps leading me into trouble."

Booster nodded soberly. "I'm beginning to think the same of *Errant Venture*."

"Next time maybe you should choose a different shade of red," Talon said.

They laughed and downed what remained in the glasses. Lando was quick to refill them, emptying the bottle.

"So what's next for you guys?" Tycho asked the four members of the Smugglers' Alliance.

"We're waiting for the dust to settle," Talon said. "And I don't mean the yorik coral dust. Everything from here to Helska and back has been given a good shaking. A lot of groups that were at the top are suddenly at the bottom, and the other way around."

"Who, for instance?" Tycho said.

Talon considered it briefly. "Well, at the top you've got the Bothans, chiefly because of Fey'lya's brave last stand and Kre'fey's heroic victory. But vying for second place are the Sullustans, Hapans, the former Imperials, the Mon Calamari."

"Who do you figure has fallen?" Wedge asked.

"Everyone Rimward of Wayland. Plus the Ithorians, Bimms, Kuati, Corellians. But more than anyone, the Hutts."

Lando nodded. "A lot of folk were forced to do without spice during the war, and have lost their appetite for it. In fact, just about anyone who had regular dealings with the Hutts has lost credibility—the Rodians—except for the Jungle Clans—Whiphids, Klatoonians, Weequays, Vodrans, Iotrans, Nikto . . . Didn't help that a lot of them supported the Peace Brigade."

"They're the ones who should be brought to trial for war crimes," Booster said.

"They will be," Wedge said. "Cal Omas has left the decision to individual worlds and systems."

"Who else is on the way up?" Tycho asked.

"Corporate Sector and Tion Hegemony," Talon said, without having to think about it. "Just about every system Rimward of Eriadu on the Rimma, and Varonat on the Trade Spine."

Lando looked at Han. "I'll tell you who's gained the most—your friends, the Ryn."

Han sniffed. "Figures Droma would come out of this smelling like a flower." He paused, then added: "Of course, knowing Droma, he's somewhere saying the same about me."

"Yeah," Tycho said. "We didn't think you could become a bigger hero than you already were, old man."

Wedge smiled. "Someday they'll raise a statue—"

Han held up his hands. "I've already heard that one from Leia. Besides, every world, every system's contributed a hero to this war." He put his elbows on the table and leaned forward. "I haven't told this to anyone, but I swear on the *Falcon* that I saw *Fett* at Caluula, and he did as much as anyone to try to save that station from the Vong."

Lando was staring at him in disbelief. "As in Boba?"

"Of course, Boba—running with a bunch of other guys in Mandalorian armor and jet packs. He even managed to come up with a new Firespray."

Talon touched his mustache. "Well, I wasn't going to say anything, but I heard that that same bunch showed up to help liberate Ord Mantell."

"And Tholatin," Crev said.

"And Gyndine," Booster added.

Lando shook his head, as if to clear it. "Hey, if Pellaeon can be considered an ally, why not a former bounty hunter?"

Han glanced from Lando to Talon. "You're the people that deserve statues. But I suppose that'll have to wait until Wolam Tser or someone does a holodocumentary about the notorious Smugglers' Alliance."

"That would be Ex-Smugglers' Alliance," Talon said.

Han rolled his eyes.

"It's true, Han. We've mended our ways."

"Seen the light," Booster said.

"Come around," Crev added.

"Reformed," Lando said.

Tycho looked around the table. "Anyone want to add another cliché?"

"How about 'gotten too old for this'?" Han said.

Wedge nodded. "That'll do."

Han glanced at Lando and Talon again. "What, Tendra and Shada are making honest men of you?"

Talon shook his head firmly. "Shada and I are business partners. That's it."

Lando grinned at Han. "Hey, it was your wife who wrote the book on the subject."

Everyone laughed, then raised their tumblers.

"To the war's true unsung heroes," Han said, "the spouses." When he had set down his glass, he turned back to Lando. "Seriously, Lando. What's the game plan?"

"Let me put it this way. With the need for so much rebuilding—of worlds, governments, trading routes—and new markets opening in the Imperial Remnant, Chiss space, even parts of the Unknown Regions, there'll be no shortage of opportunities for people motivated more by philanthropy than profit."

"To our noble selves," Tycho said, toasting with the final sip. "Few of us left."

Finishing the drinks, the seven of them slammed the tumblers on the table.

"More by philanthropy than profit," Han repeated. Taking a deep breath, he leaned his crude chair away from the table and gazed about him. "I swear, this crazy place is having an effect on everyone."

"I already know that Tahiri and Tekli want to return to the Unknown Regions with Zonama Sekot," Jaina told Jacen as they were returning from the meeting. Most of the Jedi were proceeding directly to the canyon, but the twins were taking the long way back to their temporary shelter on the cliffside. "Tekli believes she can learn a lot from the Yuuzhan Vong shapers—assuming they're willing to teach her. And Tahiri, well, I think she just wants to explore more of the Yuuzhan Vong side of her nature—of Riina."

"I know someone else who plans to remain here," Jacen said.

"Danni," Jaina said.

Jacen nodded. "Before the war, all that interested her was the search for an extragalactic species. But the one she practically discovered single-handedly she knows only as an enemy. She told me she has as much to unlearn, as learn."

"Is that going to be hard for you—saying good-bye to her?"

"I'm happy for her." He glanced at his sister. "Anyway, I'll always know where to find her."

"I didn't think of that." Jaina became thoughtful for a moment, then said, "Corran, Mirax, and the kids are going to Corellia for a while."

"You think Mom and Dad will go there?"

Jaina shook her head in uncertainty. "I've no idea what those two have up their sleeves. But what about you, Jacen?"

"I know what I don't want to do—I don't want to be part of an order or a select group. I don't want to be looked to as the guiding light of the new fealty, and I don't want to be surrounded by students who'll ask more of me that I can explain. Most of all, I don't want to be an object of fascination or admiration, because that'll only distract me from what I really need to learn. I don't have dreams of being a lightsaber master or an ace starfighter pilot, and I'm not on a campaign to change anyone or anything, except myself, maybe, just to clear away some of the confusion that's built up."

"You sound like Sekot," Jaina said. She gestured broadly to the giant trees. "You wouldn't want to stay here? Among all this?"

"I can't—because every part of me is desperate to stay, and I'm worried that I'd never leave."

"So you're going to wander the galaxy or something?"

"If that's where the Force leads me. But right now I think I'd like to spend time among some of the other Force-users—the Jensaari, the Theran Listeners, the Sunesi . . . maybe even try to find out where the Fallanassi disappeared to."

Jacen laughed, clearly at himself.

"Anakin's probably ridiculing me for even thinking of going on a quest for answers. He'd probably say that I'd do better just to plant myself under one of these boras and wait for the answers to find me, instead of roving around trying to find them." His voice took on a note of sadness. "I wish I could see him, Jaina. But I can perceive him. I carry him around with me, the way some people do a hololocket. I regret so many of the arguments we had, and so many of the wrongheaded decisions I made. But they were the best I could manage at the time. It'd be easy to say I wished we'd never gone to Myrkr. But if we hadn't gone, then none of us might have survived the voxyn. There would have been no one to find Zonama Sekot, no chance for the Alliance or the Yuuzhan Vong. It would have been a battle to the death, with no winners."

Jaina kept silent until she was certain he was through. "Anakin was such a special person that even now it doesn't seem fair that he should have been the one to die. I know that fairness has nothing to do with it, but I'll never get over his death—just like the way he might never have been able to get over Chewie's death. I never had any real doubts that I'd survive the war, but my worst fear was that I'd survive without you, Mom, and Dad. I didn't want to live after Myrkr, Jacen. If you had died there, I don't think I could have gone on. I wouldn't have just become 'the Sword of the Jedi,' but the sword the Jedi would have been sorry they'd forged. I would have made the Kyp who destroyed Carida look like a simple scoundrel."

Jacen whistled in relief. "What about Kyp? Now that we *have* survived."

"I don't know, I really don't. He's been something of a mentor, in the same way Mara has." She brought her right forefinger and thumb close together. "I thought for about this long that I could actually feel something for him, but falling in love with your mentor isn't a sane thing to do, because you're not really seeing the person. You're seeing the statue on the pedestal. You're worshiping the idea."

"The way Jag does with you?"

"Jag doesn't worship me."

"Now that he's gotten to know you, you mean."

Jaina smacked her brother on the arm. "Even though you're right. The thing is, I don't want to be at the center of anything, either. I know that Uncle Luke and Aunt Mara would like to see me mentor some of the young students— maybe even Ben—but Kam and Tionne have bonded with the kids much better than I ever could. Anyway, I don't want to be too far from the action." She looked at Jacen. "I have too much of Mom and Dad in me to give up fighting for peace and justice."

"Especially now that you've gotten so good at it."

Jaina snorted ruefully. "That's the real problem, right? When it starts to come easy?"

"You just have to avoid the killing part of it."

"Unfortunately, that's part of the starfighter pilot job description."

"So find some other way to satisfy your need for speed and action. I hear Podracing's making a comeback."

Jaina laughed heartily. "It's in our blood, anyway."

"More than the military is. I mean, Dad just about got drummed out, Mom was a Rebel, and our paternal grandparents were . . . What?"

Jaina shook her head. "I don't know. But some people say that important traits tend to skip a generation."

Streaking a cloudless azure sky, a dozen ships of motley design and capability soared high above Zonama Sekot and gradually disappeared from sight.

"Everyone's leaving, Artoo," C-3PO said in a wistful tone. "They're returning to their homeworlds or going in search of missing friends. Masters Lowbacca, Sebatyne, Katarn, Zekk, and Azur-Jamin; Mistresses Rar, Ramis, and Kirana Ti; the children . . . I already miss them."

Four days had passed since the Jedi gathering, and the two droids were standing on the simple terrace that fronted Luke and Mara's cliff dwelling in the Middle Distance. The Skywalkers were completing repair work on *Jade Shadow,* and Han, Leia, and the Noghri had gone to Coruscant on unstated business.

R2-D2 chittered a short reply.

"Of course I realize that we'll be seeing everyone again, Artoo. But under very different circumstances."

The astromech fluted in a long-suffering way, and C-3PO tilted his head to one side.

"You can be the most infuriating little droid! I am fully aware of my need to adapt to change. But that needn't interfere with my ability to express sadness over the closing of an era."

R2-D2 issued a flurry of buzzes, zithers, and hoots.

"I know it was a war, you . . . you *mechanic*! And I also realize that it was a war that threatened our existence far more than any other war has. But that's precisely the point, because for a moment *we* became as valuable as they were. As often as they fought with us, they fought *for* us."

R2-D2 made a more decorous reply.

"You're correct, Artoo. They do need us. But they need us in a good way." C-3PO listened for a moment, then said, "A far more dangerous enemy? Who or what could possibly be more dangerous than the Yuuzhan Vong?"

R2-D2 warbled.

"Obsolescence?" After mulling it over, the protocol droid loosed what amounted to a sigh. "Perhaps I am deluding myself. With all the advances that have been made in droid technology, I suppose we are in danger of being considered obsolete. But what are we to do, Artoo? Retirement isn't an option for us. We will continue as relics, of a sort, passed along to new masters until our parts can no longer be replaced, or until we suffer some irreparable system failure. Oh, it's all very . . . bittersweet, I think is the proper word."

R2-D2's response was a surprisingly cheery burst of squeaks and peeps.

"Do you really believe that life will remain as unpredictable as ever and that our adventures will continue? I hope so, my little friend, even if they don't quite measure up to adventures we've had, and even if they are lacking a dash of the old enchantment."

R2-D2 made a razzing sound.

"What do you mean, I used to say that all the time? Just what are you going on about?" C-3PO paused, then said. "I don't mind at all that it's a long story. After all, Artoo, we have nothing but time . . ."

FORTY-FIVE

Jagged Fel had been assigned to the starfighter team that escorted the Yuuzhan Vong transports from Coruscant to Zonama Sekot. Inside two Star Destroyers were the weaponless yorik-trema that would shuttle the tens of thousands to their new home in the planet's southern hemisphere. The trackless forests were severely scarred as a result of the blight the Yuuzhan Vong warriors had delivered to the surface fifty years earlier, but the first groups to arrive were already settled in the warmest valleys, and their minshals, damuteks, grashals, and crèches appeared to have taken well to their new circumstances—from what could be seen at an altitude of twenty kilometers, at any rate. Though Alliance personnel were prohibited from landing, Jag had received special permission from General Farlander to pay a brief visit to the Middle Distance, ostensibly to speak with the Solos, but in fact to one Solo in particular.

He hadn't spoken to Jaina since parting company with the *Millennium Falcon* following the pursuit of the Supreme Overlord's escape vessel. Circumstances had made for a rushed and confused conversation. Jag had returned to Coruscant to regroup with Twin Suns Squadron, and the *Falcon*—with the Solos and Skywalkers safely aboard—had jumped for Zonama Sekot. In the long weeks that followed, he had been unsuccessful at contacting Zonama Sekot through either the *Millennium Falcon* or *Jade Shadow*. When at last he had gotten through to *Errant Venture*, he'd learned that Jaina was still on the living world.

Talon Karrde had promised to carry Jag's message to her.

She was waiting for Jag on the canyon-rim landing field when he set his clawcraft down among a throng of peculiar vessels and climbed out into the cold air. Fat flakes of snow were falling, but those only made him feel more at home, for he was no stranger to frigid climates.

Jaina was wearing some sort of natural-fiber poncho and a cap of similar weave, with flaps that covered her ears. After an awkward moment of staring at each other, she grinned and hurried into his arms, hugging him tightly, then kissing him on both cheeks and once on the lips. If she hadn't let go, he might have gone on holding her right through Zonama Sekot's return jump to the Unknown Regions.

"Twin Suns Leader," she said, stepping back to appraise him.

He straightened his shoulders. "Jealous?"

"Maybe a little."

Jag gazed at the strange, triple-lobed ships that surrounded the solitary X-wing. "Are these the Sekotan fighters?"

Jaina followed his gaze. "Yep."

"I don't suppose—"

"Don't even ask," she cut him off. "They're not for sale."

She grabbed his hand and led him to a shelter that stood at the border of the field. On the way they waved to Luke and Mara, who were loading supplies into *Jade Shadow*'s cargo hold, young Ben toddling beside them.

Jaina was still holding his hand when she said, "Thank you for everything you did at Coruscant—flying support for the *Falcon* and all. Mara told me she had to stop you from searching the Citadel for me."

"I might have disobeyed if the escape vessel hadn't launched. People are saying that you and Jacen killed the Supreme Overlord."

"I don't remember a lot of what happened. But Jacen and Luke were the ones who fought Shimrra and Onimi."

Snow frosted her cap and the tops of her shoulders. Her cheeks and nose were red with cold, and she looked radiant.

"Jaina, time is scarce, so I'll come straight to the point. I'm returning to Csilla, and I want you to come with me. I know that my parents and my sister, Wynssa, would love to meet you."

Even though a light smile formed on her lips, the answer was in her eyes, and Jag felt as if he had been deflated.

"I'd love to see Csilla—really. But this isn't the right time."

"For Csilla, or for us?"

Her face wrinkled, and she took her lower lip between her teeth. "Don't make this too hard on me, okay?"

"It's your parents, isn't it? They hate the thought of you consorting with the son of a former Imperial. It goes against the Skywalker-Solo grain."

She frowned. "You're way off. After what you did for my father at Hapes, and all you've done since, they practically consider you family. And even if that was true, do you think that would stop me from going with you?"

"It's Kyp, then."

"Wrong again."

Jag beetled his brows. "I don't understand. What's made you change your mind about us?"

She shook her head. "I think it's good that you're going to Csilla. I need some time to work through everything that's happened, Jag."

"I love you, Jaina," he blurted.

Jaina made her lips a thin line, then sighed and said, "I love you, too. Someday I want a partner, and I want what my mom and dad have, and what Luke and Mara have. I intend to raise a family. I just want to be sure that I can offer my children more than what Mom and Mara have been able to offer theirs." She reached for both his hands. "I'm glad that we found each other, Jag. You made the worst time of my life a lot easier to bear. But now I'm still on the move, I'm still a Jedi and a fighter pilot. Do you understand—even a little?"

Jag blew out his breath. "As much as I don't wish to, I do understand."

"I'd love to be some kind of diplomatic envoy." Her eyes sparkled. "I'll tell you a secret: One day I want to have a seat on the Advisory Council, alongside Luke, Kyp, Cilghal, and the others. Maybe then we can think about something more permanent."

Jag smiled broadly. "Then our paths may just cross again sooner than you imagine."

She looked at him askance. "I don't think I'll be getting to Chiss space anytime soon, Jag."

"You won't have to. I've been appointed by the CEDF as liaison to the Alliance."

"You—a diplomat?"

"I can be very diplomatic when I need to be."

"Oh, I know that, all right. But—"

"Just think about it: the two of us rendezvousing on fabulous worlds, from one side of the galaxy to the other."

Jaina's eyes narrowed in delight. "You know, that doesn't sound half bad."

Gently, he pulled her back into his arms and lowered his voice. "I'll work hard at making our encounters nothing short of wonderful."

Jaina laughed. "Maybe there is a touch of scoundrel in you, after all."

They kissed passionately, while the snow continued to fall.

"Five years ago, at the signing of the accord between the Imperial Sector and the New Republic, we met aboard your ship, Captain Solo and Princess Leia," Gilad Pellaeon said. "Now I have the honor of your being aboard my vessel at the start of a new era."

"We're the ones who are honored, Admiral," Leia said.

White-haired and mustachioed Pellaeon was attired in a pure white uniform, and Leia and Han were wearing the best of the few outfits they had left to their names. The three of them were in the Grand Admiral's spacious and elegantly appointed quarters, on the starboard side of *Right to Rule*'s command tower. Beneath the viewport an exquisitely carved table was spread with bowls of food and flasks of fine liquor. In stationary orbit above Coruscant, the flagship of the Imperial fleet was central to a group of other Star Destroyers, which themselves comprised only a part of the Alliance flotilla that remained in deep-space anchor. The *Falcon*—with Cakhmaim and Meewalh inside—sat conspicuously in the docking bay of the huge vessel, amid TIE defenders and bombers.

"When do you plan to return to Bastion space?" Han asked, sipping from his drink.

"Within a standard day, Captain. Which is why I was pleased to learn that you were available to visit with me on such short notice."

"Eager to get back to your garden?" Leia asked.

"If time permits. I will have much to do, convincing some of the Moffs of the wisdom of participating openly in the Alliance. I never took the time to marry and raise a family. But I have my garden, and I tend to that as I might have my children. I may even allow a bit of randomness, a bit of 'nature' to enter, and stay my hand from culling the weak and unfit from the rows."

Han laughed shortly. "A little disorder never hurt."

"It certainly never seemed to hurt you, Captain Solo."

"That's only 'cause turmoil and me reached an accord a long time ago."

"Well, perhaps I'll attempt to do the same." Pellaeon moved to the viewport that looked out on Coruscant. "In any event, I never realized how much I missed the Core—and Coruscant in particular. Returning here after so long a time, even under such circumstances, has made me reflect on my career, and on all the events that have ensued since the Battle of Endor." He turned from the view to look at Han and Leia. "I feel that you have been instrumental in giving me back something I had lost, and I want to do the same for you."

Leia smiled graciously. "That's really not necessary, Admiral."

Pellaeon waved his hand in dismissal. "It's just a little something."

Lifting a remote control from the table, he aimed the device at a screen, which folded against the cabin's inner bulkhead to reveal the object he had been saving as a surprise. It was a moss-painting by the late Alderaanian artist Ob Khaddor, depicting a tempestuous sky sweeping over a city of pinnacles and, in the foreground a line of insectoid figures, representing the vanished species that had inhabited Alderaan prior to human colonization.

Leia stared, speechless.

"And we thought you just wanted to give us another hyperspace comm antenna," Han said in astonishment.

Killik Twilight had once hung outside Leia's bedroom in House Organa on Alderaan. At the time of the planet's destruction by the Death Star, the moss-painting had been presumed destroyed, but in fact it had been returning to Alderaan as part of a traveling museum exhibit. Hidden within the painting's moisture-control apparatus was the key to a vital Rebel Alliance spy code, which had continued to be used in the post–Galactic Civil War years to communicate with agents deep inside Imperial-held territory. Four years after the Battle of Endor, when the painting had suddenly surfaced and been put up for auction on Tatooine, Han and Leia—recently married—had attempted to retrieve it. After changing hands several times, however, Ob Khaddor's apocryphal work had ended up aboard the *Chimaera,* in the possession of none other than Grand Admiral Thrawn, whose collection of priceless artworks was already extensive.

Aside from being an emotional link to Leia's childhood with her adoptive parents, the painting had added significance for both her and Han. Khaddor's execution of the Killiks left their reaction to the approaching darkness open to interpretation. Where Leia had seen the Killiks as running from the darkness, Han saw the insectoid race as turning *toward* the storm. He had interpreted the painting as an admonition that darkness could be defeated by meeting it squarely and shattering it with light, and when Leia had ultimately accepted Han's view, it had allowed her to reconcile her ongoing confliction over the fact that Anakin Skywalker, her actual father, and Darth Vader had been one and the same person. In turn, the reconciliation had allowed her to emerge from the shadow of the Sith Lord, and decide to have children.

"Gilad," Leia said at last, "I can't tell you how much this means to me."

Pellaeon smiled. "It is one of the few pieces of Thrawn's collection that survived, and I thought that you of all people should have it."

Han put one arm around Leia's shoulders, and extended the other to Pellaeon. "I know just where to hang it," he told Leia as he was pumping the admiral's hand.

Leia raised her eyes to his. "Hang it? Han, we don't even have a home. Unless you mean—"

He nodded. "Our cozy cabin space on the *Falcon*. Right over the bunk."

Jade Shadow was the last ship to launch from Zonama Sekot, with Mara, Luke, Ben, and R2-D2 aboard. Mara took the craft to a distance of three hundred thousand kilometers, then cut the sublight engines and swung her about to face the living world. Luke ducked into the cockpit, leading Ben by his tiny hand, with the astromech trailing slightly behind. No sooner had Mara swiveled her chair around than Ben climbed into her lap.

"Won't be long now," she said.

Luke nodded and sat down. "I'll comm them."

Seven weeks had passed since the surrender. For all intents and purposes the transfer of the Yuuzhan Vong had been completed, though several dozen remained on Coruscant, and fighting continued in some of the more remote star systems. Their presence lingered also in the form of countless dovin basal mines, and in the refugees that crowded nearly every spaceport, and most tragically of all in husks of the worlds the invaders had crisped, poisoned, and altered beyond recognition.

A reply to Luke's holotransmission finally arrived. He had left the comm unit in Danni's care, but it was a diminutive and noisy image of Magister Jabitha that resolved above the cockpit's projector, and the voice of Sekot who spoke through her.

"Farewell, Skywalker," Sekot said. "With the Jedi in the known regions and myself in the unknown, we may eventually succeed in making this galaxy whole."

"We'll do our part, Sekot," Luke said. "We're greatly indebted to you."

"There can be no debt when we serve to the same design, Skywalker. May the Force be with you."

"And with you, Sekot."

Gazing at something outside the holofield, Jabitha said, "I give you to your comrades," and shortly an image of Harrar appeared.

"I leave today by airship for the far side of the planet," the priest said. "It will be interesting to see what becomes of my people. Our challenge will be to keep from giving vent to the warrior instincts we cultivated over the generations, and refrain from making war on ourselves, as we did during the transit of the intergalactic void."

"That transit brought you home," Luke said.

The priest returned a tentative nod. "When all Yuuzhan Vong have accepted that, then our circle will be closed. I hope that you will visit us, Master Jedi."

"In time," Luke said. "Until then you have our envoys."

Tahiri, Danni, and Tekli crowded into the field. "Good-bye, Luke," they said in unison. "Good-bye, Mara. Good-bye, Ben and Artoo."

Ben buried his face in Mara's chest, and R2 whimpered and rocked from side to side on his treaded feet.

"Tekli, have the shapers agreed to allow you to study with them?" Mara asked.

The Chadra-Fan nodded. "I'll be traveling with Harrar."

"What about Danni and Tahiri?" Luke said.

"Who do you think's piloting Harrar's airship?" Danni said.

"Tahiri," Luke said, "I'd like you to make it a priority to locate *Widowmaker*."

"I will, Master," she said.

Mara looked sad. "It's not too late to change your minds and come with us."

"Oh, but they have to remain here," Jabitha interrupted. "Someone is going to have to succeed me as Magister. Perhaps some three . . ."

Luke smiled in understanding. "Have a safe jump."

"The Ferroans have their shelters," Jabitha said, "the Yuuzhan Vong, theirs. The jump will go well."

The transmission ended abruptly. Luke gazed out the viewport to see engines flare to life across Zonama Sekot's northern hemisphere, their intense plasma cones propelling the planet slowly, majestically, out of the cold orbit it had adopted. It struck him that the planet had never looked more enchanting. It glowed in the star-strewn blackness like some finely wrought orb of glass.

Instinctively Luke reached out to grab hold of the console. *She's leaving,* a familiar voice said. "She's leaving," he repeated aloud.

" 'She?' " Mara said.

Luke looked at her. "Obi-Wan's words, not mine."

The stars around Zonama Sekot's circumference appeared to withdraw, then rebound. An enduring melancholy settled over Luke like a shroud, and he experienced a sudden and profound void in the Force. A wail from Ben brought him back to himself. The child was struggling in Mara's arms, stretching out toward the viewport, as if to reach for the vanishing planet itself.

"Don't cry, sweetie," Mara comforted him. "We'll visit someday."

Luke stroked his son's head and glanced at Mara. "He's meant to be there."

One of a handful of worlds along the Rimward edge of the invasion corridor to have survived attack or occupation, the Wookiee homeworld of Kashyyyk looked even more lush now than it had before the war began. Many of its tall, furred denizens had served in the war as soldiers, technicians, and couriers, but most had returned to their festive planet, and had been rejoicing almost continuously since Zonama Sekot had carried the frightful enemy from known space.

Millennium Falcon and *Jade Shadow* had arrived only the previous day and sat side by side on landing platform Thiss, the fire-blackened stump of an enormous wroshyr tree, close to the village of Rwookrrorro. Having passed the night in the treetop community, the Solos and the Skywalkers, along with their faithful droids, had trekked to the massive fallen branch where a memorial for Chewbacca had been held several years earlier, though not to the day. Accompanying them were many of the Wookiees who had attended the somber remembrance, including Chewie's father, Attichitcuk; his sister, auburn-furred Kallabow; his widow, Mallatobuck, and their son, Waroo; Ralrra, who could speak Basic; and Dewlannamapia, Gorrlyn, Jowdrrl, and Dryanta.

As on that day, fog swirled in the upper branches of the

giant trees, and a cool wind stirred the leaves and kshyy vines. In homage to the late Chewbacca, a celebrated Wookiee artisan had carved a portrait of Chewie into the trunk of one of the trees that supported the fallen branch. Han stood before the likeness, speaking as if directly to his former first mate and closest friend.

"You can relax now, pal," he was saying. "It's finally over. We fought the good fight and won, and, for me anyway, it was you who set the tone. Your sacrifice at Sernpidal was symbolic of the whole war, with millions giving their lives to save family, friends, people they didn't know, members of species they'd never seen before, even droids. Thank you, for that, Chewie, and for giving Anakin the extra time he needed to fulfill his own destiny. I'll never forget you."

Tears running down his cheeks, he turned to Luke, who had brought something that had been discovered by a demolition crew near the remains of the Citadel, on Coruscant.

It was Anakin's lightsaber, which Tahiri had dropped while helping carry Luke to the *Falcon*. Han and Leia hadn't planned to leave the lightsaber with Chewie, until the moment when the *Falcon* had put down on Thiss.

Hefting the hilt, Han looked at gray-muzzled Ralrra. "You sure the branch won't mind."

Aged Ralrra shook his head. [It won't.]

Han got a two-handed grip on the handle, as one might a staff, so that the blade would point straight down. Activating it, he raised it over his head, then drove it down, almost vertically into the flattened area of the fallen limb. The tip of the energy blade struck the hardwood and began to burn through, producing a rich, fragrant smoke. And when it had burned a hole deep enough to bury four or so centimeters of the pommel itself, Han switched it off, so that the handle stuck fast in the limb.

Luke stepped forward. "Should the need ever arise, it can be withdrawn by someone as virtuous as yourself, Chewbacca."

One by one the rest of them advanced to cover the area with leaves and vines, then they all returned to Rwookrrorro and spent the rest of the day indulging in the feast of food and drink the Wookiees had prepared. By the time the sun was setting, the wind had picked up and the chimes were tingling without letup. Like the light, the laughter, too, was dying down, and Han noticed that Luke had become introspective.

"You okay?" Han asked.

Luke smiled lightly. "Just thinking that it seems like yesterday we set out to find a place where you and Leia could take a vacation, and Mara could cure herself of the illness Nom Anor gave her."

Han nodded. "And the day before that when you and I met in a cantina on Tatooine."

Luke looked at him. "You've lost a son and a best friend, and the Jedi have been reduced by half their number. But the galaxy is more unified than it has been in generations. The years since the conclusion to the Civil War seem like an unavoidable period of transition to a present that no longer rings with uncertainty."

"There's a lot of things I'd probably do differently," Han said, "but I'm not complaining. It can be a fresh start—providing I can keep your sister from getting involved in politics."

"And providing I can keep you from adventuring," Leia interjected.

Han gestured to himself in false innocence. "Hey, I don't have the time for adventuring. I've got a ship to rebuild—practically from the framework up."

"How many rebuilds will that make?" Luke asked.

Han grinned with secret knowledge. "More than you know."

"Where are you going to perform this rebuild?" Mara asked.

"We checked out Denon—" Leia started to say.

"—but it's not for us," Han completed.

"Corellia?" Luke asked.

Han shook his head. "Not the place it was."

"Han wants to go to the Corporate Sector," Leia said.

"We're long overdue for celebrating our twentieth wedding anniversary, and I know some worlds there . . ." He allowed his words to trail off, shook his head, and began to smile.

Luke and Mara traded knowing glances. "What would you

say to having Mara, Ben, and me as company?" Luke said. "We're supposed to meet with Kam and some of the others on Ossus, but that's not for a couple of weeks."

"Ossus," Han said, "why that's practically next door to the CorpSec. No two ways about it, you've gotta join us."

[We promise not to get in the way,] someone said in Shyriiwook.

Han glanced to his right to see Waroo and Lowbacca approaching him.

[Now that the war has ended,] Chewie's son continued, [Lowie and I will be assuming my father's life debt to you.]

Han's jaw dropped and his eyes went wide. "But we're going on a *vacation*. And we've finally managed to convince Cakhmaim and Meewalh to take one themselves."

No one said a word until Leia broke the silence with an explosive chuckle, then out-loud laughter, which Luke, Mara, Jacen, Jaina, Ben, and the Wookiees were quick to amplify. Han tightened his lips and sent a scowl around the table. Then he, too, began to laugh, warmly and continuously, until tears were streaming down his cheeks and his sides started to ache.

And gradually their bittersweet laughter floated from the wooden table, up past the lanterns, the wind chimes, and the thick branches from which they dangled, meandering up through the crowns of the tallest wroshyr trees and gliding weightless into the twilight sky, up, ever up into stars too numerous to count, defying the stillness of vacuum and dispersing, vectoring out across space and time, as if destined to be heard in galaxies far, far away . . .

Star Wars:
New Jedi Order
Round-Robin
Interview

Featuring: Shelly Shapiro, Editorial Director, Del Rey
Books
Sue Rostoni, Managing Editor, Lucasfilm
Lucy Wilson, Director of Publishing, Lucasfilm
James Luceno, Author

DR: Welcome all! Let me start with Sue Rostoni and Lucy
Wilson, from Lucasfilm. Can you give our readers an
overview of your jobs and your involvement with *Star
Wars* publishing?

LW: Sure. I started my career at Lucasfilm way back in
1974. Believe it or not, one of my first jobs at the company was to type the original *Star Wars* script from
George Lucas's handwritten pages! Although I had ma-
jored in English literature at UCSD, prior to joining
Lucasfilm I had worked as a bookkeeper in the machine shop at the Scripps Institute of Oceanography in
La Jolla, so I had no professional publishing experience. At Lucasfilm, after years of working my way up
through various departments in finance, I started working with the then director of publishing on the book
program for the movie *Willow* in 1988. In 1989, I negotiated the first deal with Bantam Books to relaunch
the *Star Wars* adult fiction publishing line with three

hardcover novels to be written by Timothy Zahn. By 1990, I had transferred out of finance to head up a new publishing department full time.

SR: Compared to Lucy, I'm a newcomer. I've been employed at Lucas Licensing since the fall of 1990, when *Heir to the Empire* was first released. I began as an assistant to Lucy, who was then director of finance and publishing, and worked my way through various job titles until I was promoted in late 2001 to managing editor, which is my position today.

I was involved with the Bantam *Star Wars* books with Tom Dupree and Pat LoBrutto, the editors at Bantam. I've also edited the Berkley line of *Young Jedi Knights* novels and Bantam Doubleday Dell's *Galaxy of Fear* series, as well as numerous nonfiction titles, including the *Star Wars Encyclopedia*. For the first few years, it was just Lucy and me handling the entire publishing program.

Now, as managing editor, I am available as a resource and sounding board to the other two Lucas Licensing editors, Michelle Vuckovich and Jonathan Rinzler. I am also responsible for the editorial on Del Rey's line of *Star Wars* fiction and, recently, the Dark Horse Comics line (except for *Tales*). I review, comment, and approve every element that goes into the novels, from outlines to cover and sales copy, cover art, manuscripts, all the way to the finished product.

DR: Let me bring in author Jim Luceno. Jim, what's your history with *Star Wars,* and how did you get involved with the New Jedi Order?

JL: I was in my late twenties when *Star Wars: A New Hope* premiered. I went to a matinee screening in New Jersey with my then best friend, the late Brian Daley, who had just sold his first science-fiction novel and would go on to write a trilogy of Han Solo novels and radio dramatizations of the classic movies. The film had a great impact on both of us and became something of a leitmotif in our enduring friendship and various collaborations. Before the *Star Wars* license went to Bantam, there was a period when it looked liked Brian and I were going to get a shot at contributing new material to the somewhat stalled franchise. Brian was asked to outline a novel, and I was working on a "nonfiction" book titled *The Way of the Force*. Those projects disappeared when Ballantine Books surrendered the licensing agreement it had with Lucasfilm. Regardless, I read and enjoyed many of the early Bantam titles by Tim Zahn, Kevin Andersen, Kathy Tyers, and others. When the license ultimately returned to Ballantine, and Shelly Shapiro asked if I'd be interested in working on the NJO, I made it a point to read the entire Bantam line, in addition to all the comics and sourcebooks.

DR: That's Shelly Shapiro, the editor at Del Rey in charge of the NJO project. Shelly, what role did you play in this project, and how did Del Rey and Lucasfilm work together?

SS: I was involved in planning the NJO from the start. When I first came on board—when Ballantine first got the *Star Wars* license and we had to figure out what our publishing plan would be—I spoke with Lucy about the idea of one big ongoing multibook saga. That turned into a meeting with Lucasfilm's licensing folks out at Skywalker Ranch—a huge meeting that included some authors (*Star Wars* veteran Mike Stackpole and then newcomer Jim Luceno among them), as well as some of the guys from Dark Horse Comics. From that point on, I became the liaison between the authors and Lucasfilm— everything they did was filtered through me, and I tried to help them get their work in as good a shape as possible before passing it on to Sue for approval. Throughout the series, I continued to brainstorm and debate ideas with Lucy and Sue as we and the authors moved the growing story forward. Sue and I became a real team, supporting each other, backing each other up (and arguing occasionally over creative issues!), and just working to make these books happen.

DR: Who was responsible for what?

SS: In general, I'd say I'm responsible for the books working primarily as novels—making sure they tell a good story, are well paced, and well written and edited—while Sue is responsible for the books working as integral parts of the *Star Wars* Expanded Universe, both in terms of continuity and making sure they "feel" like *Star Wars*. But in truth, we overlap a lot, working closely together to make sure the books work as well as possible on all levels.

SR: Right. My input is generally around continuity issues, characters, story elements, what will work and what won't work.

DR: So the idea of a big multibook saga was there from the start?

LW: Even earlier. I got the idea of doing a sequential series of related *Star Wars* books toward the end of the Bantam run of original *Star Wars* novels. The Bantam books were very much determined by what each writer wanted to create and were either one-off titles or trilogy series. Very early on we had agreed that it was important to maintain *Star Wars* continuity if people were to believe the *Star Wars* universe and its history were real. That meant that all events and characters created by any author (comics, novels, RPG material, et cetera) immediately became historical and could not then be contradicted in any subsequent book, story, or comic. But as the universe got more complicated, it was clear we had to take more control over where the stories were going in order to maintain this continuity. We also knew our readers wanted more sequential stories—rather than stories that jumped around in *Star Wars* time. So when the agreements for books related to the prequel trilogy films were negotiated and licensed to Ballantine Books in 1997, we included the rights to create a new spin-off fiction program that would be one big sequential story. Originally we planned to include thirty titles in this program, but concerns about whether we could sustain one story for that many titles, combined with a desire to create new stories set in the original trilogy period of history, resulted in an adjustment that reduced what had become the NJO series to nineteen books.

DR: What role did you play in all this, Jim?

JL: My original role was to assist in the nuts-and-bolts development of the series. I attended the initial story conference at Skywalker Ranch in March 1998, then a follow-up conference in May devoted to fine-tuning the ideas that had been discussed at the first. Shelly had already written a rudimentary outline of the project, and for the next several weeks I worked closely with her and Del Rey editor Kathleen O'Shea to fashion a five-year story arc, along with individual story arcs for the principal characters, all of which would ultimately be incorporated into a writers' bible. That meant keeping careful track of plot points and continuity, creating names for new characters, and designing a social structure for the Yuuzhan Vong.

My outlines and suggestions went directly to Shelly, who would rework them as necessary and forward them to Sue and Lucy, whose comments would frequently send Shelly and me back to the drawing board. Eventually, though, we'd all find ourselves on the same page.

I was also commissioned to contribute one paperback novel to the series, though at the last minute my one book became two when changes in the publishing schedule required that Mike Stackpole's trilogy be compressed into two novels. As the project evolved, I worked with Dan Wallace and artist Christopher Barbieri to map the *Star Wars* galaxy and the Yuuzhan Vong invasion corridor, and I continued to read and comment on book outlines and manuscripts. After many discussions with Shelly, Sue, Lucy, Greg Keyes, Greg Bear, Sean Williams, and Shane Dix, I began work on the final NJO volume, *The Unifying Force,* in May 2002.

DR: Shelly, you mentioned Dark Horse Comics had people at the original meeting. What was their involvement?

SS: They had a character that we thought Bob Salvatore could use for the bad guy in *Vector Prime.*

SR: Right, Nom Anor. The original concept for Nom Anor came from the Crimson Empire II comics by Dark Horse.

LW: What we did at that meeting was plot out the major story points for a five-year book program that would be published from 1999 through 2003, with the big events unfolding in five hardcover novels; the material that would go into the paperbacks was to be developed later. That was where, for the first time, we all agreed that a well-loved *Star Wars* character would die—after all, the general story idea was a big alien invasion and galaxy war, and we wanted people to feel that there are consequences to war. Once we had agreed on the general plot, Dark Horse noted that they had invented a new character in their Crimson Empire comics who might serve as one of the invading species, so we started with the character of Nom Anor as an early concept for what was to become the Yuuzhan Vong.

DR: How was internal consistency maintained—not only within NJO but back through the entire history of *Star Wars* fiction? Who was responsible for that?

SR: In a sense, we are all responsible for continuity. Leland Chee works here at Lucasfilm maintaining our "Holocron," an archival database containing a huge number of entries. As outlines and manuscripts are submitted, Leland enters new data into the Holocron, which is then available for use by the authors and editors via CD-ROM. Initially we wrote an NJO bible for use by the authors, to give them a sense of what was going to happen in each of the hardcovers; we also included summaries of previous NJO books, et cetera. However, after the first year or so, the bible became too unwieldy to keep up, and the Holocron has been the main source of reference ever since. Leland has been indispensable as well, as he has created government flow charts, timelines of events, and various lists of characters, vehicles, locations, and so on. Leland is the "go to" guy whenever esoteric questions come up.

LW: When we first started doing original *Star Wars* publishing, the editorial group consisted of me, Sue Rostoni, and later Allan Kausch, who was originally hired as a continuity consultant. Howard Roffman, president of Lucas Licensing, was also creatively involved, and we would get input from George Lucas through a series of Q&A memos in which we asked for guidance on big plot points and ideas. In order to track continuity, both the editors at Lucasfilm and the editors at our licensed publishing houses would combine their efforts—primarily based on who had the best memory. Our RPG licensees were integral to this early on, as they tended to publish the most detailed material of anyone. The early system of tracking continuity was for a question to be called out (by phone or by yelling down the room or corridor) in the hope that someone would remember and have an answer—very high tech, as you can see. As the *Star Wars* universe got more and more complicated, I recognized the need for a full-time person to track the material in a database, and Leland was brought on board to do that in February 2000.

SS: Before Leland and the Holocron, I relied (and I still do!) on Jim, who originally came on board to help with the NJO bible and quickly became an authority on continuity.

JL: I'd like to take all the credit, but I relied in turn on Stephen J. Sansweet's recently published *Star Wars Encyclopedia,* Dan Wallace's, Bill Smith's, and Bill Slavicsek's guidebooks, and a slew of fan glossaries and compendiums. And, of course, once it was available, the Holocron!

Early on, though, the NJO wasn't intended to incorporate a great deal of Bantam continuity. We didn't want to alienate (so to speak) a new generation of Expanded Universe readers. This certainly was the case in Bob Salvatore's *Vector Prime,* and to some extent in Mike Stackpole's duology. But by the time I was writing *Agents of Chaos,* Del Rey was receiving emails and letters from fans imploring us not to abandon the Bantam continuity. The hard-core readership wanted *one story*—and we've done our best to give it to them. Given the wealth of background material, writing a *Star Wars* novel at this point is almost like writing a work of historical fiction!

DR: I've heard that the name *Yuuzhan Vong* came from a restaurant menu during an early editorial powwow. Any truth to that?

LW: You bet. *Yuuzhan Vong,* as well as many other brilliant ideas over the course of history, came from food.

SS: Lucy and some of us Del Rey people were eating lunch at a wonderful French-Thai restaurant called Vong here in New York City. I suggested using Vong for the alien invaders. But we wanted something more, and perusing the menu, I came across their list of teas, which included a mention of the "Yunan region." We tossed around ideas and came up with *Yunan Vong.* We added an extra *n,* making it *Yunnan Vong.* But a week or so later, we decided that we wanted it to sound more alien and less Asian, so we changed it first to *Yuzzan Vong,* then to *Yuzhan Vong,* and finally settled on *Yuuzhan Vong.*

DR: How much of a role did George Lucas play in shaping the series?

LW: George Lucas has been involved in all of the spin-off *Star Wars* publishing, but only on big concepts or plot points. The initial five-year NJO plot outline and early thoughts on who might die were sent to him in the form of a Q&A memo and subsequently discussed by phone.

SS: I would characterize his role as limited but important. He's the one who said the alien invaders could not be dark side Force-users, that we couldn't kill Luke, that we had to kill Anakin instead of Jacen (we had originally planned it the other way around). Other than that, he occasionally answered some basic questions for us, but that was rare. Mostly he leaves the books to his licensing people, trusting them to get it right.

JL: Several times at Skywalker Ranch, George was sitting almost within arm's reach, but I never got to speak with him. But he played a major role in giving shape to the NJO by commenting extensively on the early version of the five-year story arc, as Lucy and Shelly have said. His objection to Anakin Solo being the main series protagonist was, I think, possible confusion with Anakin Skywalker in the prequel trilogy of movies. There would be too many Anakins out there! And I distinctly recall George's taking particular exception to our careless description of Onimi as "dwarfish."

When we received his feedback, suddenly we were faced with having to create a new enemy . . . and yet somehow differentiate that enemy from the dozens already developed by various authors of the Bantam books. Worse, we were stripped of the one character from the Bantam line who was ideally set up to inherit the Jedi mantle from Luke. Even so, Shelly and I emerged with a lot to work with, and over espressos in Sausalito and pizza at Point Lobos, we sketched many of the characters who later became prominent in the series.

DR: Like the original film trilogy, the NJO, both as a whole and in its individual books, follows Joseph Campbell's concept of the myth of the hero's journey. Is that Lucas's influence at work?

SS: Not in the sense of him directing us to use it. I don't even think he knows we did it! But we wanted to use the hero's journey as a template because it is so basic to *Star Wars* and to what George has done with his mythos.

JL: We had many discussions about archetypes and mythic themes, mostly at the behest of Lucy, who would frequently have a chalkboard brought to the conference rooms and make detailed outlines of the character arcs.

LW: In order to tell the best stories, we pull ideas from a variety of sources to come up with themes that can then be woven through the various works of new *Star Wars* fiction. In our big creative meetings, we work with publishers, editors, and our writers to develop strong stories with multiple levels, including: the pacing of basic plot points (beginning, climax, resolution); themes (both mythological and biblical themes have been presented, among others); and individual character development arcs (with specific levels of development and attributes depending on whether Jedi, Sith, alien, good, bad, or other). It's the combination of these elements that makes the stories fit into the structure people associate with *Star Wars*. It's not George Lucas's decision that requires us to do this—rather, we have learned by observing his techniques and have then applied the same development process in our dealings with our print editors and authors.

SR: One of the advantages of using Campbell's template is that it's very familiar to us all, on both the minute and the grand scale, on an instinctive level. We are each challenged in ways that bring out either the hero or the villain. We each have choices and are accountable for those choices and their consequences. We are sometimes thrown into situations we thought we could never handle, and how it comes out is not the point—the point is the journey itself.

We discussed the hero's journey at length in the first creative meetings. After feedback from George, we decided on Jacen as our "hero" and the character who would undergo the most dramatic changes—in many ways, the NJO is really his series. At those meetings, we charted the character threads for each of the main characters and how these threads would interact with Jacen to show him as an indecisive young man who grows into a strong and confident Jedi. We talked about Vergere and the role she could play. We also charted other characters' journeys: how Han would react to Chewie's death, his blaming Anakin, and how something like that affects a family. We discussed how Anakin was the stronger of the siblings, and how his death would affect things, since he was the obvious choice as Luke's successor.

SS: A template such as Campbell's can be a very interesting reference for an author, a reminder of ways to keep a story exciting and keep it growing and developing. But I don't advise writers to use it as a rigid framework for a story—in other words, following it slavishly would probably result in a stiff, unlifelike story. Stories need to grow, to at least some degree, organically, with elements developing out of what has gone before. If meeting the mentor really wants to happen *before* the call to adventure, for example, it should happen that way, instead of having the story forced into a mold it doesn't want to fit. Fortunately, the hero's journey model allows for a lot of flexibility, and is terrific as a reminder that stories move up and down, forward and backward, have climaxes and crises all along the way. Although frankly, this aspect of the series didn't end up as well developed as I would have liked—probably due to the complication of using multiple authors. Individual books had it, like Matt Stover's, but I would have liked to see the mythic dimension, the hero's journey, evoked a little more, I don't know, *cohesively,* in the series as a whole. On the grand scale.

JL: I've never before been involved in a project where the template was afforded so much conscious attention. I'm aware of the template when I write fiction, but I usually rely on my subconscious to provide archetypes, and most of the time I don't recognize the mythic elements, the "heroic" elements, until I've reached the end of a book and can look at it objectively.

   Star Wars is a unique blend of romance and pulp, but what works well on screen doesn't always work on the printed page—especially when you're dealing with a series of twenty or so books, and you feel duty-bound to have not only each book incorporate elements of the template, but also the series as a whole. *Lord of the Rings* succeeds in doing that, as does *Harry Potter,* though to a lesser extent. But in the NJO we lacked clear-cut archetypes, and those characters who *were* clear-cut— Luke, Han, Lando, Leia—had, in a very real way, already completed their journeys. That said, authors Elaine Cunningham, Matt Stover, Aaron Allston, and Walter Jon Williams made terrific use of mythic elements, regardless.

DR: Probably the single most controversial aspect of the NJO was the death—some fans would say the murder— of Chewbacca. How was this decision reached?

LW: In the *Star Wars* novels published by Bantam, no preexisting *Star Wars* character ever died. It was our policy that no author could kill anyone who originated first in a script written by George. However, we knew that for anyone to really take a new intergalactic war seriously, and to realize that the New Jedi Order was not just *Star Wars* fiction as usual, someone who mattered would have to die. This was a unanimous agreement. Who would die was the subject of much debate, however. Our first thought was that the death of Luke Skywalker would have the biggest impact on the readers. However, this was not okay with George Lucas! I think it was Randy Stradley from Dark Horse who said, "Kill the family dog—Chewbacca." In our own emotional response to this suggestion (it made us unhappy just to come up with the idea), we knew Chewie's death would generate the biggest reaction from the readers.

SR: As time went by, I had more than second thoughts about this decision! I came to think that Chewie's death was a really, really bad thing. I remember going home and thinking about it and grieving even before Bob Salvatore submitted his outline. I couldn't believe we were going to kill Chewie. He was so great. So much like the family dog that everybody loves, as Lucy points out. And here we were going to kill the dog! I remember my partner's son telling me that the worst thing we ever did was to get him the book *Old Yeller*. How could we do that, have him fall in love with this dog, only to see him killed? And here we were doing much the same thing with Chewie. So I had misgivings about it at first.

SS: We didn't get George's permission to kill Chewie in particular: Chewie was simply not one of the characters George said we could *not* kill. But I think we made the best choice. Not because he wasn't a beloved character, and only partly because he seemed a difficult character to utilize in the books. Mostly it was because his death would strongly affect every other major character in the series, so it would serve as a unique emotional catalyst. And it did.

JL: Right. We wanted to throw the major characters into immediate turmoil—to shanghai them into new spiritual journeys, replete with abysses, demons, dark nights of the soul, rebirths, what have you.

DR: Were you taken aback by the fan reaction to Chewie's death? I mean, there were even death threats against the author of *Vector Prime,* Bob Salvatore!

SR: I talked with Bob often during this time. His brother had just died, with Bob at his bedside. Getting threats from fans was very upsetting for Bob, and for everyone here. It didn't make me wish we hadn't done it—Bob created the scene and wrote it with care and great insight. It was such a shock, though, that the readers had such emotion! But if you think about it, it shows the strength of *Star Wars* and of the publishing program that our readership is this invested in the characters.

LW: When Chewie died, people sat up and took notice that the NJO was going to be different from what had come before, and that the *Star Wars* galaxy was not necessarily a safe place anymore. I always felt very badly that Bob got the brunt of the criticism, however.

SS: I knew people would be sad and shocked, but I didn't expect the anger. Bob was very upset at the anger directed at him, and I felt really bad about that. He shouldn't have had to face such mean-spiritedness and nastiness. I didn't worry that we'd made a mistake, though. I thought Chewie's death was heroic and incredibly moving—exactly what the New Jedi Order needed as an emotional catalyst.

JL: I had gone through something similar when adapting *Robotech,* so I expected a flak storm. Bob, who was brought in late to launch the series, also expected as much. Regardless, he was terribly wounded by the fan criticism, and it's something we still discuss to this day. Some readers wrongly assumed that Bob had taken it upon himself to kill Chewbacca, when in fact he had been *instructed* to kill Chewbacca. There was a kind of contract out on Chewie! So, by all rights, the criticisms and threats should have been hurled at Del Rey Books, or the NJO creative team itself. Um, maybe I shouldn't have said that . . .

DR: Moving right along, how do you respond to fans who complain that they look to *Star Wars* for an escape, for entertainment, rather than for reality of this sort?

JL: I think it's a valid criticism, as far as it goes. But the fact is that the Bantam books had taken these same characters through so many betrayals, kidnappings, and David-versus-Goliath strikes against superweapons that we had nowhere else to go. For that reason, we felt compelled to shake things up by undermining Luke's ability to use the Force, testing the younger characters at every turn, having Chewbacca and Anakin die, sending Han and Leia into brief estrangement and grief, and even giving Threepio and Artoo something to worry about.

You know, what *did* surprise me was how much flak we took for having Han withdraw into himself after Chewbacca's death. From the start, the NJO was conceived as darker, more "adult." But perhaps this sometimes led to our being *too* realistic in our thinking—going beyond the sensibilities inherent in the films.

SR: Well, we wanted the NJO series to have more of the feel of reality, with conflict and emotion. By shaking up the universe, we felt we were adding an emotional depth to the stories that wasn't there before, and we were confident that our readers were up to the challenge.

LW: Again, we go back to the original stories that George Lucas was telling in the films. Good things happen and bad things happen in the *Star Wars* universe—as in our own world. Since we wanted to model the books on some of the same themes and story elements George was drawing on in the films, we did not want to always play it safe and simply provide an entertaining escape in the fiction. Had we done that, I don't think the novels would have had the same emotional response with our readers. We are always pushing the boundaries of *Star Wars* storytelling so as to not repeat ourselves or fall into a formula.

SS: Sales for the Bantam *Star Wars* books were significantly down, the books weren't hitting the bestseller lists the way they once had: clearly, readers were losing interest. One complaint that arose consistently was that it was nothing more than the same-old, same-old: someone gets kidnapped or a situation is saved by the super-weapon of the month. Nothing is ever unpredictable. There were complaints that all Leia did was be a diplomat; that Han had become nothing more than a house-husband, and Chewie, a nursemaid; that Luke was so all-powerful, authors had to find some ways to weaken him to make any fight fair enough to be even interesting. Right or wrong, we were attempting to address these concerns. The death of a character close to all the other major players was a perfect way to give those other characters a natural and believable reason to reevaluate their lives and their roles—to change and (we hoped) to revert more to the characters we all knew and loved from the movies. It also gave us the chance to grow the characters of the Solo children, who seemed to be disliked by a lot of the adult fans.

I do understand the complaints about wanting an escape, not reality. But I don't think that one major death—okay, two—is a sledgehammer of reality to an otherwise entertaining universe. Having your emotions challenged is, to my mind, part of good entertainment. When George ended a movie with Han encased in carbonite, who knew what would happen to that character? We all waited with bated breath, truly worried. And we loved it.

I do regret the relentlessness of the war against the Yuuzhan Vong—and some of the grimmer aspects of their culture. I would have preferred to make them dark side Force-users: that would have kept their darkness in the arena of magic and mystery, which, oddly enough, would have made them seem less "dark," I think. As for the war . . . Well, we had no idea when we started this series that September 11 would happen, or that we would go to war in Iraq. If we'd known that real life was going to take such a dark turn, perhaps we would have planned our story arc differently. I can't say.

DR: On to the death of Anakin. Why Anakin and not one of the other Solo children? What was the reaction of the author, Troy Denning, to the angry fan response?

JL: Anakin was our first choice as the saga's hero, not Jacen. When George nixed that idea, we were forced to rethink everything very quickly, as the first book of the series was already being outlined. For the same reasons we chose to devise dark moments for many of the characters, we wanted to have a personal tragedy accompany the fall of Coruscant. This was not something malicious on the part of the creative team, or especially manipulative, but yet another example of wanting to convey the sense that war has terrible consequences, and that no one is immune to those.

The book that became *Star by Star* was designed to be the nadir of the story arc. Like Bob Salvatore, Troy knew going in that he was taking a great risk and said as much at a story conference at Skywalker Ranch. And like Bob, Troy was bombarded by fans: all the more, perhaps, because Anakin had played such a prominent role in the Greg Keyes duology that precedes *Star by Star*. By then, though, a certain percentage of the readership had grown to expect tragic surprises, and those readers grasped that Troy shouldn't be held personally accountable for Anakin's death. My sense of it is that the fans were more forgiving with Troy than they were with Bob.

SS: The surprising thing was that Anakin had previously seemed to be a fairly unpopular character, at least judging by what a lot of fans were saying and writing. We did our best to grow him into a hero—I guess we succeeded!

DR: Which death was the most upsetting for fans?

LW: Chewie's death had the biggest impact everywhere. A lot of people, even some internally at Lucasfilm who were not involved in the creative decision, would come up to me afterward and say, "How could you!" But to counter some of the criticism, we have encouraged more Chewie backstories in comics and other publishing since his death; in a way, it's made him even more important than he would have been if he hadn't suffered a fictional demise.

SS: There's no question in my mind that Chewbacca's death was more upsetting to fans. After all, he was one of the core characters—part of the basic mythos. But there were no confrontations at conventions or anywhere else. In person, the fans were great. A huge number of people were very supportive, saying they found the death very sad and moving, and they understood why it happened and could see that it was going to benefit the series.

SR: The fans at Celebration II were quite understanding of the process. I sat on two panels with Bob Salvatore, and the fans seemed to me to be polite and accepting of the decisions that were made, even if they didn't agree with them.

JL: Even as irrelevant as he became in the Bantam novels, Chewbacca was a classic character and, more important, Han Solo's sidekick. Anakin was relatively new to the Expanded Universe, but throughout the first eight books of the NJO, he was portrayed as the "strongest" of the Solo teenagers. Either way, when a reader invests that much time and emotion in a character, only to have the character yanked away—seemingly at the whim of the creative team . . . Well, anger and disappointment are bound to surface.

DR: You've talked a little about how the NJO series was plotted. Can you give us more details?

SR: Almost from the first, we knew two things: where we were beginning, and where we were ending. We knew our heroes would succeed at the end of the series, but we really didn't know how they would overcome the Yuuzhan Vong. The hardcovers were plotted first, with major events slated for each hardcover. The mass-market paperbacks were initially designed to cover more minor events, but it soon became apparent that the paperbacks had as big a role in the series as the hardcovers. Del Rey and Lucasfilm worked hand in hand in all of this, and both sides meshed very well. There were a few areas of debate, however. The one that springs to mind is the character of Vergere. It was first decided that Vergere would give her life for her cause. Then, later, Lucy and I thought it would be better if she lived through the series. Shelly pointed out some very good reasons why her death was necessary to Jacen's growth and Luke's authority, so we agreed (after much angst). Sparks never flew—not that I can recall. We work very, very well together and have a deep mutual respect and trust.

LW: We had several creative sessions over the course of the NJO series development. The first one, which I mentioned earlier, took place in 1998 and (I believe) lasted two days. In this initial meeting, the major points of the entire story were plotted out. Subsequent creative meetings were set up in later years, each time with new authors, where more details for the individual stories were plotted out. The beauty of these meetings was that good ideas were voiced by a variety of people—discussed, enhanced, developed into even bigger ideas, and then fleshed out by each individual contributing author with his or her own voice. Not only were they fun, you could almost watch the ideas spill out and become great, which was a very energizing thing. So many authors ply a lonely trade of writing alone by themselves in a room. Having a forum to build on the ideas of a group of creative participants was, I think, very exciting for all concerned.

SS: We all meshed smoothly from the start—it's a great group to brainstorm with. Over the course of the series, we averaged one creative meeting a year, where we'd get together with a couple of the next-in-line authors and plan the next year's worth of books, continuing to develop the loose story line we'd begun with, tweaking it and adding to it—and sometimes completely changing it—based on what had actually ended up happening in the series. There was only one time I recall a serious disagreement, and I'd rather not say what that was. Suffice it to say that Lucasfilm won <g>.

JL: The story arc was little more than a blueprint. It summarized the principal action and underscored key plot points. For a time, I felt that because the NJO was shaping up to be such a collaborative effort, it would be best to plot each book and have one person serve as story editor. That had been my experience when working in collaboration with scriptwriters on various TV series, and I thought that—in lieu of George Lucas himself—someone had to uphold the guiding vision. But most writers aren't accustomed to teamwork, and who wants to do little more than connect the dots in any case?

Beyond that, carefully plotted outlines weren't going to allow for enough individual creativity and were probably going to hamper organic growth—the unexpected discoveries writers make even when working from detailed outlines. Oftentimes characters refuse to do what you figured you had planned for them! The reaction you plotted suddenly doesn't seem reasonable or consistent with the character that has emerged from the writing.

But that's not to say that the members of the creative team were always of one mind about the changes that crept into the story arc, and as we approached the end of the series, we probably had too many voices weighing in with comments and criticisms, and perhaps too many authors, as well. Some outlines went through as many as nine drafts before they were approved. Some books were canceled before they were written, and others were canceled *after* they had been completed. Had there been time enough, a lot of inconsistencies and continuity errors would have been eliminated, and perhaps some plot points would have been jettisoned entirely. But all this seems part and parcel of ambitious sagas. Even when there is a "guiding vision," it's difficult to sustain the initial vision through five years of changes.

DR: How were the authors for each book selected? How much freedom did the writers have in terms of plot, character, setting, and invention of things like technologies, names, cultures, and aspects of the Force?

SS: Some authors I knew and recommended to Lucasfilm; some came to me, and I had to read their work before recommending them to Lucasfilm. Of course, it's well known that, for a variety of reasons I won't go into here, we only use established, previously published, professional writers.

Once an author is recommended to Lucasfilm, Sue reads a sample of his or her work and makes the final decision to approve using that author or not. The writers had a lot of freedom, provided they didn't contradict existing continuity and that they hit the major plot points we required to keep the overall story arc moving along.

SR: For instance, we told Troy Denning that Anakin's demise was a part of his book, *Star by Star,* but he created the setting and action. The same was true with Bob and the circumstances of Chewie's death.

JL: At times it was like: "Start at A, go to B, then C, and make certain to wind up at D—but we don't care how you get there." Lucy, Sue, and Howard did request that we stick with existing worlds and make use of established *Star Wars* species, critters, and items whenever possible. Still, several characters had to be invented from whole cloth: obviously, with the exception of Nom Anor, all the Yuuzhan Vong. Because the invasion route had been determined early on, settings were often dictated by the needs of the story arc, but typically writers had a lot of freedom in that area. Given that we were dealing with *Episode 1*'s new revelations about the Force, as well as with an extragalactic species against whom the Force couldn't be used, there were many, many discussions about the Force, right up to the end of the series.

DR: How did your ideas about the Force change over the course of the series? How much was preplanned and imposed from the outset, and how much evolved as the series was written, shaped by the demands of plot and character? I'm thinking specifically of Vergere here.

JL: Vergere was created at the onset to serve as Anakin's, then Jacen's, mentor. At a story conference at Skywalker Ranch in March 1999, we saw a way to insert Vergere into Greg Bear's novel, *Rogue Planet,* and thus tie the prequel era to the New Jedi Order. Subsequently, Greg's novel assumed even greater importance to the NJO and became the focus of Sean Williams's and Shane Dix's *Force Heretic* trilogy. Vergere was also designed from the start to be an unorthodox teacher. Our intention was for her to serve as a voice for the Republic-era Jedi and in that capacity answer some of the questions Luke had been pondering for most of his adult life. We also wanted Vergere to *demystify* the Force, or at least convey a sense that the ability to use the Force was not simply an accident of birth. In *Traitor,* Matt Stover not only ran with these ideas, but took them beyond our wildest imaginings.

SS: I personally would like to see the Force return to the more mystical life force we saw in the first three movies, but in the end, the plot and the characters are more in charge than I am, and they moved in that direction naturally.

LW: But you know, we didn't really change anything about the Force. It's more how the Jedi understand, think about, and use the Force. That definitely evolved as the series was written.

SR: Well, it had to be that way. I mean, all the original Jedi were wiped out by Vader and Palpatine. Luke's training by Yoda was never completed. So Luke has always had questions about the Force, as have all the Jedi trained by Luke. Vergere was a bridge back to the earlier Jedi. And she'd taken her understanding of the Force in new directions, too, because of her long experience with the Vong.

DR: I'm still not sure I understand how the Vong can be immune to the Force.

SS: Me, neither <g>. They're not exactly "immune" to the Force, though—they just can't be "sensed" through the Force.

SR: This is all explained in *The Unifying Force,* never fear!

JL: Our original idea was to give the Yuuzhan Vong dark side powers and test the Jedi in a way we imagined the Republic-era Jedi had been tested. When that proved unworkable, we began to wrestle with the idea of making the Vong immune to the Force, which of course led to countless discussions about midichlorians and the possibility that the Force was *peculiar* to the *Star Wars* galaxy.

All this was admittedly muddled, and almost every writer had a slightly different take on the notion of "immunity." The basic idea was that the Vong could not be *perceived* through the Force and therefore were not susceptible to certain actions by the Jedi: very much in the same way that Toydarians, Hutts, and other species are immune to Force suggestion, and Tim Zahn's ysalamiri are capable of repulsing the Force. At the conclusion of the NJO . . . but perhaps I should leave that discovery to readers!

DR: Who came up with the idea of a biologically based technology and a culture with a fanatical aversion to machine technology and a value system and sadomasochistic theology based on conquest, violence, sacrifice, and pain?

SS: Bob Salvatore invented the biotech concept, which we liked. We built on that to come up with the fanatical aversion to machine technology. We kind of liked the flip-flopping of the way it had been in the original movies: there, the high tech was mostly in the hands of the bad guys, while the good guys wore homespun and seemed much more low tech. So here it's the reverse: the good guys are high tech, and the bad guys seem more low tech, although they're really just "different tech." The sadomasochistic theology was not planned, and while we tried to pull back on it, not stress it so much (we really wanted it only to be the extra-fanatical Domain Shai—of which Shedao Shai was a part), it took on a life of its own.

JL: At the time of the first story conference, I had just returned from an extended trip in Mexico and Guatemala, and during the brainstorming sessions, Del Rey editor Steve Saffel wondered aloud if the Aztecs or Maya might serve as models for the Vong. We began to work with this by imagining a kind of organic-tech Aztec society with a pantheon of gods, rituals of automutilation, a rigid caste system, and a hatred of machines.

We weren't out to reinvent the wheel. We were

simply trying to come up with villains who had the potential to become as interesting as Palpatine and Darth Vader. Our original conception of the Yuuzhan Vong expanded in all directions after Bob Salvatore, working from scant notes, gave them an actual look and created examples of their wondrous biotech. Mike Stackpole was largely responsible for the system of ranks, and we borrowed heavily from Central American mythology in creating the pantheon of gods. Kathy Tyers and Greg Keyes contributed immensely to this process, further defining the warrior and shaper castes and in enlarging the Yuuzhan Vong menagerie of creatures. Yuuzhan Vong words and phrases accrued as the series progressed.

DR: Were you ever concerned with the possibility that you were creating a threat far greater than Palpatine and Vader—an enemy more evil and hence, in a way, minimizing the heroism of the original series after the fact?

SR: We needed something that really strained the resources of the New Republic and could have dire consequences for the galaxy. Something that caused a rift in the Jedi Order, something overpowering. But I don't believe it minimizes the heroism of the original series at all. It expands it and shows the Jedi reacting to this enemy force in ways they never had to in the time of Palpatine.

LW: I was more worried that fans wouldn't find our alien invasion original or interesting. I've been happy to find that this isn't the case.

SS: I don't feel that the Vong are a greater threat than the Emperor and Darth Vader. Different, yes, but not more evil—in fact, it can be argued that the Yuuzhan Vong are *less* evil, because they are acting from some kind of moral stance, even though it's not a morality we agree with. The Emperor, on the other hand, was acting thoroughly without morals—out for his own ambition alone.

DR: Would you agree that the NJO series is Jacen's story—the tale of his coming of age, and the passing of the Jedi crown, as it were, from Luke to Jacen?

SR: Absolutely. It was our intention from the beginning to make this Jacen's story, ultimately.

LW: Jacen is the focus of the NJO, but I don't think that makes it *his* story exactly. Or not *only* his story. Just as the films are about Anakin's rise, fall, and redemption through his son, so, too, we wanted the books to be multigenerational, with a strong role for both the original cast from the films and the children of Han and Leia—who are, after all, the future.

SS: I would add that Jacen isn't taking the "crown" from Luke. If anything, he is serving as a catalyst to help Luke grow into his next level of leadership.

JL: To me, the NJO is about the evolution of the Jedis' perception of the Force and the rise of a new generation of Jedi Knights to be the vanguard in allying themselves with a more inclusive, more unifying vision of the Force.

DR: Looking ahead to the upcoming Clone Wars series, what are the lessons you've learned from NJO that will help make Clone Wars an even better experience for editors, writers, and, most of all, readers?

LW: We learned that collaboration is good. And we learned that it's a good idea to keep doing things that are unexpected in order to keep fans interested. But that said, Clone Wars is not going to be a rerun of the NJO—we are doing something new. Where NJO was a story that appeared only in Ballantine novels, with the Clone Wars we are coordinating a variety of stories that will be published in adult and middle-grade books, comics, and short fiction. We are also looking at great war literature for ideas and themes and are telling Clone Wars stories from different points of view—some light-hearted, some introspective, some battle-oriented, et cetera. So rather than tell one sequential story line, they will be published as a broad mix of stand-alone, but sequential, stories that reflect various facets of what war is about.

SR: The Clone Wars series is awesome! Readers will get to know the characters from the films in more depth, adding to their enjoyment of *Episode III*. The comics will have one-shot issues focusing on Jedi Masters and their place as generals in the war, as well as a monthly series going into the war in more detail. The games, eBooks, Cartoon Network animated shorts—all will tell tales set in the Clone Wars era, adding color and dimension to the characters.

LW: *Star Wars* has always been a blurring of film with print publishing, video games, toys, and a variety of other platforms from which the saga has unfolded. We can all thank George Lucas for creating a world with such depth and then allowing us to play in it! I also thank the great group of talent I have been lucky enough to have worked with, who have expanded the original *Star Wars* stories into multiple product categories and formats in such brilliant ways.

SS: Fans who experience all aspects of these projects should get the widest experience of the Clone Wars saga, but people who only like to read books, or play video games, or surf the Web will also get satisfying experiences. You won't be lost if you pick up a book but haven't played the video game!

It's going to be a huge challenge, though. How do we set all these stories during/against the Clone Wars without being relentlessly *about* war, which I suspect people are even less interested in now that we've had a real one going on? On the other hand, I think people look to art and entertainment not just to escape the events of the real world, but to help them process those events in a safer setting. That's our challenge and our responsibility—to be sensitive to the needs of our audience.

DR: Are there any plans to take up the saga again from where NJO leaves off?

LW: Unclear the future is.

SS: We're toying with the idea, but we haven't come to any definite conclusions yet. There are still lots of possibilities for tales within the *Star Wars* Expanded Universe.

DR: What was your favorite experience in working on this project?

SR: I have so many—I absolutely adore working with Shelly Shapiro! She is a rare individual, and I treasure our working relationship. I've had fun with brainstorming book titles. I think overall my best feelings came from seeing the books in print and holding them in my hand, remembering conversations with authors and coworkers, et cetera. The journey is the goal, and I really enjoyed the journey!

LW: Collaboration is exciting, fun, and what it is all about. The overwhelming fan response has been the icing on the cake.

SS: I'd say getting to actually do creative brainstorming was my favorite experience. Getting to know some new authors and becoming part of the Lucasfilm team with Sue Rostoni came awfully close, though.

JL: I'm with Shelly on this one—the brainstorming sessions with editors and authors, and getting to know and work with Shelly, Sue, Lucy, Howard, Kathleen, Mike, Bob, Greg Bear, Greg Keyes, Kathy, Aaron, Troy, Matt, Walter, Elaine, Sean, and Shane. The story conferences at Skywalker Ranch, where so much creative activity was being poured into the prequel films. The challenge of helping to coordinate such a vast undertaking. Attending Celebration II . . .

DR: What was your least favorite?

SR: My least favorite experience was reading the letters we received from the fans reacting to Chewie's death, and then talking with Bob Salvatore, trying to help him cope with the fans' vehemence while he was in the middle of profound grief over his brother's passing. I surely didn't know that our readers could be so ugly and brutal about *anything,* let alone the heroic death of a fictional character.

LW: Absolutely. The attacks on Bob for the death of Chewie are something I wouldn't want anyone to go through again.

SS: Dealing with nasty fan mail and watching my authors get bashed on various Internet boards because some fans didn't agree with the direction their favorite universe was taking. Definitely not my favorite part of the job.

JL: I'm coming at this from a different angle, although I certainly agree about Bob. Committee control can present problems for a writer: what one person might applaud, another might deride. Sometimes it seemed as if there were too many cooks in the kitchen, too many viewpoints, often at odds with one another. As you grow close to a project, there's a tendency to want to exert control. But with a series like the NJO, you can't afford the luxury of becoming too attached to your characters, your dialogue, or story lines, because you're essentially playing in someone else's backyard, where a strict set of rules apply.

I wish that there had been more time for direct contact among the authors, to ensure that characterizations remained as consistent as possible. With so many writers working at the same time—often under the gun—and the need for manuscripts to be read and approved by people at Del Rey and Lucasfilm, it was difficult to keep everyone apprised of last-minute changes.

I also wish that some of the readers had exercised more patience and trust in what we were attempting to do. Every series, whether literary or televised, may seem to have weak or unfocused installments, but that's sometimes the result of a roll of the dice when everyone is working to honor a larger design. But these are petty complaints. On the whole, the NJO was a grand adventure.

SR: You know, we had some doubts at the outset of the NJO, considering the size of the project we were taking on and everything. Would readers stick with us over nineteen books? Would the editorial team lose their minds? I'm very happy that the readers have enjoyed the books and have been so enthusiastic.

DR: What about the editorial team?

SR: No comment!

Star Wars: New Jedi Order: Rebel Stand

Aaron Alston

The bestselling series, *Star Wars: The New Jedi Order*, continues
with the second book in the *Enemy Lines* duology of military and
political action-adventure.

Luke Skywalker's daring mission to halt the Yuuzhan Vong's
nefarious plot to overthrow the New Republic is struggling on all
fronts. And time is slipping away for Han and Leia Organa Solo,
trapped on a small planet whose rulers are about to yield to
Yuuzhan Vong pressure to give up the Jedi rebels.

On Coruscant, Luke and Mara Jade Skywalker have made a
shocking discovery that is preventing the Yuuzhan Vong from
exerting complete control. But when the enemy tracks them
down, Luke and Mara are thrust into a fierce battle for their lives.
Suddenly, the chances of escaping appear nearly impossible.
And in space, another battle rages, one that holds ominous consequences for the New Republic – and for the Jedi themselves.

Star Wars: New Jedi Order: Traitor

Matthew Wooding Stover

The New York Times bestselling series, *Star Wars: The New Jedi Order*, continues with an intense, character-driven tale of Jedi teaching, life and death, and heroism behind enemy lines.

Deep in the bowels of the captured planet of Coruscant, a hunted Jedi is hidden with an unexpected mentor who teaches him new ways to understand the Force – and what it means to be a Jedi.

arrow books

Star Wars: New Jedi Order: Star By Star

Troy Denning

Written by *New York Times* bestselling author Troy Denning, *Star By Star* is the thrilling heart of darkness of the *New Jedi Order*. This is a must-read for every fan of *Star Wars* fiction and the *New Jedi Order* series in particular!

It is a dark time for the New Republic. The Yuuzhan Vong, despite some recent losses, continue to advance into the Core, and continue their relentless hunt for the Jedi. Now, in a desperate act of courage, Anakin Solo leads a Jedi strike force into the heart of Yuuzhan Vong territory, where he hopes to destroy a major Vong anti-Jedi weapon. There, with his brother and sister at his side, he will come face to face with his destiny – as the New Republic, still fighting the good fight, will come face to face with theirs . . .

arrow books